ONE APRIL AFTER THE WAR

G. S. BOARMAN

ISBN – 978-0-9600649-0-8

1 — *April Fools*

Two men rode down the crushed-stone pike that promised to be dusty in the summer, but now, in the early spring, after so much rain and with the rain falling yet again, the road was very nearly swamped. They were obliged to pick their way through the numerous depressions and scored rivulets that testified to the unusually wet weather the area had been experiencing. Without even raising their eyes to the sky, they were sure of continued wet weather, slowing them and making a long ride even longer. They both wore long heavy cloaks against the rain and the chill, so that all that could be seen of the manner of dress were the boots in the stirrups, and if these were any indication, they were fairly well dressed beneath their cloaks. One of the men was slightly taller in the saddle, with a heavier build, and thick curling black hair showing under the rim of his hat. Though both men were clean-shaven, it was the taller of the two who continually stroked an imaginary mustache. The other man appeared to be of a slight build, but this was a trick of the eye – he merely seemed slight by comparison to his riding partner. He wore his hat far back on his head – the weak and watery morning sun nearly straight ahead did not compel him to shade his eyes – completely covering the color of his hair. The bigger man was, coincidentally, the older by several years, though this didn't establish any hierarchy between them. The older man, in fact, often deferred to the younger man, in defiance of natural order.

The men rode the best horses the town behind them could provide, their own horses still stabled in Cincinnati, horses brought to that town at some inconvenience, and now temporarily abandoned as they pursued their current business down river and on the southern bank. Their primary business had been in Cincinnati, and it was that proximity to Louisville that had been the final factor which drew for them this other, dubious assignment. They could have crossed the river at Cincinnati, then continued down the south side of the Ohio on the new Short Line railroad, but they were tired of trains, and there was some concern as to whether the ramp leading to the great bridge to Covington could even be accessed after the torrents of rain that left the lower Cincinnati wharves flooded. (They had been privileged to see the very unusual sight of boats tied to the doors of stores along the swollen riverfront.) They had been spending a good deal of time lately on trains, traveling in the last month alone several times between Cincinnati and Washington City. The prospect of one more train with its numerous stations at every hamlet across the river, from Covington to Louisville, depressed their spirits almost as much as the continual rain of the last few days. And with all the rain of the past month, there were sure to be tracks washed out, not to mention muddy and damp passengers, all squeezed into a little box. Their business in Cincinnati had tired them, yet they did not favor waiting for the flood to recede to begin their next assignment, dull as that promised to be. The silly idea took hold of them to ride a riverboat downstream to Louisville, the excursion to be a sort of buffer, a small and deserved vacation, between assignments. Some of these new Cincinnati boats, they had heard, were veritable floating palaces, sporting every possible comfort and luxury. It just seemed more practical, in view of all the water lying about, to take a boat.

They had met, in the saloon of their Cincinnati hotel, the captain of a steamer, idling somewhere along Cincinnati's riverside. Like all ship's captains, John Elliott spoke with pride of his ship. He also told them of the independent packet line he operated with his two brothers, working the Memphis-White River trade in their small but growing fleet of ships. And he spoke with true fatherly affection of his daughter Emma, after whom he intended to name a ship soon to be building downriver at Jeffersonville. He assured the gentlemen it would be far more comfortable on his ship than on a train car crowded with wet and steamy passengers, and, worse, with no bar to patronize.

They were already leaning heavily towards taking passage on Captain Elliott's steamer, but what really convinced the younger man was the promise of the company of two lovely female passengers who had just stopped at their table – they didn't wish to interrupt, only to speak with the captain and to *promise* him they would be ready on time; what really convinced the older of the two men was the name of Captain Elliott's steamer – *Legal Tender.* As employés of the Department of the Treasury, it seemed only right that they should patronize a ship so named.

It was a pleasant idea — a leisurely float down the Ohio in the company of two young ladies (shockingly without chaperones) on a handsome boat with an auspicious name and offering all the amenities. The idea may have been pleasant, but the weather definitely was not. The two men joined the captain and a few other early passengers the next afternoon. It was a day ahead of the scheduled departure, but they had seen enough of Cincinnati and were tired of both it and their hotel room. They determined to spend the night on the boat and while away the hours watching the river traffic and indulging in the steamer's amenities.

It was cloudy and cool all that next day, and more than ever, there seemed no reason to remain at the hotel. Despite the chill and the clouds, they passed a very pleasant afternoon on the boiler deck of *Legal Tender*, giving passing attention to Captain Elliott's tour of his great side-wheeler, but giving a good deal of attention to the ladies who had also decided to board a day early. A moderate but steady flow of liquor kept the chill away, and by evening, they were slightly drunk. They were ashamed to admit the next day to having been greatly amused by an attempted suicide just off their port side. The silly fellow had walked the entire length of the bridge from Covington merely to throw himself from the bridge on the Cincinnati side and within rescue reach of *Legal Tender*. He was plucked from the river by better and soberer people on the boat than themselves, and then commended to the care of his friends, who succeeded in taking the man back across the bridge, only to have him attempt a second suicide at the Covington end of the bridge. It was uncharitably suggested, later in the evening in the boat's saloon, that the fellow was only half-heartedly interested in drowning himself, else he would have made a better and more successful attempt in the middle of the bridge, where the drop was longer and the water was deeper and more treacherous, and where there was no hope of rescue. Instead, he made these cowardly attempts at either end of the bridge where rescue was far more probable. It was concluded that he was probably an immigrant – they were notoriously slack in their work ethic, and it was no stretch to think they would be equally slack in other efforts as well.

The next morning broke clear and fine, one of only a handful of days in the past month to be clear and fine, and one of only three days that could charitably be called warm. A great deal of the month had been spent in rain and snow and chilly (even wintery) temperatures. Yet despite the relatively pleasant weather, the river continued to rise, as it had done for nearly a week. But now she was rising rapidly – gaining eight feet in the last 24 hours alone, thanks, they were told, to the flooded Little Miami gushing out of its own banks on its way to dump into the Ohio. Like the Lord, the Ohio was slow to wrath but great in power, and once it was aroused to its power it would not be denied its release. Nevertheless, Captain Elliott expected to depart on time at five p.m. The departure time came and went and so did the evening and the next morning and the next afternoon. Now they were told to expect the Ohio to rise yet another three feet. They would be departing the next day, positively, at five p.m., once Captain Elliott's other passengers and freight could be brought aboard.

They spent another night aboard ship and woke to yet another cloudy and damp day, a constant light drizzle of rain falling. The captain had been generous in his meals for these, his captive fares, and, of course, they had enjoyed the pleasure of the ladies' company and some fine wine. The river had indeed risen another three feet, and a rise of several more feet was expected. The cloudy and damp morning developed into a wet afternoon and evening, the drizzle becoming heavier until it became a real rain that drummed on the pilot house and the hurricane deck all night. Captain Elliott assured them they would depart, positively, the next day at five p.m.

The rain continued to gain during the night and it rained all the next day, the last miserable day of a miserable March. The river was up another two feet; at least three more feet was expected. Captain Elliott informed them at breakfast that water now stood four feet deep in the buildings at the foot of Main Street. Captain Elliott was looking a little haggard – he had been day and night rowing back and forth between his ship and the wharf to consult with the river watch of the town and to assure his waiting fares and freight. He promised them they would be leaving, positively, this evening at five p.m. But positively was becoming a relative word; the ship would leave positively only as soon as she was able.

It mattered little to the two men. They were enjoying themselves in the delightful company of the two young ladies. They were enjoying a little time spent away from their work and the hotel and the trains, and who could fault them? The weather was not of their doing, and no one could blame them for taking passage on a ship that seemed fated, by virtue of its very name, to take them to their next assignment. But, perhaps, they should have asked Captain Elliott to send a telegram for them during one of his many excursions into town. Chief Whitley could be unforgiving of tardiness and unprofitable idleness.

They did not see Captain Elliott the rest of the day, but they did not really look for him. As long as his supply of food and drink kept pace with them, he need not be present. *Legal Tender* did not leave as promised at five p.m., but she did leave, finally, late that night. All the passengers – the veterans of the past few days and the neophytes just joining the ship on the day of departure – celebrated far into the night their long overdue retreat from Cincinnati. As a result, the two men found it rather objectionable to be roused in the early hours of Friday morning and told curtly that it was time to leave, if Louisville was their destination. Captain Elliott intended to stay in Louisville but a few short hours before heading back to his home port of Memphis, and then on to his regular routes on the White River in Arkansas. He had seen quite enough of the Ohio River for the time being.

A few of the passengers grumbled at being so unceremoniously and early turned out of their accommodations; after all, for three days, the ship had promised to depart at five p.m.; why should she not stay until five this day as well? One passenger, a frequent fare on Captain Elliott's boat, explained the captain's great hurry to be gone. His ship had already spent weeks out of commission – first run aground for nearly two weeks at Fletcher's near Cairo on the Mississippi, where she almost broke her back as the river (incredibly, at that time) was receding. Then, for more than a week, she was on the docks at Memphis being repaired. This, then, was *Legal Tender*'s first trip since her near total destruction, only to find herself trapped, much as the passengers were, at Cincinnati, idling and making money for nobody.

And so the two men had been forced to leave *Legal Tender* a little earlier than planned, and with no valid reason to delay further their objective, they retired to the first hotel at which they were assured a bath and quick attention to their now rumpled clothes. Within very reasonable time, they were clean, newly shaven, and properly attired. They had only to arrange for travel to the place of their next assignment.

The duty that lay before them had always seemed tedious, but now it loomed before them as positively onerous. Despite all the delays, they had enjoyed their time on the steamer – there had been plenty to drink and some delightful female passengers had helped to ease their passage (they must be getting old, they admitted, as they commented once again on the lack of chaperones among some of the youngest ladies). But it was these two very things that initially had made the short voyage bearable that now also made the long ride from Louisville to the Warner farm very nearly unbearable. They had drunk too much and slept too little, and now their heads were fuzzy and their eyes were heavy. The roads in town had been miserable and sloppy, and the roads that led south and east out of town were not much better. Like Cincinnati, Louisville and its environs had received several inches of rain in just the last week.

This little side venture promised to be vexatious and trying. Escorting young women over long distances always carried with it both tedium and delight, but escorting old widows promised only tedium. Images of brutal afternoon teas and stultifying conversations made all the more cumbersome by the certainty of long and frequent stops, loomed heavy in the older man's mind. A simple two- or three-day trip could become a protracted odyssey of unnecessary overnight stays and constant adjustments to travel arrangements and ticket fares. And if the weather persisted in this dismal pattern – they had stepped from the boat into another cloudy, damp, and cool day – the old woman may balk at making a start at all, until conditions improved.

If the directions they had received in town were correct, they should be coming upon the farmhouse around the curve in the road up ahead. They had ridden for the most part in silence, each privately nursing his crapulous condition and resentment, but now the taller man spoke.

"I'm sure it won't be as bad as Grant insinuated. Perhaps he exaggerated."

The other man did not reply, but continued on with his lids half-closed, his body given up to the sway of his plodding horse.

"I mean, all this talk of Kentuckians and their independence and shooting the eye out of a squirrel in flight and being weaned on whiskey is all just nonsense, some myth they've devised for themselves. I never saw any of that in town, did you?" Shifting in his saddle to face his friend, the man begged to know, "Just how stubborn and intractable can any one old lady be?"

Without turning to look at his friend, without even raising his lids, the other man answered, "Grant never exaggerates. And I know how stubborn and intractable my grandmother was when she had to move out west with us." After a further moment's silence, he added ominously, "It won't be pretty."

The taller man briefly considered his friend before turning back in his saddle. He knew his younger friend's dark mood had as much to do with where they were not as with where they now found themselves. Until they had been requested for this assignment, they were to have left Cincinnati and its rains and cold behind for hopefully better and warmer weather in New Orleans. Captain Bradley of the police force there had done invaluable work investigating the sugar frauds in the New Orleans Custom House, but those cases were well – and successfully – underway in the courts. It wasn't certain what more Bradley could tell them, but whatever it was would have to wait a week or two. As would their hopes for better weather – so far, Louisville's weather had been little better than Cincinnati's.

They had passed and counted the houses along the pike, some of them quite grand, not at all what one thought of in the semi-wilds of Kentucky, and at the appropriate place described for them ("Look for the two-story stone springhouse"), they took a rough road to their right and continued on until they found themselves at the bottom of a fairly steep rise in the land.

At the top, maybe a quarter of a mile away, they saw the farmhouse. Unlike the other houses, both large and small, glorious and humble, that they had passed on the turnpikes out of Louisville, this house did not face the main road, or even its own drive, but looked south down the steeper slope of the hill, overlooking a creek below and the woods beyond. Regardless of which way it faced, the house gave the appearance of stability and a simple pride. It was not the glorified shack that they had both, independently, imagined they would find, and a twinge of guilt passed through them both.

This early in the year, the house was visible, but in another month it would be hidden by the leaves of the large shade trees that surrounded it. It was a two-story house, neatly clapboarded and painted white, with a long and deep porch that ran the length of the front of the house. The land in front wavered in gold – a huge massing of jonquils in full bloom, swaying in some breeze active at the top of the rise that the men did not feel on the road below. In their guilty reflections and reassessments, the men had unknowingly allowed the horses to stop, but now they kicked them into something of a more dignified stride to climb up the muddy, sloppy drive to the house.

As they drew nearer to the house, the land leveled out and the horses labored less, falling back into the lazy walk they had adopted from the beginning. The shorter man, who was also the younger man, began to suspect that these horses were in fact of the career carriage variety. They worked at one pace only, regardless of the commands of the rider. Apparently, despite their reputation for patriotic nobility and fearlessness in battle, Kentuckians were not above fleecing a stranger for profit. The fault was as much his own: he was a better judge of horseflesh than this – when he wasn't indisposed.

They stopped directly in front of the porch and tied their horses to the newels at the bottom of the steps. They took one last breath before wearily mounting the five or six wide steps that evenly divided the length of the porch. A slow, rhythmic creaking sound that had been slowly dawning on them now revealed its source – a long, oversized swing hung at the far end of the porch to their left. On it, a man was stretched out, with one hand flung over the eyes, one muddy, booted foot raised and resting on the chain, and the other foot, equally booted and muddy, rested on the floor, keeping the swing slowly – barely – rocking back and forth. On the floor, next to the muddy boot was a book, opened but placed print-down as a means of keeping the reader's place. The older man rebelled at such shoddy treatment of a book but relented a little when he read the title on the cover – *De Docta Ignorantia*. Though he was not familiar with this particular book, he had never known a book in Latin to be anything other than learned, despite the rather contradictory title. A man's choice in books was a clear indicator of his character, and this book indicated a man of some intellectual standing. What was sure to be a momentary lapse in book care could be forgiven in such a mind.

The swinger appeared to be sleeping, retaining only just enough consciousness to direct the foot. Certainly, this person was far enough into sleep to be unaware of the presence of the two men on the porch. The two men looked at each other. The younger man had a habit of rolling his eyes by way of rolling his head, and this he did now by way of mockery and irritation. Clearly, he had not noticed the book or did not appreciate what it indicated about the reader. He announced their presence by loudly clearing his throat.

The swing abruptly stopped and the arm that had lain across the eyes now slid slowly up and over the forehead as the head turned equally slowly to gaze at the strangers on the porch. The foot slid down the chain and the person slowly sat up. It was apparent now that this was a young woman – perhaps in the early to middle years of her third decade – wearing a man's old and worn work coat over an old white shirt and dark blue trousers, rolled up above the high mud mark on the boots. A long thick hank of brown hair hung in a simple queue down her neck and beyond. She blinked slowly, once, twice, trying to bring focus to her sight and mind. She had indeed been very nearly asleep.

"Yes?"

It occurred to both men that this was not how they themselves would have reacted to having been woken to the presence of strangers, much less the reaction one would expect a woman, alone, to have in such circumstances. Perhaps she was not yet quite enough awake to appreciate the delicacy of her situation.

"Yes?" she asked again, this time with a slight hint of impatience. She was, in fact, quite awake and, far from being alarmed at this surprising presence of men or ashamed at her state of dress, she was irritated.

The taller, older man (yet not so much taller or older) stood paralyzed with the confusion of novelty (a woman in pants, alone, unperturbed at this intrusion). If he continued in this state much longer, he would be guilty of staring. The other man broke the trance by clearing his throat again, this time less dramatically.

"Um, my name is Mr. Merritt," placing his right hand upon his chest, as if he were taking an oath, "and this is my colleague, Mr. Argent." At his name, Mr. Argent obligingly nodded his head, in case the woman should mistake him for someone else, possibly also standing there on the porch. Merritt waited for her to respond, but she only remained seated on the swing, both knees now demurely pressed together. But her hands gripping the bench of the swing on either side of her knees suggested that being demure was an unintended side effect. She sat, hunched forward, leaning on her hands, expectantly. She continued to gaze steadily at Merritt, with a look of lazy boredom that also managed to convey some latent warning. There was something that was at once mature and childish about her.

When it was obvious that her own name was not forthcoming, Merritt continued.

"We were hoping to find Mrs. Warner. Is this the home of Mrs. Warner?"

A new look came into her eyes: wicked amusement. "No, there is no Mrs. Warner here. This is not her home." Her voice was low, confident. It occurred to Argent that this woman may be older than he first thought; this was not the high, nervous voice of a young woman, but the voice of a more mature woman. Why was she dressed like that?

Then Merritt said something that visibly disturbed and angered her, and instantly the air felt as if lightning had struck nearby. "Is your father or husband at home? We'd like to confirm directions with him."

The young woman on the swing rose slowly and threateningly; the change in her demeanor was so sudden and drastic that it startled both men into a small step backward. She was taller than most women and broader in the shoulder than most, and this must have given her some deluded belief that she was physically equal to the men. Without knowing who these strange men were, beyond their names, she seemed actually prepared to fight them. Merritt had to admire the confidence and courage that allowed her to challenge opponents so obviously overmatched to herself. Her eyes were half-closed in insolent disdain for these men, and she drew a deep breath to speak. But whatever speech it was that she intended to hurl at them was preempted by a shout heard coming from beyond the other side of the porch.

Merritt and Argent moved across the porch to look out over the railing behind them. A small, thin, colored woman in a faded red cotton blouse and a white apron covering a worn-out gray skirt was running breathlessly up the hill just back of the house. A shawl had been hastily thrown over her shoulders, the corners tucked into the waistband of her apron. With her left hand she was holding up her skirts to keep from tripping as she ran, while her right hand she held up, waving wildly as she shouted between heaving breaths, "Wait! Wait!"

The men indeed waited, watching the woman finish the last few yards of her run until she reached the porch. There was a large hydrangea bush flanking this side of the porch, so that she had to stop a few feet away. She bent over at the waist, breathing heavily, her right arm still outstretched, as if in supplication. Every so often she looked up to make sure the men were still there.

While the black woman recovered, the men turned in unspoken unison to look back at the woman standing before the swing. Another change had washed over her. The anger and defiance were gone, receded, and in their place was a mild dread.

"Now look what you've done!" She was hissing at them across the porch. "Miss Carrie's seen you and now she's all riled up and hell-*bent* on having things her way."

Both men were astonished. They looked back at the smaller colored woman, still catching her breath in the drizzling rain, and then to the taller young woman, who had only moments before appeared to be ready to offer combat to two grown men, but who now appeared nearly terrified of the hornet's nest this other woman apparently presented. A desperate and truly ridiculous plea was issued by the young woman: "I'll pay you each $10 for your trouble, if you tell her you made a mistake and you go away right now."

"Are you trying to *bribe* us?" Merritt spoke with equal mixture of incredulity and amusement. All this time, Argent remained in confused silence, but no longer paralyzed. In fact, he was almost dizzy from turning to look at first one woman and then the other.

Miss Carrie had recovered enough to reach the stairs in the front, still holding her skirts, now to facilitate mounting the steps, her right arm still outstretched, now to reach for the railing at the top of the stairs. Before the young woman could respond to Merritt's allegation, Miss Carrie scolded her. "Miss Mary, don't leave your guests standing on the porch in this damp and chill. Invite them in."

Before there was any further discussion of guests or invitations, Mary quickly retorted, "They are not guests. They were just leaving."

Mr. Argent casually remarked, "Well, there was just now some mention of compensation for the long ride. I'd be pleased to have a drink of water." A decidedly wicked man.

"Water! We can do better than that." Carrie was at the front door with her hand about to turn the knob, when Merritt addressed her, hoping for a better answer than Miss Mary had given.

"Yes, ma'am, I'm sure." The thought of any drink other than water, however, was causing some disquiet in his person. "But we were hoping to find Mrs. Warner. Is this her home?"

Miss Carrie stopped turning the knob and twisted back to her right to look up at Merritt with a curious look on her face.

"Mrs. Warner!?! No, sir, she doesn't live here anymore. She's gone to her rewards. Nearly four years now."

Merritt turned slowly and deliberately to face Miss Mary and looked at her with open appraisal and challenge. Still watching Miss Mary, he asked – no, stated – "But there is a Mary Warner living here."

"Why, yes, sir. You're looking right at her." Twisting in the other direction, but still for some reason retaining hold on the doorknob, she scolded Mary. "Fifteen minutes that I know of, these gentlemen been kept at the threshold and you ain't even told them your name?" Carrie's grammar always lapsed when she was in high dudgeon. "Shame on you! Your mother and I both taught you better than that. And what would your father think of you? You know how he felt about the way you treat eligibles."

The smirk that had been growing on Merritt's face and the bemused enjoyment that Argent had been indulging at Miss Mary's expense as she was publicly reprimanded on her own porch quickly faded from both men as the portent of the word 'eligibles' sank in.

Mary enjoyed watching the table turned on these two interlopers on her morning nap. The whole morning, now that she thought of it, ruined because of these two, with the very real probability that the rest of the day would be spent in ridding herself of them. It could have been handled quickly, if Carrie had kept to her own business. Just how was it that Carrie seemed to know every time one of these land-miners came up the lane? Carrie's house was out of sight of the lane; she couldn't see the comings and goings on it. In a flash the answer came to her: Thea. Betrayal, that's what it was, pure and simple. And on today of all days. Thea knew it was Randy's birthday, and that Mary wanted to be alone, more so, today. Mary would make sure Thea felt the full weight of her disappointment and anger.

Argent's words broke in on her revelation, and her anger at Thea was tagged and filed away for later. Mary returned to her enjoyment of the situation. Argent was awkwardly explaining something, while Merritt alternately nodded or shook his head in agreement with Argent's statements.

"I think there has been a misunderstanding." Merritt nodded solemnly, casting a glance at Miss Warner. There may be hope yet of an early ejection of these two. "We aren't here for any . . ." – Argent was desperately casting about for the proper word, the dignified word – ". . . sort of . . ."

"Fishing expedition," Merritt suggested.

Mary slowly closed her eyes; *Can anyone really be that clumsy and course?* She opened her eyes to find Merritt smiling broadly at her, teasing her – the way Randy used to do. A small lurch in her heart at the thought of Randy was swiftly followed by a hard, cold anger at this man who had triggered the memory.

Argent spared Merritt a brief glance of irritation before continuing with renewed effort, "Any sort of social activity." Merritt emphatically shook his head.

It was beginning to dawn on Carrie that she had run herself to near collapse up that slippery, wet hill in the hopes that two fresh eligible bachelors were interested in Miss Mary. She had promised Mr. Warner that she would take care of his daughter, but, really, a husband was what was needed for Mary. A strong hand, a man's hand, any hand but hers. Now Carrie's hand left the doorknob and placed itself on her hip. It seemed the offer of a drink was being withdrawn.

"What other kind of activity is there when gentlemen come to call at a lady's house, so far from town?" A challenging and warning edge had entered Carrie's voice. "And what gentleman," it suddenly occurred to her, "comes calling at a lady's house, unannounced and without having made sure of a chaperone?" Now it was Mary's turn to smile broadly. She raised her eyebrows in a saucy approval of Carrie's questioning.

"This is an official call." Argent was smiling confidently, now that he had entered familiar territory. People usually responded with all due respect to this type of pronouncement. For added gravity, and to truly lay to rest any idea of marital prospecting, he added, "We have come at the request of President Grant."

Merritt and Argent were both smiling, anticipating the flurry of gasps and excitement and professions of received honor that are the usual reactions of women when they are visited by the representatives of the highest office in the land. It was because of the eminence of their patron that they had paid such particular attention to the manner of their apparel this morning. Argent pulled from his best coat the letters of introduction and other papers proper to assuring the people they called on of their respectability and validity. The papers and letters, however, remained in his outstretched hand, neither woman moving to accept them.

The dead silence that followed caused their smiles to fade rapidly. Once again, the balance of power on the porch had shifted. Carrie now looked fearfully, truly fearfully, at Miss Warner. Merritt and Argent followed her gaze to see Miss Warner standing stiff and white with small patches of red beginning to blossom and spread over her whole face. For a moment, Argent feared that she had suffered some kind of attack. He realized, however, that she wasn't ill, but furious.

With a visible effort to contain herself, Miss Warner said with deadly calm, "Leave."

Carrie – brave woman – spoke equally softly. "Mary, no matter who sent these gentlemen, they don't deserve such treatment after such a long and miserable ride. We'll feed them and tend to their horses, then send them on their way." She said this with more hope than with any real conviction that this is what would happen. She quickly opened the door and frantically motioned the gentlemen inside, giving each in turn a look that said, 'Say nothing.' She continued to hold the door open for Mary and asked probingly, "Mary, honey, aren't you coming in?"

"I'll see to the horses."

Carrie breathed a sigh of relief and walked through the door, shutting it quietly behind her. She took the men's cloaks and disappeared behind the broad, plain staircase in the middle of the hall, then returned to show the gentleman to the front room on the left of the wide central hallway. She absently asked them to sit and also if they would like anything in particular to drink. But she was lost in thought, and didn't hear the gentlemen tell her, twice, that water would truly be enough.

"Miss Carrie?" Carrie realized she had been directly addressed, and acknowledged, for the first time in some minutes, the gentlemen's presence. "Miss Carrie, are you unwell?" It was Mr. Argent speaking to her with some amount of concern in his voice.

"Oh, no, sir. I'm just trying to remember where all the guns are kept. I don't think there's one in the barn. I'll be sure and check her before she comes into the house."

Merritt mouthed the word, *Guns*. Argent took Carrie's hand and guided her to sit on one of the two short sofas in the room. The upholstery on all the seats was a little worn, but it was still a handsome room in all. Perching himself next to her on the couch, he said, "Maybe you had better tell us what just happened."

"Maybe you had better tell me what the General wants with Miss Mary."

Argent started to correct her as regards to Grant's title, but Merritt cut in before Argent could do so. "President Grant has sent us to escort Miss Warner to Washington. To meet with him."

"Oh, well" – and here she gave a little laugh – "that won't happen." She patted Argent's hand that still held hers and said appeasingly, and with a little pity, "I'll be as quick as I can with some food for you boys, so you'll be able to get back to town as soon as possible." She moved to get up, the matter obviously closed to her, but Argent would not let go of her hand. She sat again, looking at him quizzically. She felt a little naughty at letting a white man hold her hand for so long and with such politeness. What would her Henry think if he saw her right now?

Even though it was Argent who held her in place and pinned her with his gaze, it was Merritt again who spoke. "We won't be leaving without her. The President insisted. In fact, he gave instructions that we were not to take 'no' for an answer and to use any means possible – including throwing her over our shoulders and carrying her, bound, to Washington."

Argent was watching Carrie's face, and was a little surprised to find no alarm or indignation at the thought of Miss Warner's casual abduction. "Oh, Lord, do not tell her any such thing, or she'll dig in her heels and then it may just come down to gunplay. Tell her anything else you need to convince her, but do not mention the General again."

This time Argent did correct her. "He's the President now, Miss Carrie."

"And for heaven's sake do not correct her on that. Not unless you want an earful and then some of how he isn't her president since she was denied the opportunity to vote for him or anyone else. The thought of her rights denied will sour her mood for days. You mention the President, especially this one, and it's on your own heads what follows."

"Miss Carrie, can you tell us, why is she so angry with the Presi, – with the General?"

She looked at Argent, clearly wanting to tell him, but some strange code of honor she apparently shared with Miss Warner held her tongue.

"It isn't my place to say. But you should know – if you're to spend any time with her – that she is an angry child, in an ailing woman's body, hobbled by a crippled soul. Surely the General told you of the tragedies that have befallen and smothered this house?"

"Only that Miss Warner is the last of her family." Here Argent looked truly regretful at the sad situation. Then his regret gave way to vexation. "But we were allowed to believe that Miss Warner was Mrs. Warner, the mother, a widow."

Carrie laughed heartily but covered her mouth with her apron at such unseemly conduct. "Oh, the General was wicked to leave you with that idea. But, how would you have thought to treat her if you had known how young she is? No, the General knew what he was doing. If you had come in here giving commands and expecting obedience because she is young and unattached, she would have shredded you on the spot. It's a vicious and quick tongue she has. Or worse," Carrie laughed anew at the emerging picture in her mind, "speaking softly and cajoling-like to her, as if she were an addled old woman, why you'd be just an oily spot on the porch wall. It's hard to know which she hates more – being told what to do or being molly-coddled." Carrie was still shaking with laughter at the thought of innocent gentlemen being flayed alive by Miss Mary's acid tongue. Merritt and Argent looked at each other in high disapproval of such blood sport among the ladies. "No. No, it was better the way it happened, that she thought you were just two more men come to try their luck with her hand."

Now Carrie did rise, wiping her eyes with her apron, Argent finally letting go of her hand. Carrie sighed. "Her father died six months ago, leaving her alone in this big house that used to have so many in it. She spends too much time alone, and she's becoming peculiar . . . more so than usual. I don't know how you can manage it, but the General is right: don't you take 'no' for an answer. I'll help you as much as I can, but she must go and face the General. She must get out of this house, away from this farm and all the ghosts that walk it. She needs to be among the living."

When she entered the room, Mary knew instantly something had changed. Merritt and Argent were sitting, speaking quietly, sipping tea.

Out of her mother's good china tea cups, she noted. She glanced to the short china cabinet, to which Carrie had the only key, and saw the empty places where not only teacups were missing, but also plates and serving dishes. So, Carrie was putting on the dog for Grant's men. That meant some agreement had been reached between them.

The men looked up casually, then stood politely as she moved from the doorway into the room. "Miss Warner," they said by greeting, as if they were merely meeting on the street, touching their hats to her. She hated the superficiality of it all – it just made her sick – but if she was to dispense with these men, she had to let them play their parts.

That didn't mean she had to participate in the ritual. Without responding, she took the seat farthest from where the two men had just been sitting, each one on separate sofas that opposed each other, separated by the width of an occasional table bridging their armrests. They regained their seats after making sure she had taken one. She sat on the edge of her chair, both knees together, leaning forward with her elbows on her thighs, her wrists lying on her knees, her hands clasped together – very unladylike. She sat this way watching them for a minute or two. They alternately sipped their tea and gazed placidly at her. They just made her sick. Finally, she raised her hands and rearranged them into the formal prayer position, index fingers to her lips. Almost immediately, she lowered them again, and announced, "I've unsaddled your horses, brushed them dry, fed and watered them, turned them out to the field. As soon as dinner is finished, I'll fetch them and re-saddle them for you, and bring them up to the house." All her mother's training screamed for her to say something apologetic about the situation – 'I'm sorry you came out all this way for nothing' – but Mary didn't want to extend any further courtesies to them or, worse, create an opening for them to refute the fact of their leaving after dinner.

Argent replied in the even, unhurried tones of the formal parlor, "I wish you had not taken such pains, but I thank you. And we couldn't possibly allow you to saddle our horses for us. We'll be quite able to handle them ourselves . . . when the time comes."

Mary's eyebrows arched slightly. Was that a challenge? Did he think he could name the hour of his departure? Mary held her tongue. The conclusion of dinner would settle the matter. The men alternately sipped their tea and gazed placidly at her. She hated them more and more with each passing moment.

"I shall see about dinner." She was going to make Carrie pay dearly for this gross intrusion on her time and solitude, and she would never forgive her for her obvious participation in whatever was happening in the front room. She rose to go to the kitchen, and the men rose with her, smiling like idiots. She thought she might scream.

Carrie entered the room carrying a tray of small biscuit and ham sandwiches, and a pot of more tea. She sat the tray down on the low table in the middle of the room as if she were serving royalty. Carrie loved playing lady of the house with Mary's mother's things. Normally, Mary didn't care – Miss Carrie, Mr. Henry, and their children had been like family as far back as Mary could remember – but some subterfuge was going on here and it angered Mary that even her mother's china, now her china, was conspiring in it. Worse, Mary had planned on living off those very biscuits for the next week. Now she would have to spend another morning making dough, cleaning and stoking the stove while the dough rose, rolling it out and shaping the biscuits, then cleaning up the dishes while she watched over the biscuits as they baked. Since it was only herself now that needed feeding, cooking had become an enormous, exhausting task and she rarely bothered with it. But she had been wanting biscuits and she had made the effort to make them, and now Carrie was parading them around on fine china for anyone to eat, as many as they liked.

Carrie must have read her thoughts, for she whispered as she passed on her way out of the room, "I'll make you some more tomorrow, I promise. By the way, they're a little overcooked." Mary lowered her eyes at this last comment. When Carrie reached the doorway, she turned and spoke to Mary as if she were some dull child who needed indulging, "Now, run upstairs and put on something proper for dinner. And I don't mean changing out what you have on for more of the same. Put on a dress. The occasion calls for it." From the hallway, Carrie added, "And for heaven's sake, put on some shoes."

Mary, from long habit established in childhood, had removed her muddy boots before entering the house, and now stood in stockings, her legs exposed to the calf, her pants still rolled up. The gentlemen, she noticed, had walked into the front room in their muddy boots, without any consideration of her mother's best carpet.

Mary raised her eyes and studied a spot on the far wall just above the closed door to the room beyond, behind and above Messrs. Merritt and Argent, mastering the smart reply that came to mind. She realized the men were still standing in deference to her. She sat back down, this time her clasped hands hung at the knees, slightly parting them. She was losing control of the situation. The truth was, she wasn't quite sure what the situation was or how to handle it. Suitors were easy enough to dispatch. In most cases – and she knew this was a particularly ugly stratagem for a woman – she could easily shame a man's intellect, challenging their knowledge on any number of subjects. If she found herself outmatched in a subject, she fell back on the tactic of shaming a man for showing away. She never stooped (never intentionally) to coarse speech or crude displays of any kind. Sometimes she drove them away without even trying.

But these men, these were not suitors or salesmen or creditors, all of whom she could best. She wasn't really sure what they were, other than that the General had sent them. She wanted nothing to do with the General and nothing to do with these men. Silence was the best course of action. She knew that women were expected to engage in, even initiate, light conversation, especially as hostess, as she now found herself. Her sisters had learned this somehow without being told, but Mary's mother had had to pointedly instruct her in this. It was one more disappointment to her mother, one more lesson in which she had failed to provide a proper example for her younger sisters. Well, there were no more little sisters to mislead, no mother to disappoint. If mindless chatter was how a woman kept guests happy, the opposite was how a hostess inspired guests to leave. Mary maliciously ignored the two gentlemen. She slid to the back of the chair, crossed her legs and clasped her hands around her top knee, the way her father always sat. This was patently unladylike, probably even considered lewd, but she was in a foul mood, her sleep interrupted, Randy's memory disfigured, her bile stirred by news of the General, her time usurped by convention, all on account of these two men, unannounced and unbidden. She could out-wait them. She could sit this way for hours, while her mind roamed and skipped and explored. It had begun to rain again, and the soft patter on the porch roof provided a soothing background to her thoughts. She stared at the blue cloth of her pants and felt herself float away from the room.

She went to the cemetery with its unfinished stone wall and the opening that still needed a gate. Turning east, she walked along the creek, between the trees that lined it. Suddenly, an image of a vast terraced garden erupted and settled against the slope of the hill. Stone by stone, it constructed itself, a perfect cyanotype in motion, like one of Randy's flip-drawings – a practical guide to a fantastic structure. She saw it completed – an enormous walled-in, terraced garden – carved into the hillside, overlooking the creek. Eventually, she could connect it to the family cemetery situated farther west along the curve of the hill. There was plenty of creek rock for the walls and even the walkways. Digging into the side of the hill would be work, as would hauling the rock from farther and farther up and down the creek, but work was comforting as well as tiring; she needed the physical exhaustion to help her sleep. And she had all the time and freedom she needed to complete the project. She could even work far into the winter on a project like this. Once the foundations were laid, it wouldn't matter if the ground was frozen; she'd be working above ground. Winters were brutal for her. When the weather kept her from her projects and distractions, from the work of the farm, she crawled the walls with frustration, depression, and loss. This past winter had nearly claimed her sanity, this first winter truly alone, even her father gone.

She heard "Miss Warner?" and looked up. She had actually forgotten these two were in the room with her. She often heard and saw things in a kind of delayed echo, and looking at the men now, she saw that idiotic, placid gaze on their faces, but a delayed image in her mind had seen – for an instant – concern and pity. When Argent saw that he had her attention, he commented, apparently repeating himself, "I said, these little ham biscuits are delicious. Do you cure your own ham?"

Mary gazed back at him with what she hoped was the same bland expression she saw on his face. "You will ruin your appetite." She returned to her study of the blue cloth of her pants, grasping at the threads of her vision. But Merritt pulled her back from her reverie before she could dive back into her thoughts.

"I've often told Mr. Argent the same thing. He usually agrees with me, but invariably it is after the dinner that he has indeed spoiled." He smiled idiotically at her.

Well, this was just deplorable conversation, even for mixed company. Grown men discussing ham biscuits and sharing delightful tales of dinners spoiled. Moreover, an exercise in rude silence, originally intended to punish the General's agents, had unintentionally produced an idea, a goal, a distraction, a pleasurable pursuit of the mind that she could translate to her hands, work that in its mindless repetition and exertion could, in turn, calm and even stop her jagged thoughts. She wanted to get back to it, but now Merritt and Argent were bombarding her with inane observations and glimpses into their everyday interactions that made her cringe. Somehow, somehow, they were grinding her down. She had lost her touch – it had been some time since the last suitors had come out to the house – the weather had mercifully kept them warm and dry somewhere else – and now she found herself slow and rusty in her handling of such men. She unconsciously put her head in her hands, then slid them up over her forehead and down to the nape of her neck. Where did Grant get these men?

Her hands still on the back of her neck, she turned to look at them. They were watching her intently. Merritt asked, "Is something wrong? Can we do anything for you?" Of the two, she despised him the more.

She stared dully at him, then blurted out, "Why did the General send you two?" She had just broken two of her own rules that she had set for herself while tending the horses: don't mention Grant, and don't ask about his reasons for sending them. The question as she meant it, did not inquire as to Grant's reasons for sending them, but as to Grant's reasons for choosing them.

To his credit and her surprise, Merritt asked, "Do you mean why did the General send anyone at all? Or, why did the General send us in particular?"

"Answer how you will." It galled her that he had found the same flaw in her question.

Argent intercepted Merritt's reply, suggesting, "Perhaps this is a discussion that could wait until after dinner."

"But that would interfere with your plans to leave after dinner. Just after dinner." Conversation during dinner would be tedious enough; heaven forbid there should be further tedium afterwards as well.

"Well, not to put too fine a point on it, but those are your plans, and not necessarily ours." He said it genially enough, but there was just enough force to it that he must have truly thought he had a say in the matter.

"Putting a fine point on things is the noble and ultimate goal of higher speech and language." Here, Mary's voice became glacial. "And the point

I want to make – crystal clear – is that this is my house and I make the plans in it."

For the first time, Mary saw a stiff anger rise in both men. She had gone too far, had been too rude, and they rightfully bridled at the open disrespect. Mary felt the color rise to her face at her own shame. But rather than causing her to soften her demeanor, her shame brought to the surface even more bile. Mary was never uglier in her thoughts and words than when she was undeniably, inescapably wrong. She was like a cornered possum, spitting and snapping with sharp, jagged teeth; a possum refusing to play dead.

Into this caustic atmosphere stepped Althea. Thea. The traitor. Carrie's second youngest child and only daughter and, until this day, the only human being in this last year that Mary had suffered to be near her. In Thea, Mary had found both a kindred soul and a growing, living creature that she could nurture. Though Thea was a mere child, Mary and Thea got along as if they were of the same age. They spent hours together, roaming the woods and wading the creeks. Mary was teaching her to read and write, and they both were learning to play the piano, something Mary was supposed to have learned long ago, but she had balked at the hours of practice that mere scales required. Now, like so many other things, she regretted the lost opportunity. Carrie allowed Thea the freedom to spend so much time with Mary; they both needed and benefitted from each other's company.

Thea was a beautiful child, with large round eyes that were always bright with amusement. She was rarely seen without a smile, and she rarely walked anywhere; she skipped to all her destinations. Thea, therefore, didn't step into the room, but rather skipped in to announce that dinner was, finally, ready. She fairly twirled over to Mary, brimming with eagerness to tell her something, anticipating the excitement her news would bring.

"Miss Mary! Do you know what? I saw a turtle today! The first one this year!"

Turtles were a passion they both shared. Normally, such an announcement would have indeed been received with great excitement, as well as an immediate removal to the place of discovery. Nothing was normal about today, however, and Mary, fresh from her fault and stinging with guilt and the ghosted reproaches of her parents, rounded on Thea.

"You're quite the little intelligence gatherer, aren't you? What else do you see, from your perch in the tree?" Usually, Thea would have giggled at the unintended rhyme. Mary, herself hearing the ridiculous rhyme in a question intended to wound – it was like throwing a spear with a ribbon and bow tied on it – quickly added, "Besides a turtle."

Miss Warner had never raised her voice or changed the tone, not any that the two gentlemen could hear, yet the pronouncement had an immediate effect on the little black girl standing before her. Thea's large eyes widened even more, seeming to threaten the delicate skin around them. She had been found out and called out. True remorse flooded her heart. Miss Mary had been her friend, a close companion even, and Thea had betrayed her. Thea saw that now, and also saw the wonderful hours spent together dissipating, like clouds swept before a tornado.

Mary was watching her and saw with satisfaction that the message had been received. But new realizations were occurring to Mary, realizations she intended to expose. "I see," she said, though Thea had not spoken at all. "Tell me this, then. Where are the boys?" She had asked the question almost musically – Mary herself tried to trace the notes on piano keys in her mind: A, F flat, E, F flat.

Thea broke easily. "Caleb took them hunting – when I first saw the gentlemen." She nodded at Merritt and Argent. She was not going to suffer this alone. She had lured the boys – Jack and Morty, two oversized puppies – away from the house, and Caleb had kept them away. Jack and Morty – Mary's big, beautiful hounds who always warned her of anyone's approach with beautiful, melodious baying. Until she had been given these dogs she had never understood the stories she had read of hunters and their joy at the sound of their baying partners. Her boys truly made a joyful sound, and Mary found simple pleasure and pride when they gave voice.

"I see," she said again. She was unaware that Carrie, wondering why her dinner was going cold in the dining room across the hall, had come herself to announce a second time the advent of dinner. Merritt and Argent's righteous indignation had been transformed into an awkward sympathy for the little black girl obviously undergoing some kind of inquisition. They were uncomfortable observers of some private altercation. They looked to Carrie for release, both for themselves and for Thea.

"And while Caleb was out hunting with the boys, two strange men were able to bring themselves with stealth and ease to my very front door, while I lay unaware and unprepared for their coming."

Merritt took offense at the word 'stealth,' and also at being somehow involved in this very private spat. "There was no use of stealth involved. We are," gesturing with his hand to include Argent, "by nature, very quiet men. And the soft earth," he looked to Argent for agreement, who nodded enthusiastically, "from all the rain, we're told," (now nature had been implicated as well), "dampened the horses' steps." The horses were not invited to defend themselves.

"Oh, Miss Mary! You were never in danger! Papa was watching from the trees along the creek, all the time." Thea was giving it all up now; everyone involved was being dished up to share in Thea's disgrace. In the spirit of complete capitulation, Thea pointed out the window behind Mary in the direction of the creek and swung her pointing arm wildly from right to left, to show the expanse of the area under surveillance.

"And was he armed?" Some of the anger was ebbing. She was enjoying Thea's discomfort and her ready willingness to sacrifice even her father in the hopes of mitigating Mary's wrath. She was also enjoying the developing scenario in her mind: that so much coordination had been executed – was required – to ensure the safe arrival of 'eligibles.' From the periphery of her mind, she was also aware of the discomfort of Merritt and Argent. That was an added bonus, like bourbon in her tea.

"Yes, ma'am." Thea was eager to reveal all aspects of this covert operation. "He had his rifle and another gun, and some ammunition."

Another realization now dawned on Mary. "Did he get this other gun from the *barn*? Did he take *my* gun from the *barn*?" The gun that Mary had looked for and found missing, just a short time ago.

"Oh, praise the Lord!" Carrie had finally found an opening to rescue her daughter from Mary's bullying questioning. "I wasn't sure if that gun was still there or not."

Mary completely ignored Carrie's interruption. This was all too much. She was enjoying herself for the first time since Grant's men had connived their way into the house. For the first time, really, in months, maybe even years. "Do you mean to tell me," she enunciated slowly, "that your daddy is lying in wait down by the creek, right now, in case there's trouble? From *them*?" She was trying so hard not to smile or laugh, but the thought of burly Mr. Henry, positioned among the wet underbrush and slippery rocks, waiting and at the ready for some trouble from these two dandies, was delicious. "Tell me." She patted the air in excited anticipation. "Tell me, what is the sign for danger? How was he to be alerted that he was needed? That *guns* were called for?"

This was the excitement that Thea had hoped for, and though the first turtle of the year had not produced it, she was relieved to see that Miss Mary was still capable of it, even in the midst of her righteous indignation and anger. Thea clapped her hands and danced in place with the thrill of the conspiracy and its secret passwords. "I was to go to the front porch and say as loud as I could, 'Oh, no, the turtles have got out.' That was my idea. Papa said it had to be something I could remember, and I remembered how you and me is going to build a new turtle pen, so I got to pick."

During the course of her interrogation, Mary had slowly been inching forward in her seat, unconsciously bringing her presence forward to bear down on Thea, but now she rocked back in her seat, clapped her hands in glee, and said, "Of course you did!" She jumped up, grabbed Thea's little hand, and pulling her from the room, she laughed, "Oh, Thea! Let's go and do it now!" Merritt and Argent heard from the porch two female voices, both seemingly children's, saying loudly and dramatically, over and over again, "Oh, no, the turtles have got out."

Dinner was not as tedious or trying as everyone privately expected. Miss Warner's temper had moderated, and she had adopted a resigned patience during the meal. Carrie had prepared a creditable dinner on impossibly short notice. Carrie was in no way responsible for Mary's dinners or any of her other domestic needs, but she had always helped Mrs. Warner, and Mr. Warner had always quietly paid her for the help. Carrie felt a strange obligation to continue helping. After the Great Tragedy – as Carrie referred to it in her mind – had taken Mrs. Warner and the last of her children, save Miss Mary, Carrie had assumed the role of mistress of the house. Mary had been woefully unprepared – she had resisted all efforts to prepare her for running a household – as well as too grief-stricken to assume so much responsibility. Both Mary and Mr. Warner, in their shared shock and grief, would have allowed the house to fall down around them, and never would have noticed. Carrie, then, had seen to the running of the household and Mr. Warner had rallied enough to acknowledge her efforts with regular and fair payments.

After Mr. Warner's death, Carrie began to feel as if the household were truly hers to run. Before his death, Mary had developed slovenly ways, even getting out the fine china whenever she ran out of everyday dishes to use. Carrie put a stop to that by taking possession of the key to the china cabinet in the front room, as well as to the top doors to the linen press in the serving pantry off the dining room. Mrs. Warner had always kept these locked against curious little hands tempted to handle pretty things. The Warners had not been cash rich and could not afford to replace anything of value, so Mrs. Warner was vigilant about what she had called her 'vanities.' Mary never commented on the locked cabinets, or why the dishes were suddenly washed and put away.

Both Mary and Mr. Warner had shied away from food in the wake of their losses but Carried had scolded Mary that she must put aside her own regards for food in order to care for her father. Mr. Warner had been a big man, unusually tall at six feet and four inches. He also had a large frame and was well-muscled. He had the large hands of a workman, though he made his living with his mind. When he returned home that last time to bury his wife and children, he was already a shrinking man. He continued to fade in weight and strength in the following months, until Carrie took matters into hand. She cooked full meals, three times a day, and admonished Mary to eat, whether she was hungry or not, in order to encourage her father to do the same. Mary complained, privately, that nothing had taste, but she kept up the ruse of an appetite for her father's sake. She stopped losing weight, but despite everyone's best efforts, her father looked more and more skeletal as the months pushed on. By the time he gave up his ghost, the big, quiet man who could lift anything, build anything, fix anything, had dwindled down to a mere armful of skin and bones.

With the death of Mary's father – the last of her family – all pretenses of eating or wanting to eat disappeared. Nothing had taste for her. Hunger didn't visit her. She was too tired and dispirited to cook for herself, and she didn't keep anything in the pantry anyway. During the last two years of Mr. Warner's life, Carrie had cooked for both her own family and the Warners in the Warner kitchen cabin, just behind the house. Eventually, Mr. Warner had invited her family to join himself and Miss Mary at the great table in the dining room on Sundays and holidays. Ultimately, the two families shared evening meals together as well. Mr. Warner had welcomed the company – he had always loved children, enjoyed teasing them and hearing their views on the world, and Carrie's young family had given Mr. Warner some pleasure. At Mr. Warner's death, however, Henry had instructed his wife to leave Miss Mary to her mourning, and the shared meals had stopped. Carrie returned to cooking meals for her family in their own small kitchen cabin behind their own small home. But Carrie always made a little extra for Mary when she made meals for her own family, one of her sons carrying it up to the house on the hill, but often the dish came back merely picked at. Carrie suspected that Mary was drinking, and that this was dulling her already low appetite. Curiously, Mrs. Warner had never seen the need to lock that cabinet, and Carrie didn't know where the key to it might be.

Carrie began to stock the Warner pantry with simple food items that would keep and be available for Miss Mary to eat whenever hunger finally struck. Carrie kept a wrapped platter or two of small oatmeal cakes and sweet cornbread in the pantry, along with apples and nuts and hard cheeses, and she noted with pride and satisfaction that these items needed restocking on a fairly regular basis. This is all Mary had lived on for the last several months since her father's passing – until a few days ago, when Carrie had noticed (as she noticed everything about the house on the hill) that smoke was issuing from the kitchen cabin just to the back of the house. Carrie had sent Thea up to find out what was going on, and Thea had reported back that Miss Mary was baking biscuits and was carving up the last of the hams that had been hanging in the smokehouse. Carrie's genuine delight at Mary's reawakening appetite and attempts to cook for herself was paired with a disappointment at the loss of a ham she had been planning to use for their Easter dinner next month.

Carrie, in fact, had been making liberal use of many of the Warner stores —justifiably in her mind, since part of it was going to Mary's meals and since Carrie thought it was just compensation for her cooking and cleaning efforts, now that Mr. Warner was no longer making payments. Her husband had forbidden her to bring up the subject of payment with Mary, until at least a year had passed after good Mr. Warner's death. Henry had been devoted to Mr. Warner, and now he was devoted to Mr. Warner's daughter. He would never have asked for money from Mr.

Warner. There had never been any need to ask for money; Mr. Warner had always thought to preempt the need for asking, and paid Henry promptly for any work he did for the family. Sometimes, Mr. Warner even paid in advance. It was likely that Miss Mary was not aware of any of these arrangements, and Henry was not going to burden her about them during the time of her grief.

As word of the Great Tragedy spread throughout the county and beyond, it was realized that Miss Mary, Mr. Warner's odd first daughter, would eventually, if not soon, be in sole possession of a large chunk of land, ideally situated near Louisville, Kentucky's biggest city and river port. Mr. Warner soon learned that questions were being asked in town about the land and matters of solvency, and even about his own health. Although the tactics disgusted him, this flurry of interest in his first and last daughter made him realize that, if he was to have any say in her choice of a husband, he had better form a strategy. Initially, suitors who simply showed up at the farm were summarily dismissed as being unforgivably forward. Mr. Warner then engaged in a letter-writing campaign to invite the sons of old colleagues and war friends to visit Louisville – conveniently located on the Ohio, very nearly in the middle of the country, he would mention – one of the few 'southern' cities to roar back to economic health after the war. He encouraged them to come try their fortunes in this booming city, and, while they were in the locale, to ride out to his farm for dinner on a Sunday afternoon. It would give him great pleasure to see the sons of his old friends and hear reports of their fathers.

Sons of friends came, and sons of friends went. Some reported back to their families that, while Mr. Warner was very likable, Miss Mary was very odd. She performed as was expected of her – presiding over dinner and then sitting demurely in the front room after dinner, at which she had largely remained silent. Some thought she played her role a little too well, that she seemed mechanical, as one modern man prone to modern industrial metaphors called her. Others squirmed under her silent stares that preceded answers to questions that apparently took her some time to comprehend. She was correct, she was polite, but she was odd. Her father seemed to take no notice of it, nor of the discomfort of the young men in attendance. Afterward, he would comment that it had been a pleasant afternoon well-spent.

When all the sons of all the old comrades had proven uninterested, Mr. Warner began inviting to dinner those suitors who simply showed up at the farm. When this was learned in town, there began a steady stream of men of all kinds coming to the Warner farm – young men, old men, the merely curious, and even Protestants (who obviously hadn't conducted even the slightest research into the matter). Mr. Warner's judgment began to fail alongside his health, and he began to see this steady stream of 'eligibles' (as he called them) as a testament to his Mary's beauty and charms. In truth, very little credit could be attached to any charms, and there was nothing truly memorable about her looks. It could be said with perfect honesty that her face was proportioned, her eyes neither too close nor far apart, neither large nor small, of a color green that was unremarkable. In fact, there had been some dispute, among those men who compared notes, as to whether her eyes were blue or green. Only three of the Warner children had inherited their father's crystal blue eyes (and they were all the older sons); the rest had inherited their mother's brilliant emerald green eyes. Except for Mary, who seemed to have absorbed a little of the color, but none of the brilliance, of both parents. The result was eyes of a dull green, except when light hit them at the right angle, at which time they flared into a sapphire blue. Had she been aware of the effect and had she been almost any other woman, she would have endeavored to always present her eyes to this magical angle of light.

Mary would liked to have improved her looks – she wasn't as disinterested as she would have people believe – but it was all so much work and, ultimately, false, a kind of personal counterfeiting. At night, when all the corrections or enhancements were undone, she would see herself for what she was, and so would any husband. It would all have been a bother for nothing.

The one thing she could do nothing about was her height. She was unusually tall for a woman. Her mother had also been tall, as well as her younger sisters, but Mary stood taller than them all. She was as tall as many men, and taller than a few, and this was a source of distress for many prospective suitors. She did nothing to soften the effect of her height – for instance, she did not bend her head low and to one side, so that she seemed to look up to men of equal height, as Carrie had suggested – and many men found her physically threatening or challenging.

The one thing about her she could control to some degree was the complexion of her skin. But she found the effort required to ward off the sun far too much trouble. And, in the end, even total abstinence from the sun did not result in the pale white skin so favored in women. Her complexion was simply naturally dark, and when withdrawn from the sun, it looked sickly rather than fashionably pale. She was not fair-skinned, like every other child but one in the family – the third oldest brother had his father's blue eyes and black hair but, like Mary, had a complexion that tanned deeply and quickly. Even her father and mother were fair, and where this aberration in Mary (and her brother) came from was a matter of amazement for her parents and a matter of uncharitable speculation for others.

Regardless of her looks or her height or her reputed eccentricities, men kept coming down the dusty pike and up the drive to the Warner farmhouse. All these men needed feeding, and they needed to be fed well, if they were to be impressed enough to return. Carrie firmly believed that good cooking could overcome a whole host of other shortcomings in a woman. While it would be Carrie's cooking that would overcome Mary's shortcomings, the effort had to be made, in the hopes that one man more devoted to his stomach than any other matrimonial requisites would come back for seconds.

Carrie had learned from this brief interval in Warner family life – the unproductive courtship of Miss Mary Warner – to keep something handy, if not actually cooking, in readiness for unexpected company. This was especially true for Sundays, and that was why Carrie had been caught off guard this day, a Friday. All vestiges from last Sunday's dinner were long gone. Preparation for this Sunday's main meal would not start until tomorrow. Nonetheless, Carrie had already started a few scrawny chickens for their Friday dinner, and she always had something canned or preserved in reserve. Mary would not eat the chicken or ham, it being Friday when she abstained from flesh, but that left more for her guests. And there was the fortunate availability of biscuits and ham to stave off true hunger while Carried finished dinner. It was by the merest good luck that Thea had espied the two men as they rode far down the road. And luckier still that they had taken their pokey time getting here.

Carrie did not believe in gambling or the idea of chances in any form; indulging in such things was sinful and destructive. But it did seem that luck was playing a very strong hand in the happenings of the day, and if she didn't tend to believe in it or rely on it, she certainly was willing to let it fall where it may, and she would never say a word against it. She had only needed someone (Thea, it turned out, along with her brother Bill) to run from the big house on the hill to Carrie's much smaller one a short distance away, to fetch what foodstuffs she needed to cobble together this meal for these gentlemen – gentlemen, it was becoming apparent, who could be something much more valuable than mere eligibles, the supply of which was rapidly dwindling in both number and quality. These gentlemen might – had to, by explicit order – take Miss Mary from this mournful house to the city of Washington, where even she might find a suitable husband. Surely men in Washington, men who made a living of squabbling and arguing, would find in Miss Mary a suitable sparring partner.

After dinner, Carrie began to clear the table and Mary moved to help her. In the small serving pantry next to the dining room, Carrie took the dirty plates from Mary's hands, and whispered, "You take those gentlemen back into the front room and you sit and listen to what they have to say. Give them that much of your time. You know you'll rest better if you treat them right, before you throw them out the door. In this weather."

Mary looked closely at Carrie, and from her height, Mary's scrutiny bore down on her, but Carrie returned the gaze in equal strength, until at last, in exasperation, she shooed Mary out the door. "Go on, now. It's rude to keep them waiting." As Mary walked along the length of the table, she noticed the stains from dinner. Looking back over her shoulder to where Carrie stood watching her, Mary whispered at her with vicious sass and a curt nod at the table, "I am not washing that table cloth."

There was never any danger that she would. Carrie treated the good linen the same as she did the good china – as if it were her own. Carrie didn't trust Mary with any of the finer things in the house. Carrie would, without a doubt, be the one to wash the table cloth. Then she would iron it, fold it, iron it some more, then lovingly lay it, along with its brood of napkins, in the large linen press in the serving pantry. Then she would quietly and reverently shut the doors. Mary thought of Carrie at those times as like a priest, performing his duties after Holy Communion, gingerly placing the Holy Eucharist in the Tabernacle, then carefully guiding the door closed and, with a tender turn of the tasseled key, lock Jesus away for another meal at another Mass. When Mary was younger, she would sometimes sneak into the pantry and open the drawers of the press to smell the clean, starched linen. It made her think of birthdays and Christmas and Easter and First Communions when the linen was allowed to take the air. But she doesn't do that anymore; she no longer trespasses on the holy domain of the linen press. The smell now reminds her of her mother, and of the many, many times Mary had shirked her share of washings and ironings, and the problems it had caused with the other girls. After a while, her mother had quit asking her to help.

In the front room, Mary resumed the same seat she had occupied before dinner. Merritt and Argent had stood upon her entering and had remained standing, like the puppets they were, until Mary was settled. Then they did an unexpected thing. Rather than take their same seats as Mary had done, they moved to take seats on the other end of the couches. Whereas before, they had been seated at the far end of two opposing couches separated by a table, now they were seated at the near ends of these same couches, putting Merritt to her left, separated from her by a small round table, and Argent nearly directly across from her. Mary had always hated the summer arrangement of this room, but her father had been so ill last summer and fall that rearranging the furniture for winter – with the sofas perpendicular to the fireplace, channeling the heat between the two seats – had been abandoned for the time, and probably forever – Mary could not bear to change a single thing from the moment he had died, even if that meant sitting with her back to the window. She hated it even more now that all the occupants were huddled together in one small corner. She felt unbalanced; the room seemed top-heavy, as if someone had tipped the room up at the far end, and they had all slid forward and down to lay in a tangled heap near the door.

She tried to call up the image of Carrie's face just a few moments ago. Did she miss something there? This all smacked of Carrie. She was far too agreeable on the matter of dismissing Grant's men.

Argent began, "Miss Warner, we hope you'll give us the opportunity of explaining the nature of our visit." He was smiling at her patiently, as if she were addled. A disgust and anger, long her natural reaction to such smiles, was threatening to rise.

"I would be remiss if you came all this way and left without the courtesy of a fair hearing." She sat straight in her seat, with one hand lightly resting in the other in her lap. Her feet were crossed at the ankles and tucked behind one of the legs of her chair. She was wearing a dress now. Not her best dress, but her best-fitting dress. After she and Thea had worn out "Oh, no, the turtles have got out" on the front porch, Mary had fairly run upstairs to dress for dinner. She owed Mr. Henry that much. The poor man had crept from his surveillance, damp and sheep-faced, and headed to his own home, where there was no dinner waiting for him. If wearing a dress would make Carrie happy, then things would go that much easier for him at home.

She looked a good deal different in a dress, almost pretty. Argent decided she could be very pretty, with a little attention. It would certainly help if she were to wear a dress that fit properly; this one was loose and bunched awkwardly as she sat. Occasionally, she tried to surreptitiously adjust the left shoulder of the dress, which continually threatened to slip, an imbalance that had no consequence on her modesty, but which irritated her greatly.

"Well, that is all anyone can ask, especially since we came unannounced." Mr. Argent was speaking, and Mary was favoring him with all the attention she could without seeming to stare, but she was also aware of Mr. Merritt to her left, unabashedly staring at her. How could she pay proper attention to Mr. Argent in front of her, when she was being visually assailed by Mr. Merritt to her left? She felt her dress on her left shoulder begin to slip off. She wanted desperately to grab it and yank it back in place, but there was Mr. Merritt, to her left, watching her. The situation with the dress was maddening, like the itch of poison ivy.

She realized that Mr. Argent had been watching her, possibly expecting some response. She wasn't about to prolong this back-and-forth of polite one-upmanship. She tried to block out Mr. Merritt in her periphery and gazed steadily at Mr. Argent. Apparently satisfied that she truly was listening to him, Mr. Argent continued.

"As Mr. Merritt said before, President Grant has sent us to speak with you on his behalf." Argent had already begun poorly, forgetting the thorny issue of Grant's title.

Immediately, Mary pounced. "He is not my president. I was not extended the right and privilege to vote. And I should think that the General, having a wife and a daughter of his own, would be sensitive to the political disabilities that female citizens must suffer. Yet, to my knowledge, he has made no effort to advance the political standings of women. I wonder at a man who cannot even bring himself to champion the rights of his own female relations."

Argent's practiced smile had slowly faded during Miss Warner's response, until he looked lost and dejected. Mary was smugly satisfied; he had been far too cock-sure of his charms.

Merritt, however, was not deterred by this tirade, and suggested, "Why not move to Wyoming? I hear women have the vote there."

"And why," Mary grated at him, "should I uproot myself from my home to live in some foreign territory with a ridiculous name like Wyoming, just to claim the right as a tax-paying citizen to participate in the choosing of my president? I will stand my ground here."

"The people of Wyoming don't think the name is ridiculous." Merritt was deliberately focusing on the wrong point.

"Well, they can't be held responsible, if they don't know any better."

"They seem to know better as far as the vote goes."

Merritt was pointedly baiting her, and from the look on his face, enjoying it. Just the sight of him was raising her hackles. Argent, realizing that the almost genial tone of dinner was under assault (and at the instigation of his partner – what was he doing?), intervened.

"I think we're losing sight of our topic. We are merely representing the president in a private matter, outside the scope of politics."

"If you insist on his presidency, how can it be outside the scope of politics? And if I don't acknowledge the president, how can I acknowledge his emissaries?"

Argent, after his first clumsy attempts to open the discussion, finally had an inspired thought. "Would you acknowledge emissaries of the General?" Merritt smiled at him, tapping the side of his nose with his finger.

"Certainly. I could treat with you under those terms."

Argent dipped his head slightly and smiled above his irritation. Miss Warner presented a grating mix of quick intelligence and stubborn childishness. He began again. "The General – as a private citizen —"

Mary quickly interrupted. "Are you then being paid as private emissaries? That is to say, with private money? His private money?"

"No, ma'am, we're being paid by the government." Merritt cheerfully responded with complete honesty. Argent thought he could have been more circumspect in the matter, as it clearly was going to be yet another point of contention for Miss Warner.

"The General is using taxpayer money to fund his private correspondence?"

"Taxpayer money was going to be spent regardless – either in attendants and traveling staff and communication costs, if the President were to come here personally – a great expense – or he could send a personal emissary, as you call us – at far less expense."

This was unassailably rational. Argent condescended to explain further, "Even when acting as a private citizen, the President is, in fact, no longer private."

"I grieve for his trying circumstances. Tell me his message and I will give him my reply by mail. That will free you to return to your normal duties, whatever they are, and perform functions of real benefit to the weary taxpayers."

"There seems to be some problem with the mail in this part of the country. In this particular part of the country."

Mary had burned every communiqué sent by the General since her father's death; the last two had never even been read.

"The General's many attempts to reach you by mail or telegraph have all failed to produce a reply. Thus, he felt the need to relay his message through more reliable means. Because of all the mysterious delays of the mails, this is more of a mission than a message."

Merritt was looking at Argent with a wild question and warning in his eyes. Argent was about to disclose the ultimatum that Miss Carrie had promised would create the greatest resistance. It was Merritt's turn to wonder of his partner: what was he doing?

"Oh?" There it was, the challenge already rising.

Argent pushed ahead, heedless of the direction. "The Presi-, the General would like for you to accompany us back to Washington where he would like to meet with you, personally and privately."

There was a short pause, as if she were still listening to the words hanging in the air. Then she gave a sharp, incredulous laugh. If this is what Carrie was hoping to facilitate, she had gone too far in her assumptions about her place in this house.

Without any anger or indignation or emotion of any kind, Mary simply stated, flatly, "That won't happen. That can't happen." Gathering strength from these simple truths, she explained with a little testiness, "This is a farm. Farms succeed or fail on the profitability of the crops. And crops succeed or fail depending on any number of factors – too much or too little rain, unseasonably cool or hot temperatures, pests both footed and winged. The only factor I can control to any degree is the timing of the planting, and the planting begins later this month, if the rain stops and the temperature moderates a little." It had been an unusually cold and wet March; it seemed like it had been unusually cold and wet since her father had died.

Argent spread his smile and arms wide. "That should be plenty of time for a quick jaunt to Washington and back."

The testiness was replaced with weariness, as she led, by the nose, these ignorant dolts to the trough of farming facts. "The planting starts in a few weeks. Preparing the fields has hardly begun because of the wretched weather, and will take all of my time from now until the planting . . . in a few weeks." She added this last, since they were obviously untutored in farming. Repetition, she found, was helpful in learning new things and absolutely essential to teaching idiots.

"Surely you don't do all the plowing yourself?" This was Argent, at least showing some interest in the subject. Merritt seemed to be brooding about something. She liked him better that way – quiet and suffering.

"The plow does the plowing, the horse does the pulling, and I merely guide them both. But no, I don't do it all myself. Mr. Henry helps when he can take time from his own work, and his sons help when they want to earn a little money. Even then I need to hire men from town to finish all the work."

Argent brightened considerably and suggested, a little condescendingly, since he thought of it all on his own and apparently when Miss Warner had not, "Then you could just either hire more workers or hire them earlier to relieve you of some of the plowing and preparing . . . and planting." A bright student, showing away what he had learned.

"I could, but that would eat into any profits I spoke of earlier – you recall? – profits that I would need to buy next year's seed, replace or repair tools, and make repairs to fencing and the barns. And to pay my taxes, which we have also spoken of . . . previously." She heard the nastiness in her voice and regretted it somewhat. She sighed heavily, to expel her sarcasm. "Besides," she added, "how can I call this farm mine if I don't contribute to its running?" Moreover, she heard her father's oft-repeated maxim: *There is no room in the budget for laziness.*

This was the first thing she had said to them all afternoon that seemed to Argent natural, uncalculating, and open.

"I'm not as fast as Mr. Henry or as strong, but I can average an acre and a half a day. If the ground is just right – neither too wet nor too dry – and if the horse is not too tired and if the day is not too hot, I can put two acres under the plow in a day. But I am already behind." She rubbed her temples unconsciously and said, almost to herself, "I should not have left off the work today."

This was, strictly speaking, her first spring in full charge of running the farm. The last four years she had been learning from her father. Even when he was physically no longer able to direct and oversee in the fields, he was constantly reinforcing what she had already learned and adding odd bits and pieces of advice as they occurred to him. In truth, she had been directing the plantings and harvestings solo for the past two years. This, then, was her third spring planting under her sole supervision, and she knew exactly the time and labor it would take for a successful beginning.

But Merritt and Argent were unaware of all this. They suspected that Miss Warner overstated both her involvement and the vicissitudes of farming.

Seeing the patronizing doubt on their faces made the old familiar disgust rise suddenly. The fight returned to her voice. "Does the general think I can ignore the seasonal cycles of this farm simply because he crooks his finger and bids me come sit at his knee? If he wants to apologize for the sins of his past, he will have to do so with a good deal more consideration as to the time and place. And his first apology should be for this outrageous and arrogant summons."

"We don't know about any of the General's past sins," Merritt said quietly, and for once, without any attempt to tease or bait her.

Mary flushed and stood abruptly. "I see that I owe an apology to the General for assuming he has revealed something private, and I owe an apology to you both for assuming you had knowledge of it and were complicit in this venture of his. But now you've had your dinner, relayed your message, and your horses are rested. You'll be wanting to head back now to reach town before dark. If you follow the path from the porch, you'll find the steps that lead down to the barn. Your horses are in the field behind the barn." For all her other social failings, she had mastered the art of the polite and firm dismissal.

She moved to the door that led to the hall and stood there, unmistakably inviting them to leave. At the front door, she left them only long enough to gather their cloaks. Returning these to them, she then said, as she was supposed to in these situations, "I am sorry you have travelled so far to find so little success in your endeavors."

With that final course of her dismissal served, she turned to re-enter the house. Argent saw as she closed the door that she was wearing no shoes, but only stockings. She had not completely capitulated to Miss Carrie's dress code. She had covered this act of defiance by tucking her feet under the chair, behind its leg.

Merritt and Argent had no choice but to reclaim their horses. They descended the porch steps, waded through the jonquils, top-heavy with the intermittent rain that had fallen all day and, subdued by the late chill, bending over the stones of the walk. Some distance from the porch, the walkway fell off into rough stone steps that descended to the horse barn. Part of the barn was built into the side of the lower hill, so that to their left, only a few feet of wall (mostly stone at this end) and the roof peered above the ground, but to their right, nearly the entire wall showed, the stone foundation tapering with the decline of the ground. Behind the barn, the ground leveled out again. What looked like a small corral attached to the right of the barn actually wrapped around the back for the entire length of the structure. Their horses, however, were in the barn; either someone had retrieved them from the field, or the horses had availed themselves of the warmer, dryer barn. Inside the barn, they found one horse standing, spiritless, held in cross-ties in a large stall. The other stood, equally spiritless, in a smaller stall. (Whatever made them think these were acceptable mounts?) The man they had earlier seen emerge from the underbrush now emerged from the back of the barn and came towards them. "One of the horses has thrown a shoe," he said heavily. (What kind of horses were these that could throw a shoe while merely standing in a field or a stall? How long had they been in the barn?) Mr. Henry led the men out of the barn to return to the house.

From the porch window of the dining room, Mary had been watching the progress of the men's egress. She had momentarily lost sight of them as they descended the stone stairs but picked it up again when they moved beyond the hide of the hill. She saw them disappear into the barn, and then emerge moments later, without their horses, but with Mr. Henry. She continued to watch, her stomach lurching, as the three men moved towards the stone steps. They disappeared briefly from view, but then their heads, jerking with each step, rose above the cut of the hill.

She bolted from the house and down the porch steps to intercept the trio, not caring that this would reveal that she had obviously been tracking their movements. Mr. Henry held up his hand in a gesture that not only meant 'halt,' but that also meant there would be no arguing.

Mr. Henry preempted her question. "One of their horses has thrown a shoe, Miss Mary."

She regarded Mr. Henry suspiciously. "Just standing in the field? Those horses don't have enough energy or ambition to toss their own manes, much less throw a shoe."

Mr. Henry gave Miss Mary a look that said, all at once, that he heard the suspicion in her voice, that the suspicion was unfounded, and that he didn't deserve the suspicion.

Merritt and Argent, aware of their good luck, remained silent, letting Mr. Henry handle Miss Warner in her disappointment. There was some Morse code by which they communicated, and Merritt and Argent knew better than to distract an operator when working the key.

Mary, in growing desperation, asked, "But you can re-shoe her? I'll help. I'll get the tools."

She started past Mr. Henry but came back to face him when he told her, wearily anticipating the coming storm that was brewing both in the sky and Miss Mary, "I can re-shoe the horse. Of course I can. But not in time for these gentlemen to reach town before dark, and not in time for them to reach any shelter before more rain comes in. They can't be expected to ride in this rain, and it isn't right to risk the beasts on these roads that can only have gotten worse." He looked up to inspect the sky. It had rained off-and-on all day, and though it was not raining at the moment, there was no doubt that more rain was moving in.

Mary refused to be distracted by meteorology. She stated defiantly what Mr. Henry knew to be true. "These are Mr. Edwards' hack horses.

They know the way home. Even in the dark. Even in the rain. Is that my gun?"

Mr. Henry had been cleaning and oiling it before replacing it in its oilcloth wrap when he had seen Merritt and Argent enter the barn. He forgot he had it in his hand. Mary grabbed it from him and stalked off to the barn to replace the gun herself, and to see just what was the situation with Edwards' nags.

Mr. Edwards ran a stable near the river, where he was able to almost exclusively attract the business of people departing the riverboats, now finding themselves in need of horses or carriages. Most everyone in town knew to avoid Edwards' Stables; only the desperate and uninitiated contracted with Mr. Edwards. He had perfectly good horses, but these he kept in reserve for those customers whose return business he insured by renting to them first those horses sure to disappoint. When these hapless creatures were returned, Mr. Edwards greeted them with loud lamentations and sentiments of concern and surprise, and he greeted his customers with assurances of satisfaction in the replacement horse, which rented at a higher price; it was all he had left to offer. Other stables in town publicly deplored his tactics and privately begrudged him both his success and the prime real estate he occupied that guaranteed such success.

Customers with a more discerning eye for horseflesh were rented a perfectly serviceable horse – maybe not the most responsive or flexible, but perfectly serviceable – but with a guaranteed replacement strategy: Mr. Edwards kept one or more shoes on each of these serviceable horses loosely nailed. It wouldn't take much walking on cobblestone streets or the increasingly disappointing Nicholson paving to completely loosen the shoe, and the horse would lose it. Sometimes, the horse simply walked out of it. Locals, seeing horseshoes lying about the streets, knew the source. Children were given a penny or two for every shoe returned to Mr. Edwards. Some of the more enterprising urchins were practically employés, surreptitiously or casually following his horses as they left the stable, ready to claim the shoe and the additional commission paid for leading the customer back to the stable for the inevitable up-grade, unless, of course, the customers were willing to wait for their horse to be re-shod.

The horses usually threw their shoes within a ten-block radius of Edwards' Stables, so that Mr. Edwards could predict with amazing accuracy the time of any customer's return. This was crucial to timing his lunch and supper hours. Such were the horses Merritt and Argent, in their fatigue and vestigial alcoholic haze, had contracted for use. Mr. Edwards waited for their them, expecting the pleasure of their return business well before lunch. He even delayed lunch, much to the distress of his very regular stomach, to no profit. Eventually, he conceded the lost revenue, saying, "I'll be damned. That shoe held."

Mr. Henry at length followed Miss Mary back down to the barn. Merritt and Argent shrugged at each other and also retraced their steps to the barn. They not only had a vested interest in the outcome of Miss Warner's inspection, but they found themselves looking forward to her next parry and thrust in her determination to thwart their mission. They were observing some kind of play, in which the audience literally follows the actors from scene to scene, occasionally being asked to contribute to the dialogue. It was more diversion than they had hoped for on the steamboat, and it was certainly shaping up to be less dreary than they had anticipated.

Carrie suddenly appeared at the barn, wiping her hands on her apron. She was again wearing her shawl with its corners tucked into the waistband of her apron. She, too, had been watching the interplay, first at the barn, then at the top of the steps. Carrie missed nothing. "What's the trouble?" she asked, and Mary had to silently applaud her for the expertly contrived sincerity of her concern. If Mr. Henry didn't help that shoe along, it had to have been Miss Carrie. Edwards' shoes always came off before a horse left his commercial sphere of influence.

"No trouble. Mr. Henry needs to re-shoe this horse, then the gentlemen can resume their travels." Now it was Mary who was absent-mindedly holding the gun. The shoe had indeed been thrown, and it looked like one on the other horse was ominously loose; it would take only a few steps in this sucking mud to pull it off. How had they made it all the way out here on those shoes? She was lost in thought, staring at the horses, the gun hanging loose at her side.

On cue, Carrie protested, "But surely it will be too dark to ride by the time Henry is finished?" The time required to solve the problem of the shoe and the timing of the approaching dark were dovetailing perfectly. That kind of perfect coincidence was unnatural. Carrie silently thanked the luck of it.

"Horses know the way." Even the heavens were conspiring against Mary. There was more wet weather coming, a storm blowing in; they could all smell the approaching rain.

"Mary –"

"Don't you say it!"

"– Warner!"

Whatever name Miss Carrie was saying was completely covered in practiced and perfect synchronicity by Miss Warner's interjection. Apparently, she had had occasion to drown out Miss Carrie in the past.

"You can't send them out in the night, and it sure to storm, to boot."

'To boot' was something her father said, and Mary resented hearing Carrie appropriate it, especially now as Mary felt a trap closing in on her. Miss Carrie and Mr. Henry (she couldn't believe it of Mr. Henry!) working so hard to send her away to Washington. Thea's complicity. The incredibly bad luck of Edwards' nags. And those two government men, stupid enough to rent these rundown old flea traps (she was not usually so uncharitable towards beasts) in the first place. They were standing there, taking it all in, gawping like a couple of rubes at some carnival or county fair. She didn't like her misfortune and humiliation being put on display like this. She replied savagely, "Well, they can't stay here."

"Mary!" This time it was Mr. Henry. He only dropped the 'Miss' when he was truly astonished at her. A look crossed between him and his wife.

Merritt and Argent finally broke in, to assure Miss Carrie that they were quite capable of taking care of themselves. They were old campaigners, and often endured the elements in the course of their work. Mary found that truly hard to believe. Nothing about their behavior or dress or in the course of conversation with them indicated anything of the sort. That made turning them out all the more delicious. She was feeling spiteful, and it seemed to intensify with the growing energy in the air. The sky was oppressive, the atmospheric tension was building, and Mary thought it would have to burst soon. Her own storm was coming; she could feel it – an oncoming sick headache that was a vise on her temples. She was beginning to discern around the people standing here a growing glow that would eventually obliterate their faces, so that all she saw was searing colors. These men had to leave soon, or she would burst as well.

Carrie headed back up the stone stairs, and Mr. Henry followed an obviously ailing Miss Warner into the barn. He and Carrie both recognized the hollow stare that had come into Miss Mary's eyes. There was nothing to do for what was coming but to leave her alone and wait for her to ride it out. A look also crossed between Merritt and Argent, a realization that perhaps Miss Warner wasn't just spoiled and willful, but troubled and sick as well. Grant did not prepare them for this, and it was becoming clear that convincing Miss Warner to accompany them would not be the end of their duty.

Mr. Henry found Mary in the barn almost in a panic, trying to gather together all the tools and materials Mr. Henry would need to shoe the horse.

She turned to find him behind her with an apologetic look in his eyes. She rushed to say, "Did you find the shoe in the field? If not, I found a shoe that should fit and some nails, and I've gotten the tools together for you. I can bring the horse out here near the workbench if you need more room. I can hold her steady while you work." She was talking rapidly, almost frantically. Her eyes were wild and unfocused, though her mind was completely turned over to the task at hand.

"Miss Mary." Mary stopped at his voice. Mr. Henry released the horse from the cross-ties. "Miss Mary, I can shoe this horse, and I will check all the other shoes as well, so these gentlemen don't have any more problems. It's been a hard afternoon for them, too. But, Miss Mary, it can't be done in time."

She was dirty from her efforts. Her face was black in places where she had smoothed back the wild escaping hairs at her temples with dirty hands. Her dress was dirty, too. The bottoms of her stockings were black. A fine sweat had broken out on her face, even though the weather was decidedly chilly. In her rush to halt the tide of events, she had bolted from the house without any kind of cloak or other covering. Mr. Henry waited patiently while what he said was entirely understood. She was tired, exhausted by the visitors, by the effort it took to listen to them, to Carrie, and to the voices of her parents that Mr. Henry knew were never far from her mind. She was exhausted by her own efforts to stop the stampede of change she felt charging toward her. She stood before him in her moment of defeat.

Merritt and Argent had followed Mr. Henry into the barn, determined to help with the horses, and to assure Miss Warner of their very real intention to leave. They did not understand the nature of her problem, but it was clear that the distress they were causing her was not mere irritation at unannounced guests. They would not give her further cause for distress this night. They would return to town, storm or no, and telegraph Washington asking for advice. They had never asked the director to be excused from an assignment, and certainly they would never turn down an assignment from the President. But it was possible that he had recruited the wrong men for the job. It was possible that the President should have come in person.

Standing just inside the barn, they were guilty observers to Miss Warner's disarray and dismay. She was dirty as no woman should allow herself to become, and certainly not in the presence of guests. But rather than be embarrassed for her, they were full of pity. She was standing, but slouched, in front of Mr. Henry with a pleading and defeated look. She looked like she would collapse. Then from outside the barn, Miss Carrie called, "I've made up beds for the gentlemen for the night."

At that, Mary tore her eyes away from Mr. Henry, unbelieving what she was hearing. Then she saw Merritt and Argent standing there eavesdropping on her and Mr. Henry, and white-hot shame washed over her. She turned back to the work bench where she had been gathering together the impotent armaments of her final assault and grabbed the gun she had laid there.

She pushed past Merritt and Argent and strode to where Carrie stood at the top of the stairs. Looking up from the bottom Mary ordered, "They. Are. Not. Staying."

Merritt and Argent had followed Miss Warner out of the barn, alarmed at the volatile mix of her mood and the gun. Mr. Henry slowly rejoined them. He seemed unperturbed by the powder keg in front of him: a visibly upset Miss Warner, challenging his wife, and a loaded gun in Miss Warner's possession.

Anxious to diffuse the situation, Argent said with finality, "We can no longer trespass on your hospitality. We will be leaving as soon as we are able. We will send to ask if we might be received at a later date."

Mr. Henry looked steadily at Mary's back, so that when she turned at the sound of Argent's voice, she found his eyes on her. He never wavered in his gaze.

The first rumbles of thunder sounded in the distance. Carrie said to Mary's back, "It's coming on to rain."

Mr. Henry continued to hold Mary with his gaze. Cornered, she desperately suggested to Carrie, although she was still looking at Mr. Henry, "They can stay in the barn."

"Mary! What would your father say?"

That was quite enough from Miss Carrie. Whirling back to face Miss Carrie, Mary demanded, "What would my father say, indeed, to two strangers, two men, staying in the house with me and no one else?"

There was more than a little merit to this question, and even Carrie realized it.

Mr. Henry looked to the two men standing a little to the side. He felt sorry for these men, trying their best to do their duty and to do right at the same time. Usually, those were one and the same thing, but as always, where Miss Mary was concerned, things rarely followed the norm. The men had no way of knowing that when they crossed the boundary to the Warner farm, they crossed into a place apart. For Miss Mary, it was a sanctuary from the normal and expected; for visitors it often proved chaotic, disorienting, and unredeemable. He said apologetically, "I mean no disrespect, but I'll be staying in the front room tonight. With a gun."

"Not my gun." Mary turned back to the stairs and mounted them until she and Carrie were at eye level. She met Mary's glare with a steady and confident gaze.

"Whose . . . room . . . did you . . . make up?" Though Miss Warner was facing away from the men standing below, they could hear the words coming from clenched teeth. Merritt and Argent again wondered at Mr. Henry's composure at the seeming threat to his wife.

In a level voice, unintimidated, she answered, "No one's, Mary." She was sure of her decision and sure of her knowledge of Mary. "I've made up the cots in the back room."

The back room used to be her mother's sewing room. It used to be full of pieces of material, spools of thread, all sizes of needles and embroidery hoops, and an oversized table to lay out patterns. Mr. Warner himself had made the clever and beautiful cabinet for Mrs. Warner's prized sewing machine, the whole contrivance so heavy that it had never been moved from its original spot against the long outside wall. Carrie commandeered most of these sewing things, a little at a time after Mrs. Warner's death. She appropriated the remaining items last year, after Mr. Warner's death. She repaired Mary's clothes and darned her stockings. It would never get done, if it weren't for Carrie, so it seemed only natural that these things should reside with Carrie in her home, where they could be of most use. If Carrie had room in the little cottage, she would have contrived to take the table and the sewing machine as well. Miss Mary now used the table to stack books and spread out maps and her father's mechanical drawings to study. It bothered Carrie to see that good sewing table used for the wrong purpose.

Two low cots now accompanied the large sewing table in the back room. Mr. Henry had knocked them together, one for himself to be on hand when Mr. Warner began to fail, and, later, one for Thea when she spent the nights with Mary late last summer and early fall. It was cooler than the upstairs where Mary normally slept, and Mary's nightmares didn't seem to follow her to the back room.

The back room, then, was where Merritt and Argent would spend the night. Mary, having fought a losing battle all day and now having to admit total defeat, could not deny the propriety of it all – she couldn't send them out into the night that threatened to storm, and she should offer them proper beds and shelter – but she hated admitting it and being forced to accept it. Barely stifling a scream in her throat, she whirled away from Carrie and shot the gun in the direction of the barn. Merritt and Argent instinctively flinched and ducked at both her movement and the report of the gun. Mr. Henry had moved to lean with one elbow on the wooden railing of the corral off the side of the barn. With his other hand Mr. Henry wearily pushed his hat back off his forehead.

A large clap of thunder answered the gunshot. Mary strode off away from the house – away from Carrie, away from the stupid horses and their stupid shoes, away from the stupid men who had picked the stupid horses. They had ruined her day, and, because they were too stupid to know when they were being fleeced, looked to ruin the next day as well. Mr. Edwards was losing his touch – that shoe should have been thrown long before these men ever got out of town.

Miss Carrie shouted after her, "Where do you think you are going in those stockings and in this rain? You come back here, right now. They'll be black as soot and you'll catch the pneumony walking around in this rain and cold!" Carrie's penchant for exaggerating the elements was undeniable in this statement – there had not been the first drop of rain since she had first predicted that it was sure to storm. Mary did not answer. She was quickly disappearing on the horizon.

"I wisht she'd pick a target closer to the ground." Mr. Henry heaved himself away from the fence. "I'm getting too old to climb up there and fix that whirligig." Merritt and Argent looked up to see that Miss Warner had shot the crude weather vane perched at the peak of the barn roof.

A delayed breath of relief escaped Argent. But then the possibility of Miss Warner returning for more target shooting crossed his mind. "Is it safe for her to have a gun?"

Mr. Henry laughed at the question, but not unkindly. "The real hazard would be in trying to take it from her. You might want to conduct whatever personal business you need to before you take to your beds. Miss Mary will sleep with that loaded gun next to her tonight. It's best you not leave the back room until morning."

Merritt asked, "Will she be all right?"

Argent was suddenly ashamed that his first thought had been of his own safety. Miss Warner had stalked off, alone and angry, into the cold dark and an approaching storm, with nothing to cover herself, and no one had seemed to care.

"Yes. She just needs her time alone. She don't like change, and you two hauled it in by the wagonload today. I'll start after her and bring her back before the storm hits. But there's no need to worry about her in the dark – she knows every inch of this land, where to shelter. And where to hide."

Mr. Henry started towards the stairs with what looked like weariness but was instead deep sadness. As he approached his wife still standing at the top, Carrie said with just frustration and exasperation, "I can't do this anymore! She needs someone else caring for her!" In a voice low with admitted defeat she added, "She needs an institution."

Mr. Henry patted her on the shoulder and kissed her lightly on the cheek as he moved past her on the top stair. "You don't mean that, Mother."

"I know it."

Merritt and Argent saw to the poor horses, the unwitting cause of so much trouble for Miss Warner and a reprieve for themselves. Merritt released the horse from its ties – surely Mr. Henry would not start the work of shoeing a horse this late, or now that he would be holding vigil with a shotgun in the front room. Argent led it to the stall next to the other Edwards horse, then hooked the rope across its stall.. Other horses had obviously occupied the stalls towards the front of the barn, but where they were at the moment was a mild mystery; there had been no other horses in the corral. Merritt and Argent then did indeed take care of their personal business, each taking one of the outside stalls of a truly convenient and elegant four-door outhouse, some distance from the back of the house. Too many children and too many instances of multiple people ill at the same time had impressed upon Mr. Warner the wisdom of such an arrangement. Mr. Warner and his bowels had shared a deep need for privacy. He was just about to add a fifth installment, when the boys began leaving, and then dying, and the need died with them. The men washed up at the pump just off the back of the house, then let themselves in the backdoor at the end of the central hallway, calling softly to Miss Carrie.

They continued down the hall, each one taking a side, looking into rooms as they passed. On the right, the first room Argent passed had served as the birthing room, a downstairs nursery, and the sick room, but now seemed to be a mere storage room for old or broken furniture, books, and what looked to be surveying equipment. A door to another room beyond this room was directly opposite the door to the central hall. This door was flanked by windows that no longer opened to the sun and wind. Behind that door lay the back room, their bedroom for the night. Next came a room crowded with mismatched chairs, a scratched and water-stained piano, small tables piled with books and toys, and a tall clock. On the piano were pictures of the family, each one taken as each new child was born. Mr. Warner had insisted on chronicling the growth of his family. The old daguerreotypes depicted a young Mr. Warner and Mrs. Warner and their oldest boys. The daguerreotypes gave way to modern photography in the last three portraits, with the births of their last three children. Mr. and Mrs. Warner were old by then. The last and third room on the right was the front room where the day had started, so long ago.

On the left side of the hall, Merritt had looked into the large pantry and store room, that the family called the cold kitchen, where any food that did not require a large open fire could be prepared. Mr. Warner had been adamant on this point. Like the room across the hall, there was a door on the far wall, opposite the hallway door, with two windows flanking it. The windows did not look onto the outside, but into the serving pantry, out of which Carrie had served dinner earlier in the day. Merritt knew from that earlier dinner that the next two doors opened onto the large dining room with its simple but massive table and chairs dominating the space. The middle of the hall was taken up by the wide and sturdy staircase that led to bedrooms upstairs.

Merritt and Argent reunited in front of the stairs, Argent looking towards the front room on his right, Merritt looking into the dining room on the left. Merritt flung out his arm to both warn Argent to remain quiet and to attract his attention. At Argent's questioning look, Merritt nodded at Carrie sitting unaware at the big table.

"Miss Carrie?"

Carrie started, embarrassed at being caught staring into space, and said hurriedly, "Mr. Merritt, Mr. Argent, I didn't realize you were in the house. I didn't hear the front door."

"We came in through the back. Forgive us if we startled you."

It was obvious Carrie had been crying, but she was practiced at covering these rare lapses of indulgence into tears. Getting up and still speaking quickly, she defended herself, "I was just taking a moment between storms, so to speak. Caleb just left. I packed him up with enough food to hold them until I can get supper ready later tonight."

"Miss Carrie, I think we owe you just as much an apology as we owe Miss Warner. You've worked yourself ragged to provide dinner for us under trying circumstances, and I fear we've kept you from your own family. Please do not fuss anymore on our account."

Such unexpected kindness and acknowledgement of her own family very nearly made Carrie cry afresh. Instead she blurted out in frustrated sorrow, "She's a good girl, Mr. Merritt! She tries in her own way. You can't take notice of what she says. She don't mean the half of it. And I know she regrets most of it. As soon as she says some of these crazy and rude things, as soon as the words fly from her mouth, I know she wishes she could call them back. But once she's let them loose, her pride won't let her disown them. She's a good girl, and she does try."

Merritt went over to the chair where Carrie had been sitting and held it for her. "Miss Carrie, please, sit."

Carrie regained her seat while Merritt and Argent moved around the table to take up seats across from her.

Merritt regarded her kindly. "Miss Carrie, you said you'd help us if you could. I don't know how you managed it, but we're grateful for the problem with the horses. We really didn't know how we were going to convince Miss Warner to return with us when we had been so summarily dismissed."

"Oh, I didn't manage anything at all!" Carrie was slightly alarmed that they would think her capable of such direct action. "No, I think that's more of God's doing than Mr. Edwards'. God has been moving things along little by little all day, and the horseshoe was just His way of telling you boys you need to stay and finish your work." Carrie giggled a little. "And He used a horseshoe – for good luck. Ain't that just like Him."

"I'm sorry, who is Mr. Edwards?" This was the first that Argent had spoken since Merritt had first flung out his arm.

"Why, didn't you rent those nags from Edwards Stables? It's no shame on you; he does it to all customers new to the city."

Argent could not, with certainty, say from whom they had rented their horses. They had simply gone to the stables by the wharves as suggested by one of the ladies on the boat. Argent, at least, had never bothered to read the sign above the door. "Does what?"

"Well, in your case, he gave you a horse with a faulty shoe, knowing you'd come back and have to take a more expensive mount. I wonder, though, that it took so long to throw. It does him no good to have you make it all the way out here."

Suddenly, the strange looks and odd comments at the toll booths made sense: 'If you find you need help, just apply to this farm or that house along the way'; 'You boys look like you could use a little walking.'; 'Would you like a little something to eat – you don't know when you might reach the Warner farm.' Luck was indeed with them this day.

"Well, we shall have to have a talk with Mr. Edwards on our way out of town, but for now we'll have to consider it a favor to have been defrauded. It has bought us more time to convince Miss Warner. We cannot go back empty-handed. We would appreciate any help you can give us. Can you tell us of anything that would induce her to leave with us? Some place, on the way, that she has wanted to visit? A desire to travel at all?"

"Did you switch seats in the front room after dinner like I told you?"

"Yes, and it did upset her, but I don't wish to capitalize on any more of her vulnerabilities."

"You poor man! She'd 'capitalize' on your 'vulnerabilities' as soon as she found them. She likes to keep the upper hand. But, no, she don't care to travel. She hasn't even been into town in over a year now. Whenever my Henry goes into town for our family shopping, he always asks Miss Mary what can he fetch for her. It usually isn't much."

"I'm afraid the General didn't prepare us for such resistance. Is there anything at all you can tell us about Miss Warner? Anything that would help us to convince her of the determination of President Grant's invitation."

Carrie regarded the men critically, gauging their worthiness to receive such information. It had not been her place of speak to the rift between Mary and the General, and the private woes of this family were hers to guard. Then, reaching her decision and choosing her words carefully, she said, "It isn't all her fault. The way she is. She was the first daughter after six sons, a daughter the Warners had prayed for. But there was sickness the first year, and no one thought she would live to see her second birthday. Mr. Warner took the care of that sick little baby while his wife gave birth to their seventh son, little Randy. And then right on the heels of Randy there was Mary Margaret."

"So, there were three Mary's? Mrs. Warner, Miss Warner, and her sister?" From habit developed in his work, Merritt was merely confirming facts, and was surprised by her response.

Miss Carrie looked at him quizzically, and explained, "They were all Mary's. Catholics hold great store by the Virgin Mother. Mz. Mary tried to explain that they don't worship the Virgin – that would be blasphemous, like saying there are two Gods – but that they venerate her. It all sounds the same to me, but they seem to understand the 'distinction,' as Mz. Mary called it, so it's all right for Catholics. One of the ways they venerate the Virgin Mother is to name all their daughters after her. Only Mz. Mary was called 'Mary.' The girls all answered to their middle names."

"Then, what is Miss Warner's middle name?" Argent also wanted to express his interest in the story.

"Only the family called her by that name; she fairly hates it. But she answers to Lally. Lally is how . . ." Carrie thought better of what she was about to say, and settled for, "Lally is sort of a pet name, a family name. Only the family calls her that." One could almost hear the capital 'F' whenever Carrie spoke of the Warner family. "Everyone else calls her Miss Mary."

Satisfied that she had cleared any confusion on the point of names, Carrie began again. "Mr. Warner was working on one his of his projects – I don't remember which; he was an engineer and always gone, working for some railroad, mostly – when Mz. Mary sent word that Lally wasn't expected to live. The poor man was devastated, but he devoted himself to her, thinking it would be his last days with her. Mr. Warner took care of his little Lally. I told him, 'Mr. Warner, you let me help you with your girl.' But he wouldn't let go of her. He said he couldn't waste a minute, if she was to leave. He sat and rocked her for hours. The only rest she could get was when she was rocked. I'd come into the room to look in on them, and they'd both be asleep in the rocker, her lying on his shoulder. One big hand of his nearly completely covered her back, he was so big and she was so little. He sang to her and talked to her. He prayed over her.

"For three days he had the sole care of her. On the fourth day, she began to rally. She seemed to listen to her daddy when he spoke. When he ran out of silly things to say to her, he started telling her about his work, about railroads and bridges, dams, steam engines, pressure valves, whatever came into his mind. He just kept up a steady talk, speaking softly, and all the time she was staring into his eyes. Whenever he would stop to rest his voice, she would put her little hand on his lips and try to move them.

"In the evening he said, 'Now, honey, Daddy's got to have a little something to eat and drink. Would you like to join me?' He fed her tiny bites of food off the plate I took into him. She tried to drink from his cup. She was too weak to hold it, but she would rare back and squeal if he tried to help her. So he let her think she was holding the cup – she'd put both hands around it, and he'd put his hand under a towel so she wouldn't see, and he held the cup in place. 'She's an independent little thing,' he said, and I think he knew then that she had made up her mind to stay. And make no mistake about it, he said, staying was her decision.

"For two days she grew stronger and slept and ate better. But no one could do for her but her daddy. He still rocked her for hours at a time – reading to her from his trade journals – but now he could coax her to sleep in the bed. He would lie down with her until she fell asleep, and then he would take a few minutes for himself, look in on his wife and new baby boy, but he always went back to sit with Lally, and rock her if she waked. He built that great swing on the porch for her, so he could rock her outside, and so she could rock herself when she got older. I expect you found her there this morning, swinging herself to sleep.

"The doctor had been to the house several times, to see to Mz. Mary and little Randy, but Mr. Warner wouldn't let the doctor see Lally. The doctor had said the child would die, and Mr. Warner said, 'Tell him to take care of those he can and leave Lally to God and me.' I told the doctor how Lally had started eating and noticing the world again. He insisted that he see for himself. At first Mr. Warner, in his joy, allowed the doctor in, but as soon as that doctor touched Lally and tried to examine her, she began screaming. He kept trying to make his examinations, but Lally began to rare back and make a gurgling sound. She was purple in the face. Mr. Warner took Lally from the doctor and told him, 'I don't expect she likes doctors. You've made her angry,' and he sent the doctor from the room. We never knew what it was that set her off, but to this day she says that she doesn't like the way doctors smell. Can you credit it? She still won't suffer a doctor to see to her."

"It must have been a very difficult time." Argent had grown up in a family dominated by older women, the only boy in a coterie of aunts and female cousins. He knew the appropriate response expected at the telling of these stories.

"The difficult times were to come. The doctor told Mr. Warner not to expect much of Miss Mary's mind. He said the long and frequent high fevers had damaged her brain. And it seemed at first that he was right. She was nearly three before she talked. She seemed to be able to understand what was said to her, but she didn't seem to be able to speak herself. She would point at what she wanted and scream at what she didn't like. Mz. Warner talked of finding an institution for her, but Mr. Warner wouldn't hear of it. But Lally, she watched and noticed everything, storing it away somewhere. When she did start to talk, it was as if she'd been talking all along. In fact, she spoke as well as her brother four years older than herself. And she was reading before she was five."

"There doesn't seem to be anything wrong with her brain. Mr. Warner had to have been happy to find the doctor so much in error." Although Argent found some of the effusions of Miss Warner's brain somewhat acidic, he knew from long practice with female relations that a compliment, no matter how convoluted, was always well received. Merritt gave Argent a look that expressed both admiration at Argent's deft remark and questioning of such generosity of the remark.

If Carrie saw the look, she ignored it. It was enough for her that these men were making the effort to listen. "No, there's nothing wrong with that brain; there's too much right with it, in fact. She's too smart for her own good. No, it's her mind that worries me, and worried her father and mother, too."

"How do you mean? Her mind?" Merritt was genuinely interested now. If they were to escort this woman over hundreds of miles and several days, they needed to know any problems that might arise, both for her sake and theirs.

"She just can't seem to understand her place in the world and her place among other people. So, she has just given up her place; she doesn't leave the farm, she doesn't willingly entertain people," which earned a reflexive 'Humph' from Argent, "and she doesn't hope for anything better. She will sit and stare for hours, and never know anyone was in the room with her. She'll rock on that porch swing for hours, no matter the weather, staring into the distance. She forgets to eat; she forgets what day it is; she forgets where she is even walking. My Henry has seen her far down the lane on the way to town, and when he asks where she is going, she has been surprised to find that she had wandered so far.

"She's exhausted all the time. She was never a good sleeper, but at least her parents could keep her in bed. Now she's up at all hours of the night. She used to keep a lamp or two lit at night, but I made the mistake of remarking on it, and now she wanders the house in the dark. I asked her what keeps her awake and she told me she couldn't stop her thoughts. She said her thoughts were like frogs as far as you could see, and all of them croaking and jumping. She said that if she could catch one and hold onto it, that would make the others stop jumping and croaking, but the frogs are slippery and quick."

Merritt's concern was rising. If she wandered at night, they'd have to take turns watching her. It was at least two days, under optimum circumstances, to Washington, but it could very well become three or four or even more days if there are problems with the trains or trestles or bridges; and in between those days would be nights. Grant had done more than allow them to think Miss Warner was Mrs. Warner; he had withheld information about their charge that could jeopardize her safety, and possibly theirs as well. A little testily, he asked, "Was the General aware of all this?"

Carrie saw his worry and the anger behind it. She answered honestly that she thought he knew some of it but did not know to what extent. "Mr. Warner valued the General's opinion on just about everything, as the General did Mr. Warner's, but I don't know if Miss Mary was something Mr. Warner would discuss, even with the General."

Argent shifted the conversation back to Miss Warner. "Is there anything that can be done for her? At least, as far as sleep? The trip to Washington is such that we can be very regular in our meals, so it will be easy to see that she eats, but there is no safe place or room to roam on a train or in a hotel at night. We would have to lock her in her room, for her own safety."

"Mrs. Warner would get some drops from the chemist in town, and Mr. Warner would bring home other medicines that doctors in Washington or Baltimore were sure would help. But she said they made sleeping even harder. And like everything else about Miss Mary, after a while they just left her alone." This was the first time Carrie had spoken with anything other than complete respect and affection for the Warners. It was obvious that she held the parents responsible for some of Miss Warner's eccentricities, for the way she is. "She won't go see a doctor for herself. But, don't you worry – she won't cause you any trouble at night. She knows to keep quiet at night. And she's awake; she isn't wandering in her sleep."

Carrie paused for a moment, then said with weary sadness, "She's an odd creature, and she knows it. I know that sometimes she wishes she could be different, and sometimes she wishes it didn't make such a difference. But she accepts it – the oddness, the stares from people, the judgments, and even the punishments. She says it is her penance."

"Penance? For what?" There was no one else in the house but the three of them, yet Argent felt the necessity to speak softly.

"For living."

2

Both men slept fitfully. The intermittent rain of the day finally broke into a heavy rain far into the night, the deep thrumming on the roof over the back room first waking, then lulling them back to sleep. At another time they thought they heard movement in the room next to theirs, towards the front of the house. There was no door between the back room where they slept and the room to the front of the house, the locked room off the parlor, so they could only lie in their cots, straining to decipher the sounds. When Argent woke after finally sleeping soundly in the early hours, it was later in the morning than he would have liked. Merritt was already gone from the room. He found Merritt on the front porch, drinking coffee with Mr. Henry. As he passed through the front door, he noticed the rifle leaning in the corner next to the front room.

"Mr. Henry, did you sit up all night with that rifle?" Argent posed the question as if it were more about the quality of the firearm than the length of the vigil.

"Well, sir, I tried. Not because I thought you gentlemen might give trouble. I just know Mr. Warner would rest better if I did. And I'd have to answer to Carrie if I didn't. I hope you slept well."

"Very well, thank you." It was the expected lie to tell, and they both knew it. "I wouldn't mind some of that coffee, though, to chase away the cobwebs."

Merritt and Mr. Henry were standing, watching another cloudy, damp, and chilly morning develop, drinking out of substantial ceramic mugs. Miss Carrie would not allow the fine china to leave the house.

Coffee was in the cold kitchen, one of the few things allowed to be heated there, on a small but heavily fortified stove. This stove was placed against the outside wall, which was tiled all the way to the ceiling. The floor for three feet in all directions around it was bricked. Two covered buckets, one of water and one of sand, stood at the ready on either side, in the case of runaway fire. In truth, the stove was so little that not much of a flame was needed to warm the cook top. Coffee could be brewed and soups heated at the stove, but not much else. Mr. Warner had a long repertory of sad stories of houses and families in flames because of precautions not taken or stoves left unattended. And never, never, was anything more flammable than a match to be used to start a fire. Mr. Warner had read far too often of children horribly burned and dead because they wanted a quick way to start a fire, using kerosene or some other incendiary material.

Argent filled a mug for himself and rejoined the other men on the porch. Henry was saying, "I found Miss Mary soon enough and we had a talk. We come to an agreement about hearing you out and giving it due consideration." Argent was amused at the slight emphasis Mr. Henry and Miss Carrie placed on certain words and phrases, as if they were borrowing them and great care had to be taken in their custody. "She came in after me, but ahead of the storm. She slept in Mr. Warner's study, though I don't think she really slept. Always been a poor sleeper. She is crafty quiet when she wants to be. I never heard her slip past me in the front room, but she was gone when I got up this morning. I expect she's taken Emmett for a ride – Emmett gives her great comfort, and the weather this last week or so has not been conducive to riding."

Both Merritt and Argent were about to enquire about Emmett when Mr. Henry nodded toward the woods to the south below them. Miss Warner was just coming into view from the southwest, riding at a slow walk on a huge horse, one of the draft horses that had been very slowly gaining popularity in the country. A Percheron, Mr. Henry informed them, in a terrible French accent.

They all stood, with mugs in hand and watched – Henry with a wry pride on his face, and Merritt and Argent with astonishment on theirs. Miss Warner was tall and of middling frame, but even she was dwarfed by this brute of a horse.

"That's Emmett!?" Merritt finally asked in understandable disbelief.

"Yes, sir, he is." Mr. Henry was enjoying the shock that the sight of Miss Mary on Emmett always brought. "He was a gift from Mr. Warner for Miss Mary's eighth birthday. Or was it her ninth? I lose track of these things, but Carrie, she would know. She keeps a ver-i-ta-ble calendar in her head." 'Veritable' was not a word on loan, just one that needed extra marshaling.

"Mr. Warner gave his daughter that . . . beast!?" It was Argent's turn to question the credibility of this horse and Mr. Warner's parenting judgment. Merritt and Argent were practiced partners, often working in unconscious tandem even in the simplest conversations.

"He was bound to, by his own promise. The Warner children – all of them – were smart, like their father. There were times when they would all be together, and the words would fly back and forth between different ones and different groups of ones, all at one time. Many times, they didn't even need to finish what they were saying, because they could anticipate what the other intended. And every word they said – even the little ones – had two or three meanings to it at once, and almost always meant to tease, or worse. Mz. Warner was lost to most of it, but Mr. Warner would just sit and watch and listen and smile at the things they said and didn't say. He could follow them, but I think even he was surprised sometimes at the things they said." Henry was smiling at the thought of the happy chaos that used to burst from the doors and windows and roll down the hill. In happier days.

"And the promise?" Argent prompted.

"Oh. Mr. Warner didn't like laziness in body or mind, so he made those children use their minds whenever he could. It was his opinion that their schooling was just the beginning of their learning. He would have the boys go over the accounts. Each of them had their own set of books, and each of them had to reconcile to Mr. Warner's books. He had the girls do something of a kind with Mz. Warner's budget, so they wouldn't get soft in their numbers.

"Now, for their birthdays, they could have anything they wanted if they submitted a requisition and Mr. Warner approved it. Mr. Warner wanted them to learn how to write with pre-cision, to think with the logic and to consider every point, from every angle. He wanted them to think and write like engineers. They knew how to write polite letters and thank-you's and such, and they all were quick thinkers, but he wanted them to know how to write with deliberate thought and rationale. He told each one, as they got old enough to understand, that whenever he needed anything for his work, he had to submit a requisition. He had to explain why he wanted the material or the tool, why it had to be this thing and not that, what he expected it to cost, where it could be got, and the future value it would retain, and a lot more of what he called 'specs.' 'Specifications,' you understand."

Merritt and Argent nodded their solemn understanding of requisitions and the specifications required.

"So, they could have anything they wanted if they could convince him of its need and value and cost and so on and so forth. Miss Mary wanted a horse in the worst way. The boys all had horses. Now, Randy had just gotten his a few months earlier, and she was pickled with jealousy. Randy was normally so generous with Miss Mary, but he wouldn't let her near his new horse, and worse, he began to parade around in front of her and tease her. He'd say, 'It sure is useless to be horseless.' He'd say, 'Com'on, Lally, lets us go hunting,' or over to the south fork, or somewhere or another. She'd get all excited at being invited, then he would say – the little devil – 'Oh, I forgot, you don't have a horse; I hope you can keep up.'"

Merritt and Argent were smiling broadly at the image Henry was painting for them. Thinking of Miss Warner as a sister being teased by her brother made her seem more approachable, their mission more attainable. She couldn't be so different and difficult as they had first thought.

"Now Randy didn't get a new horse, mind you, but the oldest horse on the farm, just about past its use in the fields. That horse had been handed down from boy to boy, as his particular horse to care for, either when Mr. Warner got a new horse for the farm or when one of the older boys bought a horse of his own. In this case, it was both. Anselm had just gotten his own horse, so Mr. Warner's three work horses shifted down one boy, so that now Randy – the last boy – had a horse. And it was just about time for Mr. Warner to get a new horse."

Down below, Miss Warner and Emmett had stopped. Miss Warner, who Argent just now realized was riding *astride*, turned in her saddle, her attention held by something behind her.

Mr. Henry was also scouting in the same direction as Miss Warner. He continued to scout while he returned to the story. "So, Miss Mary, she asks for a horse for her birthday, and she writes up her requisition. Mr. Warner told me, 'Henry,' he said, 'that requisition was better written and better reasoned than most communiqués I see from people who make their livings by them.' She had researched in town at every opportunity how much a horse cost – a new horse, a second-hand horse, a young horse, different breeds of all kinds – and how long they can work or how much they can pull, how much feed and care they need and those costs, and so on and so forth. Mr. Warner said he could not in good conscience deny the request. But, now, Mz. Warner was dead set against it. 'You just give her a horse,' she said, 'and there will be no reining her in. A horse is the last thing that girl needs.'

"Well, like I said, Mr. Warner was bound to give her a horse. But he was determined to respect Mz. Warner in the matter as well. So, he took me with him over to Lexington, and we spent nearly a week looking for the best horse for the occasion – that is to say, the worst horse we could find. Finally, Mr. Warner heard of a horse over in Paris that seemed to fit the bill."

Merritt's curiosity was piqued. "Pardon me, but what do you mean by the worst horse you could find? Why would Mr. Warner want to give to his daughter anything but the finest he could afford?"

Mr. Henry chuckled at the question. "That way, Mr. Warner could keep his promise to Miss Mary and keep his peace with Mz. Warner. But it had to be the right kind of worst horse, you see. If we just brought back a broken-down old nag, like you two gentlemen were pleased to ride" – Merritt and Argent smarted under the casual ridicule – "she'd know what he was up to. So, Mr. Warner decided to go in the opposite direction, so to speak. When we first saw Emmett, he was biting his stall mates and kicking at the stable hands. He was too tall and too wide for Miss Mary. He was too stubborn and too much work in the upkeep. He was too much everything; he was too much horse. Mr. Warner said, 'He's perfect.'

"Mr. Warner's thinking was that this horse was so ornery and oversized that Miss Mary would concede defeat. How he ever came to entertain that thought, I'll never know. Anyway, Mr. Warner could then put Emmett to the plow and make use of that powerful body. We liked to never get home, though, trailing that beast behind us. He bit our horses and he tried to bite us. He ran ahead of us on his lead, or he pulled hard to the rear. He wouldn't eat when we fed him or drink at the creeks with our horses. He didn't like his old home and he was already sure he wouldn't like his new home. When we stopped in Midway for the night, no stable would take him. Other buyers had already been through the town with him, as he was sold from farm to farm in the area. Everyone who bought him thought they could break him to the harness. Everyone thought they were more horse expert than the rest. Everyone ended up selling him. I said, Mr. Warner, I think we've been de-frauded with this here horse. But, Mr. Warner just laughed and said, 'Well if no stable will have him, then he'll just have to be hobbled and left to his isolation in the field.' And he laughed again and said, 'The more I hear of this horse, the more I like him for our purposes. I may get out of this conundrum yet.'"

Though neither Merritt nor Argent was married or fathers, they nonetheless felt a true brotherly sympathy for Mr. Warner's conundrum. There weren't many men who had not at some point in their lives found themselves between a rock and a hard place, where women were concerned, and poor Mr. Warner found himself between a wife and a daughter.

Miss Warner, apparently satisfied with her observations, had urged Emmett to resume his walk. Mr. Henry continued staring into the southern distance, then he, too, seemed satisfied with what he saw, and turned to give his full attention to Merritt and Argent.

"We finally got home and pulled Emmett into the yard below there. Of course, Miss Mary had been on the lookout for us, and she came flying down those stone steps to see her birthday horse. Now, I have to emphasize here that there has never been a man I admired or respected more than Mr. Warner, nor a smarter man to my mind, but sometimes he seemed a little addled where his children were concerned. There was never any doubt in my mind that no matter what horse Mr. Warner brought home Miss Mary would claim it and cherish it in her own peculiar way. Mr. Warner sometimes relied on other people being as reasonable and practical as he was. When it comes to her pets, though, there is nothing reasonable or practical about Miss Mary.

"She loved that monstrous mount immediately. And the funny thing was, he loved her right back. That cantankerous horse, so much trouble on the road with two grown men to handle him, bent his head and let Miss Mary kiss him and stroke him and look him right in the eye. I was afraid for her. That horse was so big next to Miss Mary – his head alone was almost as long as she was tall. But that never gave her pause. She kissed her daddy over and over again, and he just stood there, amazed at all his scheming come to naught. At the top of the stairs stood Mz. Warner, equal parts amazed and angry. Mr. Warner just spread his hands and shrugged his shoulders. He was honor-bound to give that to horse to Miss Mary."

"But at eight? How could she possibly have ridden it at such a young age?" Argent was mesmerized at the sight of Miss Warner on Emmett as a young woman; he could not imagine her on such a horse when only eight.

"There were what Mr. Warner called *caveats* attached to Emmett. She was to understand that Emmett was a work horse first and, like he told all his sons when they were given a work horse for their own use, the horse was not to be ridden on days when it had been in the field. But Mr. Warner had no fear of Miss Warner riding Emmett – she had no saddle. The older boys owned their own saddles, and the younger ones shared two old saddles that had been handed down with all the old horses."

Mr. Henry turned back to see Miss Mary reach the barn, Jack and Morty, the objects of both their scrutiny, finally catching up to her. As she dismounted, her dress caught on the bullhorn, pulling her skirt up in the back so that the men could see the backs of her bare legs well above the knee. She gave a savage yank to free her skirt. Mr. Henry quickly turned away and gathering in Merritt and Argent with a look, suggested, "Breakfast should be on the table soon."

Breakfast was not yet on the table, but there was a fresh pot of coffee on the stove in the cold kitchen and the men, by unspoken consent, refreshed their mugs there. They had lingered there, admiring the efficiency of the arrangement between the kitchen cabin back of the house, the cold kitchen, serving pantry, and dining room. Mr. Henry was proudly recounting the additions and improvements Mr. Warner had made (and with which Henry had helped) to the home over the years. They had moved into the hall, standing before the first of the two dining room doors, where Mr. Henry was explaining how the dining room had at one time been two separate rooms. The expanding family needed ever larger tables, which usually were mere trestle tables – at one time an old door had served as the table top – until there was no more room for a larger table. Mr. Warner and Mr. Henry tore down the wall that separated the dining room from what used to be a second front room, where Mz. Warner would invite female friends to take tea with her. Female friends stopped calling as they, too, had broods too large to trail behind them. Taking down that wall created the large dining hall as it was now. It also required moving the fireplace and chimney, that the two rooms had shared, to the outside wall, by far the greatest work to be done in the renovation. Mz. Warner insisted that a proper table invest the space, and so Mr. Warner had some fine table legs turned for him at the mill, as well as great slabs of wood cut and sanded to his specs. When they were all delivered to the house, he put the table together inside the dining room, the long planes of wood entering through the window that looked out onto the porch. "That table," Mr. Henry assured Merritt and Argent, "can only leave the house if the room leaves with it."

The heavy front door opened and closed, interrupting Mr. Henry's tour of the first floor. Merritt and Argent ducked around the back of the staircase to emerge on the other side of the hall. Miss Warner was walking toward them, but looking down at her mud-splattered skirt, holding a long rip together with her right hand. She was still wearing the dress from the previous day, but it was now hopelessly stained with the black film that seemed to cover every piece of metal in the barn and with the dirt of the barn and with the fresh mud from her morning's ride. Although the color in her face was high, the skin under her eyes were bruised from lack of sleep.

From the dining room, Carrie called out, "Did you sleep in that dress?" Walking into the hall from the dining room door at the front of the house, she continued, "Did you ride that devil horse in that dress?" She finished with, "I am not washing that dress."

"You don't have to. I'm throwing it away. It doesn't fit anyway, and I just ripped it on the horn. This is why I don't wear dresses when I ride."

Enlarging the dining room had given that room two doors, indistinguishable from each other, as were all the other doors in the great hallway. The family early on abandoned clumsy attempts to distinguish one dining room door from another by simply retaining their original designations: the parlor door (nearest the front door) and the dining room door (in the middle of the hallway). Mary had already passed the parlor door but turned to answer Carrie and to flash Carrie the long tear in the front of her dress. She was smiling at Carrie's wondering dismay as she turned to continue on her way. She was surprised to see Merritt and Argent standing to the left of the staircase, watching her, and Mr. Henry to the right of the staircase, studying the floor. She recovered quickly from her surprise, and acknowledged each man, beginning pointedly with Mr. Henry. "Mr.

Henry. Mr. Merritt. Mr. Argent." She looked at each in turn, then said placidly, "You'll excuse me," and walked up the stairs to her room, revealing stockings that had pooled around her ankles and were completely black on the soles. Whatever shoes or boots she had worn had apparently been abandoned on the front porch before she entered the house.

Carrie called after her, "I'm not darning those stockings."

"I didn't ask you to," came singing down the stairs.

"You can't keep throwing away good clothes just because you're too lazy to wash or mend them." The returning silence said that she very well could.

Thea had come to stand in the parlor doorway, drawn by her mother's exasperation. Carrie turned to Thea, instinctively knowing she was there, watching everything. With a look and a nod up the stairs from Carrie, Thea went out the back door, filled a pewter pitcher with water from the pump, then carried it – very carefully – up the stairs. Miss Carrie announced with the anticlimax heavy in her voice, "Breakfast is ready."

When Mary came down, she was clean, with her hair tied back tightly, still wet from her morning ride's sweat, despite the morning chill. Apparently, her stock of male clothing was deep enough to provide a clean pair of pants (black) and a clean pale blue shirt. She wore shoes today, some kind of moccasin or slipper.

Mary poked her head through the dining room door to wish Merritt and Argent a pleasant ride back to town and a speedy return to Washington. The door to the pantry opened directly across from her. Carrie came in carrying a tray full of bacon and sausage, biscuits and toast. Already on the table, Mary noticed, were the fancy little jam dishes of her mother's, sitting in their silver baskets joined two at a time by a simple silver arch. Even when her mother was alive, these dishes rarely left the china cabinet where they seemed to be in perpetual curtsey to the world. In them were strawberry and blackberry jam and peach preserves. Each little crystal dish had its own little silver spoon. Mary also noted that the good china was being called into service again, and that the silver coffee service was sitting at the end of the table nearest the pantry door. For the first time she realized what had been tickling at the back of her mind ever since she had entered the house: the smell of coffee. There had been no coffee in the house since her mother died. Only her father and mother ever drank coffee, and her father couldn't bear the smell of it after the death of his wife. Mary noticed it all, as well as Carrie's pride in presenting it all. A cold, black thick tar began to form and spread just under her scalp. She turned to leave, but Carrie called her back, cheerfully announcing, again and with more spirit, that breakfast was ready.

"I'm not hungry this morning. You all enjoy your meal."

She turned to try and escape a second time, but Carrie insisted, "But, Miss Mary, I know you didn't eat last night, and I got up early to fix you my pancakes you like so much. All this good food is going to waste. Sit down, now, and eat something."

Miss Carrie knew Mary was required to fast during Lent, but she was showing away – full of good morning humor and concern – in front of these two dandies, who were sitting with complete ease at the family table, when they should have been gone last night. Mary felt the tar begin to drip down the back of her throat.

Argent, smiling, said, "No successful enterprise ever started on an empty stomach." He emphasized this grating platitude with an expansive gesture that said, *Please join us at your own table; we hope you'll accept our invitation.*

"I shall have to write that in my diary tonight."

From the far side of the table, Carrie slapped hard the side of her thigh. From behind her in the hallway, Mr. Henry coughed gently.

Whatever message was conveyed in that cough, Mary understood it, and in a tone meant to conciliate agreed, "Perhaps I should eat a little something after all."

As if he had put a hand on her shoulder, Mr. Henry gently guided her into the room, both following her and blocking her retreat.

Merritt and Argent were standing by the same seats they had occupied yesterday, a small source of comfort to Mary. That she was already considering these seats as their seats was a little disquieting. No one had eaten breakfast in the dining room since the Great Tragedy, Mary and Mr. Warner taking morning and midday meals together at the rough table in the cold kitchen, where large amounts of food had once been prepared for a large family. Likely it was Miss Carrie who had decided on the seating arrangement at the mid-day meal yesterday. Carrie liked her meals to go smoothly, so for Miss Mary's sake and the sake of her meal, she had placed the settings in the middle of the table; Miss Mary liked visual balance.

Mary resumed the seat she had held yesterday, as well. In fact, she had sat in that same seat all her life, for every meal, until there was no one left to sit with her. When her father died, Mary never bothered to keep up any meal-time ritual, once so central to the family. If she ate at all, she ate food that did not need cooking or, sometimes, even plates or utensils. Nuts and apples and cheese by the fire in the winter, or on the porch in better weather, with the dogs.

There was no tablecloth this morning, only place mats and trivets under the plates and dishes. She was becoming familiar again with every scratch on the table and every line of pattern on the wallpaper on the wall across from her seat. This was the only room that had wallpaper, a great gift from her father to her mother one Christmas. Until yesterday, it had been months since Mary had sat in this room, for a meal or for any other reason. Now, dining here once again, memories of all the rebukes she had received sitting in this chair came darting into her mind, like mosquitoes, diving and buzzing, but unable to escape as one by one they were claimed by the sticky black tar pooling and spreading in the back of her mouth.

Thea brought in a large silver platter with an ornate top. Mary followed its progress to the table – it seemingly floating in the air – to settle on the middle of the table nearest Mr. Argent. This was all too much for any morning but a Sunday or holy day, and an affront to the dignity of the dish. That dish was always used for asparagus and only on Easter, and here Miss Carrie had filled it with common potatoes and onions fried in bacon drippings. Thea, unaware of the cause of Mary's scowl and brooding, looked at Mary, worried, and tentatively offered, "I'm sorry for yesterday, Miss Mary."

Mary looked up and saw Thea for the first time, standing there. With real effort, she tried to smile for Thea. "We will speak of your treason no more. Except to say: let it not happen again." Then Mary patted the chair next to her and Thea, happy at such generous forgiveness, bounced into her seat between her two most favorite people, Miss Mary and her papa. Carrie poked her head around the pantry door, obviously looking for Thea who had failed to report back for further duty. Henry looked at his wife and gave a little shake of his head, and she withdrew, feeling put upon for having to both cook and serve.

Merritt and Argent were obviously enjoying their breakfast, and Mr. Henry, as always, ate at a slow and steady pace. Eating was a mere duty to the body for him and he performed this duty like any other — with deliberation and exactitude, and with no comment. Carrie was an excellent cook, but he rarely told her so. Argent broke from his conversation with Merritt to remark that Mary's plate was still empty. "Here, try these potatoes. They're really quite good." He had the audacity to drop a large spoonful onto her plate, reaching far across the table. To her right, Thea was piling bacon next to the uninvited potatoes; Thea knew Miss Mary loved bacon above all meat. Mary was watching it all as if from a distance. The scratches on the table were beginning to lift themselves off the table. She felt the tickle in the back of her throat, from the drip, drip, drip of the tar. If breakfast didn't end soon, she would scream.

Carrie – martyr Carrie – finally joined the group for breakfast, sitting at the head of the table near the pantry door. No one could really fault her for sitting there – it gave ready access to the pantry if anyone should need anything – but it rankled; that was her mother's place. Before Carrie even took the first bite, she took aim at Mary's clothes.

"Mary, honey, why would you wear those clothes down to breakfast? I know yesterday you weren't expecting guests, but now you know they're here, you should dress properly."

The tar was choking her. "I had intended neither breakfast nor guests this morning. If my present state is so alarming, please do excuse me."

Mary rose, but Thea tugged on her sleeve. "Mama, no one can see her pants when she's sitting, just her nice shirt. Please, Miss Mary." Thea tugged harder, until Mary sat again. But, by now, any inclination Mary had to acknowledge Carrie's breakfast had evaporated. She sat watching the scratches on the table rise and fall; some of them seemed to move like busy little worms. She closed her eyes to shut out the squirming scratches.

Merritt and Argent regarded her closely, unsure what to make of this odd breakfast with the formal tableware, the casual food, and at which the neighboring colored woman sat at the head of the table. Most confusing of all was the strange woman sitting across from them. As they watched, she closed her eyes against some unknown irritant.

Mr. Henry took no notice of any of this. He kept up his steady pace of eating, but stopped long enough to ask, "Miss Mary, what have you got planned for the day? I doubt we'll be able to get into the fields, but if you need any help in the barns or sheds, I can find some time."

Merritt pounced on the opening. "We would welcome a chance to earn our bread, so to speak. Please, let us make some amends for our intrusion, and lend a hand."

Mary opened her eyes to find both Merritt and Argent looking at her hopefully, but also with that maddening concern that usually heralded talk of doctors, purgatives, and restful stays in faraway 'spas.' Across the table from Mr. Henry, his three boys looked up hopefully at the possibility of help.

Ignoring Merritt's offer, Mary said, "Thank you, Mr. Henry, but I won't be working in the fields or the barns today; I have other matters that need tending."

"Then I'll be going along with you, if you plan on tending matters on the back end of the farm."

"There is no need."

"What is on the back-end of the farm?" It was really impertinent for Merritt to be asking such questions. Mr. Argent cleared his throat.

"There's an army captain that's sweet on Miss Mary." Mr. Henry gave Thea a soft slap on the thigh with the back of his left hand. Thea looked down at her plate, chastised.

Mary shot an angry stare at Thea, then amended Thea's statement: "An ex-army captain that's sweet on the right-of-way through my back end."

There was the slightest pause on the other side of the table, which Mr. Henry covered smoothly with the explanation, "Captain James wants to lay tracks across the back of the farm to connect with tracks on the other side of Jeffersontown, coming from Shelbyville, with the L&N's tracks west of here. He wants to buy land from Miss Mary for a right-of-way for a train. For the facilitating of fares and freight, you understand. A right-of-way through the back end of the farm." Mr. Henry had looked straight ahead during this explanation, then calmly resumed eating.

"It will be over my cold, dead body before he, or anyone else will defile this land with railroad tracks and all the dirt and noise that goes along with them. Think how the cattle will react."

"Captain James would like to buy your cattle, too. Then you wouldn't have to think about any reactions. And do not speak of cold, dead bodies at table."

"Ex-Captain James wants to steal my cattle. He wants to feed his railroad crews prime beef at wartime prices. I'm not in such a need to sell my cattle. It was a crime – and never punished, either – the prices they paid for pigs in the war."

"Let sleeping pigs lie. You may not be in need now, but it just takes one bad harvest, or not even so bad a harvest, and you'll be begging him to take your cattle. It won't hurt to have a little store set by, even if it is from Captain James."

"He said the railroad has a right to her land if it needs it." Thea was defiant and defensive for Miss Mary. "But that isn't so, is it?"

Though Thea had addressed no one in particular, it was assumed that these men, both new to the subject at hand as well as connected with government matters, would respond.

"Well, once a railroad has decided upon a course of action, it tends to pursue that course of action to its successful completion."

Argent supplemented Merritt's words with an action of his hand – fingers together, thumbs up, his fingertips dividing the air like the prow of a ship — the railroad pursuing its actions. He let his hands fall with a thump on the table, and made a half-turn, half-nod of his head that said, 'Yessirree bob!' All during this pantomime he was smiling at Mary and chewing. And people said she had bad manners. Usually she had trouble understanding the subtleties of people's words, but these two were easy to perceive; perhaps because their thoughts were un-evolved and unsophisticated. "It's all part of the glorious expansion of our times."

"Well, it is a slipshod way to oversee an expansion, allowing railroad companies to run wild all over the nation. Grant will never see a second term." Mary said this with satisfaction and vengeful anticipation.

"Miss Mary, it is unkind and unChristian to hope for the ill-luck of others."

"Yes, Mr. Henry." Though Miss Warner had spoken submissively, the eyes that swung slowly between Merritt and Argent were anything but submissive.

This time it was Argent who pounced on the opening. "Perhaps we could help. The government is very interested in the workings of the railroads. We could let the President know of the situation. I'm sure he could direct you to the proper authorities to contact, to help find a solution to your liking. We might even be able to present your case directly ourselves.

We are, after all emissaries of the President; we could look the situation over and hopefully find a solution to your liking."

"I couldn't possibly ask you to do so." Mary delivered this refusal slowly, though she was considering the advantages to their intervention.

"There's no need to ask; we'd be happy to do it."

Though it was very tempting to have such men – with apparently easy access to the power centers of Washington – find and make the necessary contacts for her, Mary decided against it. She would not place herself in debt to the General, no matter how far removed. The threat of the railroad was not urgent, not yet. Moreover, these two men were finding too many reasons to extend their unwelcome stay. "I thank you, but, no. I'm sure the General is expecting you back soon. And, as I said, Mr. James is a mere mercenary, a land speculator for some railroad that doesn't even exist yet."

"It exists enough that he has laid tracks practically to your western property line."

Mary ignored Mr. Henry's last comment. Looking over Thea's head to him, she half-stated and half-asked, "The horses are ready?"

Mr. Henry nodded in reply, though he never turned to look at Mary. "All the shoes have been checked. The gentlemen can leave as soon as they are ready."

Carrie had left her seat at the table to refill some of the dishes, though no one could possibly be in danger of going hungry for want of food. She returned at this last question.

"Well, they can't leave yet. I've got a roast cooking for dinner. Who's going to help to eat it, if these gentlemen leave after breakfast?" She said it in a cajoling way, expecting a cajoling reply – 'Why, we couldn't possibly leave Miss Carrie under such a burden. Of course, we'll stay.'

Instead, Mary said, lifting her eyes slowly to meet Carrie's as she sat at the head of the table, "Perhaps the family you have been neglecting these two days will be glad to eat it." Mary tasted tar in her mouth. Carrie needed to be taken in hand. This house was Mary's and Carrie would do well to remember it. Miss Carrie did not set policy here, decide on dinners or dinner guests, or comment on Mary's dress, habits, or duties. And she certainly could not be allowed to do so in front of guests in Mary's own house.

Carrie sat impossibly still, staring at Mary. Then she looked to Mr. Henry. Surprisingly, Mr. Henry said nothing, but kept eating in his slow, steady pace, his eyes straight ahead.

Argent was giving Mary a very stern, disapproving stare, which she pointedly ignored. Merritt spoke up in the stunned silence. "We've been very grateful, Miss Carrie, for your labored attentions. We've never enjoyed a better breakfast."

"Yes, Mama, thank you for breakfast." Thea looked frantically from her mother to Miss Mary, but even she could not bridge this widening chasm between them. Carrie rose slowly mumbling about seeing to some other dish, no doubt waiting to make its debut in another of the china serving dishes. Mary continued to stare at the place where Carrie sat, even after she had retreated into the pantry.

He was a guest and it was not his place to comment on the shortcomings of his hostess, but Argent could not let such cruel treatment of a woman who had invited him in, fed him, made a bed for him, and whom he knew to have Miss Warner's best interests at heart, go unanswered. He said reproachfully, "That was uncalled for."

Mary slowly shifted her eyes from the pantry door to the man who had looked so concerned only a moment before. She seemed to look beyond him, though she locked eyes with him. "That is not your call to make." Then Mary also rose, slowly, and left the room, and then the house. In the dining room, they heard the soft click of the front door being gently closed.

Mr. Henry said to Thea, "Go help your mother." With a nod to his boys, they gathered up what they could carry from the table, and also left through the pantry. When the children had disappeared behind the pantry door, Mr. Henry said to Merritt and Argent, "Don't judge Miss Mary too harshly in this matter. I know my wife – she takes liberties with this house and with Miss Mary. Carrie can't stand to see something go undone – the laundry, the cooking, the cleaning, sewing, or nursing – so she does it. Miss Mary truly don't care one way or another whether the house is clean, or the clothes are washed, or even if she eats and sleeps regularly, or gets sick. She never asks Carrie to do these things or to help her in any way. It's no way to live, but Miss Mary can't be expected to live by someone else's rules in her own house. And it is her house. I see it build up in Miss Mary, and there is a battle coming. Right now, Miss Mary and my wife are in a dance they don't know the steps to, or who's supposed to lead. My wife has known this house longer than Miss Mary and she loves it like Miss Mary loves the land, but it is Miss Mary's house.

"This isn't their first go 'round, and it won't be their last. I'll tend to my wife later, and I know Miss Mary will apologize in her own time and in her own way. Right now, I think I'd better see what Miss Mary is up to. Sometimes she needs direction when she's in a state."

Merritt and Argent left the house with Mr. Henry and found Miss Warner re-saddling her enormous horse in the barnyard, the missing 'boys' of yesterday lolloping and trotting around her efforts. The boys were her two foxhound puppies, though at only nine months they were already tall and close to ninety pounds. These were lovable hounds, litter mates, though one was a gorgeous golden red and the other had thicker fur and a dark mantle across his shoulder and down his spine. They were gifts from a nearby farmer, sent during Mr. Warner's final illness – sent, Mr. Henry told her, to soften the blow of her father's passing, but in all likelihood, the farmer had enough hounds and merely needed to find a home for them. Jack and Morty had been her salvation. If she hadn't needed to feed and care for her puppies, she likely would never have fed or cared for herself.

Jack and Morty barked happily at Merritt and Argent and made free to smell and investigate those parts most telling to a dog. Mary saw it but didn't call them back. Emmett was shifting and rolling his eyes warningly as the men came down the path; he was very sensitive to Mary's 'states.' Mr. Henry stayed at a respectful distance, keeping the possibility of an open retreat at his back. It was never good to find yourself between Emmett and the barn wall. "Give me five minutes and I will ride out to check on the tracks with you."

"I am not going to the tracks."

"Can I ask where it is you're going?"

"Into town. I have business."

"Into town!?!" This was the first time Merritt and Argent had heard any scale of emotion from Mr. Henry, and now they heard pure surprise. "You haven't been to town in more than a year! Do you still know the way?"

He asked this by way of a joke, but Mary looked up and with all seriousness asked, "It's still where it always was, isn't it? I just follow the pike west, then north at the toll house?"

"Lord, child!" Mr. Henry exclaimed in open despair. "Here, finish your breakfast." Mr. Henry handed her a large biscuit, split, with thick slabs of ham in the middle. Merritt and Argent never saw him take it from the table; he must have pocketed it early in the meal, knowing it would be needed later. Mary took it, grateful at Mr. Henry's thoughtfulness, and took a bite to show her appreciation, though, truly, she wasn't hungry, and, of course, she should not be eating at all this early in the day during Lent. One more sin to confess. The taste of tar was still with her. Then, with a wicked look at Mr. Argent, she chanted "No successful enterprise ever started on an empty stomach," and took a second, smaller bite, slowly chewing with exaggerated delight.

"Where is your hat?" Mr. Henry was trying to make sure all her basic needs were covered – food, shelter from the elements, proper directions.

"I don't need a hat. There's not much sun or heat today, and it is only April."

Merritt and Argent looked at each other – when had the calendar turned? The sky was, in fact, a silvery grey, a great creeping slag of clouds, slowly trailing last night's storm. There was the promise of more rain.

"The sun is not the only reason to wear a hat. It is very chilly this morning." Merritt and Argent noticed that not only was Miss Warner without a hat, she was also without gloves or scarf, and the coat she was wearing had seen better days. Getting no response, Mr. Henry added, "Well, maybe it's a good time to buy a new one while you're in town."

"I shall take it under advisement." This was a new favorite phrase of hers, and Mr. Henry and Miss Carrie were heartily sick of hearing it. Last year, before Mr. Warner passed, it was 'I shall relish the opportunity.'

Mary was ready to mount Emmett. Placing hands on both front and back of the saddle, she instructed the horse, "Hold, Emmett," and Emmett braced himself for the momentary unbalance that was to come. Mary placed her left foot in the stirrup that was left long for this purpose, then heaved herself up into the saddle. Now that she had control of Emmett, Mr. Henry came forward to shorten the stirrup.

While he worked the leather strap, he murmured, "How far into town are you going?" How Miss Mary dressed on the farm was of far less consequence than how she should dress for town, and no matter how clean, no matter the value of the cloth, or the cut of the pattern, trousers were unacceptable in town.

From her great height, Mary looked down on Mr. Henry's head. Preoccupied with the ceremony of the stirrup, Mr. Henry had not looked up. She answered Mr. Henry's unspoken question. "I am prepared." Mr. Henry nodded; she must have a skirt in a saddlebag or secreted in her oversized coat.

In a low tone, Mr. Henry suggested, "It is not only in town that you need to be prepared; there is a lot more traffic on the pike these days." When Mary did not respond, Mr. Henry knew that she intended to take the shorter route – the shorter and more isolated route – through neighboring farms than the open road where she was certain to be seen inappropriately dressed. He asked in a normal tone, "How is that?"

"It's fine, thank you."

Henry took three strides of obeisance backward to his original position – the distance that Emmett seemed to demand for respect. Merritt and Argent had circled around the back of the horse to confirm what they thought they had seen: Miss Warner had her "barn" gun in a holster on the right side of the saddle. In doing so, they had foolishly placed themselves between Emmett and the barn.

"Is a gun necessary in town? Louisville looked very civilized."

What did Mr. Argent know of Louisville? His appearance, along with Mr. Merritt, on her porch yesterday morning bespoke very recent intemperance; despite their fine dress, they had looked rumpled and ill. Now that Mary considered it, their choice of horses possibly spoke more of sodden, impaired judgment than of true ignorance. Whether besotted or sober, she didn't need advice from him. "Louisville is very civilized, but I might meet a panther between here and town, and I want to be ready."

Mr. Henry was intensely observing a spot above the barn door but was slowly shaking his head.

"Miss Mary." Mary looked sheepishly at Mr. Henry. "Slowly, if you please."

Mary had intended to kick Emmett into a gallop, hoping that a thick spray of mud from his massive hooves would rain down on Merritt and Argent. Somehow, Mr. Henry had known her intention.

She started off slowly and picked her way along the puddled wagon path to the lane. Jack and Morty followed her, tongues hanging out and ears flopping, giving them a ridiculous girlish look.

"Boys, stay." When they didn't obey, she brought Emmett to a halt and stared hard at the puppies until they looked away from the awful fact and height of her domination. "Stay," she said quietly. She threw them the remains of the biscuit and moved on. At the point where the drive to the house met the wagon path from the barn, she kicked Emmett into an easy trot, disappearing around the bend. Jack and Morty set up a mournful barking that quickly escalated into loud, lamented baying, both dogs throwing their voices to the sky in a kind of rondo.

Mr. Henry laughed with sheer pleasure. "They sure can sing."

Merritt and Argent watched with a kind of panicked dismay as their quarry went to ground, ironically to the very destination that was their immediate goal. They looked at each other and then to Mr. Henry, who was still laughing at the musical distress of the hounds. After both the puppies and Mr. Henry had settled down, Merritt waited another respectful moment, then asked (knowing, he thought, the answer), "Should we follow after her?" He hoped this would prompt Mr. Henry to assure them that their horses were ready, despite his comments at breakfast. They had wondered to each other, as they struggled to sleep in the back room, just when Mr. Henry would have the time to fix the errant shoe and any others that might need attention. After all, he had followed Miss Warner into the darkening evening, and who knew how long it would take to find her in the dark in the woods that she knew so well.

Their fears proved to be unfounded, however; the horses were indeed ready for the return trip to town, but Mr. Henry persuaded them that their hurry to leave was inefficient. He, too, had learned to think like an engineer. In answer to Merritt's question, Mr. Henry replied, "No, I expect that's what she wants you to do. She'll get you in town, then find some way to keep you there while she slips back home. And she won't be caught napping this time when you come chasing your own tails back to this house." He paused, looking thoughtfully down the lane, as if he could still see her. "No, she may very well have business in town, but I suspect she also means to foul the trail. She may stay the night when she finds you haven't swallowed her bait. She has a place to stay – the family of her best friend. The mother loves Miss Mary like one of her own. She'll take care of her and will send word if she can."

Argent thought he saw a way to salvage the situation, and maybe even bring about a happy solution. "Maybe we could meet this friend and ask her help in persuading Miss Warner to accompany us back to Washington. We could even offer to take her friend as well. She might find the prospect less distressing if she had a traveling companion."

Mr. Henry thought that was a fine idea, but it would not *yield to execution*, as Mr. Warner would say. Miss Mary's best friend no longer lived in town with her mother, since she had married two years ago and moved to Memphis where her new husband had farmland inherited from an uncle. Mr. Henry thought well of this man, though it was obvious he was no farmer ("didn't know a mule from a jack") and he had abandoned engineering to take up work as a cotton agent, so it was a puzzle to Mr. Henry why he would bother to inherit such land. Most of Mr. Henry's regard for this young man – one Coulter Hammond – stemmed from the fact that Mr. Hammond was something of a protégé of Mr. Warner's. Mr. Hammond had been a junior engineer on one of Mr. Warner's bridge projects, and Mr. Warner had taken an interest in him. Mr. Warner was like that; he liked young people, and always wanted to help move them along. Mr. Henry reflected privately that he had been one of those young people himself, once. Mr. Hammond had been invited to stay with the Warner's and try his prospects in Louisville, and Mr. Hammond had then courted and married Miss Mary's particular friend.

"I know Miss Mary is lonely and I wisht Mr. Hammond hadn't taken Miss Gerda to Memphis." This was possibly the real reason for Mr. Henry's disapproval of Mr. Hammond's rightful inheritance. "They miss her, too; they invite her all the time to visit them in Memphis. Miss Gerda writes and says, Come and see the new baby. They tell Miss Mary that they want her to be godmother, but Miss Mary can no more be godmother to that child than the Gen- . . . well, Catholics have very strict rules about these things. They have very strict rules about everything. Praying is about the only thing they can do without tripping over some restriction or other; that's why they do it so much." Mr. Henry remembered how the family had knelt every night in the front room to count their beads. Every inch of couch and seat was used to lean elbows on while they knelt. Even the little ones; they fell asleep on their knees, and Mr. Warner and the older boys would carry the little ones up to their beds. Rules for everything. Even their prayer is powerful regulated. "It's a very regimented religion."

Mr. Henry was speaking faster than usual, and even after such a brief acquaintance, Merritt and Argent realized that the change reflected nervousness. They also had listened to him enough to wonder at the sudden diversion into the regimented lives of Catholics. This abrupt shift away from the General was a dodge, and they strongly suspected that they had almost been allowed to see into the mysterious rift between Miss Warner and the General.

"Miss Gerda's absence has been hard on Miss Mary. It was a good plan to include her, but Miss Gerda isn't here to include."

Argent felt a silly pride at Mr. Henry's approval of his idea. But now that his idea had not borne fruit, he felt the need to fill the void. "Well, if we can't follow Miss Warner and we can't talk to her friend, then there's nothing more to be done at the moment as regards Miss Warner. If we're to wait for her inevitable return, then let us help with some work in the meantime, to earn our keep."

"Oh, no, sir. There is nothing Miss Mary would hate more than if she felt beholden to anyone in any way, especially emissaries from the General. No, but let's saddle up these old nags of yours and I'll show you what you're asking Miss Mary to leave, what you're up against."

With several good meals and one night's rest distancing them from the unfortunate bender on the boat, the last crapulous fumes had dissipated, and they realized just how sorry their mounts were. Nevertheless, they had developed a kind of miserable pride and affection for their nags.

As they followed Mr. Henry to the pasture behind the barn to catch their horses, Merritt said to Argent, "I can't believe I let you talk me into renting these wretched creatures."

"I beg to differ with you. I always indulge you in the arrangement of our mounts. You are, after all, as I am constantly reminded, the better judge of these things. As I remember it, I was wavering between the smell of the stables and the smell of the riverside and had taken up a precarious position between both. I was nowhere near the actual point of negotiations."

"As I remember it, you had taken up heaving in the alley." This was an uncharitable reminder of Argent's after-effects of their pleasure cruise, but it also neatly plucked Argent from the hook regarding responsibility for these horses. Merritt was remembering something else now: he had patronized Edwards Stables at the promising suggestion of their female companions. A suspicious man by nature and trade, he wondered if it had all been some confidence scam from the start.

Merritt and Argent were almost celebrated in the narrow circles of their trade as unnaturally successful at their jobs – ferreting out and shutting down the rampant counterfeiting operations that were plaguing the nation and bringing the culprits to justice. But they seemed to be just as nearly celebrated for their lamentable failures in their judgment of women. It was true that they operated a colorful carousel of female companions, waiting in nearly every city in the east. But the women were just like the horses on a carousel, a little too brightly painted and striking ridiculous poses, taking Merritt and Argent in circles.

Mr. Henry took them on a tour around the property, and like the interrupted tour of the house, he took great pride in the improvements Mr. Warner and his older boys had brought to the land. He spoke wistfully of the plans Mr. Warner had for the distribution of his land among his children. To his original tract of a few hundred acres, at the time considered far from town, Mr. Warner had added over the years, other smaller parcels of land. But the bulk of the added acreage came to him through what Mr. Henry called "mournful inheritance," at the death of Mr. Warner's only and younger brother.

The two brothers intended to live side by side and raise families together. They had helped each other build log cabins, temporary homes to dreams of better and bigger homes. Mr. Warner's first home was now the kitchen cabin. It had been arranged that the younger Warner – Emil Warner – was to act as overseer of the older brother's farm during his absences, for which Emil was to receive a small share of any profits. At the time of the younger Warner's death, both men were fathers to three children – Mr. Warner's all sons, his brother's all daughters. The young widow, never enthusiastic about living on a farm in Kentucky, had taken her three daughters and returned to her family in Baltimore. Though the land had come to him as an inheritance (his brother had died intestate, and so the farm had descended to him, the next oldest male in the family), Mr. Warner had paid the widow for his brother's land, paying a handsome price out of obligation to his dead brother. The widow had taken the money, and Mr. Warner had never heard from her again, though he attempted to resume ties with her often.

Thus, at the time of his death, Mr. Warner controlled a tidy number of acres. He had not been a rich man, except in the land he held outright, or controlled for his young sons. The expenses of raising and, most importantly, educating such a large family considerably strained the budget. But even when money was desperately tight, even in the face of the occasional unexpected, budget-shattering crisis, he had never considered selling any of the land. It was too sacred; it was his children's legacy, both his sons' and his daughters'. It had been Mr. Warner's fervent dream to keep his children near. His sons were already, at their separate births, the owners of ten, up to fifty, acres of land each (under their father's custodianship). Mr. Warner's own father purchased these lots at the birth of each son wherever such lots could be found. Originally, these lots were scattered all over Jefferson County and even in Bullitt County, but as land closer to home became available, Mr. Warner sold the old lots to buy ever closer ones, until he had managed to collect all the present acreage, nearly all of it contiguous to his original purchase. His oldest son was to have inherited the house and the surrounding 100 acres. The remaining acreage, after the boys had attained their age of majority, was to go to each daughter, upon the occasion of their marriage or upon the occasion of his death. In this perfect future, his children and their families would live together on this property. That dream, of course, had cracked with each son's death, and had shattered completely with the sudden deaths of nearly the rest of the family just a few years ago.

Henry had met Mr. Warner not long after the younger Warner's death. Henry had been a common laborer on the old Louisville and Frankfort Railroad and had answered some of Mr. Warner's questions about the project. Mr. Warner had thought nothing about consulting Henry, since Henry's foreman was absent at the time. The foreman, however, had taken exception to what he considered an insult, and had fired Henry. Somehow, Mr. Warner had heard of it, and had hired Henry on the spot as a kind of secretary. Mr. Warner had seen in Henry a basic aptitude, someone who could understand Mr. Warner's work and help facilitate it. Henry traveled extensively with Mr. Warner and had often stayed at the Warner house in the back room, much against Mrs. Warner's wishes, though nothing was ever said directly to Henry. After a while, Henry began to stay in

Louisville, while Mr. Warner continued on to his home in the country. He met Carrie in Louisville during one of Mr. Warner's visits home. It was when he mentioned marriage that Mr. Warner suggested Henry make his home near the Warner homestead. Mr. Warner had a little land to sell and the need for some help on the farm, until his own sons were able to assume their share of the responsibility. The two men worked well together, and Mr. Warner never assumed that Henry's help would be free.

Mr. Henry had been working fifty of the front 100 acres, closest to town, for nearly twenty years. Mr. Warner had helped him build a very decent cabin for Henry and his wife, though the cabin had grown small with the arrival of their five (now four) children.

It had been Mr. Warner's intention to sell outright to Henry those fifty acres, as soon as Henry could afford it. In the meantime, Henry worked the land rent-free, in exchange for help as Mr. Warner needed. This was the arrangement between the two men before Henry had married, while Mr. Warner's sons were too little to help. As the boys grew, Henry's help was needed less and less, except for large projects such as the house additions or during planting and harvest. He had nearly saved enough when crop prices fell in '58 and then the war came. Mr. Warner travelled in his job more than ever during the war, and Henry often travelled with him, as he had from the start. Henry put in fewer and fewer acres of crops, and so had less and less to sell. Crop prices in Louisville held up during the war, farmers in the area benefitting from fat government contracts, drawn up to feed the hordes of Union troops moving through Louisville. But all the while his savings dwindled. Even though demand for produce for both man and beast soared as the Union army numbers swelled in Louisville and crop prices rose, any profits he made were eaten up by war-time inflation on goods and products the farm couldn't provide his family. He didn't know how Carrie managed to pinch the rips in their budget together, but she had done it. Still, it would take him years to recover his savings. Now, nearly 20 years since he had come to this land, he was back at the beginning: putting in long hours at both his place and the Warner's, and slowly putting away for the day when he would buy what he already considered his land. The difference now was that Henry was the one with sons coming on to work, and Mr. Warner was gone. But he told Merritt and Argent none of this.

The entire farm, then, belonged to Miss Mary. No one loved this farm more, but it would be a lonely inheritance: no sibling neighbors, no common woods, no nieces and nephews visiting the big house on the hill.

Most of it, Mr. Henry explained, was still in woods. Every year, Mr. Warner had the older boys gird trees he had marked, adding to the pasturage and the arable acreage. Some parts – he seemed to apologize for it – were only good enough for goats and coyotes. Curiously, those seemed to be the parts Miss Mary loved the most.

"She knows every inch of these woods. I caught up with her last night over there in a bend in the creek. There's a tree root that curves out over the water and she likes to sit in it. Whenever she needs to be alone, it's water she'll go to – a creek, a river, a pond. Remember that if you ever lose sight of her."

"If we can ever get her on the train, we won't lose sight of her."

Mr. Henry smiled indulgently at them. "I'll remind you one day that you said that."

They returned from their leisurely and very thorough tour late in the afternoon. Mr. Henry was apparently in no hurry to return to the work that awaited him in his own fields and barns. The hounds, who had eagerly followed them at the start of the tour, had soon veered off to follow their own pursuits. Evidently even these had proved unsatisfactory, for they had returned to the stables before the men and were now stretched leisurely across the opening to the barn. Their fatigue, as always, was deep and incapacitating; they could not be persuaded to move. Merritt and Argent thought a swift kick might sharpen the persuasion, but Mr. Henry would not hear of it. He did manage to push – gently – with his foot the hind end of Morty forward, so that they could just squeeze the horses past and into the barn. Morty's hind quarters ended up nearly at a right angle to his chest, looking very uncomfortable, but Mr. Henry had managed the maneuver without ever waking the dog. In the dark of the barn, they unsaddled their horses, wiped them dry of the patchy rain that had dogged their tour, then led them into separate stalls, pitching in a flake of hay as a sort of apology for taking them out into the chilly damp of the day. The horse Mr. Henry rode either belonged to Miss Warner, or Mr. Henry kept his horse in her barn, for he left it with the others, in its own stall.

Merritt and Argent followed Mr. Henry up the stone steps – "Mind your step; they get slippery" – then followed his lead in scraping the worst of the mud from their boots, using the edge of the porch steps to do so. However, at the front door, Mr. Henry stopped them from removing their own boots as he had done. He had merely shaken his head and held open the door for them. They entered the house to the mid-day meal that had been waiting for them for some time. Although the table was still set with the good china, all the silver pieces had been retired. Miss Carrie may have realized, upon reflection, that the silver was a bit much. They were surprised to find that Mr. Henry would join them at the Warner table, especially in the absence of Miss Warner, but nothing about this farm was conventional; they were already learning to expect and accept the peculiarities that surrounded Miss Warner. It was a quiet meal, Miss Carrie and Thea having already eaten. In any event, Mr. Henry was not much given to table talk. Or perhaps he was reflecting on the statement he had given in the barn about Miss Warner. Merritt and Argent were certainly preoccupied with it.

As they had busied themselves with the care of the horses, Argent had asked if there was any information Mr. Henry could give them that might help them in their mission. Mr. Henry had never looked up from brushing his horse, but had replied quietly, and at length.

"There's no family left to tell me to hold my tongue, so I will tell you what you need to know. It aint all her fault, the way she is – everyone let her run wild and free with those brothers of hers because they were too tired or busy or just wanted to indulge her; then they turned a blind eye when she became troublesome or a might embarrassing. And when she needed help the most, they hauled her in, court-martialed her, and reprimanded her. During the war, there was no one here that could manage her. She was alone without her brothers; she had never made any kind of friends with her sisters, or even her mother, and she was bereft of company. She tried twice to run off after her brothers, tried to enlist as a boy over in New Albany, but both times she was recognized and sent home. She went to town without her mother's permission, watching the soldiers coming and going. She was beyond controlling; she was beyond caring about the consequences. Mr. Warner would receive letters from Mz. Warner about

Miss Mary's behavior. She finally wrote that she could no longer handle Miss Mary, Mr. Warner would have to do something. Mr. Warner never told me any of this – I heard it from my wife. Mr. Warner never talked about bills or sons dying in the war or crops dying in the field, but after this letter from Mz. Warner, he said, 'I will make her understand, even if it makes her hate me.'

"Mr. Warner made time for us to come home, and he took her in hand. He drove her down to the cloister at Nazareth, near Bargetown, spoke to the nuns, with her present, about taking her in as a permanent novitiate, in exchange for donations and support from Mr. Warner. She came back wild-eyed and pale and sick, unable to hold down food. It was too cruel, the threat to cage that wild soul behind the bars of a convent, locked behind walls, hog-tied in black robes and habits, like manacling her hand and foot in a hotbox. I told Mr. Warner as much – it was the only time we ever had harsh words between us. That threat broke something in her, but Mr. Warner was unmoved, cold and set like ice. The day we returned to the war, Mr. Warner gave his terms – he would find Miss Mary changed upon his return home or she would find herself at Nazareth.

"We heard she disappeared for days at a time; came home to sleep, no one knew she was there. Then she would leave again for more days and nights. No one could follow her; all that hunting and roaming the woods with the boys taught her how to hide and cover her tracks and remain free. My wife told me that Mz. Warner broke down and cried one day, and said, 'Leave her be, she's happier in the woods with wild beasts than she is with us.' That was the day she gave up on Miss Mary. Carrie would send Caleb to a favorite rock in the creek where Mary liked to perch, to leave a pail of food. No one ever saw her take the pail, but it was always empty when they went to replace it. After weeks of this, Mary returned home and was the perfect daughter, but she was stiff and unnatural, with no spark at all."

Merritt had asked, "What had she been doing all this time?"

Mr. Henry had turned to stare off towards the southwest, deciding how to answer. Finally, he had said, "It doesn't matter now; there's no one left on the farm who can threaten her now."

When Mr. Warner and Mr. Henry came home on their next leave, Mary put on her best dress, made up her hair, and was completely formal and exact in her behavior towards her father. She had changed, and Mr.

Warner hated it. He had changed, too. He saddled Emmett and his own horse, and they rode out over the land, were gone almost all day. Mary stopped leaving the farm, stopped trying to enlist, stopped disappearing. She took on the work the boys used to do. Mr. Warner had made her overseer in his absence; showed her the books, left the list of merchants he dealt with, left a letter granting her authority for all of them.

"She has pretty much been running this farm ever since. He told me he had treated Miss Mary wrong her whole life, trying to make her something she was never meant to be. He said it broke his heart to think how alone she has always been and probably always will be. It was time to admit that she was different, but he would never again consider that she was a lunatic or should be put away. He would never let anyone tell him that again.

"It cost him; he and Mz. Warner were estranged after that. She had expected Miss Mary to be gone, but instead, she became Mr. Warner's manager; and, of course, there was never any hope after that that Miss Mary and her mother would reconcile. Miss Mary knew that it was her mother who pushed for her to be sent to Nazareth. They never again spoke as mother and daughter.

"Her father repented the threat, but she still lives in fear of it, that it lays just beyond the boundaries of this farm." Mr. Henry had then turned full towards the men and had stated, almost challengingly, "She aint afraid of you and she aint afraid of travel or any of the hardships that might go with it. She's afraid to leave the farm, afraid of the hotbox waiting for her, of the people who want to put her there. There's one somewhere in every family, that needs putting away, that needs different kind of care. People told the Warners that Miss Mary was that one in their family, and for years Mr. Warner denied it and refused to consider it. She somehow knew of the whispers and that the only thing that stood between her and the lunatic asylum in Lexington was her daddy. That trip to Nazareth showed Miss Mary that even her own father – her one supporter and protector – had been ready to step aside and allow her to be dragged, to watch her be dragged, to a pit she could never escape. It broke something in her; she was never one to trust freely, but after that she didn't trust anyone at all."

Henry had reflected that perhaps he had told the men too much of what Miss Mary would certainly consider a personal nature. But he could not send her off with strange men, even if they were emissaries of the

General, without giving them some notion of her peculiar character, without warning them how she might view the ultimate meaning of this trip. These past few months had been particularly trying for her, not only because of the loss of her father, but because of the constant fear of the loss of her home as well – there were rumors of plans afoot, put in motion by some members of the Warner clan to 'relieve' Miss Mary of her inheritance. Old insinuations of insanity and new predictions of incompetence were being circulated. He didn't know how Miss Mary had become aware of these machinations, but she had mentioned more than once these past few months her fear of shadowy outside forces taking aim at her, taking aim at the farm. The family lawyer was, of course, maneuvering to block all such maneuvers, and Mr. Sawyer had hinted at other outside forces working to help him in his endeavors. That Miss Mary was peculiar was painfully obvious upon first acquaintance, so Henry did not feel too guilty in extending to these men a further acquaintance with that particular aspect of her existence, but perhaps matters of inheritance were best kept within the family. Nevertheless, they needed to be aware of her current state of mind. "You can wave your papers and credentials with the seal of the United States of America all you want – she won't trust you, and you'll have to watch her every minute she's with you. She'll bolt if she feels boxed in."

After the meal, Mr. Henry excused himself to return home to look in on the progress of the chores he had assigned his boys. Merritt and Argent asked if they might tag along, to stretch their legs. If they continued to indulge in the pleasure of Miss Carrie's cooking, they might have to beg the favor of her seamstress skills as well, to let out the seams of their waistcoats. Mr. Henry hesitated, not wanting to deny guests such a small request, but also keenly aware of the difference between his home and this one. He nodded his assent, retrieved his boots from the front porch, then led them out the back door. They followed a well-worn foot path that led past the kitchen cabin on their right, across the deep back yard, past the huge kitchen garden on their left, and through a small patch of woods where the path began to gently slope downhill, before they finally emerged to meet the muddy drive that arced from their right to pass within feet of Henry's cabin.

The drive, which was little more than a wide path, would be shaded completely by late spring. Had they followed the drive to its conclusion,

Merritt and Argent would have found that it re-connected with the lane that led to the pike, after arcing widely west, creating a large lemon-shaped island of woods between the lane and the drive – Thea's private haunt. In better weather, it would have been a pleasant ten-minute walk, but the heavy rains had made every step a slippery hazard. How had Miss Carrie run through all this yesterday, without mishap?

As soon as they cleared the woods, they could see a handsome cabin, a cottage, really. It was a simple but large box with a deep porch. It was not tall enough to accommodate two full stories, but a single window above the porch suggested the presence of a loft, at least in the front of the house. On either side of the two steps in the middle, the porch was fronted by a narrow flower bed, lined in rocks. This, then, was the den of treason that had propelled Miss Carrie down the path and up the hill – was it just yesterday? – to ensnare two hapless gentlemen into her web of dining and detainment.

They passed the cabin (though more than a cabin and less than a house) and in a few minutes came to the barn, which was far larger than the cabin. Inside, Henry's boys were busy working the tackle for the two mules, who were placidly chewing hay in their stalls. There were two empty stalls, but if Mr. Henry owned any horses or more mules, they were currently absent. Matthew, the youngest, was making a show of working, but was accomplishing very little.

Mr. Henry excused himself and walked over to speak with Caleb and Bill. When he returned, Merritt and Argent asked if they might help. Again Mr. Henry rejected any offer of help from the men. The heavy rains of the last week had made working in the fields impossible, so Henry had brought the work inside. For several days, he and the boys had been cleaning out the barn and the hay shed nearby, cleaning and sharpening the plows and other tools, and generally getting ready – a second time – for the coming season. They were down to odd jobs here and there, so really there was nothing Merritt and Argent could do to help. As they walked back towards the cabin, Argent said, "Well, I am not certain what we are to do with ourselves until Miss Warner decides to return." Argent was truly at a loss – he was rarely idle, and he wasn't sure how to fill his time, especially at someone else's house.

Mr. Henry laughed a little at such a ridiculous problem – he was quite happy to sit and do nothing on those rare occasions when there was nothing to do. "You remind me a little of Mr. Warner – he did not know how to be idle; even if his body was at rest, his mind was always whirring." Time on trains was spent in study of upcoming projects or just thinking about them; he often stared ahead without expression, motionless, for long periods of time. Mr. Henry would have to rouse Mr. Warner whenever the train stopped for the night or it was time to disembark. Mr. Warner often had no idea of the passage of time; he would be working on schematics and materials lists and other specs in his mind the whole time, so that when they reached a hotel or other destination, it was merely a matter of writing out, as if from dictation, his ideas, sketches, requisitions or other forms of correspondence.

Mr. Henry turned to Merritt and Argent as they walked. "You'll find Miss Mary often acts the same way – she will stare off into the distance and you will be tempted to think she is sleeping with her eyes open, but you will find she has been deep in some excursion of thought. It may be days before you find out what she was thinking. Mr. Warner had his work to occupy his thoughts, but I am not sure what keeps Miss Mary so fixed in her mind."

Merritt said, "I think we saw her in such a state yesterday – she seemed to have completely forgotten we were in the room with her, and then seemed agitated when her reverie was interrupted."

Mr. Henry nodded. "She can leave whatever room she is in whenever she wants to, just by retreating into her own head; always been dreamy that way. I think this habit of hers kept her from breaking under her grief these past few years, but now I think she employs it too much – she would rather live in her mind than in this world. She spends too much time rocking herself on that swing and staring out across the fields." Mr. Henry tended to talk and walk with his head down, but now he raised his head, himself looking off into the distance. "She won't like Washington City – it is far noisier and chaotic than anything she has ever seen – but it will do her good to go there, to break this habit, if only for a few days."

Merritt and Argent realized that they had passed Mr. Henry's cottage and were on their way back to the Warner house, but by a different route; they had passed the little footpath through the woods.

"Should we return to Louisville for the night and ride back out tomorrow? With Miss Warner gone, I feel it is improper that we stay at her home."

"No, no." Mr. Henry waved off any impropriety Mr. Argent may feel. "It means nothing. It was Miss Mary who rode off and left guests unattended. I'll need to speak to her about that. And it appears as if it means to rain yet again tonight. I would not send you out on the road in this weather. But, in the meantime, make yourselves at home." When Merritt started to protest, Mr. Henry held up his hand and shook his head. "Mr. Warner would want you to stay; he would never take no on this from any representatives of the General."

Privately, Merritt and Argent were a little astonished at Mr. Henry's assuming such power of decision over someone else's house, but everything about this farm and the relationship between Miss Warner and Henry's family was a little astonishing.

They had reached the point in the drive that connected with the lane leading in one direction to the Louisville-Taylorsville pike and in the other direction to the Warner's long uphill drive. By way of explanation, Mr. Henry said, "This way is a little less sloppy."

A rider came towards them, pushing his horse as quickly as the rain-soaked road would allow. Mr. Henry evidently was familiar with him, for he stepped out into the lane and expertly received a pouch from the rider as the horse curved to begin its way back to town. The rider evidently was familiar enough with Mr. Henry, that collecting a fee or tip was not immediately necessary. Merritt unconsciously made note of it. The timing of the message was incredibly lucky, or, the thought tickled in the back of Merritt's head, that Mr. Henry was expecting the communication.

Opening the pouch, Mr. Henry pulled out several telegrams and two letters. He handed to Merritt and Argent the two telegrams marked for their delivery, then returned at least one more telegram and one of the letters to the pouch, unread. The remaining letter he opened and announced, "Miss Mary will be spending the night in town with the Müllers, and possibly tomorrow night as well."

"Is that from Miss Warner?"

"No, from Mrs. Müller; I would have been surprised if Miss Mary had gone anywhere else; there is really nowhere else for her to go. There is a small note at the bottom here, though I cannot read it – Miss Mary writes in such a small hand."

Argent offered, "May I?"

Mr. Henry handed the letter to Argent who, despite good vision, still had difficulty reading the small script. Eventually, he deciphered, "Tell the federal underlings they need not wait on me."

Mr. Henry snorted at Mary's impudence, then realizing the insult to the gentlemen, quickly reclaimed the letter from Argent.

Argent smarted at the word underling, and Miss Warner had somehow managed to make the word federal an insult as well.

Merritt only smiled at her barb. "It seems we have been dismissed again."

Mr. Henry countered, "No, don't you mind her. Carrie tells me you have a mandate to take her with you to see the General. I once saw the General angry when his orders had gone unfulfilled – it surprised Mr. Warner, so perhaps that was a rare thing – but I won't be party to throwing you to his sometime wrath. Miss Mary will go with you; I will see to it. You gentlemen know your way back? Carrie will see you have dinner before the evening is out." Then Mr. Henry slung the pouch over his shoulder and returned down the narrow trail to his home.

Carrie brought them some dinner a few hours later, and though she employed the good family china, she did not set out dinner in so grand a fashion as she had done before; she did not use any of the ornate serving dishes that were on display in the cabinet in the front room, but merely set the table with the china plates that were stored in the serving pantry. She pattered around in the serving pantry and the front room while Merritt and Argent ate, two men alone in a large dining room at a long empty table. Then, when the men had risen from their meal, she gathered the dishes, washed them in a large pan on the rough table in the middle of the cold kitchen, then dried them and carefully returned them to the cabinet in the serving pantry.

Carrie was largely silent and absent during this dinner. Merritt and Argent were sure she was still smarting under Miss Warner's cutting remark of the morning. They had hoped to hear more of Miss Warner and her family – the current assignment almost demanded they probe further – but, unlike the night before when Carrie seemed relieved to tell someone of the burdens of her heart, this night she was unapproachable, closed.

When she left for the evening, she asked if they needed anything, then bid them goodnight before they fully answered, no, thank you.

Merritt and Argent spent the evening roaming, respectfully (they had been careful to clean their boots before entering the house), through the house. They explored all the rooms on the first floor – all, except the room whose only entrance was through the front room: that door was locked. In the middle room, where they had seen the piano, they picked up books and pictures and reverently handled the toys of children now lying in the nearby cemetery. Argent pulled the weights on the pendulum clock in the room and reset the time. (Though he had uncharacteristically neglected to reset his watch to L&N, and therefore Louisville, time while in town, he knew the difference from Cincinnati time was negligible.) Later, during the night, he regretted the chimes that sometimes woke him every 15 minutes. At the 2:30 chime, Merritt turned violently on his cot and cursed Argent. At 3:00, Argent went into the middle room and stopped the pendulum.

They also briefly explored the upstairs. On either side of the open stairwell were three large bedrooms, the configuration matching the rooms directly below. Though no one had slept or lived in them for several years (there were no mattresses on any of the beds), it was apparent that the two of the rooms to the right of the stairs belonged to the boys – on each bedpost was hung with evident reverence and love, some memento of the boy who had once slept there. Several of the bedposts sported Union army hats, and one lone Confederate army cap. A bridle on one bedpost must have belonged to Randy or George, the only boys not to have fought in the war. On simple dressers there were other small items of immense sentimental value – books, pocket knives, playing cards. The windows in these rooms looked east over the steep hill that led down to the wagon path to the barn, the creek and the overgrown field beyond. Somewhere past that field was the turnpike that led west to Louisville and east to Taylorsville.

Continuing on towards the front of the house and past the boys' rooms there was a large open space with a wide bank of windows that looked over the front of the house, the roof of the porch just below. Underneath the windows, running the full width of the space, was a storage box with a wide lid in four sections. Cushions along the back spoke of its dual use as a bench. It must be pleasant to sit here and look out over the yard, down to the barn and even to the creek below. There were toys and books here as well, and a few chairs and stools. There was no order, as if the children had played here one moment, and then left forever the next.

Continuing around the banistered stairwell, Merritt and Argent looked into what must have been Mr. and Mrs. Warner's bedroom – there was a single large bed that dominated the room. In the corner nearest the door and the window, facing east, was an old prie-dieu, the cushion on the kneeler well-worn. And against one wall sat a beautiful carved cradle, long since unused. The men did not linger long at the door.

Opposite the boys' rooms, across the stairwell, were the girls' rooms. Like their counterparts, these bedrooms had been stripped of their mattresses, and the precious possessions of the sisters who once slept there were also carefully preserved. Handbags as well as bonnets, now hopelessly out of style, hung from several bedposts. Gloves were carefully laid out on the dressers, and in the room where the youngest sisters evidently slept, there were intricately carved toy beds and cradles, but no dolls or small linens; like the girls' beds, the doll beds had been stripped bare (were the dolls also lying in the cemetery, eternally held by their young 'mothers'?). The windows here were just above the one-story addition below, part of which housed the back room with their cots, and the other part belonged to the locked room off the front room.

"I don't know how she bears to look at this every day and night." Argent's voice was an awful assault on the silence and the preserved memories of the upstairs.

Merritt asked, "Where does she sleep? All the mattresses are gone."

Both men realized at the same time that the only mattress they had seen had been in the parents' room. Miss Warner, then, could not bear to stay in a room where she had known others to sleep with her. Looking into this room again, they found that the mattress on the bed was not the only one in the room – another could just be seen where it lay on the trundle bed, which had not been fully replaced under the larger bed. Miss Warner and her father, of course, had needed new mattresses. Grant had told them of a great sickness that had taken most of the daughters and Mrs. Warner, but not the name of the sickness; regardless, it was common to burn anything the diseased had touched. Perhaps Miss Warner had dragged her mattress into her father's room as his health failed, to be near to his needs, even in the night. Apparently, she had never moved out, and the rumpled linens implied she still slept there.

3 — *Passion Sunday*

Both men woke to the smell of coffee, but when they reached the cold kitchen, Carrie was already gone, leaving behind her a hearty breakfast, but without the gilding. On the simple table in the middle of the room were covered dishes of fried eggs, bacon, and potatoes, biscuits, a scoop of butter and a small covered bowl of strawberry preserves, and, of course, the coffee. Carrie had also left out a few of the everyday plates, mugs, and utensils for their use. Either their status as mere government agents had lowered the level of hospitality, or Miss Warner's comment made Carrie re-evaluate her approach to the men.

Rather than eat in the cavernous dining room, Merritt and Argent opted to eat in the cozier cold kitchen, pulling two chairs from either side of the fireplace. For a kitchen, the fireplace was relatively shallow, as was the mantle above it; but, like any kitchen fireplace, it was hung all around with pots and pans, dried herbs, and long-handled utensils. After breakfast, Merritt heated some water at the little stove where the coffee was brewed, while Argent rummaged as respectfully as he could for a mirror. He found a small hand mirror in one of the girls' rooms, and guiltily borrowed it for their purpose. When he presented Merritt with the mirror he admonished him, "Be quick about it; I want to return it as soon as possible." Merritt merely nodded, shaving first and quickly, then handing the mirror back to Argent. Argent cut himself in his eagerness to return the mirror, but he counted it a small price to be able to replace the mirror on the little girls' dresser. He also, in his distracted hurry, shaved off the beginnings of a dearly missed mustache.

Merritt remarked upon Argent's return to the back room, "I thought you intended to let your mustache grow back in. Or are you planning to take up again with the dear widow?"

Argent scowled at him. He had only shaved his mustache at the insistence of a woman whose interest he had needed to cultivate during their last investigation. Argent was shocked to find out that apparently many women did not care for whiskers of any kind. There was even some silly rumor bantered about among women that whiskers, beards in particular, were nesting grounds for consumption. Argent had never cared to wear a beard, but that women feared such danger even from a mustache much disquieted him. It could possibly explain a great deal of reluctance on the part of several women to kiss him. With these thoughts in mind, he replied, "That even a criminal like the Widow Rogers finds whiskers repellant suggests that women of higher status may also find them distasteful. This is the beginning of an experiment – I shall determine if a clean-shaven face attracts more kisses."

Merritt had never subscribed to the convention that a man's whiskers were his badge of virility. "There is no need to put your theory to the test. I can give ample testimony to the truth of the matter." It was true – Merritt was never at a loss for female companionship, and he was as clean-shaven as a priest.

Dressed and fed and completely without direction, Merritt and Argent walked down to the horse barn to tend to their horses, but found them already fed, watered, and even put out to the field behind the barn. The day promised to be a decided improvement over the last several days: the sky was clear, and the sun was already warming the air. Henry's tour had taken them far and wide on the farm, but they had not really seen the area closest to the house. They were not really so bored as to explore the henhouse or sheds or any of the other support buildings that dotted the lower hill and were connected by well-worn paths, some of them even set with stepping stones. Instead, they followed the narrowing path that took up where the drive to the front of the horse barn left off.

This path was well-worn, too, though as much by animal traffic as by human feet. This was the path on which they had seen Miss Warner return from her morning's ride, just yesterday morning. Following the path as it led westward around the base of the higher hill upon which the house perched, they came across the family cemetery. There was a gaping entrance framed by five-foot high walls on either side, but a look through the opening revealed that the two side and back walls were much shorter, in some places only one stone high. The variation in the incomplete walls gave the cemetery the appearance of being destroyed or shelled, rather than unfinished. But inside the enclosure, the graves were maintained, laid out in a grid fashion, with well-manicured paths separating the individual graves. There were even small garden plots in various geometric designs, full now with jonquils.

Merritt moved among the headstones, none of them old enough to show weathering, introducing himself to M's family. Argent disapproved of this seeming intrusion, and remained just inside the opening, until Merritt beckoned him over. Merritt said nothing but pointed to the death dates on several of the headstones. The earliest death was ten years ago – Randy, the younger brother whose horse had caused such jealous longing in Miss Warner that her father had given her Emmett for her birthday. The other deaths were more recent – there were two in 1863, one tombstone with the single word 'Chickamauga' chiseled under the name and dates; two in 1865, both with the word 'Sultana' as their final epitaph; a single death in 1864, but no more information than a name and dates. But the greatest number of deaths occurred just four years ago – six children and their mother all succumbed within days of each other in October 1866, the victims of some great epidemic or fire or some other tragedy that could consume life so quickly. One of the graves held two sisters, twins, born together and now buried together. And, of course, there was Mr. Warner, the newest headstone, announcing his death mere months ago.

They left the cemetery and continued on the curving path past the stone walls until they found themselves eight or more feet above the creek. The water was running fast and high after all the spring rain, but it was evident that a series of wood steps leading down to the water extended even farther than they could see, suggesting the true depth of the creek, once the spring freshets were over. The steps appeared to be old railroad ties wedged into a corner of the descending bank. A rope swing hung from a heavy branch that extended over the water. The seat of the swing was submerged under the water, jerking to the coursing creek.

Not far past the point where the chunky wood ledges led down to the creek, the path veered away from the stream and entered woods that became increasingly dense. Occasionally, they would come across a bench or some other structure, such as the crude platform high overhead in a tree, accessible by boards nailed into the trunk. A small shed, or more likely, a playhouse, was quite a distance from the house, and the men wondered at its distance. Where the path crossed small rivulets or ditches, old planks of wood had been thrown across to reach the other side.

There were other paths darting off from the main way, but Merritt and Argent ignored these. After some time, the path stopped abruptly as the woods gave way to rocky ravines and rough terrain. To their right they heard the angry rush of water forcing itself through a channel too small for the volume. At last following one of the offshoot paths, they re-entered the woods until the path ended at a long ledge of unbroken stone. Looking over this ledge, they saw the source of the rushing noise – six or seven feet below them a great stream of water was gushing from an opening in the stone wall, to splash several more feet lower near a decent-sized pool completely surrounded by trees growing on a lower floor of the woods. The falling water must have collected in some other, separate channel, for the pool was absolutely still, unperturbed by the chaos of the cataract nearby. The pool was not large, but almost perfectly round and the water in it was the most curious shade of blue Argent had ever seen in water, except perhaps the color of the ocean seen at some distance. Usually ponds appeared muddy or murky, but this pond was exceptional in its color and clarity.

Argent placed a hand on a nearby tree – an almost affectionate gesture of appreciation. "This must have been a wonderful place to grow up."

Merritt was crouching by the stone ledge, turning something in his hands. He observed with uncharacteristic melancholy, "So many of them never got to finish growing up." Standing, he added, "I think she was here last night," and handed Argent a nail used in shoeing horses – it was unused and without weathering.

Argent pocketed the nail, and said wonderingly, "She ran into the woods at dark with a storm coming on, in stocking feet to the edge of this cliff. She must know these woods like the back of her hand, indeed, to make it here and to brave this ledge in the dark."

"She would rather take her chances out here in the dark than have to play hostess to two uninvited guests. Giles, if she ever consents to return with us, it will be a hard three days traveling. We will have to watch her every minute of every day and night until we deliver her safely to the White House."

"Unfortunately, the last thing she wants from anybody, but especially from us, is a watchful eye. How can we grant her the privacy she so obviously needs without also extending to her the opportunity to bolt like she did last night? Grant should never have sent us with so little understanding of the task."

"It is not the task that is confusing, but Miss Warner. I begin to think President Grant has no more understanding of Miss Warner, the task, and how to complete it than any of us, including Mr. Henry and Miss Carrie. The White House is our ultimate destination, but first, we need to get to Parkersburg."

One of the two telegrams they had received last evening contained the cryptic message "Help is waiting for you in Parkersburg." Argent had remarked cynically, "We need help in Louisville, if we are ever to get to Parkersburg."

There had been no assumption of failure to lure Miss Warner from her farm, and no further explanation as to what help would be waiting for them. Argent had speculated that Grant was sending a female servant or attendant of some kind to accompany Miss Warner and to see to her needs. As Argent had expressed this possibility, it occurred to both men that a female attendant should have been provided from the very beginning. It was well-known, and amply documented that, by virtue of their very sex, women were subject to frequent maladies of varying degrees. They had already seen that Miss Warner was indeed subject to some kind of fit, that Mr. Henry euphemistically referred to as a 'state.' Mr. Henry seemed to think that all she needed was time alone to emerge from these states of hers. The more they thought about this, the more the men had become alarmed at the prospect of attending to Miss Warner on their own.

Argent's father had been a doctor, as were his two uncles, and it had been assumed that Argent himself would follow in their footsteps. Accordingly, he had begun his studies of medicine and was advanced enough at the start of the war to be assigned as a field surgeon's assistant. Then as the slaughter of the war had escalated, so had his responsibilities, becoming a field surgeon in his own right. He had subsequently changed career paths, but still had learned enough to act as *de facto* doctor among his colleagues in the Service, when out in the field of operations. Last night, he had both horrified and fascinated Merritt with his store of possible female maladies – which were legion – that could strike Miss Warner. With all these medical snares before them, the three-day trip began to stretch out farther and farther in their minds, the number of days to reach

Washington escalating well into double digits. They had gone to their sleep adopting the certainty that Miss Warner would carry them from one female emergency to the next during the trip. The only help that Grant could possibly be sending them was a full complement of medical specialists and equipment.

In the light of day, of course, this seemed somewhat silly. While there was no denying that women were frail and disposed to more illnesses than men, they had both had enough experience with women to know that, at least when young, women could be healthy for weeks, even months, at a time. There was also no denying, either, that Miss Warner was somehow not well, in both mind and body – Miss Carrie had said as much and they themselves had witnessed her coarse outbursts and seen the fatigue in her eyes. Her demeanor was altogether unnatural.

Reaching Parkersburg became the burning goal for the men, and they were eager to start. Returning to the Warner house, Merritt and Argent first looked for Mr. Henry at the horse barn, then in the house itself, then in the back of the house where there was the pump and, even farther back, the outhouse structure. Mr. Henry was nowhere to be found near the Warner house. Merritt and Argent then made their way back down the small trail that led to Mr. Henry's house, but it was the same here – completely empty of people.

Merritt remarked, "Someone was here earlier today – someone left us breakfast and saw to our horses, but where are they now?"

"It is as silent as the grave, as if someone died."

"It always seems that way in the country – you know, the cathedral of the soul, or something."

Argent suddenly realized, "It is Sunday! They have gone into town to attend services." Argent smarted a little at another realization – chasing counterfeiters and other revenue criminals respected no Sabbath or holiday, and he had slowly left off attending services himself.

"Is it Sunday again?"

Argent could never tell if Merritt had any religious leanings at all. He was certainly a moral man – he believed deeply in the mission of the Service to protect the money supply, not only because it was a matter of national honor, but because he despised what the trade did to families and communities, initiating even the very young into a life of crime. He was passionately patriotic, which for him included extending help to anyone who needed it. There was no one more honorable, Argent felt, but whether Merritt ascribed to any denomination, Argent was not certain.

With everyone gone to town and nothing to do, Merritt and Argent returned to the house on the hill. Argent took a seat on the front porch swing and began to jot down notes that he would use later when writing out a full weekly report. Merritt let himself into the house, then brought out the last of the morning's coffee, handing one mug to Argent. Argent muttered his thanks, then hissed as Merritt dropped onto the swing, causing him to spill the coffee on himself and his notebook.

Argent's irritation, however, was lost in curiosity as he watched Merritt open an envelope. "Who is that from, and where did you get it?"

Merritt answered absently, "It was sitting on the table in the little kitchen."

He handed Argent the envelope. Scribbled on the back in pencil was the note: 'This letter came yesterday but did not see it until late last night.'

When Argent looked up from the envelope he saw Merritt smiling broadly as he read the letter; when he had finished, he passed the letter to Argent. "Help is indeed waiting for us in Parkersburg."

Argent also smiled as he read the letter from Grant himself explaining the nature of the help. Knowing Miss Warner's penchant for privacy and natural aversion to crowded situations, Grant was sending to Parkersburg a small train on which Miss Warner may travel in comfort and safety. She was to have her own guest car, while Merritt and Argent would share a similar car, outfitted for sleep and dining. This would allow Miss Warner the option of staying on the train and not in a hotel, if this should cause her any distress. The train, the President wished to stress, is a government project, too long left unexplored, that will allow the objective trial and evaluation of the rapidly developing field of train technology. This was a project that Mr. Warner himself had advocated, being greatly disturbed by the fatal trial and error methods of testing new steamboat technology (particularly the boilers). As the goal of this project is to test new technologies and not to aggrandize the government itself, the cars themselves are not new, but have been completely refurnished inside for their present purpose. Grant ended with, "Please be advised that nothing considered dangerous is being tested on this, the train's maiden run. Please extend to Miss Warner my best wishes for a safe and pleasant trip to the nation's capital."

"This is perfect. She need never leave the train, and we need never worry about her running off."

Merritt agreed. "A separate car for her will afford her all the privacy she wants, and I'm sure we can manage some system of securing her there during stops for water and fuel. It is only sixteen hours between Parkersburg and Washington."

Argent's smile faded a little as he remembered last night's worries. "I am still concerned about escorting a young lady without an attendant. I wonder that the President did not address that issue."

Merritt took the letter from Argent and scanned further down the missive. There were the usual exhortations for speed and care and the stern reminders of the importance of Miss Warner's happiness and comfort, and the honor which the President is sure Merritt and Argent feel for this task, but there was nothing about a female attendant. There was a short line about a stock car for the transport of their own horses left in Cincinnati, with the cryptic mention of any other livestock that might need transport as well.

Merritt sighed, but only slightly. "If we leave tomorrow, we will be in Washington City early Wednesday morning. Parkersburg is a bit of a wait, but we can grin and bear it until then."

"That is, of course, assuming that Mr. Henry can bring about a reversal of Miss Warner's adamant rejection of the trip."

"I think Mr. Henry can bring about just about anything where Miss Warner is concerned."

When Carrie arrived at the house to begin the big Sunday meal, she found both men napping on the porch – Argent stretched out on the swing and Merritt braced, back and feet, between the two newels on the top step. She had come through the back door, trailing Thea, Caleb, Bill, and Matthew, everyone carrying something needed to prepare the largest and most elaborate meal of the week. She had sent Matthew in search of the men when her halloos to announce their arrival had gone unanswered. When Matthew returned with a story of both men drunk on the porch, she had gone to investigate herself.

Regarding them in their repose on the front porch, Carrie doubted very much that they were drunk, but they had been drinking. She had disapproved of her husband's allowing these men – trusted government operatives or not – the freedom of the house when neither owner nor hostess were present. Her disapproval turned into suspicion last evening when she looked to the house on the hill – as she always did in the evenings – to see lights going from room to room, even to the upstairs. They had no business poking around the sad remnants of the family's bedrooms. When she mentioned this to her Henry, he said that it was good that they should see the cause of Miss Mary's fierce grief – it could only help them understand her better. And, now, fast on the heels of last evening's trespass, these men had helped themselves to some of the Warner's whiskey, and on the Sabbath!

Carrie's disapproval was deep enough that she allowed her children free run of the house and, though she did not encourage their loud play, neither did she attempt to curb it. She, herself, was unusually loud in the cold kitchen and the dining room, and she slammed the back door shut every time she left the house to check on the true cooking in the kitchen cabin behind the house.

Merritt and Argent were, in fact, not drunk, but they had taken the liberty to toast the good news contained in President Grant's letter. It was an admittedly selfish toast, not only celebrating the great relief to themselves, but also supporting the hope that these new travel arrangements could allow them to adopt the shorter two-day express schedule. The toast was shallow, and so was the drink, relatively speaking, especially for men who were experienced in the art of social drinking, both in the gambling dens where their work often took them and at the more moral and elegant events they sometimes attended. But the wild and unpredictable rhythms of life on this farm (and the reverberating chimes of the tall clock) had kept them from achieving true sleep for the last two nights. The beautiful quiet of the morning and their long walk easily gave even this modest drink the power to subdue the men into a drowsy state, and then into deep sleep.

Argent was the first to emerge from his Sunday morning nap, to find that it was now Sunday afternoon. He had been awakened by a good deal of slamming – the back door, cabinet doors, and, if he was not very much mistaken, a window being slammed shut. Argent grew up in a household of women. Even before the death of his father, during the war, leaving

Argent the sole male in the house, the household was decidedly feminine; though he was an only child, three female cousins, their widowed mother, and another aunt all lived with them. And, of course, there was his own mother. Argent, therefore, instantly recognized the unmistakable timbre of the slamming that anger brought out in women. Sitting up and pulling his hand down his face, he found Thea and Matthew solemnly observing him while they sat on the porch floor, nibbling on cornbread. A moment of disorientation engulfed him as he tried to place where he was. As he looked around to get his bearings, he remembered not only where he was, but why he and Merritt had come to be there.

Suddenly awake, Argent gathered up the bottle and the glasses, under the somber watchful eyes of the children, and thumped Merritt brusquely on the shoulder as he passed by. "Shaw! Up! I think Miss Warner is home."

From behind their cornbread, both Matthew and Thea shook their heads, no. Matthew asked, "Are you drunk?"

Though Thea elbowed him hard, she looked inquiringly at Argent, also interested in the mysterious state of being known as 'drunk.' Merritt, rudely roused from what must have been a very pleasant dream, also looked at Argent, almost perfectly mimicking Matthew and Thea's innocent and expectant curiosity. Argent answered gruffly, "Certainly not." Immediately regretting his surliness, he asked in a much lighter tone, "You say Miss Warner is not yet returned?"

Thea spoke up. "No, sir; she won't be home 'til later. She's hoping you'll be gone when she gets back."

Matthew asked, "Will you be gone?"

Merritt had still not risen from his place on the step and smiled openly at Argent's discomfort. He neither rose to stand by Argent nor offered any help in responding to the children's direct and honest comments and questions.

Argent looked long at the children, who never wavered in their patient expectation of replies, except to nibble at their snack. Finally, Argent said, "We will be gone when your father has convinced Miss Warner to go with us. If Miss Warner is not here, who is in the house?"

"Mama is making Sunday dinner. It is Sunday," Matthew observed, pointedly looking at the bottle hanging limp in Argent's hand.

Thea added, "Mama sent us out here to make sure you didn't fall in your drunken stupor."

A jolt of clarity explained the anger behind the slamming. This, then, was the source of the anger – not Miss Warner's disappointment to find them still in her house, but Miss Carrie indignant to find them suspiciously asleep with empty glasses and a bottle of the red liquor nearby. Then Matthew's comment echoed in Argent's mind: It is Sunday. There were few things more reprehensible to the female sentiment than the alcoholic blasphemy of drinking on the Lord's Day.

Merritt at last rose at Thea's comment, and said, "Thank you for watching over us," and flipped them both a penny for their trouble. The children were delighted at such largesse and, stuffing the last of the cornbread in their mouths to free up their hands to carry the precious coins, ran off the porch and down to the barn to show their father. Merritt asked Argent, "Just how much did you drink after I fell asleep?"

Argent favored him with a cold glance before entering the house. He replaced the bottle of whiskey – very good whiskey, they had both agreed – in the small cabinet to the left of the front room door. Then both men spent a few minutes re-tucking their shirts, straightening their coats and neckties, and running fingers through their hair, before presenting themselves to Miss Carrie. A slam from the back of the house indicated that Miss Carrie had either just left or just returned. They found her in the cold kitchen, plating buttered boiled potatoes, to join a small host of other, already plated, side dishes, all of them covered with layers of cloth to keep them warm and free of flies, already numerous this early in spring.

The men offered their subdued good days, to which Carrie responded, "I hope you enjoyed your morning activities and your nap." She never looked up from her work. "I am glad you are finally awake. Dinner will be ready very soon. I hope your hunger has not been too blunted."

Argent looked wearily to Merritt, who surprisingly exposed himself to possible further barbs from Miss Carrie's quiver of moral rectitude. "Miss Carrie, there is nothing that could blunt my appetite for your cooking. In fact, it was the delicious aroma – all the way out on the porch – that woke us. We wore ourselves out this morning walking off the breakfast you left, and it looks like we'll have to take an even longer hike after this meal."

Miss Carrie spared a look for Merritt to judge the sincerity of such comments. Whatever she saw there, satisfied her, for she was noticeably less aloof. She covered the potatoes with a lid then slid the dish under the blanket of cloths with the other dishes. She took the two dirty glasses from Argent's hand without a word.

Argent offered, "We don't normally indulge in drink so early in the day or on a Sunday, but we were celebrating, perhaps prematurely, leaving with Miss Warner tomorrow morning."

Miss Carrie gave him a leveling look, then patting him on his sleeve, said, "I understand – Miss Mary can drive the best of men to drink. I have been sorely tempted myself on occasion. Now you two go on out of here – there's not enough room as it is. I'll have Thea call you when dinner is ready, but don't go far."

Merritt and Argent were thrilled to have been so lightly upbraided for their Sabbath transgression. They left Miss Carrie without any further prompting. Even so, they felt it best to leave the house completely, and so headed down to the horse barn, which seemed to be the heart of the farm, at least for everyone but Miss Carrie, who seemed to rarely leave the kitchen or dining room.

At the barn they found Matthew and Thea, still clutching their pennies, and skipping around their father. Mr. Henry was working the leather on an elegant set of harness and saddle. Nearby was a trunk whose interior was partitioned in two. One side was full of neatly-packed apples still edible from last year's crop; the other side was obviously in progress of being packed with odds and ends of horse tack, including shoes, stirrups, and lengths of leather strips. At Merritt's and Argent's entrance, Mr. Henry casually closed the lid of the trunk, and bid them good afternoon. He also mentioned his disapproval of giving his children money for doing what their mama had asked them to do, though he said it without any real feeling. He occasionally looked up from his work to regard the men, finally observing, "You don't look to be in a drunken stupor to me."

Merritt and Argent shifted in their shame before the children, but also sighed a little defiantly at the charge. Matthew said in his piping voice, "That's what Mama said."

Mr. Henry continued working the leather on the saddle and replied to Matthew, "Well, that's what makes your mama a lady – she doesn't really know what a drunken stupor is, and that a little nip before dinner upsets her so much shows how genteel she is."

This made both Thea and Matthew giggle loudly, and as they both circled over and over again one of the support posts, Thea said, "Mama isn't genteel, she's gentle; *gentle*, Papa."

Mr. Henry gave his children a rare smile, and said, "You may be right, at that. Now go on up and see if your gentle mama has dinner ready yet." After the children had run out of the barn, Mr. Henry said, "I do enjoy Sunday dinner, but it comes far too late in the day for my likes."

Argent moved closer to inspect the saddle under Henry's hands. "Thank you for delivering the letter this morning, and for the care of our horses."

Mr. Henry waved off thanks for the horses, but asked, "I hope you had good news?"

Merritt inclined his head. "We did. We need only your help in convincing Miss Warner to accompany us."

Mr. Henry returned to the saddle that Argent was beginning to wonder at; it was far too fine a saddle for everyday use on a farm, and it had unusual customizations that he could not place. He was pulled from his observations by Henry's words. "Oh, she will go. She will sputter and buck, but don't you mind that. I suspect she knew even before Edwards' nags pinned you here that she would have to go. She doesn't like to admit defeat. She rarely loses a contest of words or ideas, so she isn't used to it, but she'll go."

Mr. Henry gave up on his work and began to clean up. He was as meticulous in this as he had been in working the saddle: the oil was carefully capped and placed in its appointed spot on one of several shelves above the workbench; the rags he had been using were put in a pail, that he closed tightly with a lid, keeping the oiled rags from drying out; a few detail tools that he had employed were returned to their places with deliberate care. While he was conducting this finishing ritual, he added, "Miss Mary is trying to fight too many fronts at once. She is trying to run this farm as if nothing had happened; and, of course, the farm has to be run as if nothing had happened, but she can't do it alone, not this year. She is trying to find her footing with my wife, as mistress and owner in her own home. She is trying to salve her grief with work, and too much of it. And she is trying to find a way . . ." Here Mr. Henry stopped, then continued, "No, I think it is permission . . . she is trying to find permission from someone, somewhere to find a little happiness for herself. And now you gentleman bring news to her of movement at a front she thought she had conquered. She thought that ignoring all that correspondence from the General had closed the conversation, that she could suffocate that fire by turning her back on it."

Argent was indignant for Grant, though he tried to keep it out of his voice. "You and Miss Warner seem to labor under the mistaken impression that President Grant has something unpleasant in store for her. I don't know the cause of the rift between the two, but I assure you, President Grant wants nothing but to speak with her, and is very solicitous of her happiness and comfort."

If Mr. Henry heard any rebuke in the statement, he ignored it. "You and I know that, but until she meets with him and finds out for herself, it is war between them. And I think she has finally figured out for herself that she can't fight all these other fronts here at home and be distracted by the General in Washington, too. She'll go, if for no other reason than to rid herself of that distraction."

"If you can tell us without betraying any confidences, what is the rift between Miss Warner and the President? Perhaps in the little time we are traveling with her, we can work to ease the tension she feels." Merritt had heard the muffled snit in Argent's voice, and though Mr. Henry had not reacted to it, Merritt still felt obligated to support his partner.

Mr. Henry fixed Merritt with a penetrating stare, much like Carrie had done last night. "It is not my place to reveal the private disagreements of others, especially of two people I hold in particular affection. But I will tell you this: in this matter, I find the President in the wrong. Whatever other conclusions you may come to about Miss Warner, know that her grievance is real, and it is deep."

From the top of the stone steps, a lazy Thea shouted, "Dinner is ready."

Mr. Henry ushered Merritt and Argent from the barn as if he were showing them to their carriages at a fine mansion, then he led them up the stairs. Thea waited for her father on the top step, and when he reached her, he lightly scolded her. "I'm sure your mama didn't tell you to holler at us like you were cheering at a three-legged race. Next time, you walk down to the barn like you're supposed to and give me your message in a simple voice."

"Yes, sir." Then she whispered, "Dinner is ready."

Dinner was very pleasant. It was truly a huge affair, with three kinds of bread – cornbread, biscuits, and loaf bread – and a myriad of side dishes: buttered, parsleyed potatoes and mashed potatoes, pickled cabbage, deviled eggs, green beans preserved from last year (cooked to almost mush with a huge hock of ham), lima beans, three bean salad, jellied peppers, two huge roasts sharing a platter, and some of yesterday's ham slices. There were also sauce boats of gravy and bowls of strawberry and blackberry preserves. There were pitchers of tea and jugs of water and milk. The china had remade its appearance, though probably in deference to the day rather than to any change in the status of the guests.

Not only was the food appetizing and plenty, Miss Carrie had regained her former good humor at the table, and Merritt and Argent found the children an amusing diversion from the heavy subject of Miss Warner and her war with the President. Merritt seemed especially amused with the children, teasing them about one thing or another. It was apparent that Thea was especially taken with Merritt, though she conspicuously included Argent in her comments and inquiries. She always added, "And you, Mr. Argent?" in quite a ladylike fashion. Argent found Thea's heartfelt goodwill towards him sweet, but he was a little put out that Miss Carrie also seemed overly solicitous to Merritt. Mr. Henry occasionally joined the banter at the table, but mostly he chewed his food deliberately and slowly, and his contributions to the conversation usually took the form of a mild rebuke at the table manners or speech of one of his children.

The meal was finished, and dessert had just been brought to the table when Miss Warner appeared in the doorway. She was wearing a somewhat dingy skirt that apparently had seen better days. Carrie was certainly familiar with it. "That skirt is hardly fit for a workday, much less the Lord's Day."

Her shirt, however, was new to everyone. Thea exclaimed, "Miss Mary, I really like your new shirt!"

It was a very handsome article, a wraparound blouse with long trailing shirt tails at the front that, when crossing each other and wrapped around to the back, were tied to create a small bow; the collar was very simple, perhaps even unfinished – a simple fold of fabric on each side that created a soft V at the throat. Oddly, Argent thought it was the most feminine thing he had seen Miss Warner wear, even more so than the dress she had deigned to wear at their first meal.

Miss Mary replied pleasantly, "Thank you, Thea. Mrs. Müller made it for me. It is my Christmas gift." Miss Carrie sniffed, rather audibly.

Thea patted the seat next to her, just as Miss Mary had done for her two days ago. "Come sit with me," she said brightly.

Carrie had stopped cutting the pies that were serving for dessert, but now she resumed. "We've just finished dinner, but you can fix yourself a plate back in the kitchen — I haven't put anything away yet."

Mary waved her off; she had already had her meal with the Müllers, but admitted she was never too full to turn down pie. This was said with such honest goodwill that Carrie's initial stiffness relaxed, and she passed Mary a large wedge of apple pie. Mary had not acknowledged Merritt and Argent, even to glance in their direction. She had, of course, noted Edward's two nags still occupying the field behind the barn.

"It is good to see you again, Miss Warner. You are looking well."

Mary glanced briefly at Argent, and thanked him, but offered no further conversation.

Thea, a natural conversationalist, asked, "Miss Mary, what did you do in town?"

"I stayed with Mrs. Müller."

"Yes, but what did you do?"

Mary was loath to give an accounting of herself in front of Merritt and Argent but saw no graceful way out of answering Thea. "I visited with Mrs. Müller and Mary and helped in her dining room a little. Then we all went to confession" – at which Carrie sniffed again – "last evening. I left after Mass this morning."

M knew that mentioning Mass and confession, and in the same sentence, was likely to dispel from Miss Carrie's mind her usual query when anyone returned from town: What was the talk? This week, and likely for a long time before and a long time in the future, the talk was of the passage of the Fifteenth Amendment. Most of Mrs. Müller's customers were Republican in politics, but not all, and M had heard rather loud lamentations, from some diners, of the destructive "nigger vote." It was a word never allowed in the Warner house, though Mary was aware that certain relatives on her mother's side employed it often. The *Courier Journal* had thoroughly denounced the amendment as an overthrow of representative government, but given its pre-war and wartime vitriol, it was surprisingly diplomatic in its urging calm and dignified compliance with the detested Republican "perversion" of the Constitution.

Mary's diversion took its effect. Carrie asked in alarm, "You didn't wear that awful skirt into the church?" Almost immediately, a worse horror occurred to Carrie. "Or those awful trousers?" Although she did not approve of much of the Catholic faith – confession seemed particularly odious to her – she nonetheless would be mortified if Mary had entered a house of God dressed as carelessly as she was now. Carrie had many friends in town who might think she approved of such disrespect.

Though the question obviously aggravated Miss Warner, it was also obvious that she enjoyed taunting Carrie into believing she was just disrespectful enough to try it. Mary settled for a simple, if exasperated, retort: "Of course not – they'd turn me away for a heretic. Mrs. Müller had made a dress for me as a Christmas gift, so I wore that, and she let me borrow a veil."

Argent was privately amused at the thought of Miss Warner in a veil, outwardly devout, but surely thinking of everything but church.

Mary continued excitedly, "In fact, she made three dresses for me – two for this past Christmas and one for my birthday, but she gave them to me all at once."

Thea asked, "What's a heretic? Does it mean to wear pants?"

"No, that's a visionary." Merritt and Argent both grunted. Mary ignored Grant's men. "It is all St. Paul's fault, the blowhard."

Miss Carrie put her spoon down hard on the table. "Mary!"

"It doesn't make him any less of a saint, just an irritating one."

Argent heard a strange sound come from Merritt, and he realized that Merritt was stifling a laugh. Although Merritt smiled often, it just now occurred to Argent that he rarely heard Merritt laugh.

Mary continued, "He must have been unbearable at dinners or parties. You can just tell he loved to hear himself talk, if his epistles are any indication."

Carrie exclaimed again, "Mary!"

"And because he couldn't keep his thoughts on God in Church —"

"Temple," Argent corrected, though under his breath.

"— if he saw a woman's hair, we all have to wear these ridiculous veils. I think wearing a veil should count towards penance."

Argent could not remember how the conversation had tilted so violently against St. Paul and veils. At any rate, Miss Warner was voluble on the subject. "I don't think God really cares what one wears to Mass. We're born naked" – Carrie gasped at the mere word, as well as the thought, and on Sunday – "and He liked us just fine then, and probably prefers us that way."

Argent could not tell if Miss Warner really believed this or if she was enjoying shocking Miss Carrie or, the thought occurred to him, if she thought she was shocking himself and Merritt, hoping to scare them off. Miss Warner was concluding, "If God had intended clothing all along, He would have made us born in full dress."

Thea countered, "God couldn't make us have clothes, just born."

"Certainly he could; it is blasphemous to say otherwise. It is like saying God has limits. God can do what He likes when He likes. That's how we can be sure God is male."

Mr. Henry joined Merritt and Argent in harrumphs.

Carrie cut in with the real question on her mind. "Where are these dresses Mrs. Müller made for you?"

The sudden shift in topic made Mary blink, but then she answered, "Oh, they are in the saddle bags."

Miss Carrie gasped. "The saddle–! I can't believe you did that!"

Mary agreed. "I can't either; it was difficult enough to force one in a saddle bag, but it was almost impossible to fit the other two in one saddle bag together."

Carrie stared at Mary in utter horror of the treatment of three new dresses. "They will be hopelessly wrinkled." Then in righteous condemnation, Carrie added, "Well you can just spend the evening ironing them yourself."

"Why? I'll hang them up for a while, then lay them flat on a sheet and put some books on top. Eventually, they'll lose their wrinkles. I have no immediate plans to wear them."

Carrie intoned, "Lord, give me patience."

"Exactly. With a little patience, one need not iron at all."

The children had continued to eat pie during this careening philosophical discussion, but only Thea had tried to follow with any real interest. Mr. Henry moved to redirect the conversation before Miss Mary drove his wife to utter despair.

"Miss Mary, were you able to complete that errand while you were in town?" When Mary regarded him with a blank look, Mr. Henry prompted, "The business you said you needed to tend to, when you left yesterday morning."

If Mr. Henry had thought to call some bluff of hers, he was disappointed. Mary replied, "Oh, yes; I forgot." She had brought into the room with her a small satchel, that lay on the chair next to her. Suddenly remembering its presence, Mary turned to root through the sack. When she finally found the object of her search, she turned to Thea. "Here, I thought you might like this."

Thea gasped at the huge blue silk bow that Mary presented to her. When Thea looked up at her, Mary said, "Look, it stays tied just like that, and there is a clip on the bottom, so you can just clip it into your hair." Mary reclaimed the bow from Thea, commanded, "Turn around," and clipped the bow nearly on the top of Thea's head. Without asking to be excused, Thea jumped up from the table and ran into the serving pantry, from which was heard her squeal of delight.

Argent asked the room at large, "Is there a mirror in there?"

Miss Carrie answered, "Yes, and now I'm afraid that's where she'll spend the rest of the day."

Argent muttered, "I wish I had known," but no one but Merritt heard him.

Despite Carrie's dire predictions, Thea soon returned to the room, beaming in her new bow. Caleb could not let the opportunity pass. "That bow is as big as your head."

Mary leaned over and whispered to Thea, who promptly said, "Not as big as your mouth."

Miss Carrie sighed. "You are not home five minutes and you have already managed to disrupt dinner."

Mary returned to her satchel and brought out a large spool of lace trim, placed it on the table, and with a practiced push, slid it across the table to land neatly near Miss Carrie. Carrie wiped her hands on her apron twice before she picked up the spool, and said, though without much animosity, "This doesn't excuse you."

Mary shrugged her lack of care, then gave the satchel to Thea. "Take this to your brothers over there." She watched with simple satisfaction as the boys decided between them who would get the small leather pouch and who would get the small penknife and who would get the toy horse. As expected, the decision was a hierarchical one, wherein Caleb, the oldest, claimed his prize first (the leather pouch – he already had a penknife), Bill claimed the penknife, and little Matthew claimed (though he had no choice) the leather toy horse with real horsehair mane and tail. Thea's thorough search of the satchel had also turned up a bag of candy, which Miss Carrie confiscated, and a large envelope. When Mary saw the envelope, she instructed Thea, "That is for your father." Thea handed her father the envelope, which he opened, briefly scanned the paper within, then replaced, and nodded either his agreement or thanks.

Though she had pointedly ignored himself and Merritt, Argent was amazed at the difference in demeanor Miss Warner now displayed. She seemed relatively relaxed and almost happy. Merritt asked with wicked amusement, "Did you bring us anything?" Argent closed his eyes in exasperation; why must he taunt her?

Miss Warner never wavered in her attention to the children at the far end of the table, but she answered, "I am sorry, but no. I had thought you would be gone. I hope you are not too disappointed."

Merritt returned the taunt. "I was just about to say the same thing."

Mary slowly moved her eyes to regard Merritt, then moved her head to match her gaze. Before this sparring match could develop, Mr. Henry said, "Boys, Thea, take your pie out onto the porch."

"Not on those plates." Mary closed her eyes at Carrie's constant guardianship of the china. Merritt could swear she was rolling them beneath closed lids. After Carrie had traded the good china for sturdier stoneware and the children left the room, Mr. Henry began.

During meals, Mr. Henry rarely looked at anything but the wall in front of him, but now he turned to Miss Warner, demanding her attention. "Miss Mary, you know where my loyalties lie as to this unpleasantness between you and the General. But these gentlemen here are not the General, yet you have treated them as such. You know in your heart that they have not received the welcome due them as simple guests or even as messengers from the General. They have been ill-handled merely because of their connection with General Grant. They have been witnesses to and victims of heated exchanges and rudely left on their own, while you retreated into town. I never thought I would have to remind you, but what would your father think?"

Miss Warner began to respond with evident heat, but Mr. Henry held up his hand. Merritt and Argent were almost spellbound by Henry's handling of Miss Warner. "I know you have a legitimate grievance and that it is difficult to separate your feelings from the grievance. But you have tried and convicted General Grant in your heart without giving him the benefit of a trial. You need to let the General have his say, and if he is still guilty after you have heard all the facts, then no one will support you more than I will in your right to sever all ties with him. Put out this fire, and you may just sleep a little better."

Miss Warner had lowered her eyes at the catalogue of her inhospitality and had remained silent throughout. When she did not reply, Mr. Henry asked, "Miss Mary, are you listening?" Mary raised her eyes to meet Mr. Henry's gaze, and he knew he had convinced her of the fairness of his argument.

Mary drew a deep breath. "I will write the General my apologies and accept future correspondence, but I do not want to go to Washington."

She held Mr. Henry with a look that Merritt and Argent could not see, but that had an effect on him. Something like sorrow and sympathy crossed his face. Even so, Mr. Henry said softly, "It is too late for that. These men have come a long way with a command from the General. They cannot go back without you."

Miss Warner briefly gave Merritt and Argent a sidelong glance. Argent wanted to assure her of their very best intentions to make her trip as comfortable as possible, but he was afraid to intrude in this oddly public-private reprimand and quiet encouragement that Mr. Henry had delivered to Miss Warner.

Mary knew Mr. Henry was right on all accounts. She began to feel the walls close in on her as she realized she could not escape this trip. She suddenly sagged as she dropped her head into her left hand and leaned on the table. Merritt and Argent were not without feeling for her predicament, and Merritt breathed out his dissatisfaction at having so corralled Miss Warner. Mr. Henry, too, regretted that the young woman in front of him had been cornered into defeat. He offered a small inducement to help her more easily swallow the inevitable.

"Washington City might be the best place to contest the railroad right-of-way that Captain James plans to settle on your land. He has already begun a spur off the main tracks and has almost reached the southwest corner of the property. The General could help you meet with the right people who can help you keep him off your land. Railroad companies are powerful, and they are hard to beat alone."

Mary did not seem to hear him, seemed completely defeated, but she suddenly raised her head and asked, "What of Emmett?"

Mr. Henry said distractedly, "Oh dear Lord, I forgot about Emmett."

Argent thought there was something a little flat about Henry's response. Though he had known him only a short time, Argent had seen Mr. Henry step outside a very narrow range of expressed emotions once – when Miss Warner had asked to confirm directions to town. That time, Argent had seen genuine surprise surface, but this time seemed less spontaneous. Then his mind went back to the barn before dinner, when Mr. Henry had been working on a fine saddle and had quickly closed the lid on a trunk full of apples and riding gear. In another flash, Argent remembered the odd addendum to President Grant's letter about room for additional livestock. Mr. Henry knew about the train and the stock car. The letter had come to them sealed, but late; had Mr. Henry read their correspondence?

Next to him, Merritt's lowered eyelids told Argent that Merritt had come to the same conclusions but did not trust himself at this moment to look at either Mr. Henry or Miss Warner. Probably Miss Carrie and Miss Warner were the only two in the room who were unaware of the help awaiting Merritt and Argent and Miss Warner in Parkersburg.

Miss Carrie said with true dismay, "No one can do for that horse but Miss Mary."

Mr. Henry added, "I've been kicked once by that brute and don't plan on trying my luck again."

Miss Warner was quick to defend Emmett. "He didn't mean to kick you, at least not so hard. He has a real fondness for you."

Mr. Henry snorted his doubt but offered a solution. "You will only be gone a week or so. Emmett can stay in the fields. The weather is finally turning, but if it gets wild, I'll make sure he gets to cover."

Mary could not believe Mr. Henry's casual attitude towards Emmett's comfort. Then a worse idea struck her. "Someone may steal him! And he has to be brushed at least once a day; you know that, Mr. Henry!" Mary was becoming alarmed at Emmett's fate in her absence.

Merritt thought it was time to relieve Miss Warner of her anxieties regarding Emmett. "I think we might have the solution. We received word while you were in town that the General has sent a private train of sorts for your personal use. The train includes a car for our own horses that are stabled in Cincinnati. There will be room for Emmett and anything he may need to bring with him."

It was Henry's turn to lower his eyes in salute to Merritt. Grant's men had found him out and were playing their cards perfectly.

For the first time since she had entered the room, Miss Warner gave serious attention to Merritt and Argent. She regarded Merritt with suspicion, sure he must be teasing her. Finally, she said, "Emmett is not a warhorse – he has never ridden a train before; how will he be stabled? What if the train stops suddenly; how will he be protected? How can you guarantee his safety?"

Argent was amazed at the level of anxiety Miss Warner displayed regarding her horse, never once asking about her own accommodations. Merritt was careful to keep any amusement out of his voice when he replied. "Emmett will not only be safe but comfortable. Each horse has his own stall. The stall allows the horse just enough room to stand, so that if there is an unexpected movement in the train, the horse is kept secure in one place. There will only be our three horses, so there will be room between stalls in case any of the horses is inclined to bite. There will also be enough room for hay and apples" – Merritt looked directly at Mr. Henry – "and riding gear."

Miss Warner continued to inspect Merritt for any sign of trickery or mockery. "The train is here? In Louisville?"

Merritt answered her levelly. "No, it will be waiting for us in Parkersburg. There is currently no bridge across the Ohio at that point, so the train can't come any closer. But the trains we plan to take between here and Parkersburg can also accommodate horses. Horses are transported regularly on trains. We'll get a berth for Emmett on the Short Line, as well as on the Marietta night train. Once we're in Parkersburg, our three horses will have their own stock car. The ride is only for three days, at most, and regardless of which train we are on, each evening the horses can be let out for exercise and grazing. There is plenty of water along the way."

Mary continued to observe Merritt, long after he had finished speaking. After a moment's pause, Argent added with a little exasperation, "Emmett will be as comfortable as you will be, if you are interested in your own accommodations."

Mary shifted her gaze to Argent, and mused, "If there is all that much room in the stock car, I can just stay with Emmett."

Merritt and Argent both held their breath. This was the first indication that Miss Warner was actually considering making the trip to Washington. Argent said cautiously, "That idea can certainly be entertained."

Mary realized that Argent had spoken to her, and that she had all but agreed to return with these men to Washington. The realization and the finality of the decision made her flush. She looked down to the untouched pie in front of her to hide her reaction. She was cornered and committed, and she was terrified of leaving home.

Mr. Henry must have known something of the turmoil in her mind, for he said softly, "I have been so impressed these last few years, watching you hold this farm together under the worst conditions possible. And if you don't know it already, your daddy was bursting with pride to see how well you did on your own. He told me often he was glad to be leaving it in your hands. But, Miss Mary, you know I always helped your daddy in the past, and I know how he liked things done. I'll keep the care of things while you're gone."

Again, Argent felt like he was eavesdropping on a very private conversation. Miss Warner seemed completely unaware that she was not alone with Mr. Henry. She did not look at Mr. Henry but fixed her gaze on a point past him. It was clear she was struggling to come to some decision. When she spoke, her voice was thick with emotion and pitched low for Henry's ears only. "I don't want Dad to think I can't do the work, or I don't care about his farm."

Mr. Henry closed his eyes for a moment and pitched his own voice low. "Honey, your daddy is gone. This is your farm now, and no one can accuse you of shirking your duty or not loving this land as much as he did." Raising his voice just enough so that Merritt and Argent could also hear, Mr. Henry added, "Now, I want you to go on to Washington and conduct your affairs; but don't dawdle — I can't do this all myself for long."

Miss Warner was still staring at some point past Mr. Henry. She nodded slowly at Mr. Henry's words. She seemed to be in some kind of trance. She asked of no one in particular, "When do I have to leave?"

But it was Mr. Henry who answered. "They want to leave in the morning. Can you be ready?"

Again, she nodded slowly. Finally, Mary sighed and looked at Mr. Henry, seeing him. With a hollow voice, she said, "I'll go look in on the children." She rose and turned to leave without acknowledging anyone else.

Before she had reached the door, however, Carrie called to her. "Mary, honey, don't you want your pie?" Mary returned to the table and slowly slid her plate with the untouched pie across the table, until it sat in front of Carrie. Mary never took her eyes off Carrie, who returned the gaze. In a smooth and uninterrupted motion, Mary retraced her crossing of the table, only this time she was pulling towards her the pie plate that was missing only the smallest slice. Only when she was in possession of the pie, did Mary break eye contact with Carrie, pick up a fork, and say, "Thank you," then left the room.

Argent asked incredulously, "Will she eat all that?"

Carrie answered with a snort, "No, most of it will go to those hounds. It is a sin the way she wastes food. I cooked her a nice piece of meat last month, and I found the dogs tearing it apart behind the house. I was furious, but she refused to apologize. She said, 'They only have ten or so years to live on this earth, let them have their pleasures.' She does it just to aggravate me."

Mr. Henry soothed, "That's not true, Mother."

But Carrie wasn't finished. "She cares more about those dogs and that horse than any person on this earth."

Mr. Henry repeated, "That's not true, either." Mr. Henry got up and made a point of leaving the room by way of passing his wife. "Supper was fine, Mother." He kissed her on the cheek, then he handed her his empty dessert plate and left by way of the serving pantry.

Merritt and Argent carried the dirty dishes, over Miss Carrie's vigorous and loud protests, to the cold kitchen. Though they did so in a very sincere effort to help for its own sake, the greater impetus was to save little Thea from the punishment that Miss Carrie had threatened after her husband left the room. In sending Thea and her brothers outside, Mr. Henry had unwittingly left Carrie without the help she expected from her daughter, help she apparently didn't expect from Miss Warner, even though the privilege, the obligation, and the house were hers.

In the hallway outside, Merritt opened his coat and offered Argent a slender cigar, but Argent shook his head and pushed Merritt's coat closed. "It is Sunday," he said quietly.

"Oh. Then shall we join the others on the porch?"

But there were no others on the porch – all the children had gone home, and Miss Warner had slipped off somewhere. Jack and Morty were pushing around the empty pie dish with their noses, hoping to find some crumb or smear of filling that had previously eluded them.

The two men sat on the swing. Sometimes they spoke quietly in the dark of Miss Warner and the trip they would begin in the morning. Sometimes they rocked unconsciously in silence. After a while, the soft glow from the dining room window was extinguished, and the porch became even darker. Still the men sat, until they heard footsteps approach the porch stairs.

Mr. Henry called, "Is that you gentlemen on the swing?"

Merritt answered, "Yes, sir. We were just waiting for Miss Warner. We want to assure her of our every intention to make this trip as comfortable and enjoyable as possible for her."

Argent added, "And to thank her for agreeing to return with us. We know it was a very difficult decision for her."

Mr. Henry had ascended the stairs and was standing before them, though they could hardly make him out in the dark. "You'll be sitting here a long time before she'll be back. I was just going in to make myself comfortable for the night." He stood there waiting for them to take the hint. Finally, both men rose from the swing, and followed Mr. Henry into the house, also dark except for one small lamp left burning on the bottom step of the stairs. Mr. Henry took it to light his way to the front room; once he had lit a lamp or two for himself there, he handed the lamp to Argent. "Once you're finished with that, please to replace it on the stairs, so Miss Mary can find her way."

Argent took the lamp, asking, "Where is Miss Warner?"

Mr. Henry sat wearily on one of the couches. "I expect she's making her goodbyes."

Merritt prompted, "Her goodbyes?"

Mr. Henry positioned his shotgun on the floor by the couch. "She's down to the cemetery. She'll come home when she's ready. Don't wait up on her – she'll be ready to go in the morning. I hope you spend a restful night."

With that dismissal, Merritt and Argent found their way to their cots in the back room, lit a lamp there, then Merritt returned the lamp to the bottom step in the hallway. Both men listened late into the night, but they never heard the front door open.

4

Merritt and Argent were up early the next morning, but Miss Carrie was up even earlier; breakfast was ready and on the table within minutes of their appearance in the hall. They ate alone, wondering at it. When Carrie brought in a fresh pot of coffee to set on the table, Argent asked, "Will Miss Warner be joining us?"

Carrie set the pot down, saying almost defiantly, "She gave her word that she would leave with you. She will join you as soon as she can."

Merritt rescued his friend from this misunderstanding. "We do not doubt the honor of her word. We were wondering if she would be joining us for breakfast. It is a long trip to Covington, and we can't guarantee we will have time to eat during any of the stops."

Carrie showed no remorse for jumping to conclusions; in fact, she seemed ill-tempered in general this morning. She was curt, then, when she replied, "Miss Mary is not hungry this morning. I will pack a little something for you all to share on the train." She left them to their breakfast, their coffee, and their confusion.

They were taking the last of the coffee on the porch in the earliest light of the day, when Jack and Morty were immediately roused from their deep slumber and ran to the window that looked in on the front room, their tails wagging vigorously. Both men followed the dogs and peered through the window, then immediately resumed their positions at the stairs, looking out over the horse barn and the fields and woods below.

"It looked like she had been crying. She may be entertaining second thoughts."

It looked very much like she had been crying. In their brief glance, they had seen Miss Warner emerge from the study beyond the front room, Mr. Henry behind her. Merritt took in a deep breath. "She may be entertaining second thoughts, but she won't pull out now. I meant what I told Miss Carrie – I don't doubt the honor of her word; but I also don't doubt the degree of dread she feels towards keeping it."

Argent stiffened a little at the rebuke he perceived in Merritt's defense of Miss Warner's honor, but he had to agree with the sentiment. "I agree that her reluctance is real and deep, and it isn't entirely due to her anger with the President, but I don't understand it. It is only for a week or two. Most young women would be silly for the chance to travel, and to the capital, no less."

Merritt tossed the rest of his coffee, gone cold, out into the dirt beyond the porch. "I think the first thing we need to do is to stop thinking of her and treating her like any other young woman, or any other young man, for that matter. I think it is a mistake to assume anything about her."

Argent also tossed his coffee, and asked, a little testily, "Then how do we treat her?"

Merritt turned to him and answered, "From minute to minute, and this minute we treat her for what she is at this moment – a terrified and grieving daughter leaving home with two strange men on a trip she doesn't want to take to a city she doesn't want to visit to see a man she hates. This afternoon, we may have to treat her as a willful woman determined to make us earn our pay. We learn as we go and pray that we don't have to treat with her as the escape artist or the skilled woodsman we have heard she can be or the person we first saw on the porch three days ago who was quite willing to fight one or both of us."

This was a Merritt that rarely surfaced, and Argent was confused at his attitude toward Miss Warner. Merritt had been nothing if not an ardent admirer of the fairer sex in her expected role. He was as passionate in his disgust for men treating women with anything but the utmost respect. In their dealings with counterfeiters and other criminals, nothing made Merritt more aggressive in apprehending a suspected man than when it was learned that man had beaten his wife or children, or left them penniless, while he drank or gambled away his earnings, even his counterfeit earnings. Merritt had surprised Argent that first night as they lay in their cots waiting for the storm to break. Merritt had said, "I wonder how many other women hate their dresses and would rather roam the woods than sew or sit in parlors and take tea?"

As Merritt walked back towards the front door, Argent wondered, "How many people can she be on a three-day trip?"

Before turning the knob, Merritt returned the question. "How many Miss Warner's have we seen in the last three days?" Then the Merritt that

Argent knew returned; with a wink he said, "Regardless of which Miss Warner we see, this promises to be a lot more interesting than escorting an old lady and her trunk of lace and mothballs."

Merritt and Argent found Miss Warner in the dining room, not so much eating breakfast as hoarding it. She was not sitting but leaning over the table dropping stacks of bacon and biscuits onto an oversized napkin.

"Good morning, Miss Warner. We have good weather for traveling. There is no need to eat on the run; we still have time."

Though they rose early, it was not to catch the early Short Line out of Louisville. The early train to Covington left at a very reasonable 10:05, but as they discussed it last night on the porch swing awaiting the return of Miss Warner, they opted for the afternoon express train at 3:55. It would have been difficult to catch the early train, since Merritt and Argent still needed to return their mounts to Mr. Edwards, near the wharf, which would add an extra hour or more to the morning's schedule. And one of them would have to go to the hotel, settle the bill and gather their bags. Moreover, Miss Warner was already dreading the trip and they did not wish to add to her anxiety by pushing for what would be a truly early departure from the farm. And there was, of course, the matter of her baggage – Miss Warner had retired later than anyone in the house and she had done no packing. Their experience of female packing did not bode well for the early train.

Mary finished loading the napkin, then neatly tied it into a bundle. She mumbled good morning to the men and a belated "glad to hear it" some moments after Argent's comment about the weather. She was avoiding looking directly at either man.

Merritt asked, "May we help you with any baggage?"

At that Mary straightened up with some alarm and repeated, "Baggage?" Turning to the serving pantry, she called out, "Miss Carrie, am I supposed to take baggage?"

From deep within the pantry, or possibly from the cold kitchen, Miss Carrie answered, "I packed for you this morning. Ask Mr. Merritt and Mr. Argent to carry it down to the wagon for you."

At last Miss Warner turned fully to Merritt and Argent and looked the question at them.

"We'd be glad to take care of your baggage; where may we find it?"

Miss Warner turned back towards the direction of the pantry door, apparently ready to shout this question through the walls as well, but Carrie arrived through the hall door, wiping her hands on her apron. "Mary, honey, please don't shout."

Miss Warner whirled around, less at the surprise to find Carrie at her back and more to hide the cache of food she had secured in the napkin. She deliberately stepped sideways to hide her work.

"Mr. Merritt wants to know where they may find the baggage."

Carrie looked suspiciously at her, but then directed Merritt and Argent to the top of the stairs.

The trunk was rather large, an old trunk with a brass plate with the name H. H. Warner engraved on it, but it was lightly packed. When they reached the bottom of the stairs, Miss Warner asked Miss Carrie, "What is in there? I have already packed my grip bag." Miss Warner seemed dazed and a little wild.

The irritation Carrie had directed at Merritt and Argent earlier was completely absent as she answered calmly, "Your clothes. I've ironed the dresses Mrs. Müller made for you, and added a few others, but if they are too loose, don't you wear them in front of the President. Maybe Miss Julia can take you shopping for something that fits proper. Your veil and gloves are in there, and your winter cloak." At Miss Warner's objecting look, Carrie said, "I don't know what you did with your light cloak, so you'll just have to make do."

All the while Merritt and Argent stood holding the trunk, but when Miss Warner commanded, "Wait!" and bolted from the hall, Carrie sighed and told them, "You might as well set it down for the moment."

A few moments later, Miss Warner reappeared with a small stack of books in her arms. Argent obligingly opened the trunk for her. She dropped the books on top of the ironed dresses that Carrie had so carefully arranged. Carrie cried out, "Mary! I just ironed those dresses!"

Miss Warner closed her eyes, not in exasperation at Carrie, but at her own stupidity and at the distress she had caused Carrie mere minutes before she was to leave. The composure she had assembled in her father's study was threatening to break. She opened her eyes to see on Carrie's face her own regret at causing a stir so close to departure. Miss Warner said, quickly, "I'm sorry, I'm sorry," and she redistributed the books so that the entire top dress was pinned down with equal weight. "Hopefully, that will keep the dresses from shifting."

Carrie began, "But that —" then checked herself and said instead, "That's a good idea."

Mr. Henry had entered through the front door during this exchange, but at the sight of his wife and Miss Mary seemingly entering another battle, he ducked into the dining room by way of the parlor door. Merritt chanced to look up during the exchange at the trunk to see Mr. Henry deftly stow the napkin full of food under his coat. When Mr. Henry looked up to find Merritt watching him, he motioned to let Miss Mary know he had her package. Merritt nodded his understanding.

With the trunk at last packed, closed and latched, and Miss Warner's smaller traveling bag on top, Merritt and Argent again lifted it to carry it down to the wagon waiting at the barn. When Argent began to start off with the trunk, however, he felt a tug as Merritt stood, unmoving. Merritt was watching something in the dining room.

"Shaw," but Merritt merely held up his free hand. Eventually, Merritt said to the dining room doorway, "Mr. Henry has it," then he nodded, and turning to Argent said, "Let's go."

They were not privy to the goodbyes between Miss Carrie, Miss Warner, and little Thea, but judging from Miss Warner's expression, it had gone hard. She came slowly down the stone steps, in one of the new dresses Mrs. Müller had made for her, a dress that fit her better than that she had worn out in the rain and torn on the bullhorn. Her hair was pulled back in a tight chignon, but the early morning wind was already loosening the hair at her temples, giving her a wild look.

Though Miss Warner herself had expressed her dislike of riding in a dress, Mr. Henry could not shake her from her determination to ride Emmett into town. Therefore, while Merritt and Argent saddled Edwards' nags, Mr. Henry fitted Emmett with the saddle he had been conditioning and readying yesterday. Merritt and Argent occasionally glanced towards Mr. Henry as he prepared Emmett, but Mr. Henry did not acknowledge them. Finally, Argent asked, "Is Miss Warner planning to ride Emmett to town?"

Mr. Henry never looked up but waited until Miss Mary had passed them and entered the barn. "Yes; I will drive the wagon, and she will join me at an appropriate moment."

Merritt offered, "I could drive the wagon and hitch my horse to the back. I know how busy you are, this time of the year, and now taking on extra duty. I'm sure we could persuade Mr. Edwards to return the wagon – at no cost." Merritt added this last with relish.

Mr. Henry gave a final tug on Emmett's saddle. "I thank you for your concern, but I will see Miss Mary on her way as far as I can."

While Mr. Henry rounded the back of the barn to catch the farm horse that would pull the wagon, Merritt and Argent stepped into the barn to retrieve the trunk that Mr. Henry had been packing yesterday, fully knowing it would be needed. They found Miss Warner just closing and latching the trunk. Without looking at them, she said, "It is ready." Outside, the trunks were loaded and secured, and the workhorse backed up and hitched to the wagon and all made secure. Argent checked his watch; there was still plenty of time for a leisurely drive into town, time to address Mr. Edwards, and time to reach the station for the 4 pm train. But the sooner they had Miss Warner on the road the better, before she found reason to reverse her decision.

Merritt and Argent followed Mr. Henry back into the barn to let Miss Warner know that all was ready, but she was not readily seen. Mr. Henry called, "Miss Mary? It's time."

From an empty stall, she said shakily, "Will you whistle for me?" Merritt and Argent looked at each other with confusion, and then started when behind them, Mr. Henry whistled loud and clear two simple long notes, the sound amplified into a blast within the cavernous barn. Within moments, Jack and Morty came rounding into the barn at an impossible speed. They ran past the men standing in a cluster, then rounded again at the back to return to Mr. Henry.

Behind them, Miss Warner said quietly, "Boys," and the hounds shamelessly abandoned Mr. Henry for their true pack leader. Without regard for her new dress, Miss Warner knelt down and hugged each dog fiercely, accepting in return their rough affections. Finally, she said, "Sit," and both dogs dropped onto their haunches. Rising, she walked to the workbench and retrieved the napkin of bacon and biscuits that Mr. Henry had secreted from the house for her. She gave each dog a full slice of bacon. Despite all her efforts to train them otherwise, they nipped her fingers as they greedily grabbed the offered bacon. The men watched as she fed them piece after piece, each time asking them to move a little further into the barn. As she moved away with them, they could not clearly see her face, but could clearly hear her sniff as she tried to bear down on her wretched tears. Finally, she opened a rough plank door to some storeroom and coaxed the puppies in after her. She remained with them a few minutes, allowing herself to cry softly her goodbyes to them; before she closed the door and latched it, she threw the last two biscuits to the back of the room and then the napkin in after it. Locking her puppies away nearly broke her heart. She stood by the door a long time listening.

"Miss Mary." Mr. Henry spoke softly. "Come away; don't torture them or yourself any more than you have to." When Miss Warner rejoined the men near the front of the barn, she was a mess – her dress had paw prints and other dog smears, her hair was in complete disarray, and her face was streaked with tears and dirt. Mr. Henry suggested gently, "There's a pail of fresh water and a clean cloth on the side of the barn. Go straighten up and then we need to be going."

After Miss Warner left the barn, Argent offered, "I am sorry this has caused so much distress for Miss Warner. President Grant warned us of her likely obstinance, but he did not advise us of the level of anguish we would encounter. I confess, I am at a loss as to how to reduce her anxieties; the trip is perfectly safe."

"There are things she fears, but not the trip. And she would no more confide in you her fears than she would confide in you her dreams; both are," – Mr. Henry searched for the right word – "intimate to her. But she is taking leaving hard. People who don't know her think she is cold and heartless and unfeeling. The exact opposite is true – she feels all too deeply, everything. These great bouts of anger are not always childish outbursts; for Miss Mary, there is no degree of being wronged – all her grievances are monstrous in her mind. But she is not selfish in this – wrongs against others are often of more magnitude to her than to the person wronged. And the same is true of her other feelings, though she is far better at keeping a tight rein on those. She is far more tenderhearted than most people would guess, and more than she would like to admit."

Mr. Henry had been looking out the barn door as he spoke, looking towards the house on the hill. He turned towards Merritt and Argent.

"I have particular affection for Miss Mary. I have watched her grow up, from the day of her birth, and it would grieve me to know she was unhappy. I know your job is merely to put her on that train and ride with her to Washington, but I ask of you, as gentlemen, to extend whatever kindness you can, even when you may think she does not deserve it."

Both men found themselves without words to answer Mr. Henry's plea. Usually, it was Argent who handled the more delicate aspects of diplomacy in their work, but Argent had merely nodded and turned away, making a show of studying Mr. Warner's collection of tools. Merritt finally said, "It was never our intention to treat Miss Warner or anyone else under our care and protection as mere cargo, but I promise you, Miss Warner will have our every attention and effort to make this as painless for her as possible. I hope she appreciates what a true friend she has in you."

Mr. Henry nodded his thanks. "Miss Mary and I have our understandings."

What was originally a ruse to escape the intensity of Mr. Henry's plea had become a real source of interest for Argent. As he scanned Mr. Warner's workbench, he realized that his collection represented a tidy sum of money tied up in tools of all kinds. Everything was neatly organized: there were awls of several sizes, cleverly hung – in descending order of size – through small tin loops; there were levels of all kinds – horizontal, vertical, right angle, long levels and short levels, bearing the mark of Edmund Draper; there were saws of every degree, from making simple blunt cuts on undressed lumber to making fine cuts on cabinet grade wood; there were three hammers and several screw-drivers; he had a T-square, files, rasps, boring tools and bits, and more. Unbelievably, there was a transit made by the famous William J. Young, late of Philadelphia. The maker alone made this tool a prize, yet here it hung in a barn, just one more tool on a peg. Argent reached to inspect it closer. From the doorway, Miss Warner said with dead calm and fury mingled, "Don't touch that; those are Dad's things." Argent turned to find her glaring at him.

Mr. Henry quietly chided her. "Miss Mary, he didn't mean anything by it; your father's tools are of interest to him, that's all. They are very fine tools."

Miss Warner made a visible effort to blunt her anger. "I know; please forgive me."

Argent lowered his hand. "Not at all; it is quite understandable. A man's tools are sacred, and you were quite right to protect them."

Mary was sure there was condescension somewhere in the reply, but she had promised Mr. Henry early this morning in her father's study that she would try to assume the best from these men, and accept their help and attentions, even if she felt they were not necessary. She would make the effort, for Mr. Henry's sake.

Argent was asking, "The transit – it is a Young transit?"

Mary answered almost mechanically, "Yes. Grandpa gave it to Dad when he graduated from engineering school. He bought it from one of the retired B&O engineers; Latrobe, I think."

Argent gasps. "Benjamin H. Latrobe?"

"I believe so. Why? Did you know him?"

"Only by reputation." Pointing to the transit, Argent advised her, "That is a very valuable transit."

"Yes, I know; it belonged to Dad."

Argent smiled. "Of course."

Jack and Morty were beginning to realize that more bacon or biscuits were not forthcoming, and they were beginning to whine and paw at the rough plank door of their confinement. Miss Warner's eyes went to the back of the barn, but before her feet could follow her gaze, Mr. Henry said, "Miss Mary, it is time to go." He managed to turn her towards the wagon without touching her, but merely making the gesture of guiding her shoulder.

Behind Miss Warner, Mr. Henry mouthed, "We need to hurry." Outside the barn, Merritt and Argent immediately mounted their horses, and Mr. Henry climbed onto the wagon. He motioned Merritt and Argent to move ahead. They hesitated, noticing that Miss Warner had yet to mount, but they kicked their horses into a walk anyway. Argent heard the wagon lurch into motion but could not resist a look back to check on Miss Warner. She was very cautiously mounting Emmett, arranging her skirts as she did so, to avoid damaging her new dress. He noted with slight amusement that she wore riding boots beneath her skirts. As he turned back in his saddle, he caught Mr. Henry watching him, and felt slightly guilty, but for what, he was not sure.

Behind them, Jack and Morty had decided that something was definitely not right, and began to bark, then to bay. Mr. Henry snapped the reins on the back of the workhorse, urging a quicker pace. Without looking back, Merritt and Argent also urged their horses into a quicker walk, knowing that Jack and Morty could undo the hard-fought work of the last three days. Merritt chanced a look behind and saw that Miss Warner was keeping up, but her head was down. Argent asked quietly, "How is she doing."

"Miserably." Merritt almost sounded miserable himself.

Jack and Morty were reaching their crescendo. Unlike their slow warming from whining to barking to howling, the hounds would stop suddenly after reaching a fevered pitch, and Merritt thought they were near that point. In this, he was mistaken — their baleful baying followed the group well after they had turned from the drive onto the lane and even after they had passed the little turn-off that led to Mr. Henry's cabin.

The ride into town was silent. Though Miss Warner was no longer staring at her hands, neither was she looking ahead; she stared listlessly at some distant point to her left, trusting Emmett to keep to the path, her body limp in the saddle – seemingly, no horsewoman at all. Merritt and Argent took their cue from Mr. Henry, and remained quiet, leaving Miss Warner to her solitude. After some time, however, Mr. Henry asked, "Stirrups too short?"

Merritt and Argent both turned to see Miss Warner shift uncomfortably in the saddle. She replied with a simple, flat "Yes."

Mr. Henry offered, "We can stop and lengthen them."

"No, I'll take care of it when we get there." Though Mr. Henry nodded his understanding, neither Merritt nor Argent knew if 'there' meant Louisville or Washington. Argent didn't think she knew either but was moving and speaking in a kind of stupor.

The easiest and most efficient route would have been to go to Ormsby Station or even Anchorage, several miles east of Louisville, and though not much closer to the Warner farm, they would not have had to contend with the crowds and traffic of Louisville. However, there was the matter of Mr. Edwards's nags, which needed to be returned, and the matter of Mr. Edwards himself, with whom Merritt and Argent intended to thoroughly acquaint their disapproval of his tactics as well as acquaint him with whom he had been dealing. So, they rode into town, the long length of the Louisville-Taylorsville Pike, until it ended at the Bardstown Pike, where they would turn north towards town.

At the toll house at the end of the Louisville pike, Mr. Henry dismounted and spoke briefly with the keeper; when he returned, Mr. Henry led the horse and wagon just beyond the toll gate, indicating that Merritt and Argent should continue through with him. He continued to lead the horse to a small clearing where he stopped. When Miss Warner reached the same place, he asked, "Miss Mary, will you ride with me now?"

Mary replied without looking at him, "Not yet."

Mr. Henry reminded her, "There is a lot of mud and filth from here on in; you don't want to ruin that dress Mrs. Müller spent so much time and thought to make for you." Louisville, or any other town, had its sloppy hazards, even in the driest weather, and, as everyone knew, it had already been a wet spring. Standing water (filthy with horse manure and other refuse) and muddy rivulets in the roads were still possible, even several days after a rain.

Mary did not reply but she began to slowly dismount, being careful not to repeat the incident of Saturday morning that had left that day's dress hopelessly ripped down the front. Merritt and Argent also dismounted. Merritt held Emmett steady until Mary had safely reached the ground, then offered to take Emmett's lead. Miraculously, and to everyone's surprise but Merritt's, Emmett consented to be led away by him and tied to the back of the wagon. Argent waited at the wagon to help Mary up into the seat next to Mr. Henry. She was at first confused by his presence and his offered hand, then blushed at this simple attention. Argent was astonished at her reaction and began to understand the enormity of this undertaking for her – she had left behind her world that operated under different rules and was entering a world of which she had little experience or even knowledge. She was supremely ignorant of the simplest interactions between men and women, unsure of her proper role. She may as well have been entering a foreign country, where she did not know the language nor possess any of the currency.

With Miss Warner firmly seated next to Mr. Henry, Merritt and Argent were not so conscious to keep their group close together. In fact, it would have been impossible to keep a wagon and two horses completely intact as a group on increasingly crowded city streets. Merritt and Argent therefore pulled ahead and lost sight of Mr. Henry's wagon, but without alarm. They picked their way to the wharves and piers where they had disembarked only three days ago. At the waterfront, it took them some time to work their way to the esteemed Edwards establishment – there was always a great deal of activity and noise at the waterfront, but it was heaviest on Monday, after the Sunday lull, and heavier still on this Monday after so many days of depressed business during the long rains.

Argent noted several steamers bobbing on the swollen river. "I never want to ride a steamer again." Then a thought occurred to him. "I wonder if Miss Warner would have preferred the steamer to the train."

"It is best not to give her any options in our travel arrangements. A steamer, especially, can only encourage her to jump ship, and I have no doubt she would try it. At least on a train, there are four walls and a roof to contain her."

Mr. Edwards was happy, though a little curious, to see them so lately returned from their excursion outside the city. He asked if they had enjoyed themselves and asked also if they had been satisfied in their mounts. Merritt answered lightly, "Very satisfied; they answered our needs very well indeed. In fact, we owe you a great debt — rhetorically speaking."

"Oh? I am certainly happy to have been of service, especially if the service is rhetorical; it costs so little to provide services of that kind."

"I'm afraid in this case, it will cost you – at least the amount of the refund you will be extending us."

Mr. Edwards' good will began to dissipate. "Now, gentlemen, refunds are only for dissatisfied customers, and you yourselves have admitted to being not only satisfied but indebted. And now you insist on refunds? Shall I send my boy here to bring the police?"

Argent had taken a seat on a hay bale, settling in to enjoy Merritt's little tutorial. There had never been any spoken or formal agreement or arrangement between them, but by natural consent Merritt usually handled those situations that required an adjustment in perspective of suspected counterfeiters, reluctant or greedy informers, disrespectful colleagues in law enforcement (especially those arrogant U. S. Marshals), or, as in this case, merchants, hoteliers, railroad ticket and baggage agents, or ostlers attempting to profit unduly from the taxpayers. It was true that Merritt and Argent rarely announced themselves as operatives of the federal government to the various agents of commerce, but that piece of information, properly and timely announced, always seemed to shed a stronger light on the dubious practice that had offered offense.

Merritt smiled and encouraged Mr. Edwards, "By all means; it will save Mr. Argent" – Merritt gestured towards Argent, who nodded courteously – "and myself" — placing his hand on his chest — the gesture that had irrationally irritated Miss Warner – "the trouble of finding the precinct station and filling out the inevitable paperwork. However, I would much rather settle our differences outside official means."

Mr. Edwards showed a considerable amount of confusion and a small but growing concern that a financial threat was looming. "Our only difference is in the honoring of the commercial contract we consensually entered when you rented my horses last Friday."

"Then we are agreed on the point of honor: we agreed to pay you for the use of two horses, properly tacked and able to carry us to our destination and back, and you agreed to provide said horses. Instead, however, you provided us with two horses of questionable quality – which I admit to misjudging – but also horses that had been intentionally slipshod to perpetrate a fraud against us."

Mr. Edwards began to protest both the falsehood of these allegations as well as the impossibility of proving such allegations, all in the smoothest and surest tones. Merritt and Argent were not the first travelers to realize the nature of Mr. Edwards' business nor the first to threaten action against him. Mr. Edwards had been down this road before, and he knew every obstacle in the path and how to sidestep them.

Merritt let Mr. Edwards continue with his well-worn refutations until finally Mr. Edwards observed that neither Merritt nor Argent seemed impressed, much less intimidated, with the legal barricade he had constructed before them. When Mr. Edwards' voice trailed off into confused alarm, Merritt began casually, "As operatives of the United States Treasury," – at which Mr. Edwards visibly paled – here was an obstruction in the path he had never before encountered – "we are entrusted to protect the currency of our fair nation. Mr. Argent" – again Merritt gestured towards Argent, who nodded courteously – "and I" – placing his hand on his chest, suggesting a sacred oath was in progress – "believe that this duty extends to protecting the taxpayer's money that we spend in our efforts, and also to promoting a healthy attitude toward commerce in general, where money is so vitally involved. Now, imagine our dismay when preparing to return to town last Friday evening, we found that one horse had lost a shoe and the other threatened to lose one, if not two shoes, as well. Then imagine our disappointment to hear that this sort of calamity often befalls first-time patrons of your fine establishment."

Mr. Edwards had become deathly still as Merritt calmly peeled back the veneer of his operations. "As I said, the delay caused by this unfortunate situation worked to our advantage but caused a great deal of distress for our hostess and a great deal of work for the man who had to properly shoe these horses. I think you can agree that a refund is due, since it is manifestly evident that you intended to defraud representatives of the United States government, and thus the United States government itself. A refund will go a long way to proving your sincere efforts to provide honest service to your fellow taxpayers."

Mr. Edwards assured Merritt that he could clearly see the justness of the settlement thus proposed. The refund was retrieved from the deep coffers of Mr. Edwards' profits, along with profuse professions of regrets and offers of future service, diligently extended. As Merritt and Argent emerged from the stables, Mr. Edwards incredulously called after them, "Be sure to recommend me to your colleagues and fellow passengers."

They found Mr. Henry waiting for them on the wagon, a package – apparently a new wrap for Miss Warner – on the seat next to him. Miss Warner, however, had rejoined Emmett and led him a short distance from the wagon, stroking his great neck and speaking softly to him. At Mr. Edwards' exhortation, Miss Warner looked up, then walked Emmett over to the wagon. Merritt took the reins from her, and she watched with something like jealousy as he mounted her horse without the least resistance from Emmett. She hurried to regain her seat in the wagon before Mr. Argent could again offer her his hand. Argent followed her onto the wagon, crushing her between himself and Mr. Henry. She was extremely conscious of the physical proximity of both men, and sat stiff and unmoving, desperately trying to avoid touching either man, but especially Argent. She was grateful for the package in her lap, to occupy her hands.

Making their way to the depot proved maddeningly slow, and, as Mr. Henry predicted, the streets were filthy, especially as they approached the little one-story brick station. This was the station the Louisville Cincinnati & Lexington had inherited from the failed Frankfort & Ohio railroad, which had languished for more than twenty years from lack of business and never-ending repairs, as well as from failing hopes of reaching the Ohio River at Covington. The fairly new LC&L, a merger of the Louisville and Frankfort and the Lexington and Covington railroads a few years earlier, found more patronage as the Short Line to Covington/Cincinnati. The older, longer route had required traveling first to Lexington, then transferring to the Lexington and Covington. The Short Line bypassed Lexington, despite that city's name in the company's title. Lexington was reached indirectly, via the old Louisville and Frankfort tracks, joining the LC&L at Lexington Junction, just past Lagrange, a mere 28 miles outside of Louisville.

However, the LC&L was dangerously flirting with Louisville's grip on southern markets. As Louisville saw its monopoly on southern river trade slip away to trains in general, it was loath to see Cincinnati enjoy any advantage over Louisville, especially through one of Louisville's own railroads. The railroad bridge that was already building across the Ohio at Newport across from Cincinnati – connecting the Little Miami Railroad with the LC&L – was little removed from blasphemy as far as Louisville's warehouses and commercial agents were concerned, and where warehouses and commercial agents were concerned, so was the tax base. The LC&L was inviting southern trade into Kentucky not at Louisville, where all southern trade should enter, but at Cincinnati, that vile hotbed of anti-southern, anti-Kentucky, and above all, anti-Louisville, sentiment. It was insult upon injury, and the Louisville city council made the LC&L suffer for its dishonor. Therefore, the LC&L depot was relegated to that stinking part of town known as Butchertown where distilleries and porkhouses and stockyards vied to belch the most convulsive odors. Moreover, passengers wishing to travel beyond Louisville to points south had to, upon quitting the LC&L, engage carts and wagons or carriages from LC&L's humble station to take their persons and possessions to L&N's grander facilities at Ninth and Broadway, nearly two miles away, through congested industrial streets. The same would be true for passengers wishing to travel north into Indiana and west to Illinois and Missouri and beyond, catching trains crossing the new (only weeks-old) bridge to Jeffersonville, the longest iron bridge in the nation.

All these carts, carriages, and wagons needed mules, horses, and even oxen to pull people, baggage and freight from the LC&L to the L&N, or the Jefferson, Madison and Indianapolis, or the Louisville, New Albany and Chicago railroads. Whether these animals and their conveyances were standing idle at the little station or in performance of their trade, they were a constant and concentrated presence in this area of town, and their copious droppings and evacuations were concentrated near the depot, adding yet another layer to the proprietary smell of the Butchertown area.

Miss Warner was no stranger to animals or their natural proclivities, but the concentration of their smells coupled with those of the breweries and slaughter houses was overpowering, especially on an empty stomach and a sore heart. Even in her swelling misery, Mary felt ashamed that these two men should see Louisville in such a disgraceful state.

A block before the depot, they passed St. Joseph Catholic Church. Mary had been unaware of this church; the family had always attended Mass at St. Bonifacius. A silly thought crossed her mind: this must be where River Catholics worshipped. If there were River Catholics, what was she? Every description of herself – farmer, country dweller, defiant – seemed ludicrous when paired with "Catholic." River seemed to lend itself to everything – riverboat, river trade, river rat, river snake, even river Catholics. All this silly speculation merely served to distract herself from the stinging guilt that, until yesterday, she had not attended Mass for months – she simply had not been able to bring herself to go into town. Mr. Henry advised her every Saturday night that his family would be going to services in the morning, and she was always welcome to travel with them – he'd be happy to take her to whatever church she wanted – but she always thanked him, saying, "Not this week, maybe next week." Miss Carrie always regarded her with a mixture of disapproval and pity. It suddenly occurred to Mary that on this trip – away from everything familiar and safe – she could very well die unshriven – confession this past Saturday could only last so long, or as long as she did not commit any new sins. She must make the effort this Holy Saturday, so that she may receive Holy Communion on Easter; she simply must make herself do it. She could not die unshriven – she would never see her family again. Mr. Henry had assured her she would reach Washington City well before Palm Sunday, and so be able to return home in time to attend Easter services at home, but more importantly, share the Easter meal with Mr. Henry, Miss Carrie, Thea and the boys, as she has done these last few years. What if she did not return home as promised? The thought of attending confession or Mass at strange churches was a new source of anxiety for her. She had made it through months of ignoring confession and her Sunday obligation, but now the thought of missing just the next one or two, especially as Easter was approaching, was inspiring a kind of dread in her. The thought made her shiver. Shiver and shriven – the similarity in spelling must mean something, but before she could explore this any further, she heard from her right, "Are you cold?" She shook her head, not trusting the bitterness and sarcasm that was welling up in her. If I die it will be Grant's fault, and if I die in a foul mood, it will be Mr. Argent's fault. He was very likely to inquire of her on her deathbed, *Are you dying?*

At the depot, Mary could not avoid Argent's proffered hand as she stepped down from the wagon onto the pavement. Mr. Henry and Merritt left the group – Mr. Henry to inquire into the stowing of her two trunks and Emmett's accommodations, while Merritt headed for the ticket agent's office to purchase their tickets. Argent found the station disappointing and oddly out of place for a city in size and prominence as large as Louisville. It was a small station – a single-story brick affair, with little more than an overhang to keep passengers out of the weather. It was little better than most country stations far from cities; Louisville could do better than this.

Mary had not been to this station for years, since the last time the family had gone to visit relatives in Cincinnati, just before the war, when the station was the terminus for the Louisville and Frankfort Railroad. The last time she had ridden the train, she and her father had gone to Ormsby Station, outside the city, to board it. The Louisville station had not improved over the years.

There was not much opportunity for privacy on the small platform. Mary had reclaimed Emmett's lead from Mr. Henry, and now held the reins at the edge of the platform, while Emmett stood on the ground just below. Gathering her skirts, Mary jumped down to join Emmett and walked as far away as the limits of the station would permit. She stood near his head, leaning against him. Argent could just hear her softly talking to Emmett but could not make out the words.

Merritt and Mr. Henry returned at the same time. Merritt slapped Argent jovially on the shoulder as he passed. "Mr. Henry has recommended a restaurant for us," and began to walk off.

Argent followed, with only the slightest hesitation. After a few steps, Argent reached Merritt's side and asked, "What is happening?"

Merritt replied with less good humor than his friendly shoulder thump had implied, "We are going to order lunch for the group in the hopes that Mr. Henry will deliver Miss Warner in time to join us."

They passed the International Restaurant, directly across from the depot. Argent observed, "That establishment looks likely enough." Indeed, it was heavily patronized at that hour.

Merritt explained, "Miss Warner objects to the Newfoundland there," which explained very little to Argent.

Miss Warner did join them in time, being escorted into the dining hall by one of the waiters. Argent stood as Merritt seated Miss Warner and noticed again the extreme discomfort this small gesture caused her. Though Mr. Henry had earlier declined his offer to dine with them, Merritt asked, "Mr. Henry will not be joining us?"

"No, he is colored, and is not allowed in."

Miss Warner said this with such finality and lack of indignation for the man who had acted in every way as an intimate guardian that Merritt felt offended. "Had we known, we would have patronized a less objectionable establishment."

Mary looked at him in wonder. "You would be hard-pressed to find one, especially with all the ex-slaves in town – the rules have become even harsher since the war. Mr. Henry knows this."

Argent probed, "It must rankle when he cannot join you in such places."

If Miss Warner suspected she was being tested, she did not show it. "Of course, it does. The only thing that should matter in a restaurant is if one keeps one's elbows off the table, doesn't slurp the soup, and doesn't tie the napkin under the chin." She hesitated, making sure she had not forgotten any of the major "don't's" constantly admonished at home. "And as long as you pay," she added; it was, after all, a business, and not a home.

"Of course," Merritt agreed. "It is, after all, a business, and not a home."

Mary looked up sharply at him, but he merely gazed back at her. She did not like to find herself in such complete and eerie agreement with Mr. Merritt. "I say, God made him and therefore let him pass as a man."

"You say that?" Though Merritt seemed amused at Miss Warner's plagiarism, Argent could not let it pass.

"I parasay that."

"You mean paraphrase."

"No, I'm fairly certain I quoted Portia word for word, but I quoted her for my own meaning: I paraquoted her." Having explained her position, Mary continued in another vein. "Of course, it is no different than when I am excluded from bars and saloons and smoking rooms and reading rooms. I wonder if Mr. Henry is rankled on my account for these things."

Argent regarded Miss Warner with something close to shock. "Why would you want to visit such places? And you cannot possibly compare exclusion from these places to the injustices born of slavery."

Now Mary regarded Argent with shock. "I never made such a comparison. Nothing can compare to such humiliating, vile, and ungodly bondage. It seizes my heart with terror to think it could have happened to Mr. Henry or little Thea or any of his family."

Argent sputtered an apology, but he had touched a nerve and it would take more than a polite retreat to calm it. She continued: "I have no desire to visit bars or saloons or smoking rooms, but there are other things denied me on the basis of my sex that make as little sense as barring Mr. Henry from dining with us here. It is all the grossest nonsense to deny colored people the right to ride street cars or eat in restaurants or shop in any store. And it is also the grossest nonsense to deny people, who happen to be female, the right to vote or own their own land or dispose of their income as they see fit without permission from husbands or other fatherly relatives." Her anger compelled her to speak rapidly, and now she continued without pause, "Tell me, how can the federal government reconcile advocating the right to vote for freedmen, men just recently thought incapable of making an informed decision of any kind, and yet still deny the vote to their very own daughters and wives, most of whom have more education to their names than most of the freedmen? No, I do not compare these injustices to slavery, but they are injustices nonetheless and they are all the more infuriating because they are validated as some kind of protection or welfare for the *ladies*, and they are more invasive because, colored or white, women represent half the population. I will say this for the rebels – as despicable as they were, they stood up and fought to the death for their beliefs. The federal government didn't fight for anything but against the South, mere reaction to a threat against union. The federal government says they want equality for all men, but what do they do about it? Pontificate and debate and legislate laws that they lack the will or intention to enforce, while they turn a blind eye to every other kind of injustice. The government won the war, then retreated from the aftermath. It killed the beast, only when it became expedient to do so, then left the carcass to rot and stink to high heaven in the southern heat, and now jackals pick at it and tear it apart and drag it to all quarters of the nation, and we all suffer the noxious, putrid fumes."

Anti-federal sentiment was known to run high in Kentucky. The problem had become so troublesome that there were even calls to enforce reconstruction measures on the state, though she had never declared for the Confederacy. Ex-Confederates held the highest offices in the cities and state, molding a new Democratic Party that was particularly bitter towards the federal government. The days-old Fifteenth Amendment was certain to stir up even more anti-federal sentiment and even more resentment against ex-slaves and other blacks, who it was justifiably supposed would vote Republican. Merritt and Argent did not often operate below Cincinnati and so had no real or personal experience with the deep disappointment, distrust, and sense of betrayal that Kentucky held for Washington, or the surprising resurrection of Confederate ideals in this border state *after* the war had ended. They had, of course, read the Cincinnati papers when in that town, but had thought the condemnations of Kentucky, and Louisville in particular, were exaggerations born of an old rivalry between the two cities. Even so, to hear Miss Warner – whose father had worked so closely with Grant, and who had several brothers die in the effort – to hear Miss Warner express such sentiment was shocking. Both Merritt and Argent had fought for the Union – *for* union – and not merely against the South, and it was with great effort they did not respond to Miss Warner's tirade. The merest look between them acknowledged the need to say nothing.

Dinner was set on the table and Merritt and Argent both prayed that this interruption would redirect Miss Warner's agitation. Instead, she seemed to simmer just below the surface. She at first ate angrily, attacking the food on her plate, but then she abruptly abandoned eating. She refused to be pulled into any light conversation, and only answered when directly addressed, and with the briefest reply possible. Finally, Merritt said, with terseness, "I am sorry the world is not as you would have it."

"You should be sorry the world is not as it should be, that the world does not hold in equal value anyone who is not a white male. No, you are sorry that you have to sit next to someone in such a foul mood, and I am sorry that such basic desires and rights of even the least among us are beyond your comprehension."

Before Merritt could respond, she leaned across the table and fairly hissed at Argent, "And I am insulted that you would hold me in such low regard as to think I would equate the foolish denial of my desires with the barbarities of slavery. I am sick near unto death of being reprimanded by ex-Confederates for holding to the Union and in turn being reprimanded by Northern victors for living so close to rebels that I must have absorbed their blasphemy. My family was shunned by people we once thought friends when we applauded the Emancipation Proclamation. And despite my brothers in the Union army and my father's close association with General Grant, we were under constant suspicion by federal forces in Louisville. A marshal even came to our house, near the very end, and threatened to take all we had – our house, our horses, even the very guns we used to patrol our land when Morgan's marauders came so close we could smell them, while Union soldiers stayed safe in town – threatened to take everything on the merest acquaintance of my father with Judge Bullitt. It was no picnic being a 'border' state during the war, and it has been no picnic in the wake of the war. We have been held guilty nearly as much as the rebels themselves. And now you sit across from me, knowing nothing of me, and accuse me of such a callous sentiment? The only callous sentiment I carry with me is bitterness at having agreed to this trip and the prospect of speaking with the General."

She abruptly stood. "I will see you at the station." She turned and strode from the room before either man had fully stood at her rising.

"I will follow her." At a look from Argent, Merritt assured him, "She won't know. And I'll take care of things at the hotel." Then Merritt, too, left.

Argent sat, stunned at the turn the dinner had taken, at the strange convictions Miss Warner held so deeply, at the fury she apparently held in constant check, at the tongue lashing he had just endured, at the simple, innocent question he had asked that had touched it all off.

On the street, Argent heard his name called from behind, as he walked toward the station. He turned to find Merritt waiting for him a few steps away. Argent looked at Merritt, confused, then turned to look behind himself. "Where is Miss Warner? Have you lost her?"

"Not a particle. You seem lost, though; that was the third time I called your name — you walked right past me." Merritt retraced his steps to join his partner.

"Yes; I have been re-visiting our lunch with Miss Warner. Where is she, did you say?"

"She is at the station, as promised; Mr. Henry is with her. She has some interesting thoughts about rights, desires, and men and women, and the war."

"Interesting, strange, but only vaguely justifiable; possibly why she remains unwed, despite a healthy dowry. But what concerns me most is this volcanic anger that is so easily ignited. She does not know what is permitted and what is not permitted in polite society. She may touch off her volcano at the wrong moment to the wrong person."

"Surely, between the two of us, we can keep her out of volatile situations for three days. We shall keep her to ourselves and solely reap the benefits of her interesting thoughts. I found her personal appropriation of Latin intriguing. I shall have to remember it."

"You mean her bastardization of 'paraphrase'? It is Greek; and your memory of literature is already in a perilous state of decomposition. I advise against it."

Merritt chuckled. "She would not call it bastardization, but a turn of phrase, a paraturn of phrase." Merritt chuckled again, this time at his own cleverness.

Argent thought Merritt was entirely too pleased with himself and at the prospect of more of Miss Warner's interesting thoughts. He seemed completely unaffected by Miss Warner's assessment of him. "You are in a tolerably good mood."

"I am."

When Merritt was not forthcoming with an explanation, Argent prompted, "Do you intend to share the font of your good humor? Surely it is not merely the prospect of our impending travels with Miss Warner?"

"I find that Miss Warner has her charms, after all; but, you are correct – she is not the source of my good humor. Once I had determined

Miss Warner secure at the train depot, I took the opportunity to visit the telegraph office, and sent our happy and successful news to the President, and happy news met me there – our mail have caught up with us." He handed Argent a small packet of letters addressed to him and waved his own packet of letters before returning them to his coat pocket.

Argent brightened considerably. "The mail has been a long time in catching up with us. It will be a pleasure to have these to read on the train. I hope one of these" – patting his chest – "is from Miss Kayes."

"I had forgotten about Miss Kayes. She is the lady in Rochester?"

"No, you are thinking of Miss Meiners. That was exploded long ago."

"A bullet dodged, my friend."

"Indeed. No, I made acquaintance with Miss Kayes in Buffalo. You recall – she gave testimony on behalf of her brother, who worked for Tom Ballard."

"That was never proven. But I remember her – she cried a great deal at the trial."

"She is very devoted – however mistakenly – to her brother."

"A sister's devotion is a noble thing to behold, but women with brothers sometimes are confused in their affections. It is best to pursue women who are brotherless, and preferably also without sisters."

"You are describing an only child."

"No, that would not do, either. An only child – especially daughters – are cultivated and guarded nearly beyond hope of attainment. The ideal woman would also be fatherless – one less man to claim her affections."

"Tsk, tsk, Merritt. Afraid of a woman's natural devotion to her father."

"Mothers, too, present problems. I have a cousin whose mother-in-law lives with him. Half the time she berates him for perceived faults of his, and half the time she mock flirts with him, and the other half of the time she intimidates his wife, her own daughter."

"Your cousin's household exists in some strange environment where they enjoy time and a half. But what you are describing now is an orphan, and there are not enough orphans to go around, God be praised."

"God be praised. But orphans are the ideal, being completely unattached."

"This is a perfectly grisly topic to be discussing, even more so when I think it began with my sunny hopes of a letter from Miss Kayes."

"Miss Warner is one such."

"One such what?"

"Orphan; unattached."

Argent considered Merritt's words. She was certainly parentless and presumably unattached, but an adult woman, no matter how young, can hardly be thought of as orphaned. Nearly everyone finds themselves parentless at some point in their lives, but not all are orphans. She was no longer a legal infant – she was surely beyond the age of majority; otherwise, she would not be permitted to live alone and own and work her farm. Merritt regarded Argent with open amusement as they threaded their way through the crowds. He was not going to engage Merritt in one of his pointless semantic debates.

Conceding both the points of orphan and unattached, Argent asked drily, "And are these the charms Miss Warner possesses that you have so recently discovered?"

"Certainly not; these are her status, not her charms. One must not confuse the two. For instance, the natural response to an orphan, especially one so manifestly and recently orphaned as Miss Warner, is to apply pity, because of her status, and then mistake that for affection, which should be applied to her charms."

"You seem to have given this a great deal of thought, but the question is whether it has been given to the status of orphans *in toto* or to the status of Miss Warner in particular."

"I began with Miss Warner in the particular, then found myself considering lady orphans in general. It occurs to me that we should exercise the same induction process in our professional labors – begin with the crime in particular, then consider the greater expanse of crimes. Perhaps there is some underlying clue that could help propel us to the offensive position, rather than, as we are, always on the defensive side of things."

"Merritt, sometimes your convoluted theorizing makes my head spin. Nevertheless, I have learned to stake my original position, and so I return to the anticipation of reading my letters on the train. And here we are at the depot."

They found Mr. Henry and Miss Warner in back of the depot, standing together, in silence, Mr. Henry holding Emmett's reins and Miss Warner clutching a book. Her new wrap was nowhere in sight – Mr. Henry must have packed the wrap and retrieved the book from the trunk that had already been stowed. From long experience riding trains, Argent knew that doing so had not endeared Mr. Henry to the baggage handlers. Emmett had been divested of his saddle, which presumably was now packed in Miss Warner's second trunk. At their approach, Mr. Henry said something to Miss Warner and she slowly raised her eyes to meet them. There was an awkward silence, then Mr. Henry asked, "Did you enjoy your meal?"

Argent answered, a little too convivially, "Indeed, the recommendation met all our expectations."

Another small silence, then Emmett nudged Miss Warner, and she said, "I am very sorry for my behavior and rash words at table. I in no way meant to denigrate your own service during the war, which I am sure was exemplary."

Merritt smiled; Miss Warner was sure he was enjoying her discomfort. "Not at all; your passion is commendable, and your arguments are not without validity. In any case, it is always desirable to hear the thoughts and ideas of places other than Washington and New York."

Or Cincinnati, Mary thought.

The train blew its first whistle, giving notice of its impending departure. Mr. Henry handed the reins to Miss Warner, then stepped forward to shake hands with Merritt and Argent. "I will be heading back now. Take care of our Lally." At the sound of her family name, Miss Warner turned in towards Emmett's neck. Mr. Henry stepped back to lay a hand on her shoulder, but she would not turn around. With his other hand, he stroked Emmett's nose. Quietly, he said, "Remember what we talked about, now." Miss Warner nodded her head into Emmett's great neck. Mr. Henry let his hands fall from both the horse and the woman, then slowly headed toward the yard where the wagon waited for his return trip.

It was apparent to Merritt and Argent that Mr. Henry's heart was as full at this parting as Miss Warner's. As he watched Mr. Henry walk away, Merritt felt shame that he had assumed there would be no tender feelings on his part upon leaving Miss Warner or that it would not have been a burden to him to convince Miss Warner to leave her home.

Beside him, Argent had lowered his head, not wishing to intrude upon the exchange between Mr. Henry and Miss Warner, even though the noise and general confusion attendant upon departing and arriving trains and the traffic around the station virtually insured such privacy. Neither man, then, realized that Miss Warner had also walked away, leading Emmett toward the stock car. They reached the stock car as Miss Warner was pleading with the handler to let her load Emmett. The man was rude and even disrespectful; to her protests he snarled, "It is your bad training of this horse, missy, that has given so much trouble. I mean to teach this horse to behave." Miss Warner was at once furious and terrified. She desperately grabbed at the handler's jacket to pull him away from Emmett who was indeed misbehaving and threatened to rear and kick.

Suddenly, Mary felt the jacket give way and the man stumbled backward. Argent had neatly plucked him from the fray and was dragging him backwards some distance from Emmett. On the horse's far side, she heard Merritt cooing at Emmett, calming him. Merritt asked, "How should we proceed?"

Merritt's generous acquiescence to her opinion was lost on Mary. "The car is already full. The other horses are strange to him and he has never been on a ramp. He does not like it."

"It is that brute that he does not like. He'll load quietly if he is treated properly."

Miss Warner walked beside Emmett, constantly talking to him, while Merritt, walking backwards, led him up the ramp. In the stock car they worked together to secure him in the only open space. Miss Warner thanked Merritt but resisted leaving with him.

"I'm going to stay here with Emmett. I don't want that man mistreating him."

"I promise you, Emmett will suffer no more from that man. Mr. Argent is at this moment explaining to him Emmett's preferred status. Come, the railroad company will not allow you to stay here."

From the far end of the car a man spoke. "I, too, am solicitous of my horse. Perhaps our two horses could travel together and lessen their tedium and anxiety." A well-dressed man approached from the shadows, and with a tip of his hat said, "With your permission, I will speak to the handler to treat your horse as if it were my own." Without waiting for an answer, he moved smoothly past Mary and Merritt and disappeared down the ramp. Though a man of obvious wealth had offered to include Emmett under his aegis, Mary felt less confident of his efforts than those of Argent; she had overheard some of Merritt's conversation with Mr. Edwards, and if the mere mention of their status as U. S. operatives could quell Mr. Edwards, then it would surely carry great weight with the handler.

She followed the stranger from the car, descending the ramp at a curious angle, completely unaware that she had left Merritt standing at the top of the ramp with his offered hand empty.

At the first of the passenger cars, the conductor helped Miss Warner up the first step to the platform, and even she had to admit help was necessary up such a high step. Upon entering the car, Mary's heart sank – the car was full, mostly of women and children, and the air was already stifling and slightly odorous. Children were sniffling and coughing off the last of the winter illnesses or taking on the first of the spring colds. She turned to find herself blocked by Argent.

"There must be a less crowded car further down the train."

"Doubtless," he answered, "but this is the ladies' car."

"Are the other cars barred to ladies?"

"No, but we cannot guarantee the behavior or the character of the other passengers, male or female. And one of the cars is the smoking car, which even Merritt and I have found wanting after an hour of constant cigar smoke."

From behind Argent, Merritt said, "We need to move on; there are ladies waiting behind me."

Mary turned back toward the seats and found even more cause for dismay; there were no two seats open next to each other. They would have to split up. For the first time, she found herself wishing to be with these two men. A light touch on her shoulder from Argent made her move forward, and she took the first open seat. Argent and Merritt moved forward to find seats for themselves. She marked where they sat, on the other side of the aisle, one in front of the other on the two-seat benches that all faced forward.

If it had not been for that atrocious man at the stock car, she might have reached the passenger car in time to at least claim a window seat, but all the open seats were on the aisle. With no passing scenery to pass the time, her only option was to read the book in her hands. Reading while the train moved was sure to make her nauseous, so that was truly no option.

Nearly every seat was taken, and then some; many women had children perched on their laps. At a request from a few women, the conductor reversed the backs of two seats, directly across the aisle from each other, so that four benches faced each other creating a small private island for their inhabitants. On the floor between these seats were even more children – apparently friends or an extended family of women traveling together with their children. This was how her family had traveled, that last time, to visit relatives in Cincinnati, her father leading them all onto the car as soon as was permitted, then commandeering several seats grouped together, as these women had done. Each of the older Warners held on their laps one of the younger Warners, so that each brother had a corresponding sister. Only Randy had been without a sister, but he was unable to sit still anyway – he spent the trip wandering the aisle and making friends with many of the passengers. She had sat on Wim's lap on that trip, a long time ago.

Despite all the children, there was little noise or talk, just the common noises of people shifting in their seats, clearing throats, accidentally banging into the seat to the front.

There were some men on this car – chaperones of the ladies who needed them or husbands with their wives. Mary refused to think of Merritt and Argent as her chaperones. She adamantly rejected the need for such an escort, though she had found herself profoundly grateful for their help with Emmett just now. She looked to find the backs of their heads. What were they, then? Escort seemed too refined a term for the task they were performing. Abductors was too harsh, especially since she had agreed to accompany them. Though her goal in these thoughts was to find the worst (but fair) label for Merritt and Argent and their assignment, she found that any attempt to cast opprobrium on them, rebounded on her. The most accurate description of her relationship with them was that of a horse or some other cattle being herded from one place to the next, or to slaughter. She certainly felt like some beast in a herd on this crowded train that promised to grow even greater in its crowd.

There were now people standing in the aisle. Both Merritt and Argent gave up their seats for women. She saw them consult briefly, then Argent made his way back to stand near her seat, while Merritt exited through the other end.

"Mr. Merritt has gone to take a seat in one of the other cars. He will rejoin us when this car has cleared out a little."

Mary merely nodded her head. They had been stupid to take a train on a Monday, when so many people resumed their mobile schedules after the Sunday break. She had been goaded into this trip without any time to consider the exigencies of travel. On top of homesickness was a growing sense of being trapped, of suffering the consequences of someone else's bad planning or ignorance. She should have locked herself in the stall with Emmett on the stock car. Merritt, of course, had escaped; she would gladly have taken a seat on another car – the need for a chaperone or escort or drover on a train was grossly over estimated. She anticipated three days of pounding headaches, the first of which was spiking behind her right eye.

The woman next to Mary, the woman who occupied the coveted window seat, said, "It looks like to be a very full complement today."

Other than mothers speaking softly to their children or the very low whispers between companions, these were the first openly spoken words on the train. Mary nodded without turning to her, then added out of a sense of politeness, "Looks like," but she spoke quietly, hoping that would end the conversation.

But the woman, an older woman with an older woman's body – large and mostly shapeless, except for an immense bust – was happy to continue her observations. "I always wonder where so many people go every day. Here there is a loaded car – and doubtless the other cars are just as full – and it is only one of several such trains leaving the city."

Mary did not respond; she in no way wanted to encourage this woman to prolong an unwanted conversation.

The near silence that had characterized the car slowly began to crumble as passengers began to check their watches and wonder aloud to no one in particular, "When will we begin?" The woman next to her, said, "The train is already ten minutes late." After another ten minutes – time known to Mary only by the comments of other travelers – Argent bent low to speak to her. "I am just going to inquire about the delay." Then he was gone, before she could ask to accompany him. She was worried about Emmett, and more than ever regretted leaving him. She much preferred the stock car to the ladies' car.

Argent returned almost immediately with the news that the train is being held, waiting for through passengers to New York. The feeling of being trapped intensified and with it came a growing sense of suffocation. The ladies' car took on the apparition of a cage, which in turn became the scaffolding, the frame, the skeleton, of a coffin. She had been robbed of time; time spent here in this stuffed and stuffy car was time taken away from Emmett in the stock car, time taken away from home. They need not have left the farm so early, only to sit in idle, useless company with complete strangers.

The whistle finally blew, after nearly an hour's agonizing wait, and the cars one by one lurched forward against the phenomenon known as train resistance, as her father had called it – the force needed to start a train moving from a stopped position. There was a formula for it, but she could not call it to mind. The distress at no longer being able to ask him questions, the feeling that she had not paid close enough attention, that she had wasted opportunities, flooded through her. These government men had distracted her for days with this ill-advised trip to Washington, and now this feeling that had been an almost constant companion for more than a year, and then abruptly denied, bore down on her with the strength of a dam broken through. What else had she forgotten that Dad had told her? She took a ragged breath and closed her eyes.

The woman mistook Mary's reactions to be those of an unseasoned traveler, of a distress born of inexperience. "The first lurch of these great engines is always the worst – it nearly brings my stomach to my mouth, but you'll get used to it." She gave Mary a motherly pat on the knee. "Tell me, dear – where do you travel?"

Mary answered, "Cincinnati," but offered nothing further.

"Well, I won't be going that far, but we'll have each other's company until I depart at Campbellsburg."

Mary eased open the cover of her book and glanced at the train schedule she had slipped there: Campbellsburg – past the Lexington Junction, after Sulphur, but before Carrollton. The train was scheduled to stop at Campbellsburg at 5:41. Mary slowly closed the book. They were already late in starting, but regardless of their departure time, the travel time remained the same – nearly two hours (two more hours) of this woman's company. The train was hot and thick with the odors of two score or more people. Her back promised to ache with the hardness of the bare wood bench and the effort to sit erect and still. At home where there were none to chastise her, she sat comfortably in comfortable clothes; she often slouched. And now she must endure the unwanted ramblings of a total stranger. How had she managed to sit next to the only passenger intent on talking?

The woman was addressing her. "We might as well get acquainted. I am Mrs. Blaiser. I have been visiting my sister here for some weeks. I was supposed to return home last week, but I have been so enjoying myself that I decided to stay a little longer. This foul weather has also given me pause about traveling. I have scoured the local papers, but I have seen nothing about any washed-out bridges or mud slides or what have you when it has rained so much."

Mary nodded slightly; she couldn't risk any more movement of her head. "I hope you enjoyed your stay."

Above the women, Argent listened as Mrs. Blaiser did her best to engage Miss Warner. It was evident, however, that Miss Warner was barely attending to the conversation. He thought it would do Miss Warner good to have the company of an older woman. He in fact began to plan a strategy to find similar passengers to act as *de facto* chaperones for her; then perhaps he and Merritt could ride together in one of the other common cars. He could join Merritt at the next stop – Anchorage, if memory served, or perhaps he could have a closer peak at that train schedule Miss Warner had secreted in her book – then perhaps Merritt could join Miss Warner at Campbellsburg, staying with her until she could be seated with another such matron. This could solve a whole host of problems associated with escorting a woman, at least as far as Parkersburg. After that, the train that President Grant was sending would completely answer any traveling concerns for Miss Warner.

Below him, the conversation was faltering. Miss Warner had not risen to the name bait, and Mrs. Blaiser was teetering between considering offense or adopting an even more patronizing attitude. Finally, she prompted, "And your name, dear?"

Miss Warner hesitated, as if she may have forgotten her own name. Argent's hand was on the back of the bench, and with the slightest motion, he moved his thumb across her shoulder blade. He immediately apologized, as if it had been an accident. "Please excuse me, Miss Warner. I felt a cramp in my thumb."

For the first time since he had taken up his position in the aisle, Miss Warner looked up at him. Her face was strained with obvious pain and flushed with heat; she looked truly miserable. "Not at all. But, please, if you are cramping from standing, allow me to take your place, if only for a little while."

Argent did not know what the trouble was, but he could not count himself a gentleman and sit while a lady stood. "I thank you, but the spasm has passed; I am in no discomfort."

"Oh, are you traveling with the young lady? It was unthinkable in my day to travel alone without the protection of a man. But trains are changing everything. Young women whisk here and there without a thought for their reputation. I hear they even stay in hotels unchaperoned." Returning to Miss Warner, "You are wise to have made this arrangement with Mr. —?"

Again, Miss Warner left the question hanging in the air; though, in truth, the air was so thick, mere thought could hang there. Argent answered for himself, "Mr. Argent, ma'am."

"And is Mr. Argent a relation of yours?" Mrs. Blaiser had briefly given her attention to Argent, but she returned to Miss Warner; she was determined to engage the young woman next to her.

Even through her headache, Mary could not resist saying, "No, not at all; he is a complete stranger. We only just met a few days ago."

Above her, Mary could feel Argent stiffen, and next to her she could hear Mrs. Blaiser take in the smallest breath. She also thought she could feel a sudden deeper quiet descend on the benches nearby.

Argent quickly stepped in to dispel any unfavorable ideas forming about his relationship with Miss Warner. "We are strangers, though, beginning, I think, to understand each other better. I am an employé of her late father's colleague and have been dispatched and entrusted to escort Miss Warner to meet him — a reunion long overdue."

The train was just passing the Fairgrounds on the far eastern reaches of the city. Mary thought desperately, *I could just jump off and then walk home; I have not yet gone too far.*

Mrs. Blaiser was satisfied with Argent's explanation. "You are lucky indeed to have someone so interested in maintaining ties with you as to send an escort to ensure your safe arrival. Have you no brothers or other male relatives that could fulfill this function?"

Miss Warner stared at her book and feigned to have not heard the question. Miraculously, Mrs. Blaiser did not pursue the subject; Mary did not see the gesture Argent gave to Mrs. Blaiser indicating this was a delicate subject. This information seemed to inspire in Mrs. Blaiser an even greater maternal approach to Miss Warner. She launched conversations on dress and hair and proper diet and rest and guarding one's reputation as one guards the soul.

Mary dared to look in Mrs. Blaiser's direction to look longingly out the window as the train passed first Woodlawn, then Ormsby's Station, each outpost marking more miles separating her from home. It was when she had looked up at Ormsby's Station that Mrs. Blaiser had begun her discourse on diet and rest.

"If I may say so, dear, you need to look to yourself; you look tired and dispirited and lusterless. A man will not be interested in a young woman who might appear too frail and thus a greater burden to him."

Argent had listened with growing sympathy for Miss Warner, and thought this last observation was going too far. Miss Warner had spoken as little as possible, even to the point of being rude. She remained obstinately silent at this last comment. As Mrs. Blaiser was softening her observation with, "Not to worry, though; once you are feeling better and amend your hair and clothes a little, I'm sure plenty of men will find you an acceptable prospect," Miss Warner carefully cracked open her book to a page with a small piece of paper to mark it. Written on the scrap of paper in careful lettering was a list of rules of some sort:

Ask people about themselves, but nothing personal
Ask where their trip is taking them
Ask if it is business or pleasure
Only make comments that are pleasurable or complimentary
Keep comments short
Avoid comments with any sort of 'not' in them
Only look at people's eyes and nowhere else on the face

With a flash of understanding, Argent realized this note was from Mr. Henry and his admonition at the station to "remember what we talked about" referred to this list as much as to anything else discussed this morning in Mr. Warner's office.

Mr. Henry had, in fact, given the note to Mary in her father's study as he explained certain situations she might face on the train – like entering and exiting the train politely, dealing with crowds and noise, enduring hours sitting in a moving box with strangers – situations her father had always seen to and sheltered his family from. Henry had suggested she take a seat next to a window, if at all possible – it would give her something to look at and eliminate a fellow passenger on that side.

It was the final suggestion or rule in the list that affected Argent deeply. There was an arrow pointing to it, underscoring its place in the hierarchy, despite its lowly position in the list: whenever possible, just say nothing at all. This young woman sitting below him was dreading even the simplest of conversations and was trying so hard to remember rules that would be instinctive to most anyone else. He could almost feel emanating from her the dread of misspeaking and the hopelessness of remembering so many things at once. A wave of pity washed over him. He was ashamed at plotting to foist her onto someone else, submitting her to the very thing that would make this trip unbearable. He and Merritt had promised Mr. Henry they would do their best to make the trip as least unpleasant as possible. He had already miserably failed both her and Mr. Henry in his mere thoughts.

A last-minute inspiration or realization had been hastily scribbled and crammed at the bottom of the page. Mr. Henry advised Miss Warner to keep Mr. Merritt and Mr. Argent between her and other people as much as possible; in all likelihood, they wouldn't bother her with conversation and could act as a buffer from other passengers.

Mary closed the book after reviewing the notes Mr. Henry had given her. She felt nauseous and dizzy. She had always heard accounts of women fainting at dances or funerals or other gatherings, and she had arrogantly considered herself above such weakness, but she was very concerned at fainting herself, here and now. Her head was pounding, she was hot, even perspiring, and the smell in the car was overpowering – human sweat and other body odors and, over it all, competing perfumes and colognes. If she did not get air soon, she would faint – or scream.

When the train pulled into its first stop at Anchorage, Miss Warner stood abruptly, her head only narrowly missing cracking into Argent's jaw. Mrs. Blaiser gently scolded her, "This is not your stop, dear."

Miss Warner turned to Argent and said quite defiantly, "I need off this train; I need fresh air," and without waiting for a reply she pushed past Argent as well as a great many others to reach the door.

Argent heard his name called from the door at the other end, and turned to see Merritt looking at him with the question: where is Miss Warner? Argent gestured outside, then refined the gesture to include the other door. Merritt left before Argent was finished waving his signals.

A great many people left the train, but before more boarded Argent was able to secure two benches together. Being a veteran of train travel, Argent knew how to turn the back of one of the benches so that the two benches faced each other. Mrs. Blaiser followed Argent forward in the car to this new arrangement, assuming herself now to be a member of the party. She immediately claimed one of the window seats, but Argent refused to allow her to keep it. He explained that Miss Warner was not feeling well and really needed to have one of these seats, and that his partner was also of the same traveling constitution as Miss Warner, and he would be needing the other window seat – he was sure she would understand. Mrs. Blaiser understood, but was not happy about losing what she thought of as her prerogative, especially since her last seat had already been taken by a new passenger. Her mood lightened considerably, however, when Merritt appeared with Miss Warner – not feeling much better from the looks of her – and Mrs. Blaiser began to realize that her benchmate would be Merritt, a handsome young man with a somewhat saucy look to him.

Merritt and Argent had been together long enough that Merritt did not question when Argent directed him to the window seat for his "motion problems." Argent took his seat next to Miss Warner, who had the window seat opposite Merritt. And Mrs. Blaiser sat happily next to Merritt, across from Argent. Miss Warner stole another look at her train schedule; against all hope to the contrary, it still said that Campbellsburg was 29 miles away and Mrs. Blaiser would still be with them until 5:41.

The whistle blew, and the train lurched forward, the motion momentarily worsening the pain in Mary's head. Mrs. Blaiser immediately set forth on her views of their new seating arrangement. "It is so much nicer to face one's companions than to be forever twisting this way and that to address each other." She admitted to having noted a little stiffness in Miss Warner and hoped now she could more easily join the conversation. Mary looked up and met Mrs. Blaiser's eyes to satisfy that woman that she could do so, but she did not offer to join the conversation, one-sided as it was.

Argent welcomed Mrs. Blaiser to their little group, introducing Merritt and Mrs. Blaiser to each other. Merritt was charming, as he was to all the ladies, big and small, old and young. He would be honored if Mrs. Blaiser would consider him as her personal escort for as long as she was on the train. Mrs. Blaiser was properly flattered but was sorry to inform Merritt that he would only have that honor until Campbellsburg, where she would depart for her home.

Mrs. Blaiser was an indefatigable source of chatter and curiosity. Argent kept up a steady stream of conversation with Mrs. Blaiser, deftly fielding questions meant for Miss Warner; but sometimes the questions were so directly worded that Miss Warner was required to respond. Merritt noted this strange interplay on Argent's part, but assumed it had something to do with the mysterious "motion problems" he had assigned Merritt as well as with Miss Warner's blooming headache, that was reflected on her face for all the world to see.

By the time they reached the Lexington Junction – where passengers wishing to go east to Lexington departed and those wishing to go north embarked – even Argent's patience with Mrs. Blaiser was strained. Without asking, he extended his hand to Miss Warner, which she gratefully took, the matter somehow settled between them that Miss Warner would be needing more fresh air. On the platform, Miss Warner moved as far away from the milling crowds as possible and leaned against a pole, drinking in cooler, fresher air. At the sound of the whistle, she rejoined Argent, who had waited for her almost where she had left him.

They returned to their seats to find Merritt gone – to inquire about someone named Emmett, Mrs. Blaiser informed them. Merritt returned just as the train pulled forward once again.

"And how is Emmett?" Mrs. Blaiser asked. This, more than anything, made Mary intensely dislike Mrs. Blaiser. Emmett was none of her business, and she had pre-empted Mary's own inquiry.

Merritt replied that Emmett was just fine. He looked impishly at Miss Warner. "He has just had an apple to carry him through the next few miles."

"An apple?" Of course, Mrs. Blaiser had no way of knowing that Emmett was a horse; even so, Mary found the question a marker of ignorance.

"Yes, and he will have another later still, to keep him until he can have his hay in Covington."

"Hay! Good heavens! Is Emmett a horse, then?"

"He is Miss Warner's horse."

"Oh, indeed; and do you take him to visit your family friend, Miss Warner?"

Mrs. Blaiser was stumbling into very dangerous territory, and Miss Warner looked to be descending into a very nasty mood. Argent answered for her. "Miss Warner is an accomplished horsewoman. She takes Emmett everywhere."

Mary felt wretched – she had made such a poor impression on these two men that they felt obliged to shield Mrs. Blaiser from her. Mary fingered the edge of her book until she located the note. She opened to the page just enough to review her notes. She gave a quick thought to St. Jude, though, truthfully, he had been a disappointing saint for some time. Even so, she unthinkingly fingered the place on her dress near her breast where St. Jude was pinned underneath.

Mrs. Blaiser was intrigued. "In my youth, I was quite accomplished myself. Everyone said I was the very picture of grace and decorum on a horse. I still have my side-saddle, though I am afraid my days arranging my riding habit are long gone. Mine was a great gift from my father, made especially for me in England, but I understand side-saddles can be obtained here now, as well. Is yours English or domestic?"

Mary tried to find a way to answer this question without a negative – "avoid any comments with any sort of 'not' in them" – but every answer involved the negative and the black truth: I don't ride side-saddle. Mary was truly trying to formulate a proper answer, but in her efforts, she was staring at Mrs. Blaiser. Finally, she blurted out, "I ride my brother Wim's saddle. It is the best in the barn, and the most comfortable." There were, sadly, quite a few saddles in the barn; neither Mr. Warner nor Mary could bear to part with them, even though they represented a fair amount of money. Occasionally, she would take one or another of them from their place and work and condition them as if they would one day be ridden.

There was a slight pause before Mrs. Blaiser stumbled, "I'm afraid I don't understand – surely your brother did not ride side-saddle. Or was he infirm?"

Merritt stepped in to save Miss Warner from weary explanations. He felt obliged – a topic he had thought would ease Miss Warner into an enjoyable conversation had instead become a multi-headed hydra ready to attack everyone in their little covey. The subject of Emmett had somehow spawned references to the detested General Grant (the family friend), a favored and dead brother, and her peculiar penchant to ride astride, sure to strike horror into the bastion of proper female behavior such as Mrs.

Blaiser represented. Though Merritt thought there was nothing more noble than the sight of a woman properly seated on a horse and side-saddle, he had seen enough women during the war and during trips out west riding astride to find the practice acceptable, when necessary. Miss Warner's habit of wearing pants was still a shocking novelty to him, though the shock lessened with familiarity; but that topic had to be kept close to the vest.

"Miss Warner does not ride side-saddle. Nor, I am sure, did her brother."

To this Mrs. Blaiser said, "Well, I am at a loss for words, only to say that it is shocking, shocking. It cannot be good for your prospects."

Before she even realized the thought had occurred, Mary said, "As long as I don't ride my horse astride down the aisle, I don't see why any prospects should care." She immediately regretted the comment, but it could not be recalled. Mrs. Blaiser stared at Mary, who returned the gaze, but without rancor. Mrs. Blaiser excused herself and relocated to another seat.

Surprisingly, neither Argent nor Merritt reprimanded her. Nevertheless, Mrs. Blaiser's indignation spoke for itself – Mary had failed Mr. Henry and his notes, and had likely embarrassed Merritt and Argent, as well as herself. She laid her head against the window and closed her eyes. They had just passed Pendleton. If she could only have held her tongue for eight more miles, she could have counted herself successful in her encounter with Mrs. Blaiser. *Oh, God*, she thought; *we have only gone 34 miles, only 34 out of 600 and more miles total.* She felt herself overwhelmed at the enormity of the misery ahead.

She remained this way until the train pulled out of Campbellsburg. Slowly she had become aware that Merritt and Argent were speaking quietly, but their voices were merely low hums to her. Even so, she understood that they were discussing hotels in Covington; one more bad decision she would leave to these two men. Her headache had begun to subside as the train continued its sinuous path northward. The track had been laid with so many curves, in fact, that engineers referred to the line as the Rat Hole. Despite all the curves, the westering sun stayed either behind the train or on the other side of the car. With the shadows on her side, she could watch the scenery without aggravating her headache. Although new passengers continued to occasionally board, far more passengers disembarked along the way, so that the car gradually became less crowded, hot and smelly. The quiet also took on the quality of a nursery at naptime. The days were still short, here at the start of April, and at this hour the shadows were already long and the sky purpling.

Out of the corner of her eye, she saw Argent remove his pocket watch to check the time – it was just coming on to seven o'clock. She was surprised at the time – it meant that they were more than halfway there. This encouraging thought was quickly followed by the realization that the delay in Louisville had put them an hour behind schedule. It had only been two hours. Doubtless, Argent was just as disappointed as she, snapping closed his watch with a sigh.

They were in the middle of the tedious run of the schedule where the train was required to stop on average every ten minutes. She recited the stops in her head, no longer needing to consult the schedule in the front of her book, all the times adjusted for the delay: they would soon stop in Carrollton at 7:07 (the half-way mark), then Worthville (7:18), Eagle (7:30), Liberty (7:40), Sparta (7:50), Glencoe (8:05), Elliston (8:20), Zion (8:28), Verona (8:45), and Walton (9:00). Then would start a long run of 45 minutes where there would be no stops, past Bank Lick, Independence and Maurice. They would finally reach South Covington on this, the "fast" train, at 9:45, after less than five hours' travel.

She did not know when she fell asleep, but Zion was buzzing around in her head when she first became aware that she had slept, and unbidden the verse came to her: by the rivers of Babylon, there we sat weeping when we remembered Zion. She did not so much truly wake as interrupt her sleep. The book she had held so tightly began to slip down her lap as her hands relaxed. She briefly opened her eyes as somewhere her brain registered a change. Merritt was just catching her book as it slipped completely from her hands. Looking up to find her watching him, he said, "I'll hold it for you, if you like." Her brain having been satisfied as to the cause for interruption, signaled her to close her eyes and return to her slumbers.

She slept through the greater number of stops, with all the lurching each time the train pulled away from a station or depot, and all the screaming breakings as the train approached the next stop, sometimes only three miles apart. She slept through several re-coalings and re-waterings, an incredible feat given all the deep thumping of the coal as it slid down the chute to the tender car, and the grating release of the water from the tower after the great chain was pulled. She slept through the piercing whistles blown at each stop and sometimes as the train rounded one of the sharper curves, warning any cows that couldn't yet see or hear the train to vacate the tracks. When she woke later, she could not say how long she had been awake, but simply became aware that she was staring out the window again.

It slowly dawned on her that her hands were empty. The book served not only to give her something to read (and to hide the suggestions and the schedule Mr. Henry had gathered for her), but also to employ her hands. It seemed like everything she wanted to do with her hands was considered unladylike: placing one or another on her face or head while she thought, especially if this involved bending elbows and leaning on anything; crossing arms was completely unacceptable, as was chewing a thumbnail. But simply laying one hand in the other in her lap for hours on end (as this trip promised) was untenable; eventually, being unoccupied, one hand or another would unconsciously make its way to her mouth or forehead or chin or even to twisting her stray hairs out of mere boredom. A book seemed to answer all potential problems, but now it was gone. She glanced down to her lap and opened her hands, as if somehow the book had diminished itself and was lost in her lap.

The book slid into view. She looked up to find Merritt leaning forward with it. "It slid from your lap. I kept it for you while you slept."

Mary took the book from him, and merely nodded. In the shadowy light of the car, Merritt could just make out her bloodshot eyes.

From her left Argent asked, "I hope you had a pleasant nap?"

Mary nodded absently, then returned to the window. The morning when she had left the farm and then Mr. Henry seemed a long time ago. She was still homesick, but sleep had dulled it somewhat. Now she felt a weary determination to finish this trip as quickly as possible, but even her determination felt dull. After a moment it occurred to her that she had been rude; she should have made an effort at conversation with these men. She turned away from the window and began, "How far away . . ." then halted. She had started to ask, *How far away from Louisville are we?* She began again. "How far from Covington are we?"

Argent answered. "We have just passed Independence, so perhaps eight miles to Covington. The train has been fairly true to its run time – another 20 or 25 minutes."

Passed Independence. A surge of relief that she had slept through the crossing of the terrifying trestle works at Independence was followed by a sickly anticipation of an equally terrifying crossing of the Bullock Pen viaduct and the trestle works across Banklick near Milldale. Last summer, before his last illness, her father had seemed almost his old self again. He had become enthusiastic about base ball and closely followed the Cincinnati Club. He announced one day that he was going to Cincinnati to watch the team – *his* team – and he was taking his daughter with him. It was her first time on the recently finished Short Line, and her father proudly pointed out the engineering achievements and his own small contributions to them. The Bullock Pen viaduct was one of them. Her father had consulted in some manner on this viaduct. He had wanted to stay close to home after the last burials, and Mr. Fink had recommended her father to Messrs. Smith and Latrobe. Her father had held her hand as they crossed nearly every bridge and trestlework, but even so he could tell her fear overshadowed any pride she should have felt for her father's work. They had greatly enjoyed the game – the Red Stockings had won by only one run, the closest any team had ever come to beating them last year – and her father had treated her to dinner at the Burnet House. The next day as they had walked the old haunts of his boyhood, he had grown increasingly distant from her. On the trip home, he had hardly said a word, not even to point out some difficulty in the terrain along the tracks or to give the dimensions or amount of material used on any of the line's structures. Soon after their return home, he had begun the last decline in his health. It had been disloyal to fear something her father had helped build, and Mary wondered if her father had felt betrayed. Perhaps her loyalty would not be tested this time; perhaps she would sleep again.

It was completely dark outside, but Mary continued to stare out the window, looking for flickering glimpses of contours in the landscape in the low light of a rising moon only a week into its waxing. She thought of Jack and Morty alone at home, wondering where she was, thinking she had abandoned them. She should be home with them, sitting on the porch, watching the moon rise, listening to the evening wind ushering in, little by little, warmer weather.

It occurred to her that Argent had spoken her name. She turned from the window to regard him. He began again. "Miss Warner, I know this has been a trying day for you."

Lamps had been lit in the car, though the candles gave hardly any light at all. Oil lamps were now forbidden on all trains – oil was simply too flammable – so the night was dispelled by mere candlelight. It was difficult to make out Argent's expression, but what might have been kindness in his voice, was distorted in the darkness as polite pity. She returned to her study of the night outside, and said wearily, "Just call me Mary; I don't mind. 'Mary' is strong enough to stand on its own. It will also save you one syllable each time you address me. You can save them up and use them for something more important than saying 'Miss Warner' all day and night; something like prayer, for instance, always a worthy pursuit, especially for unCatholics." She vaguely wondered if they had attended services yesterday, whatever denomination they were. She had thrown the barb about prayer at them because she was still somewhat annoyed at them for eating some of the last of her ham on Friday, when she herself could have none.

It was an outrageous comment to make, though it was said with neither bitterness or condemnation, but much as if she were commenting on a fact of nature. And it was just the kind of remark that Miss Warner was notorious for, and that very probably inspired the well-intentioned suggestions on the scrap of paper secreted in her book. Miss Warner had, of course, determined the gentlemen to be "unCatholic" at their first meal together, when she abstained from flesh on Friday and they did not. Argent chose to ignore the sweeping review of Protestants and focused on the generous offer of her Christian name. "That is very kind of you. I'd be equally pleased if you addressed me as Giles, and Mr. Merritt, I'm sure, would not take it amiss if you addressed him as Wrenshall, or even Shaw, as I know him."

Instead of seconding Argent, Merritt asked wryly, "Why don't we save even more syllables and just call you M?"

Argent turned to Merritt with a look of absolute confused horror. "One cannot simply call a woman a mere initial. Really, Merritt, I had thought better of you."

To his further distress, Argent heard Miss Warner consent. "I do like that; it is so simple and unique. I had not thought you capable of such elegant compromises." Then, as if she remembered something, she raised her head from the window to regard them. "That is very kind of you, as well." She said it slowly, trying to mimic Argent's polite response, but also a little disturbed at their gesture. She had no intention of calling them by their Christian names.

"Mary," Argent began again.

Mary looked at him, then blinked, retracing the last few minutes back to his 'Miss Warner,' and remembered he had been about to say something. "I'm sorry. You were saying?"

Argent truly felt for her. She had obviously slept little last night and the distress of leaving home, leaving her 'boys,' leaving Mr. Henry at the depot, and leaving Emmett in someone else's care had all put a further stress on her reserves. And the failed attempt at polite conversation had taken some of the fighting spirit out of her. She could be irritating and even cruel when she was without restraint, but she was abjectly pathetic in her failed efforts to conform. He hesitated, now worried how his next comment might be received, but moved ahead anyway. "I did not mean to pry, and I only caught the briefest glimpse as I stood in the aisle next to your seat, but I saw the list in your book." Though he could not see her face clearly in the imperfect light, he saw her jaw tighten and he felt her stiffen in the seat beside him. He felt her anger but hurried forward. "I hope you do not feel the need to withhold conversation when in company with us."

Merritt, too, had seen the scrap of paper in her book. As she slept, Argent had indicated to Merritt to open the book. Merritt had found the note between the pages, had read the suggestions, and had burned with indignation for Miss Warner as he read the admonition to say as little as possible. From the other bench, Argent had watched Merritt return the paper to the book and slowly close it. He held it in his lap for a minute or two, then gently laid it next to him on the bench. He only briefly looked at Argent before he turned to the window; it was some time before Merritt pulled his attention from the scurrying scenery outside.

Both men braced for the explosion expected at the incursion into her privacy, the exposure of her faults. Miss Warner, however, merely breathed out heavily. She returned to the window, now a perfect black square. "I can hardly be angry that you saw on paper what you have already witnessed in person. I can do a great many things that no one would expect of me, but I can't seem to do what is expected of me. I don't know how to converse with people. It should be the easiest, most natural thing in the world – women, especially, are expected to excel at it – but I find it a burden. I dread it. I avoid it whenever I can, and when I can't, I always meet with disaster and walk away with a headache." She thought bitterly, *Why couldn't I be more like Randy, always happy and pleasurable and so easily sociable? He was made for this world; he should still be here.*

Then she turned back to the men and wondered, "I should have thought that after our lunch, you would have had enough of conversation with me."

"Not at all. When you are not completely loathing me, I have found you to be an engaging conversationalist." From across the small divide, Mary could only see shadows around Merritt's face, but she heard the amusement and tease in his voice. For the first time, she did not find his amusement at her expense irritating. She hesitated a moment, then came to a decision.

Bending her head conspiratorially, Mary volunteered in a low voice, "Mr. Henry made it for me, but it isn't complete. There are things he didn't tell me about."

"Perhaps we can help." Argent had also lowered his voice. "Mr. Merritt and I travel quite a bit, and there aren't many situations we haven't encountered. May I show the list to him? And then the three of us can work out what is missing."

Mary hesitated a moment, then carefully removed the paper and handed it, still folded, to Argent. He glanced over it briefly, though he had already seen it once, then handed it to Merritt. Merritt, too, looked briefly over the list he had already seen. The shadows on Merritt's face exaggerated his features, made his eyes black and hollow and turned his mouth into a grimace. Mary thought him angry at having yet one more chore to assume in this unenviable assignment. She took it from Merritt, and said, "Please don't bother; I don't want to be any more trouble than I already have been."

Merritt said quite honestly, "It is no bother at all. As Mr. Argent has said, we have had to learn ourselves over the course of our travels how to handle social situations of every kind." He had put his hand on his chest at the word "we," as he had done at his first introduction. It was a pointless gesture, but it was already familiar to Mary, and it relieved her in some way. She also noted in some recess of her mind that his hand was absurdly huge on his chest, as if it belonged to another man.

She felt truly relieved to learn these things were not solely her trial, but she nonetheless thought that plotting strategies would prove fruitless.

"Well, I don't expect to travel much at all after this, so maybe writing lists is unproductive. I can't remember it all at once anyway." Looking down at her list, at the last suggestion – just say nothing at all – she added absently, "It is probably best to avoid all conversation, especially avoid initiating one. But," and here she lowered her voice to an almost hoarse whisper, leaning left and forward to gather both Merritt and Argent into her shame, "what do I do when someone else insists on talking? How can I answer the first question, to be polite, then politely tell them I have nothing more to say? And here's a question no one has answered to my satisfaction" – she was leaning forward, looking intently, imploringly at Merritt – "why is it impolite to want to be left alone? Why am I always the one to be impolite? Why isn't someone else impolite for starting unwanted conversations?"

Merritt was overwhelmed with her intensity and the sincerity of her naïve confusion. Argent rescued his friend. "It isn't at all impolite to want your solitude. There are ways to signal others to that end. Reading a book is an unassailable signal to be left alone. Anyone who interrupts someone at their studies is the impolite one. But sometimes, you are expected to participate in the conversation. The way to fulfill your duty with the least effort is to join in briefly with simple answers, then divert the conversation to another in the group. Here, I'll show you. Merritt, start a conversation with me."

Merritt felt foolish, but M was watching with all seriousness and he found that he couldn't see her abused by such a list again. "All right," he said, but he found himself in empathy with M, as he also found it difficult to start a conversation on queue. Merritt felt Argent's impatience. "All right," he said again, looking to the ceiling. Then lightly clapping his hands, he said, "The day looks like it might rain."

Even in the low light Argent's look clearly relayed disappointment in the effort, but he rallied to use even this most banal of conversation starters. "Yes, it does," he agreed, then turning to Miss Warner, he said, "I've heard there has been considerable rain in your parts this spring. Is that true, Miss Warner?"

Mary was warming to the exercise, and exclaimed, "And here is where I have to answer, and you don't have to talk about rain anymore!"

"Exactly."

"And what if I divert back to you?"

"Then I possibly divert to Mr. Merritt."

"So, then it could become a game of keep away. Diversion seems to be a very useful strategy, but it lacks permanence."

"Maybe so, but in those cases, it then becomes a contest of diversionary tactics, and could be quite challenging." Argent's inspiration was burning bright today. It was apparent from their first meeting that Miss Warner was a competitive creature, and the best way to gaining her compliance in anything was to make it challenging. It was certainly gratifying to see her distracted from her misery.

"Well, it is certainly a strategy to keep in reserve for the most unavoidable situations, but I still think the best course is to avoid it altogether. You can't drown if you stay away from water."

Argent admonished, "But you will also never learn to swim."

"The benefits outweigh the hazards." To forestall any more talk on the subject, she asked quickly, "Will the ride be as long and crowded tomorrow?"

Merritt took this question. "It will be a good deal longer – nearly twice as long – but the accommodations are more comfortable; and I think we can find seating outside the ladies' car that will be just as inoffensive."

Mary fairly gushed with gratitude. "Yes, that would be so much the more preferable. I am still perfectly willing to stay with Emmett. Perhaps the porter in Cincinnati will be more agreeable."

Argent said a little indignantly, "You needn't sit with the beasts merely to avoid discoursing with people. I'm sure we can find an agreeable arrangement."

As Argent predicted, the train was (relatively speaking) on time, pulling into its temporary station in Covington, leased from the Kentucky Central Railroad. The Louisville Cincinnati & Lexington Railroad had yet to establish permanent termini at either end of its line. In Louisville, a powerful L&N component on the city council jealously guarded that railroad's southern monopoly, rebuking LC&L efforts to establish its own depot within the city; thus, the LC&L was relegated to that small station just east of Louisville on Beargrass Creek. At this, the other end, competing interests to establish a bridge at either Covington or Newport kept the LC&L from finalizing its terminus across from Cincinnati. So, for the moment, the LC&L rented facilities from Kentucky Central in Covington.

Though Miss Warner had slept deeply and long, in the stronger light of the depot, it was apparent that the miseries of the day had left her exhausted and stunned. She stumbled more than stepped from the train, then became almost frantic in her desire to see to Emmett's retrieval and comforts for the night. Merritt assured her that he would see to Emmett, while Argent fairly pulled her along after him to the hotel where they would spend the night. In the morning they were to take the first of the Marietta & Cincinnati trains, which would take them, ultimately, to Parkersburg, far up the Ohio, where help was waiting.

5

Merritt woke grudgingly from the best sleep he had had in over two weeks, despite the chill in the air. He had learned early to take sleep when and where he could — first as he accompanied his father from post to post as a military family, and then during the war, when sleep was always a premium for the intelligence corps. But these past two weeks had proven problematic even for him, and he suspected, for Argent as well. Their covert operation in Cincinnati had required long days in disguise and long nights in reconnaissance before its successful conclusion. Then there was the ill-advised trip on the packet steamer to Louisville that, while accommodations were comfortable, had left them crapulous and unprepared for the disorienting events at the Warner farm. And it was not the rough cots in the back room of the Warner home which had disturbed their sleep, but the strange person of Miss Warner that had kept them wondering and listening far into the nights.

Now Argent was roughly rousing him. Argent had turned up the gas lamps, so that the room was lit. It was still dark outside, but the sun would be up by the time they crossed the bridge to Cincinnati. Merritt heaved himself from his bed and wearily slipped on his pants. Argent, he noticed with a lazy irritation, was already shaven and fully dressed.

"You're bright-eyed and bushy-tailed this morning."

"We have an early train to catch, and before that, we have a horse to retrieve, a bridge to cross, and a woman to tend, but not necessarily in that order."

"A woman to tend." Merritt was coming to full alertness at last. "That sounds vaguely disturbing: a woman to tend, a woman to tender, tender an offer, to superintend. That makes us tenders. You had better find another word; M is sure to take exception."

Argent made a small gesture of disapproval. "You surely do not intend to proceed with that ridiculous manner of addressing her?"

"If she is agreeable, why do you disapprove? She apparently does not think of herself as Miss Warner, and she clearly resents any usurpation of her family pet name —"

"Lally."

"— yes, that is it – and if I am not mistaken, to use Miss Mary would be an intrusion on her relationship with Thea, Miss Carrie and Mr. Henry. I think she was relieved to have a name specifically for the purpose of this trip – one that she can dispose of once she is back home."

Argent sat at the small table in their room and regarded Merritt as he finished his toilet. "I was just about to see if Miss Warner is awake and readying herself, but you seem to have a deep understanding of her. Perhaps you should tend to her."

"The honor falls to you, since you are so fully and immediately presentable. M diverges in a great many ways from most women I have known, but she has so far proven herself very much the woman in her inability to be ready on time, or at least completely ready. Even with Miss Carrie and Mr. Henry packing for her, she still managed a few last-minute delays."

Argent thought of her collecting her books, saying goodbye to her dogs, a last-minute wash-up afterwards. He sighed and stood. "I don't know what possible delays she could conjure this morning – there is no packing to be done or partings to be made – but Miss Warner is nothing if not surprising."

Argent left the door open as he crossed the hall to Miss Warner's room. Merritt buttoned his vest as Argent knocked softly on Miss Warner's door. He shrugged into his jacket as Argent knocked a second time. He raked his hair with his fingers as Argent spoke firmly, "Miss Warner, we are on a schedule this morning." Stepping out into the hall, he closed the door behind him as Argent stopped a chambermaid passing in the hall. "I cannot rouse Miss Warner. Could you please look in on her?"

Merritt and Argent moved down the hall a polite distance to wait, but the chambermaid never fully entered the room. She turned to the men and said a little apologetically, "Miss Warner is not in her room." Then looking into the room again, she added, "It does not appear that she has even slept in here."

Alarmed, the men entered the room to find that the bed was still made, but contrary to the chambermaid's assessment, Miss Warner had at least lain on the bed. Merritt turned up the lamp for a closer inspection of the room. Looking around, he found her book on the bedside table; the train schedule was still inside the front cover, and the note from Mr. Henry still embedded between pages 71 and 72. "Well, she is still in the city, then."

"Day Two is not beginning auspiciously." Argent said this more dispiritedly than with any real irritation. Last night, Argent had seen Miss Warner to her room and had instructed the desk clerk to send some supper up to her. Though it was long past the supper hour, many hotels near major train depots were used to accommodating guests' needs at most hours. The LC&L had been held up before, waiting for passengers from tardy trains to make their Cincinnati connection, and the Covington hotels were prepared to accommodate their guests. Argent had waited for Merritt in the lobby of the hotel, and when Merritt arrived with the news of Emmett's satisfactory stabling, the two men had visited the hotel saloon for a congratulatory drink (or two). Argent had toasted their success so far: "Morning came and evening, the first day."

The toast was not the callous countdown it may have seemed to an uninformed observer, nor did it accurately reflect Argent's familiarity with the Bible. (Even Merritt, lazy at all forms of literature, had recognized the mistake. "I think you have that backwards," to which Argent had replied, "Not at all – everything seems to be backwards with Miss Warner.") With guilt, both men had observed that same toast would have been given and heartily approved with a far different intent had it taken place under circumstances first suspected. They would indeed have been counting the days (if not the hours) to the end of their assignment had the Mary Warner in question been the elderly lady of their first suppositions. Now, however, the toast took on a different meaning. Merritt and Argent were determined that the next two days of Miss Warner's trip to Washington would be matron- and headache-free. Anticipating Argent's complete approval, Merritt had already procured tickets for one of the luxurious (but more importantly, less crowded and more private) parlor cars for the next leg of their trip on the Marietta & Cincinnati Railroad. After seeing to Emmett's accommodations, he had just made it to the M&C ticket agent's office before it closed for the night.

"At least she ate a little something." Argent nodded at the remains of last night's meal, being carried away on its tray by the retreating chambermaid. Returning his attention to the bed, Argent said, "If she slept it was not for long or very well."

"She was much more agreeable after that long nap on the train."

"Who wouldn't be? To sleep that well and that long amid all that commotion, she must have truly needed the sleep. I wish something could be done for her in that respect. She might find the world a little less irritating and burdensome."

"The world will always be irritating and burdensome for her, but sleep would go a long way to helping her to endure it with less aggression."

Argent looked up wonderingly at Merritt. "You seem to be full of insight into Miss Warner's character this morning. Does that insight suggest to you where she might have gone, leaving behind her trusted book of schedules and suggestions? What is she reading, by the way?"

Merritt turned to the title page and intoned, "Elements of Practical Hydraulics for the Use of Students in Engineering and Architecture. Part I. With numerous woodcuts."

From the hall came the sounds of frantic beating on someone's door. Even before they saw her, Merritt and Argent heard Miss Warner plead, "Wake up! Wake up!" followed by more open-palmed slaps on their door.

"Miss Warner, what is wrong?" Mary whirled at the question behind her. She was as frantic and wild as they had ever seen her.

"He's gone!" Then, as if suddenly realizing Merritt was there, she furiously rebuked him. "You said you would take care of Emmett, and now he is gone! How could you have been so careless? How could this have happened? I should never have trusted you!"

Before a stunned Merritt could react and before Miss Warner's anger found its true pitch and volume, Argent grabbed her by the elbow and steered her into his room, none too gently. "Please, Miss Warner, sit, and tell us what has happened."

Argent led her to the only upholstered chair in the room, and she had briefly sat, but she was up immediately. Her face managed to be both white and red at the same time. The room was too small for her anger and her terror. She began to pace between the window and the door, but at the open door she found Merritt standing in her way, so she changed her route to pace along the wall with the window.

"I have been looking for Emmett all morning." As day was only just breaking, Merritt wondered when M's mornings began. "I went to all the livery stables, even the boarding stables on Madison. He wasn't at any of them."

"He is stabled at Moreland's just down the street, as far from both the chaos of the tracks and the activities of the hotel as time last night permitted."

Mary stopped her pacing long enough to glare pure hatred at Merritt and to spit out, "Was stabled; on my second round of stables, that idiot groomsman remembered that Emmett had been there, but was put on the morning train to Paris, per instructions. He is on his way to Paris. Paris!"

"I am sure he meant Paris, Kentucky."

Now Argent was the target for Mary's searing contempt. "I am aware of that. And what do you think will happen when he is unclaimed, whether it is at Paris, Kentucky or Paris, France? He will be sold to cover the cost of his passage and his feed, sold to one of those mule hagglers, sold to someone who won't understand him, who will likely beat him or sell him to the next person and the next person, like he was sold before he came to me."

She turned to include Merritt in her condemnation. "Mr. Henry made me promise — *don't give these gentlemen any trouble; consider their position; they are good men in a bad situation*. I half believed that yesterday; I half-believed I could count on you. And now I find that you have sent my horse away." She was near tears. "He is the last living thing I have of my father's."

From the door, Merritt reasoned, "Miss Warner, why would I want to send Emmett away?"

"Because he is more work, because he might interfere with your schedule."

Argent was losing patience with her hysterics. "And what would that schedule be, pray tell?"

Mary turned a slow and deadly eye on Argent. She quoted, "Morning came and evening, the first day."

She glared at Argent, daring him to challenge the truth of his words. Merritt began, "Miss Warner, you misunderstood the meaning of the words."

"I understand perfectly the meaning of the words: one day endured of a three-day trip, before you can return to more pleasant pursuits. I am counting the days, too, and I don't care how many days I have to add to your misery and mine — I go no further until Emmett is retrieved."

Argent finally found his voice. "I assure you the sentiment behind what you heard is not at all what you think. It was a clumsy toast, and I deeply regret that you heard it. But as to Emmett, it is a mere matter of wiring ahead to Paris to have him returned to Covington."

Mary closed her eyes slowly to master the retort that came to mind. Instead she said, "I am aware of that as well. What I am not aware of is the location of my baggage, wherein I keep my money. Apparently, no matter how noble the message, the Western Union will not send one without first being paid."

In the dark and sleep-fogged departure from the train last night, Mary had neglected to retrieve her money from her father's large trunk. Carrie had secreted it there against M's notorious neglect of her possessions – she often laid down something (a handbag, a scarf, gloves, her rosary) only to leave it behind, and Carrie was not about to leave money to the doubtful safety of Mary's grip bag. Mary, therefore, had only the barest necessities and the smallest change in her grip bag.

Argent was chastened somewhat. He had managed to insult her intelligence and pride with every word he uttered. The best thing would be for him to excuse himself from her presence and try to redeem himself by coordinating Emmett's safe return.

Merritt, however, had long before seen the prudence of vacating the room, and was waiting for the appropriate time to do so. "I will see to the telegram and arrange for Emmett's return on the next train." He turned and slipped from the room before Argent could object.

Miss Warner also left, closing the door quietly (surprisingly) after herself. After a moment, Argent went to the door himself and slowly turned the knob. He crossed the hall listening at Miss Warner's door. He had almost decided that she had not returned to her room when he heard the creak of the bed as she must have dropped onto it. He retreated to his room, leaving the door ajar just enough to watch Miss Warner's door, from the chair he had dragged into position.

Merritt nearly slammed the door into Argent's knees when he returned from his errand to the offices of the Western Union. Merritt was gone so long that Argent had fallen into a kind of reverie as he sat vigil by the door and did not hear Merritt's approach until the very last second.

Argent was irritated with Merritt for so much more than this near collision. "Where have you been? And the next time there is to be any cowardly retreat from Miss Warner's anger, it will be mine, especially when you are the cause."

Merritt smiled at Argent's indignation. As Argent repositioned the door and the chair, Merritt said, "And the next time we assume a cowardly surveillance of said lady, the honor will be mine."

Argent softened at Merritt's lame rejoinder, but defended himself nevertheless. "It was bad enough that I dragged her into our bedroom, I didn't think it proper to sit with her in hers until you decided to reappear."

"But neither did you want her slipping out on you, as she apparently did last night."

"No. What was she doing out of her room last night? How did she manage to hear us?"

"I suspect she couldn't sleep. That seems to be her perennial problem."

"What of Emmett? And what were these mysterious instructions Miss Warner mentioned?"

"It turns out that Emmett has never left Covington. But he had been transferred to the yards of the Kentucky Central in anticipation of departing for Paris on the 7:55 train, which is not due to leave for another 90 minutes."

"But you have restored Emmett to his proper stable?"

"I have requested he be transferred to the passenger depot on Pike."

"Good. You've also made arrangements with the transfer company regarding Emmett? If we hurry, we can still manage the 7:30 out of Cincinnati."

"Emmett is awaiting the pleasure of the transfer company, but I have made no immediate arrangements. Giles, perhaps hurrying is not the answer in this case. She is already wrought up and is convinced our only goal is a dash for Washington to push her out of the train at the first convenient depot. Let us prove her wrong."

Argent considered the floor at his feet for a moment, then agreed. "Perhaps we could spend the day in Cincinnati, show her some of the sights. With the elections yesterday, the good sheriff and the police force will surely have gathered up the criminal element, and the streets of Cincinnati will be as safe as they can ever be. We could take an early dinner, then take the night train. Yes, that might be preferable, after all. We know she can sleep on a train, and if she finds sleep unattainable, at least she won't be able to slip out anywhere; at least not while the train is moving."

"We should still alert the porters to that possibility at any stops."

"That goes without saying. You should advise her of Emmett's good luck and our revised plans as soon as possible."

"Certainly, but I had thought you might like that task."

"Nothing would give me more pleasure than to deliver a bit of sunny news to Miss Warner, but I have an errand of my own that needs prosecuting before we leave Covington."

Argent's errand took longer than he had anticipated. As such, upon his return he found Merritt and Miss Warner gone from the Clinton House, that excellent establishment where they had spent the night. Merritt, however, left a note for Argent, directing him to the book store just up the street. Looking through the windows, Argent easily found Merritt at Yeaman & Graves. Upon entering, he eventually spotted Miss Warner slowly wandering among the tables and stacks, occasionally picking up a book to examine, but in general she seemed to be merely enjoying the atmosphere of a library. Argent approached Merritt near the front of the shop, deeply intent on Beadle's latest dime novel, *Prairie Pathfinder.* Merritt was so intent that he did not perceive Argent at his shoulder until Argent coughed, rather loudly, in his ear. Merritt turned to greet Argent sheepishly. "M is enjoying her meditations among the tomes."

Argent grinned wryly at Merritt. "As ever, Merritt, you have coupled your slipshod detective work with an equally slipshod literary reference. I shudder to think where Miss Warner would be now if you had been reading something truly engrossing. Have you breakfasted?"

"No, M insisted on waiting for you."

"Did she?" Argent was genuinely astonished.

"Yes. One of M's charms is her determination to apologize for her outbursts. She talks constantly of penances to be paid – apologies being one of the worst, and most frequent, penances required of her."

Argent looked past Merritt to Miss Warner. "I hope there will no more occasions for her penances."

"There is always hope, but there is also habit. Probability says there will always be more occasions."

"For the next few days, I hope to help her lower that probability." From his pocket he withdrew a stoppered vial. At Merritt's questioning look, he said, "I have been to several physicians this morning and have consulted with them on Miss Warner's sleeping problems. Each one prescribed this medication."

"It was a noble errand, Argent, but you know M will not appreciate the gesture, and she will defiantly neglect its use. Miss Carrie said the family had tried everything; M will see this as one more deadend."

"This is a new medication, just come into common use this year; certainly more recent than Miss Warner's last attempts at relief. And I don't mean to advise her of my nobility or the medication. We need merely add a dose to an evening drink. If she can sleep, perhaps she will be less likely to indulge in these explosive tirades, no matter how valid. Perhaps she will simply feel better."

"If she finds out, she will certainly view this as an attempt to dose her into compliance, to make our task easier."

"Once at night, for two nights is all we have to manage. I won't deny that I will sleep easier myself if I do not have to worry about Miss Warner wandering about with insomnia. But I truly hope this can bring her some relief."

Mary had spotted the two men whispering conspiratorially, and despite the implication that she had eavesdropped on them the previous evening, she had no desire to intrude on their private conversation. Though she could not hear their conversation – and pride dictated that she should not care to – she could not help but see Argent carefully place something in his inner coat pocket. It seemed he was always stuffing something in there. One day he must surely run out of room in that great breast pocket.

She had decided to place an order with the clerk, but she again came up against the pesky problem of payment; she still did not know where her baggage had been stored. She inquired of the clerk about placing an order for payment on delivery. Behind her Argent offered to make the purchase for her, but she adamantly refused the offer. To the clerk, she said, "Thank you for your trouble," then headed out the door before Argent could make any more uncomfortable offers or arguments.

Mary's insistence on waiting for Mr. Argent had less to do with penance and more to do with her obligation to fast until the midday meal. That the two needs coincided was merely an efficient happenstance. At the late breakfast, it was learned the origin of the mysterious 'per instructions' regarding Emmett's near-exile to Paris. The wealthy gentleman at the LC&L station in Louisville had, as promised, instructed the stock car handler to treat Emmett the same as his own horse. Whether from sheer stupidity or malicious vengeance, the handler had taken the man at his word, including sending Emmett with the other horse on to Paris. After Merritt had settled Emmett at Moreland's last night, the stable manager had received word from the depot to forward Emmett to the stock pens at the freight station, which location Emmett had just left.

Likewise, Mary revealed how she came to overhear the unfortunate toast. Wanting to retrieve something from one of her trunks, she realized she had no idea where they were. She had knocked at the men's door with no result, then had inquired of the desk clerk, who had then directed her to the attached dining saloon. She had not actually entered the saloon, but she was close enough to hear the toast, and had immediately left. More professions of misunderstandings and heartfelt apologies followed, and Mary knew it was her Christian duty to forgive them, but suspicion nagged at the very back of her mind. She had been trained to forgive, but her nature was to remember, to never forget.

Emmett, of course, was foremost in Mary's mind, and it was to Emmett she headed after their meal. Though there had been a satisfactory rapprochement at 'breakfast,' Mary was not at all interested in their company while she visited with Emmett. She, in fact, intended to ride Emmett out into the countryside for an hour or two, knowing it would be the last such chance for either of them, for at least the next two days; and after a rapid engagement with the General, there were another three days on the home trip. She hated the thought of Emmett standing for so long in his train stall. And now that their plans had changed, and they would be taking the night train, she had time to exercise him a little before his long incarceration.

Merritt and Argent would not take the hint, however. All her protestations fell on deaf (stubbornly deaf) ears as they walked from the hotel to the passenger station. After a few moments, Mary again realized the absence of her trunks. Upon applying to the gentlemen as to their whereabouts, Argent assured her that she need not worry on account of money; she had only to tell him what she needed or wanted, and he would be happy to oblige. In fact, he assured her that any expenses incurred during her travels were the responsibility of the President, but that both he and Merritt felt it both an honor and a pleasure to fund anything necessary to her health and happiness.

This man was so obsequious in his attentions, it very nearly made her sick, especially on a stomach full of the rich foods of the restaurant. She found herself teetering between disdain and gratitude for these men, but especially Mr. Argent. He, in particular, had urged food on her, and she had spent a good deal of the meal fending off his efforts with the repeated assertion that her plate was full enough.

"I don't like to be in anyone's debt."

Argent ignored Miss Warner's rejection and returned to his offer at the publisher's. "I wish you had allowed me to help you in your order."

Regarding Argent with weary acceptance of her dependence on these men for information, Mary said, "I have more than money in those trunks, and I have more than enough money to support my needs and wants on this trip. While I do appreciate the offer, it is not necessary. What I want at the moment is my saddle, which is in one of the trunks. Where may I find the trunks?"

"Your saddle? Surely your intention is not to ride this morning?" Mary was becoming familiar with Merritt's penchant to begin nearly every exchange with a question.

She regarded Merritt with a measuring look, then stalked off toward the offices of the LC&L. Merritt and Argent fell in line with her, one on either side. Merritt said, "I take it that you are in search of your trunks?"

"Yes."

"It is a long walk to Cincinnati and the M&C offices, and an even longer walk on the return, carrying a saddle."

Mary stopped, bringing the men to a halt as well. "Why is my saddle in Cincinnati? And what do you mean by *walk* to Cincinnati?"

"The baggage was forwarded to the station in Cincinnati last night, as a convenience – one less detail to manage on a busy morning." Argent had adopted a tone meant to soothe, but as Merritt watched M's reaction, he was certain Argent had excited a different reaction. Merritt intervened before M's swelling indignation engulfed them all in another fireball.

"You, of course, may hire a personal carriage or take one of the street cars across the bridge, but even so, by the time you return, there will be little time left for a ride."

"Bridge?" M began to pale. This was not the reaction Merritt expected, though he was gratified the subject of a ride had been superseded. "They finally finished it?"

"Why, yes – three years ago this January, just past." Argent held in his voice astonishment that Miss Warner should be unaware of such an architectural and engineering accomplishment so close to home. "I have always wanted to cross it, but we never seem to have the opportunity. It is the longest suspension bridge in the world, you know."

Three years ago – no, three and a half years ago – Mary and her father had stood by the fresh graves of her mother and remaining siblings. Three and a half years ago she had begun the long goodbye to her father, as he began to slowly and irrevocably slip into decline after the final deaths had brought him home permanently from his work travels. Her father had, of course, spoken of the bridge, of his admiration of the engineering involved, including the ingeniously simple method Roebling devised for displacing the water during the construction of the massive piers. He had looked forward to its completion, after so many stops and starts in its construction. Each time he had come home from one of his travels, almost always going through Cincinnati where he could observe the construction, he had updated anyone who cared to hear of the bridge's progress or its setbacks. He looked forward, too, to being able to cross one of the wonders of the world. But he had been called home, three and a half years ago, before the bridge was completed and put into use. He no longer traveled to Washington or Baltimore or any of the other cities and construction sites that had once called him from home. And last year, when she and her father had traveled to Cincinnati to watch the Red Stockings, they had taken the ferry across the river. How had she missed the bridge in its operation? With shame, she realized that her father had shielded her from the bridge, had gone immediately to the ferry (on both crossings), and her willful ignorance had kept her blind to it all. Her childish fears had denied her father a last desire, a final wonder to behold, before his death.

It was not this sad remembrance, however, that made Mary pale and fall silent. Nothing inspired fear in her so much as bridges – not the pleasant stone arches over small rivers and large creeks, but the arrogant spans over vast valleys and broad, deep rivers, depictions of which she had seen in the newspapers and magazines her father brought home over the years. One in particular rose before her mind – the Tray Run viaduct on the B&O.

Argent's words hung in the air, and he was confused at her lack of enthusiasm, both as a citizen of Kentucky and the daughter of an engineer. Merritt, on the other hand, had a dawning suspicion of the problem.

They had reached the station and, accepting Merritt's receipt for Emmett, the ostler nodded towards the big horse standing by himself on the far side of the corral. But Mary didn't need to be shown her own horse and was already striding off to reunite with him. Emmett was glad to see her, as well as Merritt, though it grated to acknowledge that.

Once he and Merritt caught up with Miss Warner, Argent returned to the subject of the bridge and crossing it. "We thought we could cross over into Cincinnati now and spend the day there before boarding the night train."

A perfectly innocent and well-intentioned suggestion reignited Mary's intention to ride Emmett.

"Spend the day there!?" The horror of crossing the bridge was quickly supplanted by the prospect of spending time in the city across the bridge. "Have you ever been in Cincinnati?"

"Our work, unfortunately, takes us there often."

"Then why on earth would you want to return there for pleasure? The air is unbreathable, and every drink of water is a roll of the dice, not whether you will fall ill, but which illness will fell you. No, I thank you. This is Emmett's last chance for any real exercise for the next two days, and if I can't ride him, I will walk him."

She abruptly resumed walking, trailing Merritt, Argent, and Emmett behind her. Merritt asked, "Have you ever been in Cincinnati?"

"Some years ago." Her recent realization about last year's trip made her ashamed to think on it, and her last days with her father was private. "We accompanied Dad as far as Cincinnati on his way back to Washington or Baltimore or some other such city. He stayed with us a few days, then we returned home, and he went on."

"Perhaps things have changed in the meantime."

"No city changes for the better – they just get bigger, dirtier, and smellier. And more expensive," she added as an afterthought – she was somewhat concerned at the price of breakfast this morning (the men had paid over 50 cents each for their meals; she would truly have to marshal her funds to last the next week until she returned home). More than ever, the unknown land north of the Ohio was forming in her mind to be a wasteland of dizzying bridges, mounting filth, and noxious odors. And then there was Washington waiting at the end of the line.

"That is a fairly grim pronouncement from someone who has not been in a city in over a year."

"Your information is obsolete; I was in Louisville just yesterday, as well as the two days before that. And it was my lengthy absence that allowed me to more objectively assess the changes wrought over that time, changes that a resident so ensconced in the city could not readily notice."

"Perhaps Louisville is the exception to the norm."

"You will have to enlighten me on that account. You seem to have traveled a great deal; how does Louisville fare when considered among other cities?"

Merritt and Argent had been following Miss Warner during this discourse – she had taken Emmett's reins and was leading him from the muddy and manure-filled yards of the station. Argent noticed she still wore her riding boots from yesterday. In fact, nothing about her attire had changed – she wore a simple dress, more of a work dress than something appropriate for travel: there was no bustle or overjacket, and her upper chest was somewhat shockingly exposed. The only factor that suggested her attire was for other than working in the home or on the farm was the quality of the material – a very fine cotton, light blue, with a matching silk or satin lining that showed itself at the collar. Mrs. Müller knew exactly what would suit Miss Warner and what might mitigate her more shocking preferences.

It was Merritt who had been speaking with Miss Warner while Argent followed quietly, absorbed in Miss Warner's boots and dress (and where was her new wrap? — the morning was chilly), but he instinctively sensed a change in Miss Warner's tone in her last comment. Merritt's response had to leave Louisville with honor, but realistically so, or Miss Warner would smell the deception. No people were more jealous of their city's and state's reputations than southerners, including the hapless border state of

Kentucky. It occurred to Argent that perhaps border states, being neither northern or southern, were even more solicitous of their honor.

"Favorably, I assure you. I have only ever passed through Louisville, and only during the war, until this past week, of course. But what I have seen of Louisville is the equal to that of any eastern city. Louisville need not blush for any lack or any excess. Her problems are those of any city her size, but her accomplishments and refinements are worthy of her boasts."

Argent held his breath – Merritt had laid it on a little thick, and Miss Warner was not fond of flowery speech.

"Thank heavens I wore my riding boots this morning. I don't know how else I could have waded through such complimentary observations."

Argent slightly sputtered out his held breath at Miss Warner's coarse implication, but Merritt chuckled his approval. Argent began to suspect that Merritt intentionally baited Miss Warner in hopes of hearing such outrageous comments. A jolt of disapproval followed as he realized that Miss Warner had become something of a private amusement for Merritt. While Merritt may enjoy Miss Warner's unconventional musings and behavior, encouraging her will only cause her trouble among other, less amused, company. It suddenly occurred to him what a fish out of water Miss Warner will be in the suffocating social restraints and expectations of Washington. Perhaps her intention to immediately return home after meeting with President Grant was the best course, after all.

They had reached the gate leading out onto the street. Argent hurried forward to open it for her, but hesitated. "Where do you intend to walk Emmett?"

"I have no destination in mind, except to remove him from this disgrace of a field. I don't even see a water trough or feed of any kind available for these poor beasts." It was really an unjust comment on the corral – horses were never meant to stay here for any great length of time, and Emmett had only been accepted by way of apology for the mix-up of the morning. Mary suddenly recalled Merritt's promises of water and feed and evening exercise. "So far, accommodations for Emmett have not lived up to your promises."

Argent hoped that Merritt would not make the distinction . . . but the hope died before it was fully formed in his mind. Merritt said, "If you will recall, those promises were made when we intended to take the Marietta night train, last night. I could not anticipate that we would be held up in

Louisville and too late to catch that train, or that Emmett would be the victim of mixed instructions or end up in this regrettable pen." Argent sighed inwardly; why would he remind her of that?

"Flowery dodges and deceiving sophistry. You are in the wrong branch of government, Mr. Merritt. You should be running for office somewhere."

Mary had pressed ahead of Argent through the gate and headed south down the street. She was obliged to defer to the numerous carts, wagons, and street cars that congested the streets near the depot, but eventually she broke through to quieter parts of the town. Her concentration on negotiating the traffic was such that she completely forgot about Merritt and Argent and was thus somewhat surprised to find that they were still with her.

"And where will the day take you gentlemen?" She was fairly certain she knew the answer but did not care to launch into a foregone aggravation.

Merritt was sauntering beside Emmett, on the other side, hands clasped behind his back. "Oh, wherever the wind blows us."

"Well, I wish you well. I like to walk into the wind myself – it keeps the stray hairs out of my eyes. What time shall I meet you for this evening's train?"

"The train leaves at seven. We will need to be at the depot somewhat earlier, but we should cross the bridge long before that. There are some excellent restaurants where we could take our evening meal."

"Meals seem to be ever upward in your mind, Mr. Argent." Mary didn't mind the regular meals, especially since she did not have to prepare them herself, and the food was some of the best she had ever tasted, and with that thought she realized her taste and appetite were returning. But she loathed the over-attention, the lengthy times spent at table to merely eat. It was especially distracting while she was obligated to fast for Lent.

Merritt and Argent usually ate when and where the opportunity arose, but when the time or the locale allowed, they enjoyed a decent or even a refined meal at the better eating establishments. Though neither man had deeply probed the other's background, both knew the other had some higher education and at least a nodding acquaintance with some of the finer pursuits in life. They were therefore doubly suited to each other's company – both in their passion for their work and their preferences in their pleasures. The time and the locale were certainly presenting themselves for finer dining, but more than this, Argent was determined to keep his promise to Miss Carrie to see to it that Miss Warner ate well and regularly.

They continued walking southward out of town. Merritt and Argent smiled and tipped their hats to passersby and shopmen standing in their doorways, but M seemed oblivious to the curious stares the three of them attracted as they walked a huge unsaddled horse through town. After some moments in silence, M asked, "The train leaves at seven tonight? How long will we be traveling in the dark?"

"This is the express train; it travels all night. We'll reach Scott's Landing just before 4 a.m. Then we'll have some connections to make before we actually reach Parkersburg across the river at Belpre."

M did not respond to this information. Merritt and Argent exchanged looks over Emmett's back and shrugged. At length they came to a cemetery near the edge of town. M somehow directed the group to it, though she rarely looked up from her study of the ground passing beneath her feet. This was one of the first habits Merritt registered about M – she nearly always walked with her head down. At the entrance to the grounds, even M seemed surprised to find herself there, but accepted the destination, and without hesitation, she led Emmett through the gate. The path was too narrow for all of them to walk together. Merritt and Argent fell in line behind Emmett, though far enough back to avoid his casual evacuations.

The cemetery wasn't one of those grand affairs outside of the larger cities which attracted leisurely Sunday drives and quiet Saturday picnics. It certainly was no Cave Hill, in Louisville, or Spring Grove, in Cincinnati. Moreover, Miss Warner didn't seem to have any particular grave in mind to visit but stopped often to read the tombstones. She never remarked on what she read, but sometimes she would look up from reading to look out across the cemetery, lost in thought.

Argent whispered to Merritt, "I don't know why she came here, but surely it does her no good service to brood among the dead."

"I think the only service she is seeking is to rid herself of us and to delay crossing the bridge." At Argent's quizzical look, Merritt immediately regretted alluding to M's suspected fear. He felt he had somehow betrayed a confidence, though none had been given. "She isn't used to company and for so a long a time, and the crowds near the bridge must have given her pause."

"Ah, you are probably right. I thought something bothered her when we discussed the bridge earlier. Well, I shall do my best to keep her distracted from the crowd as we cross over to Cincinnati. But she may as well accustom herself to crowds – Cincinnati and Washington are full of them."

Privately, Merritt thought that he would have to distract M from Argent's well-intentioned efforts.

Miss Warner did not follow any particular path among the tombstones, but upon the third time passing the entrance, Argent decided it was time to head back to town, the bridge, and Cincinnati. Miss Warner looked up at her name, hesitating only the slightest when Argent called for her to leave the cemetery. She had not spoken since her last inquiry about the night train, but once they left the cemetery behind, she returned to the subject.

To neither man in particular, she asked, "Have you traveled at night? On a train?"

"Many times; it is quite convenient – one boards a train in the evening in one city, then wakes in the morning in another city." Convenient was probably not the word that would pique Miss Warner's approval. Argent amended with, "Very efficient."

Merritt added, "There are sleeping accommodations."

On one of the rare occasions, Mary looked up and over to Merritt. "Sleeping accommodations? I cannot picture it. Does one sleep with complete strangers?"

"No, nothing of the kind. We will retain a private sleeping berth for the three of us" – M's eyes slightly widened – "that is to say, a private compartment with three separate beds, separated by heavy curtains."

Mary continued to watch Merritt, obviously weighing the efficacy of curtains, no matter their weight, against a private compartment shared with two strange men. She came to a decision. "I would prefer not to ride the night train."

Argent countered, "You will not even know you are on the train, once you are asleep, and, as I said, you will awake with nine hours of travel behind you and a final day of travel before you. We would be in Washington tomorrow evening, that much closer to the end of your affairs."

Mary mulled this over, studying the ground just in front of Emmett as they walked. Finally, she said, "I prefer to see what's coming."

"Pardon?" M's shift from her obvious distrust of the sleeping arrangements to this new tack had taken Merritt by surprise.

"If you travel to Cincinnati with any kind of regularity, then you must know of the M&C's sad litany of wrecks and fatalities, especially at night."

She particularly remembered the last miles of the road after Athens to be considered unusually dangerous – gradients were steep, and the line required a great number of trestles and tunnels. Even her father had found that stretch of the road somewhat unsettling.

Her father had been a voracious reader of newspapers, and he had subscribed to quite a few of those published in the towns along his route to and from Washington – Cincinnati, of course, as well as Chillicothe, Marietta, Grafton and Martinsburg (mainly for news of the great machine shops there), Cumberland, and Baltimore. Oddly, newspapers from Washington itself never came to the farm. Most of the newspapers were in English, but a few were in German, which helped her stay current in that language. She still received them – she could not bring herself to cancel his subscriptions. She read what interested her from each paper, then used them, as her mother had, in the kitchen garden to retard the growth of weeds under the vegetable plants. These papers had kept the family informed during the war, informed of opinions and interpretations from a purely northern perspective. Though 'north' was only a few miles from Louisville, it was sometimes surprising to see the differences in views so short a distance could generate. Occasionally, the delivery of some papers had faltered in consequence of paper shortages, especially in those towns along the tracks, where the voracious appetites of the early locomotives had stripped the nearby forests of trees and therefore had denied the presses of paper.

Those papers had paraded a fairly constant report of accidents on the M&C, though that worthy line was rarely found to be at fault. Moreover, her father himself had told her that only those who were absolutely obliged to ride that line did so, and that it was his professional opinion that much of the line simply needed to be rebuilt.

Merritt and Argent had indeed been present at several incidents, not only on the M&C, but nearly every railroad they had ever ridden. It was, unfortunately, the price of mass and rapid travel – there would always be drunks passing out on the rails or falling off trains, and there would always be horses and cows unfortunate enough to be on the tracks and too paralyzed by fear to get off in time (poor dumb beasts). There would always be mudslides and rockslides and bridge failures and engine troubles, and workers injured and killed in the execution of their jobs. But one could not dwell on these things; no one would ever go anywhere, if such thoughts were indulged. Trains and railroads would never have pushed ahead to give the nation its growing access to nearly every destination or commodity desirable.

"I think 'litany' indulges a certain sensationalism that is undue to the actual facts. And witnessing any in the light of day can hardly make them less regrettable."

Mary largely disregarded Argent's patronizing remark about litany, except to say, "I know what I read." Then she added, "A death or injury does not need the light of day to afford it the proper regret, but if that death or injury involves myself, I want to see it coming. The only regret for myself would be such a surprise in the dark, with no possibility to react or prepare."

"Do you always give such consideration to minimally potential catastrophes? Argent, perhaps we regard our own travels far too lightly."

The amusement in Merritt's voice angered Mary; she had voiced a concern he found lacking in merit, and it made her doubt herself. She did not answer Merritt; she would give him no further reason to laugh at her opinions or thoughts. When will she learn to hold her tongue? If she was not insulting someone with her comments, someone was insulting her because of them.

Mary intended to continue to agitate for continuing by rail during the day, even if it meant adding time to an already onerous travel schedule, but they were deep in town now, and Argent was speaking to Merritt. "I shall take Miss Warner to the hotel and gather our few things. You see to tickets for the street car." Then to Miss Warner, "Or would you prefer to walk?"

Argent was angry with Merritt for teasing Miss Warner as he did, and he thought this the reason for her hesitation in answering. Mary, however, was deep in calculations weighing the benefits and liabilities of walking a mile across the river – which would extend the time but leave her a free agent should the bridge collapse – or riding across the bridge, which would be quicker, exposing her to less chance of calamity, but which would make her a prisoner of the streetcar, should anything happen. In the end, she opted for the quicker streetcar.

"No, the streetcar will do."

Merritt asked wickedly, "Are you certain? We know how you enjoy a leisurely walk."

Mary glared at Merritt. Did he suspect her fear and was he teasing her? "My short but sad experience has been that walking with you is anything but leisurely."

Argent had the distinct feeling that something had passed between these two, but he couldn't understand what, only that Merritt had enjoyed it at Miss Warner's expense. Merritt smiled at Miss Warner as he relieved her of Emmett's reins. Miss Warner said nothing, merely turning away as she headed back to the hotel. As he turned to follow Miss Warner, Argent glared an open warning at Merritt. Merritt merely smiled, but he judiciously waited a few moments before following Argent and Miss Warner down Madison, not to the hotel, but to Moreland's Livery to give Emmett a quick brushing and a long drink of water, and to settle the bill with Mr. Moreland.

Merritt and Emmett rejoined Argent and Miss Warner at the corner of Fifth and Scott to await the street car that would take them across the Suspension Bridge to Cincinnati. Seven street cars traced the several loops of rails throughout Covington, Newport, and Cincinnati every day, and the patronage of the railway companies plainly cried for ever more cars. As they waited, several people joined them. The bridge was in plain sight; it was, in fact, in plain sight from nearly every point in Covington. Mary was almost panicked at the thought of crossing the bridge. She had decided on a proposal that would offer an alternative to the bridge. In as casual a manner as she could manage, Mary suggested taking the ferry.

"I have been thinking of Emmett. I am certain he will give trouble on the bridge."

"Nonsense – horses cross it every day without incident. The street car horses cross it and recross it several times a day. Emmett will do well." Argent spoke absent-mindedly; he was eagerly eyeing the bridge towering above the buildings of the intervening streets, watching in his mind the pedestrians and street cars entering and exiting that engineering marvel.

"Argent has long wanted to cross this bridge; I would hate to see him miss the opportunity."

Argent tuned to glare at Merritt. His wishes had nothing to do with the matter at hand. Miss Warner was very naturally concerned about her horse, and he was determined to see her worries for Emmett allayed.

Miss Warner, however, seemed determined to accommodate Mr. Argent's wishes to cross the bridge, while keeping Emmett off the same structure. "As would I. Please enjoy your crossing; Emmett and I will take the ferry and meet you in Cincinnati."

Argent seemed without answer to this and was happy to let Merritt make the reply. Argent returned to his giddy anticipation of their ride.

"That we cannot do – it would be a complete dereliction of our duty." Moreover, Merritt argued, though M may have once visited Cincinnati, he was certain it was under parental supervision, and that M simply did not know the city as well as they themselves (at this point Merritt looked to Argent for agreement, but Argent's mind was elsewhere engaged) and M could easily find herself lost and at risk – the riverfront was notorious for rough workmen and smooth pickpockets.

Mary offered what she considered a completely equitable solution – that one of the gentlemen could accompany her on the ferry – but Mr. Merritt seemed to become irritated at the suggestion.

After having delivered to M the good news regarding Emmett this morning, Merritt had sent an errand boy to the ticket offices of the trains here in Covington to change their arrangements from a parlor car on this morning's M&C fast line train to a Silver Palace sleeping car on tonight's express train. "All arrangements have been made, and the street car is almost here." The street car pulled up just as Merritt finished speaking. He was not without feeling for M's fears (he was now certain that bridges and possibly heights in general were the problem), and though he would like to accommodate her, he also realized the need to set precedent – they simply could not argue every aspect of the trip that M disagreed with or which caused her discomfort.

As a few people exited the street car, Argent realized the tone of the conversation had taken a rather authoritarian turn, something he rarely heard from Merritt, even when dealing with criminals. Argent recalled

Merritt's enjoyment of Miss Warner's concerns regarding traveling by night. It had obviously angered her into silence. Hoping to both salve her pride and to assure her of the safety of train travel, especially at night, Argent had returned to the topic at the hotel – in Merritt's absence. Rather than assuring Miss Warner, Argent himself had been somewhat alarmed at her reply: "You wouldn't take your travels so lightly if you were aware of just how much mere glue is used to hold these cars together." Nevertheless, Argent was determined to keep Merritt from further antagonizing Miss Warner, whether her concerns were valid or not. "What is the problem?"

Merritt opened his mouth to speak, but Miss Warner spoke first. "Not a thing. Mr. Merritt has assured me of a fair crossing."

"Well, certainly he has. This will be wonderful. This is the longest suspension bridge in the world, almost half a mile, and we'll be crossing it in style and while it is still in its infancy."

Argent was far too excited at his good fortune to notice M's paling complexion. Merritt noticed it, not without sympathy, helping her to her seat on the trolley, making sure she was situated between himself and Argent.

Emmett was tied to the back of the car, over the objections of the driver, but not over the handsome tip Merritt offered him for the privilege. Merritt also convinced the driver the seats nearest the back should be reserved for the owner of the horse in case that massive animal should find the crossing unsettling. When Merritt had nodded at Miss Warner as she stood next to Emmett stroking his stout neck, the driver had seemed doubtful that any woman could restrain such a beast, but Merritt had indicated, also with a nod of his head, that control by the owner included efforts from himself and Mr. Argent.

Sitting in the back shielded Mary from the view from the front – a long stretch of road across the river, a road suspended by wire cables above and all around, creating a kind of spidery tunnel. Quite naturally, Argent and Merritt sat on either side of her, thus blocking much of the front and rear views of their crossing. But Mary had a clear view looking out the window opposite her; she would be facing west and would watch their crossing of the bridge with a full view of the river and their height above it.

Mary sat straight in her seat, staring at the hat of the woman seated across from her. She need only endure thirty minutes, at most, in the complete crossing of the bridge. They stopped at every street corner on the way to the bridge, taking on more passengers. As the car turned onto Fourth Street, Mary had a fair view of the bridge, despite the intervening buildings. The two massive stone pillars that bespoke the entrance to the bridge loomed ahead. Rather than give her comfort, their heavy presence filled her with dread – she imagined them collapsing as the street car crossed the bridge, being both crushed by falling stones and drowned in the river over one hundred feet below. This image would not leave her, even as Argent pointed out the Custom House that slowly rolled across her view. Distantly, she heard the woman whose hat she had been studying remark to apparently no one in particular of the recent escape from the jail that was now to Mary's back. It occurred to Mary that it was a stupid arrangement to have a jail so close to a bridge that led to another state and therefore another jurisdiction. Perhaps she had given voice to her thought, for the car seemed to become silent. She could not be certain of either thing, for her ears were now filled with a roaring that only the beating of her heart could overcome. They were crossing a street at a strange angle, and with that turn of the car, Mary had a lightning-quick view of the entrance to the bridge.

There were the two massive pillars guarding the long arching avenue across the Ohio. As if to confirm her fears, the sign above the ticket office and toll entrance to the right announced in bold letters: *Fine for riding or driving faster than a Walk. Processions must break step in marching.* From far away, she heard her father tell of a suspension bridge destroyed decades ago by a fiddler. It had almost seemed like a fairy tale at the time – a fiddler about to lead a wedding procession across the bridge had challenged that he, and he alone, could bring down the bridge, simply by playing his fiddle. The fiddler had been cheated by the same family when the elder daughter was married just the year before and was determined to get his due. The wedding party, of course, was furious at the interruption, as well as at the eclipsing of the wedding itself, by his proclamation. The father of the bride, angry at the dismay this caused his daughter and also smelling a path to cheating the fiddler yet again, answered the fiddler's challenge by promising to double the fiddler's fee if he could prove the claim, but paying the fiddler nothing if the claim proved false. The fiddler bowed his acceptance of the conditions, took one step upon the bridge, and began to fiddle, striking one note after another, until he hit the sweet note, the fundamental tone, that set the bridge to vibrating. The vibrations grew and grew until the wedding party begged the fiddler to cease, for their destination was the other side of the river. Finally, the engineers were called, and only their earnest entreaties succeeded in saving the bridge.

It had seemed like a fairy tale, but of course there were no suspension bridges in fairy tales, only solid stone bridges under which hid trolls and other such unsavory characters. But bridges could be brought down by oscillation; that much of the story her father had said was true. Bridges vibrated and hummed under the lock-step of armies, and there were bridges in Europe that had indeed fallen under the tonal burden of marching men. Armies could break their step, or the bridges would break under them. Mary looked around and was alarmed at the number of soldiers from the Newport barracks, across the Licking River from Covington, who were on the bridge or milling about the entrance. They were not in formation – they were likely on leave – but still she did not trust them. Soldiers were creatures of enforced habit; they could not help themselves. Any minute now they could break out into the thrumming step of their training. She kept a wary eye on them while straining to hear the tell-tale humming of a bridge dirge, heralding death and destruction. She willed the driver to go faster, though he himself was constrained by the rules – their car could go no faster than the pace of walking. There were, in fact, pedestrians passing them on the walkways that flanked the wide middle avenue of the bridge.

M looked straight ahead and endured the long ride in utter silence. Argent was looking around and smiling like an idiot at a fair, oblivious to the terror seated next to him.

"It takes your breath away, doesn't it? All this iron and steel cable, the massive stone work? And the magnificent Ohio surging below us. It leaves one speechless."

M was speechless for another reason. Merritt had the good grace to look ahead and not tease her. He worried, however, how she would fare crossing the far higher bridges, trestles, and viaducts (as well as the long tunnels) to come on their rail trek through Ohio, West Virginia, and Maryland.

Finally, the street car descended to its terminus in Cincinnati at a small depot on Front Street. Every single passenger exited the car, since the Covington Street Railway Company was not allowed to penetrate further into the Cincinnati economy. However, that did not mean that a

Cincinnati street car would be waiting to take passengers from that point to their ultimate destinations. Instead, grumbling visitors from Kentucky could either hire a hack at the stand near the Custom House or walk to the closest street car stand on Fifth Street. Despite Cincinnati city council's perennial applications to the notorious Route No. 9 to honor its legal obligations to run between the Ernst Street bridge and the Suspension Bridge, that route went no further south than Fifth (and no further north than the Mohawk street bridge).

Merritt took charge of Emmett, leading him away, without permission from Mary or any explanation as to why. When she began to follow, Argent gently pulled her by the elbow away from the crowd disembarking the street car and those waiting to board for the trip back over the bridge into Kentucky.

"Merritt will install Emmett at the M&C depot. I assure you Merritt will be making absolutely clear how Emmett should be treated, both before and during our trip." Miss Warner neither agreed nor objected as she watched Emmett walk away, but Argent added for good measure anyway, "We simply cannot be trailing a horse behind us all through Cincinnati."

As it was, Argent and Miss Warner eventually followed Emmett and Merritt west on Front Street, then north on Vine Street. Merritt, however, would leave Vine at Second Street to take Emmett to the Plum Street Depot where the Marietta & Cincinnati shared facilities with the Indianapolis, Cincinnati & Lafayette Railroad. Argent and Miss Warner continued on Vine until Argent ushered her into an establishment a few blocks away from Front Street.

Mary was surprised to find herself in a restaurant. Surely it was not yet the dinner hour, and what about the promised tour of Cincinnati? After they were seated, Argent explained that the morning's unscheduled activities precluded the possibility of any touring of the city. There was enough time for a leisurely supper before their train departed at 7:05, hardly two hours from now.

It was not long before Merritt joined them at Hunt's Dining Saloon, one of the few decent restaurants that served meals at all hours of the day and night. Hunt's was able to serve a great many people at one time in two dining rooms, one for gentlemen and one for ladies and their escorts. Once again, Mary found herself between escorts and exile – without escorts she was without respectability. Remembering the rude and domineering handler at the LC&L depot in Louisville, she realized that without escorts she was also without power. For the first time, it occurred to her that she might have to endure escorts – perhaps even these very same escorts – on her trip home from Washington. The return home, she was determined, would be made on her terms. She had already learned a great deal about travel in these last few days, and she would not be caught unawares next week when she would be the one planning the routes and times and manner of conveyance. The ferry will do quite well in place of the bridge.

At dinner, Argent continued to gush about the great accomplishment of the bridge. His enthusiasm was such that he, for once, did not comment on Mary's seeming lack of appetite. He spoke of John Roebling and his studies abroad, and of how Roebling used as his guide the design of French bridges over French rivers.

"French! That bridge comes from the same minds who gave us the guillotine!? Are American Rivers designed after French Rivers? It is my understanding that, with very few exceptions, the Ohio River is one of the largest rivers known. Can French rivers compare? Then how can French engineering possibly stand up to the rigors of American rivers? You can't possibly expect me to cross that bridge again knowing the design could be faulty, that is to say, French."

"If it makes you feel any better, the steel cables are from England." Merritt couldn't tell if Argent honestly thought he was helping, or if he enjoyed Miss Warner's distress. Merritt was at least grateful that Argent declined to correct Miss Warner on her inflated sense of the Ohio's global standing.

"God help us all! Our vital commercial and personal interests are held hostage to European standards! I suppose the train you expect me to board is from Spain?"

"No, no, no, no. It was built in Massachusetts. But I am given to understand that a good deal of the machinists and designers who work there are of German stock."

"Well, we at least have that to be thankful for – you can't beat a German for engineering or machine work."

"You approve of the Germans, then?" Merritt sounded slightly disapproving himself, though Mary suspected it was of herself.

"I do not disapprove of the French or English, just their engineering. But, yes, I approve of Germans, being German myself."

"Really! 'Warner' is such a pronounceable name; I had thought it English. Or is it your mother who is German?"

Mary ignored Merritt's observations on German pronounceability, especially since there was some private amusement lurking behind his words. "My father and his father worked on the L&N. Grandpa was a division superintendent. He travelled a lot, like Dad. He took Dad with him to different places and made him attend college to become a proper engineer. Dad stayed with family in Germany while he studied, and so I know German engineers are the best." Miss Warner seemed to be loquacious for two reasons – when angry and when speaking of her family, especially her father. "My brothers would have been engineers, too – most of them."

"Did your farm, then, come through your mother or grandmother?" It seemed impossible that a man could pursue a career in engineering if he already had a ready means of livelihood, such as a farm, at his disposal.

"No; Dad acquired the acreage on his own and built the house himself, though Mr. Henry helped sometimes. Grandpa never had a farm, though he had some land attached to his house; he lived here in Cincinnati. So do his sisters, Dad's Aunt Ada and Aunt 'Scella. We used to visit them sometimes; but Grandma and Grandpa lived with us in the end."

Merritt and Argent were both stunned at this piece of news, but Merritt spoke first. "Do you mean to tell us that you have relatives here in Cincinnati? Why have you not come to live with them, rather than run that farm by yourself?"

"I have lots of relatives in lots of places, but none of them happen to live where I live. I have cousins of every degree in Wisconsin, and I have first cousins in Versailles and Knoxville and Indianapolis. There may be cousins in other places as well – all the Warners have ten or more children, and some of them are married by now and with children of their own, no doubt."

"But, Miss Warner, can you not find a home – at least until you are married yourself – among one of them? Are they aware of your situation?"

Mary's relatives of course knew of her father's death and knew also of her "situation." Only the most strenuous rejections to their offers of hospitality had prevailed. There were a few serious attempts by distant older male cousins to assume control of the farm – of course, in her best interests – but, unbelievably, mysteriously, they had one by one abandoned the attempt. Mr. Henry had hinted of an outside benefactor whose legal resources had kept threats to her inheritance at bay, but he would not or could not give any particulars. It was a constant worry of hers that she could, through inheritance laws and other legal maneuverings, lose her home, or worse, live there under someone else's rule. Merritt's and Argent's interest in relatives set her already jangled nerves further on edge. A truly unpleasant and fantastic thought flashed through her mind – that Merritt and Argent represented the vanguard of some effort to separate her from her home, gathering the information necessary to prove her unequal to running the farm on her own. Upon further reflection, she realized that she had no real proof that these were, in fact, Grant's men. She had taken them at their word, and now found herself over 100 miles from home with them.

Miss Warner had been silent for so long as she considered these facts that Argent needed to prompt her. "Miss Warner?"

Mary pulled her mind back to the current moment. She blinked slowly at Argent – once, twice, three times – before answering. "I'm sorry, I'm afraid I was woolgathering, thinking about Dad's family." This was strictly true, and it covered her growing fear of entrapment from men who might be operatives of a scheme waged against her. "Of course Dad's sisters and cousins know he has passed, and most have offered to take me in, I believe is how it was put. But that dust has settled to everyone's satisfaction."

Before either man could refer again to her 'situation,' Mary continued. "But I am neither out in the cold nor in the least interested in pursuing marriage. I could never leave my home, and certainly not just to wait until some phantom bachelor should come along only to assume control of everything that is rightfully mine. Spinsterhood is not so bad when you have land and an independent means of support."

"But what of children? Surely you would like children someday."

Mary considered Argent as she considered her answer. She thought she might want children — she should want children — but she knew what pregnancy and childbirth could do to a woman. She had seen her own mother stripped of her health with the arrival of each succeeding child; and Mary had no idea of what each child before Mary's own birth had cost her mother; certainly her youth was long gone by the time Mary arrived. Her mother's life had been one of endless meal preparation and laundry and cleaning; Mary did not think she could give up her own freedom — to hunt with the dogs, to ride Emmett, to sit idly on the porch swing, to walk the planted fields as they matured throughout the spring, summer, and fall — for the sake of children, for the promise of so much more work. Beyond all this, she was growing concerned with each passing birthday that children would be an impossibility for her — the clues of nature did not visit her on anything like a regular schedule; it had been nearly two years now. "It is not something I would care to pursue." To share the guilt she felt for rejecting future children, she added, "I think it very selfish of men to expect so much of women, when they themselves have to give up so little."

Diners nearby were beginning to steal glances at the table where the men's voices were rising in surprise and shock and the woman's voice was rising in anger, and where the topic under discussion – at dinner, in public! – was the *option* of children.

Merritt deliberately lowered his voice. "You can't possibly be serious in making such comments. You might as well suggest the sun revolve around the moon."

Mary lowered her voice as well and said quite honestly, "I like men, I like children. I don't like the law – either civil or moral – that determines my place among them. I have accepted that – through my own fault, through my most grievous fault – I will very likely never marry or have children. I just wish everyone else would accept it as well. I have seceded from society peaceably; I wish society would peaceably let me go."

"If you're going to use the language of treason, I must point out that this line of thinking is treasonous to your sex and blasphemous before God and nature."

Somehow, this seemed strange coming from Merritt. Perhaps she had shocked Argent into silence.

"Treason? Secession isn't treason. This nation was built on secession, as well as treason and disobedience. It is arrogant, specious, two-faced, and ironic for the very government that was itself founded on secession and treason to turn around and impose sanctions on its member parts for invoking the same right to self-government."

"Self-government that includes slavery?" Mr. Argent had found his tongue.

"I have already made my views known on the issue of slavery; but you mistake me – the member parts to which I refer are women, or at least myself among them. I would very much like to secede from the government that regards me with so little value."

Mary cut across whatever reply Argent was about to make. "But if you insist on returning to slavery, let me say this: in theory, I think the rebel states had every political precedent to secede, but no moral standing to do so. I hope you don't think so little of me that I could support such a heinous practice. Of course slavery had to die, and it would have been better if it had died long ago. This war should have happened long ago, and we'd be fifty years further ahead, and our brothers and fathers and sons and husbands would be with us here today. But there was so much regard for tradition and status quo and preservation of political power that slavery was allowed to burrow deeper and deeper into the culture. So it is with marriage – generations upon generations of tradition have become law with no real natural basis. Why do you suppose a woman needs a husband to manage her affairs? Because no one has bothered to teach her how to do so herself. Certainly men are useful for their strength, and only women can bear children, but the difference ends there. I can think as well as you, and if there is a lapse in my intellect it is because of a lapse in experience or education, experience that I have been denied and education which has been limited. I can shoot as well as the next man, and ride as well, too. If I can't run faster than most, that is a mere matter of limb length, but it doesn't mean I can't run at all. You, in turn, can sew just as well as the next woman; if your stitches are clumsy, it is a matter of experience. You can clean as well as the next woman, or launder or even care for children; you've never been given the opportunity, it has never been expected of you. And as for nature, there is nothing unnatural at all in my retreat from marital bondage; not every woman marries. A woman remains single usually because men have excluded her from the opportunity – either because of her looks (which is the basest of animal criteria, hardly reason to celebrate the merits of matrimony) or her lack of dowry (which is unforgivably mercenary). I simply choose to remove from any man the opportunity to dismiss me on either grounds, or the opportunity to pursue me on either grounds which would make me little more than an investment of an unknown depreciation."

"You have such a low opinion of men; did you think of your brothers and father in such light?" Argent seemed personally offended.

"They were men of clay, as are we all; but they were of the very best clay – they were marble. But they were like you, afraid or unwilling to peer over the wall to see what might be in the next field."

Mary realized she had just alienated the two men who could make her trip less miserable. She wasn't so entrenched in her opposition to marriage as her speech had just suggested. But she was angry with Merritt and angry with herself that she had let him see her fears, and she had allowed herself to speak with far more vitriol than she truly felt. She had wanted to discomfort them, as she had been discomforted on the bridge, but she had gone too far. More than ever, she wished the trip would be over; more than ever, she wished she had stayed home. She made the effort to make peace with the men. "I don't reject the sacrament of marriage; I don't completely reject the possibility for myself. I don't reject the benefits – both social and personal – of marriage. I reject the liabilities that accompany it. It may be that I reassess the balance in years to come, but at this moment, the liabilities far outweigh the benefits. I know what I can live with and what I can live without." She paused, but when neither man replied, she added, "I don't apologize for my position and views – I have spent the last year fending off male relations and dubious suitors who would 'relieve' me of my father's farm – but I do apologize for displaying them at dinner and to the discomfort of those who do not share them with me." After the merest pause, she added, "You see why I should avoid conversation with others; it never ends well."

Merritt relented in his disapproval. "The fault lies equally with us. The subject of marriage and children is, of course, a private matter, and it was not our intention to delve into family affairs, also a private concern."

"Still, I should think you would like to visit while you are here?" Argent simply could not believe that Miss Warner could be so completely estranged over the matter of her inheritance that she would eschew the possibility of visiting relatives while in their very midst.

"I would very much like to visit." Though Mary put much effort into this lie, Merritt and Argent recognized it as such immediately. "But I could hardly call on them at such very short notice, especially since we are leaving so soon. Which begs the question, when are we leaving?"

"Everything is in order at the station – our bags are checked and berths for our horses have been reserved. We can take a short stroll after our meal, then board the train."

Though Mary still harbored misgivings about traveling at night, she ventured, "Should we not board the train as soon as possible, in order to secure favorable seating?" By favorable, she meant, of course, seating near a window, seating with each other, seating without matronly neighbors.

Both men knew the source of her anxiety, but Argent answered quickly in order to forestall any further teasing from Merritt. "Our seats – our berths – have already been reserved; our arrangements are perfectly favorable." Though he had meant to staunch Merritt's ever ready reservoir of teasing, Argent's own comment had the tint of a smirk to it.

Mary noted the perceived jeer, but merely nodded. She should never have shown them Mr. Henry's note, or invited their help and comments. Now she would always be subject to their mockery.

Merritt repeated his suggestion for a walk around town after dinner. The town, though populous, was not very large geographically, being hemmed in to the north and east by steep hills and by swampland to the west, and, of course, by the Ohio to the south. Mary was eager to stretch her legs, but first insisted on looking to Emmett's accommodations, and privately she wanted to see what kind of horses these men brought with them. She wanted to confirm what their choice in nags at her farm had suggested – that they were no judge of horseflesh. She uncharitably relished the chance to ridicule them as they seemed to be ridiculing her, but the pleasant prospect of a walk was abruptly brought to an end before they even left the front room of the restaurant. As Mary returned from her personal business in the wash rooms of the saloon, she walked into the vestibule to see Merritt and Argent receive a note from a courier of some sort. She remained at a discreet distance, but they received the note without comment or payment to the deliverer. Argent spoke to Merritt even as he read the note. Though Argent's head was down, it was obvious, even from a distance, that he was angry, and Merritt mirrored his partner's anger in placing his hands forcefully upon his hips. As he did so, Merritt looked up and chanced to see Mary watching them. He spoke a single word to Argent, and Argent, too, looked up.

Mary watched as Argent handed the note to Merritt before joining her in the back of the vestibule.

"You have had disagreeable news?"

Argent could not help but think the question was asked with the slightest tone of hope and enjoyment. "Not so much disagreeable as inconvenient. But we hope to neutralize the inconvenience. I ask your patience for a few moments while we attend to this unexpected irritation. We may have to cut short our walk."

Mary nodded. "I hope you come to an agreeable, convenient solution." She was, however, hoping for the opposite. A problem for these federal men would mean an honorable retreat for her. This trip – never truly hers to plan – was slipping out of control, from even Merritt's and Argent's control. Despite his disclaimer to the contrary, it was evident the news contained in that little note was far more than merely inconvenient. Across the room, Merritt's countenance had grown darker as he obviously argued with the courier. Why did he not merely dismiss the man? It was pointless to blame or barter with the bearer of bad news.

Argent rejoined Merritt in time to hear the district attorney's junior clerk regretfully inform them that District Attorney Bateman was adamant on this point: the cases needed to proceed immediately. Moreover, the District Attorney had Chief Whitley's assurances that Merritt and Argent were at his complete disposal. Normally, Merritt and Argent would have readily complied with both Mr. Bateman and Chief Whitley, but the matter of escorting Miss Warner to Washington to meet with the President presented an unusual facet to the situation.

Argent argued for the obvious, a continuance in the case, but the courier was ready for this objection: Bateman had, of course, applied for a continuance, but the judge had somehow learned of the men's intended immediate return to the city, and the judge saw no reason for continuance when the star witnesses were so readily available.

Merritt offered, but without much hope of being accepted, "We would be happy to give thorough, detailed depositions. We could have them to Mr. Bateman first thing in the morning." Beside him, he felt Argent slightly slump at the thought of yet another delay in their departure, another night in a hotel with Miss Warner free to wander at will.

"I am sorry, sirs, but Mr. Bateman must insist you testify in person, especially given the intimate nature of Mr. Argent's participation in the investigation. He is concerned that the judge would want to hear such testimony himself, and that he might delay the hearings and trials to an even further date until he is able to do so. We have already lost several witnesses. Mr. Bateman is afraid a later date on the docket will only result in the loss of more, if not most, of the remaining witnesses."

Merritt and Argent and every other operative of the division had come to expect the sudden disappearance or unavailability of witnesses. It was no secret that many witnesses, whose reliability and integrity were shaky to begin with, were often bribed by defendants or friends of defendants or even counsel for the defendants to simply vacate the area of jurisdiction at the time of the trial. And if the date of the trial proved inconvenient to the defendants, other bribes and other inducements were brought to bear upon the judicial system, greasing the wheels of that increasingly sluggish engine to facilitate later and later trials, which in turn facilitated acquittals, more or less by default of any witnesses. Many counterfeiters simply paid their way back to freedom and back to counterfeiting, earning them more than enough money to thwart convictions. Arrests for them were merely an inconvenience to be endured.

The case which Merritt and Argent had been working in Cincinnati had been one of long standing and of particular interest to Mr. Bateman. The counterfeiting gang under investigation had been working quite effortlessly in the city and had so far evaded all attempts to infiltrate or thwart their work. The target of their investigations was so shrewd that Merritt and Argent had taken the unusual precaution of bringing their own horses to Cincinnati. As Argent was to present himself as a man of some means, he could not be caught renting a horse; nor could he lend himself to investigation by anyone in Cincinnati, including the owners of and those employed at the numerous livery stables in the city. The leader of the counterfeiting ring they hoped to break – one Catharine Rogers – commanded deep loyalties throughout the city, but no one knew exactly where these loyal conspirators worked or lived in the concentrated population of Cincinnati. Argent had worked particularly hard and under personally objectionable circumstances, but they had caught the culprit red-handed and their convictions were assured. The case, however, was not to have come to court for two weeks yet. The trial had, in fact, been purposely given a rather late date in the hopes that the ring of shovers out on bail would lead the Service to bigger fish – the engravers, manufacturers, boodle carriers, etc. – most likely in New York, and maybe even reveal the mysterious source of capital and other resources behind so many of these illegal ventures. Other Service operatives and detectives in the Cincinnati police force were to maintain surveillance in these hopes.

The newspapers, of course, printed what Chief Whitley wanted printed – that the capture of Catharine Rogers and her clan was a coup, an important and significant arrest in the Secret Service's war on counterfeiting. Almost all of their arrests were presented in this manner. Sometimes it was true, but in this case the arrest was something of a disappointment – while the Widow Rogers was indeed a major player in the pushing of the queer in Cincinnati, she was only a part of a greater national network of counterfeiters operating out of the eastern centers, but slowly moving westward. So far, her arrest had yielded nothing pointing to this greater network.

This sudden change in the court schedule was also puzzling because the Widow Rogers had initially asked for her own continuance, in order, so she said, to secure witnesses, prepare for the trial, and to find and hire replacement counsel, since her counsel of choice had competing commitments. Everyone in the courtroom recognized the request as a delaying tactic – the passage of time tended to result in the 'disappearance' of witnesses or dulling in the clarity of the memory of witnesses. Some of the more resourceful counterfeiters continually delayed their trials employing a succession of counsel, first firing one, then needing time to hire another, all to astounding good results. In short, defendants rarely requested that cases be moved *up* on the docket.

With Argent's true identity exposed, as well as that of Merritt (who had participated in the arrests), the men had been both available and in the area when the particular errand for the President had been presented to them; and as soon as Miss Warner was safely delivered in Washington, they were to return to Cincinnati for the trial. Now, according to the note from Mr. Bateman, the trial had been mysteriously and almost silently moved up on the docket. Very soft rumors had suggested that it was known that both Merritt and Argent, the most important witnesses in the case, were engaged elsewhere for some few days, and it was in the best interest of the defendants to proceed forthwith. The trial, in fact, was already underway. The District Attorney's office had used every possible delay over the last two days and could stall no more: the prosecution needed to present its prize evidence as told by its prize witnesses.

Mr. Bateman had been sending frantic telegrams to Merritt and Argent in Louisville, but without response. He had set men to watch for them in both Covington and Cincinnati for first word of their return. As the junior clerk explained all this, Argent kept a watchful eye on Miss Warner as she wandered about the room. Noticing his distraction, the junior clerk assured them that they would suffer no consequences because of the delay as regards their exclusive business for the President. District Attorney Bateman had taken the liberty of wiring Washington to inform President Grant of the inevitable delay; he all but suggested the President appoint new escorts. The inconvenience that Merritt and Argent had felt at this sudden change in court dates erupted into true anger at the public knowledge of their work for Grant. Their assignment for the President was to have remained private, and in all their previous communiqués they had never referred to Miss Warner by name or by purpose. And after only a brief time with Miss Warner, they were certain she herself would have preferred to keep her reasons for travel private. As for new escorts, both Merritt and Argent realized that they had become somewhat attached to Miss Warner and, though it was unlikely that Miss Warner returned the sentiments, it was equally unlikely that she would accept overtures from two more complete strangers. Mr. Henry had told them that she did not like change and changing escorts now would bring out all her old objections with renewed vigor. And, unless the President could find suitable escorts immediately and in Cincinnati, it was likely that Miss Warner would return to Kentucky and her farm and entrench against future incursions. As Mr. Henry had said, she would not be caught napping a second time.

Merritt's demand for the source of Mr. Bateman's information regarding both the President and Miss Warner was met with stiff disapproval from the clerk. "I'm sure you will need to consult with Mr. Bateman in the matter. In the meantime, I shall report to Mr. Bateman that I have found you and relayed his message to you."

Upon hearing of the delay – which Merritt and Argent presented as a matter of two to three days, but which they full well knew could last much longer if government representation was weak, or if the accused's representation was strong, as it promised to be in this case (the widow had great financial resources with which to defend herself and her errant family) – Miss Warner at first stared (as she always did), then merely said, "Very well, then. I shall return home until such time as you are able to accompany me to Washington."

Merritt attempted to intercept this, casually mentioning re-crossing the Suspension Bridge, but Mary handily dodged the ploy – she was familiar with the ferries here, was certain that Emmett preferred the ferry to the bridge and intended to regain Kentucky soil in that manner. Merritt then tried another approach: the return train ride would be difficult alone – he knew how stressful it had proven on her initial trip. But Miss Warner proved to be resilient and a fast learner. She had determined to henceforth pretend to both deafness and muteness in order to secure refuge from future fellow travelers. Argent found her willingness to lie and deceive somewhat alarming, but more importantly he saw their precarious hold on her willingness to travel with them evaporating at an alarming pace. She was no longer the frantic, cornered victim, but a determined and confident adversary to their success. She now held the reins, and she knew it.

It was too late for her to return this evening (even the chance to escape this trip, which she found increasingly irritating, did not trump her concerns about traveling at night), but she would leave in the morning. "You may contact me when your work here is completed, and I will arrange to meet you at my earliest convenience."

"That sounds very much like 'when it suits you.'"

"It is exactly that – unless I am your prisoner, I am under no constraint to remain with you or conform to your schedules."

Merritt stepped in before Argent's rather stuffy objections could escalate. "Mr. Henry will be disappointed."

Mary resented Merritt's attempt to shame her. "I undertook this trip for two reasons only: on the promise that it would be a quick one, and because Mr. Henry wished it. Even before this latest interruption, the trip was already spinning out of time – by your first estimate, we should already be in Washington, and I would have already met with the General, exchanged our salutes and salvos, and with, admittedly, the greatest luck, be on the next train to return. Yet here we are only in Cincinnati. The schedule is in ruins, and it was only my promise to Mr. Henry that has kept me on this journey so far. Even Mr. Henry will agree – asking me to sit in a hotel room for days on end while you conduct courtroom business is asking too much." When Argent began to protest the length of time, repeating the two- to three-day estimate, Mary held up her hand in an imperious gesture that rankled – dignitaries, foreign nobility, government officials and the very wealthy could avail themselves of such a gesture, but farm girls from Kentucky were overstepping themselves. Miss Warner superseded him, "It is no stretch of the truth to say that federal projects of any kind are rarely accomplished on time or on budget."

In the end, the best Merritt and Argent could elicit from Miss Warner was a very hollow promise to reconsider her intention in the intermittent hours until morning. Merritt retrieved Emmett and their own horses, and Argent escorted Miss Warner to a hotel as far from the river as was practicable – that is to say, as far from the river and its ferries as possible while still being located somewhat close to the court rooms in the Post Office where the trial was being held. When Merritt rejoined them after settling Emmett for the night, Argent insisted they seal Miss Warner's promise with a final drink before ending the evening.

6

The morning presented Merritt and Argent with their first bit of luck since leaving Louisville: their baggage was lost. More accurately, it had been sent ahead on the Marietta & Cincinnati overnight train, the train they had themselves planned to take. Receiving the unwanted summons from Mr. Bateman, learning that their quiet assignment for the President had been exposed, and arguing with Miss Warner over her plans for the immediate future, had all converged to produce in both Merritt and Argent an uncharacteristic lapse in responsibility – though Merritt had retrieved the horses, neither man had thought to alter the arrangements yet again for their baggage or themselves. As a result, the baggage had gone on merrily through the night without them, an especially important piece of it sharing their paid-for berth with a rather bold but seasoned second-class ticket holder.

Their clothes, their razors and combs, and other sundry articles of travel lay waiting for them at the small depot at Scott's Landing, just below Marietta. That was merely inconvenient, but the absence of the large locked trunk with their stash of counterfeit money used in the course of their work, their field notes and formal documentation for both Whitley and the court, in short, the absence of everything they had left in Cincinnati while extracting Miss Warner from Kentucky. It was a critical blunder in the prosecution of their case. Evidence was sometimes kept with lawyers, sometimes kept by defendants and plaintiffs, and sometimes kept in more official depositories like police offices and court houses, and sometimes evidence was kept in the offices of the district attorney. But in this case, and in many counterfeiting cases involving the Secret Service, evidence was closely held by the Service itself. Chief Whitley had amassed quite a collection of past and present evidence at the division's office in New York. Both Merritt and Argent were very conscientious of the importance of such evidence and they rarely let it out of their sight or control, and so the locked trunk of evidence had been specifically singled out to be placed in the private berth assigned to them on the train, and not in the baggage car.

The only luck lay in the fact that Miss Warner's baggage, too, was languishing far upriver, nearly opposite Parkersburg, where help was awaiting them all. It was unlikely that Miss Warner would chance returning home without first regaining possession of her baggage which contained precious books from home and dresses made for her as gifts. Most importantly, however, Miss Warner could not go anywhere without her money, also left in her baggage, and though neither man would ever deny a lady monetary help, especially in regaining the safety of home, neither would they, in this case, offer it without being asked, and Miss Warner was loath to ask anything of them. They may just manage to wriggle out of this conundrum yet.

Luck also seemed to be with the new drug Argent managed to slip into Miss Warner's drink the night before: for the first time since they met her, they woke before she did. In fact, she slept so far into the morning that they were obliged to leave without wishing her good day. The district attorney had summoned them to an early morning pre-trial meeting, and so they left a note to Miss Warner, informing her of the matter of her baggage. They also left instructions with the hotel clerk to accommodate Miss Warner in anything she should want or need, especially as to meals.

Merritt and Argent returned to the hotel after dark, frustrated and resentful at the proceedings at the Post-Office and Custom-House Building. The Widow Rogers, the leader of the elusive counterfeiting gang flooding Cincinnati with spurious scrip, presented herself as a wronged woman, preyed upon by the unscrupulous Argent masquerading as a gentleman caller. Not only did Mr. Argent knowingly mislead her as to his true identity and his true regards for her, he was caught in the act of violating her very person at the time the other detectives burst through the door and into the room. She did not know if she could ever escape the shame and humiliation of that moment (though she was quite willing to parade it before the court). Argent had squirmed uncomfortably in his seat, so much so that Merritt had to rap him, backhanded, on the thigh to quiet his agitation. Mother Rogers had even been able to produce what appeared to be real, wet, and copious tears as she recounted the infamy of Argent's reconnaissance and penetration of her home and clothing. Likewise, Mother Rogers' daughter and sons condemned Argent's pretensions and behavior towards their mother, the sons especially incensed at the violation of her honor.

The prosecuting attorney spent a good deal of time asking elementary questions, repeating the answers, and asking the same questions a second time as a constant check of verification. It was Merritt's turn to twist and turn in his seat, constantly casting his gaze to the back of the courtroom. At Argent's fiercely whispered admonition to sit still, Merritt petulantly returned his attention to the trial in progress. After a moment or two of self-imposed calm, Merritt leaned towards Argent and burst into whispered complaints. "What is this man doing? When will he stop confirming her name and address and get to the meat of the matter? This is not the level of expertise or experience Bateman promised us in prosecuting this case. Who is this man? He isn't one of Bateman's assistants." It was all the more galling because District Attorney Bateman was himself in the back of the courtroom, witness to this dull display from his hand-picked prosecutor, and had not intervened somehow to move things along. At this rate, the case would be held over to the October session. The judge also seemed disinclined to move things along.

At the end of the court day, Bateman met Merritt and Argent outside the courtroom and led them to a quiet room deep in the heart of the Custom-House, where he explained to them the reason for the obvious stalling on the part of his colleague. It had become known to the defense team that Merritt's and Argent's evidence – their notes, copies of reports sent in to Whitley, and other documentation, including the counterfeit money confiscated at the Widow Rogers' house – had all left Cincinnati last night. It had become known to the prosecution that the defense therefore intended to skip their intended attack on Argent's character and integrity and instead demand to have produced in court the evidence held against their client. The prosecution had therefore stalled such requests, holding the floor until the end of the day. As to the expertise and identity of the prosecution, Bateman would only say that the man enjoyed all Bateman's confidence and that he could assure Merritt and Argent of a winning outcome. Bateman himself and his star assistant district attorneys were busily engaged elsewhere, concentrating all their efforts on the so-called "Cincinnati whiskey-ring," bringing unpleasant notoriety to Cincinnati from as far away as San Francisco.

In the elegant vestibule of Walnut Street House, they removed their hats, handing them to the waiting attendant. Argent was looking forward to a deserved drink or two before dinner, before meeting with Miss Warner, with the hope of a short smoke afterwards. Without consulting Argent, however, Merritt inquired at the front desk as to Miss Warner's movements for the day. The various desk clerks throughout the day had kept accurate watch on Miss Warner, the current clerk providing Merritt with a detailed and timed report, which Merritt found vaguely intrusive, but which Argent found admirable. There was no exact time of her rising, though the general consensus among the staff was that it was shortly – very shortly – before her rather disheveled appearance at the desk at 9:45. She left the hotel – Argent raised his eyebrows in disapproval and alarm – to 'evaluate' accommodations for her horse. Merritt regarded Argent with a look that conveyed both vindication and understanding of her motives for venturing out alone. Upon her return, she asked that tea and toast be sent to her room, but since the hour for breakfast had passed, she was resigned to wait for lunch. She made several trips downstairs, inquiring as to her missing baggage and consulting ferry and train schedules.

Argent interrupted the clerk's report to ask, "Schedules for the Short Line?" Turning to Merritt, he added, "I would think she has that line memorized by now."

"No doubt. No, I suspect her inquiries regarded the routes west, presumably to North Vernon, then south to Jeffersonville." At Merritt's questioning glance, the clerk confirmed Merritt's speculations. Returning to Argent, Merritt continued, "A short ride on a familiar ferry from there would see her on blessed Kentucky soil without the terror of crossing a bridge at Cincinnati."

Merritt had last night acquainted Argent with his suspicions regarding M's fear of bridges. Keeping surveillance on suspected criminals, male or female, was a necessary and almost daily part of their work, but neither man was certain how such surveillance could be conducted as regards a lady in their charge, or even if such surveillance could be socially validated. Merritt had suggested they set watches at the ferries for any sign of Miss Warner's departure there, but Argent had countered that was pointless when she could far more easily slip across the bridge. Upon learning of her likely fear, Argent had been abashed at the thought that any words or actions of his had caused Miss Warner even further cause for fear.

"There are ferries here, as well as at Louisville."

"Ah, but the ferries here would be the first places we would look."

The clerk continued with the recapitulation of Miss Warner's day. Her last trip to the entrance hall showed her to be restless, even agitated – she circled the room, looked into the great dining hall, and wandered in and out of the main floor halls and offices. After apparently surprising a wealthy patron at his business in one of the back rooms reserved for such things and such people, she was politely asked to vacate the main floor, which she did.

"Miss Warner, then, is in her room?"

"Oh, no, sir. She stepped out, sir, presumably to visit her horse." Argent did not at all like the smirk that was forming on the young clerk's face but liked even less the prospect of retrieving Miss Warner from the stables two blocks away, where Merritt had stabled the horses, thinking a little distance might dissuade her from leaving the hotel; Merritt had told Miss Warner that the stable on Fifth Street was superior to the hotel's own facilities. It was an odd fact of experience that work in the field that sometimes meant chasing criminals through streets, buildings, and other environs was somehow less tiring than a day sitting in court or conferring with lawyers on cases pending in court.

To his relief, Miss Warner entered the hotel from one of the back hallways. Merritt breathed out his relief. "I did not fancy fetching M from the stables after finally being released from the courthouse."

Guilt at harboring the same sentiment made Argent censor the younger man. "Your relief should be at her safe return at a decent hour."

Unaware of the men at the registration desk, Miss Warner turned to mount the stairs, and would have remained unaware if the clerk had not called out, "Miss Warner, you were asked not to visit the back rooms of the ground floor."

Mary turned around, ready to level the young clerk with some withering reply, but whatever it was died on her lips when she caught sight of Merritt and Argent leaning against the front desk, clinically observing her. "I came through the back so as not to track muck across the carpets." Though the rains had stopped several days ago, the streets – especially in areas around the stables – were still in a precarious state, and Mary felt that she had carried two to three pounds of mud and muck on each shoe on her walk home. "I promise not to take the state of the carpets into consideration again."

Merritt thought he detected an undercurrent of dislike on Miss Warner's part for the young clerk, and turning to look at the young man, Merritt was sure he detected derision on the clerk's part.

Miss Warner acknowledged Merritt and Argent with a nod and a weak smile, then turned once again to mount the stairs. Argent caught up with her as she reached the third step. "You'll join us for dinner?"

She was obviously chilled – why did she never wear her wrap? – and obviously disappointed with the day, but she managed a pleasant reply. "I look forward to it. When shall I meet you?"

"Whenever you are ready. Look for us here or in the dining hall."

At dinner, Miss Warner asked of their day in court; Argent studiously avoided any details regarding his involvement with the Widow Rogers. Miss Warner seemed genuinely interested in their work protecting the money supply from counterfeiters. She seemed equally interested in counterfeiting itself. And she was absolutely enthralled as Argent and Merritt told – in a see-saw fashion, swapping the narration back and forth as if planned well in advance – the story of the capture of one of the most dangerous counterfeiters in the nation. Charles Ulrich, masquerading as Charles Henderson, was caught in the express office of this very hotel just two years ago by Colonel Wood. M was disappointed to learn that neither Merritt nor Argent were among the detectives present at such a momentous occasion. Even learning that both men, while on assignment in Philadelphia, were the first to rouse suspicion that Ulrich was working in Cincinnati did little to blunt her curious disappointment. Even more curious was her instant dislike of Colonel Wood, the division's chief before the current Chief Whitley. She thought it was selfish of Wood to steal Argent's and Merritt's investigation from them; people who must prop themselves up at others' expenses were certain to have defects of character.

Miss Warner shivered at the end of her pronouncement on Col. Wood, whether from the heat of her words or because she was chilled. She had shivered on occasion throughout the meal, and at this last demonstration, Argent admonished her for going out without proper clothing. He insisted she promise to dress better tomorrow.

"I did wear proper clothing for the weather of the morning, but the weather of the afternoon made a cloak superfluous, and I abandoned it at the stables. I will retrieve it tomorrow on my way out of the city." Privately, she thought, if it is still there. Probably this is what happened with the light cloak that Carrie could not find – likely she left it somewhere when it became a nuisance to wear or carry, and then forgot about it.

Merritt fixed Miss Warner with a peculiar stare and entreated that she give them one more day's indulgence. Argent baldly lied that closing arguments were expected in the morning (which earned him a barely concealed look of censure from Merritt – the only thing truly expected tomorrow morning was the return from Scott's Landing of the evidence in the locked trunk). Furthermore, Argent hoped the prosecution's position was strong enough to render a quick and successful conviction by the jury. There was the very real possibility of making the M&C train tomorrow evening.

Miss Warner rejected the notion out right. "I nearly crawled the walls with inactivity today. I won't spend another day studying the four walls of a hotel room."

"You could visit some of the sights here in Cincinnati. I would be glad to arrange a tour and proper escort for you."

Once again Miss Warner promised to give it thought, and once again Argent suggested a drink to end the evening. Merritt prided himself on catching the slightest and most secretive movements of the criminals they pursued, but he never knew when Argent introduced the medicine into Miss Warner's drink. Yet, for the second morning in a row, they rose, breakfasted, and were gone before Miss Warner woke for the day.

7

Mary descended the staircase of the hotel very carefully, her head swimming with the dull fatigue that seemed to dog her these days, as well as with the dose of laudanum she had allowed herself to stave off the headache she felt lurking in her neck when she awoke. She needed to walk in the cool morning air, both to clear the fog in her head and to arrest the threatening headache. She no longer needed to consult with the clerk at the desk in the vestibule – she had become familiar yesterday with the few blocks around the hotel, and she knew where to find Emmett, and that was all she needed for the moment. Just before she reached the door, a strange man carrying a cloak approached her, holding out to her a letter or card of some kind. He introduced himself as Mr. Hamper, assuring her she was safe in his presence, as she read much the same in the note from Argent. This man, then, was the proffered, but never accepted, chaperone.

Mr. Hamper insisted upon escorting Mary to the dining saloon for a late breakfast, draping across her shoulders the cloak – which she now recognized as her own; no doubt Argent had sent him to the stables to retrieve it for her. He drank only coffee himself but seemed intent upon what and how much Mary ate. She was determined to rid herself of the man as soon as possible. Mr. Hamper was equally determined to remain at her side; moreover, he assumed to determine their destinations for the day. He announced (recited came to mind) a list of places most favored by tourists, none of which suited Mary's needs. She suggested (commanded came to mind) a visit to Forepaugh's Great Zoological and Equestrian Aggregation. She had seen a poster announcing the arrival of the circus in town on Monday and seeing it had caused a twinge of regret – she had promised Thea to take her to the next circus to come to Louisville. The poster tacked up outside the hotel had included the announcement that it was to go next to Louisville for a 'short season.' She would be in Washington when Forepaugh's was in Louisville; Thea would be disappointed. She would not go to the circus without Thea, but she would use the circus to rid herself of this Mr. Hamper.

The poor man looked almost panicked when he realized he could not persuade Miss Warner to attend any other attraction – other attractions that Mr. Argent had emphasized were appropriate and safe for Miss Warner to visit. Mr. Hamper had been called to the rooms of Messrs. Argent and Merritt at the Walnut Street House last night and charged with the safety and entertainment of Miss Warner (after first being sent to find her missing cloak at the stables). He had worked for the two gentlemen occasionally in the past, usually as a mere messenger, but once he had been asked to follow and record the activities of a particular man. It had been the most exciting thing he had ever done. The pay was low, but Mr. Hamper was willing to labor for the gentlemen for free if it meant a chance to join the permanent ranks of the Secret Service. And now they had entrusted him with the safety of a lady, an important acquaintance of theirs, if their intensity was any indication. He would not fail them, but they had neglected to mention the stubborn nature of the young lady. How was he to impose his will upon a woman who was someone else's particular lady, not was his wife, sister or mother?

Mary understood instantly, though without any intentional observation of the man, that Mr. Hamper would take her to the circus, though it was clearly against his own wishes or, more likely, the wishes of Argent and Merritt. She set a brisk pace to the site of the circus, at 8th and Baymiller, which happened to be in the direct opposite direction of the more traditional tourist sites in the center of the city that Mr. Hamper had suggested. As they walked, Mary sought to calm the man by talking of her desire to see the great war elephant, Romeo. She had, of course, seen elephants in magazines and books, but to see one live and one so massive as to be called 'mastodon' must be a true experience. But she did not want to dominate the day – she would see any show Mr. Hamper wished to attend. In fact, she insisted that they should attend one of the shows first and save the glory of the elephant for the last of the day; the image would then be fresh in her memory, and she would be forever grateful to Mr. Hamper.

There were two immense tents – one for the exhibition of the animals (in thirty emerald cages) and one for the circus and the equestrian shows. The crowds were like nothing Mary had ever seen; they were obliged to slow their pace long before they reached Baymiller. She had counted on the crowds to help her slip away from Mr. Hamper, but she almost faltered in her plan when she saw the throngs pushing their way through the streets and into the tents. She was somewhat comforted that most of the people in attendance at this time of the day were children and women; there were very few men. It was not until they reached the ticket seller that Mary truly felt defeat – there the perennial problem of money confronted her. Mr. Hamper, however, paid for her 50-cent ticket seemingly without a thought and then ushered her into the circus tent.

The crowds in the streets and outside the tents had been oppressive, but inside the tent the press of people was overwhelming. Not only did Mary want to escape Mr. Hamper, she now also wanted to escape the wriggling, excited horde squeezing onto the hard benches of the stands that were crammed against the canvas walls of the tent. Mr. Hamper was gallantly trying to open up a space for her on a bench with an advantageous view, but the women and their children that he was trying to displace were growing indignant. Mary desperately wanted to leave – she felt panic creeping into her chest.

The fear of disappointing Argent and Merritt finally overcame Mr. Hamper's fear of irritating other patrons of the show. He forced a wedge between two groups of people who foolishly sat too loosely together and seated himself and Miss Warner on one of the front benches, though far to the side of center. Mr. Hamper attempted conversation, but she was not in the mood; she had not yet seen Emmett this morning and she resented more and more the presence of this latest escort. She stood, excusing herself, but the man stood with her, insisting he accompany her wherever she might be going. Mary actually blushed as she considered the only place Mr. Hamper might be barred from going. Mr. Hamper understood the blush, merely nodded, and said that he would be here waiting for her.

Once outside, M plowed her way through the crowds, returning to the stables. She stayed there long enough to reassure Emmett (and herself) that all was well, then returned to the hotel, where she asked that a message be sent to Mr. Hamper at Forepaugh's circus. In this note she merely stated that she had decided to leave but hoped he had enjoyed the show. She regretted any inconvenience Messrs. Argent and Merritt might have imposed upon him. The day had warmed considerably since the morning and the skies were fair; she was not about to spend such a day in a hot, crowded tent with a complete stranger at her side. By the time the messenger found Mr. Hamper and Mr. Hamper had returned to the hotel, Mary was long gone, revisiting some of the familiar places of earlier visits in that area of town known as Over the Rhine.

In the courtrooms of the Post-Office and Custom-House Building, the prosecution presented testimony from Merritt and Argent as to the means of discovering the Widow Rogers' counterfeiting success, countering the defendant's testimony of yesterday. There was no outrage visited upon the person of Mother Rogers, nor any other impropriety engaged. On the contrary, the discovery was voluntarily and enthusiastically offered by Mrs. Rogers herself. Believing that Argent was a new addition to her family of shovers of the queer, she had demonstrated to Argent – in the privacy of her parlor – the means by which she could pass counterfeit notes yet never seemingly have any about her person when questioned by the police. On the stand, Argent had the uncomfortable job of describing the ingenious method of stashing the counterfeit notes in the article of female clothing usually stuffed with horsehair, creating the alluring bustle that men so enjoyed watching bounce as women walked away from them. By means of a simple drawstring around her waist she was able to access the contents of her bustle, taking only a note or two at a time, then re-closing and repositioning her bustle with a simple tug on the string. Thus, whenever she was confronted by police or shopkeepers, she could open wide her reticule and show that she had only honest money, and that she had herself been the dupe of some unscrupulous person who passed the counterfeit onto her and she, innocently and unknowingly, had passed it on to the latest shop she had attended. When so caught, she always offered to repay with legal tender.

Argent's obvious discomfort in describing such intimate female apparel was kept from blossoming into full embarrassment by the anger he felt at the ridiculous show Mother Rogers had presented, and at Merritt's obvious enjoyment of his discomfort on the witness stand. Argent's discomfort became a barely contained mixture of indignation, exasperation, and anger when his honor, both personal and professional, was challenged during cross examination. He was asked how he presented himself to Mrs. Rogers, and upon giving his alias, was instantly attacked for dishonorable behavior towards a widowed and vulnerable lady, as well as for deceit in general. Argent countered that it was standard practice to assume a false identity when conducting detective work, but this only inflamed the defense counsel to greater indignation for both Mrs. Rogers and the morals of the federal government. 'False' was not how the people wanted their national government to behave and 'false' was not the type of evidence courts required for convictions; 'false,' however, was the only way to describe how Mrs. Rogers had been portrayed in this whole, unsavory matter. Mr. Argent had assumed, by his own words, a false identity in order to lure Mrs. Rogers – and one could assume countless other unsuspecting, innocent people, using other false identities – into sinning against herself and her government. It was hardly a laudable manner in which to protect the nation's sovereign currency.

Merritt, however much he enjoyed Argent's squeamish recounting of his very personal encounter with the Widow Rogers, did not enjoy seeing a friend and fellow detective so vilified in open court. When on the witness stand himself, he exonerated Argent of any improper actions, not only as regards the Widow Rogers, but in any instance of his life. From somewhere, Merritt had produced testimonials as to Argent's character from a wide variety of sources, including a clergyman that Argent was fairly certain he had never met and several Washington society ladies whom he had only briefly met at a charity ball. With the imprimatur of the gatekeepers of both this world and the next on Argent's character, the day's testimony closed.

Argent railed in whispered tones, as they traversed the halls of the Post-Office and Custom-House Building, against the flagrant assassination of his character by one of the most perfidious women he had ever known. He spoke in righteous resentment, as they waited for a carriage in the foggy dark, of the ease with which damning judgment is passed upon the merest misperception and in complete ignorance of circumstances. In the carriage, he gave full vent to the frustration of the restrictions, "the virtual handcuffs," under which they were forced to pursue the female element of crime – "They are all 'Hands off! Hands off!' They weep before the judge and plead their weaknesses and throw scandalous accusations at their captors, all to muddy the waters and inflame the pity of the courtroom. And it works! A woman need only cry, and her sentence is reduced, if not abrogated altogether. And I, an officer of the law, must defend myself in open court against baseless and outrageous claims!" Merritt listened to it all patiently, until Argent's indignation had spent itself a half block from the hotel. Argent finally looked at his friend seated across from him, and with renewed irritation, thought he could detect Merritt rolling his eyes. But the carriage was dark and its rollicking motion and effect on Merritt's head may have only made it seem that way.

At the hotel, Merritt retrieved from the desk clerk the report of Mr. Hamper as to his day spent with Miss Warner. It was curiously long on his late breakfast with her but short on the rest of the day, which essentially said they had gone to the circus, at Miss Warner's insistence. If his services were needed tomorrow, Messrs. Argent and Merritt need only reply by note. Merritt accordingly left a note with the desk clerk to be delivered to Mr. Hamper engaging his services for one more day. Argent joined Merritt at the desk, scanned Hamper's report with a surprised eyebrow, and was about to ask the clerk for any information he wished to add when Miss Warner entered the hotel, this time through the front door.

Argent immediately noted Hamper's absence and Miss Warner's high color. Wherever Hamper had taken her, it had included some amount of time out in the sun and wind. She stopped abruptly upon seeing the men at the desk, and her color deepened. She then moved further into the room and waited for the men to join her. Merritt thought she was studying them a little more intensely than usual.

"Miss Warner. You have enjoyed your day?"

Mary studied Argent for any signs of sarcasm but found none. "Yes, very much so. I will not ask in return if you enjoyed your day, but if you enjoyed success in your day."

"That remains to be seen; we cannot count success until it is announced to us from the jury foreman." Argent hurried to add, "Which we hope to hear tomorrow."

To stave off any of M's reproaches, Merritt himself hastened to add, "We can tell each other of our separate days at dinner."

Merritt was relieved when M did not wave before them her usual intentions to leave their company and head for home – her perennial war flag – but was dismayed when she waved off his invitation to dine with them. It was not M's absence at dinner that dismayed him, but the inevitable remonstrance from Argent that would surely ignite M's anger.

"I wish you would reconsider – Mr. Hamper tells us you ate very little this morning before you left for the day." There it was, and now Merritt waited for M's excessive response.

"You have spoken with Mr. Hamper?"

This was not at all the response Merritt expected, and had but little time to wonder at it when Argent blundered in his own reply. "Not spoken with him, no, but he has left us a note." And with a single innocent wave of the note, Argent fanned M's ire and indignation.

Mary stared at Argent, trying to remember if she had said anything or done anything (other than slip away from him) that Mr. Hamper might put in his report. She would have to make certain, before she entered the lobby tomorrow morning, to look for and avoid the man with the striped vest and calfskin boots. "He has reported to you? I understand that you felt the need to assign a chaperone to me, but not a spy!" Merritt rubbed his forehead and prayed that would be the end of M's explosion. She had more to say, but at least she lowered her voice for her next salvo. "I am not your prisoner or some suspicious character under investigation. I will not be treated in this matter. And Mr. Hamper need not bother to report here tomorrow, as I will not be going with him, or anyone else, anywhere." With that, M stalked off, and Merritt rubbed his eyes.

It was as Argent was drifting off to sleep that he realized that he never heard the clerks' reports of Miss Warner for the day, and also that Hamper had left Miss Warner unchaperoned, but for how long after leaving his note? A momentary concern disrupted his drifting until he reasoned that Miss Warner had probably gone to see her horse, of course, of course, of course . . .

Mr. Hamper received the note from the Walnut Street House with apprehension. He had been intentionally vague about his time – his short time – with Miss Warner, and he feared his subterfuge had been somehow revealed. He knew Miss Warner would not expose him, not without exposing herself as well – it had become apparent to him her intention to deceive him from the very first moment of their meeting – but he also knew the clerks at the hotel were charged with monitoring Miss Warner's activities, and it was their exposure he feared. He also worried, if he had somehow escaped exposure, how he would manage Miss Warner tomorrow. But he need not have worried – the note said bluntly that he would not be needed again. Payment for the day was included, but nothing extra to cover the one dollar spent on tickets for a circus neither he nor Miss Warner saw.

8

In the court rooms of the Post-Office and Custom-House Building, the closing arguments were given. Merritt and Argent were satisfied that the government's counsel had presented an iron-clad case and were certain they would be free by late afternoon. Their hopes were dashed, however, when the time came for the judge to dismiss the jury for deliberations. His instructions included the rather inflammatory if not leading caution to weight the Secret Service operatives' testimony accordingly. By this he meant, and explained, "These operatives are men who, as part of their duty, often adopt false identities and even oftener entice their targets into committing the very crimes they purport to halt." In short, he suggested, the operatives of the Secret Service were little better than criminals themselves in the employ of the government; and, really, how trustworthy can the testimony of such men be?

As the jury deliberated not only the case at hand but the learned words of the judge as well, Merritt and Argent stepped outside to find the weather had turned very fair, though more than a little blustery. A court courier ran to hand them a note – which they almost lost in the wind during the hand-off – then dashed back into the Post-Office Building to attend to the next errand. Merritt opened the note and smiled. "M has decided to afford us this day to conclude our business – she is curious as to the outcome of the case – and is enjoying reacquainting herself with the Cincinnati of her childhood visits. Wishing us success in court, &c. &c." Merritt noted M's avoiding mentioning Hamper and smiled at her childish peevishness. He had argued long and hard with her last night (alone, without Argent, the sole author, in her mind, of the day's spying) to accept Hamper's company one last day. She agreed only on condition that he would take her where she wanted to go, and not where Argent dictated. Merritt had only agreed himself when she promised to agree to Hamper's decision as to appropriateness. It was all bluster on M's part, in any case, since her baggage had still, mysteriously, failed to return to Cincinnati.

Argent smiled broadly around the slender cigar in his mouth. After taking a deep draft and blowing the smoke ahead of the wind, he patted his stomach and said, "As I had hoped, Miss Warner, when less fatigued, is more reasonable." He added, "I find it gratifying that she has taken such an interest in our work – we can count one more citizen as forewarned against the plague of counterfeiting."

"It is a pity we can't count that judge among them."

In the end, however, the evidence against the Widow Rogers and her family overwhelmed even the reservations of the judge. Perhaps her money (counterfeit though it was) could have been better spent in bribing the jury than in bribing the witnesses. The government secured its convictions, though the sentencing was over-light where the women were concerned. One woman was even acquitted, the only true disappointment in the case. She was the only defendant without blood ties to Mrs. Rogers, and perhaps this confused the jury. The case was concluded only slightly later than Merritt and Argent had hoped, but still with time enough left to indulge in a celebratory drink with the district attorney. The Widow Rogers had long been a target of the Secret Service and a burr under the district attorney's saddle.

It was as they were in the private rooms the District Attorney kept at the Burnet Hotel (so conveniently located next to the Post-Office Building wherein were housed the United States courts), quietly sipping the attorney's private stock of whiskey – private, because it was Kentucky bourbon and not the native and therefore more patriotic Cincinnati whiskey so reviled in Louisville – that another courier brought to them another note. Argent remarked a little condescendingly as he accepted the note, "Miss Warner probably intends to hold us exactly to the twenty-four-hour extension she granted us." The mild curiosity on his face quickly transmogrified into alarm and even terror as he read the note.

Merritt carefully placed his unfinished drink on the desk. "What is in the note? Is it from M?"

"No," Argent breathed, but Merritt wasn't sure if it was in answer to his question or in response to the contents of the note. "No," Argent repeated more forcefully, then, "No, no, no." Argent had risen from his seat as he said this, and Merritt followed him to his feet. Argent left without a word, leaving Merritt to excuse both himself and Argent from the attorney's hospitality.

Argent was striding ahead of Merritt, heedless of the looks as he brusquely pushed passed people in his path. Merritt hurried to catch up with Argent, asking, "Shall I hail a carriage?"

Argent never slowed in his pace or softened in his determination to shoulder past the other pedestrians. Merritt often had to step behind Argent to avoid toppling on-coming passersby into the street. Finally, there was an opening in the sidewalk traffic, and Merritt was able to walk abreast of Argent and hear the news.

"This note," Argent said between gritted teeth and fiercely waving the note at Merritt, "this note was written more than three hours ago, and it was just now delivered to us."

Merritt retrieved the note from Argent's angry waves and read it as Argent simultaneously explained its content. "Miss Warner was arrested nearly four hours ago for disorderly conduct and indecent exposure."

Merritt rarely expressed real surprise or astonishment, but in this instance, he repeated rather loudly, "Indecent exposure?!" earning him suspicious looks from several passersby. Lowering his voice, he said, "There must be some mistake. M can hardly bring herself to speak to other people, much less engage in lewd behavior."

"No, I can't believe it of her, either; but she has been in custody these four hours, and according to that note, she was due to be transferred to the workhouse an hour ago, if she could not find the means to pay her bail."

"And her baggage wherein she keeps her money is at Scott's Landing."

"As are our own." They had elected to deceive M into staying ever longer in Cincinnati by feigning problems with the luggage retrieval. The truth was that, other than the locked trunk with its evidence, they had never requested the return of their baggage (though they had insisted on its security), certain they could still get Miss Warner on the M&C and on their way to Washington. They (and M) had been living out of their grip bags ever since. Their deceit was coming back around to trip them. "Hopefully between us we can manage her bail and get her out of there. If she has not already been sent ahead to the workhouse."

"The Workhouse." Though they were striding at a very fast pace, Merritt managed to say the ominous words slowly. The wind blew dust and grit into his mouth and eyes. Merritt now understood Argent's repeated 'no' – someone with M's pride would find the shame and humiliation unbearable – almost anyone would. And Merritt saw a great cascade of repercussions for her in Louisville from such ignominy – the event, of course, would be printed in the papers; and certainly, least of all for themselves, her quite understandable desire to return home, and never, *never* leave again.

Argent said, "She will never forgive us for taking so long to come to her aid."

They arrived at the Hamilton County Jail, where Miss Warner had been taken hours earlier, transported through the streets from Police Court in City Park to the jail, some eight blocks away – a shameful ride often escorted by rock-throwing boys and saluted by jeering men and women along the way. Though the Court House (and the jail behind it) were several blocks away from the Burnet House, it is doubtful that a carriage could have made better time than the brutal pace Argent had set. Upon applying at the sheriff's office on the ground floor of the county court house, Merritt and Argent had been relieved to discover that Miss Warner was still there. By the mercy of God, the sheriff had been busy processing the backlog of the usual surge in criminal activity that always followed the cessation of bad weather. In this case, though the bad weather ceased several days ago, the unusual length and severity of the bad weather was reflected in the protracted incidence of crime afterward, filling the jail and police stations. And though this year's election had been one of the calmest in recent memory, there were still those miscreants who took advantage of the confusion of the polls to commit their crimes or those who overindulged in drink, either to celebrate their party's win or to lament their party's loss. Though Miss Warner was processed fairly quickly in Police Court on an unusually light docket-day, after an unusually orderly election a few days earlier, she was still at the mercy of the perennially overcrowded jail. Miss Warner's crime, despite threats to the contrary, was given attention in due order of occurrence.

Once the sheriff was satisfied as to their names and characters and responding with the appropriate alacrity when presented with the name of the resident district attorney (who was unaware at the time that his name had been invoked in this matter), the jailer was summoned, and Merritt and Argent were shown to Miss Warner's cell. They followed the jailer through the familiar hall, past the great spiral iron staircase that led to the rotunda three stories above, then down the stairs to the tunnel that connected the jail with the courthouse.

The jail was indeed crowded with the latest miscreants; many of the one hundred fifty-two cells housed two or more inmates, waiting to be processed and sorted and assigned to Hamilton County's labyrinthine court system – police court, mayor's court, court of common pleas, United States Court, Commissioner's Court, etc. – or were awaiting transfer to the Workhouses or the state penitentiary, or were simply serving out smaller sentences in these cells. Most (the drunkards, whose numbers always increased with the onset of bad weather and the elections) would dry out a little, pay their fines, then be on their way. Only those inmates whose stay was of a more permanent duration held cells in solo.

Miss Warner was the sole occupant of her cell. She sat incredibly still and erect on the middle of the bench against the wall, her eyes closed. Her hands were clasped tightly in her lap and her jaws were clenched. Merritt could not discern even the slightest indication of breathing. In the cells to either side of her were men in different stages of inebriation, though of a like mind as to their appreciation of Miss Warner's presence. Several men lined the barred walls shared between the three cells, leering at her. A few hands were slung through the bars, hoping for a pinch should the tall woman venture close enough to touch. Probably this is why she sat so perfectly centered on the bench, equidistant from the threat of violation on either side of her. One man said over and over, "Com'ere, darlin'. I'll make you feel better; com'ere."

Argent was furious to see Miss Warner detained in such a manner and subjected to such vulgar behavior. The stench was overpowering, a noxious commingling of urine, vomit, a medley of alcohols, and unwashed bodies. And the high wall around the back of the jail did little to block the smell of stagnant water and rotting vegetation that wafted from the canal's Lockport and Cheapside basins less than a block away. It was only April; the air inside the jail must be truly stomach-churning in the heat of summer. Argent wanted to cover his nose and mouth with his hand, his lapel, a handkerchief, but resolved to suffer at least this much with Miss Warner. He could see Merritt, too, was affected by the smell, casting his nose this way and that to find some pocket of air less foul.

The jailer languidly unlocked the cell door, calling to Miss Warner, "Your custodians have come to claim you. Up with you." Miss Warner remained unmoved. The jailer turned to Merritt and Argent. "This is how she has been all afternoon. What she needs is a good thrashing to bring her to a proper sense of respect." Miss Warner's plain dress, a work dress with none of the frills and fineness of a woman of any means, was not the only barometer by which the jailer measured her: she did not even carry with her a handbag, nor did she wear a hat or cloak or gloves. She gave all the appearance of a woman of the lower classes, and therefore not worthy of any special consideration.

The sheriff had accompanied the jailer to Miss Warner's cell, mildly curious as to all this fuss over such a woman as she. He had, in fact, delayed sending the message that Miss Warner had asked him to send; he simply did not believe a woman of her apparent stature and committing such a crime could claim patronage at such high levels of Cincinnati's judicial system or of the federal government.

Merritt pushed past the sheriff and jailer, and, standing before her, spoke her name quietly. At his voice, Mary opened her eyes and rose, but did not acknowledge Merritt. She walked out of the cell, past the sheriff and jailer, past Argent, and continued down the hall towards the outer chamber. The sheriff neither hurried to escort her from this vile place nor censured the inmates for the lewd comments that both preceded and followed her. Only occasionally did the jailer strike the bars of a cell if an inmate's hands reached too far in a quest to grab Miss Warner. Some show of concern was required when the district attorney was involved.

Mary waited patiently at the end of the corridor until the sheriff reached the door and unlocked it. After they had all passed through and the sheriff had re-locked the door, she waited wordlessly and seemingly sightlessly, moving only when it came time to follow the sheriff to his office.

Merritt and Argent also remained silent, in equal parts fury and disbelief and – if they had been honest with themselves – in wary anticipation of the explosion of anger that was surely brewing beneath Miss Warner's own silence. No matter what she had done, or how she had come to be in such disgraceful circumstances, she was their responsibility and she had trusted them enough to stay while they conducted their business. Now they had let her languish in a jail in the hated city of Cincinnati while they had taken a little pleasure in a celebratory drink with the district attorney.

The sheriff led them not to his office in the front of the Court House, but to the jailer's much smaller office, not far from the cells. Much as the sheriff had followed the jailer to the cells out of curiosity, the jailer had followed the sheriff to the small office for the same reason. As the sheriff closed the office door, he invited everyone to sit, but Miss Warner remained standing and mute. Merritt and Argent remained standing in deference to her, but the sheriff shrugged his shoulders and took his seat behind the jailer's desk; the jailer sat on a corner of the desk, which seemed to irritate the sheriff.

Argent asked, "What, specifically, are the charges against Miss Warner?" Mary stared straight ahead.

The sheriff cocked his head to inspect Miss Warner, then directed his answer to Argent. "Miss Warner has been charged with disturbing the peace, specifically, with inciting a riot by means of indecent exposure of person and disorderly conduct." Despite her best efforts, Mary's face burned with embarrassment at the accusation.

Merritt removed his hat and scratched the back of his head. "I can say with almost positive certitude that Miss Warner is incapable of such behavior."

"Then you have not been privileged to see her riding a horse in a manner unbecoming her sex, as well as wearing trousers while doing so. The sight of a woman acting contrary to natural laws and God's design provoked visitors at Spring Grove – hallowed ground here in Hamilton County – to understandable heights of righteous indignation and condemnation."

Argent shifted uncomfortably; they had indeed been privileged to see Miss Warner indulging in such behavior, but, like Merritt, he was certain she neither considered it lewd or intended to incite a crowd by doing so. Argent was confused on one point, though – Miss Warner knew the proscription against this behavior. She understood the need to avoid it in public and he had seen her follow Mr. Henry's direction to dismount as they neared Louisville several days ago. Merritt was speaking again.

"I assure you that disturbing the peace was not her intent. She is only guilty of a momentary lapse in judgment. She often rides in such fashion on her farm, where it is more efficient for her to do so in the management of her property."

"The privacy of one's home has never been protection from the law. Morality knows no jurisdiction."

Merritt had to concede the point. He also pursued criminals and expected them to be prosecuted to the very letter and punctuation of the law.

Into this silence, Argent asked, "I take it, then, that she has already been arraigned? Then there is only the matter of providing surety for her bail."

The sheriff considered Argent for a moment. "Bail was set at the maximum – $500."

Mary closed her eyes against the impossible amount; hearing it a second time did not reduce the shock. On either side of her came the sound of caught breaths.

When Argent found his voice, he remarked, "That is considerably higher than one would expect for a first offense."

Merritt asked, "What was the judge's reason for such an unusual bail?"

The sheriff leaned back in his chair and studied his hand on the desk. "In addition to her indecent and disorderly conduct, there were other charges." He waved off Argent's obvious intent to question him regarding these other charges. "In addition, it was learned at Miss Warner's arraignment that her very near plans include leaving Cincinnati and the state for some purpose she declined to reveal. Moreover, when pressed, she gave conflicting answers – she was returning to Kentucky or she was heading to Virginia. The court was of the opinion that if Miss Warner did not know her own mind, Hamilton County could be even less sure of it. The bail was set to help insure that Miss Warner fulfill her obligation to appear in court at her appointed time; and if she chooses not to comply, by vacating forever this jurisdiction, her bail would cover the fines that would have been assessed her, as well as salve the injured honor of the court. That, of course, would not protect her from any jail time she might receive for her absence and contempt of court, should she ever again find herself in the state of Ohio."

"Her arraignment, then, was also her trial and conviction?" Merritt's voice was soft, but Argent heard the angry challenge and the frustrated impotence of the situation. Of course she would be convicted; she had in all probability done just as she was accused.

"Her conviction is assured – there were a number of witnesses and victims who are willing and ready to testify to the event. They have already made their statements in Police Court."

"Victims?" Merritt had asked the question, but it was Argent who looked with growing alarm and dismay at Miss Warner.

"In the understandable agitation of the riot, several missiles were thrown – rocks, a few bottles, and someone threw an umbrella. Several persons were hurt in the confusion."

Argent allowed himself a second's relief that Miss Warner had not actively and personally accosted anyone, but this was followed by a realization that she could still be held accountable for those injuries that resulted from the riot she inspired. Another thought occurred to him – "Was Miss Warner injured?"

Mary never wavered in her stare straight ahead or broke her silence. She was a thing, an object to be discussed by her superiors and custodians. She often stood thus when receiving punishment at school and home. From experience, she knew that offering defense only aggravated her punishment; claiming victimhood while guilty was an intolerable affront to authority.

"Not that we could see or determine, or that she has mentioned. She has remained mostly uncommunicative."

Suddenly, Argent realized something that had been gnawing at him since the sheriff first spoke of her offense. "You say Miss Warner was wearing trousers in public? Yet here she is, in appropriate dress."

"Miss Warner was arrested after the fact, at the stable where she boards her horse. She had ample time to change her habit."

Looking at her, Merritt observed, "That does not appear to be the case. Her clothes are clearly mud-spattered from her ride." Had he looked even more closely, he would have seen a tear near the back of her collar where one of the missiles did indeed hit her as she sat atop Emmett, struggling to maintain control of him in an increasingly hostile and enclosing crowd.

The sheriff, however, had had enough of answering questions about Miss Warner. He disapproved of her – she had appropriated male attire and now had appropriated male behavior, standing aloof and disdainful of her accusers and of the very office of the sheriff himself. He had been told she had acted the same way in Police Court, standing mute and challenging before the judge, in effect waiving her right of examination. A plea of 'not guilty' had been entered for her, though there was no doubt of her guilt. The sheriff could have sent her straightaway to the Workhouse, but he had wanted her to absorb the full experience of being a man. So, he had let her sit in a jail cell surrounded by men. He would send her to the women's section of the workhouse after she had developed a proper appreciation of her behavior. Occasionally, he had looked in on her progress, but he had always been disappointed to find her sitting perfectly still, her eyes closed, learning nothing.

But now she was being rescued by these seemingly upright gentlemen, and so he was ready to wash his hands of her. "The state of her person at this time is neither my concern nor my obligation to record. If you gentlemen are possessed of the amount of bail, I will be happy to accept such from you and release Miss Warner to your custody. The fines, of course, can be paid by yourselves or someone else, but I strongly advise she be allowed to work to pay them herself at the Workhouse; she has shown no remorse for her actions. On the contrary, she appears even now to be defiant. I am not clear what your relation is to Miss Warner, but at the very least her father should be advised of her behavior, if you are unwilling to make corrections with her."

Mary held her breath; it was impossible to hope that these men would have on their persons such a huge amount of money, but it was possible that their positions as government agents might prove a boon to her in this situation. She hated the thought, but hated more the prospect of the Workhouse, where she was told she could work off her debt at the rate of 70 cents a day. In her head she calculated 100 days was $7, 1000 days was $700. No, back up – 700 days would make $490; ten more days would make another $7, and another five days would make $3.50; 700+10+5 = 715 days. She would not be debt-free and out of the workhouse until after 715 days. Another calculation – 365 days a year divided into 715 – two weeks shy of two years – years! – at state labor. Plus, another 104 days for the 104 Sundays – days of rest – during those two years for which she would not be paid. For the first time, Mary felt her legs lose their strength. Without realizing it, she threw out her right hand to clutch at Merritt for support. An undercurrent in her brain threatened to wash her off her feet, but the current moved on, and she released Merritt's sleeve.

Argent hated his next words. He spoke them slowly, punishing himself as they grindingly and completely revealed his impotence before the law. "We do not have the required bail at this time."

The sheriff stood and said, equally slowly, "Then I will be returning Miss Warner to her cell in anticipation of her removal to the Workhouse." Argent knew the sheriff could do no otherwise, even if he were so inclined.

Merritt said in a restrained voice, "We respectfully ask that Miss Warner be given a cell more appropriate to her situation."

"And what would that situation be?" The sheriff could not believe that a woman wearing a work dress and riding a horse astride as she did and keeping such rude silence could claim any station that deserved his consideration. The jailer, who had remained perched on the corner of his own desk, raised his eyebrows.

"A young woman with no experience of jails and the inmates that generally inhabit them." Merritt's exasperation and anger had shown in this last statement, delivered more as an outburst. But he moderated his tone as he continued, "We also ask, respectfully, that you delay Miss Warner's transfer to the Workhouse until we return with the required bail."

The sheriff was enjoying this elevation to grant-giver, and made Merritt wait a long moment while he considered both requests. He exchanged a brief glance with the jailer before finally agreeing to posit Miss Warner in a less populated part of the jail. "I cannot, however," he said with perfect honesty, "hold her here indefinitely. The jail is already full, and more lawbreakers are admitted by the hour. If bail is not received by midnight, she will be transferred."

By way of acceptance, Merritt for the first time since they had all entered the jailer's office turned full to M. "You will not spend the night here, nor be transferred."

Argent thanked the sheriff for his forbearance and nodded weakly at Miss Warner as he and Merritt left the office to beg and borrow the necessary funds for her release.

Outside the court house, Argent ran a hand through his hair, gripping it tight in the back, then yanking on it before replacing his hat. "The banks are closed for the day. Even if we somehow pull together enough promissory notes or checks from I-don't-know-what sources, we won't be able to present them for redemption until the morning."

"I could give surety for the bail."

Merritt's offer was tentatively given, though not because he worried about the loss.

"As could I, but verification of any assets pledged would not be received in time to help Miss Warner tonight. And any inquests to those assets would only provoke speculation for the wrong reasons, and invariably it will come out that it is to assure bail for a woman jailed for lewd and disorderly conduct. Any hope of sparing Miss Warner further scrutiny or invasions into her privacy will be completely dashed."

Merritt nodded. "I'll telegraph the President – maybe a telegram from the White House with a promise to pay in the morning will carry enough weight for the sheriff."

Argent groaned. "The President. What will he think when he is advised that his intended guest is sitting in a Cincinnati jail for lewd and lascivious behavior?" Argent removed his hat and ran his free hand through his hair a second time. "Why would she do that? If we get her out of this, we need to keep her on a tether."

"If we get her out of this, I don't think a tether will be necessary. Did you not see her in there? She's terrified, mortified, and humiliated. And it is obvious the jailer was enjoying her humiliation. No, if we get her out of this, she will either bolt straight for the Kentucky shore, even if she has to swim the river, or she will keep her promise to Mr. Henry and continue on to Washington, but I doubt she will speak another word on the way. What are your plans between now and midnight?"

"I am returning to Mr. Bateman to plead his assistance. Perhaps there is some thin membrane in the law through which Miss Warner may pass without consequence. Otherwise, we may be discussing at breakfast tomorrow morning whether we remain in Cincinnati for a speedy trial in Police Court, if her case can be returned to that court, or we continue on to Washington with the caveat that we must return with M to Cincinnati in time for her court appearances. The latter will probably appeal to M."

Merritt did not realize Argent's switch from Miss Warner to M until he was well on his way to the telegraph office.

After much scrambling between the district attorney's hotel retreat and the Post-Office Building – and by a great piece of luck the judge was still in his office – Argent was able to have the bail reduced substantially. He shamelessly invoked President Grant's name in the matter, so that both the judge and the district attorney were assured that bail need not reflect Miss Warner's impending absence from the city and state. Merritt was equally successful, procuring from somewhere a draught for the full amount. He had also sent a telegram to the White House but knew he could not expect a reply any time soon – the President was this day in New York, attending the funeral of General Thomas. He did not know the President's travel plans after the funeral or if the staff at the White House would even try to locate him during such a somber event. But even as Merritt was about to enter the Burnet House, a messenger brought to him a reply from the White House assuring Cincinnati officials they need not fear Miss Warner's absence from court when due to appear. Somehow Grant had been located and advised, and he had all but promised that he would escort Miss Warner himself to assure her presence.

The district attorney looked up in some surprise when Merritt presented both the presidential telegram and the money draught for his review. "This is very impressive." Whether he was impressed with the source of the telegram or the ready money that Merritt had procured, was uncertain.

"The President desires very much that Miss Warner be released as soon as possible. The draught, of course, cannot be drawn until the opening of the banks tomorrow, but it is hoped that Hamilton County and the State of Ohio will honor the good faith that instrument implies."

"I am certain such will be the case. I will send a note to the County Attorney's office to that end. If I may ask, what is Miss Warner's relationship with the President?"

"Miss Warner's father was an engineering consultant for the President during the late war. General Grant not only valued Mr. Warner's expertise in engineering, but it is our understanding that he valued Mr. Warner's friendship as well. Mr. Warner passed away several months ago, and the President has invited Mr. Warner's last surviving child to visit Washington. This is the reason for her being in Cincinnati – we were escorting her to Washington when we found ourselves obliged to testify in court. While waiting for us to conclude our business and in our absence, unfortunately, Miss Warner has somehow managed to run afoul of the law here." Argent was speaking quickly, running his hands along the brim of his hat.

"Well, I won't keep you any longer. I am sure Miss Warner has had quite enough of Cincinnati's hospitality, and I am sure you are anxious to return to your proper duties in the field."

Word of the presidential telegram evidently preceded Merritt and Argent to the jail – the sheriff had not only reassigned Miss Warner's temporary accommodations but had improved them so that she was kept in a small (locked) room not far removed from the sheriff's office. After the sheriff was satisfied as to the bail (and encouraged by the county attorney to accept the draught), Miss Warner was once again brought to his office where Merritt and Argent waited for her. The sheriff offered a weak comment on the situation, regretting the necessity of subjecting Miss Warner to the realities of the jail, but he ended with the suggestion that perhaps Merritt and Argent could school her in the inappropriateness of her actions and bring her to a proper understanding of a woman's place in society.

At this last comment, Mary raised her eyes from staring at the floor to glare at the sheriff, and for the first time she spoke. "If the bail has been satisfied, I am not required to linger in this place any longer, and I certainly am not required to endure the morality lectures and censures of any man who is neither my father nor a priest." Without waiting for a reply or any other word of dismissal, she left the room.

Merritt followed her out of the jailhouse, but did not step in stride with her, instead following close behind. Only when Argent caught up with him did both men fall into step with her, one on either side.

They had been able to keep Merritt's promise to Miss Warner, gaining her release long before midnight. It was well after eight o'clock, however, by the time they reached the hotel. The fair weather of the afternoon had been replaced with clouds and a fine mist was falling, making it feel cooler than it truly was. Miss Warner had resumed her silence on the walk from the jail and was heading up the stairs without bidding them goodnight, when the desk clerk called to her. She turned to acknowledge the hail, but the clerk instead spoke to Merritt and Argent. "I regret that we can no longer accept Miss Warner's patronage at this hotel, given her conduct at Spring Grove this morning."

The clerk had made no attempt to keep his voice low, and at this time – in the very middle of dinner service – the lobby was fairly full of diners coming and going. Merritt walked slowly towards the desk and in tones so low that neither Mary nor Argent could hear, evidently convinced the clerk to ignore hotel policy in this case. When it became apparent to her that her lodgings would not be denied to her – at least not this night – Mary turned and resumed her climb up the stairs to her room.

In their own room across the hall, Merritt and Argent reviewed the day. Merritt dropped onto the side of his bed, his hands clasped loosely between his knees. Argent considered his friend's slumped posture. "It has been a long day; perhaps a drink is not out of order."

Speaking to the floor, Merritt said, "If it has been long for us, consider how long it must have been for M."

Argent sighed. After a moment he said, "It promises to be even longer for her tomorrow." When Merritt raised his head at this, he saw Argent holding in his hand an unfamiliar gun. "Miss Warner's gun," Argent explained.

"She had a gun?"

Argent handed the gun to Merritt. "At the time of her arrest, that gun was found to be in her possession." Argent thought back to Mr. Henry in the barn readying M's saddle, and the customizations he could not place at the time. But Miss Warner had rented a saddle from the stable (giving Merritt's name for payment). She had carried the gun in some other manner. He also thought back to Monday morning — as he, Merritt, and Henry were entering the barn, M was closing the trunk, the trunk that was waiting for her at Scott's Landing.

Merritt turned the gun over in his hands. It was a handsome piece and a quality piece, made with expertise and an eye to beauty, not factory-made. But it was somewhat dated; there were certainly better and more powerful guns to be had. On the butt was engraved 'H. Warner. In gratitude.'

Argent retrieved the gun from Merritt and laid it on the top of the dresser. "She must have put it in the trunk with Emmett's apples and tack. I don't know how it got from there to Miss Warner. She has not had access to those trunks all this time."

"Henry did. At the station in Louisville, when he retrieved her wrap and book; he must have retrieved the gun for her as well. It has probably been in her grip bag, sitting next to her, always with her."

"Why would Henry feel the need to give her the gun?"

"I suspect it was a compromise of the moment. M probably demanded it in exchange for a last-minute condition of going to Washington, and Henry probably agreed to keep the peace. Perhaps he doesn't trust us anymore than M does; he slept with a gun in the front room only when M was in the house."

Argent returned to the discovery of the gun here in Cincinnati. "The sheriff asked me if she had a permit to carry it. I demurred, but I'm sure she does not. She is at least facing additional charges and fines regarding the gun, if not another arrest. She did herself no favors speaking to the sheriff as she did."

"Why did he release the gun to you?"

"I explained that Miss Warner was only passing through the city and that perhaps a permit was not required of her. I am almost certain that is the case, but I am equally certain this gun will be reason enough for a second arrest, if only to prove before the court her right to carry it. The good people of Hamilton County are understandably protective of the sanctity of Spring Grove."

"But M said she was not yet in Spring Grove when she was accosted." In the time between sending and receiving telegrams, Merritt had learned from friendly sources at the jail a few more details of the events of the morning.

"Whether in Spring Grove or merely near its entrance, M was seen to be riding Emmett astride in full view of the street cars and carriages full of visitors to that sacred site. She was also seen to be wearing trousers under her skirts, and by all accounts, was making no effort to hide this fact." In the brief moments that Argent had remained behind after Merritt and M's departure, the sheriff had acquainted Argent with a few more details of the events of the morning, in addition to the presence of the gun. "The sheer audacity, as the sheriff put it, of her behavior incited the crowd to unruly heights."

"Unruly?"

"One gentleman, in righteous indignation, approached Miss Warner with the intent to pull her from her horse. She grabbed his cane, pushing the gentleman either with his own cane or her booted foot – the details have yet to be established — causing the gentleman to slip in the mud, ruining his clothes and wounding his dignity. He intends to bring charges against her. At this monstrous defiance of all propriety, some boys in the crowd threw rocks at her, and other men charged at her to bring her to justice."

"Was she hurt?"

"The sheriff repeated his earlier statement: not that he could determine or that she had mentioned. He also repeated the jailer's suggestion regarding corporal punishment."

Merritt did not reply to the jailer's suggestion. "Was that the end to it?"

"No; when the good Christian men on the road attempted to detain her until one of the sheriff's men could be summoned to deal with her properly, she turned her horse towards the crowd, and according to witnesses, threatened the safety of the people with its sheer size. She caused her horse to rear and circle while doing so, then effected her escape by galloping eastward. One brave citizen planted himself at the bottom of the bridge over the creek, attempting to bar her way. In what can only be described as a reckless and possibly intentional disregard for the man's safety, she caused the horse to jump, intending, one supposes, to jump over the man. The intended hurdle himself jumped out of the way, just as Emmett was landing, dangerously close to him. In this way, Miss Warner fled the scene of her iniquity. The sheriff is considering adding resisting arrest to her charges."

Merritt ran a hand across his face, then let it fall back to his knee. He sat this way for a moment. "I am tired and hungry, and I cannot think properly, but something seems off about this whole affair."

"What is 'off' is Miss Warner's skewed since of propriety and her complete want of judgment. One day she will say the wrong thing to the wrong man, and it will cost her more than a mere fine or the inconvenience of an arrest." Argent sat down heavily in the chair by the armoire. "Forgive me; I, too, am tired, more tired than I realized. Dinner and a drink or two sounds like the very thing."

Merritt looked over to Argent and waited. It was apparent that Argent was indeed more tired than he realized, or else he would not have neglected the obvious. Merritt suggested, "It is a fair bet that M is hungry as well and may very much need a drink . . . or two."

Argent looked blankly at Merritt for a moment, then shook himself of his reverie. Standing, he said, "I am ashamed to not have thought of her comfort beyond her hotel room. I shall see if she would like to accompany us to dinner."

Merritt stood, too, but halted Argent before he reached the door. "After that reception downstairs, she will not want anything to do with a public appearance of any kind. I'll see to having some dinner sent up for all of us."

When Merritt returned from his errand, he found that Argent had not moved, but still stood in the same spot where Merritt had halted him. "Are you unwell?"

"No, not at all; just confused. I have been trying to understand Miss Warner – a young woman, not altogether unpleasant to behold, with the privilege of a decent education, a healthy inheritance, and the good will of the highest office in the land yet determined to undermine it all with an unaccountable desire to swim against the tides of both man and God. She could choose her own husband, who would free her of the responsibilities of the farm, and perhaps cultivate a profit that would support a maid and cook for her. She need not live as she does, alone and helpless."

"Whatever you may say of her, M is not helpless."

"Of course not. I meant that she was without proper help on the farm."

"Perhaps everything we have seen is a temporary aberration, a kind of madness of grief. Her father only just died within the last several months; perhaps it was wrong of the President to disturb her so soon."

"No, I disagree; she should have been disturbed much sooner. It is unhealthy to dwell on one's sorrows. She indulges herself too much in her grief, and see the state of her health and her mind. She lacks self-control in her grief and her anger and her eccentricities. I fear that if she is not restrained in some way, she will come to true personal grief."

Merritt cocked his head at Argent, a gesture Argent knew well, like a dog who hears one or two known words in a procession of words and is trying to build understanding around those few known words. Merritt was considering his friend as a puzzle to be solved, and Argent hated giving him the reason to do so. Finally, Merritt answered, "Whatever disappointment or anger you harbor for M has no place at the dinner table. Shall we go?"

Argent followed Merritt across the hall and stood behind him as he knocked on Miss Warner's door. She was a long time in answering, and Merritt had just raised his hand to knock again, when she opened the door, but only wide enough to show her face; the room beyond her was in complete darkness.

Merritt hesitated at the sight of the lightless room behind M, but then forged ahead. "I hope we haven't woken you, but we were hoping to have the pleasure of your company for dinner."

She was still dressed in the mud-spattered clothes of the day. If she had been asleep, it was not the repose of bed. "I am afraid my company would be anything but pleasurable tonight; but I thank you for the invitation."

She started to shut the door, but Merritt placed his palm on the panel, applying just enough pressure to hold the opening. "Then let our company be pleasure for you."

Mary hesitated, stumped by Merritt's refusal to accept her refusal. "I could not possibly join you tonight; I have prepared nothing to wear to the dining room." Again she moved to shut the door, and again Merritt matched pressure for pressure. Merritt merely stared at her, neither challenging her nor acceding to her. Mary had the feeling he was studying her and waiting to study her at one and the same time.

Behind Merritt, Argent said, "We are not prepared to dine downstairs, either. We have taken the liberty to have dinner sent to your room. I think we could all do with a quiet meal."

Mary made the mistake of shifting her gaze from Merritt to Argent, and in that instant, Merritt gently pushed open the door, exclaiming, "Your lights have gone out; allow me to relight them." He pushed past her and, striking a match, began to light the lamps in the room. As she turned to object to Merritt's intrusion, Argent slid past her as well. Almost immediately, hotel staff arrived to set up a temporary table, dress it, and lay it with their dinner.

Mary backed away from all the frantic preparations, and stood, her back to the corner near the window, silently watching. Argent directed the staff, and Merritt stood, much as M did, off to the side, silently watching. What he saw angered him, as each staff member took pains to observe the notorious woman who had defiled Spring Grove and now their hotel. One hotel employé in particular pointedly leered at M as he passed by, tray held in front of him. M did not flinch from him, but Merritt was sorry to see that neither was there any challenge in her eyes; she was submitting to her punishment.

Argent followed the last servant to the door, but did not close it, instead leaving it ajar a good foot or more. Merritt retrieved M from her corner, seating her in the chair that would leave her back to the door. As she sat down he noticed the tear in her dress at the collar and the bruise spreading just above the tear. "You were hit, at least once. Are you hurt anywhere else?"

Mary covered the back of her neck with her hand. "No, and it is only a bruise." To herself she thought, *They had remarkably bad aim.* Merritt remained standing behind her a moment. Mary twisted to look up to him. "I am not injured." The testy aggravation then left her voice. "But I do not know about Emmett. I know he was hit several times, but they came for me before I could see to him. I don't even know if he has been unsaddled yet, and I'm —"

She almost let "I'm afraid" slip past her lips. "I'm not sure if I am welcome at the stables."

Merritt circled the table to sit across from her, with a clear view the open door afforded. Argent was seated between them, to Merritt's right. "I will see to Emmett after we have had our meal."

Argent began serving from the dishes, filling not only his own plate, but Miss Warner's as well. "That includes you, Miss Warner; you nearly fainted in the sheriff's office, and I am sure it was as much from want of food as it was from excitement. I do not plan to spend the remainder of our time together keeping you from falling in a faint. I don't think I have ever seen you eat a full evening meal."

Merritt was pleased to see a glimmer of anger and defiance pass across her eyes. Mary was furious that a momentary weakness should play so easily into his hands. She ate at first so that she would indeed avoid the unpleasant possibility of fainting and relying on either of these two men. The small dose of laudanum she had allowed herself for her daylong headache was not sitting well on her stomach; perhaps food would settle it. Then she ate because she truly was hungry. She had been offered food at the jail, but her agitation was such that food held no appeal. The food at the jail could justifiably be said to hold no appeal to any but the absolute starving. Despite her Lenten obligations to eat only a small evening repast, she validated this evening's full meal as recompense for her missed midday meal.

Merritt and Argent spoke to each other of their day in court, and of the successful conclusion of the government's case against the counterfeiters. Mary ate and drank and paid them little attention, other than to will them to eat faster and end their dinner talk. She was anxious for news of Emmett. She was also anxious for Merritt and Argent to be gone. Now that the numbness of arrest and jail was wearing off, she wanted to strip out of her clothes and wash up. There was no question of sleeping this night – unwanted images of the day's events would not leave her mind – but she would like the luxury of lying down while sleep evaded her.

Abruptly she realized that she was sipping from a full glass of wine, when she was sure she had already finished her glass, signaling for her the end of the meal. She looked questioningly at the wine in her glass then looked up to see both Merritt and Argent watching her expectantly. From long experience she knew that she had been addressed and that a response was expected, but she could not pull from any echoes in her mind what had last been said.

Setting down her glass, she asked, "I'm sorry?" A little of her old exasperation at social requirements found its way into her question. The last thing she wanted tonight was after-dinner conversation. Argent looked down at his plate, a gesture she was sure indicated his disappointment at her role at dinner. Remorse followed her exasperation; these two men had, after all, extricated her from the jail, and at no inconsiderable expense. "I'm sorry," she repeated, with true contriteness. "Would you repeat that?"

Argent repeated, "I know it is an unpleasant topic for you, but we must discuss the events of the day." He looked up from his plate to find utter incomprehension on her face.

For a brief moment, Mary thought he wanted to discuss the details of the counterfeiting trial, but how could that be any of her concern? Then with a shock that tingled her scalp, she realized he wanted to discuss her humiliation and shame. She opened her mouth long before she was ready to speak, but finally she managed to say, "I beg you to leave that out of any conversation. I am well out of that jail, and I don't wish to revisit it in any form. I am very aware of your part" – and taking in Merritt with a glance – "your parts in my release, and I give you my word I will repay you every last cent, but, please, can we let it die?"

Merritt pulled her attention from Argent. "We find no pleasure in the topic or in asking you to recount the memory. But in order to help you when you are called to court, we need to know exactly what happened."

Again, Mary regarded him with a look of utter incomprehension. This time, however, it was replaced with one of horror. "Called to court? You mean I have to go back?! Didn't you pay the $500?" She did not think she could bear another session before the crowded lobby and court room, full of strangers and spectators there merely to gawk at the unfortunate accused being paraded and processed through the Cincinnati judicial system. The leering audience and the chaos and the disorientation of events had left her stunned into silence. It was not until long after she had left Police Court and was on her way to the county jail that she realized she had not entered a plea of any kind. She did not remember being asked for her version of the events. Perhaps these things were not allowed in Cincinnati. She thought she had already been convicted.

It was Merritt's and Argent's turn to regard Miss Warner with confusion. Then Argent shook his head. "I am sorry; we spend so much time in and around courts and jails that this is all second nature to us. Of course you would not understand the procedure."

Merritt continued, "The money paid today was mere bail, a surety against a promise that you will appear in court at the appointed time. That money – and it was greatly reduced from the original $500 – is forfeit only if you fail to appear. Otherwise, it is returned to the bondsmen – in this case, Mr. Argent and me – once you have stood before the court on your court date. So, there will be no need to repay us."

"My court date." Her voice had dropped to barely a whisper.

"Yes." All Argent's authoritarian railings on her lack of control and judgment melted in the face of her complete naiveté of the legal system. "At that time, witnesses will testify as to the events of today, before a jury. It is the jury who will decide your innocence or guilt. If you are convicted, the judge will pass sentence." Argent hesitated. "Or you could avoid the public spectacle of a jury, plead guilty before the judge, and accept his sentence."

Mary, quite against her upbringing, placed an elbow on the table and cradled her head in her hand. "Sentence," she repeated dully. "I can't go back to jail." Then she closed her eyes in utter dismay, while her mouth filled with bitter saliva; she was going to be sick.

Argent quickly added. "Please understand, this is a misdemeanor; jail sentences are rare, especially for first offenses. In all likelihood, you will be fined – with court costs – and then be free to go on your way."

Mary dropped her hand from her face, suddenly too tired to hold it in place. "When is my court date?"

Argent paused; she should have been told this at her arraignment, but it was obvious that she had understood little of what was happening. "The next session of Common Pleas, where your case likely will be held, begins

June 6, though we are trying to have your case returned to Police Court for an immediate hearing."

If she heard, she gave no indication. She sat, staring dully, her shoulders slumped. No one at that time could have called her "not altogether unpleasant to behold" – her hair had not seen a brush since the day began, her clothes were dirty, disheveled, and torn in places, her eyes were pinched and hollow, her posture unbecoming.

"Miss Warner?" Mary turned a dull face to Argent, and said harshly, "Don't call me that; that's what the jailer called me . . . all day." She thought of how he repeated her name every few words in every sentence, lingering on the 'Miss,' as if the designation were in question: *Miss* Warner.

Merritt said, "I thought we had agreed on 'M.'"

"Or nothing at all." More than ever, she wanted to be left alone. There couldn't possibly be anything more they had to say to her; she prayed there wasn't anything more to be heard.

"M it is, then." Merritt was struggling hard to lighten the atmosphere, and he looked expectantly at Argent.

Argent cleared his throat and began again. "M, if you could start from the beginning and tell us all that you did."

"If I had started earlier, maybe none of this would have happened. I hate Cincinnati's air – these last few mornings, I have been very stupid, unable to fully wake until well past sunrise."

As she sat in the county jail, she had reviewed the morning and realized with a jolt of guilt that she should have attended Mass this morning to commemorate the Seven Dolours of the Blessed Virgin Mary. She had seen the trials of the moment as her just punishment for ignoring her obligations. She had then begun to recite the rosary, without her beads, giving an entire five decades to each of the Seven Dolours, but she found that she could not remember the second Sorrow. She had moved past it and on to the third Sorrow, the loss of the Child Jesus in the Temple, and then the fourth and so on, but the second had still eluded her. Reciting in her mind the decades of the Hail Mary over and over again had silenced in her mind the crude men in the jail all around her.

Argent shifted in his chair. "You must have needed the rest."

"But I don't feel rested – just stupid."

Merritt prompted, "You went to Spring Grove with Mr. Hamper."

"No, not with Mr. Hamper. He never came. I went to Spring Grove on my own."

Both Merritt and Argent stared at M, disbelieving.

Some of M's natural combativeness returned. "I know the way there, I know the back roads and the covering fields."

But Merritt returned to Hamper. "Mr. Hamper never came? You're certain of that? Is it possible you merely missed each other?"

"I am certain of it. I asked the register clerk if Mr. Hamper was waiting for me in the dining rooms, and he said Mr. Hamper had not been there all morning."

After the slightest pause, and careful not to look at Argent, Merritt prompted M once again. "You went to Spring Grove."

"Yes. Dad had taken us there when we were young, and I wanted to see if it . . . I wanted to see it again." She suddenly shifted her narrative and her tone. "I know the prevailing sentiment toward certain habits of mine. I know what is acceptable and what is not. I know what may be done in public and what must be kept private. It was never my intention to incite a riot. It was never my intention to be seen riding astride or wearing trousers in public."

Merritt answered calmly, "I am certain of it. But how came you to be seen thus?"

"I remembered the route we took from Grandpa's house, the last time we were in Cincinnati. There were footpaths through the woods; there were hardly any houses or other buildings. It is well east of Spring Grove and the way is not generally crowded. It crosses several dairy farms and streams. I walked Emmett out of town and did not mount until we were in woods. Whenever I met someone on the path, it was easy to swing my right leg over the saddle until they had passed. It was my intention to approach Spring Grove from the east, dismounting once I lost the cover of the woods." In truth, however, M had become disoriented by the immense changes in the area since last she roamed the outer woods with her brothers some years ago. There were still woods, but they were in patches, the once large forests scored by new paved and gravel roads; the hills were now all shorn of their glory, and large mansions now sat on the crowns. As a result, she had not been able to ride Emmett as much as she had thought. But the greatest change had been at Winton Place – once nothing but vegetable farms and woods, there were now large estates, with wide-open views. She should never have mounted Emmett in such an open place; even so, she thought herself alone when she had been surprised by what seemed to be a roving crowd.

Argent asked with some embarrassment, "And what of the trousers?"

"I was wearing trousers, but under my skirts."

"But, M, why wear them at all?"

If Argent was embarrassed before, he was completely put to the blush at her answer. "The trousers keep my inner thighs and calves from chafing against the saddle and Emmett's sides." If Merritt's complexion was any indication, Argent was certain his own face must be beet red. Yet he was also as certain that M spoke from a complete innocence of the effect; she was utterly unaware of the impropriety in her words.

M did, however, note the change in the men's faces, but it did not move her to any embarrassment of her own. "Whether I wear them or not, or for what reason, is no one's business but my own." M was forging ahead, gathering indignation in the retelling. "I did the right thing and covered them with my skirts. I did the proper thing and swung my leg across the saddle – against my better judgment and in all defiance of safety – whenever anyone approached. I did the considerate thing and followed the longer and more circuitous route to spare others the wounding of their pious and prissy sensibilities. And what do I get for all my trouble? An ambush of voyeurs, of ill-behaved tourists, throwing rocks and sticks and bottles. And when Emmett reacts quite naturally to being surrounded and pelted from all sides, they cry 'foul' to the sheriff, and accuse me of threatening them with my horse. Emmett had never been so agitated – it was all I could do to remain seated. And while I was trying to regain control of my horse, boys – young boys! – ran up and pulled my skirts up over my knees. If they saw trousers, it was because they wanted to." She thought angrily of the crowd, incensed at the sight of her trousers, when they should have been incensed at the actions of the boys. Her father would have whipped her brothers raw if they had done any such thing to any woman.

Her indignation receded as the memory of the attack was replaced by the memory of her arrest. "And then to be arrested in front of so many people on the street."

Her voice broke, and Merritt could see it took a great deal to master herself, to deny herself the pleasure and release of crying. Suddenly, Merritt realized what had been nagging at him.

"You were arrested here in town?"

"Yes!" She nearly spat at him. "That vile desk clerk pointed me out as I neared the stables. Pointed to me, then turned and left, the great coward! The petty coward!"

"M, listen to me; this is important." Merritt paused until he was sure he had her attention. "Did the arresting officer present you with a warrant?"

"No. I don't know. What does it look like?"

"It is an official document that specifically names you in a complaint. Someone at Spring Grove at the time had to have made the complaint in writing before you could have been arrested . . . unless the officer was at Spring Grove himself. Do you remember seeing him there?"

Argent was shaking his head. "If he was there, he should have arrested her on the spot, and not waited until she was back in town; he would not need a warrant. And why would he need to have her shown to him?" Another thought occurred to Argent: "M, is there some ill will between you and the clerk here?"

For the first time, M looked truly guilty, but not about the trousers or riding Emmett or inciting a riot – she was defiant in the face of those charges. But Argent's question about the clerk had caused her discomfort.

"I was rude to him."

Both men waited, but she volunteered nothing further.

Merritt asked, "What prompted this rudeness?"

M remained silent. Argent warned, "If he has insulted your honor, he has more to fear than mere rudeness."

M sighed. "No, not my honor, just my pride, and I reacted poorly. I overheard him make a comment about my dress, the dress Mrs. Müller made for me." In utter exasperation she blurted out, "There is no pleasing anyone – trousers or dress, it is never to anyone's liking."

Merritt brought her back to the clerk. "You reacted poorly, you said."

M refused to look at either man as she confessed, "I insulted him."

They waited again. This time, Argent prompted her. "M?"

"I told him 'My dress may be plain now, but I can change it at any time and with ever more costly materials. You, however, will always wear the glazed suit of a hotel clerk and your fingers will always be stained with the ink of the register.'"

Argent sat back in his chair and observed the woman who shied from every courtesy extended to her, but who also was unafraid to confront with unchecked vigor the slightest insult.

"Dad always told me, one day you'll say the wrong thing to the wrong person, and it will cost you. Thank God he isn't here to witness the truth of it." But, of course, he knew; her father knew everything now, saw her every flaw with perfect clarity; death granted the righteous truth and exposed the living.

Argent both nodded in his agreement with M's father, and grimaced at the unpleasant sensation of having spoken with Mr. Warner's mouth.

Merritt offered a salve and caveat. "Trading insults with a hotel clerk should not lead to this kind of retribution. Did the clerk know you were going to Spring Grove, and by what route?"

"He may have. I asked one of the other clerks the cost of a ticket to Spring Grove, but he thought I meant the cost of fare on the street car. I told him I intended to ride to Spring Grove, that I knew the back roads and the countryside from earlier trips to Cincinnati."

"He could have easily learned this from the other clerk. Do you remember seeing him there? At Spring Grove?"

M shook her head. "All was confusion. I cannot even say how it all started. I wasn't even in Spring Grove – I was not even near the entrance; I did not think I was, yet a group of visitors surprised me. I don't know where they came from. All of a sudden, they were behind us, then all around us. I had not the time to dismount or change my position."

She stood and made a dismissive motion with her hand. "It makes no difference why or how it happened. It did; and now my name is on a record somewhere, forever more, and it will be known in Louisville before the week is out. Much as I would like to, I can't even cower in my own home town."

She had moved to stand by the window. Pulling back the drapery, she placed her forehead on the glass, black and cold with the night and the rain outside. The headache that had pounded all afternoon in the jail had abated with the meal and the laudanum, but the dull thud was becoming sharper. The cool glass helped a little.

Merritt saw for the first time Argent slip the chloral hydrate in M's drink. Picking up the glass, Merritt took it over to M and asked,

"Headache? I'm not surprised." He handed her the wine. "Sometimes it helps."

M took the glass but did not immediately drink. "I hate the winter, but sometimes I wish there could always be ice. Cold helps more than anything."

From the table Argent offered a kind of cold comfort. "I doubt the dull proceedings in police court in Cincinnati will be of interest in Louisville."

M turned from the window and regarded Argent with something like disbelief and pity at his ignorance. "Of course it will be of interest in Louisville. Louisville newspapers are full of gossip from near and far. Everything goes downstream, and everything that goes downstream stops at Louisville. Even if only long enough to negotiate the canal or the falls, it is long enough to shout to shore."

In answer, Argent raised his glass and bowed his head to her tutelage. She drank in return.

Merritt and Argent stayed long enough to see that her room was properly restored after dinner. Without any further prompting, M finished her glass of wine, placing her glass on the last tray as it left the room.

In their own room, Merritt said, "It could very well be that the arrest was improper, though I did not want to give M any false hopes."

"Yes, I am furious with myself for not asking the sheriff to produce a copy of the warrant for my own inspection. But even if we can have these charges dismissed, there is the probability that any one or more of these 'witnesses' can swear out a warrant, and she will be arrested, properly, once again. And the sheriff, of course, has the right to detain someone while waiting for such a warrant, if one is indeed already being processed."

Merritt had moved to the table and was hefting M's gun. "Can the discovery of the gun be considered illegal, since it was made at the time of the false arrest? Or can she still be charged with carrying a gun without a permit?" Then he took a breath and said, "It is a hard lesson for her to learn."

"I have been so much among men and women for whom arrest and detainment are a mere inconvenience that I had forgotten what a genuine reaction looked like. She needed to be taken in hand, but not like this. I hated to see her in such distress."

Merritt put his hand to his head, just as there came a knock at the door. Before Argent even reached for the doorknob, Merritt said, "I promised to look in on Emmett."

Indeed, it was M at the door, swaying with fatigue, wine, and drugs, but nevertheless intent on Emmett's welfare. As he guided her back across the hall to her room, Argent assured her that Merritt was just on his way to the stables. Argent left her sitting on her bed with the promise to bring her news of Emmett soonest. But when he returned only twenty minutes later with the news that Emmett was in fine shape, Argent found her asleep in the awkward position of one passed out – she had simply slumped over from where she sat. Argent had seen enough women drunk and incapacitated in his work that he was not so prudish that he could not help her to a better position. He removed her boots and noted wryly that she was still wearing her trousers.

As she had drifted off into sleep, it finally had come to Mary the second of the Sorrows of Mary: The Flight into Egypt.

9

Argent's prediction of a long day for M proved correct only for the morning. It began with an early summons at the hotel for Merritt and Argent and Miss Warner to meet a Mr. Stallo at City Hall. Along with the summons from Mr. Stallo was a package for Miss Warner, explained in Stallo's summons – he understood there was some issue with her trunks, and he hoped she would see such a forward gesture as necessary for her appearance in court.

Merritt and Argent were easily ready in short order to answer the summons, but Miss Warner proved less able to respond to the urgency of the request; she really was quite stupid in the mornings, almost as if she were crapulous from too much drink. The chamber maid Merritt tipped to waken Miss Warner reported success only with difficulty. After several minutes of inquiring at M's door if she was ready, Merritt paid a different servant to help Miss Warner dress (handing her Stallo's package) and to bring her to the lobby. It was nearly thirty minutes before M appeared on the stairs, slightly groggy, but clean and appropriately dressed. Argent briefly entertained the idea of reducing her dosage but decided to wait until after this business in Cincinnati was concluded.

As she reached the floor of the lobby, Merritt and Argent each took an elbow and practically lifted her from her feet, hurrying her out of the hotel and to Police Court in City Hall.

District Attorney Bateman had been busy on M's behalf after Merritt and Argent left him last evening. The interest of the President in Cincinnati's legal proceedings had proved impetus enough to engage Bateman's aid, if not his mere curiosity. Bateman had thus sent for the particulars of Miss Warner's case and engaged the counsel of Stallo & Kittridge to represent her. There was really nothing for them to do – there was no doubt as to the outcome – but it showed good will on the part of his office to offer her what help he could. John Stallo was a good man, understood Cincinnati's court system and had good rapport with almost everyone in it (having served a few years as judge of Hamilton County Court of Common Pleas), and would see to it that Miss Warner's case was expedited as quickly and smoothly as possible. And Stallo was that *rara avis* in the political world – a Republican Roman Catholic. The paperwork forwarded from the jail had included the preliminary information needed to admit Miss Warner to the workhouse, including her religion. Bateman thought Stallo was tailor-made for this case: as a Republican, Stallo would be keen to help Grant avoid any nasty publicity his relationship with the young woman might generate, and as a Catholic, he could help a fellow communicant pass through the legal gauntlet looming before her. Good man that he was, Stallo had offered to represent Miss Warner *pro bono*.

Stallo immediately and successfully argued to have the charges against Miss Warner dropped in the police court for lack of a warrant. Once out in the corridor, however, a warrant arrived from the Court of Common Pleas for Miss Warner's proper arrest, and the group proceeded to that court (several blocks away) where she was arraigned on the charge of breach of the public peace as well as the additional charge of carrying a concealed weapon, and the rather dubious charge of assault and battery. Stallo challenged this second charge, successfully arguing that Miss Warner's status as a mere traveler passing through the city allowed her to carry a concealed weapon.

The assault and battery charges were also dropped, Stallo arguing the charge as specious, and as the 'victim' had failed to appear at the hearing, the judge agreed. Later, Mr. Stallo warned M that she could still face legal action from that gentleman, should he wish to pursue compensation for the damage done to his clothing or any bodily harm she may have inflicted. But Mr. Stallo had told her this in such a manner that it was obvious he thought the claims of the 'gentleman' ridiculous. Bail was levied a second time, also for $500 (out of mere mulishness, Argent thought), which Stallo successfully challenged and had reduced. This time, however, M was not detained in county jail while awaiting bail to be paid. Stallo was somehow able to circumvent the tedious process of requesting a refund of her previous bail from Police Court and was instead able to have that bail directly delivered to the proper officials in the Common Pleas court. M walked out of the Hamilton County Court House with her dignity somewhat intact.

All this was done without Stallo having ever spoken with Miss Warner, other than to introduce himself briefly outside City Hall. Once out of the Court House, however, he asked her indulgence to return with him to his offices, where he could discuss her case with her. M's chloral cloud was finally lifting. With evident gratitude and relief, she said, "I would relish the opportunity to have someone explain to me what is happening. This seems to be a bad dream that won't end, and I can't make myself wake up."

Stallo held out his arm for her to take, and after only the slightest hesitation, M took the proffered arm. Merritt and Argent fell in behind them, but Stallo stopped, and looking back, advised them, "I wish to speak with Miss Warner alone. I will escort her back to the hotel when we have finished." With that, Merritt and Argent were dismissed, and Stallo and M moved on down the street, seemingly a father out for a walk with his daughter.

Argent did not care to be so summarily dismissed. "We are, after all, charged with her safety and well-being. We report to the President himself in this matter."

Merritt at first was equally indignant, but as he watched Stallo and M fade from view, he mused, "Perhaps this is what M needs, and Stallo knows it – to be in public in a respectable activity in the company of a respectable man, and not being escorted in an official capacity by two government agents from one court and hotel to the next."

Argent harrumphed his grudging agreement, but inwardly he balked at being described as merely an official escort. Nevertheless, Mr. Stallo's usurpation of their duty freed himself and Merritt to explore yesterday's mysterious absence of Mr. Hamper. As was often the case with them, Argent found that he and Merritt – without having spoken – were already walking in the direction of the St. Nicholas Hotel, where Mr. Hamper currently boarded.

Mr. Hamper, however, no longer boarded at the St. Nicholas Hotel. The clerk at that noble bastion of male boarders explained that Mr. Hamper had been recalled home for some family emergency. No, he did not leave a forwarding address, and No, the clerk did not press for one because Mr. Hamper had settled his accounts in full – there would be no need for the St. Nicholas to contact him and neither, apparently, did Mr. Hamper expect anyone else to contact him.

Argent and Merritt also, on occasion, kept rooms at the St. Nicholas; it was, in fact, how they had met Mr. Hamper, and where they had stayed during this most recent investigation regarding the Widow Rogers. The clerk this day was unfamiliar to them – a recent addition to the staff, no doubt – but many of the regular boarders were not. They availed themselves, then, of the gentlemen's sitting-room, where many, if not most, guests of the hotel eventually found themselves, if for no other reason than to admire the celebrated painting of Pauline Bonaparte in all her gauzy beauty, modestly arrayed in silk stockings and slippers (though little was left to the imagination in this painting, the lady's feet were covered – few gentlemen found the feet of ladies appealing).

Despite a lengthy appreciation of the Princess Borghese and a rather healthy patronage of Catawba champagne (both wine and painting were legacies of local millionaire Nicholas Longworth, God rest his soul), Argent and Merritt learned little else of Mr. Hamper. Old St. Nickers familiar to them could only support the clerk's statement of a family emergency – Mr. Hamper had indeed seemed upset about something yesterday before he left. A stealthy (and somewhat unsteady) search of Hamper's room also failed to reveal any further information.

Argent and Merritt returned to Walnut Street House, a little less flushed and a little steadier for the walk in the cool air. The intermittent rain of the morning had stopped, though it could be argued that a little splash in the face would have done both men some good. They had only been a short time in the hotel and were taking a bracing cup of coffee in the dining rooms when Miss Warner and Mr. Stallo joined them. Stallo seated Miss Warner, but then immediately excused himself. From his position at the table, Merritt was able to watch Stallo approach the registration desk and be promptly admitted to the back office. He emerged after only a few moments to take his leave. Merritt and Argent could not convince him to stay and share coffee with them, but he promised to keep them apprised of Miss Warner's case. Then he lightly kissed Miss Warner on the cheek, whispered a private word in her ear, and left.

M was calmer and happier than Merritt and Argent had yet seen her. They asked after her time with Mr. Stallo, pointedly omitting any mention of her case. Surprisingly, M herself broached the subject. Mr. Stallo and M had discussed her current situation over the mid-day meal, but not in his offices and not immediately. Stallo had first escorted M to see some of the finer sights of Cincinnati. He had taken her to the observatory at Mount Adams, where she had been treated to a breathtaking view – despite the clouds and hanging mist – of Cincinnati and the surrounding hills, as well as of Covington and Newport across the river. They had then taken a walking tour of a few of the architectural delights – the Mozart Hall, St. Peter in Chains Cathedral (though M found this uncomfortably close to Police Court in City Park), and St. Xavier's Church (which Appletons' Railway and Steam Navigation Guide ventured to call "one of the handsomest specimens of Gothic architecture in the West," excepting, of course, its missing spire and towers). After a sumptuous lunch at the Burnet House (at which they both restrained themselves, in obedience to Lenten regulations), they had strolled down Vine and stopped at Pearl Street to admire the life-like Bengal Tiger in the store windows of William Dodd & Co.

His coffee finished, Merritt stood, excusing himself to keep a previous engagement. To Argent's surprise, Miss Warner also stood, announcing her need for some fresh air – she found the confines of these hotels and dining rooms stuffy and sometimes unbreathable. Argent, of course, had stood with her, and agreed that hotels could indeed be stuffy, especially on days such as these. Argent saw the slightest hesitation on Miss Warner's part – and he detected a slight mixture of disappointment and resignation as well – but she agreed to his company.

Out on the sidewalk, Argent asked M if she would like to visit some shops. M said without thinking, "I can think of nothing I'd rather do less than spend a perfectly pleasant day shopping." Then she blushed. "Forgive me, I did not consider that you might care to shop."

"Not at all; I find shopping without a stated need to be tiresome."

"Exactly; if one needs to shop, then it is a chore. Shopping for the mere sake of looking is an exercise in frustration – I always see something I would like but could never afford or justify the purchase of, so I avoid it altogether."

"What sort of things do you like but can't afford or justify?"

"Oh, the usual entrapments of vanity – a pretty dress or piece of jewelry."

"Really?" Argent was genuinely surprised to hear that M was possessed of such natural feminine desires.

"I'm like everyone else – I like to have nice clothes to wear and something sparkling on my wrist. Men have their vanities, too – you and Mr. Merritt are always well-dressed and well-groomed. But you mistake my appreciation of trousers for a dislike of dresses. It is what is underneath dresses that I dislike, and it is the impracticality of dresses that I dislike."

Once again, M's casual mention of what lies closest to her body was threatening Argent's comfort. He cleared his throat. "What other things catch your interest in shops – other than dresses and baubles?"

"Gadgets and puzzles, almost anything in miniature, and objects made of glass, especially cut glass."

"Why glass, so much?"

"It just seems clean and stays clean. I can sweep the floor and never really tell if it is clean, but I can wash something made of glass and I can see right through it."

"And why cut glass?"

"For the prism effect. My mother's best vase is made of cut glass, and when the sun hits it, the opposite wall and part of the ceiling are dappled with small razor-sharp bands of intense color." M paused, considering, then decided to speak of her father. "We had an ice storm two years ago. Every branch of every tree and shrub was perfectly coated and outlined in ice. It was almost a holy beauty in its own right, but when the sun came out two days later, every tree and shrub was covered in brilliant drops of rainbow. I had never seen anything so beautiful. Dad and I sat for hours on the front porch swing, watching the sun move across the sky, igniting the rainbows."

M remembered how they had sat there, side by side, bundled against the cold, in utter silence, unaware of the passage of time. Suddenly, as if defending some inward challenge to the silence, her father had said, "This is not a time for words, but for wonder." It was one of the few times she felt that he had put aside his grief for a moment to spend only with her. But when she had helped him into bed that night he had spoken to her as if she were her mother, his wife. He had spoken softly, in a tone she had never heard before, but which she instinctively knew to be the tone of the bedroom, of midnight talks long after the children and the demands of the day were put to bed. M had cried that night, lying on her pallet at the foot of the bed; had cried for the intimacy her father would never again share with his wife and for the intimacy she was certain would never come to her – she would hear no man speak soft and low to her in the deep of the night as her father had spoken to her mother.

M had sunk into one of her reveries, and Argent did not press her further for conversation, only speaking a quiet word here and there to guide her among the crowds and carriages careening between shops on a Saturday afternoon.

Merritt found Argent at the small table in their room, working on the endless reports required of them, even on this, an assignment completely divorced from the Treasury. Come to think of it, Merritt mused, perhaps these reports were not intended for Chief Whitley. Argent looked up at Merritt's entrance, but immediately returned to his writing.

"What are these lengthy communiqués you are scribbling? What could Whitley possibly need to know of our time spent on this assignment?"

Without breaking the stride of his pen, Argent answered, "Not only does Whitley not need to know of our movements, but he most emphatically said he did not care to know about them, except when we should be available to return under his direction. President Grant, however, has asked me to give an account of both ourselves and Miss Warner." Laying down his pen and stretching forth his legs, Argent continued, "I admit I did not think I would need so much ink and paper to record the accounts."

"You are providing exhaustive detail, then?" There was something of disapproval in this question, but Argent would not be baited, especially since it was he, and not Merritt, who was providing the written reports.

"Force of habit," Argent replied blandly. "Also, the President requested detailed reports. I confess, I had fallen somewhat behind these last few days, being pressed by Bateman at one end of the court and Miss Warner at the other. What of your previous engagement – did you learn anything of Miss Warner's time with Hamper?"

Merritt hesitated; he hated to give Argent further details to include in his reports or further reason to curtail M's movements, but Miss Warner had not spent the day with Mr. Hamper two days ago, or, at least, not the entire day. But Merritt would not withhold information from his partner. "I spoke with the clerk who was on duty that morning. M did indeed leave the hotel with Mr. Hamper, but returned not long afterwards, alone."

Merritt paused; the next bit of information would surely anger Argent. "She sent a note to Mr. Hamper, excusing herself from his company, hoping he would enjoy the circus, where she had apparently abandoned him. She then left the hotel for parts unknown. She did not return during the rest of the clerk's shift."

"And none of this was in Hamper's report." Argent said nothing more, but it was apparent that he was disappointed in both Hamper and Miss Warner.

Merritt was surprised at Argent's mild reaction; perhaps M had confessed to her deception of Hamper. "How was your walk? Were you able to inquire after her time with Mr. Hamper?"

"It was a quiet walk. Miss Warner had little to say; she was in a contemplative mood and I did not wish to disturb her, so I did not raise the subject of Mr. Hamper. All the day's excitement and walking has tired her; she is resting in her room."

Again, Merritt hesitated – M had not been in her room resting. She had been instead at the stables, preparing to take Emmett out for a walk; all the day's excitement and walking had not tired her – she seemed in a perpetual state of excitement. Merritt was beginning to disapprove of this chloral hydrate – it didn't seem to be delivering the rest that the Covington doctors had promised. She seemed more fatigued by the day, and yet restless, at the same time. Finally, Merritt said guardedly, "Miss Warner has only just now returned to her room to rest."

Argent gazed steadily at his friend for several long seconds. "I take it that Miss Warner was intent on riding Emmett, and you happened to intercept her before she embroiled herself in a second incident."

This time Merritt held Argent in his gaze before answering. "She was intent on walking Emmett, and she had a viable plan to do so."

At this, Argent exploded from his seat. "She has no sense of boundaries, no real sense of propriety or responsibility or of the burdens she places on others because of it. If she had caused another scene, even the vaunted Judge Stallo could not help her and it would be weeks before we could break free of Cincinnati." Merritt let Argent expend his justifiable exasperation, and when he had done so, a considerably calmer Argent sighed. "Thank heavens we are leaving tonight before she can manage more mischief for herself."

Merritt was washing up at the washstand, his head bent over the bowl as he rinsed his neck and face. Argent took his silence as a mere inconvenience of the moment.

When Merritt was properly washed and dressed, they gathered Miss Warner from her room and proceeded to an early dinner. Merritt suggested a different venue for their meal, and M proposed they walk to their destination, to justify their appetites. Argent commented rather sullenly, "Your rest this afternoon seems to have been restorative." Argent's tone clearly revealed he was aware of M's deception. Merritt noticed that M wisely (uncharacteristically wisely) ignored the gibe, sensibly avoiding the patristic lecture lurking behind the comment. Merritt sighed inwardly — it promised to be a long and contentious dinner.

They did not have far to walk, however, and Argent's mood lifted considerably when a one-time female companion called to him just as they were being seated at the St. Nicholas restaurant and cafe. Argent excused himself and sat for some time with the lady and her party at their table.

M was grateful once more for Mr. Stallo's thoughtful and prescient gesture to provide her with a proper dress to wear while in Cincinnati. Otherwise, she would have felt supremely self-conscious in such a crowd as took their meals at the *bon-ton* St. Nicholas dining saloon. Even so, her dress was not flush with the full hoops and petticoats of even the least dressed of the women in these rooms. When M pressed to know what she owed him for her clothes, Mr. Stallo had explained that her outfit was a vanguard sampling of what Mr. Shillito hoped to offer very soon at his store here in Cincinnati. Mr. Shillito had offered it freely, as a gesture of goodwill from the city of Cincinnati. He hoped to corner, in this city, a market expanding in the bigger cities of the East, something called ready-made clothing. Ready-made apparently did not mean fully equipped. That was ungracious of her, and moreover ignored the reality of her situation – smaller hoops and fewer underskirts left more yardage for her dress to reach the floor. A tall woman could not complain about readily available clothes, especially when those clothes miraculously meet the necessities of her height.

Argent returned in time for the delivery of their meal. As he placed his napkin in his lap, he asked lightly, "What have you two been discussing in my absence?"

"I was trying to discern if that was Miss Breen or Miss Sayler who called you away. I was telling M of your many female acquaintances here in Cincinnati." Turning to M, he said with wicked enjoyment, "We almost lost Mr. Argent to one of Cincinnati's more celebrated sirens."

"Oh? Pray tell, what kind of woman is it that Mr. Argent can so thoroughly approve of as to lure him into danger?"

Argent shifted uncomfortably in his chair, saying in a low and warning tone, "Shaw."

Merritt was anticipating far too much fun to acknowledge Argent's warning. "She is a widow of both substantial means and morphology."

M giggled, the first such time either man had heard her make the sound. Despite the cause being at his expense, Argent found that a little amusement went a long way in transforming Miss Warner from a tired, angry, wary woman to a pleasant table-mate. M caught Argent watching her, then lowered her eyes. "Excuse me."

"Why excuse you? You didn't belch or stick your fingers in the sauce."

Argent flashed Merritt a quick wondering and disapproving glance. M said, "No, but I should not have laughed at Mr. Argent's expense or at the objects of his desires."

Merritt laughed genially and spread his hands expansively. "Oh, there is no need to worry on that account. Mr. Argent is perfectly willing to sacrifice his dignity for the right cause."

"And what, pray tell, is the cause at the moment?" Argent did not mind helping to ease Miss Warner's troubled mind, but he did not like Merritt catering the event.

"Why, the prospect of an entertaining meal."

M seemed nearly as disapproving of Merritt as Argent. "I don't think it right to ridicule this widow for her looks, her age, or her experience, or to ridicule Mr. Argent for the nature of his desires. I understand many men prefer a more mature woman to younger prospects, especially if the dowry is commensurably mature." If M was being facetious or even sarcastic, her face nor her voice showed it. She was thinking of the suitors who used to come frequently to her door, willing to overlook her looks, her character, her peculiarities, even her obvious distaste for the whole business, willing to overlook all in deference to the acreage of her inheritance, so suitably perched near an expanding Louisville. It would appear that Argent was of like mind as a suitor. "Perhaps it was not so much Mr.

Argent who was nearly lost to the widow, but the widow who narrowly escaped Mr. Argent."

Merritt suspected something of the turn of M's mind. "Giles, it seems you are in danger of being assigned to that disreputable species of bachelor known to beguile women of particular enrichments." Argent's look of suffering victim quickly turned to one of alarm as he, too, realized the meaning behind M's comment. "I think we had better explain to M the nature of your relationship with the Widow Rogers."

In deference to public propriety and in some sympathy for Argent's dignity, Merritt gave a very abridged version of their investigations of the Widow Rogers, revealing only that Argent was the object of the widow's affections. Merritt withheld from both M and Argent, for the moment, that other men involved with the investigation had begun referring to Argent as 'Ardent' Argent. He would save that little *bon mot* for a more appropriate time and audience.

M confessed, "I'm relieved to know that Mr. Argent's disapproval of me does not rest on anything so superficial as looks or money. It must be a deeper and more profound disapproval, and therefore of a more worthy and lasting nature."

This time, there was no mistaking the teasing behind the words, but Argent was genuinely concerned that his disapproval had been so obvious. His judgment of Miss Warner's character had no bearing on the task at hand, and he was ashamed that he had let his personal views intrude.

Miss Warner, as she had since their first meeting, ate little at her evening meal, despite the opportunity to sample some of the best cuisine in the West, certainly among the best in Cincinnati. She still looked tired around the eyes, but the day spent walking in the open air suited her complexion. Argent urged her to take more food, to take the opportunity to try something new, but she assured him that she was still full from her midday meal with Mr. Stallo. For himself, Argent regretted that time and circumstances did not permit retiring to the bar for a slow drink and a languid pull or two on one of the fine imported cigars offered at the hotel.

As it was, they were somewhat pressed for time. Argent suggested they ready themselves to reach the depot well before departure. Merritt had strangely lost his tongue, and M looked a little sheepish. Argent looked from one to the other, with growing apprehension. "Has something happened?"

"I know it is in complete opposition to my earlier position, but I would like to delay our departure until tomorrow evening." At Argent's stunned look, M hurried ahead. "Mr. Stallo has invited me to attend Palm Sunday Mass with his family, and then to dine with them afterwards at his home. He has invited the both of you as well." Then with a sudden side-long glance at Merritt, she added, "I had thought Mr. Merritt would have told you."

"The opportunity did not present itself in the brief time we were together before dinner." Argent also favored Merritt with a sidelong look.

Argent suddenly sighed. "If you will excuse me, then, I will need to reschedule our arrangements at the depot."

Merritt stood ahead of him, however, insisting that it was his turn to make the arrangements. After he left, M confessed, "I feel so burdensome — everyone making arrangements of every kind on my behalf. I am used to doing for myself."

It was the first admission of hers that was not attached to some outrageous act or inflammatory remark. She seemed genuinely uncomfortable and uncertain in the face of these simple acts of courtesy. Other women would graciously take them as a foregone assumption, but M moved awkwardly in the social world. She was pitiably clumsy in her engagements with other people and easily embarrassed at attentions paid to her and at the mistakes she made. She had been kept too long from the world and did not know how to navigate its currents.

"Come, think nothing of it. We are so practiced at making these arrangements for our own travels that we could almost do it in our sleep. And, to completely dispel any discomfort you feel in the matter, consider that it is our duty to make all arrangements on this trip."

"Still, I should know how to do these things for myself, for my return trip."

"Oh, I shouldn't think the President will allow you to return home unaccompanied."

M's face became hard at the mention of the President. "What the General allows or thinks he can allow and what I allow may well be two different things."

Once again, Argent was astounded at the level of animosity Miss Warner displayed when the subject of President Grant entered the conversation. His curiosity in the matter very nearly overcame propriety, but he bit back any questions he had as to the source of her anger.

Argent and M returned to the Walnut Street House. Argent was not inclined to let Miss Warner out of his sight, given her earlier misrepresentation and her unauthorized foray into the stables. He suggested they wait for Merritt in the hotel's restaurant, where they could take coffee together on this, their last night in Cincinnati. Surprisingly, M gave little resistance. She did, however, absolutely refuse what Argent called their "customary evening drink." Palm Sunday services began at dawn, and she couldn't be late, not when the kind Mr. Stallo had invited her – she would not repay his kindness and generosity with tardiness on such an important day. Even as she made this pronouncement, Merritt joined them, handing one note to M and one note to Argent, having received them from the clerk as he passed by the register.

Both notes were from Mr. Stallo, both stating his intention to retrieve Miss Warner at an early hour in the morning. In Miss Warner's note he expressed delight in her attending Mass with his family, and in the note to Merritt and Argent, he assured them of Miss Warner's safety while in his company and hoped they could join his family for dinner. M bid them both a good night, even though the hour was early. After M left the table, Merritt observed, "She did not once ask after Emmett's accommodations or his evening comfort."

10 — *Palm Sunday*

Argent woke to find both Merritt and M up and gone before him. He breakfasted alone, and then began the task of making arrangements for their departure that evening. Argent procured a private berth for the three of them on one of the Marietta & Cincinnati's sleeper cars. And, unlike M's incomprehensible omission of yesterday, Argent remembered to make arrangements for Emmett (and their own horses) as well. He was looking forward to returning to his usual duties in the Secret Service. Although it was, of course, an honor to be in the personal service of the President, escort duty had proven less glamorous and far more nerve-racking than one would have thought. While Miss Warner's circumstances were certainly tragic and worthy of compassion, she had behaved poorly for a woman her age and apparent upbringing. Argent reflected with some surprise that on occasion she acted just like a child. But what woman didn't occasionally revert to that state?

Merritt rejoined Argent sometime before noon, with no mention of where he had been or what he had been doing. Argent knew it would be useless to ask – Merritt had the annoying habit of turning questions inside out in wordplay that was sometimes childish and sometimes absolutely inscrutable. Merritt often, but not always, eventually revealed his secrets, but it was always of his own time of choosing. He handed Argent another note from Judge Stallo, and laughed as he buttoned a freshly starched and pressed shirt at Argent's groan. Merritt redeemed himself however – at least part of his time away from the hotel had been in altering the arrangements Argent had made just this morning. Judge Stallo had very kindly offered Miss Warner and "her party" the use of his railroad pass and the accompanying reserved accommodations; the pass was at their disposal, but there was no guarantee the reserved accommodations would be available on the night train. Merritt had cancelled Argent's tickets for travel this evening and had then told the ticket master that accommodations reserved for court officers would be needed on the early morning train.

He and Argent need only obtain the pass from the judge before leaving his house tonight. Arrangements for Emmett and the other horses were also changed. Both the ticket master at the depot and the manager at the stables were weary with the ever-changing instructions emanating from Messrs. Merritt and Argent. Neither had any hope that the gentlemen would actually leave on the morrow.

Merritt and Argent joined M at the Stallo home for a late afternoon meal. M had left early in the morning with Mr. Stallo to attend Palm Sunday Mass and all the ceremonies attendant with it in the Catholic Church. Consequently, they had not seen her leave the hotel in her best dress. M had been wearing, of necessity, the same dress for the greater part of this past week and had been wearing a dress and overcoat provided by Mr. Stallo for the past two days. Merritt had telegraphed to Scott's Landing yesterday afternoon, while M was with Judge Stallo, finally (and for the first time, despite what they had led M to believe) requesting the return of their baggage. That baggage had arrived at the hotel sometime during the night, and M had evidently taken charge of hers as soon as she was aware of its presence. Merritt and Argent also retrieved their trunks from the offices of the hotel and were grateful to have clean shirts and trousers to wear to Judge Stallo's house.

It was evident that Mrs. Müller was a seamstress of some skill: for one thing, Merritt wryly noted, the dress fit – it did not sag at the shoulders or puddle in her lap when she sat. It was modest without being prudish, and M seemed comfortable wearing it. Argent also appreciated the change in M's appearance and decided M deserved a better epithet than 'not altogether unpleasant to behold.'

The dinner was pleasant, and moreover, M seemed completely at ease in the household. She was used to children – she had helped to raise her youngest sisters and spent a great deal of time with Thea – and the Stallo children responded well to M's teasing. After dinner, Mr. Stallo invited Merritt and Argent to his study, where he presented a written report detailing the events surrounding M's arrest, her appearances in court, and his considered approach to her upcoming trial.

"I have, of course, discussed everything in this report with Miss Warner herself, and although she appears quite capable of understanding it all, it has been my experience that many clients – especially those who are making their first acquaintance with the law – are too overwhelmed to retain all that I have told them. She seemed particularly distressed over time to be spent at the Workhouse, should her bail somehow fall through. I gave up trying to assure her that her bail was secure, so I instead informed her that the state of Ohio does not require any inmate of the Workhouse to remain for more than one year on this account. She had worked up in her mind some fantastical calculation of relinquishing to Ohio nearly two years of her life in order to pay her debt to the court. I don't know what distracted her more – the distress at spending so much time at forced labor or the relief at finding the ordeal to be merely half what she expected. I do not know if you will be escorting Miss Warner on her return trip to Cincinnati, so I have prepared this for you to pass on to whomever shall be with her at that time. She is under the impression that she will be returning on her own, but I hardly think the President will allow that."

"No, sir," Argent responded, but Merritt noted the response lacked certitude.

They left the Stallo house soon after an early dinner. M had been pleasant company and had seemed completely at ease at dinner, unlike the meals they had shared with her in her own home. And she had proven to be a delightful conversationalist, both with the adults and the Stallo children. Argent had been amazed at the difference between Miss Warner in her own home and Miss Warner in the home of a complete stranger.

Once they entered the carriage, however, M had become quiet. Argent and Merritt discussed their strategy for attacking the preparations for riding the coming train ride, divvying up the errands between them. M only half listened in the carriage as Merritt and Argent informed her of the arrangements, only giving her full attention when Emmett's accommodations were discussed. She was dreading this next leg of their trip – despite Argent's promises of privacy and comfort, she held no real belief that either of those things could be had on a train. And much as she feared crossing bridges in the light of day, doing so at night was promising to hold a special terror for her. She had never been farther than Cincinnati and had little knowledge of the lands beyond. The only information she had was several years old, snippets of conversation from her father, and none of it reflected charitably on the M&C. She desperately wanted to know the terrain they would be traveling through, but she could not bring herself to ask these men, and possibly reveal the real need behind the question.

She decided on a flanking offensive. “It is a shame,” she said as their carriage came to a halt in front of the hotel, “that it will be too dark to see the countryside. I have never been beyond Cincinnati.”

As he handed her down the steps of the carriage, Merritt smiled knowingly at her, but did not respond. Argent, however, answered: “It is a much longer trip than from Louisville to Cincinnati – more than twice as long – and even you could not stare out a window for that long. It would have been better to sleep through the trip; by morning we would have been in Parkersburg, and nearly halfway there. After Parkersburg, our trip will proceed apace, no more changing trains or tracks.”

M halted just outside the door of the hotel. “Would have been?”

Merritt smiled again at her. “An early Happy Easter, M.”

Looking to Argent, M saw that he was smiling as well. “We have taken the liberty of changing our tickets for tomorrow morning.” Then, to assert some control over the situation, Argent added, “Very early tomorrow morning.”

Perhaps she was tired, but she revealed far more relief than she intended. “Thank you.” The words came out on one long release of breath.

At the look of utter relief on M’s face, both Merritt and Argent regretted having insisted on taking the night train. Her gratitude was sincere and deep; they had never seen or heard anything so genuine from her and they were ashamed that such a relatively small favor, withheld by them, should be the occasion of such thanks.

In the lobby, Argent made his usual suggestion of a drink to end the evening. Merritt was frowning his disapproval and had opened his mouth to voice it, but M declined Argent with good cheer. “Can’t; I have an early morning tomorrow.” Merritt swore he could hear her skipping as she spoke.

Argent and Merritt, had they stayed in Cincinnati, would have been surprised to learn that the U. S. courts, after a curious and unusual spate of activity, were now entirely idle, the halls and courtrooms empty.

11

They splurged on a carriage to take them to the depot at Plum Street, though it was only a few blocks from the hotel. M was prepared to walk (and to carry her own bag), but in the end, there was not enough time for it. Despite the cloudy skies, M had lost none of her good cheer from last evening when she had learned that she would not be compelled to ride the M&C night express.

The train did not, in fact, leave so very early (departure at a reasonable 7:30), but taking breakfast, taking care of Emmett, including having him sent ahead to be boarded (though not sent ahead too early – M was concerned for Emmett's long duration on a train, and there was no need to add to it), and sending, receiving, and replying to communiqués between the men and the district attorney's office, took some little while, but it was all completed in time. If M hadn't herself been so difficult to wake these last few days, she would have smirked at what Mr. Argent considered "very early" – a 5:30 rising (as they did this morning) was a luxury on the farm, except during deepest winter when the sun rose far after 5:30.

Merritt exercised Emmett himself in the morning and arranged for the exercise of their own horses as well, and Argent sent their trunks ahead to the depot, so all was ready. They needed only to see to the last-minute distractions that always seem to crop up, especially where women were involved. However, this morning, the last-minute distractions all belonged to the men. Just as Argent was offering his hand to M to help her into the carriage (possibly the real reason M was prepared to walk), a note arrived for the men, and though Argent received it and Merritt read it, M was left in ignorance of its contents, only that it caused a short flurry of activity. The carriage was asked to wait (and M was asked to wait in it), and while Argent scribbled a hurried note in his pocket notebook, Merritt returned to the hotel lobby and was back with a young boy as Argent tore out the page. The note was handed to the messenger boy, who sprinted off down the street in the direction of the river. M had already seated herself in the carriage, and Argent stuck his head in to ask her forbearance for just a moment longer, then he and Merritt both disappeared into the hotel, reemerging within a very short time, trailing two more young boys, each clutching a note, presumably written on proper stationery obtained at the hotel desk. These boys also sprinted off down the street, in the same direction.

With the dispatch of these last two messengers, Merritt and Argent joined M in the carriage, and they were finally on their way out of Cincinnati. The carriage let them out at the Indianapolis, Cincinnati & Lafayette Railroad station on Plum Street. The station was crowded and noisy, and M relied on Argent to guide her through the chaos.

The last-minute delay denied M the chance to inspect Emmett's situation on the train. She could not count on the fortuitous presence of a wealthy and influential stranger to ensure Emmett's well-being and happiness on this new train. Merritt assured her that Emmett was receiving the treatment of a prized thoroughbred, though this did more in the way of insulting Emmett's heritage (and M's pride) – Emmett did not need to be coddled, but merely respected – than it did to allay any of her fears. Nonetheless, she accepted Merritt's assurances amid a growing jealousy that Emmett was fond of Merritt and *vice versa*. There was a hurried conversation between Argent and some menial of the railroad, with lots of head-bobbing and an occasional pointing of the finger to a particular car on the part of the menial, ending with a single, final bob of the head on Argent's part. They finally stepped onto the train at 7:28.

Argent led them down the aisle of their appointed passenger car. M noted that the accommodations on this train were far nicer than those on the LC&L, and that the car was far less crowded. She also noted the ever-present spittoons placed along the aisle; she was careful to keep her skirts well clear of them. M spied a perfectly acceptable seating with room enough for all three of them and, most importantly, an empty seat next to a window. M cleared her throat, but neither Argent in front of her nor Merritt behind her took notice. At the end of the aisle, Argent opened a rather ornate door, then moved aside and waved M through. On the other side of the door was a private apartment of sorts. No hard benches here; no children sniffling, nor women fanning their sickly-sweet perfumes throughout the car, nor big-busted matrons, intent on enforcing their neighborly good will. The space occupied about a third of the passenger car in length (though not as wide as the common area they had just left), room enough for a handsome table and chairs in the middle, as well as comfortable single chairs, well-upholstered and with arm rests. There was a thick carpet covering the entire floor and a separate carpet overlaid, under the table. There were indeed thick curtains, but they were at the windows, where curtains belonged. Though the entire space was handsomely and comfortably appointed, M found it chaotic, even to distraction. There was a myriad of wood types and finishes, and the fabrics used ranged widely from silky to velvet to rough, with all manner of patterns. Her mother had been given to this style of decor, but her father had managed to restrain her to some degree. These last few years, at her father's direction, M had given quite a few items to Miss Carrie that her father either could not bear to see and be reminded of his wife or that he had never approved of in the first place. The house therefore gave an unfinished or stripped-down appearance to visitors unfamiliar with its history or the occupants, both present and past.

M had not moved since entering the apartment, simply taking in the view. Argent touched her on the elbow. "Claim your seat, M."

M looked behind, guilty at holding up the other patrons she supposed were the reason for Mr. Argent's prompt; but there was no one else waiting at the door. The door, in fact, was closed, admitting no one else.

"Is no one else joining us?"

"Not without your permission or without valid reason." Merritt was smiling at her. He confused her – his smiles portended both good and ill, and she didn't care for the confusion.

"Mr. Stallo has granted us the use of his pass on this train, which entitles us to the use of this private apartment. He has not only availed us of his pass but has somehow managed to reserve this entire space for our personal and private use."

M turned from surveying the room to say with open wonder, "That was very kind of him." Then as the magnitude of the gesture sank in, her social obligations rose up before her. "It will be difficult to find thanks and repayment commensurate to the kindness."

"I think Mr. Stallo would be entirely satisfied with a pleasant thank you note. You have ten hours, ten private hours, on this train in which to compose one." Argent repeated, "Claim your seat. Mr. Merritt and I have some tedious paperwork to attend, so we will be at the table for some time."

The morning was cloudy, but M still elected to seat herself on the side of the train which would have received the morning sun. Almost immediately, the train pulled out of the IC&L station and slowly chugged down Pearl Street, crossing under several bridges that carried the earliest streets of Cincinnati over the newer railroad. The tracks brushed up against Front Street, very near the Ohio River, where another railroad, the Ohio & Mississippi, ran its tracks. After this near miss with the O&M, their train, still riding on the IC&L tracks, curved gracefully away from the river to pass behind the large buildings – the depots, train sheds, machine shops, and the roundhouse – of the Cincinnati, Hamilton & Dayton Railroad. Craning to look into the extensive operations as they passed, M was astonished at the numerous sidings on site for storing freight cars. The CH&D apparently did a goodly amount of business.

At some point the M&C – their train – would leave the borrowed tracks of the IC&L to run on the borrowed tracks of the CH&D. M expected to join those tracks as soon as the CH&D depot came into view, but the M&C did not make the switch for another four or more blocks. She might have missed such a switch, in any event, being somewhat stunned by the number of tracks pouring out of the CH&D depot grounds – at least four sets of tracks pulled smoothly into place next to their own tracks and those of the IC&L. Almost immediately – and alarmingly – this phalanx of tracks dissolved down to three lines. Surely such a waspish contour of tracks so near a depot was ill-advised, but M had no more than formed this thought before the tracks burgeoned out again to more than half a dozen tracks.

This remained the situation until they reached the base of a respectable hill, where their train finally switched over to the tracks of the CH&D. They had hardly gained these tracks when they curved north around the base of the hill to cross Mill Creek through a covered bridge with a painted tin roof. The tracks never crossed Mill Creek again, though it flirted with the creek in several places.

Once across the bridge, M had a mostly unobstructed view of the western end of Cincinnati and the hills to the east. It was obvious many of the streets nearest the creek were recently created; what used to be swampy, low land was being filled in for establishing new neighborhoods.

The view these low lands now provided would soon be compromised by houses, stores and shops, and possibly even factories.

Suddenly something to the east caught her attention – a sudden and short flash of light, above the low profile of this side of the city. She vaguely knew this part of town, but her memory was slow in responding to her inquiries. She was attentively looking east when there was a second flash, and this time she caught its origin. Though predominantly cloudy, the sun had, occasionally, muscled through the clouds for brief moments of dull sunshine. These last two moments of sun had glanced off a lone metallic structure relatively high in the sky, and the memory of what this was finally fell into place. They were passing Brighton, the section of Cincinnati that was home to the famed Brighton House and its (to some) infamous gilded cow, topping the five stories of the old hotel. Ernst and Joseph had taken her along with Henry Louis, Anselm and George to see what Ernst had told them was the golden calf of Bible repute. She had gone with her brothers without telling her parents, and was severely chastised for it, though the severity may have been caused by her defense that she had not been specifically forbidden to accompany her brothers.

The sight of the golden calf had thrilled her, a solid and real tribute to the truth of the Bible, a truth that she did not realize until that moment that she had sometimes doubted. But there it was, the golden calf that the Israelites had worshipped in petty defiance of God and Moses, and it had somehow landed in Cincinnati, precariously balanced atop the cupola of Brighton House. The reality was, of course, that it was not the golden calf from the Bible; it was not even a calf or a cow, but a steer, and it was not golden, but merely gilded. Idly, M wondered if it was also gelded – it would make for a clever pun or poem:

The slaughter houses builded,
That paid for a steer that was gilded,
But a cow as everyone held it,
Because, after all, it was gelded.

The steer was a tribute to the slaughter houses and related industries that crowded around the Brighton House and lined the Miami canal. It was these industries and the men and people who worked and lived near them to which her parents had objected (the canal was objectionable throughout its entire length), not the revelation of the golden calf. Afterwards – after the chastisement – her father had softened and understood her curiosity, and even was mildly (though privately) amused at the joke that Ernst and Joseph had perpetrated against their younger siblings. It was something brothers would do.

They stopped at little Brighton station – it had been called Ernst station, just like her brother, the last time she was here – and M remembered crossing Mill Creek on an old, weathered and worn bridge, directly across from the station. The bridge looked to be rebuilt (there were railings now) and already a line of wagons and carts waited their turn to cross it. Her brothers and she had left the wonder of the golden calf to watch the trains on the other side of the creek. Now she was riding on one of those trains, and it was the golden calf that was watching her.

The train lurched again into motion. M did not need to see it to know that they were nearing the stockyards. Though Argent had closed the windows against the morning chill as soon as the train started from the depot, the proprietary smell of a stockyards would not be deterred by the mere presence of a pane of glass. It was the effluvium from these extensive stockyards, added to the waste and discharge from the numerous slaughterhouses, breweries and distilleries, paper mills, and starch factories, that made Mill Creek such a noxious oozing flow in its last twelve or so miles on its way to the Ohio River. As children, they had been forbidden to play anywhere near the creek (it was, strictly speaking, beyond the limits set by her father, being at the time, the far western reaches of the city, but he had thrown Mill Creek in with the canal for good measure). That was ten years and more ago, and the filth could only have gotten worse in the meantime.

The route of the train was relatively flat, rising only slightly on its way out of Cincinnati; but on either side of the tracks there were noticeable hills. Though she had seated herself on the right side of the train, M knew that only a little further west of Mill Creek and the tracks, there had been hills ever since they had crossed Mill Creek. There were hills to the east of Mill Creek as well, but they were far to the east of the creek, only gradually crowding westward as the city expanded to the north. Somewhere around Cumminsville, the geography switched, and the west side of Mill Creek opened up, while the hills crowded the eastern bank. M was no stranger to hills – more than a few acres of her father's farm were tied up in hills – but the hills of Cincinnati crowded her. They were no higher than any hills back home, but they were in the city, and that is what bothered her – Louisville was mostly level. Cincinnati sometimes felt like it was about to topple onto itself.

At Cumminsville, M was startled to see several trainmen race along the side of their car, *on* the side of their car. She had, of course, noticed the diminished width of their apartment, but did not pursue the matter further. Now she asked, "What kind of car is this? There are men coming and going along this walkway outside." There was now a passenger, a man, enjoying a smoke where the walkway ended near the middle of the car, where M realized there was a door to the common area.

"It is a type of combination car; sometimes it is called a gallery car because of the walkway – the gallery – that runs along the length of this apartment. It allows privacy or security in one part of the car, while still allowing train crew and passengers access to the full length of the car. I am afraid there is nothing to be done about men smoking on the gallery; it is usually only for the duration of station stops."

M acknowledged Argent's view of smokers. "Men will always need to smoke." Turning back toward the window, she saw the man flick the last of his cigarette far from the train and leave the gallery by way of the offset door. She was fascinated with the gallery – such a simple concept, yet so useful. "If this is a gallery car, does that make us Gallerians?" It was a silly pun, probably not worth the saying, but it had slipped out before she had fully examined its worth. She did not turn to see the men's reactions, but she heard Merritt muffle a laugh.

After the stop at Cumminsville, the train approached Spring Grove Cemetery. M studiously avoided looking across the car to that place of her humiliation and infamy. The line of the CH&D sliced across the southern end of Spring Grove, so that she couldn't avoid it entirely. There were monuments on either side of the train, but from her window, there was also the nursery beyond the monuments, where trees and shrubs and bushes of all varieties, matured and patiently waited their turn and their place in the celebrated landscaping of the cemetery proper.

She could also see Spring Grove Avenue, or simply, the Avenue, as it was referred to by Cincinnatians. She could not fault the people of Cincinnati for singling out this roadway for place of honor as the Avenue. It was gravelled and tree-lined and perfectly maintained. It was very wide, even after accounting for the horse-railway tracks on one side of the central roadway as well as wide swaths of soft dirt on either side, both pathways almost as wide as the central roadway itself. A pair of horsemen came into view, obviously racing each other, one on the left dirt pathway and the other on the right. They easily overtook the train.

As they passed Spring Grove, the site of Miss Warner's infamy, Argent wondered what she thought. Under different circumstances, Argent might have suggested the view out the windows opposite where Miss Warner now sat. The Resor monument in the cemetery was a tall marble monument that could readily be seen from the car. The train always traveled at a conspicuously slow rate in deference to the cemetery, and many travelers took the opportunity to marvel at the grounds as they passed. Miss Warner, however, seemed impervious to the allure of the cemetery.

Very soon after the last of Spring Grove's magnificent monuments and orderly nursery left their view, the train stopped at another station. From M's window, she could see the multiple tracks and platforms of a freight concern. The two horsemen who had been racing were standing together, laughing; it had evidently been a friendly race, determining the winner left up to the honor of the gentlemen.

The porter knocked at the door and asked to speak with one of the gentlemen. Merritt wordlessly volunteered and disappeared into the common area of the car with the porter. He returned within minutes with a small satchel overstuffed with papers of some kind. Neither man seemed happy at the arrival of this newest batch of paperwork, and so Merritt tossed it onto the table where it lay unopened. Both men, however, took their places at the table, one on either side of the pouch, both acknowledging and ignoring the waiting work.

When the train started forward, M felt the switch onto different tracks; at the same time Argent stated, "We have just passed out of Cincinnati."

Without thinking, M retorted, "It cannot be soon enough. It is a relief to see the backside of Cincinnati disappear behind us." Realizing that she had perhaps spoken intemperately, she moderated her tone. "We are on the M&C's own tracks now? How many stations are there between here and Parkersburg?" M regretted the lost schedule she had obtained at the hotel, but given the frosty relations with the hotel desk staff, she had shied away from asking for a second schedule.

Merritt reached across the table and picked up a thick piece of paper. "I have been writing down the towns as I remember them – the schedule of the M&C."

M accepted the schedule, briefly scanning the list and times of the train's stops. His memory must have been exceptional, or he had ridden this train often enough to give very exact times for stops.

"I omitted the accommodation trains. Unless you would care to embark on an excursion through the countryside? I am told some of the scenery is unsurpassed on these lines."

Argent cast Merritt a wild look. They were already inexcusably behind schedule, and despite her repeated wish to end this journey as quickly as possible, it would not be beyond Miss Warner to accept just such an excursion to exercise her horse or merely to pique Merritt and himself.

M caught Argent's look, and she graciously declined Merritt's bait – she had seen the scenery on the LC&L and was certain it was itself unsurpassed.

Argent returned to Cincinnati. "Do your relatives live in the city, or in one of the suburbs? Loveland will be the last of the suburbs we pass through in Hamilton County."

"Some of the cousins live outside the city, but to the east. Or rather, it used to be outside the city – near Avondale. Grandpa and Grandma lived near there, but I think Aunt Ada and Aunt 'Scella live in the city somewhere now." Miss Warner had resumed her observations out the window; she sounded slightly exasperated with the subject of her relatives. On the contrary, however, M was absorbed in the subject of her relatives, just not the Cincinnati kin.

The exasperation was with the men themselves. Today was Gretta's birthday, and, as they had done on Randy's birthday, that first day they had come to her farm, they were intruding on her memories of her family. M shared April as a birth month with two of her sisters and Randy. Randy and M had been born within a year of each other, and once, while in town, someone had had the effrontery to refer to them as Irish twins, and Mr. Warner had reacted angrily, a thing M had rarely seen off the farm (and rarely on the farm, without good provocation). Agnes and Theresa, true twins, could also be considered Irish twins of a sort. They were born only minutes apart, yet Agnes was born on New Year's Eve of one year and Theresa was born on New Year's Day of the next year. Her father had been inordinately proud of this happenstance, as if he had somehow engineered it. Gretta had also caused a special pride in her father – she had been born on Grandma's birthday, her father's mother's birthday. That had made her special. So had her blonde hair, bright yellow and curly. She had been a beautiful child, happy and sparkling, like sun on riffling water. She would be … how old would she be now? It didn't matter; she would never grow older, she was perfectly preserved at the age of her death. All of them were. M closed her eyes and lowered her head.

"Miss Warner?"

M looked up to find Mr. Merritt considering her with that inscrutable gaze of his. It irritated her that she could not discern the meaning behind the gaze – was he concerned or amused? Perhaps he didn't know himself and that is what gave his gaze such an undefined character. It irritated her all the more that he could not make up his own mind.

"Yes?" Her irritation showed in her response, but Merritt seemed unfazed by it.

"If you are fatigued, you might be more comfortable on one of the long benches near the inner door. They are quite comfortable."

"I am well where I am, but I thank you. I would like to know where we are, what station we are near."

Now Merritt cocked his head; it seemed he was about to decide between concern and amusement. "We have just now passed Montgomery; Symmes is next, but this train will not stop again until Loveland." He paused a moment before adding, "If there is anything you should want or need, it can be obtained there."

Now M considered him; what was he suggesting? What had she revealed in her posture or face that suggested she needed or wanted something? She looked down at the scribbled schedule laying in her lap. The train was scheduled to stop in Loveland, perhaps four miles ahead, at 8:49, and had left the junction near Spring Grove at 7:56. She did not realize she had been so lost in her thoughts and grief and memories.

"I have no needs or wants."

Merritt left to rejoin Argent at the table, but not before giving her one last look, definitely a look of concern. But her thoughts were none of his concern. Her grief was private. All grief should be private. She detested the parades and speeches on Decoration Days. She had gone with her father to both the Confederate and Union events at Cave Hill, and it had taken all her control not to walk away, even while her father had stood at attention and tears threatened in his eyes. She had never seen him cry over any of her brothers, but this gaudy display of patriotism had moved him. It was not the flowers or the attention to the graves of those who had fallen. She planted heavily in her own family's cemetery and always brought wildflowers from her walks in the woods to add to the perennials. It was the marching and the speeches, especially the speeches. High, florid talk of noble sacrifices and the pride every family, especially widows and mothers and sisters, should feel at such honorable deaths. At Union Decoration Days, the speeches often ended with appeals to support Republican efforts to reconstruct the states in late rebellion, to further honor these dear fallen. At Confederate Decoration Days, Democratic politicians spoke to the crowds, thundering against the Republicans who would dishonor the Confederate dead with ever more radical measures against the states in late rebellion.

What did these speakers, these men, know of sacrifice? They were here, weren't they? They were whole and living. The men who talked most of noble sacrifice had very often sacrificed very little, nor had to live with the very real consequences of the deaths and infirmities of husbands and fathers, brothers and sons. And why speak to women of supporting Republicans or Democrats? Colored men could now vote, but not women, not the real victims of sacrifice. But, possibly, it was unpatriotic of her to think this way.

At Loveland, M noticed a begrimed railroad worker walk the length of the train, stopping at each wheel to duck under the train in a most contorted way, pulling with him a hand lantern and a hammer with a long handle. The windows were now open – when had that happened? – to relieve the stuffiness that had collected in their car, and through them M could hear a curious tapping. The tapping grew fainter as the man worked his way toward the engine, then it grew louder again as he worked his way down the other side of the train toward theirs, the last car, in the train. Loveland was the junction of the M&C and the Little Miami Railroad, and M saw other begrimed men performing similar inspections on other trains coming and going through the station.

There was a knock at the inner door before a shabby little boy poked his head in to inquire if the gentleman or lady would like to buy anything. Argent invited the newsbutcher's boy in and bought from him newspapers from two or three different publishers, then before paying the boy, he looked the question at M, but she shook her head.

M did not realize Merritt had left the car until he bounded through the outside door, nearly pirouetting as he closed it. He seemed in high spirits. He smiled his greetings to M, but his smile faded briefly when M asked after Emmett, the goal, she thought, of his departure.

"He is with the other horses, but I have not been to look in on him. I am sorry that I did not think to do so. I have been to the telegraph office." He made a great show of pulling from his breast pocket a small bundle of telegrams; he and Argent received a great number of telegrams, no matter where they were.

"You have no reason to be sorry; Emmett is not your responsibility. I will look to him myself at the next stop." At this Merritt looked to Argent, and M saw something pass between them.

Merritt smiled again at Miss Warner, apologetically this time, before seating himself at the table with Argent, dividing between them this newest correspondence.

The train stopped once more – a place that was truly only a stop on the line – before pulling into Blanchester. M had nearly dozed since the last stop, though it was hardly half an hour – the track had gone in a nearly perfect straight line and, despite the poor ballasting that had made the ride rougher than it could have been, M had been lulled into a kind of absence of mind. She was only vaguely aware that the engine had mildly labored on ascending grades.

M consulted her schedule again. Now began the tedious four hours of stopping at nearly every hamlet along the line. Some stops were only ten minutes apart, hardly time for the engine to get up to speed. The only respite was the forty-eight minutes between Frankfort and Chillicothe. She should not complain – she would not complain – not when she had such comfortable arrangements for the ride. She thought of her ride on the LC&L last week, and her mouth watered with remembered nausea.

There had been a lull in the conversation for some time. At first the men had thought M dozing, but a surreptitious glance told them she was still staring out the window. She glanced at the schedule in her hand each time the train stopped at a station, even when there had only passed 10 or fewer minutes since the last stop. All the stopping and starting, lurching, whistle-blowing, and tramping overhead were conspiring to spawn a headache.

A mile or so past Leesburgh, Merritt watched M sit white-knuckled as the train passed over the bridge at Lee's Creek. Almost immediately, the train entered a deep cut, and he saw M relax her jaw and hands. They would make the smaller crossing at Walnut Creek very soon. At the table, Merritt glanced across at Argent, who was, as ever, engrossed in the study of their work, both those cases winding their way through the court systems of various states and cities, as well as cases in various stages of being built – ongoing investigations, affidavits being collected, witnesses kept in view, clues being run down, etc. They had also come into possession, in that first overstuffed satchel received at Winton Place, of the new counterfeit detector, and it was this that Argent was so diligently studying. Occasionally, Argent lowered his hand from where it perennially rested against his jaw to jot something in the margins of the detector. Merritt picked up a pencil and scrawled something on the corner of one of the many papers scattered on the table between them, then slid it carefully across the table to rest in front of Argent. When Argent failed to acknowledge the note, Merritt pushed the paper even closer to Argent's line of view. Argent absent-mindedly pushed it away from him, thinking only that Merritt, as always, had failed to contain the work before him in anything like order. Merritt cleared his throat; still no acknowledgement. Finally, Merritt slopped some of his cold coffee on the papers closest to Argent, papers Argent kept neatly corralled. Argent looked up angrily as Merritt did his best to look contrite while sopping up the coffee, an unusually small amount of coffee, given Merritt's past incidents of such disregard for the paperwork. At the moment he looked up, however, Merritt pressed his note into Argent's immediate view and nodded urgently at it.

Argent looked down to read it and Merritt saw the rise of Argent's lashes that said his eyes had widened at the information there.

We are approaching Monroe and Greenfield.

Argent looked up, his earlier glance of remonstrance replaced by one of a near frantic nature. Merritt nodded again, and then with a slight tip of the head and a sidelong glance, indicated Miss Warner.

Monroe and Greenfield. Or, rather, the bridges over Rattlesnake and Paint creeks, respectively.

Both bridges were high enough to make even a seasoned traveler faintly nervous; Monroe's was the higher but shorter crossing, while Greenfield's was high as well, though much longer to endure. But it was the narrow and unadorned nature of both bridges that would add to Miss Warner's discomfort: neither bridge had guard rails or side attachments of any kind. The bridges were only wide enough to admit the tracks themselves and maybe a few inches on either side beyond the actual rails, so that from the cars it often looked as if the train was traveling on mere air. Given Miss Warner's now-known fear of bridges in general – even the massive and sturdy bridge at Cincinnati had caused her discomfort – the bridges near Greenfield could only induce palpable panic.

Argent chanced a glance at Miss Warner, sitting still and silent on the other side of the room. Soon her eyes will come to rest upon the steep valley ahead of them and then the first bridge will come into sight, and her calm repose will shatter. His first thought should have been to shield her from the fear, but he was ashamed to find himself seeking to shield himself from the histrionics one could expect from such a volatile woman. She had handled herself well on the Roebling suspension bridge (Argent had not even suspected the problem), but she had not been on a train during that crossing, and that bridge was far, far more massive-appearing in its great stone piers. How will she react to this onslaught against her courage?

Argent returned to Merritt to find himself being observed. Merritt smiled, then in a tone not at all commensurate with the smile, exclaimed, "Do forgive me, Argent. I'm afraid my breakfast has not sat well with me and the rocking of the train has made me nauseous, and the nausea has made me clumsy." He made a great show of mopping up a second time the cold coffee spilled earlier. His movements were slow and suggested great effort.

"Not at all, though you should have said something *sooner*, so that we may have *planned* for a remedy before any such accident could occur."

Despite his words, Argent seemed to know exactly what to do for the poor, ailing Mr. Merritt. He rose from his seat and beginning on Miss Warner's side of the apartment, began drawing closed all the curtains at all the windows.

Miss Warner did not seem overly concerned about Mr. Merritt's illness, though, in truth, she did feel sympathy for him. Nausea, especially at the height of one of her headaches, was not unknown to her; her own headaches and nausea could last for hours, and sometimes – to one degree or another – for two or three days. Darkness and cold helped her own nausea and she would not deny them to a fellow sufferer, but she did not care to sit in the dark for any length of time on a train.

"Perhaps a cold compress to his head might also help." Though she suggested it, she did not herself move to find one.

"Yes, I believe that might help." Merritt had moved to one of two long, padded bench seats on either side of the room, just inside the door to the common area, and laid on his back, his arm slung over his eyes, even the little light left in the room too much for his aggrieved system.

Argent dutifully dipped one of the many handkerchiefs that he kept about his person into a pewter ewer of water and, having barely wrung it out, dropped it at Merritt's waist, just below where his other hand lay, leaving a spreading wet spot on his trousers.

Merritt raised the hand that shielded his eyes to mutter "Thank you," while with the other hand squeezing the remaining water from the handkerchief onto the floor before dropping it in a wadded heap onto his forehead.

It was not long before they felt the train slow down as it approached Monroe, then come to a complete stop. These stops at the smaller stations were always brief and within two minutes the train whistle sounded, and they felt the train slowly regain its speed. As was the situation at most of the smaller towns, the railroad skirted along the outskirts of Monroe and was immediately out of the town altogether. As soon as the siding rejoined the main tracks, the line began to curve away from Monroe and towards Rattlesnake Creek. Argent felt the tracks leave dear mother earth, the tracks reaching across mere air to the other side of the chasm. He prayed that Miss Warner did not mark the difference in the feel of the ride. She did not mention it, though she chanced a peek out the window through the closed curtains. Did she see the rocks and falls directly below the bridge – far below the bridge – and the turmoil of the water beyond? Merritt did not see M confirm her suspicions, but Argent did and braced for the coming hysteria. Instead, Miss Warner folded her hands – tightly – in her lap and lowered her head. She sat that way during the entire crossing, though the bridge was not a very long one. The next bridge at Greenfield, however, was much longer. Argent nonetheless knew from her clenched hands and jaws that it was nothing short of eternity for Miss Warner.

There were a few smaller streams to cross between Monroe and Greenfield, but those did not seem to excite in Miss Warner the dread she kept just in check during other crossings. Height certainly fueled her fear, but there seemed to be something else lurking just beneath that fear that gave her dread an almost angry or challenging aspect. Argent felt he had almost grasped that deeper current in her fear – her words in Covington came back to him: I prefer to see what's coming – there was some other implication behind the words, but just as he was beginning to tease out this other implication, they reached Greenfield, and soon after they started across the bridge.

Merritt's distraction had obviously failed, so that by the time they had reached Walnut Creek, about midway between Monroe and Greenfield, he had rejoined Argent at the table. Neither man had made any move to open the curtains, though Miss Warner parted the panel nearest her and resumed her watch out the window.

As they pulled into the depot at Greenfield, Argent checked his watch – the train was fairly on time. He intended to check his watch against that of the B&O's station clock when they reached Parkersburg. While on the M&C, they were obliged to recognize Cincinnati time, but once in West Virginia – once they were on B&O tracks – they would be obliged to follow Baltimore time. He intended to be on Baltimore time until they delivered Miss Warner to the Executive Mansion, at which time he would set his watch to the time of whatever city Whitley intended to send him next. Argent was returning his watch to his vest pocket when he noticed Miss Warner watching him.

"We are making good time; we will reach Parkersburg in time for dinner, if our luck holds."

M nodded her thanks.

The whistle sounded 'Up Brakes' and the brakemen thumped along the tops of the cars releasing the brakes that had kept the train stationary at the depot. The engine itself was without brakes, except for one lone set on the tender behind it, so that as each car's brakes were let up the engine pulled a little more against its unnatural restraints. Like a horse that has been tightly reined in and then given free rein, the engine lurched ahead as the last brake was released, pursuing its natural desire to move forward. There was a jerk felt in each car as it was gathered up in the engine's desire to move forward. M's car was the last to jerk forward, the last to join the engine's harem moving eastward.

M glanced out her window, then quickly pulled the curtain closed and after the briefest pause she turned to Argent. "May I trouble you for your watch? Only for a moment or so." She seemed impatient.

Argent fished out his watch and handed it to her, curious at the request.

M mistook his expression and assured him, "I promise I will handle it carefully."

Despite her promise, she realized she was holding the watch tightly, squeezing it in her growing terror. She concentrated on holding it loosely, but that took too much of her mind from the task she had set for herself. She gingerly laid the watch in her lap, and while watching the second hand, she counted as the car ran over each joining of the rails. The train was, of course, gaining in speed as it worked its way to the next station – she shifted her glance to the schedule, now pinned in place in her lap by Argent's watch – Lyndon, four miles away.

Even as she counted, she felt the slight shift in sound and feel as the train started over the bridge. It was pointless – she could not keep an accurate tally while the bridge presented such a distraction – but she kept on counting anyway. After what seemed an inordinate amount of time – why must these bridges be so close to depots, when engines are at their slowest? – she felt and heard the train return to its tracks on land. She was just resolved to start over when Argent broke in on her efforts.

She turned to him and he repeated, "May I ask your need for the watch?"

"I wanted to try and determine the train's speed, an exercise my father taught me. But I attempted the exercise too soon – the train has not yet settled on a speed."

She offered the watch to Argent, but he suspected the purpose behind the exercise and replied, "Keep it until you can complete your exercise, then tell me of your conclusions."

Merritt, however, could not wait. He also suspected the reason behind the exercise – bless good Mr. Warner – but he wanted to see if M would admit it. There were far worse bridges and viaducts, harrowing curves that clung to cliffs, and other unpleasant characteristics of the road ahead of them, especially after Athens. It would go easier on her if she admitted her fears and allowed himself and Argent to help distract her. At the very least, it would give them plausible reason to announce each unpleasantness as it neared, so that she may prepare herself.

"What is the nature of this exercise?"

M looked up from the watch, astonished, whether at the sound of Merritt's voice or the question itself.

"Algebraic, I believe."

"Algebraic!" It was now Argent's turn to be astonished. "Are you schooled in algebra?" It was not unheard of for girls to be schooled in the rudiments of math, certainly enough to keep a household budget, but algebra seemed completely unnecessary for any woman, much less a woman farmer.

"I am schooled as much as my brothers were. I often sat with them whenever Dad helped them with their lessons." She was as quick as any of her brothers in adding, subtracting, multiplying and dividing, though she had to admit that she bested only Randy in algebra.

Merritt asked the next question. M noticed this about these two men – they often conducted conversations in this see-saw manner, taking turns at making comments, asking questions, giving replies. "Then, please, explain the algebra to me."

"I count the 'clicks' of the train as our car runs over the joining of the lengths of rails as I watch the second hand. After a minute, I stop counting. The number of joints tells me how far the train has traveled in a minute, and from that I can calculate the speed of the train in miles per hour."

"How can you be certain of the lengths of the rails?" Argent's turn.

"Any other road, I would not be so confident, but the M&C is notoriously, almost negligently, behind in renewing not only its ballast but its rails as well. Doubtless you noticed the poorer quality of our ride on this road compared to that of the LC&L. Much of this rail has been on the road almost from the beginning of its existence. Though newer rails are getting longer and longer, the old rails were almost always 30 feet long. So, however many clicks I count is multiplied by 30."

"And then what?"

M hesitated. She suspected Merritt did not so much want to know the formula as he wanted to know if she truly did. "I multiply that number by 60 — for the minutes in an hour – then divide that number by 5280 – for the number of feet in a mile." She did not like being put on display like this. She decided to challenge Merritt, as she felt he had challenged her. "Surely you did such exercises in your own schooling."

"Sadly, I did not give algebra the attention it deserved. Perhaps you could teach me sometime."

M felt him teasing her, maybe even snickering at her. She knew her interest and abilities in math – modest as they were – were unusual, but it was something her father had shared with her, and she did not care for Merritt's attitude. She decided to do a little snickering of her own.

"It isn't a complicated formula, but I shall endeavor to help you through it."

Argent heard the growing irritation in Miss Warner, but before he could step in and halt Miss Warner's escalating irritation and Merritt's obvious enjoyment of it, Merritt came to what probably was his true intent in engaging Miss Warner.

"Why bother?"

"I beg your pardon."

"Why bother counting clicks and seconds when the same goal may be obtained by consulting the schedule. One needn't even be on a train to determine its speed. The schedule provides the times of arrivals and departures at depots and the miles between those times. Rate of speed could easily be determined from the facts given on the schedule."

M blinked once, twice, three times before responding. "Sometimes the exercise itself is the goal. Doing the calculations in one's head, without aid of pencil and paper, sharpens and quickens the mind." Almost as if she had shrugged, M added, "It helps to pass the time." In truth, her father had instructed her in several such exercises to occupy her mind when crossing the higher bridges and trestled viaducts of the LC&L. She had been proud and felt particular to him on those occasions when he had explained such things to her, especially when it was remembered that for all other times of mental and emotional anguish he prescribed saying the rosary, even if one was without the beads themselves. But that was when she was young – she could not even say with certitude where her own rosary was at the moment.

Merritt smiled widely at her. "We would be glad to help pass the time, should the need arise." He had put a curious emphasis on 'arise.' Then Merritt turned to Argent. "We often find the need to pass the time once past Athens."

Argent instantly understood Merritt's ploy, and smoothly added, "Usually by that time, we find that we have need of a break from our endless paperwork. We often play cards. Do you play cards Miss Warner?"

"Only the simplest games. I am afraid you would find me a poor partner for your games." Then M became animated. "Perhaps you could teach me poker. I would like to be able to play poker, though I couldn't gamble, especially not this week."

"This week?" Argent sounded faint; the idea of teaching a young woman poker was not what he had in mind when he suggested cards to pass the time.

"It is Holy Week, and while the Roman guards were shameless enough to throw dice for Christ's seamless robe, I shall not insult the sanctity of the week in such a way. But I would like to learn to play." She had seen the hired workers on her farm often spend a lunch break throwing down cards, laughing even amid obvious disappointment. It seemed the perfect social engagement – one's hands were always occupied, it was challenging, entertaining, and there didn't seem to be a requirement to add to the conversation.

Merritt supported M in this. "If you like doing sums and such in your head, you will enjoy poker – it is a game of probabilities, as well as memory and skill." It was vaguely disquieting to have Merritt's support.

"Perhaps poker itself, even without the gambling, should be avoided in deference to the liturgical season. I am certain we can find something else to occupy our time. I shall think on it in the meantime."

M nodded to Argent, then remembering the watch, offered again to return it, but Argent again refused it. "Please, keep it as long as you like; I have no immediate need for it. There is no better way to pass the time than with a watch."

M did not bother to count the clicks or calculate the speed of the train, but she was curiously calmed by the presence of the watch. She consulted it at every stop, to compare it with the stated times on the schedule. After Lyndon (a mere scattering of buildings) they breezed past Harper's, which was a forlorn little depot in the middle of nowhere. Frankfort Station was some distance from the village of the same name, but it, too, was little more than a flag stop.

Unlike most of the other stops so far, however, the station at Chillicothe was not on the outskirts of town. Chillicothe was a sizable town, not only a station on the M&C but also the intersection of several major roadways in the county, as well as host to a small segment of the Miami and Erie Canal. After crossing the canal on the way into town, the tracks ran alongside the Scioto River, eventually crossing it at a pinched point of the Old Channel. It was an orderly town, neatly laid out on level ground. The train pulled into the station, exactly on time, by Argent's watch. They would tarry here for a relatively lengthy fifteen or twenty minutes, enough time, it was supposed by M&C's schedule, to procure a noontime meal at the Depot Hotel, a mere few feet from the depot. The Depot Hotel looked presentable enough, but the depot itself was old and worn out, in need of replacing.

Merritt offered to fetch the meals for everyone – there was no sense in bolting down a cold sandwich like animals in the dining saloon of the hotel, when they could procure something a little more substantial and enjoy it at a more human pace at their own table. M was happy to hear the arrangements, since that would give her time to visit Emmett, a visit long overdue. There was the slightest hesitation on Merritt's part to let her pass through the door after him. She saw him glance over her head, and without seeing, knew that something, again, had passed between the two men.

"I'm afraid you will not be allowed access to that car. This is the only time the crewmen who are responsible for baggage and other belongings are able to grab – literally – something to eat for themselves. There will be no one there to assist you."

"I don't need any assistance; I am quite capable of pulling open a car door and climbing up into one."

"Merritt, you had better hurry." M turned to face Argent, in time to see him nod reassuringly to Merritt. Behind her, Merritt left, pulling the door decidedly closed. "We don't doubt that you are. However, the railroads are very particular about who handles their investments, including something as simple as opening a car door. Because they are facing more and more lawsuits for injuries from passengers, they are imposing more, and ever more stringent, rules for the operating of their roads."

For a wild moment, Argent thought Miss Warner might insist on her right to see Emmett, who in fact was not on the train. Several of the many notes received and answered this morning just prior to reaching the depot in Cincinnati concerned the matter of Emmett's travel arrangements, as well as those of their own horses. The M&C fast train had been unable to accommodate the three horses – their group's last-minute change from the overnight express to the daylight fast train had left them without a berth in either of the two baggage cars. There were, in fact, no stock cars in this train. They had no intention of delaying this trip one more day in Cincinnati in order to find a mixed train, with both passenger and freight cars, that could accommodate Miss Warner's requirements for Emmett. He was, therefore, relegated to the freight train, like their own horses, chugging along slowly behind them – by now, far behind them. Emmett would reach Parkersburg long after they had themselves retired to bed this night. Instructions – strict, explicit instructions – had been given as to Emmett's care on the train. Argent had not hesitated to mention President Grant in these instructions. Miss Warner would, of course, have to be told eventually, but Merritt and Argent had agreed to delay that particular moment until they were as far as possible from Cincinnati.

For her part, M felt a little piqued at this latest barrier to visiting with Emmett, who by now must surely think she had abandoned him. But, no matter how she felt about rules that should not apply to herself, she conceded that it was wrong of her to deny these poor, underpaid and overworked trainmen the chance to eat a decent, if hurried, meal.

"His needs are being seen to?"

"Of that, you need not worry." M studied Agented briefly; he had slightly emphasized 'that' – 'Of *that*, you need not worry.' It suggested that she might need to worry about other things. She considered ignoring the possible implication of his tone; she even considered that she had misheard the tone of his voice. In the end, she decided to drop the subject in deference to Argent himself; he had, after all, allowed her the use of his watch this last hour or more.

M nodded, but added, "Emmett may have been standing all this time, but I have been sitting. I need to stretch my legs a little."

"As do I."

M sighed; there was no circumventing Mr. Argent's avowed determination to escort her everywhere. She returned the watch to him. "I have no pockets. You'll need to tell me when to return to the train."

Argent and M returned to their car just as Merritt was returning with their food. As M passed into the car, Merritt looked a question at Argent, who mouthed 'Later.'

The whistle blew, and the train started up, but before the engine had gone far enough to exert its pull on the last car, a louder, longer whistle was heard, and the train stopped again. There was a flurry of movement on the roof overhead. Merritt left the car to inquire into the delay and soon returned with the news that there was a wreck on the road. The long whistle was from the road's machine shops just ahead near the tracks, a signal that any men in the town available to answer the whistle should assemble for transportation to the site of the wreck. In this case, the wreck was to the west of Chillicothe and would not affect their own train or schedule. Once this same information was conveyed to the engineer, the train started forward again.

They ate a simple lunch at the splendid table in their ornate apartment, as the train crossed the long bridge over the Scioto River out of town. After lunch, M took up her position at the window. The curtain here was still only partly parted, and all the other windows were still curtained, despite Merritt's remarkable recovery earlier this morning. Their apartment was therefore dark, and the room was becoming warm with the advance of the day, so that M dozed in her chair, counting the clicks of the wheels over the rails, as she used to count the clicks of the beads of her rosary.

She was distantly aware of the stopping and starting of the train at the next several stations, and she could tell from the low level of noise at each stop that these were little towns with little depots, sleepy little towns like she herself was sleepy. At Hamden Junction, however, the noises of a larger town and of two railroads in close proximity eventually, thoroughly roused her. However, she woke only as the train was on its way out of town; she had missed another opportunity to look in on Emmett.

The day outside had only slightly warmed up, but inside the car had become stuffy, so much so that Argent and Merritt had evidently removed their coats. Upon waking, M had just caught the last frantic motions as the men replaced their coats, giving almost military tugs on cuffs and lapels, snapping the coats into proper place. Over Argent's confusing objections, M had thrown open her window some time ago and had sat as close to the window as her chair would permit, reveling in the weak sunshine and the breeze stirred up by the motion of the train. They were far enough behind the engine that soot was not so much of a problem and though the road was poorly ballasted, little dust was stirred up after the recent rains.

They entered Zaleski from the south, after crossing a wooden bridge. By now, M did not need to feel the crossing to know they were on a bridge, at least wooden ones. Now she listened for the engineer to cut off his engine to know when a wooden bridge was imminent. A long-ago explanation from her father had resurfaced: engines could not be engaged while on wooden bridges for fear of sparks causing fires. Bridge watchers were employed to report those engineers who did not comply, as well as to walk the bridges after each train had passed to look for signs of nascent fires. Sometimes she saw these bridge watchers emerge from their nearby cottages as soon as their car began its crossing on the bridge.

Argent had occasionally volunteered varying information he thought might be of interest as they passed through towns or places. They had crossed many creeks by this time, but for some reason this was the first creek he bothered to mention by name.

"This is Big Raccoon Creek. We will be following it for several miles and crossing it several times."

M was more occupied with the crossing of the bridge wobbling on wooden trestles than with the name of the creek. She absently acknowledged Argent's comment. "Is the creek big or are the raccoons big?" She did not realize she had spoken until she heard Merritt let out one short laugh.

After a wide bend in the road, the tracks ran almost perfectly north. The train whistled "Down Brakes" and M heard the brakemen overhead hurry to their jobs. The slowing train reduced the breeze through the window, but M was now interested in the train's shops and turntable, slowly passing by as the train continued slowing to its stop at the depot. Just past the freight car shop was the roundhouse, the structure that most fascinated her. There were tracks to and from the turntable but only one track led into the roundhouse. She would like to visit a roundhouse to watch the great engines that pulled long lines of cars be themselves moved on the great turntable that directed them to their own particular stalls.

The single track of the road had fanned out to include six or more tracks as they had neared the car shops of Zaleski, but just after the roundhouse, these tracks had again melted away to one lone track as they entered the siding at the depot. On these multiple tracks was an assortment of new cars, shiny in their first coats of paint. These were mostly flat and stock cars, although there were several 'house' cars used by different masters of the line. There were also lines of full and empty coal cars, and beyond the tracks were huge bins of coal.

M stood long before the train came to a stop, and Argent and Merritt reluctantly joined her on their feet. They had passed notes back and forth, trying to develop some reason to keep M from visiting a horse that was not on this train, but they had come up empty-handed. Now she would have to be told, but almost as soon as the train stopped, it began its slow return to speed. The porter entered, after knocking, to see if they required anything. To Merritt's inquiries, the porter answered that the train had only stopped long enough to receive its telegraph orders, handed to the engineer himself directly from the platform. There were no passengers to retrieve or to let off — a measles epidemic in nearby McArthur ("raging in McArthur," as the porter had put it) had retarded passenger traffic in the area this past week, and no one of the crew cared to exposes himself to the disease by visiting the depot grounds. All trains stopping here were receiving their orders in this manner. The porter excused himself and left, but not before pointedly looking at M's open window, letting in fresh air, air now possibly heavy with measles.

M remained standing, staring at the door; behind her, Merritt and Argent breathed a sigh of relief that would last only until the next stop – Moonville, only six miles away.

M finally turned to the men, but instead of anger or frustration at being thwarted yet again, she was obviously concerned. Her concern, however, was not for the good and suffering people of McArthur, but for Emmett. "Can horses catch measles?"

Argent's relief at keeping M unaware of the unspoken lie of Emmett's whereabouts kept him from rebuking her for her lack of concern for the children of that town who were certainly suffering at this moment, some of whom would most likely die.

It was Merritt who answered. "Not to my knowledge. I am certain Emmett is safe from this epidemic."

After the little town of Moonville, they crossed Raccoon Creek one last time, over a trestle, just before entering a tunnel. The tunnel reflected the surrounding area – eerie and remote, with echoes that distorted the senses. It wasn't overly long, but it was narrow and curved, though slightly, adding to the sense of confinement and deepening the darkness.

As they exited the tunnel, they passed a ramshackle shanty, probably the abode of some flagman, ready to warn approaching trains if the tunnel was occupied. The heavy forest continued on this other side of the tunnel and was, if possible, even more imposing. The ordinary noise of the train itself was muffled and subdued.

Within minutes they were entering another tunnel, but as M's car entered and before darkness overtook them, she noticed the portal and the walls within were constructed of timber. The portal had a basket weave look to it, but the walls looked far less whimsical – great chunks of lumber angled from the wider floor to the narrower ceiling. The size of the timber did nothing to assure the traveler of the stability of the tunnel. Instead, the tunnel had the appearance of a mine shaft, lending to the imagination a sense of impending collapse, of a crushing weight barely held in check. It reminded M of a coffin.

For the first time while on the train, Argent sat in the chair across from her. M sighed inwardly – she would have to engage in conversation. But they had been patient with her, granting her solitude, pretending, as she knew, to be deeply absorbed in their work (but she had seen them, out of the corner of her eye, passing notes like naughty little schoolboys). She looked over to him and he smiled; she nearly recoiled from the probable platitudes that perched behind that smile. She liked her seat by the window and the silence in the car. Despite what he believed, she could very well stare out the window for the duration of the trip. Why had she left her book in the trunk? She could have easily signaled the need for solitude and, by his own admission, she would have been in her rights to be left alone. She decided to pre-empt whatever he had to say by choosing the subject.

"How many tunnels are on this road?" She should have known, and perhaps at one time she did know, but she found that many things she used to know were no longer available from her memory. She felt so old sometimes.

"There are eight. We have just passed through the fourth – King's Switch tunnel."

"Fourth? Are you certain? Was that not just the second?"

"Quite Certain. You may have slept through the first two, near Richland Furnace."

M nearly blushed at being caught napping. Had she snored? She glanced down at the schedule in her lap. Richland Furnace was not there. "Where was Richland Furnace?"

"A few miles west of Hamden. They aren't very long tunnels. You did not miss anything."

He and Merritt had, in fact, done everything possible to insure she missed everything between Chillicothe and Hamden. That particular section of the road required several deep cuts. Cuts, no matter how deep, did not seem to bother Miss Warner, but where there are deep cuts there are likely to be, conversely, high trestles and bridges, as a train moves between one hill or mountain to the next. In addition, where the road was not cutting through these hills or mountains or trestling between them, it was clinging to the sides of Alpine-like cliffs. It was far better for Miss Warner to pass unknowing through such lands, and, as soon as Merritt alerted Argent that she was napping, the two men put into motion – quietly – efforts to keep her in that state. Merritt stepped into the common area of the car where the porter was given the strictest instructions to keep himself and any others well clear of the apartment – they were not to be disturbed for any reason short of murder or some other extreme calamity. As for the men themselves, all speaking (even whispering ceased), and papers on the table were moved with the greatest care. Anything that might shift or rattle was muffled with the small towels provided near the water ewer. The windows remained shut and curtained, despite the growing warmth. Eventually, the warmth had prompted them to very carefully remove their coats, placing them on the backs of their chairs. There had only been one moment of concern, when Argent's watch – never properly re-secured to his vest after M returned it to him – went flying across the table, knocked from its loose perch when Argent was removing his coat. Both men stood silent and still in panicked worry and hope that M would not be roused by the noise. They all three survived the moment, and now it only remained to keep M as ignorant of these terrors in her wakefulness as she had been when asleep.

"Of course not. There is nothing to miss in a tunnel – it is all black and sightless." M consulted her schedule again. "So there are four more tunnels. Are they also not very long?"

"Two are very modest in length, but two are somewhat longer."

M seemed to consider the tunnels on the road, but Argent had observed her as they had entered and exited the last two tunnels (she had indeed been dozing near Hamden). She had not exhibited any fear or trepidation. He suspected the true focus of her present concentration was not tunnels, but bridges and trestles. Every railroad had to grapple with keeping its line as straight and level as possible, and every railroad had its bridges and trestles and even tunnels. Argent had to admit, however, that the M&C seemed to have more than its share of bridges and trestles, and after Athens there would be even more harrowing high structures, sharper curves, and heavier grades. It would do well for M to doze those last forty or more miles. Perhaps he could persuade her to join him in a drink sometime before Athens.

"Tunnels should be listed on these schedules." What M would truly like to see listed were all the bridges and trestles.

"Because you prefer to see what's coming."

Argent almost winced at Merritt's intrusion into the conversation. Like M, Argent had thought Merritt himself was dozing in his chair at the opposite windows. M, however, met the barb head on. "Anyone with even a modicum of intelligence would. Surprises are only enjoyable for children, and possibly on birthdays and Christmas and at public entertainments." Returning her attention to Argent, she asked, "Do you find in working with Mr. Merritt that he enjoys surprises?"

"He certainly enjoys creating them."

The whistle announced the approach of another town. M consulted her schedule. "Is this Marshville already?"

"No, this is Mineral City; but we won't be stopping."

M thought Argent must have been mistaken, for the train was slowing. It did not stop, however, although it did pass a depot. M thought 'city' was a rather grand designation for the town; maybe it was a grand hope.

Marshville, the next stop, was not much bigger, but the depot facilities were somewhat better. As the train pulled onto the siding at the depot, M stood, signaling once again her intention to visit with Emmett and to personally assess his accommodations. Once again, Merritt and Argent rose heavily to their feet, anticipating the volatile reaction Miss Warner would surely have once informed of Emmett's absence. Merritt was only just realizing the folly of postponing the inevitable, of allowing Miss Warner's acerbic disappointment full play in public, as was certain to happen — she would storm from the car to the depot to demand a west-bound ticket, all the while blustering (admittedly justifiably) about deceptions and outright lies and broken promises. They would do better to tell her long before a station stop, to allow time for her anger and resentment to diminish somewhat. Merritt was about to reveal the ugly truth when Argent exclaimed with unjustifiable enthusiasm, "Oh, look, here's the prize-package boy!"

The prize-package boy. The bane of all train travelers, except possibly parents and their children and ignorant immigrants. It was not only the cheat of his trade – promising valuable prizes or even money hidden in over-priced packages of candy, cigarettes, or other sundry goods – it was also the shrill voice and sly, knowing looks of the boy himself, but most of all it was the impudent persistence in shoving his packages and bundles under one's nose at every opportunity as he prowled the aisles of the cars. Merritt and Argent, as veteran travelers of the rail, were well acquainted with these often flamboyant boys, and it had been one of the pleasures of this trip to have a private apartment on the car, the porter of which kept these boys at bay. But now, Argent had spotted one on the platform outside, surrounded not by children clamoring for candy, but by men eagerly buying the special 'literature' that seasoned male travelers liked to surreptitiously peruse in the water closet on these long through-routes.

M glanced out the window at the group of men crowding around a young boy, insisting on his attention as they waved money at him.

"What are they buying?"

Merritt leveled an almost loathsome look at Argent.

"They may buy almost anything. Newspapers, cigarettes, candy, coffee, tea – anything a weary traveler may find he needs at the moment. Usually the young man walks the aisles —"

"Stalks the aisles."

M considered Merritt. Whatever excitement Argent held for the boy, Merritt did not share it.

Argent began again. "Usually the young man or boy sells his wares in the cars, sometimes even riding the train to the next town where he will pick up a train going back to his starting point. But, see, this young man is so favored that the people have gone to the platform to search him out." Argent then looked pointedly at Merritt. "I'm certain we could persuade him to visit us here, away from the crowds and the smoke and dirt of the platform."

Merritt remained unmoved. He understood the ruse Argent was constructing, but Merritt detested the prize-package boys. He regained his seat and left Argent to make the arrangements.

M had continued watching the scene. The men were scattering as children were crowding with their weary parents, searching for some distraction for the next stretch of travel in a crowded, hot box full of strangers and bored restless children. She did not realize Argent had left the car until she saw him push his way through the children and glaring parents to speak to the boy. The boy nodded avidly, holding up one finger indicating his intention to follow in a minute (or two – the candy business was good).

Argent returned to their apartment, slightly flushed with his hurry and excitement. He nodded once at M and once at Merritt. "He will be here presently."

There was a knock at the platform door and Argent admitted the boy, laden with his wares. He saw M and then glanced at both Merritt and Argent, and a look crossed his face, a look that M could not identify. She instantly disliked this boy. For his part, the boy immediately approached M, speaking in a nasally voice and in an almost prissy, simpering manner. He did not act like any boy M had ever known, and not at all like any of her brothers.

M was showing signs of confusion and alarm as the boy pressed ever forward while M pulled as far away as possible, without resorting to taking a step backwards. He was showing her small bundles of candy and stationery, soaps and small towels. He spoke without pauses or stops, never allowing M the chance to either accept or reject his offers. Only once did he pause to pull from his filthy jacket a small bottle. "Perfume for the lady." He was almost sneering as he said it.

Argent (and reluctantly, Merritt) had allowed the boy his performance — he was, after all, keeping M from discovering Emmett's absence. But when the boy pressed M with the perfume and promised her a valuable gem inside, though he could not promise the type or color, Merritt stood and then stepped between M and the boy.

"I would like to see your Gift Enterprise license."

"License, sir?"

"You are attempting to engage the young lady in gambling – offering her the chance of something valuable in exchange for an incommensurate amount of money. You are in essence asking her to place a bet."

"She is getting something in exchange."

"You are selling chances; it is a cheap lottery. Show me your license or leave."

The boy replaced the perfume in his pocket, sneered at both M and Merritt, then left, brushing past Argent as he passed. M had never seen anyone so young act so rudely to adults, to men. She wondered that neither man offered to thrash him.

The sound of the whistle reminded M of her original intention to see Emmett, but now the train was pulling out of town and she had missed another opportunity. She realized she was still standing when Merritt spoke to her.

"I apologize for the behavior of that boy."

M nodded, then realized both Merritt and Argent were waiting for her to take her seat before they themselves would sit. M regained her chair and resumed her observations out the window. She was aware of some conflict brewing between Merritt and Argent. They were not arguing, or even speaking, but she was aware that their movements had taken on the character of anger. Papers were being pushed back and forth between them at the table, and they were being pushed back and forth with great heat. She wondered – without much real interest – how often the two men quarreled when traveling together.

Several miles later, after passing between concealing bluffs, Athens burst upon them, coming into sudden view just before crossing the Hockhocking River over a covered bridge. Athens itself sat upon a hill in a bend of the river, with a commanding view of the narrow river valley below it and the rolling hills all around it. Argent consulted his watch; they were remarkably on time.

M almost hesitated to rise, conscious of failed previous attempts to reach Emmett. As she did so, however, the disagreement that had been brewing between the two men boiled over the table to puddle at M's feet. Merritt rose and quickly moved to intercept her, and against Argent's obvious disapproval, broached the subject of Emmett.

"M, there is no need to leave the car; we are stopping only for a few moments before beginning the last stretch before reaching Belpre."

"All the more reason to hurry." M moved to pass Merritt, but again he blocked her way.

"There is no need to hurry, no reason to see Emmett. He is not on this train."

Argent had not moved from where he stood at the table, but his stance and face said he wanted to be anywhere but where he stood. M gazed at him, almost disdainfully, fully understanding his discomfort and willing to let him suffer it indefinitely. She turned, however, to address Merritt. "He is not on the train."

There was no hysteria in her voice, no incredulity, no anger. There was, however, below the flat statement a low threatening challenge.

Merritt held her with his own gaze, his own challenge. "He is not on this train."

M blinked slowly, once, twice. Somehow, she gave the impression of having held her stare. "He is on some train, then."

"Yes. He is on a freight train, somewhere behind us. He, and our own horses, will rejoin us in Parkersburg."

"How far behind us?" It was her first question, but it was spoken with that low threat that was lurking in her voice. Argent found that, perhaps, the expected histrionics would be preferable. He did not care for the slow rising fury that M was building to. He had thought her reaction would be to Emmett's absence, but he was slowly realizing that her reaction was to their duplicity in the matter. They should have told her long ago. Far past Cincinnati, of course, but long ago.

Merritt hesitated, but he, too, knew the real, the immediate, object of M's rising wrath. Lying further would make matters worse. They would let her give voice to her anger here in the car and accept the stony silence that would surely follow for the next forty miles. She had been mostly silent the entire day, but Merritt was beginning to discern the varying textures to M's silences. "We don't know. Our last-minute change in plans to take the day train upset arrangements made for the horses; there was no room for them on this train. We only know that they were to be sent on the next train with the available and proper arrangements. Conditions for Emmett's travel were made very clear to the agent. He is traveling well." Then, in a moment of exasperation over the fuss made for a horse, Merritt added, "He is traveling better than most of the people on this train."

M ignored the implied censure, but she did acknowledge the efforts behind the circumstances that made the censure even possible. "How long have you known that he would travel separately?"

Argent heard the shift in her tone and hazarded to answer her. "We were alerted to the problem as we were leaving the hotel this morning. We simply could not delay leaving Cincinnati any longer."

M realized the truth of the matter and her own part in the circumstances that led to this moment. She had been as much cause for delay in Cincinnati as had the men and their work, and her outburst in Covington over Emmett's absence then had prompted these men to delay telling her. She realized that Merritt and Argent were afraid of her reaction. She should be ashamed at having cowed them, but she enjoyed knowing that it was possible.

"No. Of course you couldn't." Her stance changed, and her voice shifted again so that there was nothing left of the challenge. "How will you know of his arrival?"

This was not at all what the men had expected. The panic and desperation of Covington had never surfaced, and the lurking anger had dissipated, rather quickly. Miss Warner may remain silent until Belpre, but it would not be stony, not because of Emmett.

"Freight agents at both Scott's Landing and Belpre have been alerted to the situation. Once at Belpre, Emmett is to be commended to the personal care of the depot agent there, at which time the agent will telegraph us in Parkersburg, and one of us will personally escort Emmett across the river. When we ourselves reach Belpre this evening, Merritt or I will confirm with the agent his instructions."

M nodded her acquiescence, but again moved to pass Merritt. Though he did not attempt to block her, neither did he give way.

"The train will be starting again very soon. It is dangerous to leave now, it is dangerous to rush to return to the train. Many of these deaths you have read about are people attempting to board a moving train."

M was perfectly aware of this; the official and most often ascribed cause of death among railroad officials was 'want of caution.' She was aware of men losing their footing as they grabbed for car platforms (or, in the case of hobos, the flooring of open freight cars) and falling under the great iron wheels in motion. She had every confidence in her own footing, but she did not tell Merritt this, nor did she intend to try her luck.

"I only wish to walk the length of the depot platform. I will return at the first whistle."

This time Argent moved to intercept her. "I assure you, there is no time for even that. We surely will be moving immediately; the train has already stayed overlong."

"I promise you I am able to return in time and mount the steps to the platform without aid – you need not wait for me beyond the comfort of the car."

Both Merritt and Argent had read newspaper accounts of men and boys and, sometimes, women being dragged under the wheels of a car while attempting to board a train, no matter how slowly it was moving. In the case of women, even if one should achieve a firm footing, her skirts often became her undoing, as they could catch on almost anything, impeding movement and becoming the means of being pulled under the car. In all instances, death was a mercy to being hopelessly mangled, sometimes dying after hours or even days in agony and after having undergone amputations of the damaged limbs. But in Miss Warner's case, Argent was almost as equally concerned with the very real possibility of her using this opportunity to conveniently "miss" the train as it pulled out of the station. She had come only very reluctantly on this trip and now that her beloved Emmett had been separated from her, she might feel justified in abandoning her promise to meet with Grant in Washington. The more he considered it, the more he thought that M had taken the news of Emmett's absence rather too well.

As these things coursed through Argent's mind, M had not moved, but considered him, a challenging look coming across her face as an unpleasant thought stole across her mind. "Am I, then, your prisoner? That I must ask your permission for all my movements?"

Argent was somewhat stunned by the accusation implied in the question, but Merritt answered instantly. "Of course not; but we are charged with your safety, you are our responsibility." Even as he spoke, however, Merritt was distracted by the scene outside M's window. A small crowd had gathered and was growing by the moment. From his few excursions beyond their apartment to the common seating of the car, Merritt recognized more than a few of their fellow travelers. Though Athens was a growing town with an expanding commerce, and therefore an expanding traveling population, the crowd outside seemed incommensurate. And the train was now long overdue to be resuming its schedule.

Now Argent was at the window. "Something is out of sorts."

M took the opportunity provided by the distraction to reach the door to the platform. "Allow me to discover what is out of sorts." She was down the steps of the platform before either man had reacted.

Just as she reached the ground, the porter reached the steps. M asked the man the cause for the delay and for the milling crowd. Rather than answer M, however, the man looked beyond her and up to Merritt and Argent, now standing on the platform of the car.

"There has been a collision on the tracks ahead. The delay is expected to be lengthy. We are asking everyone to leave the train so that it may move ahead to make room for following trains. If you will, please quickly retrieve anything you may want or need from the car. It will be pulling off as soon as I alert the engineer that everyone has been notified."

"May I retrieve something from my trunk in the baggage car?" If the wait was going to be lengthy, M would like the option of reading, somewhere alone and secluded, without Messrs. Merritt and Argent peering over her shoulder and commenting at every turn of a page.

Now the porter did acknowledge M. "I'm afraid not, Miss." And without further explanation the porter turned to struggle back through the crowd to inform the engineer that he was free to move the train.

The crowd was not so great as it was condensed. The depot at Athens was disappointingly small for the number of trains and passengers moving through it each day. It was therefore easy for a small suggestion (made by one or two hack drivers waiting for fares) to circulate quickly. The suggestion was to spend the time visiting some of the nearby attractions. Small groups were forming and making arrangements with the hack drivers to tour Athens, with the assurance that some means of communicating with the depot be put in place so that the travelers would be returned in time to board the train when it was ready to leave.

The only tour M cared to make was of a bookstore and possibly a quiet park or cemetery in which to read. Being denied access to her trunk in the baggage car had denied M the possibility of retrieving a book. It also had denied her the possibility of retrieving a coin or two with which to buy a book or even a newspaper. She was going to have to contrive some way of having money about her person without the added responsibility of carrying some handbag or reticule. She had lost enough of those already.

Merritt had apparently slipped away at some point, for he returned with news that he had procured a conveyance and driver to take them to some points of interest in the town. Argent looked dubious – not only was he aware of Miss Warner's aversion of crowds, he was also aware of Merritt's penchant for finding activities and entertainments that were off the beaten path. At both M's and Argent's hesitation, Merritt assured them they would not be following the great herds going all at once to the university or to parade past the residences of the wealthiest Athenians, although that was always a possibility after the crowds had vacated those places.

"Where do you propose we go in the meantime?"

Merritt instead addressed M. "Do you like diamonds, Miss Warner?"

She was thankful that, at least in public, he had put away calling her "M." She was beginning to regret accepting this moniker, but he had been kind after her time in jail when her proper name had left her feeling so raw. She found that she was beginning to think of herself as M, as an indefinable sound than as a definable person.

"Not in particular. I prefer a stone with color, but I do appreciate the sparkle."

"It is the sparkle I have in mind."

Argent sighed. There was no help for it when Merritt was in one of his punning moods. With his hand, Argent signaled that Merritt should lead them to their conveyance and sparkling destination.

Merritt led them across the tracks to a street corner where awaiting them was an old man holding the reins to what looked like a simple farm wagon somewhat renovated to resemble a landau carriage. Though the driver's seat was unadorned, the two opposing seats in the back were padded and covered. The exterior wood, though rough cut, unsanded, and of simple construction, had been painted a glossy black, and the spokes of the wheels had been painted red. Merritt was pleased to see M smile at their private carriage.

There was no door in the side, so Mr. Hiram Evans, as Merritt took pains to introduce him, helped M over the low side panel into the 'pit' of the carriage, leaving her to choose her seat while he took his place at the reins at the front of the wagon. Merritt and Argent clambered in after her, taking the seat opposite her, their backs to Mr. Evans.

As their wagon pulled away from the tracks, M looked down the street to her right to see one carriage or coach after another pull off in another direction. The crowd was, indeed, going in great herds to some common destination.

M was delighted with the ride – the day was mild, she was out of the train car, with both the wind and sun on her face, and they were heading to a surprise destination. After two or three turns – ever away from the depot – Mr. Evans settled on a street for a few blocks before turning northwards away from town. M did her best to ignore the two men before her, but at this last turn she noticed Argent turn pointedly to Merritt with a stern question on his face; to which Merritt merely smiled.

They reached the Hockhocking River at the north of town, where the road ended in a rough but serviceable landing of sorts. Mr. Evans led them, without a word, down to a waiting boat, where he exchanged his driving duties for those of a river pilot. Argent begged Mr. Evans' patience while he consulted with Mr. Merritt.

Pulling Merritt off some distance for privacy, Argent scolded Merritt. "We are already 45 minutes from the depot, and now we are to cross the river as well? And how will we know when to return to the depot in time to board the train? Where is it that you are taking us?"

Merritt smiled again. "We will not miss the train – we have hours to wait. I spoke to the engineer. The wreck east of here is fairly serious – two freight trains collided and most of the cars are off the track. I was assured it would take a great deal of time to clear the tracks and get at least one new engine to the site. And, Giles, even if we miss the train, we will gain indulgence from Miss Warner. If the engineer is right, we will be here long enough for Emmett's train to catch up with us."

"He will still have to travel on the other train."

"Agreed, but M will be relieved to know that he is right behind us. You know, I believe she meant to leave us after we told her about Emmett."

"She may intend on leaving us yet. Her trunk, if you will recall, is where she keeps her money. I think she meant to retrieve her funds and part ways with us."

"I had the same thought. So why tarry in town where there are stage coaches to take her to depots west of here or steamers to take her to the

Ohio where she could take passage home? Mr. Evans picks up a little extra money, when not in his fields, carrying travelers from the depot to the hotels in town. I offered a little extra if he could take us somewhere less tempting to M."

"And where is that?"

"I don't want to ruin the surprise." Merritt, confident that he had won Argent's approval, returned to the boat, where he and Mr. Evans helped M into the boat.

Argent followed only a little reluctantly. Merritt made perfect sense, of course, but Merritt should have consulted with Argent before making all these decisions.

M seemed at ease in the boat, even to dangling her hand in the water. Mr. Evans rowed evenly and without hurry. Their boat was not long in crossing – the Hockhocking was not a wide river, certainly not as wide as the Ohio at Louisville, which was M's measure of all other rivers. To her, the Hockhocking was something of a large creek.

On the northern bank was a more extensive and less primitive landing where Mr. Evans tied up their boat. He got out first, then helped M, Merritt, and Argent out in turn. He then said simply, "Wait here," before leaving them standing on a small wharf of some kind, disappearing into a small building, one of many buildings of what was some manufactory concern. He returned with a younger man, far better dressed than Mr. Evans. The younger man introduced himself, though M did not catch his name; she had been watching Mr. Evans leave their little group to sit on the low wall of the landing and to pull out his pouch of tobacco and roll a cigarette. He reminded her of her grandfather – her Cincinnati grandfather – when he would sit on the back of a wagon at his house and roll a cigarette in much the same way. He had been a railroad man and he had been injured during his working days, losing one finger and the parts of two others. It had fascinated her to watch him roll his cigarettes in one hand, as deft as if he had all five fingers. She felt Merritt touch her shoulder as the old man said to him, "I'll wait here for you."

Merritt's surprise was a tour of the Herrold salt works. Although she couldn't be certain, the salt works appeared to have its back to the river. Whatever its true orientation, the operations closest to the river is where they began their tour. Their guide took them first to the well where brine was drawn up from hundreds of feet below. The well itself was continually being deepened by means M did not understand but which required very high poles supporting great chains and ropes positioned in a tent-like fashion.

As they were led to the larger buildings M felt the ground crunch beneath her feet. She was walking on salt deposits from brine that was most likely slopped over buckets on its way to the great drying furnaces. The ground glimmered in the sunshine, and M suspected this was the sparkle that Merritt had promised her.

There were several buildings on the grounds, but they were all dominated by one very long, two- or three-story building. From the center of the roof rose a large and tapered stone chimney, belching black smoke. There were other chimneys or smokestacks throughout the works, all of them in use, pouring black smoke into the blue sky.

M was not much interested in the production of salt, but she was glad to be away from the train and the town and the crowds. She was outside on a pleasant day and she was not sitting. She had not known sitting could be so wearisome. And if Merritt and Argent were not concerned about returning to the train, neither was she; it had occurred to her that if they missed their own train, she would insist on waiting for Emmett.

M followed their guide to the various areas of the salt works. The fires that fed steam to the great pumps and breathed heat under the kettles of brine needed constant feeding. They were never blown out, even on Sundays, unless the sheriff should bring the Sunday laws to the attention of the owners. Great heaps of coal from the nearby coal mines fed these fires. Sweaty men tended the rows of kettles settled into snug openings in a hearth of some kind that stretched the entire length of the building. The heat emanating from this building kept their group from actually entering the building, but M could see the men bending over the low pots, dipping out salt with long ladles. This damp salt, she heard the guide say, was spread in large grainer pans for further drying. They next watched men pack the salt into barrels, which were made on the premises. These barrels would soon be carried on the Columbus & Hocking Valley Railroad being built into Athens. A road bed for private tracks and a spur was already being prepared between the salt well and the buildings in anticipation of the completion of the C&HV, expected sometime this summer. Until that time, the barrels were shipped down the Hockhocking to the canal for distribution from Athens.

They were about to recross this roadbed to return to Mr. Evans and their waiting boat when Merritt said, "One moment, please." He spoke privately to their guide, who smiled and nodded his assent to some favor. Merritt rejoined the group. "I believe I owe you some diamonds, Miss Warner. If you'll follow me."

The guide led them into and then up the stairs of a small two story building just across from the well. The guide beckoned her to the back window where she could look down on the well and out across the river. From this height and angle, the salt on the ground did indeed sparkle like diamonds in the sun, far brighter than the mere glimmer she had noticed earlier.

The salt announced itself before she even reached the window. The day here was bright and clear, far from the clouds of Cincinnati, and the sun struck the salty crystals in such a way that the air was dazed with their reflection. Intense white pinpricks of light peppered the air all around. The yellow sun was dull in comparison. M had to look away, but was left with, strangely, black pinpricks in her vision where there had once been the white sparkle of the salt.

M blinked once, twice, three times to clear her vision. Merritt was watching her, awaiting her verdict. It had been beautiful, but blinding and harsh. The air around it, like the ground all around, had been bleached by the sheer intensity of the reflection. It lacked inspiration. To Merritt, however, she said, "Thank you. Salt enhances everything."

It was a less than gracious response to the obvious effort to engage her, but Merritt did not seem to take offense. Argent took his turn at the window, but his attention strained to see far into Athens; he was worried about missing the train.

They recrossed the river and again took up seats in Mr. Evans' wagon to return to Athens, only a mile away. Argent was intent on discussing arrangements upon their return to the depot. Merritt listened politely, but without comment or interruption, and M disregarded the conversation altogether. She returned to her thoughts on the salt sparkle. Why had it disappointed her? Sunlight never disappointed her. Quite the opposite, it always thrilled her, even in winter when it was so muted and short-lived. Nothing inspired her to hope or gave her a sense of unbending vitality as the approach of spring, as the strengthening of the sun. The sparkling salt had not inspired her, not like the whirling dance of sun glinting off the creek at home or the ricochet of prism from her mother's few crystal pieces. The sun at those times had created movement in the air. The reflection from the salt had instead stunned the air, left it paralyzed and pockmarked with negative light; it had turned the air inside out, showing the reverse of the pinpricks. It had been a blunt beauty. Again she thought, it had lacked inspiration. She also thought of her conversation with Argent several days ago, when she had told him of the ice storm she had watched with her father. Why had that display of light so moved her? It was the same sun, the same principle of reflection. She had thought of it as a holy beauty; why? Because it had been inspired and inspiring. The very word implicated breath, a breathing into life. The ice had been beautiful, but the sun had inspired it to a higher beauty with searing colors and razor edges. It had given breath and at the same time what it produced had been breath-taking. Sunlight, of course, was inspired by God, it was the inspiration of God; sunlight was the Paraclete, the Holy Ghost, the Breath of God. If He could breathe life into mere ice, inspire it to higher beauty, then why could He not do the same for her, for all people? She needed to be inspired, she needed purpose. An unguarded thought flashed across her mind: she resented God in this. Then a proper sense of blasphemy swept the thought away with a prayer for forgiveness. She rubbed her temple.

"Have you a headache?"

Argent regarded her. He had evidently exhausted the subject of arrangements (travel? dinner? M wasn't clear on the exact topic), and had turned his attention to her

"No, a conundrum."

"Oh? What is the nature of this conundrum? Perhaps I can help."

"I was thinking of God. He makes my head spin." It was doubtful that anyone could help her to understand God's motives; after all, His ways are not our ways; His ways are mysterious.

"Perhaps that is not a word one should use when speaking of God." Argent shifted in his seat with disapproval.

"I hardly think God would care what He is called, as long as He is not called so in vain."

Merritt suddenly found his tongue. "Perhaps we could now see the usual sites travelers visit when in Athens. The crowds have by now surely thinned out." Merritt then turned to Mr. Evans to inform him of their new destinations.

"Merritt, we do not know the status of the trains."

Mr. Evans spoke from his seat without turning around. "The trains are going nowhere for some time yet. There has not been a whistle or bell of any kind for hours now."

This was true, though no one had realized it until Mr. Evans had given words to it. In a town where trains were an almost constant presence, the absence of that presence would be easily felt by the townspeople and even the nearby farmers. Given the lengthy silence of bell and whistle, it was certain that trains on both sides of Athens were at a standstill. Getting help to any wreck on a single-track road would require a great deal of maneuvering just to reach the wreck. Communication with stalled trains was only as fast as a man walking or riding a horse from the telegraph office to the engineer to relay instructions. Entire trains might have to be backed to the nearest siding before wrecking trains and crews could move forward to the scene of the wreck. If heavy equipment or a replacement engine was needed, that information would have to make its way back to the first telegraph station to be relayed back to the nearest facility that could provide those things. In the meantime, all other trains had to be shunted to sidings or stalled in towns until the wreck was cleared. Athens itself saw three to four passenger and three to four freight trains come through its depot every day. That could mean three or more trains idling on the tracks on either side of Athens, waiting to resume their schedules.

Argent consulted his watch – nearly half past five. What crowds they may have missed at the university or other places would surely now be congregating at the few eating houses in Athens. Argent preferred a late dinner, especially since it would allow him the opportunity to dose Miss Warner's drink. As in Cincinnati, it would be unwise to leave Miss Warner free to roam at all hours of the night, should they be obliged to spend the night in Athens. And should the train depart at some reasonable time this evening, it would be best if Miss Warner were to sleep through the next forty or more miles, considered the most dangerous and harrowing part of the entire line.

Argent realized both Merritt and Mr. Evans were waiting on him to either approve further explorations or to offer an alternative. "Have you any suggestions, Mr. Evans?"

"There is the tunnel being excavated under the cemetery. Some people find that of interest."

M was clearly interested. "A tunnel under a cemetery! Are you building catacombs? Is anyone buried there?"

"No, Miss. The tunnel was started years ago when the M&C was first building through here, but it was abandoned in order to go around the university hill. Now there is talk of taking up the tunnel again to take the M&C through the north part of town. The depot may be removed to near there."

Mr. Evans had never spoken so much. Clearly, he was interested, too, and wanted a chance to see the remains of the tunnel, on someone else's time. Both Merritt and Argent, however, thought that perhaps there were other points of interest in Athens that did not involve crawling through a massive hole or visiting burial sites; they both thought M had seen enough cemeteries for the time being. Argent suggested visiting the university, but possibly by way of a pleasant drive around town.

Mr. Evans drove them past the court house, a relic of some of Athens' earliest days. It was as plain a building as M had seen and clearly in need of replacing, but Mr. Evans seemed proud of it. And he drove them past some of Athens better residences – Judge Welch's place on Court Street, the home (also on Court Street) of the venerable General Grosvenor (commander of the 18th Ohio Volunteers, and a veteran of the entire war), the residence of Colonel Van Vorhes (a long-time state legislator), and a pleasant drive admiring the homes on College Street.

They passed the Presbyterian church, which prompted Mr. Evans to rate the various religious buildings in town according to architecture. The Methodist Church on College Street was the finest, followed by the Presbyterian house of worship, leaving for last "the poor clapboard shack, west, over on High Street, where the Irish carried on their prayers and rites." Without doubt, Mr. Evans was neither Catholic nor Irish.

At the end of their short tour of Athens proper – a mere four blocks that boasted, nonetheless, some very presentable buildings and homes – they at last arrived at what was arguably the most notable place in town: the university. Mr. Evans, however, was content to sit and smoke in his carriage while M, Merritt and Argent wandered through the three buildings on the college green. M seemed to genuinely enjoy wandering the open rooms of the college. Once outside, she wandered the beautiful campus green among the trees. Merritt was content to let M roam on her own, and in that vein, he joined Mr. Evans on his wagon for a companionable smoke. Argent was willing to allow Miss Warner some latitude in her wanderings, but when she drifted to the back of the Office Edifice he followed, quickening his pace until he caught sight of her again.

She was heading for the farthest corner of the campus, towards the tracks and the river and, as it happened, their own train, which had pulled away from the depot. Argent caught up with her as she was about to cross a wide, undefined area of road.

"Where are you headed?"

M continued walking, her destination fairly obvious – the South bridge over the Hockhocking, leading out of town. Without turning to acknowledge his presence, M informed him, "There is something building over there; I saw it from the university hill. I'd like to go see."

"You mean to cross the bridge?" This hardly seemed credible, given M's fear of bridges. Argent returned to his study of bridges and Miss Warner that he had undertaken at Greenfield. The South bridge was not nearly so high, of course, but why would crossing this bridge on foot be any easier than crossing the great suspension bridge at Cincinnati, with its massive piers and sturdy deck?

M turned now to study Argent. Why did he ask that? Did he suspect her terror of some bridges? She would need to more closely guard her reaction when crossing the worst of these railroad bridges and trestles. She turned back toward the bridge. It was roofed, and the sides were covered with vertical boards. It was not very high, but the presence of the siding gave her comfort. She would walk quickly across, wander among the rising walls of the buildings being constructed, then walk quickly back again. The prospect of crossing the bridge was not insurmountably daunting.

"Yes. The place of building is not very far from the bridge. I won't be gone long."

The confusion about Miss Warner and the bridge was replaced with a growing irritation. She lacked any sense of duty or propriety, making his job that much harder. "You meant to go there alone, without consulting with Mr. Merritt or myself?"

"There was no need and there is no danger. Mr. Merritt is happily engaged with Mr. Evans, and I had thought you were content to walk the grounds." The unpleasant thought of earlier returned to her: was she their prisoner? They seemed ready to block her on any attempts to be alone.

Perhaps she should consider plans for a quiet and surreptitious retreat, just in case. "Are you also interested in the buildings?"

Something had crept into her voice; she was testing him somehow. The question was innocuous enough, but he instinctively knew that how he answered it would decide something of importance to her. He knew that she was interested in the buildings; he would match her interest.

"Indeed, yes. It is a great project undertaken by the state of Ohio. What did you mean, 'there is no danger'?" M had allowed him to join her and they were walking side by side towards the bridge.

"There is no one there." For her father, danger always meant men, strange men. The real interest M had in the buildings was their half-constructed appearance and the absence of workmen on such a fine day. Was the place abandoned, to become a mystery for some long-distant future generation, like the ruins in Greece? But Argent had not spoken of the 'great undertaking' in the past tense; it was not abandoned then. "You know its purpose then?" They had reached the passage over the tracks, an open metal bridge that led to the covered bridge.

"It is to be one of the state's asylums for the unfortunate who suffer maladies of the mind. I believe the state legislature is being petitioned for enlargement to house as many as 200 patients."

Miss Warner stopped dead in her tracks. Argent himself stopped only one step beyond her, before turning back to her. "Miss Warner?"

An insane asylum. There had been talk, near the end of the war, of sending her mother to the one in Lexington, as one son's death had followed another. She would have surely been sent there after the deaths of her remaining children, had she not herself died soon after them. And M held deep in her being a fear of such a place for herself. She heard echoes of her mother's dire whispers in the night, when M could not sleep, and of her father's sharp replies. There was such a place in Washington City. That was what her mother had wanted – her father to take her with him to Washington, to leave her at that place until he could take her home, until he himself could come home to stay, to relieve her mother of the burden of such a daughter. Now her father was gone, and there were others who would like to be relieved of her, to relieve her, in turn, of her possession of the farm. M closed her eyes. Grant could not do such a thing – what would be his authority in the matter?

"Miss Warner?"

M realized that she had left Argent waiting for a reply. "I find the venture has lost its attraction for me. But, do, continue on for your own purposes. I will return to the university and Mr. Merritt."

Argent said nothing, but returned with her, neither one speaking further.

All the eating houses in Athens were busy that night; there was no avoiding crowds no matter what time dinner was attempted. M and Argent were largely silent, but they would have been hard pressed to enter into any conversation at the table. They had been obliged, by reason of the large crowds drawn from the several trains delayed at or near Athens, to share a table with some of their fellow travelers, and it seemed that their table had attracted the most loquacious of the travelers. Merritt moved in and out of conversation with ease. He was a great favorite with the ladies, but he managed not to incite the jealousy of the men among them. The talk, of course, was of the delay of the trains and the speculation as to how much longer they would all have to wait to be on their way. Of course, all this misery could have been avoided if the M&C were double-tracked. Those men with knowledge however, relayed (almost conspiratorially) that the M&C found itself embarrassed – yet once again – financially, and a second track was out of the question as far in the future as anyone cared to speculate.

M had successfully avoided most of the food, eating a bite or two of vegetables from each course but she regretted the waste of food, and occasionally she found Argent urging her to taste this or that dish. She lasted until the fourth course, when she excused herself for some fresh air. No one suspected any other reason – in truth, the dining hall was rather ripe with the commingled odors of frustrated men and women and the aromas of several sauces and soups and fish and meat entrées. She had tried her first oyster, in the first course, and did not care for it, and oyster seemed to be all she could taste for the rest of the meal. The noise, the smell, and the lingering taste, together with her thoughts surrounding the asylum crouching half-built across the river, combined to make her a little queasy.

It was still light when Mr. Evans had dropped them off at the Brown House, but the lengthy wait between being seated and being served and the multi-course fare had taken them into the evening hours. It was dark now and M really had no destination in mind other than to leave the hotel's dining rooms. She had of course seen the look, however brief, that had passed between Merritt and Argent when she had risen to leave. She was not surprised, therefore, when one of them joined her almost immediately. It was only a matter of which one, but when Merritt announced his intention to also take the air, M was not very surprised at that either – Argent was the last to escort her, and so now Merritt would take his turn.

"Shall we walk and take in the town?"

"I believe we have already seen the town."

"Ah, but not by lamplight." Merritt took out a slender cigar, thought better of it, then returned to his coat.

M saw the movements. "Please, smoke if you like. My father always enjoyed doing so just after a meal." They had begun walking, but M did not remember if it was she who had taken the first step.

Merritt silently declined the invitation, and led her up College Street, which despite the widely-spaced residences, was fairly well-lit. The lamplighter, of course, had been through here as soon as it had turned dark, but in addition to the street lamps, the homes themselves sent soft shades of yellow light from their windows. They turned onto State Street, with its curious little bend, before turning back towards the river, down Court Street. Court Street was crowded with both buildings and people, many of them, travelers like themselves, out for a walk to pass the time until the trains should move again. The trains – their train – was now a good six hours behind card time.

"Does this happen often? Are trains delayed for so long a time?"

"Trains are often delayed, though sometimes for only a few moments, and rarely for more than an hour or two. The length of this delay is unusual, especially for this line. The M&C usually runs close to its schedule."

"Then you don't know how much longer it might be. Perhaps Emmett will catch up to us."

"Perhaps, but freight trains are required by law to go much slower than passenger trains. They go much slower than merchants care for, and engineers often feel pressure to spur their trains on to faster speeds, especially if the train has itself been delayed. Then it is a matter of regaining the schedules, which is what often leads to these wrecks: one train is running on time, but another is late and speeding to regain time, and there are these collisions and derailments. Let us stroll over to the depot and see what news is there."

Just across from the university, they turned down Union Street and made their way to the depot that handled business for both the railroad and the Hocking canal, which abruptly terminated there. Other people also thought to visit the depot in search of information, so that M was obliged to wait outside while Merritt made his inquiries within. In addition to the frustration of the delay, there seemed to be some high excitement informing the crowd, but M did not tell Merritt of it until they happened upon Argent as he himself was heading to the depot.

"What news from the depot?"

"We will be another several hours yet. There is other news as well." Merritt sounded ominous, and Argent did not seem disposed to inquire into the matter. The two men seemed able to understand each other with a mere look or a few words.

M, however, was bursting to tell her news, but Merritt's mood as he had exited from the depot had suggested he wished silence. It was in deference to his mood that M did not speak of the news tossed about on the depot platform and beyond. But now Merritt had broached the subject, whether Argent was interested or not.

"You mean the escaped prisoners? One of them is quite hardened, by all accounts told at the depot."

Argent muttered under his breath, "That jail is a sieve."

M was disappointed in Argent's dull reception of her news. Moreover, and though she could not clearly see his face, a shift in his stance suggested disapproval of her enthusiasm for the story. She continued in spite of her dull audience.

"There was a fire in the northwest part of town, but when the men arrived to confront the fire, it had already been put out. Apparently, it had been little more than a campfire in someone's yard, but some of the men who had gone to help were guards at the jail. It was suggested that one of the guards lives in that area and was concerned for his property and family, naturally enough. And in the absence of the guards there was a jailbreak."

Merritt finally acknowledged M's news. "If a desperado is running about loose, we should end our walk and make arrangements for the evening."

"The hotels are all full, and even those residents willing to take in strangers can take no more."

M was secretly grateful they would not be spending the night in a hotel – she had developed a distinct dislike for them – though Argent seemed more distraught about it than she thought the situation merited. "The train is comfortable enough, surely, for one night. And when the trains are ready to move, we will already be on board, and won't have to fight the crush to leave the hotels."

Argent seemed relieved at the suggestion, or, M wondered, relieved that he had not been obliged to forward the suggestion. They all agreed to wait out the delay together in their apartment on the train. Others unfortunate enough to be denied room at the hotels had also decided to spend the night in their seats on the train. It would be a miserable night for those people in common seating, with no room to stretch one's legs, and children restless or crying, and snoring sleepers, and the inevitable war of the windows, with those who are hot opening them and those who are cold closing them. M almost felt guilty at her own, comfortable and secluded arrangements. The thought then occurred to her that, comfortable and secluded as their apartment was, she would still be in company with these men, and the thought of several more hours of conversation nearly panicked her.

Merritt returned to the depot to purchase some newspapers, and Argent escorted M to the train. The porter was not on duty, but the apartment was unlocked, so they let themselves in, Argent lighting every lamp. M immediately reclaimed her chair, but Argent remained standing, clearly uneasy. M sought for some tidbit of conversation to fill the awkward moments. "Did you enjoy the rest of your meal?" A tidbit indeed.

"Yes. I'm sorry you were unable to stay. The fresh air seems to have done you some good."

"This car could use some fresh air."

The apartment had become stuffy during the hours of delay. M stood to open the window nearest her, but this simple event seemed to intensify Argent's unease. "Perhaps night air should be avoided."

M nearly lost her patience. "Heavens, Mr. Argent! This morning's air was unhealthful and now the evening air is unhealthful. Do you approve of breathing at all? I sleep with the windows open at home much of the time."

"I am very fond of breathing, but the Hocking has only recently overflowed here, and it is wise to avoid the miasmas of rivers in general and of marshy lands in particular."

M suspected there was something else behind the desire to keep the windows closed, but she left the window closed and regained her seat. M reflected on Argent's speech – he spoke well, in a professorial manner that occasionally slipped into some regional accent and dialect, though she wasn't familiar with it (in truth, she wasn't familiar with any accent or dialect but her own, that of Louisville and Jefferson County). Sometimes he used strange words or used words in a strange way. Just now, for instance, he said Hocking, instead of Hockhocking, as if he was at liberty to alter a word to his own liking.

They were not as near to the river as Argent alluded. At some point during the day, in deference to the canal traffic which was not affected by the railroad's woes, the train had pulled away from the little station and did indeed rest quietly on the very banks of the river. Sometime after dark, however, a freight train had arrived at the depot, unloaded the appropriate freight for Athens and took on what Athens had to give, then it, too, pulled away from the depot, nudging the passenger train further along the tracks. The freight train was much longer than the passenger train, so that the latter was obliged to pull completely around the back of the university, nearly half-way around the hill, which not only blocked passage on Vine Street, but also placed the very front of the train on the Currier property. Every engineer in the M&C's employ knew of the Currier sisters and their aggressive opposition to the presence of the tracks on their property, despite a generous right-of-way settlement forged during the waning days of the war. There was no love lost between the M&C and the Currier women. The engineer of their passenger train, therefore, pulled completely around the bend to move off Currier property, finally to rest near the oxbow curve in the river.

They were nearly a block away from the river, measuring by city standards, but apparently even this distance proved inadequate for Argent's fear of miasmas. M was beginning to consider him somewhat timid, if not delicate.

Merritt returned with a basket filled with his purchases. In addition to every paper printed in Athens and brought in by the railroad, there was a small cake of some kind, a bottle of wine, and a silly gift for M – a small pouch of salt.

"Genuine Athens salt, to help you remember our time here in Athens."

"My memories should be salty?"

"Enhanced."

"I shall sleep with it under my pillow every night."

Merritt merely smiled at M's less than enthusiastic reaction. "It is somewhat stuffy in here." Neither M nor Argent said anything as Merritt opened every window in the apartment. Merritt then unpacked the basket, first withdrawing the bottle of wine before carefully lifting the wrapped cake from its secure position in the basket, and finally dropping the newspapers and the latest *Harper's* magazine in a heap on the table.

Answering Argent's unasked question, Merritt explained, "I saw the porter on the road, and explained our need for plates, forks, and glasses. He will be here as soon as he has finished his business in town," his business in town being a certain young lady, one of several young ladies he visited during stops on the road. He was taking advantage of this extended stop to make an extended visit.

Though Argent knew the point of the wine – Merritt, too, did not care for the idea of M wandering Athens at night (especially now that escaped prisoners might be lurking about, waiting for the trains to start, hoping for a ride out of town), and wine was the most innocuous way to slip M the chloral – but he was curious about the cake. "Are we celebrating something?"

"I sleep better after a glass of wine." Argent looked levelly at Merritt; he need not belabor the obvious. "And since M and I did not finish our meal, I thought we could at least enjoy a little dessert."

M was not at all averse to dessert, but this presented one more incident where she must dodge the offer of food and found that she hoped the porter's business in town would delay him indefinitely. In the meantime, M picked up the *Harper's* magazine and the men each picked a paper, and they read in comfortable silence. Little by little, however, sounds from outside began to intrude. Those people who were obliged to spend the rest of their wait in the cars were soon weary of their seats. The men, at least, left the cars and were congregating outside, some standing in circles of smoke, enjoying an evening cigarette away from complaining females in the cars, and others sitting on crates or barrels or whatever else they could furtively borrow from the baggage car, also collected in circles, playing cards. The smokers, of course, were divided between the area around the baggage cars and the area to the very back of the train, having been chased away from the intervening cars by those same complaining females who had ousted them from the cars in the first place. The card players naturally sought the back of the train as, when inside, they sought the back of rooms and the back parlors for their play.

The porter finally came, bringing with him plates and forks (and a knife) for the cake and glasses for the wine. The ate their cake at the table, with the bursts of laughter and groans from the card players and the smoke from the smokers wafting in through the windows. M made a great mess of her plate of cake, occasionally putting the fork to her mouth, but tasting as little as possible. It would have made things so much easier if she could tell the men that it was Lent and that therefore she was fasting; but her father had told them all that to announce such things was to behave as the hypocrites in the Bible, who wanted everyone to know they were fasting. She would just have to do her best to join their meals without actually eating.

Though the wine bottle was on the table with the wineglasses, where the porter had arranged them, Argent felt the need to stand to open the bottle. Moreover, he made a pointless circuit of the table to reach the wine bottle, lightly squeezing Merritt's shoulder as he passed behind his chair. After a short moment, Merritt also rose, going to one of the windows to look down on the card players below.

Argent poured the wine, but as he began to pour the third glass, M waved him off with her hand. "None for me, thank you." Wine with dinner was acceptable, but to drink afterwards during Holy Week was surely a serious breach in her fasting obligations. M idly wondered how many other breaches she had committed with drink this Lent. She must do better.

"Nonsense – it will be good for the digestion."

M shook her head, and to underscore her decision, she joined Merritt at the window. Argent poured the chloral into her glass before pouring the wine into it. In deference to her wishes, he did not fill the glass.

Merritt briefly left M to gather his own glass and the half-filled glass meant for M. "I think they are playing five-card stud poker." As he spoke he handed M her glass as if it were settled that she was going to drink it.

M absently accepted it as she continued watching the card play below, all resolution to abstain already forgotten.

"What is that – stud poker?" M sipped her wine; it tasted salty.

"It's a very popular game. I first played it a few years ago. Argent, who was it that taught us?"

"I taught you."

Merritt turned from the window, astonished at Argent's answer. "Really! I thought it was someone in the army. Who taught you?"

"Someone in the army."

M suddenly drew back from the window, blushing. Merritt looked out and saw the reason – she had been spotted at the window and now several men were looking there. Merritt waved at the men, then pulled the curtain shut. There was another burst of laughter outside, and M was sure it was at her expense. She found she needed the wine after all and took another, larger, sip.

Merritt moved away from the window and began extinguishing lights all around the car, except for those closest to their chairs. Argent excused himself, leaving by way of the inner door, and was gone some moments. Several moments after he returned, M heard the porter speaking to the gentlemen asking that they please remove to some other place, away from the train, as it was getting late and the ladies and their children were ready to try their luck at some sleep. The card games broke up and the smokers drifted away, so that there was silence outside and fresh air inside.

M drank the rest of her wine but found that it helped neither with digestion nor sleep. The queasiness after dinner had returned, though to a lesser degree, and she was curiously restless. She would like to take another walk, but even she knew it would be reckless to go out alone with prisoners on the loose and bored men from the train wandering the night. She resigned herself to read her magazine; the men were studiously reading the papers, occasionally laying down one only to pick up another.

They had been reading like this for perhaps half an hour when the inner door opened. M looked up to see a man standing in the doorway. Neither Argent nor Merritt had looked up from their newspapers, assuming it was their assigned porter come to change the water in the water cooler or to perform some other mundane function before finally retiring for the day, functions with which they need not bother themselves. The porter was one of the menials of the road who did not merit their attention, unless he was negligent in his duties.

The man stood there staring at M as M stared at him. He seemed to be waiting for something; if it was for M to speak, he would be waiting a very long time. Having initially considered him a stranger, M eventually recognized him as the first man to look up at her from the circle of card players; he had probably led the others in laughter. She was not about to play hostess to him here, where he did not belong. Finally, the man cleared his throat and said, "Excuse me, I had thought this the water closet."

At this Argent looked up from his newspaper and Merritt turned in his chair, both men astonished at the presence of a stranger in what was clearly a private compartment on the car. Only the greenest of travelers could have mistaken the ornate door for one to a water closet. There was something rough about the man, though he wore a fine suit. Somewhere in the back of his mind, Argent thought it strange that a man so well-dressed could be so ill-informed of the arrangements on a car. Perhaps the man was new to both his suit and traveling.

Merritt stood and said, almost challengingly, "You are mistaken. The water closet is at the other end of the car."

Rather than show embarrassment or humility at his error, the man continued to stand there a moment longer, locking eyes briefly with Merritt before turning his attention to Argent. Finally, he said, "Do excuse me," and left the car.

Merritt looked over to M before resuming his seat. She seemed completely unperturbed by the stranger's arrival, appearance, or attitude. She had, in fact, stopped studying the stranger as soon as his presence became known to Argent and himself. She was now studying Merritt, with some expectation in her gaze. He apologized for the intrusion of the stranger, then again took up his newspaper. Argent also apologized, with the promise that he would speak to the porter about restricting access to their apartment. Having been dismissed of all but the most basic duties in this apartment, the least he could do was to keep intruders at bay.

M tried to return to her reading, but her mind was restless, her thoughts both insistent and scattered, and she could not bring her mind to bear on what she read, nor could what she read bring any order to her thoughts. She finally gave up the effort and turned her head towards the window. No matter what Argent thought, the air was fresh and cool.

She was still awake, though seeing nothing, when she heard the outer door quietly open and shut. She waited to see if it was the strange man returned to murder them all, and it was as she waited that she drifted into sleep. Her scattered thoughts coalesced into a memory of the creek at home and in this memory was Merritt, and they played together in the creek, though they were both grown; he made her laugh, like Randy used to do.

12

The train finally left Athens in the early hours of the morning. Orders poured forth from the telegraph to each engineer and conductor of each train delayed by the wreck with precise instructions on order of movement, which sidings to take and at what time, in order to let opposing trains pass each other in as short a time as possible. The speeds of all the trains were closely monitored, calculated from arrival and departure times of each train as they reported in to the stations, those times telegraphed to the dispatchers at each end of the line and carefully entered into a time register. New orders, based on these changing calculated speeds, were issued to the stations, and relayed in written orders, one copy to the engineer and one to the conductor. Once received, the engineer and the conductor repeated these orders to each other, and confirmation of agreement was recorded on the written orders before the trains could proceed. All the trains were obliged to make their usual stops; it was doubtful that any passengers from yesterday's schedule were still awaiting their train, but regardless of passengers, engineers needed the latest information on train movements and to receive any new orders. These obligatory stops were actually mere pauses, the trains slowing down only long enough to be handed orders from depot platforms, a concessionary gesture in acknowledgement of the circumstances. Even larger towns were treated as mere whistle stops. The engineers were of course admonished to keep a keen eye out for trains moving out of order or out of time, and to keep a red lantern lit on the last car in the train. Any problems were to be wired as soon as possible to both Scotts Landing and Cincinnati. When in doubt, they were to find a siding, set out their lanterns, front and back, and wait for further instructions.

As sometimes happens, everything went perfectly. None of the sleeping passengers were aware of the intense scheduling involved in setting eight or more stalled trains back on card time. Any missed connections at either Cincinnati or Parkersburg, of course, could not be helped. And in one of those ironies that only happenstance can produce, the M&C night express, delayed only relatively briefly outside of Athens, remained on card time, and so arrived at Scott's Landing ahead of that line's day train, which had started out nearly twelve hours earlier.

M slept poorly – she was neither deeply asleep nor fully awake. She was aware that someone had extinguished the light near her chair and, later, all the other lights. She realized that a blanket covered her, though she did not know when she was covered. She was also aware on several occasions when the train was crossing a bridge or trestle and twice she woke to absolute darkness and an odd change in the sound of the train and knew that they had entered a tunnel. And throughout the remainder of the trip, there was always the slowing and the accelerating of the train, before and after whistles, as it dutifully bowed in passing at each town on the schedule.

The wild fluctuations in speed as the train hurried from station to station, breaking hard as it closed on the next set of orders, the obligatory pauses at each station, and the enforced idling on sidings in order to let west-bound trains pass, all combined to make the last forty and more miles between Athens and Belpre a much longer trip than normal. M did not know exactly when the train left Athens; she only knew that when Merritt was finally able to rouse her from what seemed her first real sleep of the night, it was well past dawn.

She allowed Merritt to guide her down the platform steps and towards a ferry landing. It occurred to her that it was usually Argent who performed this duty, but Argent was nowhere in sight.

"We have lost Mr. Argent." M was desperately trying to fully waken, but no amount of blinking was clearing her sight. M was certain, though, that her efforts had produced a clear and concise voice, but the words Merritt heard were slurred.

"Not at all. He will join us in Parkersburg. He has stayed behind to gather up our horses."

Argent would indeed be, ostensibly, waiting for Emmett and the other two horses, but he also remained in Belpre in order to interview some of the train personnel regarding the strange, rough-looking man in the fine suit who had let himself into their apartment.

Last night, after M had drifted off to sleep, he and Merritt had discussed the odd intrusion. Soon after the man had excused himself, Argent had himself left the car to locate the porter and to berate the man for allowing the intrusion, as he had only a short time before forcefully conveyed that the young lady in their charge found the smoke and coarse behavior of the men outside their car unsettling. The porter had been profuse in his apologies but did not know that anyone had entered the private apartment, and he regretted being absent at such a moment, but he had been alerted by a passenger to an emergency that, in the end, did not exist. This sounded too much like the earlier fire that, in the end, did not exist, and Argent asked the porter to identify the passenger who had sent him on this false errand. But the man could not be immediately found. Argent would have the porter help him search for this man among the passengers in the morning when there was light. However, as they later discussed this event, Merritt realized that M possibly recognized this man – Merritt had caught the briefest look at M, and her reaction to the man's presence was not so much surprise (and it was certainly not alarm), but one of anger and resentment. Argent, however, countered that such a reaction seemed to be Miss Warner's standard, initial response to all strangers. In the end, they decided that they were possibly overreacting to an innocent though odd mistake. Just in case, however, they locked both doors and closed the windows with only a small crack in a few of them, for air circulation.

At Scott's Landing, however, their plans changed. They had woken to the porter's soft knocks on the platform door. He brought news that the man under discussion last night was no longer on the train, and as the train had hardly fully stopped at any station or depot during the night, it was the porter's thought that this passenger had never left Athens, which was curious since his ticket, which the porter had asked the man to produce, had originated at Athens. Though the porter was whispering, and M showed no signs of waking, Argent and Merritt nevertheless stepped outside to join the porter on the platform. There was more news. Others on the train crew had seen this same passenger attempt to enter the baggage car earlier during the day. He had said he wanted to retrieve something from his luggage, but when pressed for his baggage check to confirm ownership, he was unable to produce one. Argent asked the porter to describe this man, and at the following description, both Merritt and Argent became alarmed – the passenger with the false rumor of an emergency and who had attempted to break into the baggage car was also the rough man in the fine suit who had violated the privacy of the apartment. The porter was dismissed, but Argent and Merritt remained on the car platform a few more minutes, even though they were without vest and coat, and quickly made new plans. During their investigations in Cincinnati – indeed, during any of their investigations – Merritt and Argent were obliged to carry with them some of the very counterfeit money they were working to suppress. It was used solely as means to enter the game, to induce would-be shovers to reveal themselves, who would in turn, it was hoped, help them catch confederates farther up the distribution chain and possibly even to the production and manufactory chains as well. It was kept under lock and key in a large trunk that was at that moment on the baggage car. It was only remotely possible, but possible nonetheless, that this man was aware of the presence of this counterfeit money and had attempted to steal it. But why return later with a legitimate ticket, enter the private apartment, only to leave empty-handed? They could tease that out later, but for now, once they reached Belpre, Merritt would escort Miss Warner to Parkersburg where they would board the private train there, and Argent would remain in Belpre, in order to talk personally with the train crew present at the baggage car incident, as well as to telegraph Athens for any information on this man, especially as to whether he was still in Athens. Depending on what was learned, they may have stumbled across the basis for a new investigation. Ultimately, however, that would be up to Chief Whitley.

The gallery car which had been their home for a day now would not be crossing the Ohio with the rest of the train; it would, instead, be heading back to Cincinnati on the next train that would allow it to tag along. The other passenger cars would be crossing the Ohio on the *Mount Clare*, a special car ferry, fitted with rails to accommodate the cars' wheels, and which aligned with tracks on the banks at both Belpre and Parkersburg. In Belpre, the cars (still carrying their passengers) would be gently let down the bank on rails that neatly met those of the ferry, and the cars would be pushed onto the ferry. At Parkersburg, the opposite happened: the cars were pulled off the ferry and onto tracks leading up the bank, where they were ultimately united with a waiting engine and any additional passenger cars. They would then be riding on the rails of the old Northwest Virginia Railroad, now owned and operated by the Baltimore & Ohio company. M and Merritt (and Argent), however, would not be continuing on just any B&O train.

Merritt and M rode the Paden ferry, a side-wheeler that allowed them to enter the ferry directly from the bank without that awkward passage over a wobbly gangplank that sternwheelers required. Overhearing M's remark that the river looked low, Mr. Paden assured her that there was river enough for steamboating, and moreover, that his boat could run on little more than a heavy dew.

A half-hour's crossing brought them past the wharf boat to the ferry landing at the confluence of the Ohio and the Little Kanawha, on the West Virginia shore at Parkersburg. The last of the river fog was burning away under the warming sun, revealing the great piers of the B&O bridge being built across the river. Though they had just recently risen above the surface of the river, to M they seemed like some ancient, undecipherable totem or a place of savage sacrifice to the great Ohio River.

They breakfasted at the Swann House at the very edge and corner of Parkersburg's plateau. M was fascinated with the view from their table window in the dining room. The bend in the Ohio at Parkersburg was far more conspicuous than the soft curve at Louisville.

Merritt was searching for some way to introduce the stranger in their apartment. Nothing had presented itself yet, though he was certain doing so in a crowded hotel restaurant was not the place to prick M's memories, or worse, her feelings.

"There is a much better view from Fort Boreman."

"Where is that?"

"Across the Little Kanawha. The bluff is much higher there, and the view more expansive. But first, I would like to send our grip bags to the train."

M weighed the promise of an expansive view against the possibility of missing Emmett's arrival. "I had better wait for Emmett; he may not have liked his ferry crossing."

"It is likely to be quite a while until Emmett crosses the Ohio – freight trains are given the lowest priority on the tracks, and freight trains travel at much slower speeds to begin with. Come, we can't stand on the ferry landing all day waiting for him. I'll leave word for Argent at the train to send for us as soon as he arrives."

In truth, M did not relish standing in one place for any length of time, no matter how noble the wait, nor did she care to spend any more time sitting. Her morning fog had lifted, and she was restless. Merritt arranged to have their bags sent to the train that was waiting for them at the outer station further down the Little Kanawha River, along with a note for Argent, and they started on their way to Fort Boreman.

They followed Kanawha Street from the Swann House. On one side of the street were the city blocks of Parkersburg, and on the other side was the long river depot of the Northwest Virginia Railroad, now known as the Parkersburg Branch of the B&O railroad. It was the longest depot M had ever seen, and entirely covered, for four blocks. At Market Street the depot ended, and Merritt stopped.

"Are you lost?"

"No, the way to Fort Boreman is here, across the bridge."

It was a much shorter and lower bridge than the one across the Ohio at Cincinnati, but it was a bridge nonetheless. The bridge was roofed and sided on either side of the two inner lanes, but those were for wagons and those crossing on horseback. They would cross on the pedestrian walkway, on the outside of the wall, in full view of the deep river below.

M studied the bridge and the far bank. She hated that Merritt suspected her fear and hated even more that she struggled so much with something everyone else seemed to accept without reaction whatsoever. There was no graceful way to turn back.

"Let us cross the bridge, then."

Merritt paid the toll – five cents, each – which M thought exorbitant, especially given the rather shabby state of the bridge; tolls apparently were not going into the upkeep of the thing. Merritt walked on M's right, keeping himself between M and the river. The bridge was relatively empty; they had missed the early morning business use of the bridge when men crossed the bridge from Parkersburg to their work at the tanneries, the tobacco factory, and the oil rectifying plants. There was still the occasional pedestrian crossing either way, and they heard from the dark tunnel of the bridge on the other side of the wall the occasional slow rumbling of a wagon hauling goods from the plants along the south bank.

There were two stores directly across from the end of the bridge, and a scattering of other structures in an otherwise heavily wooded area.

Merritt, however, knew his way, and led her up the path to the top of the rugged cliffs of Mount Logan to Fort Boreman.

"Is the fort still active?"

"No." For the first time Merritt considered that M might find a fort uncomfortable. Although women were drawn to a man in uniform, most women did not care to explore any further behind that uniform. Nor should they. "Why?"

"This path seems well used."

Despite the warm dry weather Parkersburg had been enjoying, the dirt where it was overhung by trees was still slightly damp, and the imprints of horse shoes were everywhere. "This is a favorite place for picnics and celebrations." Merritt caught himself before he added that Fort Boreman was also the place for public hangings, and thousands came up the path to witness them.

They reached the site of the old fort, to find a scattering of people there ahead of them. There had been talk in the hotel dining hall of the final and long-awaited turn in the weather – echoes of 'Let it be spring' were heard several times. Though it was long before the picnic hour, those lucky few with leisure time had come to Fort Boreman to fully partake of the fine weather.

As Merritt promised, M was indeed impressed with the expansive view, both up river and down. Military men, of course, would call it a commanding view, and thus the reason for posting a fort here during the war. M gazed down on the long depot at the very edge of the Little Kanawha. Boats and barges were lined up along the length of the depot, which extended a hundred yards over the river's water and was elevated on great posts above it. Barrels and crates and boxes of all sizes were being loaded and unloaded by means of hoisting machinery. There, also, just past the bridge they had just crossed, were the tracks leading down to the river where the *Mt. Clare* would transfer the cars of the M&C to continue on the Parkersburg Branch. It would have been important to protect this nexus of the railroad and river during the war; transshipment of coal, especially, would have to be protected, else the railroads could not run, and cities would shiver in the winter.

M was itching to ask Merritt about his time in the war. Had he been stationed here? The subject of the war, however, had become prohibited for her, a self-imposed restriction she had set for herself after that disastrous lunch in Louisville. That was days ago, more than a week now. Washington was creeping closer.

Merritt was itching to ask M what she knew about the man in the fine suit, but she seemed preoccupied with the view of Parkersburg.

"If you look down river, you can see Blennerhassett island. You know of its history?"

M turned reluctantly. "Of course. Poor Mr. Blennerhassett was ruined by Aaron Burr."

"He was hardly poor, and he had his own hand in his ruin."

M followed Merritt to a clearing near the edge. Mr. Blennerhassett's island was in plain view, the young leaves of the trees creating a green blur in her vision. It was sad to think of his fine mansion fallen into dust. Burr had come to his island garden and had spread poison; he was the snake in the grass, the snake that had bitten and then had slithered off unscathed.

"I would like to visit there one day. Does anyone live there now? Who owns it?"

"I think a few farmers work the land; they grow corn, I believe. I don't know who owns it."

It had surely passed out of the Blennerhassett family. M could not imagine any living relative abandoning family lands; it was simply inconceivable. She would never abandon her father's farm, never leave it to the desecration of some stranger with no idea of its sacredness. The dread that had come to settle on her chest these last several months threatened to well up in her. The land had passed to her upon her father's death. It was her sacred duty to keep it, to guard it, to cherish it. There were none left but her to do it.

"Aaron Burr was a snake."

Merritt was startled by M's sudden return to Aaron Burr. She had fairly spat the words; the absolute loathing that coiled between the words seemed almost personal.

"It was a long time ago, and both men are dead now."

M blinked her eyes once, twice; she did not realize she had spoken. She saw she had unsettled Merritt and regretted it. She regretted that once again she had failed to marshal her tongue and her thoughts.

"Yes. Still, it is a shame."

They wandered around the scant remains of Fort Boreman, Merritt pointing out the zig-zag trenches, dug for protection, that were slowly filling in. The forest was already reclaiming the land. The barracks were gone – burned, if memory served Merritt correctly – when the army abandoned the site. Merritt showed her where the cannon would have been placed to best effect. M wondered if Merritt had ever touched off a canon.

They returned to the spot where M had contemplated the long depot on the river. Parkersburg was a flat city, architecturally, compared to Louisville – there was no building higher than four stories; in fact, there was only one building that tall. The city itself was built on a plateau fairly high above the river. Following the tracks from the depot along the Little Kanawha, M found the second, outer depot laid out upon a second, higher plateau. Distant hills pimpled the land behind Parkersburg.

There was some excitement happening near the wharf boat. A man was gesticulating wildly, apparently very angry at the other man, who stood calm, his arms folded, resolute.

"I wonder what that is all about."

Merritt continued watching for another moment before he decided that someone's boat was being seized in default of some kind. Merritt seemed slightly amused at the man's misfortune until M wondered that anyone had the right to do such a thing.

"That is a U. S. marshal. They're allowed to do almost anything."

It was M's turn to be startled by the bitterness in Merritt's voice. M turned to him, mildly curious at his little outburst, but Merritt, too, regretted his lack of control. He changed the subject, suggesting they return to Parkersburg for a late lunch. M surprised him, by asking to remain a little longer on the bluff. She confessed that she simply enjoyed watching the ferries glide back and forth across the river, here at the bend.

Most of this morning's few visitors were women with children, though without doubt the few men present were there as escorts. One of these few men joined Merritt and M in enjoying the view. Though he stood a few feet away, and though it was really impertinent of him to acknowledge it, he had overheard M's remark about watching the ferries.

"It is a shame you were not here several days ago, when I arrived. Company K of the Fifth Cavalry came through here from Washington City on the Northwestern Virginia. Four baggage cars and five cars for their horses – all of that and 170 men transferred from their train to steamboats. It was quite a show."

The man's impertinence paled in comparison to the picture he gave. M was particularly concerned for the horses.

"Horses enough for 170 men all on only five cars?"

Merritt knew that M was imagining Emmett's own transportation on the M&C, imagining Emmett struggling to breathe, squeezed in among an unforgivable number of horses in a small moving box.

"A company has at most 100 men, so there would only be horses for that number." Merritt turned and fixed the man with a most commanding stare. Returning to M, he added, "I can assure you that Emmett is not traveling under such circumstances." He left it at that, and hoped M would accept it, at that. Merritt stood patiently while M searched him, quite openly, for any signs of deceit or dissembling. Apparently satisfied, she settled for watching the next ferry to cross, then she promised to return to Parkersburg with Merritt.

It turned out to be the most entertaining crossing of the day. For twenty minutes they watched, increasingly amused, as a ferry from Belpre belched and lurched its way across the Ohio. It was not the elegant and reliable Paden ferry they had taken earlier. In fact, it was hardly a proper ferry at all, but a small steamer that was hardly more than a mere tug boat, towing an old barge of some kind, seating provided by planks of wood fastened across it. There was no roof or sides, and certainly no higher accommodations. Just when the barge was within reach of the Parkersburg bank a mere breeze seemed to blow it off course and into the mouth of the Little Kanawha, where it wallowed about, the tug listing this way and that in the wake of more powerful and, frankly, better steamers, too good, in fact, to render any assistance. A man in the barge stood and began uselessly bawling orders to the captain of that good tug.

Merritt let out a hearty laugh, and even M was tickled at the scene below. Then M recognized the man.

"That's Mr. Argent."

"Yes." Merritt barely got the word out between fits of laughing.

They watched long enough to see the lubberly little steamer and its barge finally get the help it needed – long enough for Merritt's mirth to wind down — before they descended to once again pay the toll and cross the bridge. They met Argent half way down Kanawha street.

"Did you have a fair crossing?"

"Delightful. How have you two been spending the morning?"

"We have been enjoying the view from Fort Boreman."

Argent hesitated slightly, gathering that they had probably been witness to his less than genteel patronage of the *J. R. King*. "Then you have not yet had your dinner. Let us stop in at the Swann House, and afterwards we can board our train. Perhaps we may make some distance before nightfall." It was seventeen hours from Parkersburg to Washington (including the swing past Baltimore), but there was still the matter of the horses, which Argent had learned could still be several hours yet, and, given Miss Warner's objection to travel by train at night, it was likely they would not make Washington before morning. But Argent hoped they could at least make a start on those seventeen hours. Clarksburg, he thought, was the best they could hope for before they would need to stop, but there was a decent hotel there, and Miss Warner could spend this night in a proper bed.

M thought she showed great restraint in waiting until after they had been seated to inquire after Emmett, but Argent showed signs of fraying at the edges where her horse was concerned. It was not so much Emmett that had frayed Argent's edges, but the frustrations of his morning's work. He had spent hours trading telegraphs with Chief Whitley (growing steadily unhappy about the multiple delays), as well as with officials in Athens, trying to ferret out information on their mystery man. Time between those telegraphs had been spent hounding the clerk in charge of the time register for information as to when he could expect a certain freight train from Cincinnati to arrive. An equal amount of time was spent hounding the freight master as to when the cars of that freight train (having finally arrived at Belpre) would be ferried across to Parkersburg. Emmett, as well as Merritt's and his own horse, would ride the *Mt. Clare* to Parkersburg because every railroad man in Belpre was busy, frantically trying to clear up the long line of waiting freight caused by the night's delay, and no one, absolutely no one, had the time or the inclination to allow Argent to take personal possession of the horses. Getting to the horses was no problem – he could see the car right there, right in front of him, as he half-pleaded, half-scolded the clerk at the time – it was the inevitable filling out of forms and receipts, which, of course, would need to be signed by the clerk's supervisor, and who knew where he was in all this mess? No, the clerk in Parkersburg could sort all this out.

Argent made a visible effort to speak as calmly as he could as he explained the difficulty with the horses. At the end of his explanation, during which time Miss Warner had interrupted twice with questions and once with a belated, and therefore pointless suggestion, Argent forestalled any further discussion on the subject by telling her that at the time of his departure from Belpre, the train which carried Emmett and their own horses was next to be ferried across. Once that train was moving on the Parkersburg side, it would make a stop at the outer depot, where their horses would be released into the B&O stockyards there. Not until then would they be able to reclaim their beasts.

M accepted this with the caveat that after their meal she would watch for Emmett's crossing from the landing where the tracks ran down to the river. She, of course, was anxious for Emmett's safe crossing, but she was also intrigued by the ferrying of these great train cars from one shore to the next. Like watching the regular ferries crossing and recrossing the river, M didn't think she would ever tire of watching the tracks of the great barge on which train cars crossed the river link so cleverly and so perfectly with the matching tracks on land, and the squat little engine that pulled the cars up the bank to be united with another engine capable of carrying many cars in its train.

M did watch the crossing of Emmett's car, pointed out with great authority and certainty by Argent, but from a point which both Merritt and Argent deemed safer for such viewing. Once the car was across and coupled with a growing train, they made their way to the outer depot, less than a mile from the court house as the crow flies, but almost exactly a mile following the city's streets from the Swann House.

Even at the leisurely pace set by the men, which frustrated M, they still arrived at the depot ahead of Emmett. As it was, they need not have bothered to walk there at all. Upon applying at the clerk's desk to begin the process of reclaiming their 'cargo,' they were met with disappointing news. The boy who had been charged with delivering Merritt's and M's grip bags to their waiting train at the outer depot, had left Merritt's description, and their bags, with the clerk. Confirming Merritt's identity, the clerk explained that the strange little train that had been idling in the yard for almost two weeks now had been commissioned to run an excursion up to Grafton and back; it would not return until dark. When Merritt pressed for a time more specific than "until dark," the clerk had explained that the exact time depended upon whether the guests on the excursion elected to dine at the Grafton Hotel or on the train. Dining at the hotel, of course, would push the train's return back to 'well after dark,' or even occasion an overnight stay in Grafton.

Any hopes, however slim, that had remained of returning home by Easter were now shattered. She would spend the holiest days of the year in a strange city, full of strange people, far from home. Nothing, *nothing* had gone as planned on this trip, and each delay found her farther and farther from home, in increasingly unfamiliar circumstances from which it was becoming more and more difficult to wrest personal control. To leave now would be to make several travel arrangements, several awkward connections between ferries and trains, for both herself and Emmett. The chain of transportation between herself and home was growing longer and more complicated with each day. She was not an experienced traveler and the prospect daunted her. She should have turned around in Cincinnati, at the very first sign of delay. Her bitterness with Grant was taking on a tinge of hatred and a growing belief that so much of what had gone wrong these last two weeks was his fault, was some design of his. A headache was developing on the top of her skull.

"Miss Warner."

M turned at her name; she suspected that it was the second time that Argent had addressed her.

"Miss Warner. I know that yet another delay is not welcome news, but it is only a relatively short delay, and we are within a day's ride to Washington."

M considered Argent. In the hierarchy of delays, this was probably the easiest to absorb. It was of a known duration, unlike yesterday's frustrating wait for news of resumed activity. It was certainly shorter than the days-long delay at Cincinnati. Yet, how much more was she expected to swallow? And for some reason, Argent's soft-spoken delivery of the news rankled her. She did not like being treated as if she were brittle or addled. Why was justified and expressed anger in a woman somehow seen as a malady?

M chose to ignore the subject altogether. "As soon as he arrives, I will take Emmett for a walk. All this time on the train cannot have been good for him."

"I will see to it that he is exercised."

"You misheard me. I will see to it."

Miss Warner was in a defiant mood, and Argent declined to challenge her, but he insisted she be accompanied. At first, he thought she would argue that point as well, but after a moment's hesitation she agreed. She also agreed to wait inside the depot where there was a place for her to sit down.

In a corner of the station, Merritt quietly related the details of the fate of their train. It had been appropriated by some middling local politician who had somehow learned of the train's temporary availability as well as its taxpayer funding. Wanting to court the temperance vote in his district, he appealed to the right people with ties to both the B&O and the Grant administration to release the train for a short excursion to Grafton, which was rumored to be hosting a temperance convention in a few weeks. These potential voters were to be treated to a sort of pre-convention for temperance, to see the facilities available (although, in truth, almost all of them had been to Grafton before), and to experience the thrill and privilege of riding a private train.

"Their efforts would be better spent in Clarksburg." Despite the determination of the good people of that town to curb its liquor problems, men (and some women) openly walked drunk in the streets at all hours of the day. The last time he and Merritt had been through the town, there had been some talk of revoking the power to grant liquor licenses. Argent doubted that would have much impact – liquor was one of the easiest commodities to slip through the restraints of law.

There was nothing for it but to await the return of the train, their train, and hope for an early departure the next day.

When Emmett arrived, he was released into Merritt's custody, which irked M; she had not even been allowed near the car as Emmett was led from it. Merritt convinced her to allow Emmett a little time to adjust to being on solid ground again, so to speak; they could return later to properly exercise him. In the meantime, Merritt offered to accompany M back to Fort Boreman; she seemed to have enjoyed her time there.

M found that she had enjoyed her time at Fort Boreman, but the magic of that place belonged to this morning. Already, Fort Boreman and its beautiful views were developing a characteristic of nostalgia for her. Nostalgia was a favorite place of being for her, a sweet torture she inflicted upon herself in penance for past sins, past neglects, past opportunities, a lashing litany of remember when, remember when, remember when . . . It was a private place and a private penance; she could not indulge in it here, in front of these men.

Into the awkward reverie that had abducted Miss Warner's attention, Merritt offered, instead, a tour of the town. They could make a leisurely return to the town. M nodded absently. It was not until she and Merritt had walked westward a block that M realized Argent was no longer with them. She thought she heard a hint of sarcasm in Merritt's explanation that Argent had remained at the depot to await the possible early return of their train. Privately, Merritt thought that no amount of toe-tapping or pacing up and down the depot was going to hurry any train into an earlier arrival. But Argent was not a man to sit still for long, and if staring down the tracks towards Grafton, willing their train to appear, gave him purpose, well, then, he was welcome to it.

Parkersburg was a small city, and it did not take long to walk the outer perimeter of the city's core. They walked down to the wharf and watched, for a while, the comings and goings of the different river craft, something which seemed to rivet M's attention. Then they walked up Ann Street, then down Washington Street, once again, towards the river, this time to watch the work on the great piers. M's attention seemed equally riveted here, though Merritt had the odd sensation that her attention had the quality of challenge to it, a determination to watch, rather than any true interest in it.

When the light began to seep into the west, Merritt suggested it was time to return to the Swann, where, hopefully, they would be met with the news that their errant train had returned. As they waited for Argent at the Swann, Merritt finally broached the subject of the rough man in the fine suit. By now, Merritt was well aware of M's fondness – her preference – for window seating, and he was able to find a table next to a window. M immediately began her study out the window. Merritt waved the waiter away and began his own study of M. She was a restless person, preferring activity, even when away from her daily work, when given a chance for rest; when not on the train, she was constantly walking. He had walked a number of miles himself as he accompanied her these last few days. Yet, to look at her now, one would not suspect her restless spirit – she sat perfectly still, staring and observing.

M suddenly shifted her gaze and then turned her head to watch the entrance to the dining hall. Within a few seconds, a middle-aged woman came in, searching the room then, finding the object of her search, moved to join a friend at a table towards the back of the room. M watched the woman settle herself, then returned to the window. Before she could lose herself again in the sights of the river outside, Merritt asked, "Do you know that woman?"

M looked back at him, a little confused. "No; how could I?"

"You seemed to recognize her."

"Only in that I saw her at the cemetery on Washington Street." M became more interested in the conversation. "Don't you think it odd that the cemetery was not enclosed? Even a simple fence would be an improvement." M could not imagine her own family cemetery being left open to encroaching vegetation. It still needed a lot of work to finish the wall, but then it would be completely safe from wandering creatures and M even fancied that the shade cast by those walls and the windbreak they provided would somehow be appreciated by those within.

Merritt ignored M's preoccupation with cemeteries. "Did you also recognize the man on the train at Athens?"

M looked at him again with a hint of confusion. "Did you not? He was one of the card players outside our car; he was the first to look up as we stood at the window."

Merritt was careful not to show his concern at this revelation: the rough man in the fine suit was not lost on the train – he knew from his position playing cards outside the car that there was no water closet behind those windows. But what was his purpose in confirming what he already knew? The purpose was just that – confirmation, not of the room, but of the people in it. If this was someone interested in their secret store of counterfeit money, then perhaps he was confirming the operatives in possession of that money. If they were identified as detectives with the secret service department, then they would have to be careful about any investigations they conducted in Ohio, certainly near Athens.

Merritt, however, need not have taken care to mask his concern: M, too, realized the lie behind the man's statement. "That man knew perfectly well we were in that apartment. He was no more looking for a water closet than I was looking for a tavern that night." M was certain he had merely let himself into their apartment to more clearly view the woman he had laughed at. "Mr. Argent is here."

Merritt looked over and waved Argent to their table. That he joined them with exaggerated good humor told Merritt of some new unpleasantness. Merritt also noted that, while Argent asked after their walk and for details of their tour, M did not respond in kind; she did not ask about the train for which he had set himself to watch. Either she was no longer going to react to the vicissitudes of travel or – he suspected was more the case – she was planning her earliest departure from this trip. Merritt, therefore, opened the topic which neither Argent nor M seemed willing to discuss. It was, after all, the reason they were in Parkersburg.

"What have you heard about the train?"

Argent thoroughly surprised Merritt with his answer. "The train has arrived."

"That is good news." Merritt said it with less belief and more as a hope for confirmation. "When will we be able to board and depart?"

"I have spoken with the engineer." Argent seemed ready to end his answer there, but after a few (ominous, Merritt thought) seconds, he continued. "A passenger car that had been coupled to the train was being uncoupled as I left. Mrs. Hughes – our engineer's wife – is in the city now shopping to replace stores recently depleted." A small amount of groceries had been stocked on the train to supply them — Merritt, Argent, M and the crew – with a few meals over the course of their trip. The excursion party, or rather those lucky enough to have been invited to ride in the parlor car, had exhausted those supplies, as well as Mrs. Hughes' good will, in being asked to prepare and provide food for people who were only a few hours between meals as it was.

Argent had mentioned, as casually as possible, the need for a hotel this night, and Merritt carefully ignored the comment; he was surprised and grateful that M also ignored it. M, instead, reminded Merritt of their intention to exercise Emmett and the other horses, but Argent assured her that the care of the horses had been arranged, including being exercised. Argent assured M that he had personally seen to Emmett's accommodations, and that he was enjoying private and well-stocked quarters. Argent had also arranged for their own accommodations at the United States Hotel, including retrieving from the outer depot their grip bags, as well as all their trunks, which had been deposited earlier from the M&C baggage car, now attached to a different engine, on its way on the Parkersburg Branch. Though the Swann House was perfectly acceptable, it was a standing agreement between Argent and Merritt that the farther away from boats and trains Miss Warner could be kept the better. The United States was in the very heart of Parkersburg, across the street from the Court House. As it turned out, Miss Warner retired early, as soon as she could gracefully extricate herself from their evening meal. Indeed, Argent had to work extra hard to convince her to stay long enough for their traditional nightly drink.

13 — *Spy Wednesday*

Argent was up and gone early the next morning, but he was back in time to share breakfast, as well as the latest telegrams, with Merritt. There was no word from Whitley, which was worrisome, for Whitley was never quiet. President Grant's messages were likewise growing more terse with each new development. Everyone's patience was being tried, and tried again. Miss Warner had certainly reached the end of hers yesterday, but it was hoped that a good night's sleep would restore her to her native patience, little as that was to begin with.

M, however, found it hard to rouse herself in the morning. Messrs. Merritt's and Argent's propensity to salute with a drink every accomplishment, no matter how small or mundane, was beginning to tell on her. She did not subscribe to the ridiculous calls to abandon all drink – where would the biergartens and the saengerfests be without beer and wine? However, Merritt and Argent could possibly benefit from such restrictions – Mr. Argent in particular was fairly adamant that M celebrate with them their safe arrival at Parkersburg last night. All she had wanted was to retreat to her bedroom and pour a dose of the laudanum Miss Carrie had packed. The headache that had begun at the depot had only slightly worsened as the afternoon wore on, so she had hopes that it was not too late to stop it from developing into one of her sick headaches. She had found the bottle of laudanum that first night in Covington with a note from Carrie that said, "For your woman's troubles." M was rarely bothered by that particular problem, and she prayed she would stay free of it for the entire time she was away from home. But like her mother, M suffered from headaches, and like her mother, laudanum seemed to be the only thing that helped. M did her best to leave the laudanum only for the worst of her headaches, but she allowed herself freer use on this trip, which seemed to be the source of one headache after another. She did not want to find herself stricken in the company of these men, and so she had been taking small doses as soon as she could, once a headache seemed imminent.

She would gladly have skipped breakfast to spend a little longer in bed, but she could hardly berate Merritt and Argent for all these delays if she herself was not ready to go at a moment's notice, and she seemed to remember agreeing to meet the men for an early breakfast. She found, however, that, though the men had waited some time for her at their table, they had elected to dine without her, bowing to her need for more rest. A sudden irrational anger flared at their condescending acknowledgment of her fatigue. It took some minutes for her to smother that fire, while she gave only scant attention to their tentative plans for this next and last part of their journey.

The men regretted that there was little time for a proper breakfast, but they had taken the liberty to order some little breakfast that she might enjoy in her car. They had received word from Mr. Hughes that they would be leaving within the hour, and he asked that they report to the train as soon as Miss Warner was ready. M thanked them for their concern, secretly grateful that she need not tiptoe through another forbidden meal with these men, but she assured them she could wait until the midday meal to eat. Laudanum often reduced her appetite, but they need not know her personal habits; moreover, this one morning she could avoid altogether Argent's increasing efforts to urge her to eat. She was weary of the effort to keep her Lenten obligations, and to keep them privately, and to keep them in the presence of such determined diners. Argent, however, persisted. Finally, he cooed at her, "I promised Miss Carrie that you would eat regularly; you would not have me break a promise?"

Again, the sudden, irrational anger returned. What else about her had he and Miss Carrie discussed? An unacknowledged suspicion burst through at that moment: what was the real purpose of this trip?

Both Merritt and Argent saw the sudden rise in Miss Warner's anger and an alarming dilation of her pupils, but it was Merritt who stepped in before Argent could further fan the wildfire he had sparked in her.

"Until our midday meal, then. Shall we make our way to the train?"

Argent remained behind at the hotel to arrange to have their trunks and other baggage delivered to the train, while Merritt and M headed towards the depot to arrange to have their horses also delivered to the train.

Argent found Merritt inside the depot, having just finished sending a telegram. "Where is Miss Warner?"

Merritt nodded toward the door. "At the train. Did you know there was such a thing as paper wheels?"

"They work splendidly on paper wagons. You left her at the train?"

"She is with Engineer Hughes. They have become great friends; I have never heard her talk so much." He had never heard of paper wheels either, until M asked if the train would be testing them.

Argent lit a slim cigar as they started for the little train sitting out of the way in Parkersburg's small yard at the outer depot. He was not one to smoke excessively, and rarely so early in the day, though Merritt noted that Argent had smoked a great deal more than usual on this trip. "You also have spoken with Engineer Hughes."

"Yes." Argent released a long breath of smoke. "How often have you ridden on a private train?"

"Never, excepting the occasional excursion train."

"There is an interesting contrast of perceptions regarding a private train. Such a train suggests wealth —"

"Not our train."

"— superior accommodations —"

"Yet to be seen."

"— and privilege."

"Bedfellow of wealth and superior accommodations."

"Yet you may be surprised to find that even with wealth and superior accommodations a private train is, in fact, not privileged on the tracks."

This, then, was the immediate reason for Argent's current smoke – the status of their track rights was considerably less than they had presumed, which meant a quick departure was not likely. "A few hours' more delay won't make much difference at this point."

"No, you misunderstand me. Once we start – whenever that may be – we become that bane of all railroads, the wildcat train. We will always be at the mercy of the schedules of other trains. We will be, in fact, a train without a schedule, required to stop at every station for orders as to whether we will be allowed to go forward or sent to a siding while other, scheduled trains proceed. Moreover, until we reach Cumberland, we will be traveling on a single track, which means we will be dodging trains going both east and west. The simple eight-hour ride that most people enjoy between Parkersburg and Cumberland could easily become sixteen hours or more." Argent drew on his cigar before adding this tidbit of hope:

"Things should move a bit more quickly once we are on the double tracks past Cumberland." The smoke he exhaled drifted away, much like all the other little tidbits of hope had disappeared so far.

The final indignity that Argent did not share with Merritt was that their train would also be subordinate to even construction trains, including the gravel trains charged with re-ballasting the roadbed every spring. As Mr. Hughes said, those trains, after all, had work to do. The final cautionary advice that Mr. Hughes did not share with Argent was that the Parkersburg Branch seemed to be in a state of chronic confusion, as regards scheduling. Mr. Hughes could not make this criticism with authority, since his experience of the road was limited, but in the time that he had been in Parkersburg and the little that he had been allowed to run on that road, the schedule seemed to be always in tatters. The Parkersburg Branch men roundly denounced the Ohio trains as the seminal source of delays – the Ohio trains could not be depended upon to run on anything like card time – but Mr. Hughes knew that many delays could be put squarely on the shoulders of the branch's own trains and the accidents and other events occurring on the branch's own tracks.

Merritt considered Argent's news. Sixteen hours would mean at least one more night at a hotel, and that was just on this side of Cumberland; there was another eight- or nine-hours regular passenger travel to Baltimore. "Are the dispatchers aware of President Grant's hand in this?"

"No, and at his direction. He wanted to shield Miss Warner from any notoriety. As far as the dispatchers are concerned, we are a nuisance to be tolerated. We ride only at the sufferance of Mr. Garrett and the B&O."

Just before they reached the last car of their train, Argent stubbed out his cigar on the heel of his boot, then carefully placed it in a breast pocket of his jacket. As they rounded the back of the last car they found M bending over in a most indecorous manner, looking at and attending with great intensity something on the underside of the train to which Mr. Hughes was pointing and explaining. At the sound of her name, M straightened up, as did Mr. Hughes, and Argent heard the tail end of his explanation: ". . . since the drums need to be rewound after each use, it is only for emergencies."

Miss Warner, against all expectations, smiled at Merritt and Argent. "We have been waiting for you to begin the tour."

"You needn't have waited on us. What have you been doing?"

"Mr. Hughes has been explaining to me all the appliances to be tested on this train. My father always believed a train like this should be developed – one that tests new inventions during regular operations on the tracks. Mr. Hughes has asked me to consider naming the engine."

Mr. Hughes was beaming; M had thoroughly captivated the man. "It would be an honor to have her choose a name. She is an apt student of trains. But let me show you the train, and where you'll be staying."

They began with the stock car, which elicited exuberant praise from M. Instead of the bare and spartan stock car she had imagined with the rough slatted sides of traditional cattle cars, here was a car with full side walls and painted the same pale yellow and green trim as the other cars in the train. She had thought it was the baggage car. It was, in fact, an old freight car, but not one of the parsimonious freight cars the B&O was known to cling to, but one mysteriously acquired by Mr. Hughes from an unknown railroad, the extra expenditure approved by Grant himself. The larger size was at the heart of Mr. Hughes' renovations for the horse car.

The real praise, however, was saved for its interior. M had thought to find an open interior in which Emmett would find himself at the mercy of the jerking and swinging of the car, constantly readjusting his weight to find stability. What she found instead was a snug stable on wheels, neatly divided according to use. On either side of the great sliding doors on both sides of the car were two stalls parallel to the walls, but staggered, so that one end was close to the opening, and the other butted against the rear and front walls. This not only left plenty of room for hay, tools, saddles and other tack, but kept the horses out of reach of each other, in case any were inclined to bite or were less than neighborly.

The outer posts of the stall ran from ceiling to floor, and between these were strung lengths of heavy rope, from which could be hung blankets and other scraps of material used in wiping down the horses or conditioning saddles and other tack. There were hooks everywhere – on the posts and open wall space – some of which were already occupied with the usual tools needed in the everyday care of horses. The floor – notoriously neglected in the usual stock car – had also been given attention as to the comfort and safety of the horses. What was essentially a large tray had been built into the length and width of the floor and filled with sawdust, wood shavings, and straw. Pitchforks and manure shovels needed in keeping the floor clean were among the tools hanging from hooks.

The floor had another surprise. A concern whenever animals were transported on trains was the need to keep the animals calm. Most animals found the noises of regular train operation unsettling. It was hoped that the thick layer of material on the floor would deaden these noises. However, one of the loudest and most alarming noises was the dropping of the ramp from the car to the ground just before animals entered or left it. This violent assault on their ears sometimes caused them to balk or even rear up, in the case of horses. If Miss Warner cared to look more closely at the floor, Mr. Hughes suggested, she could perceive that the floor was in fact raised, and between this new position and the original floor, she could further perceive the ramp as it was stored there. From this place it could simply be pulled out and gently let down to the ground below.

M was nearly speechless, until something occurred to her as she inspected the ramp. Trying to sound as casual and uncritical as possible where Emmett was concerned, she asked Mr. Hughes about the trucks and the wheelbases. And then, despite her best efforts to remain calm and to allow Mr. Hughes to answer the first two questions, she immediately demanded to know why the wheels were set so far back from either end of the car. Instead of upsetting or insulting Mr. Hughes, he beamed at her observations. He had met the president only briefly, on his way down from New York to Baltimore to take possession of the little train and control of its renovations. But in that short meeting, the president had told him that Miss Warner was something of a *cognoscenti* on the matter of trains. Mr. Hughes understood that Miss Warner's father had been an engineer (though not of the train variety), had consulted for Grant during the war, and he had passed his passion for mechanics and other aspects of engineering on to his daughter. But Mr. Hughes had been strictly admonished not to reveal that Grant had spoken to him of this.

"You're very observant, Miss." The wheels were set back farther than any train M had seen so far, about four feet back from each end. "This part of the road – the Parkersburg Branch – has its fair share of tight curves, like any railroad, but once we get past Grafton and up into the mountains, they become more numerous and even sharper. Placing the wheelbases closer together like this helps us ride through those curves with greater safety. The original trucks on this car have been replaced with the same trucks on the other cars in this train. In fact, we had to do a fair amount of work to the underside of this car to make it right for the horses."

"I am so very grateful for all the attention you have given to Emmett and the other horses. You are a great credit to your vocation."

Merritt thought Mr. Hughes might burst with pride. Mr. Hughes was not too modest to mention that he had designed the car himself, but he was too modest to mention that he had been selected in part because of this very design (somehow obtained by President Grant), because of his interest and concern for the safety and comfort of the horses. A native New Yorker, he was a frequent patron of the circus there. He had cultivated friendships among those workers who were developing into a kind of transportation staff, as the P. T. Barnum's circus was beginning to take its show farther and farther afield from New York. Mr. Hughes was fascinated with how the circus transported so much equipment and personnel and animals. He had been allowed to inspect their travel accommodations, and from these experiences, he designed a very efficient, safe, and comfortable stock car, not only for Emmett and Merritt's and Argent's horses, which Miss Warner loosely referred to as 'the other horses,' but in anticipation that President Grant might choose to travel with his own horses in the same manner, on a small train such as this.

The horse car naturally rode behind the tender, where the ride was smoothest and least likely to upset the horses. It was also the most convenient for the train crew to reach the water closet built into a corner at the head of the car, closest to the tender and engine. There were, of course, in addition to the two sets of sliding doors, a door for the men at either end of the car.

Merritt and Argent trailed behind M and Mr. Hughes as he led them past the next car in order of the train to the third car. During that short forty- or fifty-foot walk, M and Mr. Hughes were heard to be discussing the brakes that were being used – Mr. Hughes did not like to say tested, as he assured Miss Warner that nothing that could possibly put her at risk was being employed on this train – but suffice it to say that nearly any braking system was preferable to the horrible old Loughridge brakes. The Pennsylvania Company clung to them yet, but Mr. Hughes assured her that that worthy railroad would abandon them soon enough, if for the noise complaint alone. M could not agree with him more, and she assured Mr. Hughes that she was entirely dependent on his expertise in these matters.

Merritt and Argent were nearly dumbfounded. M was completely at ease with the engineer; she was the most congenial that they had ever seen her. They contrasted her at this moment with the M who had barely tolerated Mrs. Blaiser on the LC&L. Merritt also reflected on her ease with Mr. Stallo in Cincinnati. He leaned close to Argent and whispered, "Clearly M prefers older men." Argent elbowed Merritt back into position.

This next car was to be Miss Warner's car. At this, M was truly surprised; she had not expected the luxury and solitude of an entire car for herself. Inside it was almost everything Mr. Henry had told her it would be. The night before she left the farm, he had found her at the cemetery and told her what she could expect on the train waiting for her in Parkersburg. He had been trying to comfort her. He had never been in what he had called a varnish car, but he had heard about them – draped in satin and velvet, with the finest wood carvings, and all the amenities one could hope for in a moving cabin. Mobile, he had corrected himself, a mobile cabin. M did not think she could say she had ever been in a varnish car either – it was not draped in satin and velvet, and there were no gold dusted tassels hanging from the tablecloths or curtains, and the woodwork, though highly polished and beautifully carved, was not inlaid with exotic woods. That was not to say that it was not a handsome car, or at least this first half of it. It was well-appointed, with a cylinder desk along the right wall a few feet inside the door, and two sofas. Just inside the door, to either side of it, were corner cabinets of moderate craftsmanship, contents unknown. Straight ahead was what appeared to be a small, shallow fireplace with a fine mantle and a mirror above it in a gilt frame that was far too fancy for a train. In front of the fireplace and to the left was a small round table with chairs. To the immediate right of the fireplace was a door, leading to another room or apartment. And covering nearly every surface and at the windows were cloths and drapings and upholstery of every shade of red, M's least favorite color. M uncharitably thought 'bloodbath,' a word she had come across last year in some newspaper article about Saxon words the English language had left behind. Only the clerestory had been left unassaulted. In short, though it had all the characteristics of a fine parlor, M found it chaotic and dark; only the mirror helped to cut through the clutter and bolster the light trying to breach the heavy damask guarding the windows.

At Mr. Hughes' gesture, M stepped farther into the car. Passing her, still with his arm held out inviting her even further into the damask and brocade den, he stopped at the ornate door to the side of the fireplace. Like the mantle, it was painted white with an almost porcelain-like finish. M joined Mr. Hughes at the door, and at his gesture, opened it. The room beyond – obviously a bedroom – was almost as awash in red as the parlor room. The bed was as large as her parents', but far more plush in its linens. There was a dresser and mirror, an overstuffed armchair, and against the very back wall, a wardrobe, cleverly inset next to what must have been the water closet, whose door matched those of the wardrobe, so that the back wall presented a uniform front. Between the overstuffed chair and the water closet was a washstand with all the usual appurtenances. Unlike the toilet ware in M's house, everything here matched — ewer, basin, soap dishes – sporting large, dusty red cabbage roses. Conspicuously missing was the headend door usually present in passenger cars.

M did not know what to say. It was all too much, and not at all to her liking. Her mother had preferred this kind of decor, but her father held a heavy hand on the household budget, and so there was little left for such frills and what he called pointless prissiness. The Warner house, therefore, had a spartan appearance, which Mr. Warner regarded rather as efficient. M tended to agree, if only because the absence of so much frippery meant far less cleaning – fewer articles of cloth to beat or shake the dust from and less time spent washing and ironing them.

In this moment, M began to panic. What was the right thing to say? What was expected of her? She turned back toward the door to find all three men watching her, waiting, expecting. Merritt was wearing his ever-present half-smirk, Argent was regarding her with what looked like stern disappointment, and Mr. Hughes was beaming with a pride that M did not understand, until he said, "My wife furnished the rooms herself." That she had been able to do so in such a sumptuous manner while only slightly exceeding the budget was the real matter of pride for Mr. Hughes.

What would her mother say? What would anyone but M herself say? The longer she remained silent the more her lack of polish, and her lack of appreciation, showed. She began to lace and unlace her fingers. Finally, she blurted out, "It is too much. I don't know what to say."

It was far less than gracious, and disappointment showed in Argent's face. Mr. Hughes seemed to accept it on face value – it was all a bit too much to him, as well. His wife would be glad to hear that her efforts had excited such an overwhelmed response. She looked to Merritt to bolster her courage; nothing steeled her like his arrogant amusement. But he was neither smirking or disappointed; he seemed almost apologetic.

Thankfully, Mr. Hughes was as ready as M to move on. Outside the car, he began to excuse himself, needing to – as all good engineers did – complete, and then repeat, his inspections of the engine, the journal boxes, the axles, and everything associated with the running of the train. What went on inside the cars was little to none of his business. M stopped him, even as he turned to go. She was curious about the rest of the train, but especially about the car next to Emmett's car.

"Oh, that is the gentlemen's car," nodding towards Merritt and Argent. "It is not fitted up as nicely as your car."

Merritt stepped in to relieve Mr. Hughes. "Why don't we let Mr. Hughes return to his true duties, and we can tour the car ourselves." Mr. Hughes nodded his thanks and moved off toward the front of the train and his as yet unnamed engine.

As they passed the head end of what M was already regarding as the parlor car, M looked back to confirm that there was, indeed, a door, with its own sagging platform, where the wardrobe had been.

The 'gentlemen's car' was simply and cleanly furbished. Moreover, it was not divided into two chambers, though the function of each area was clear. The front of the car – that is to say, the area nearest the door at this end of the car – was clearly an area intended as a sort of den or study. There was a simple but wide desk and chair, a single couch and two armchairs (though not nearly as stuffed as the armchair in the parlor car bedroom). There were identical cabinets to either side of the door they had just entered. At the far end of the car – that is to say, the headend of the car – was the water closet, a simple washstand with a metal bowl and ewer, a chest of drawers and a wardrobe, though this wardrobe did not block the door at that end. Between the study area and the dressing area were two simple frame beds, one anchored to each side wall. No carpets covered the floors, though the floors were sanded, finished, and highly polished. There was no heavy presence of reds or cloth materials. The widows were covered by simple wooden blinds. There was no clerestory in this car. The roof, however, was arched as if at one time a clerestory had been contemplated.

Argent announced that now they had seen the cars of particular interest to themselves – the other two and, of course, the caboose, were for the use of the crew as living quarters and storage – he would see to the storage of their own baggage, and he suggested that they (meaning Miss Warner) should board the train in anticipation of leaving shortly. With a heavy sigh he added that with any good luck they could make Cumberland, before nightfall.

After they had installed M in her crimson carriage, Merritt looked at Argent incredulously. "Cumberland? I'm as ready as the next man to allay a lady's apprehensions, but in spite of M's unfounded fears, shouldn't we push ahead at night? She has a perfectly comfortable and cushioned place to wait out the dark hours, and I'm sure we can speak to Mrs. Hughes about spending the night with her. And there are the double tracks to eliminate the need to dodge on-coming traffic." Privately, Merritt thought that they should also speak to Mrs. Hughes about the heavy decor in Miss Warner's car – it was obvious M was uncomfortable in the midst of so much stuff and fluff.

"I'm certain that if Mr. Hughes knew of Miss Warner's apprehensions, he would pull off onto the nearest siding at the first sign of dusk. He seems thoroughly taken with her. However, in this case, Miss Warner's fears are not a factor in the decision to avoid night travel. It is a decision of the dispatchers, with which Mr. Hughes himself approves. I am told that the only thing more begrudged on a railroad than a wildcat train is a wildcat train at night. Much of the road's commerce travels at night when there are fewer passenger trains in operation. We would be dodging almost as much traffic during the night as during the day, without the benefit of daylight to see clearly any unexpected problems or even to find the correct siding. And finally, Mr. Hughes advises against running at night because of his own lack of experience on this particular road. An engineer who knows every curve, bridge, siding, and tunnel would be less hesitant to attempt the run, but Mr. Hughes properly acknowledges his own limitations in this case."

Before he left on his errand to secure their baggage, Argent headed for the engine where he had a private word with Mr. Hughes.

Once M heard the men's voices fade away as they boarded their own car, she left the dizzying environs of the parlor car to spend some time with Emmett in the stock car. When the first lurches of the train's movements were felt, she briefly considered her luck in being on the train at all, having seriously considered gathering some tender-looking clover nearby. She felt she owed Emmett such an offering for having neglected him so much these past few days.

The little train was graciously allowed to skip Claysville, a station practically at Parkersburg's back door, but at Kanawha Station, Mr. Hughes, pulled onto the siding to dutifully report the presence of his train and to receive the next set of running orders. The stop was brief, as their train was permitted to continue on to Walker's Station, where they would repeat what would be a long series of stops – some brief and others not so brief – as they bowed to the primacy of other, revenue-producing trains.

They were making good time at the moment, but Mr. Hughes knew that would not last. The trains that operated on card time were allowed to pass by smaller stations that did not have regularly scheduled stops; but if there was a telegraph office or even merely a telegraph operator working out of a store or business on the side of the road, Mr. Hughes was required to stop to make communication with the dispatcher. At West Union, the little private train was required to idle on the siding while several freight trains (only one of them westbound) was allowed to pass. It had taken them a little less than three hours to travel a little more than forty miles.

While Mr. Hughes understood the necessity of operating under such restrictions, he was beginning to feel that these restrictions were imposed with something like professional discourtesy. He felt he was asked to wait longer than necessary, while the necessary paperwork was complete – the clerks seemed to take great care in their penmanship as they recorded the presence of the little train at each station, and to read with great intensity the dispatcher's orders before turning them over to Mr. Hughes. He reflected on these things as he worked his little train down the Parkersburg Branch. It was at West Union that Mr. Hughes realized the source of the discourtesy. Returning to his engine after reporting to the station, Mr. Hughes confided to his fireman, "I believe we are being deliberately retarded in our progress."

The fireman nodded his agreement, before spitting tobacco juice out the side of the cab. It was a notable effort, the red missile of liquid sailing on a beautiful arc before landing several feet beyond the tracks. The fireman was a little amazed that it took the engineer this long to come to this conclusion. Mr. Hughes was a fine man and an excellent engineer, but he was a little green when it came to the human side of business. The long and the short of it was that Mr. Hughes was not a B&O engineer. Nor was the little train exclusively a B&O train. Mr. Hughes had been handpicked by the President (though none but the President knew the reasons why). Mr. Hughes had then been given authority to hand-pick not only his crew, but the engine and cars that made up this private train, and, moreover, had been given complete superintendence of the renovations made to the cars and of the inventions and innovations installed for testing on the road. The only thing truly 'B&O' about the whole affair were the tracks themselves. Such exclusivity outside of the proud B&O family was bound to rankle that road's community of workers. Mr. Garrett may have given the President the use of the road, but he had not given any particular instructions to the supervisors or road masters to expedite this little excursion train. His workers responded to the presence of the President's train in strict accordance to the rules, but not at all in fidelity to the courtesy and well-mannered characteristics lauded by all as the hallmarks of B&O service.

Some kind soul, either at Parkersburg or one of the stations in between, had left a copy of yesterday's *Wheeling Intelligencer* on the gentlemen's car platform, weighted against wind with a rock. By a strange scheduling in the mail trains, news from Wheeling arrived the next day, although Wheeling was only nineteen miles from Parkersburg down the Ohio banks. Even with its route via Grafton, however, the railroad should have been able to move the mails well within twenty-four hours between Wheeling and Parkersburg, with all stops in between. Wheeling, Parkersburg, and all those stops in between were loud in their criticism of the B&O on this (and other) matters. The charge had been made that mail from New York reached Parkersburg within twenty-four hours, while mail from Wheeling took and additional eight hours. It mattered little to Merritt or Argent that the news was late, being happy to have something to read of the world outside of their little train.

As their train trundled its way to West Union, Merritt occasionally read aloud as he came across an article or editorial he thought Argent might like to hear. Argent only half-listened as he caught up on his paperwork as regarded Miss Warner and their trip thus far. At one point, Argent absently asked, "What seems to have done M good?" Argent hardly realized he had spoken.

"Outdoor exercise. Country living."

"What are you talking about?"

"The article I have been reading you – 'Health by Good Living,' by Dr. Hall. 'Outdoor exercise and a proper diet are his curative measures.'"

"M takes too much exercise and her diet is anything but proper."

"Nonsense, she is merely off her feed because of the stress of this trip. A woman doesn't grow to be that tall if her diet is historically destructive. And anyway, she seems to have the right idea about doctors."

"How do you mean?"

"Have you not heard any of what I have read? A person living in the country 'has it in his power to avoid or cure almost every malady with but the slightest medication.' I, for one, did not know my health was in peril merely by living in the city, or outside of the country. I think it would be in our best interests if we occasionally visited Kentucky."

"The environs just outside of Louisville, perhaps."

"Yes, you understand me exactly."

Argent regarded Merritt for a moment. "And how is it that Miss Warner seems to have the right idea about doctors? It is the accepted understanding of all who know her that she universally rejects them."

"I think she rejects abdicating any authority to them. Here, Dr. Hall seems to agree with her: 'Physicians are a useful class of individuals and would be much more serviceable than they are if all who employ them were well informed and sensible. It is not they' – doctors, you understand – 'usually, who are fond of dosing with drugs. They are obliged, or think they are, to give medicines, because so many believe in their efficacy.'"

"The efficacy of doctors?"

"No, the efficacy of drugs."

"And which does M believe in?"

"Neither! She is the perfect patient."

"How so?"

"She would only consult with a doctor if it was absolutely necessary, so any doctor she consulted could be assured their assistance was needed and that their time was nobly employed, and not wasted by these whining hypochondriacs. And she would never pester a doctor for a drug, so that if a doctor prescribed some nostrum or other, they can be assured she would not abuse the substance."

"I think any doctor can also be assured she would not take the nostrum in the first place." Argent laid down his pen as a thought occurred to him. "Merritt, do you disapprove of the chloral I administer to Miss Warner?"

Merritt regarded Argent for a moment. "I am in no position to disapprove of a drug so unanimously prescribed by doctors in Covington. And I certainly do not disapprove of your best intentions. But it does seem like the drug does not help M in the manner promised. She seems to be sleeping more, but also seems to be less rested with each passing day."

"Yes, I have noticed that as well. I have considered increasing the dose, but I will only do so upon the advice of an experienced chemist. If we are detained long enough in one of the larger towns, I will visit a chemist and consult with him."

Merritt nodded, and returned to his newspaper.

Mary, by the time the train reached West Union, had dozed, despite all the stopping and starting of the train. She had comforted Emmett through three tunnels and over numerous bridges and trestles before she realized he didn't need comforting. Though that third tunnel had seemed exceedingly long, the bridges were short affairs – the train was already across most of them before M even realized they had been on one. Consequently, when she began to feel drowsy, she did not feel guilty in leaving Emmett on his own; she slept through ten or more tunnels, unaware of the lengths of any of them.

Had she been fully asleep, she would have found the abrupt slamming back of the side doors of the stock car as rude, but she had been drifting in and out of a light sleep since the last stop, when all the noise attendant with a water stop had first woken her. Still, she had only enough time to stand as Merritt and Argent half-jumped, half-hauled themselves up into the car, but in that strange manner of hearing she heard the echo of the men speaking outside the car.

"Whatever Miss Carrie thinks to the contrary, I think we will need to lock Miss Warner in her car at night. We have spent enough time indulging her in these wild sorties bereft of planning or even of common sense. We should not need to verify her presence at each and every stop." Mr. Argent's usual equanimity was still absent, or newly retreated, at M's supposed transgressions.

Compared to Argent's strident tone, Merritt seemed calm and composed. "Hopefully, she is still in Parkersburg; I'll have Mr. Hughes telegraph there to determine the fact. If she left the train during any of the intermittent stops, she can't have gone far on foot. We'll split the stations between us; maybe someone saw her leave the train."

M stood dazed by the conversation that recalled itself to her. They intended to lock her in the car, intended to restrict her movements, her access to Emmett, her freedom. And they had consulted with Miss Carrie in the matter. Was Mr. Henry involved as well? Why, oh why, had she agreed to come on this trip?

At the sight of Miss Warner, both Merritt and Argent stopped in their movements. She showed obvious signs of sleep interrupted – there was hay in her hair, her dress was rumpled, and her gaze was unfocused, even as she stared at the men.

"Miss Warner." Argent's tone, though restrained, still carried a measure of anger. "When did you leave your car?"

"In Parkersburg. This morning."

Merritt regarded M. Her initial stupor seemed to have been replaced by a wary reticence that somehow also conveyed hostility.

"We must insist that you remain in your car until we are available to accompany you."

Argent had stumbled slightly in this command, and M was certain that he had almost said, "until we allow you." M neither agreed nor contradicted Argent, though it was clear she did not like being so pointedly directed.

Merritt stepped into the silence before Argent could demand a response. "Mr. Hughes tells us we will be delayed here for a short while. Not knowing our immediate schedule, it may be the only time available for a proper meal."

M had not moved at all since the men's entrance, but now she sat down on the hay bales where she had recently lain sleeping. "I would be much obliged if you could send a little something to eat in my car. I think the time would be better spent – not knowing our immediate schedule – in exercising Emmett and finding some fresh water for him." She pointedly did not mention the other horses; if these men chose eating over the care of their own horses, that was their business. She immediately regretted such mean thoughts about two of God's innocent creatures – the other horses certainly deserved more charity from her. *Cogitatióne, verbo, ópere et omissióne.* She hastily added, wanting to avoid cause for contrition later, "I would be happy to see to the other horses as well."

Argent began to splutter in advance of well-worn objections that Miss Warner, frankly, should both understand and accept, but Merritt stopped him in mid-splutter. Argent, in his turn, should have, frankly, observed and recognized the increasingly entrenched attitude Miss Warner was adopting. Merritt, frankly, for his part, was quite willing to let M eat alone in her car. Argent apparently felt the same way for he replied that she could suit herself, he would not bother her with his concerns for her welfare any more.

Merritt ignored Argent's unusual snit. "That won't be necessary. We intend to see to our own horses. And you make a valid argument for a better use of our time." Turning to Argent, and deliberately speaking slowly and firmly, Merritt suggested that Argent either direct that the midday meal be delivered to "our separate cars," or kindly ask Mrs. Hughes to do the same. Merritt, in the meantime, would exercise his own horse while Miss Warner did the same for Emmett; Argent could possibly join them later. For a moment, both M and Merritt thought Argent might not accept the compromise, but after a deep breath, he nodded and left the car.

Separate meals were delivered to the gentlemen's car and to Miss Warner's car, but not from any establishments in West Union. Merritt and Argent enjoyed a hardy, hot and large meal through the good efforts of Mrs. Hughes. She, too, had been up long before the train started from Parkersburg, and after having spent a long night cleaning up after the unexpected and unwelcome guests of the day before. It had been her understanding that her job on the train was to provide hot meals for both the crew and the guests, and, towards that end, she had been busy early in the car she shared with her husband and which also housed the cooking facilities. She, frankly, had been a little hurt when Mr. Argent had asked her to solicit meals for himself, Mr. Merritt, and Miss Warner from whatever sources she could find in West Union. She would cook their meals and take care of whatever needs and wants Miss Warner should have – as her husband had explained was part of her function on the train – but she would not degrade herself so much as to procure and serve inferior food on her own train.

"That won't be necessary. Dinner is making here and will be ready shortly. I will deliver it to you as soon as possible."

Argent left feeling he had somehow managed to insult Mrs. Hughes, and realized Mrs. Hughes had spoken to him in that same slow and firm manner that Merritt had spoken to him in the stock car.

Another three hours saw them at Grafton. There had been a second water stop, at Cherry Camp, as well as the forced idling on what seemed like every siding along the way. They passed through four more tunnels, the last one just after Cherry Camp, the longest of the four. M counted at least ten bridges, though she dared not look out the window to confirm, even though none of them was very long. Business on the road picked up as the day advanced, and they spent nearly three quarters of an hour at Clarksburg, waiting for their turn to dart between scheduled trains.

M had defiantly left her car at each stop without waiting for either Merritt or Argent to grant her permission. The first time she had done so, she had practically marched to the head end of the train, surprising both Mr. Hughes and the fireman. But once he had understood the reason for her visit, Mr. Hughes happily received her at each succeeding stop. M solicited from Mr. Hughes his comments on the different trains that passed them. They had taken to keeping track of the number of cars in each train, and M wrote in a journal, as she stood next to Mr. Hughes, the number and types of cars, the type of engine, whether eastbound or westbound, and the location of the observation. M was aware that she herself was being observed by Merritt and Argent. Argent was certain she joined Mr. Hughes at each and every stop merely to flaunt her defiance and to pique them; Merritt thought that M simply wanted to escape the confines and scarlet miasma of her car; and Mr. Hughes was simply delighted at her interest in his work and her attention to his comments. M, however, and despite her genuine liking for Mr. Hughes, was gathering intelligence for a possible – a probable – escape from this train. The overheard conversation about locking her in her car had truly frightened her, and she did not intend to be at anyone's mercy or submit her freedom to someone else's discretion.

At Clarksburg, however, Mr. Hughes was not immediately available for their usual tete-a-tete. Instead, as soon as the train came to a complete stop, she opened her door to find Merritt standing there, hand raised in the very act of knocking.

"I must ask you to remain in your car, at least until we are settled further up the siding. Clarksburg is busier by far than any other stop we have made, and there is a great deal of construction at the depot at the moment. I will advise you when it is safe to exit." M merely nodded and closed the door.

It was some minutes before the brakes were released, but instead of advancing on the siding to the right of the main tracks, their little train was backing up, the fireman ringing the bell all the while. When the whole length of the train had backed up and onto the main track, there was a moment's stillness before the train began moving forward again, this time to pull off to the left on one leg of a Y track behind the depot.

One of the things M regretted omitting from her packing was her father's pocket watch. She had argued with herself considerably over the benefits (and comfort) of keeping the time and the overwhelming dread of losing such a cherished heirloom. In the end, dread overcame desire and she left it in the safekeeping of her father's desk. She also regretted having antagonized Argent, who might have been willing to lend her the use of his watch, especially now that she occupied a separate car. She wondered if Merritt had a watch; she had never seen him consult one but seemed content to follow Argent's lead in matters of time. Now, without a watch, M waited for what seemed like a deliberately extended amount of time before there was a knock at her door.

Mr. Hughes greeted her pleasantly and almost eagerly, asking if she would like to observe the coming and going of the trains. He promised quite a few more trains here than they had seen anywhere else heretofore. He also apologized that their wait would be longer here than anywhere else heretofore.

M graciously accepted his hand as Mr. Hughes helped her down the steps of the platform. She followed him, not to the front, to the engine, where they usually took up their watch for the trains coming and going, but to the very back of the train. Their position on the Y gave them a clear view up and down the tracks. Mr. Hughes had taken the liberty to have a comfortable chair brought out onto the platform of the caboose, should Miss Warner want to sit as she recorded the business of the Parkersburg Branch. M was genuinely grateful, and promised Mr. Hughes his efforts would not go unappreciated, but for the moment she preferred to stand, after so much sitting on the train. After some time, Mrs. Hughes joined them, and M insisted that Mrs. Hughes take the chair, thanking her for such a considerate midday meal. If M had calculated that such a gesture would endear her to Mrs. Hughes, she had done so with great accuracy. If Mrs. Hughes had come thinking she would find any impropriety between Miss Warner and her husband, she was grossly in error. She found instead two people who could have been an older brother (or uncle) and younger sister engrossed in their play or some game, the score of which was kept in Miss Warner's journal. Miss Warner's interests were not confined to the cars, engines, and a rating of the depots, however, but included the terrain along the tracks and even the county roads that intersected with the railroad. Mr. Hughes was sorry to admit that he had little knowledge of the roads in West Virginia, though it was his understanding that they were generally considered poor. Except for the National Road, of course; that was a fine road, and well-kept. Perhaps, if time allowed, he would be pleased to show it to her when they stopped in Cumberland.

The depot and the tracks were on the northern outskirts of Clarksburg and at the far east end of town. In between the loud sounds of passing trains or trains stopping at the depot, then moving on – the whistle-blowing, bell clanging, the pumping of the pistons, and the sound of the wheels on the rails – there was the sound of construction, rising from almost every sector of the city. The nearest sounds of construction, of course, came from work being done on the new depot, very near to completion. M would like to have gone to the depot, and to the city beyond, maybe even to wander along Elk Creek, but Mr. Hughes would hear nothing of it, unless she were accompanied by Mr. Argent or Mr. Merritt. That caveat closed the discussion for M.

M and Mr. Hughes stood for quite some time – Mr. Hughes, as a matter of professional habit, checked his watch at the passing of each train – as they watched local freight trains, coal trains (and empty coal trains), and stock trains pull in and out of the Clarksburg station. After the passage of what would be the last train in their vigil, Mr. Hughes said, "That's our train," and crossed the tracks, heading for the depot.

Almost immediately, M found Merritt at her elbow, suggesting that it was time to return to her car. Ever the gentleman, he helped Mrs. Hughes down from her perch, then to the platform of the car she shared with her husband and the kitchen. Though M assured Merritt she knew the way back to her own car, Merritt equally assured her that her car was on the way to his own and he was happy to see her safely settled. Unlike with Mrs. Hughes, whom Merritt had merely helped up to the first step of the platform, Merritt followed M up to her very door, wishing her pleasant travels until their next stop. M knew that Merritt remained on the platform for a minute or two after she had closed the door. He made no attempt to conceal his movements on the rickety steps.

M heard Mr. Hughes shout to his crew as he walked past her car, then heard the brakeman run down the tops of the cars to release the brakes. Again, the train backed up along the curve of the Y track, returning to the main track, before starting forward and resuming their trip to Washington City.

In her car, M pulled from her grip bag the annual reports of the B&O that she had brought along as a sort of guide. Her father, as a (small) stockholder and an engineer, had assiduously read these reports. But he had also begun to keep a sort of engineer's journal or apology in the margins of the text – explanations of the technology, machinery, and engineering of the railroad and its rolling stock. These notes were not for him, but for Lally, assurances that he was safe in his travels. Sometimes he wrote short observations of the land, some of them almost poetic, though that was generally very unlike him. There were also little drawings or sketches accompanying explanations of mechanics or engineering or of the topography of the route. The reports themselves, of course, provided great detail as to bridges, tunnels, sidings, and other structures, as well as to their exact positions on the road. Originally, M had intended to consult these as a sort of homage to her father as she followed the same route he had taken for years, whenever he left home to consult on some project or other. Now, she furiously copied notes onto the back pages of her journal, creating a prosaic map of a possible route home, following the railroad, while also avoiding it.

With her head bowed over her work, her eyes strained in the dull candlelight of a darkened car whose windows had all been covered against the spectacle of bridges, M ignored, as she had since West Union, the spectacular scenery whirling past outside that other travelers had praised in lofty rhetoric ever since that great railroad excursion thirteen years ago celebrating the opening of the M&C and the Parkersburg Branch railroads, as well as the Ohio & Mississippi railroad, creating one continuous route from Baltimore to St. Louis.

M may have missed the grand pageantry of nature along the Parkersburg Branch, but she was aware of the changes in the topography of the railroad. She was aware of when the tracks were carried over bridges and trestles and, of course, when they were ushered through the numerous tunnels. She had been aware, even as she dozed on the hay bales in the stock car, that the train had occasionally labored uphill. Shortly after Clarksburg, the train entered into yet another tunnel, this one the longest tunnel by far, and the heat and trapped smoke of all the engines that had passed through it this day made breathing nearly unbearable for several minutes until her car cleared the eastern end of the tunnel.

They stopped briefly in Bridgeport, where they were, thankfully, told to continue on to Grafton; there was no need to stop at Webster. At Grafton, however, they were obliged to endure another extended wait, as Grafton was even more choked than Clarksburg with trains coming and going. Grafton was the nexus of the Parkersburg Branch and the Main Stem of the B&O. From this point travelers could either continue to northern and eastern destinations, via Cumberland, or turn northwest to Wheeling. In fact, in addition to regular, express, and fast line trains, there was the Grafton Accommodation which sole purpose was to run between Grafton and Wheeling. Likewise, there was the Cumberland Accommodation, running between Cumberland and Wheeling, with a stop at Grafton in between. And there were, of course, the myriad freight trains filling out the schedule. In short, there was hardly a time of day or night in Grafton when the tracks were not busy diverting trains here and there in the yard, where freight was loaded or unloaded, or passengers boarded or disembarked, shifting the business of the road between

Parkersburg, Wheeling, Baltimore, and all points in between. It would be difficult for Mr. Hughes' train to pull away from the frantic magnetism of the hub at Grafton.

As the train began to slow on its approach to Grafton, M left her writing at the cylinder desk to peak out the windows. On one side of the car, the view could have been almost anywhere near her home in Kentucky. On the other side, M looked out over the precise rows and uniform headstones of a military cemetery, so necessary in so many places after the slaughter of the late war. She crossed herself, thanking God her brothers, but one, had been brought home to rest in the family cemetery. Belatedly, and with what she hoped was the proper amount of shame, she prayed for the men in the passing cemetery that did not make it home.

Mr. Hughes stopped at the depot only long enough to allow Merritt, Argent, and Miss Warner to disembark, then he pulled the train to some designated spot among the intricate tangle of tracks and switches, that only engineers and station masters could understand. It was not a good sign that the expected wait would be long enough to at least allow for one of Merritt's and Argent's involved meals at the station, which also included a fine hotel. M had briefly pleaded to stay in her car, claiming a lack of hunger – briefly, because neither Merritt nor Argent had time for her objections and obstructions. It was as rude as either man had ever been to her, though M had to admit, as she watched the trains pull in and out of the depot, that there had been little time for a full discussion – no train lingered long at the platform, and conductors were almost as rude in ushering passengers into and from the cars as Merritt and Argent had been to her. M was, in fact, hungry, but she had wanted to continue taking her notes. Argent, however, had forcefully grabbed her elbow and pulled her down from the car's platform.

The station hotel sat snugly between the fork of the tracks of the Parkersburg Branch and the B&O Main Stem. The building almost seemed to squat defiantly in its little nook, the only building dedicated to human use on a crowded, narrow, flat strip of land almost exclusively claimed by railroad tracks, equipment, and shops. Beyond the tracks, the town struggled up the sudden rise in the land. On the other side of the river and the creek, there was more room to spread out. Across the tracks from the hotel rose the magnificent sixteen-bay roundhouse of the B&O. M thought the roundhouse the far more attractive of the two buildings.

Inside the hotel, however, all the feeling of being cramped and crowded disappeared. The main hall was large and open. On either side a parade of washstands stood at the ready, and hotel employés also stood at the ready with clean towels, immediately replaced after each use. This was something no train ever offered its passengers. Towels and cups at the water cooler on trains were for common use, and only the very thirsty dared to drink from cups covered with the patina of former parched passengers, and most men and women would rather dry their hands on jackets and skirts rather than soil their hands anew using towels neither dry nor clean.

Beyond the main hall was the dining room, extending far into the building. It seemed impossible to believe that so many people could eat at one time in one place, yet the number of tables said this was possible here. It was hardly the dinner hour, yet Merritt indicated to a waiter the wish to be seated. A *maître d'hôtel* of some sort led them to a table near the middle of the immense room, but at a quiet word from Merritt, they were led to a table near a window. The *maître d'hôtel* returned to take up his station at the entrance to the room, ready to take the next party to the table in the middle of the room that was once theirs. M watched the man as he made several such trips between the door and the tables and was surprised when a young female voice addressed her. M looked up and was even more surprised to see that the very young woman who addressed her was their waiter. That M had never seen such a thing before was understandable – she had not traveled beyond Louisville for years, and never ate at any establishment in town but Mrs. Müller's – but she had never heard of such a thing, either. M was not about to play the rube for Merritt and Argent, and so made her request with as much nonchalance as possible.

In a rare reversal of mealtime habits, M ate from a plate of fruit and cheese and crackers, while Merritt and Argent merely sipped at coffee; occasionally one or the other man would take a morsel from the plate, which M had placed in the middle of the table, indicating it was to be shared. Yet despite the lack of a full course meal and the usual time it took to consume it, this small collation was as exhausting as any other meal with these men had been. Merritt and Argent took turns asking questions that, if treated honestly, would be very poor topics at table: How do you find your car? Are you comfortable? Have you been enjoying the scenery? And the like. To which M would have answered honestly that her car sometimes made her nauseous, that she was as comfortable as could be under threat of being locked in, and that she had closed the shades on her windows to avoid seeing just how high were these bridges and trestles that they crossed. Of course, honesty in conversation, she was learning, was the least thing people wanted, and so she answered almost every inquiry with some variation of "It's fine, thank you."

Other than Miss Warner's more than usual level of fidgeting, Argent thought the interlude at the hotel restaurant passed off well. There were no gawking hotel employés, no crowds of weary and stranded passengers, no awkward tensions at the dinner table. There was no talk of the late war or present politics – he had been particularly grateful over the course of their entire journey thus far for the avoidance of the thorny topic of the Fifteenth Amendment, being put to the vote in several of the cities they had passed through, a subject certain to ignite Miss Warner's outrageous views of universal suffrage. The late afternoon coffee and tea this day could arguably be called their best meal yet. Argent was worried, however, about the coming evening meal. Miss Warner had rejected last night – for admittedly reverent reasons – their customary evening drink. But this morning's shock at finding her gone from her car had pressed upon Argent the need, Holy Week or no, for Miss Warner to imbibe in some form the chloral that had proven to keep her in place well into the morning hours. He did not know what drink other than alcohol could conceal the bitter taste of the drug. He would consult with Merritt on the matter; they had all the way to Cumberland to devise a strategy, and Cumberland would be the last night such a strategy would need to be employed.

Merritt dutifully telegraphed both Whitley and Grant as to their progress. He did not relay in these telegrams, as Argent suggested, a projected arrival in Washington of Thursday afternoon or evening – their projections had fallen far short of reality so far on this mission. A fair assessment of the situation spread blame equally between themselves, Miss Warner, and the vagaries of travel by train. Argent was no stranger to these vagaries, nor to the unexpected twists and turns in their investigations (which included delays, postponements, setbacks, and a good deal of simple waiting), but this particular assignment seems to have brought out in Argent a naïve hope for, and even an expectation of, a perfect coordination of timing, circumstances, cooperation, and luck. Merritt had already sent too many revisions of their expected arrival. At this point, he was content to leave Whitley and Grant both to their private speculations.

This proved both prescient and wise on Merritt's part, for he was required once again – twice in one day – to advise his superiors of unforeseen delays. This second notice, however, was particularly galling because the cause of the delay was the result of a completely avoidable combination of human vice and petty retribution. It was M, however, who provided an unassailable reason for the continued delay, so that Merritt was able to avoid reporting the unbecoming particulars.

At almost every stop, Merritt and Argent noticed that both the fireman and brakeman, and sometimes Mr. Hughes as well, disappeared together into the surrounding woods for several minutes at a time. They could not say that this was unusual among train crews, since they had not previously had occasion to so closely observe any. But Miss Warner's insistence on leaving her car at almost every stop had required Merritt or Argent or both to leave their own car to be in attendance, and so they had been witnesses to the strange ritual among the crew. Merritt's and Argent's initial explanation was the obvious and understandable call of nature, but after the third such incident, the fact that the crew so often answered that call together was curious, if not troubling. Nevertheless, Merritt and Argent did not give it any great attention until Grafton, when the absence of the crew, Mr. Hughes included, left the train unattended when a runner from the office brought news of a small window for departure, should the train be able to leave immediately. Unable to deliver the news, the runner returned to announce that the train was in no way prepared to leave.

Argent was almost purple with indignation and frustration when this was revealed to him. He had kept a young boy employed for the past hour and more, running between the station and the hotel, to keep him informed of the movement of the trains and of any indication that their own train might be ready to depart. It had been difficult persuading Miss Warner to remain at the hotel, against her wishes to visit the soldier's cemetery just across the river. They had kept her with them with the ever-thinning prospect of an imminent departure. The young boy had finally come with the news that their train might be able to slide in between two freight trains. M was visibly relieved; she had walked through every part of the hotel at least once, had spent a good deal of time standing at the windows of the restaurant watching the trains, and had swallowed more than one retort at Argent's promise of a request – at any minute – from Mr. Hughes to return to the train. No sooner, however, had they reached the water column with the great swinging spout that pivoted between the tracks, when this same boy returned, breathless, to say that they had missed their chance – Mr. Hughes could not be found, and the dispatcher could not wait for him.

"I will speak to Mr. Hughes, and I will know why it is he was not at his engine, and, furthermore, why it is that he and his crew are habitually absent from the train at nearly every pause on the road."

"He smokes."

Argent whirled around at M's voice; in his anger, he had forgotten her presence. "What?"

"He smokes – like you. They all smoke."

"And he leaves the train to do so? Why can he not indulge himself at the train, or near the train, somewhere within shouting distance of the train?"

"It isn't allowed."

"Miss Warner, I appreciate your unusual understanding of engineering and technology, of railroads in particular, but I'm afraid you are out of your depth here. Of course, it is allowed. There is, after all, a smoking car, and, moreover, many gentlemen – like myself, as you say – merely step outside the cars at the depots and stations and have our smoke. There is no need to run and hide in the woods, like some green schoolboy."

M blinked slowly at Argent, once, twice, a third time. "It isn't allowed for train crews." And in direct response to Argent's condescending remarks about her "unusual understanding," M slowly enunciated, as if to a dullard, "Smoking near the engine and tender is dangerous." It did not need to be said that members of the crew, the engineer included, would not be welcome to partake of their smokes near where paying customers did so.

Merritt coughed behind her. "That seems to be a reasonable restriction." Neither his cough nor his agreement with railroad policy broke M's staring at Argent.

Argent, realizing – too late – the error of his words, but not wanting to cede the field, countered that if smoking was restricted, Mr. Hughes *et al* should take up the chew instead.

"It isn't allowed." As Argent spluttered out, "Oh, come, now!" M qualified, "Mrs. Hughes doesn't allow it. She has stepped in one too many puddles of juice near the engine when she brought Mr. Hughes his lunch or a drink or just to visit." M wondered if her own father had been similarly denied that dubious pleasure. She was thankful he did not chew – she could not imagine her father spitting long-tailed balls of amber juice in the yard or the barn where they had all played barefoot. Her father liked to smoke, and she had dim memories of him doing so in the house and of sitting in his lap in the piano room while he smoked. But she knew that he had been banished to the front porch, along with her older brothers, as they had, one by one, begun to smoke. She had very vivid memories of her father and brothers all standing at the railing, the smoke curling around their heads as they smoked in silence, staring at some unknown mesmerizing spot in the yard. Her mother had banished him to the front porch, and he had complied.

Merritt broke in on her thoughts. ". . . understandable, but the fireman and brakeman also observe this restriction?" Merritt seemed almost indignant at the authority Mrs. Hughes apparently wielded at the front end of the train.

"She suspects the fireman chews, but she has never caught him at it. I have seen him spit – Mrs. Hughes would have to wander wide of the tracks to encounter any of his efforts."

Mr. Hughes, when confronted with the news, was mortified. He rarely joined the others in their clandestine jaunts into the woods; he knew his duty. But the realization that he was perhaps not as respected as much as other engineers of like or even less experience on this road had somewhat decomposed him, and he had sought solace in his tobacco and among his crew. He walked away, shame-faced, and, in a great show of atonement, refused a cigar offered him by the fireman.

There may have been other opportunities to leave Grafton – and the engineer would have been glad to leave the scene of his shame behind – but as the late afternoon stretched into evening, M announced that she would be staying the night in Grafton, so that she may attend the first night of Tenebrae at St. Augustine's. No one could deny her right to attend sacred services, especially in view of the repeatedly broken promises that she would be back in time to attend these very services at home. Both Merritt and Argent, however, found their feathers more than just a little ruffled that M had chosen to inform Mr. Hughes of this development. Mr. Hughes had then reported the change in circumstances to Merritt and Argent, with the added information that he would be escorting her to the church.

Thus, when Merritt telegraphed news of a second delay at Grafton, he was able to clothe it in the somber justification of a lady's devotion to her religion.

14 — *Maundy Thursday*

Merritt had briefly considered pouring a little of the chloral hydrate into Argent's drink last night. It would be so much easier this morning if he had been induced to sleep a little later. Mr. Hughes had accompanied M and his wife to Tenebrae at the church up the hill, while Merritt had sent his telegraphs (including one to Mr. Henry, who, after all, might be interested in whether Miss Warner would be returning in time for Easter dinner). Argent had taken the time to complete his reports and to sift through such information as he had kept with their inventory of counterfeit money, half-finished plates, and other items (including clothes, dyes, and even false whiskers for disguises) used to convince targets of investigation that Merritt and Argent, too, were of the criminal brethren.

They had dined together last night without Miss Warner, a rare circumstance these last two weeks. Argent had slipped a note under Miss Warner's door asking her to join them for dinner, but when he had returned some time later to repeat the invitation, he had been told by the brakeman (the only member of the crew still at his post) not to expect Miss Warner back in "any decent time" for dinner. When pressed, the man had confided that "these Catholic circuses" were lengthy on any given day, but were especially so near Easter. Argent had stared at the man before repeating "Catholic circuses?" But the brakeman had insisted he had said 'services.' Circuses or services, Miss Warner was indeed too late in returning to join the men for dinner.

Argent had informed Merritt that Miss Warner would not be joining them for dinner, and why. Now Merritt found himself in the similar position of informing Argent that Miss Warner would not be joining them for breakfast, either, and for the very same reason. And so, it would have been easier if Argent had been induced to sleep a little later.

Merritt himself had become acquainted with Miss Warner's religious duties when he had crept away from locking Miss Warner's car door and had been met by the fireman, waiting for him at Merritt's car. It was the fireman who had informed Merritt of Miss Warner's intentions to attend Maundy Thursday Mass in the morning. Merritt had therefore risen very early this morning to unlock Miss Warner's car well before she would need to leave for the day's services. He and Argent had briefly considered having Miss Warner stay at the hotel, but there was no guarantee that they could safeguard against her wandering at night. It was especially worrisome that the hotel was so intimately located near the tracks, which could prove fatal even in the day. Ironically, it was decided to keep her in the very midst of the tracks, in her own car, but locked in against any inclination to indulge in a midnight walk. Merritt found the action distasteful but understood the necessity of it. He would rather withstand M's fury at being locked in than face the prospect of returning her body to Kentucky. Even seasoned trainmen were killed in these busy yards.

The little train finally extricated itself from the confusion of Grafton's schedules and tracks in the middle of the afternoon. Some change had come over the B&O dispatchers during the night, a change that Merritt suspected ultimately came from President Grant, but immediately came from B&O's own president, John Garrett. For the first time since their private little wildcat train had stumbled back into Parkersburg from the temperance excursion on Tuesday night, they had been given an exact and assured time for departure.

Before their departure, however, a fair amount of time had been spent in sober discussion between Mr. Hughes and the yard master as to whether the little train would need the efforts of a second engine in scaling the demanding grades east of Grafton. Mr. Hughes had, of course, descended two of these grades – the Cranberry and Newburg grades – when bringing his train to Parkersburg more than two weeks ago, but he had climbed both the Seventeen-Mile and Cheat River grades; he was hardly ignorant of these tests of engine strength. The yard master had critically eyed Mr. Hughes' engine – one of the early Mason eight-wheelers converted from wood- to coal-burning, but not otherwise converted for use on this part of the B&O; it clearly did not come from B&O stock. The Masons were fundamentally commendable engines, and even elegant, if that really mattered on the road, but on this, the third – the mountain – division of the

Baltimore & Ohio Railroad, what was needed was raw, brute power; what was needed was a Perkins engine. In the absence of that, what was needed was a helper engine. However, it had to be conceded that this Mason was not pulling a heavy load; it was possible the engine was up to the job. The decision required a trip to the depot offices by the yard master, who returned long minutes later, to continue the discussion with Mr. Hughes, who then accompanied the yard master to the depot offices a second time. Eventually, Mr. Hughes emerged with the yard master, each then heading in opposite directions – Mr. Hughes to his engine, and the yard master to find a second engine for the little train. It had finally been decided that in the best interests of keeping this wildcat train at speed, a second engine was necessary. The yard master had left Mr. Hughes with the parting shot that "the Camel will help you keep your front foot down," as if Mr. Hughes did not know his own engine. (He had been sincerely surprised, as he ascended the Seventeen-Mile Grade, at the feeling that the front of the engine was somehow not fully engaged on the tracks; the Mason's relative light weight was, he had to admit, a liability on these steep gradients.)

One of the Winans Camels, older even than the Mason, was assigned to the private train, to help pull it up the punishing climb at Cranberry Grade; but before that there was the grade beginning at Newburg, or Simpson's Water Station, as the yard master insisted on calling it – one more gibe at Mr. Hughes' status on the road as a novice. It was becoming more and more clear – even to the genial Mr. Hughes – the acute resentment held by B&O employés toward the wildcat train cobbled together from distant yards, and toward the foreign engineer chosen over loyal and experienced B&O engineers or hopeful-engineers; such play-work as this 'excursion' could launch a deserving B&O lad into an engineering career. As for the grades, Mr. Hughes had to admit (to himself) that he had indeed needed help up the dreaded Seventeen-Mile Grade between Piedmont and Altamont as he came west, but he would be descending that ultimate, reputation-making grade as he moved east; these other slopes could not compare in length, though he could see where Cranberry grade would surely give loaded freight trains – the great bulk of them heading east (and, therefore, up the grade) for the biggest markets – great trouble.

There was no shame in needing help on these storied slopes, but Mr. Hughes could not help but feel that his engine and his own reputation was somehow, even deliberately, diminished by the presence of the Camel, taking place of honor at the front of his train. It would not have stung so much if the Camel had taken a position in the back of the train, as was the case usually with longer, heavier trains. It stung all the more when, arriving at Newburg, Mr. Hughes found that helper engines (almost universally 'pushers') were usually assigned here and not at Grafton.

Merritt and Argent stood at the windows of their car and watched the discussions between Mr. Hughes and some manager of the yard. They stood in silence for some time as the conversation that began in the yard abruptly ended as the manager left for the depot, then returned to resume the conversation, which apparently required that both men leave the yard for the depot offices. As Mr. Hughes and the manager both returned to the yard but not to their conversation, Argent said, almost under his breath, "I wonder what that was all about?"

Merritt, pulled from his reverie, which had nothing to do with what was happening in the yard, regarded Argent for a moment. "I'm certain it is merely the mystical musings between two engineers, of which you and I would understand very little. There are probably secret handshakes and the like which need to be conducted in private. Thus the reason for their removal to the depot office – there is probably a dark closet there where these things are practiced." As Argent turned from the window and favored him with a disapproving glare, Merritt asked a question of his own. "What did you and Mr. Hughes discuss before we left Parkersburg?"

Argent's disapproving look was replaced with one of surprise – he had quite forgotten the 'little word' he had asked of Mr. Hughes yesterday. "I wanted to confirm something Miss Warner had said to me in Covington."

"And was it confirmed?"

"Yes, but not in the way Miss Warner intended. After you had ridiculed her concerns about traveling at night on the M&C" – at which Merritt cocked his head in dubious agreement with the term 'ridicule' – "Miss Warner said, 'You wouldn't take your travels so lightly if you were aware of just how much mere glue is used to hold these cars together.'"

Merritt was smiling broadly. "And Mr. Hughes confirmed this?"

"Yes, but as I said, not in the way, I am certain, Miss Warner intended. A great deal of glue is indeed used in the construction of passenger cars, but far from being a cheap and dangerous method of construction, glue – as it dries – substantially adds to the strength and rigidity of the car. Only those cars with a sagging appearance are of any concern. Miss Warner, I think, took great pleasure in implying a rickety and unsafe character by mentioning 'mere glue.'"

Merritt laughed. "She gave you enough information to inflame your concerns, but not enough to quench them. She is too clever by half. I wonder if glue is used in paper wheels?"

"Mr. Hughes would be the man to ask."

M returned to her reports and notes. Mr. Hughes, of course, could not add anything to the information her father had provided in his glosses, but he had given her information that was neither in her father's comments nor the reports themselves – the importance of the schedules and the great number of trains on the road at any given time. Between the pages of the reports, M had placed, as her father had given them to her, pictures from *Harper's* and other publications, of towns or scenes along the road. She had also placed there a schedule her father had given her, but it was several years old now; she would need to procure a recent schedule. She had no doubt either of Grant's men would find one for her, but she would prefer that they remain completely ignorant of any knowledge of the road she might have. Mr. Hughes would find one for her; she need only ask and give the desire to follow their progress on the road as her reason for wanting one. He may even let her copy his time card — it may have more information than a simple passenger schedule. Perhaps at the next extended stop, she could approach him about it.

As soon as the train left Grafton, it began crossing a series of small bridges, some of them so short as to escape M's notice. They were obliged to pull onto the siding at Independence, having traveled little more than ten miles. It was hardly worth the stop, as Mr. Hughes was gone only long enough to report his presence to the station master, and as they were obliged to stop at Newburg, hardly a mile or two away. At Newburg, however, the stop was more than for the mere technicality of reporting to the station. Both the Mason and the Camel and their tenders topped off their water and coal, in preparation of the climb up the first grade. The road had, in fact, already begun its climb at Independence, doing so gradually in soft curves. Both Independence and Newburg were busy little places, but not on the scale of Clarksburg or Grafton, and so the little train was able to escape after little waiting.

M only stopped her frantic copying (she was dismayed to see how much her handwriting had been sacrificed to speed) when the train entered a curving tunnel very soon after leaving Newburg. She had not even stopped to step out of the car during the waits at Independence and Newburg, though she was aware that either Merritt or Argent were outside her door, neither knocking nor calling to her, merely waiting to forestall her should she open the door. With the Camel's help, M could not feel any strain as the train climbed the steep grade, though from the reports laid out before her, she was aware of the climb – 500 feet elevation in five miles. The curves, as her father assured her, right here in his notes, helped to compensate for the steep rise.

The train entered a second tunnel – long and straight – fairly soon after clearing the first. This must be the great Kingwood Tunnel. Even as M leafed through the reports to find the gloss that told her to expect it, she felt the warmer temperatures trapped in the tunnel from earlier trains, and her car began to fill with the smoke from the two engines pulling this train. As soon as they cleared the tunnel, M opened the windows, and the smoke was quickly pulled from her car.

After a relatively long stretch of uninterrupted travel, the train pulled onto a long siding at Tunnelton, a mile past Kingwood Tunnel, and then again, a mile past that onto a shorter siding, with only a few minutes to spare before the lone passenger train – the Fast Train due at Tunnelton at 4:08 – passed them on its way west. They waited for some time as freight trains passed, going both east and west; but it was the western-bound trains that were given priority – they could not be asked to step aside, while working their way up the grade, in order to let any downward train, much less a wildcat, to pass. There were great gaps in the times between the passing of these western-bound trains, but these were the trains working their way up the Cheat River grade, and even with helper engines these trains, some of them quite long, moved more slowly.

M paused in her work to glance out her window for the view from the top of the grade. They were truly in the mountains now, with the promise of even greater peaks in the distance. The immediate area, however, was level enough, and they had stopped at what appeared to once have been a sizable town but had dwindled down to a mere hamlet. It made her sad for some reason. After passing through the warmth of the tunnel, the air felt cool, and M shivered at the change in temperature as much as at the deserted town.

Again, M was aware of the presence of one of the men outside her door, and knew the train was about to move forward when she heard him descend the steps of her platform, though it was obvious that he tried to conceal his movements.

Now began the descent down the Cheat River grade, where the road would cross that unfortunately-named stream (though the road would meet and parallel it long before) as both road and river made their way down the slope. Her father had given two reasons for the name of the river, enumerated 1. and 2., as if these speculations were facts that had to be kept in order and separated:

1. pioneers had mistakenly thought they had reached the Ohio River, and so had felt cheated when it was realized they had not

2. the water was a dark color and the depth of the river changed a great deal; the color concealed the depths, so that some drowned unfortunates were "cheated" of their lives when they thought they were crossing in shallow waters.

M tried to imagine dark-colored waters but could only see in her mind the Ohio River, which seemed perpetually muddy, but not truly dark. It must be a sinister river, indeed, to have dark waters. Before this cheating river, however, M re-read a well-worn section of one of the reports, from the year of her birth. Her father had not always been a stockholder, but the reports of the Baltimore & Ohio were highly prized by engineers of all roads for their detailed accounts of bridges and viaducts built, tunnels bored, and all other manner of obstacles overcome. The B&O had become a proving ground for railroad engineering, technology, and mechanics, and other roads had watched and reaped the benefits.

It had been the discovery of the Tray Run viaduct in the reports that had first ignited M's fears for her father. She had cried every time he left on one of his extended trips to the east. Her mother had become aggravated, even sarcastic, at M's behavior. She had forbidden M to read the reports, had locked her father's study to deny access to them. This was the very reason, she had told M, that girls were not fit for the study of such subjects, and why M should devote herself to those activities and studies God had intended for girls. But her father had instead provided M with ever more information, in the hopes of allaying her fears of roads she had never traveled. Over the years, he had brought home images and sketches from different sources of all the viaducts and bridges and tunnels, pictorial testaments to their sturdiness. All these were carefully placed between the appropriate pages of the reports. In the reports themselves, he had provided facts and figures, his own drawings and diagrams, and referrals to books in his study (sometimes, from his great memory, even the exact pages had been numbered) for explanations of engineering theories, proving the scientific safety of the structures.

She had followed his glosses and studied the images, but instead of reassuring her, they had developed in her a kind of protective penance, paid in exchange for her father's safety. She had repeatedly studied the Tray Run viaduct – to her eye, dizzyingly high wire-thin trestling balancing on an even higher stone wall, suspended for hundreds of feet between two great spurs of the mountain, upon which a tiny train was expected to keep its footing, looking neither right nor left at certain destruction below. Each time she tortured herself with the possibility of disaster, forcing herself to imagine the terror of crossing the viaduct, and begging God to let her father pass safely. She believed that living the terror herself somehow kept it from her father.

Now she leafed through the pictures again, but her father no longer needed her protection. Now she would be the one crossing the tight-rope, and the terror would be real. She paused at the last picture in the bundle, the last picture her father had brought home, sometime early in the war. She was always slow to realize the magnitude or importance or sacrifice of any kindness or gesture, and now she realized, years too late, that in the middle of a war, with sons dying and stretched between the demands of both the farm and his duty to the Union, her father had stopped for a moment to collect this picture for her. More and more, with each year added to her age, she was beginning to see herself as perhaps others had always seen her – selfish and ungrateful and incapable of natural feelings.

Looking more closely at this last picture, and despite her entrenched fear of such structures, M for the first time saw the trestling as something beautiful. Iron arches shouldered the roadbed above as they stepped across the tops of the columns below. In the picture, these arches looked small, though M knew that the distance from column to column where the arches touched down was several yards. The vertical bents and the inclined posts were united and cinched at their throats by metal bands, and from that union sprung the graceful arcs that met between columns to create full arches. At the base of every second arch, a third arc sprouted forward to shoulder the weight of the walkway that extended beyond the tracks. And all of it – 50 feet high and 445 feet long – resting on a stone wall, itself one hundred feet high, built across the mouth of Tray Run as it trickled down the mountain and into the Cheat River. It was beautiful; the trestling even brought to mind cathedrals, for some reason. But it was a terrible and arrogant beauty, bracing itself against and competing with the even greater terrible beauty of the mountains.

She began to pray for a safe crossing, but she found she lacked the same intensity that she had brought to her prayers for her father. She found instead a dogged resignation to merely endure the passing.

Some change in the sound of the air as the train passed through it alerted M to a change in the road. Leaving the written terror of Tray Run on the desk, she chanced a peak out one of the windows, and immediately drew back at the sight. The Cheat River was far, far below, seen at a very steep angle. The train was crossing one of the B&O's celebrated masonry walls, Buckhorn Wall, ninety feet high; the wall itself was built into a cliff far above the river. From this point to Rowlesburg, the tracks clung to the mountainside, sometimes on a ledge hardly a few yards wide, often on curves, and always going down on a 2% grade, so minuscule on paper, yet so challenging on tracks.

Four miles, only four miles, and Tray Run, and then Buckeye Run, would be behind them, and they would be past the first of the two wretched mountains that the wretched B&O crossed. The only saving grace to this section of the road was the complete lack of sidings – they would not be required to pull off on some piece of track tottering on the edge of a precipice.

It would have been reckless to proceed down this slope at a normal speed, but even so, M found their rate of travel almost agonizing. It was only five miles down this side of the mountain, and even at freight train speeds it would take little more than thirty minutes. She only had to wait and endure.

M stood in the middle of her car, eyes closed, concentrating on the passage of time, counting the clicks of the wheels rolling on the tracks. She had achieved some measure of calm when a loud crack followed by a series of thumps broke her thoughts. The car rattled slightly, curiously intensifying as the train slowed, then stopping abruptly when the train stopped. M remained standing, her mind stalled. She strained to hear anything that would indicate the reason for the stop. She did not think enough time had passed for the train to have reached Rowlesburg, though she would have been happy to find that to be the case. No; the whistle had not blown its announcement to the town. They were somewhere suspended in the mountains between Buckhorn Wall and Rowlesburg.

She heard someone run past her car towards the rear of the train. Then she heard Mr. Hughes and the engineer of the Camel talking, quite close.

"It will go hard on Miss Warner. There have been all manner of delays on her trip."

"It's what comes of pulling together a bastard train." Perhaps the Camel's engineer regretted speaking ill of another man's train, for he added, "Still, it could happen to any train and it could have been worse."

There were more footsteps, then she heard Argent ask, "What's the trouble?"

"Broken axle." M did not like this Camel engineer; she was certain that Argent had addressed Mr. Hughes, but the other engineer had answered quickly, assuming primacy. There was really no need for a helper going down the mountain; why hadn't he uncoupled at Tunnelton?

M wondered at the calm deliberations of the men as they doubtless stood at the site of the broken axle. Broken axles were reported constantly in the newspapers, sometimes with deadly results. She moved to the side of the car away from the sound of the men's voices. She wanted to see where they had stopped, but she did not want to chance any of the men seeing her at the window; as long as they were busy discussing the broken axle, she might be able to slip out onto her platform, if only to prove to them that she intended to do as she wished. As she pulled aside the curtain, she heard Merritt offer, or rather state his intention, to go to Rowlesburg for help. They must be close to Rowlesburg, then.

M's mouth suddenly filled with saliva – they were stopped on the Tray Run viaduct. She knew it with complete certainty, without consulting her father's notes or the B&O reports, without seeing the cathedral-like trestling, without knowing their speed or the time passed since Buckhorn Wall. There was the Cheat River, over two hundred feet below, its dark waters made almost black in the shadow of the gorge. Her heart skipped a beat, then began beating out of time, an erratic rhythm that reached her ears and held there, blocking out all other sound, confusing her mind. She felt her body sway and her legs almost gave way, but she managed to hold herself upright until the wild drumming in her ears passed, and her balance and hearing were restored.

She found herself back in the middle of the car, a childish strategy to keep the train balanced. The men were still outside talking, calmly, as if they were on a flat plain, on a safe siding next to double tracks, as if they were not stranded on a narrow strip of road, perched high atop a mere weaving of iron threads. The brakeman had been sent back up the road to warn oncoming trains of their predicament, and the fireman had been sent ahead of the train for the same purpose. Merritt was on his way to Rowlesburg. For the first time, a terror seized M for Merritt – he would be walking the tracks, the only route to Rowlesburg, and the tracks were infamously built along the cliffs of the mountain. If a train did come from Rowlesburg, was there anywhere safe to step off? It was only a mile, a fifteen-minute walk, shorter if Merritt ran. She began to pray for Merritt's safety. More than ever, she missed her father's watch; in twenty minutes, Merritt would either be safe in Rowlesburg or dead; prayer would be pointless after twenty minutes.

At some point M sat on the floor, though she could not say when she had done so. She became aware of the fact when she heard Argent call her name, rather forcefully, the tone people usually took with her when she had not responded to first, second, and even third attempts to gain her attention. When she looked up she found that her neck was stiff. Argent was standing just inside her door, the door still open behind him. He was watching her with that look of concern that sparked in her an instant, seething anger.

"Yes?" She refused to acknowledge anything more than his mere presence; she pointedly remained as she was, on the floor. In truth, she found that her legs were nearly asleep, and she didn't care to struggle to her feet in front of him or to accept his assistance in rising. She sat gazing up at him, as if sitting on the floor in the middle of a train car was acceptable behavior, possibly even preferable behavior.

Argent paused, confused, then delivered his message. "Doubtless you are aware we have stopped." Argent paused again, but Miss Warner merely looked up at him, expectantly. "We have suffered a broken axle, but expect the arrival of help very soon, and hope to experience only a short delay."

M, by now, had acquired something of the language of travel with Argent (and Merritt), and understood a short delay to mean nothing short of several hours', if not an entire day's, delay. Moreover, she knew a broken axle, as well as being almost commonplace and vexatious, was also a great devourer of time. And usually, now that she thought about it, a broken axle was usually discovered when the train was thrown from the tracks as a result. The great Angola disaster was precipitated by a merely bent axle. The thought of such an event at such a place as Tray Run made her scalp prickle and the color ran from her face.

In the darkened car, with all the windows curtained, Argent did not notice her color, though he sensed some change in her. "Every precaution has been taken; we are in no danger."

She noticed that he had not mentioned their location. "Has Mr. Merritt returned?"

Again, Argent paused. How much had she heard? They had taken great pains to keep their voices low and had even moved the conversation to the very back of the train. He had explained to both engineers Miss Warner's fear of heights and had enjoined both men to refrain from referring to their present position. Argent had, frankly, been surprised that Miss Warner had not attempted to exit her car; he had been standing guard, so to speak, near her platform to intercept her at the earliest signs of her emerging. "No, but I did not expect him to return. He will wait for our arrival in Rowlesburg."

M hated herself for what she said next, for the cowardice of it. "Have you been to look in on the horses?"

Argent knew then that Miss Warner was very aware of their position on the road. She would never have asked his appraisal of the horses but would have insisted on seeing to Emmett herself; she would have done so long before now. She was apparently, however, unaware of the particulars of the broken axle – it was the axle to the front of the stock car that had broken, the axle that ran under Emmett's stall. It seemed to Argent a small miracle that the car had not left the track, or that the following cars had not piled into each other. Miss Warner was apparently ignorant, as well, of the suggestion to remove all the horses from the car. The engineers had expressed some surprise at the position of the break along the axle. Each man had taken a turn under the car to examine it for himself and each had said with peculiar wonder, "Snapped in two – in the very middle."

"Emmett is unharmed, as are our own horses." Argent hesitated, knowing his next words would be taken as a command of sorts, and Miss Warner did not respond well to commands. "There is little room to work here, so I must ask you to remain in your car while repairs are effected." To his astonishment, Miss Warner nodded her understanding and agreement. Before he left, Argent held out his watch. "It will not make the time pass any more quickly but knowing the time may offer some comfort."

The watch ticked slowly as they waited for help from Rowlesburg. Eventually, M was aware of the presence of more men on the viaduct as new voices were heard. Each man examined the situation, and all agreed that a broken axle was the cause, and that such a perfect break so perfectly placed was unusual. She heard the sounds of repair, though she did not know what repairs were made or, rather, how they were made – one more thing she had forgotten to ask her father.

Mr. Argent knocked on her door once more, to announce that they were at last ready to move. Without opening the door, M thanked him. She felt her car taken up in its turn as the slack in the couplings disappeared under the pull of the engines. Only then did she realize that she had not returned the watch to Argent.

They arrived in Rowlesburg after dark, though it may still have been light in places out of the deep shadow of the mountains. As soon as the train came to a stop, M gathered up her reports and journal, replaced them in her grip bag, and headed for her door. She was more than ready to feel terra firma under her feet. She was also determined to escape her car for the night and sleep in a hotel room, whose key she commanded; she was aware that she had been locked in last night.

Upon opening her door, M found Argent standing on the platform, as if keeping some appointed time to meet her. Any other time, it would annoy her, but she was worn out with worry and praying over these last four miles, her neck was sore, and a pricking behind her eye promised a sizable headache. If Mr. Argent wished to escort her to the hotel, he may well do so, but his presence would be dismissed for the night once she had a room.

Argent noted the grip bag and the unmistakable signs of one of Miss Warner's 'states.' He said nothing but relieved her of her grip bag. This was the first time that she had let either man help her with this bag, and he was struck with its weight. He had not returned her father's gun to her; he and Merritt had agreed to withhold it from her and had prepared a response whenever she should ask its whereabouts. They had referred to the gun only obliquely and sparingly and had gingerly indicated that it was still in Cincinnati, awaiting her return for her court date. Incredibly, she had never mentioned the gun, though it must have held great sentimental value for her. Now Argent wondered if the unusual weight of her bag indicated a second or third gun. Miss Warner displayed a decidedly unfeminine taste for guns.

M was grateful to step off the train but admitted that she did not know where to go. It was a dark town, little more than a village – there were few lights seen (and the nearly full moon had not yet shown itself), indicating a mere scattering of buildings. As he had done before, Argent barely touched her elbow, guiding her down the tracks a short way, until turning down one of Rowlesburg's few actual streets. After a short block they reached a very broad street, evidently the main street of the town. They turned right, heading towards the river and the bridge their train would cross tomorrow, before beginning the climb up Cranberry grade.

"Merritt is waiting for us at the River House. After dinner, we will return to our respective cars, so that we may get the earliest possible start in the morning."

M did not initially respond to Argent's statements, turning instead to Emmett's accommodations for the night. Once she was satisfied as to these, she informed Argent that she would not be traveling on the morrow – she would not, could not, travel on Still Friday, one of the holiest days of the church calendar, and certainly the holiest day of Karwoche, of Holy Week. She would be attending any services the town's church provided or spending a good part of the day in prayer and reflection.

Argent had the good sense not to argue with M, or any woman, over religious practices. Once again, he was uncomfortably reminded that his own religious practices had slipped somewhat these past few years. M must have felt Argent's consternation, for she added, "I regret the interruption to the schedule."

The River House was an indifferent hotel with indifferent food; Argent could not fault M for picking through most of her meal. Any intentions M had of staying the night here were left at the door.

Mrs. Hughes had apologized, upon their arrival in town, for not having dinner ready, but the incident on Tray Run viaduct had somewhat unsettled her and, moreover, had confused her cooking schedule. Argent had told her to think nothing of it, but it was regrettable nonetheless, given the alternative.

After dinner, M announced her intention to locate the Catholic church in town; perhaps tomorrow's services were posted on the door. Merritt looked to Argent, who shook his head.

Merritt and Argent had been through Rowlesburg many times but had never tarried there longer than the usual time involved in an ordinary stop on a train's schedule. They had never, in fact, left the car while in Rowlesburg. Still, it was a small town, and it wouldn't be too difficult to find the church. M seemed confident in her search as well, leading the men down the hotel porch steps, and heading down the main street and away from the river.

M thought of Randy, as she did every Holy Thursday. Nothing ever dulled his wit, not even the solemnity of Lent in general or of the Triduum in particular. One Holy Thursday – his last, she realized – as the family was bouncing along the Louisville-Taylorsville Pike, in the cold dark of the morning, on their way to commemorate the Lord's Last Supper, Randy had quipped that if Mass were being held in the morning, it should be called the Lord's Last Breakfast. Several of the older boys had laughed, and M was sure she had even heard her mother's soft chuckle coming from the front of the wagon, but her father had not been amused. Randy had received rather harsh punishment afterwards, as had the older boys, who had not only laughed at Randy's near-blasphemy but had also failed their duty as older brothers to set the example for proper piety.

She wished she was like Randy – bright and laughing, irrepressible, even in the cold and the dark. But some flaw in her character was drawn to the darkness and heavy foreboding of Maundy Thursday and Good Friday, to the plaintive chants of Tenebrae. On those days and in those services, everyone – every man, woman and child, even her tall, strong father – was a child, whimpering and huddled in a dark corner, trembling in suspended dread of deserved punishment and pain. There was an unnatural thrill at laying bare her fundamental guilt, the Original Sin that somehow marked her as both damned and saved. *O Felix Culpa!* Oh, happy fault that sent Christ to the Cross, the guilt of that Crucifixion which inspired such wrenching prose and poetry and such mournful music.

M was obviously lost in thought, and Merritt hoped to save her from becoming lost in the town. "How do you know there is a Catholic church here? It is a very small town."

It was a question, now that it was asked, M thought Argent should have asked. "Dad told me. He was very fond of Father Meurer, the priest at Grafton. He said Father Meurer rode up and down these mountains, ministering at towns along the railroad – Newburg, Tunnelton, Rodemer, Cranberry. Rowlesburg is a very small town, but there are a lot of Catholics here, working for the railroad."

"What is the name of the church? Perhaps we could ask someone."

"I don't know the name; it had not been built the last time my father was through here."

"Then how can you be certain it has been built now?"

"Dad told me."

Merritt was touched by the simple faith M had in her father's words; he hoped M would not be disappointed by them here. Argent, on the other hand, found M's parceling out of facts tiresome. After a few more questions, it was learned that Mr. Warner had enjoyed a correspondence with Father Meurer and had donated towards the building of a church in Rowlesburg, though he had not lived to see it realized, the church being hardly a year in existence, and Mr. Warner had spent the last of his days in 1869 ill and dying.

After a moment's quiet walking, M suddenly said, "Thaumaturga."

"Beg pardon?"

"It's Greek."

"Yes, I understand the word, but what prompted you to say it just now?"

"Mr. Merritt asked the name of the church, and I had said, 'I don't know,' but it has come to me that I do know. The church was to be dedicated to St. Philomena. Pope Gregory called her the Thaumaturga. It's a beautiful title, though, of course, not as beautiful as Theotokos. I find I like Greek, or the few words of it I know."

They reached the church, and there was indeed some service in progress — very faint light could be seen coming through the windows. M waited by the door, listening, then announced, "Tenebrae is finished." She sounded disappointed and cheated.

"Someone is in there – I see a few candles lit." Argent sighed at the thought, but offered, "We could wait until one of them leaves and ask about services tomorrow."

Merritt had a better idea. He moved to open the door, but M intercepted him and forcefully removed his hand from the handle.

"What are you doing?" M fairly hissed at him.

"I thought to go in and quietly ask the person closest to the door for information."

"No one will talk to you now; they are at perpetual adoration. People will be coming and going all night to pray before the Holy Eucharist. People are there to pray, not to talk or hand out schedules. I will return here tomorrow, early in the morning, and hope to be here in time."

M had relieved Argent of her grip bag after dinner and had occasionally transferred it from hand to hand as they walked. She shifted it once again as she led the men away from St. Philomena. It was a small church for a small town, and she wondered where such a church would prepare an altar of repose for the Sacred Host this night. She selfishly thought of her own repose.

"Are there any other hotels in Rowlesburg?" She was tired, she wanted to get out of her dress, wash up and work on her notes. She had to be prepared for Cumberland.

"One – the Virginia House." M felt Argent stiffen at Merritt's response. Merritt must have sensed it, too, for he was quick to add, "But it is no better than the River House."

"Is there something wrong with your car?"

"No, nothing."

In their own car, Argent explained M's determination to remain in Rowlesburg for the whole of Good Friday. Merritt agreed it was an understandable delay but disagreed with Argent's assertion that M would be able to celebrate Easter in Washington.

"That is a rather dim view of our prospects. Despite the aggravations of the road so far, I feel our luck is about to turn, and that once we are on the double tracks beyond Cumberland, our humble status as a wildcat train will not be such a burden to the dispatchers."

"It is not the double tracks or the dispatchers that I fear will further slow our progress. We have orders from Whitley to look into a matter in Cumberland, since we are practically there. That telegram was sent yesterday, long before today's delays and mishaps and not knowing of Miss Warner's religious practices. He expected us there last night."

"What is this matter in Cumberland? I did not know there were any concerns there. Whitley can't expect us to look into any counterfeiting or other such crimes – not with any proper attention – while we are in company with Miss Warner. There must be someone he can send in our stead, and with greater speed, I might add."

"He did send someone, or rather Nettleship did – one of his Philadelphia boys. There was some rumor of a new partnership being formed near Cumberland, with heavy financing from an unknown but prominent politician connected with the canal."

Despite his aggravation with Whitley, Argent could not help considering the puzzle. "The good Senator Spates, perhaps."

"Perhaps; but Maryland has exonerated Senator Spates of those other charges."

"That is so, but you and I both know that once a man is accused, suspicion clings to him, no matter who has exonerated him. And after being accused of embezzlement and forgery, it is no great leap to suspect him of counterfeiting, especially when such a convenient vehicle as the very canal he had allegedly cheated is at hand, to float bad money downstream."

It was not clear whether Merritt agreed with the conjecture about Senator Spates, but he understood the value of the canal for counterfeiting – it had been used in this manner before. "These little towns on the canal, and the even smaller ones in the country, would not know they had been paid in the spurious stuff until long after the pushers were gone."

"Are we to help in confirming this rumor? Again, the presence of Miss Warner is no small obstacle. She is all but ready to leave us now. She will certainly abandon this trip if we ask her to wait while we conduct our investigation in Cumberland."

"I wouldn't give too much weight to her inquiries about hotels – after enduring several hours perched high atop Tray Run viaduct in that car that she clearly does not like, and no doubt gritting her teeth and praying all the while, she simply might have liked to sleep somewhere else tonight. We should consider allowing her to stay with Emmett in his car for the duration of the trip."

Argent stared at Merritt until he returned to the matter of Cumberland. "We are simply to find Nettleship's associate, retrieve what information he has found, and bring it with us to Washington."

"It can't be relayed in any other way, by any other courier?"

"If Senator Spates is indeed the subject of the rumor, I can only imagine that these investigations are being carried out with the greatest of discretion. Information of such a delicate nature would need to be safeguarded during its travels as well as during its collection."

"Have we a name by which to search for this man?"

"No, but we have a location. The Slack Water."

Argent closed his eyes a moment. "In Shantytown? We will likely bring back not only information but vermin of every type as well. And what are we to do with Miss Warner while we visit the most disreputable part of Cumberland?"

"I'm sure there is some Catholic ritual or service happening the day before Easter. We'll escort her to the Catholic church there, arrange for Mr. Hughes to escort her back to the train, while we conduct our business."

"If this Saturday service is as long as Tenebrae last night or the service this morning, we will have plenty of time to conduct our business and return to escort M ourselves back to the train. And we leave earliest – earliest – Sunday morning."

Merritt cleared his throat and presented an unwelcome fact. "She will, of course, want to attend Easter services."

Argent at first seemed surprised, then covered his obvious lapse in planning. "Of course. Certainly. Then at our first opportunity afterwards, we take our leave of Cumberland, making good time on double tracks, leaving her with President Grant well in time for Easter Sunday supper."

Merritt mulled over this a moment. “We promised to have her back home for Easter. She will not want to spend any part of the day with President Grant, a day she had thought she would spend with Miss Carrie and Mr. Henry and little Thea.” Argent sputtered an interruption, but Merritt continued. “Let us celebrate the day with her, dine with her – a proper feast in honor of the day – and possibly take a walk around town, to the Narrows perhaps — she would like the view, I think. And then we take our leave of Cumberland, at the earliest – earliest – opportunity Monday morning, making good time on double tracks, leaving her with President Grant well in time for Monday supper.”

Monday. Argent nearly groaned. Monday would mark two full weeks since they had set out from Louisville with Miss Warner.

Merritt guessed at Argent’s silence; he sought to soothe his friend’s disappointment. “One day more won’t matter.”

Argent merely harrumphed. How could they be assured there would be only one more day? How could it have possibly taken this long to reach Rowlesburg? The trip so far had presented an amazing variety of delays; Miss Warner’s religious duties may prove to be the only truly understandable one.

In her car, M searched and scoured her mind for a way to quietly leave the train and Grant’s men at Cumberland, liberate Emmett from his car, lay a false return trail on the B&O, and all with a long enough start to frustrate the inevitable chase. M shuddered at the thought of returning by the route she had just traveled.

She could not think about that. She should not be thinking about anything but the solemnity of the evening, of Christ’s Agony in the Garden. She should have dismissed Argent and Merritt at the church and entered to offer prayers before the Blessed Sacrament. But she was tired and needed to make her plans. Christ’s reproach rose up before her – *Una hora non potuistis vigilare mecum?* Too many demands for her attention were crowding her mind, and she felt the first tightening of her skull that heralded a headache. She found the laudanum in her grip bag, and with a prayer asking forgiveness for seeking relief from pain while Christ was about to undergo his yearly crowning of thorns and scourging at the stake, M swallowed a dose. She needed her sleep these next two nights – between the Mass of the Pre-Sanctified in the morning and Tenebrae in the evening, M intended to finish her preparations for escaping from Merritt and Argent, this train, West Virginia, and whatever was waiting for her on the other side of Cumberland; and on Saturday she had a long day of walking ahead of her.

Sometime during the night, her hard-won sleep was disturbed by a click and a soft step on the platform. Argent or Merritt had turned the key and locked her door.

15 — *Good Friday*

M was up early, but not earlier than the man who had unlocked her car door. Upon descending the steps of her platform, Merritt joined her as if he had been watching for these very movements. Normally, this would merely rankle her, but after having been locked inside her car these last two nights, coupled with the earlier revelation of Miss Carrie's involvement, this constant attendance of one or the other of these men began to assume a sinister form.

Merritt greeted her pleasantly, but she merely nodded at him. He didn't ask her destination and she didn't offer it; he simply walked by her side until they reached St. Philomena. Merritt then tipped his hat before taking his leave.

M dropped her veil into place, then entered the church. Despite her early arrival, M was not the first to enter the nave. There were several other people already at their devotions, mostly women saying the rosary, but there were a few men as well. And there were, of course, those participating in the perpetual adoration of the Most Blessed Sacrament since yesterday's Mass, when two Hosts were consecrated, instead of the usual one. In the church in Grafton, as in all Catholic churches the world over, the second Host had been reserved for today's services, when a true Mass would not be celebrated – there would be no celebration of any kind on Good Friday or Holy Saturday, the Church being in solemn mourning at the death of Jesus Christ. After yesterday's Mass – after the elevation of the two Hosts – there had been a last pealing of the church bells before utter silence reigned, to be broken only by the celebration of Easter. The second Host, the Presanctified Eucharist in the form of bread only, had been escorted in a chalice with great ceremony to its altar of repose, especially prepared with the costliest fabrics and precious metals and gems that each parish could provide. There the Host would reside, in constant attendance and perpetual adoration throughout the night, until unveiled and consumed by the celebrant on Good Friday during what was erroneously called 'Mass' of the Presanctified.

M knelt in one of the pews in the back of the church, but though she prayed, she paid little attention to the words. Cumberland rose before her. Cumberland would either offer her freedom or be the final bolt in her prison – once they reached the double tracks past Cumberland, there would be no more frequent or protracted stops; she would be locked in her car until delivered up to Grant's plans. What were those plans? Why was he so adamant that she travel to Washington City?

She did not know when Mr. and Mrs. Hughes joined her, only that she had been smelling for some little time the tell-tale oil and coal and smoke odors of a trainman that no amount of scrubbing could eliminate from body or clothes. M already knew Mr. and Mrs. Hughes to be Catholic – they had attended both Spy Wednesday's Tenebrae and Maundy Thursday Mass with her – but the presence of the fireman was unexpected. M chanced a glance to the left of Mr. Hughes, and now that she saw the fireman, mostly wiped clean of coal dust and grime, she knew him to be the Hughes' son.

The priest (whom M assumed was Father Meurer, of her father's acquaintance) entered silently, as they all had, without song or greeting or genuflection. Everything was changed from yesterday's Mass; everything bespoke mourning, desolation, and terror. The priest and his deacons wore black today, whereas yesterday their vestments were white. The tabernacle door had been left open yesterday – God was gone, His people's sins too much, for the moment, for even Him, and parentless, the Church felt the loss. The altar here, as in the church at Grafton, had been stripped bare yesterday, and the Cross had been veiled by a black cloth. There was no music, except the voices of the choir, and the bells had been silenced. Even the candles reflected the somberness of the day, the pure white wax candles having been exchanged for those of yellow wax. They were no longer in a church, but a tomb, dark and lifeless, and they were themselves but shadows, searching and scratching along the rough walls, looking for the way out, hoping for the light.

While Father prayed in silence before the altar, its forlorn nakedness was covered with a single cloth, then he rose, and the lengthy morning services of Good Friday began.

First there were the two lessons, prophecies from the Old Testament. Then, for the third time this week and the second time in as many days, M heard the Passion from the Gospel of St. John. Each time she heard it, she was struck with the strangeness of it, the dream-like narration. There were so many men there in the garden, yet so few words spoken. It was as if the scenes were being played out in an awkwardly edited play on a poorly lighted stage; or maybe it was the olive trees and torches that distorted the scene in M's mind. There was the confrontation in the garden of Gethsemane with its strange negotiations between Jesus and the guards (Jesus protecting his friends, like any friend would, telling the guards to 'let these men go'), and Peter's sudden violence against the poor servant, with the equally sudden appearance of a sword among the disciples (why had Peter attacked a servant and not one of the guards, and why slice off the servant's ear? Did that mean something to Jews, or perhaps Peter was simply a very poor swordsman – after all, how much opportunity would a fisherman have to use a sword? And John had made a point of identifying the servant as Malchus; why?) There was also the sudden flare of Jesus' anger. But Peter seemed to bring out the worst in Jesus – Jesus had been angry with Peter on other occasions: planning some festival of booths after witnessing the Transfiguration, admonishing Jesus for talking of his coming death (*Retro vade, Satan!*), and now for using a sword to protect Jesus himself. M reflected that in some ways she was very much like Peter, always misunderstanding things, always mis-stepping.

Then there was Peter's crisis in the courtyard, the long night of terrified, shivering vigil while Jesus, culled from his friends and constant companions, underwent his examination by Annas, then by Caiaphas. There was the crowing of the rooster, such a common sound at home. It was strange to think that there were roosters in the Holy Land and Kentucky alike; perhaps Kentucky was a Holy Land in its own way.

Jesus seemed more human in the hours before he was to die than in any other story about him – he had asked his friends to be spared, he had barked an order at Peter, and now he seemed prickly, even antagonistic, in his interview with Annas: "Why question me? Ask those who heard me" and "If I have spoken wrongly, testify as to the wrong. But if I have spoken rightly, why do you strike me?" (M reflected, however, that if she had spoken to her father or any authority as Jesus had, she could well expect to be slapped.) He was almost taunting as he answered Pontius Pilate about being a king: "Do you ask this on your own, or did others tell you about me?"

Then there was the unimaginable violence done to Jesus, which should have filled pages, but which was reported with a few words, in the most ordinary tones: Pilate had him flogged (John might have said with equal composure, Pilate had his carpets beaten); the soldiers struck him in the face; here, they crucified him.

There was the crucifixion itself, with its carnival-like atmosphere – the people gathered to watch, the soldiers gambling over Jesus' clothes, the chief priests haggling over the inscription above Jesus and their whining directives to hasten the crucifixions of Jesus and the two thieves (so that the Sabbath may not be fouled by the very corpses of their own making). Did Jesus hear any of it through his suffering?

At the words *Et inclinato capite, tradidit spiritum*, they all knelt, just one of many such times the Church would kneel this day, in mingled shame, supplication, and adoration. After the reading of the Passion, there came the intercessory prayers, with the strange formula of standing and kneeling – *Oremus. Flectamus genua. Levate.* – over and over again the congregation was invited to kneel, then immediately told to stand again. These were prayers for the Church, the Pope, the bishops and clergy and catechumens, for the end of disease, famine, and worldly errors, prayers even for heretics, schismatics, pagans, and Jews. The prayer for the Jews was the only time during these extensive prayers that the congregation did not kneel. In kneeling in mockery before Jesus during his Passion, the Jews had defiled the gesture of deep deference, respect, and humility, and so the Church would not kneel for the Jews, even when praying for them. The prayer even referred to them as *perfidis Judaeis*, though it seemed harsh to call them all perfidious, when Jesus Himself was a Jew, as were his disciples, and it was very probable that not all Jews had knelt in mockery. It was a point of theology M had once raised in school, but she had been punished for the thought and words.

The bleak barrenness of the room was a fit setting for the desolation, despondency, sorrow, and grief relived in the Passion. All statues had been covered with a purple veil these last two weeks, since Passion Sunday. But the Cross, which had been covered with a black cloth, was now slowly revealed to the congregation. As an act of humility, Father had divested himself of his chasuble, the vestment that marked him as a priest. Beginning on the Epistle side of the Altar, he received the veiled Cross from his deacon. Little by little he unveiled the Cross, first the part of the upright above the crossbar; then, after each step, as he moved closer and closer to the people in the pews, he revealed first the right arm of the Cross, and finally, as he stood before the middle of the Altar, he removed the cloth entirely. At each exposure of the Cross, it had been elevated, the second time higher than the first, and this third and final time, highest of all. Now Father removed his shoes and, genuflecting three times, he kissed the Cross.

Now the Church was confronted with the improperia of Christ, the awful Reproaches in which Christ laid bare the ingratitude of his people. M heard the priest intone the ancient, plaintive censures – *Popule Meus, quid feci tibi? Aut in quo contristavi te? Responde mihi* – and she answered with the other worshippers, *Sanctus Deus, Sanctus fortis, Sanctus immortalis, miserere nobis*, as they shuffled closer to the Cross, to venerate it with a kiss as Father had done. But she could not keep her mind on the service; she could not say at any time to which of the twelve reproaches she was responding. Good Friday was like that – time almost stood still inside the church, the service moving at a glacial pace, the repetitive nature of the back-and-forth between congregation and priest lulling M into a kind of trance.

Having sat in the rearmost pew, M was one of the last of the congregation to be reseated after venerating the Cross. And as such, she missed seeing the Corporal spread upon the Altar. It was a silly thing, but she was captivated by the ceremonies of linen that occurred on the Altar, even though – possibly because – she could not actually see the ritual. The priest, of course, stood in front of the altar, blocking what transpired there, but M saw in her mind, intuited it from watching the motions of the priest, the reverent unfolding of the Corporal – first to the left, then to the right, then it was unfolded away from the priest, and finally the last fold was opened towards the priest. Such unyielding and unchanging exactitude, however, could be expected for the fine cloth that would receive the Blessed Sacrament, pre-sanctified at yesterday's Mass. But today, only the priest would partake of the Holy Eucharist. By the time M regained her seat, Father had resumed his chasuble, the candles had been lighted, and the Chalice containing the consecrated Host had been retrieved from its altar of repose.

And now came a point in the ceremony that had made her mother choke, but which M found almost intoxicating. The Sacred Host was removed from the Chalice and placed upon a Paten, and wine and water were poured into the now empty Chalice. Father Meurer then censed the offerings and the Altar with the thurible, but in acknowledgement of the grief of this day, did not thurify himself. The small church was filled with the aroma of incense, heady and salty and full of smoldering mystery. M was so entranced in the moment that she began the reply *Suscipiat*, responding without thought to the priest's *Orate fratres: ut meum ac vestrum sacrificium acceptabile fiat apud Deum Patrem Omnipotentem*. Fortunately, her mistake was covered by Father's immediate singing of the *Pater Noster*. After this and a following prayer, the Host was elevated on high, high above Father's head so as to be seen by the congregation at his back, and the congregation bowed deeply before it. M then watched the movements of Father's back with an almost clinical observation as he broke the Host into three pieces, dropping one into the Chalice while reciting some secret prayer that only priests knew. The other two pieces Father held in his left hand, saying three times, *Domine, non sum dignus ut intres sub tectum meum; sed tantum dic verbo, et sanabitur anima mea*. The congregation watched in envious reverence as the priest consumed the Host and then drank the water and wine blessed with, but not transubstantiated by, the Particle of the Host dropped into the Chalice. And thus ended in a somewhat unsatisfying manner, the Mass of the Presanctified.

But it was not the end of Good Friday services. As soon as Father Meurer left the Altar and returned to the Sacristy, the small choir immediately began reciting Vespers. Small as it was, the immediate town could not have produced the choir, not with two other denominations vying for vocal talent. These were most likely railroad men and farmers come in from the surrounding countryside to both attend and serve in Good Friday services. And with them came their sons, the younger boys supplying the higher voices of the choral music. These Vespers, however, were simply recited, and M felt something had been lost because of it. Certainly her attention wandered, though it was not completely lost – she was able to respond at the appropriate moments, and she fully listened to the *Magnificat*, that inspired explosion of praise, thanksgiving, humility, and obedience spoken by the Virgin Mary upon learning of her divine purpose. Eventually, the last prayer of Vespers was said, and M, along with the Hughes family, emerged from the darkened church into the lazy sunshine of early afternoon. The air was unusually warm and strangely still, a brooding atmosphere appropriate for the solemnity and latent excitement of Good Friday. Unbidden, the phrase, 'Something wicked this way comes' came to mind, and she crossed herself for such a wicked thought on such a holy day. Still, the weather promised an unfavorable change.

Apparently, Merritt was completely agreeable to allowing Mr. and Mrs. Hughes (and their son) to escort M back to the train, but he did not trust M to make it on her own from the engine to her car. At her door, he informed her that the train would be leaving soon, and that a meal had been left for her inside. Then he tipped his hat, as he had at the church. M noted, however, that he did not leave the platform of her car until she had entered and closed the door.

Almost immediately, the train started for the bridge over Cheat River, both engines having been kept stoked and ready for departure while Mr. Hughes and his family were at their devotions. Once again, the Camel led as they worked their way up, Cranberry Grade, the next grade in their trip through the West Virginia mountains. This was even steeper than the Newburg Grade they had climbed, as well as the Cheat River Grade they had cautiously descended. Only Seventeen-Mile Grade was steeper, but they would be going down that harrowing hill, on their descent into Maryland.

Once M felt the train regain land on the other side of the bridge, she looked out one of the windows at Rowlesburg. From this perspective, the geography of the town appeared as a tongue outlined by the river. The image made her think that Rowlesburg was somehow turned inside out, that the town – the tongue – was lapping at the river, instead of the water lapping at the land, as water was always portrayed in stories and travelogues and accounts of excursions. As the train drew further away from the town, she saw the quarry at the east end of the bridge, and little dots far along the riverbank that she eventually realized were tombstones in the town's cemetery. Her final sight of Rowlesburg before she left the window was that of little St. Philomena, Thaumaturga, at the far end of town, holding back the mountain.

M was grateful for the meal that had been provided for her – she had not had time for breakfast (such as was allowed) and there had been the usual restrictions regarding supper, a supper that had been disappointing to start with. Despite her hunger, however, she was unable to finish her dinner – the constant pull of the train up the grade, as well as the sharp curves, turned her hunger into a crouching queasiness, not fully recognized but ready to rise up. She dared not look out the windows for fear of igniting a complete paroxysm of her stomach. Even so, M was aware of the train's passage over a bridge or viaduct, and, of course, she knew when the train entered the two tunnels on this grade. She almost preferred the tunnels to the open-air scaling of the mountains.

M felt slightly uneasy at traveling on Good Friday – the family had always spent the day in Louisville, attending all the services of the day; travel was only accepted as a means to reach the place of services. But Mr. Hughes had told her that he had spoken with Father Malone (it was not Father Meurer, after all) about their circumstances, and Father had assured him that work could be done on Good Friday, but always with the suffering of Christ in mind. Mr. Hughes assured her that they would be stopping at Cumberland in time to attend Tenebrae there, as well as the Easter vigil Mass on the morning following, and that he had made this clear to Mr. Merritt and Mr. Argent; he had found them unusually receptive to the delay. Mrs. Hughes had then pressed into M's hands a prayerbook – a loan from Father Malone that M must return to him when she herself returned to the town on her journey back home. The prayerbook contained the Stations of the Cross, which, when said while clasping a blessed crucifix, would gain her indulgences. M was ashamed to say that she had not brought with her any blessed crucifix, not even her rosary, lost somewhere in the house or barn or lands of her home. She would have to recite the Stations without the aid of a crucifix and hope that God would grant her some recognition, some slight indulgence, for the effort. But then she thought of the faithful in Cincinnati, on Good Friday, praying up the wooden steps on Mt. Adams, ultimately reaching Immaculata Church and the great wooden Cross Archbishop Purcell had erected there. Her father had told her that many of them knelt all the way up the incline. M was kneeling in her crimson and carmine car, but she was gliding on rails up Cranberry grade. How could her poor prayers, said in comfort, contend with those said on hard wooden stairs, in the elements? She wanted to offer any indulgence she might gain for the dead of her family, if God could be persuaded to spread such a small indulgence equally over so many souls. She was being pulled up Cranberry, while Christ was being pushed up Calvary. Things were getting muddled in her head.

Though she recited the Stations of the Cross, contemplating the awful price Christ paid for her sins, M was also aware when the train had reached Cranberry Summit, and knew from the reports that there followed about twenty miles of level travel through lush glades. Here, between the Sixth Station, when Veronica wiped the face of Jesus, and the Seventh Station when Christ fell a second time, M allowed herself to enjoy the scenery and the uninterrupted sun. She even opened a window to allow fresh air into the car. It was much cooler here than in Rowlesburg, but even so, M intuitively knew that it should have been cooler still – the strange weather of Rowlesburg had followed them up the mountain. The trees were still bare here, though at home, the leaves would have been nearly at full growth.

The train stopped long enough for Mr. Hughes to receive his orders. M was surprised to find that the train was passing a long siding – the presence of a siding had almost always signaled a delay of some kind for their little train. When the train began to climb again, she shut her window and pulled the curtains closed. After crossing two bridges, M expected the train to stop once more for orders at Oakland, but the train only slowed before continuing on the road; Mr. Hughes must have been waved on. Neither did they stop at Altamont, the very summit of the B&O and the watershed of the Potomac and Ohio waters – the Potomac flowing east to Washington, and the Youghiogheny flowing west to the Monongohela, and ultimately to the blessed Ohio. They crossed a succession of bridges before pulling into Piedmont, but, again, only long enough to report their presence on the road and to receive orders to proceed to the next station. If all their stops were as short as these, M had good reason to hope to reach Cumberland in time for the last of the Tenebrae services this year. They stopped once more, to take on water at Rawlings, and then after crossing several more bridges – they had crossed at least thirty since leaving Rowlesburg, but M had stopped counting – the train pulled into Cumberland, something of a record run for their little train.

There was the usual consternation at the depot in Cumberland as regarded the little wildcat train. The depot itself was little more than a glorified shed, something of a lean-to attached to the Revere House, the tracks running through the eastern half of the building, with a brick, arched opening.

M had her bag ready, intent on staying in a hotel, whether the men liked it or not. She could not afford the possibility of being locked in her car at night; she needed the relative freedom of a hotel to effect her escape. She would not be denied this. She was pleasantly surprised, therefore, when Argent knocked on her door and informed her that they would be leaving the train for the time being. If she did not have her things together, Mrs. Hughes could send them to the hotel later. But M was ready, her grip bag in one hand and Argent's watch in the other, which she held out to him. Argent reclaimed his watch, then relieved M of her bag, handing it to James, a porter from the St. Nicholas Hotel posted at the depot. M noticed that James already had possession of Merritt's and Argent's bags as well. As soon as they were off the platform, Mr. Hughes backed the train out of the depot and back to the tracks around the roundhouse they had just recently passed. There it would stay until both the gentlemen and Miss Warner were ready to depart Cumberland.

Argent led Merritt and M down Baltimore Street to the St. Nicholas Hotel at the end of the block, at George Street. M wondered why they simply had not stayed at the Revere House, next to the depot, but it did not matter where they stayed – she would be gone tomorrow night. Merritt stood with M while Argent made the arrangements at the hotel desk; the porter stood nearby with their bags. Argent seemed particularly pleased when he rejoined them, and when they reached their rooms on the third floor, M knew why – their two rooms were connected, a mere door separating the two. The St. Nicholas was progressive enough to provide locks on the doors and keys to the guests, but not so progressive as to think that the woman in the group should have possession of any of them. The porter had led them into one of the two rooms, placing M's bag on the bed before taking Argent's and Merritt's bag into the next room, through the connecting door. Upon returning to what had been decided as M's room, the porter held out to Argent the three keys – one to each room and one to the door between them. M smoothly intercepted him and took all three. She took her bag into the next room, and returned with the men's bags. Only then did M return the room's key to Argent. She thanked the porter for his help, then retreated into her new room, and closed the door. Merritt thought that M had somehow managed to make locking the door louder than was actually possible.

She was equally successful in her efforts at silence as she left her room almost immediately afterwards. Merritt and Argent both, however, were familiar with her tactics, and Argent was waiting for her in the hallway as she slipped out of her room and quietly turned the key in her door. Argent adopted his most congenial tone.

"Miss Warner! Well, this is a happy coincidence! I was just about to descend to the lobby to finalize arrangements and inquire into other matters. We may descend together. What are your plans?"

M knew very well that Argent's presence in the hall was no coincidence, happy or otherwise. "I was just going to see about Emmett's arrangements – information about him was glaringly absent in your room just now. I was also going in search of Mr. and Mrs. Hughes. We had agreed to attend services together, if we arrived in Cumberland in time."

Argent held out his arm, indicating she should join him. "Mr. Hughes has informed us the intention to attend Good Friday services; he and Mrs. Hughes will be joining you here as soon as the train is settled. I would be happy to sit with you in the dining room until they arrive. As for Emmett, he is being boarded at the hotel stable, in the back of the lot. Instructions – written instructions – were sent along with Emmett as to his particular care. I know Emmett will be happy to see you, when you are free of your religious duties."

Religious duties. What did Argent, or Merritt, know of religious duties? She had not seen either man attend church at any time these last few weeks. It occurred to M that she had now known these men for two weeks, two weeks today, but it seemed far longer.

They had reached the landing on the second floor. M noticed closed double doors on the outside wall, doors she had not noticed the first time passing them. It was a curious place for doors, a full story off the ground, especially such grand doors and especially when, M knew, the hotel occupied a corner lot – there was no other building attached to the St. Nicholas. Argent noticed her distraction, and his first inclination was not to answer the obvious question on her mind. She would find out on her own, however, so he volunteered, "Those doors lead to a covered passage to the Windsor Hotel across George Street. When there is overflow at either hotel, guests are escorted across the passage to the hotel with available rooms." He took the opportunity to caution her, "That is for staff use only." That may or may not have been true, but Argent preferred that M believe it to be so.

M doubted that Argent truly had final arrangements or other business to conduct in the lobby, but she was not given the opportunity to catch him in any lies or deceptions. Mr. and Mrs. Hughes were waiting for her by the registry desk. Mrs. Hughes was very agitated – didn't Mr. Argent tell Miss Warner of the great need to hurry? Tenebrae services at St. Patrick were about to begin and St. Patrick was several blocks away. Mrs. Hughes grabbed M's elbow and hurried her to the door, but not before M thought she saw a look pass between Mr. Hughes and Argent.

St. Patrick Church reminded M of some Greek temple, with its triangular pediment spread over Corinthian columns. Only the cross at the top of the pediment redeemed the structure for Christian worship. The inside was far more adorned and polished than that of sweet little St. Philomena. As Thaumaturga, the Greek outer architecture would have been better served for St. Philomena. M preferred the back pews, but Mrs. Hughes led them almost to the very front of the church, where they managed to squeeze in just before the last Tenebrae of Lent began. M had noticed the absence of the fireman, the Hughes' son, but now found that Mrs. Hughes had gone unerringly to the pew where her son had managed to stave off other worshippers and reserved a short space of the pew for his parents and M.

Though the church was fitted with gas lighting, candles were still lit. The most important of these were the six on the altar and the fifteen on the hearse, seven ascending on either side of the fifteenth and highest candle. They were all made of unbleached wax, funeral candles. As a child, M had been able to judge how much was left of the service by these candles. After the reading of each psalm (nine psalms of Matins and five psalms of Lauds), but before the accompanying antiphon, a candle was extinguished, first on one side of the hearse and then on the other, beginning with the lowest candles, until only one candle – the fifteenth and highest candle in the triangular formation, the Christ candle – was left lit. This candle was then removed from the sight of the congregation and hidden behind the altar – a people bereft of their Messiah, his death temporarily leaving his people in darkness. Then would begin the extinguishment of the last six candles, on the altar. Like the candles on the hearse, these were extinguished alternating from side to side, one after every second verse of the Canticle of Zachary. Any other candles still lit in the church would also be extinguished at this time.

Counting candles was something she had done as a young child, a way to endure the lengthy Tenebrae services, especially at a time of year when the weather was changing for the better, when her pagan soul longed to be outside in the sunshine and warmth and rebelled against the somber and weighty intonations of the priest and choir and the dark confines of the church. Then, during the war, Tenebrae had taken on a new meaning, or, rather, a new feeling. The slow and steady darkening of the church, even as the world outside was also slowly darkening with each slaughter of the war, had a curious effect on M. Rather than dampening her spirits, something was ignited in her, something that quickened her pulse and made her chest tight with excited expectation. There was some dark allure to death and disaster and calamity, to the anguished anticipation before it struck. There was an intensity in those moments that did not exist in even the happiest and most exciting moments of life. The joys of Easter could not match the terrible thrill of Tenebrae.

She came to prefer Tenebrae to weekly Mass, even High Mass. She especially preferred Tenebrae on Good Friday. This was M's first Good Friday alone. She made a good effort to truly pay attention to the psalms and lessons of Matins and the psalms of Lauds, and the canticles of Zachary and Ezechias (*I said in the midst of my days: I shall go to the gates of hell*). She was particularly drawn to the Lamentations of Jeremias – "Our inheritance is turned to aliens: our houses to strangers" – but her mind wandered, as always, during the Epistle (to the Hebrews) – St. Paul had that effect on her. And she could not help but feel that the Psalms sometimes spoke of her: *Deliver me not over to the will of them that trouble me: for unjust witnesses have risen up against me and iniquity hath belied itself*; and *I am counted among them that go down to the pit: I am become as a man without help, free among the dead*. She could not help but think of Merritt and Argent when she heard, *But they have sought my soul in vain, they shall go into the lower parts of the earth: they shall be delivered into the hands of the sword, they shall be the portions of foxes*. 'The portions of foxes' was a particularly pleasing image for her. She also liked, *I will meditate like a dove*.

Finally, the last candle remaining lit was removed from the hearse and hidden behind the altar, and the *Miserere* was said one last time. Then there came the Great Noise, the *strepitus*, a representation of the earthquake that rent the sanctuary curtain in two, released the holy dead from their graves, and split the earth at Golgotha, separating the crosses of Christ and the Good Thief from that of the Bad Thief. The Great Noise also signified the closing of the tomb and the loss of Christ's light. The *strepitus* continued until the priest retrieved the Christ candle from behind the altar and replaced it on the hearse. M thought the effort to produce the noise – men banging books against the pews and boys (and some girls) stomping their feet – showed overzealousness on the part of the congregation of St. Patrick, but, then again, the Irish were animated in all things they did; they were especially devoted to their religion.

It was dark when the Hughes family and M emerged from St. Patrick. M and Mrs. Hughes walked behind Mr. Hughes and his son. Everyone who left St. Patrick left in silence, and that silence lasted until they were well away from the church. M very much wanted to explore the streets, to get her bearings for the moment when she would leave Cumberland, but the somber mood of Tenebrae kept her from asking Mr. Hughes to accompany her on a walk. As it was, Mr. and Mrs. Hughes separated from M and the fireman, and headed back to the train near the roundhouse. Mr. Hughes said, "We'll see you in the morning, then." The fireman escorted M to the hotel, where Merritt awaited her. The fireman left without a word, and without a word Merritt walked with M up the two flights of stairs to her room. At her door, Merritt said, "Sleep well, M," and stood there until she entered the room and closed the door.

16 — *Holy Saturday*

When M emerged from the darkened church the next morning, she found both Merritt and Argent waiting for her. The presence of both men did not bode well for her, but she greeted them with unusual good will – this would be the last time she would find them haunting her every step, and it made her generous. She was enjoying the obvious displeasure on Argent's face; she even found that she was enjoying the usual smirk on Merritt's face. She immediately reproached herself for indulging in pleasure – no matter how private – on Holy Saturday.

"Miss Warner. It was our understanding that you would be attending services at St. Patrick with the Hughes's." Argent was definitely not happy with her.

"That was the understanding yesterday, but I wanted to attend the Easter Vigil where my father had attended services, on his travels through Cumberland. I'm sure you understand."

The rejoinder that both M and Merritt were certain was forthcoming from Argent was interrupted by the appearance of a young boy carrying a smallish pumpkin, somehow preserved from last fall's harvest, which he offered to M. M accepted it as if the boy had handed her a bouquet of roses. She thanked him profusely, underscoring her gratitude with a coin pressed into his hand. The boy ran off to join a small group of friends who gathered around to admire the coin earned for such a simple errand, with many suggestions as to how to spend it.

M walked with the pumpkin held low at her waist, pleased with her acquisition and either ignorant, or devilishly defiant, of the looks she was garnering as she and the two men made their way to the hotel. Both men pointedly refrained from asking M about her pumpkin – neither man was in the mood for anything so silly as any story M was likely to give. Instead, Merritt asked what was ever uppermost in his and Argent's minds: "What are your plans for the day?"

Though the question was distantly expected, M had not thought beyond the discomfort her pumpkin was causing for the men, and therefore paused some few seconds before answering. "I had thought to walk the town, to sample its charms, and to avail myself of the health of the mountain air, which Mr. Argent so readily recommends." This morning upon waking, M had discovered a note slipped under the connecting door between their two rooms, a note evidently deposited sometime last night. In it, Argent had expressed his understanding of the religious importance and significance of these next two days and was completely reconciled to staying some little time in Cumberland should Miss Warner wish to attend any other religious services. Argent then conveyed his admiration for the mountain city, its beauty, but especially the health of the mountain air, which many travelers pursued by taking walking tours into the mountains. He would understand if Miss Warner would like to perhaps spend a day or two here. The note had not been signed by Merritt.

For a moment, Argent thought Miss Warner had somehow seen through his ruse to pause in Cumberland, but then she became genuinely enthusiastic when she continued.

"I would really like to see the canal and basins and watch the boats come and go. And the manner of their loading." Her father had talked of the ingenious loading mechanisms being built in Cumberland, and she felt it her duty to observe them in operation in his stead.

Merritt readily agreed. "I can certainly accommodate you in that request."

"That is very kind of you, but I have already spoken to Mr. Hughes about it, and he has agreed to explore the city with me."

Merritt, however, was not inclined to leave M to the suspect supervision of Mr. Hughes – he had, after all, misplaced M this morning in merely escorting her to church. Merritt merely smiled and inclined his head, but he had every intention of joining M and Mr. Hughes. He would send a quick note to Mr. Hughes advising him of that fact.

Argent then startled M by asking her to accompany him to an exhibition that happened to be showing this very afternoon.

Again, M paused; she was not expecting such an invitation. She had, of necessity, been in the constant company of one or both of these men during these two weeks or more, but to her best recollection, it had never been at the suggestion of one of them — usually, one or both men had accompanied her to a destination of her choosing or desire. This sounded suspiciously like a personal engagement. In her confusion, she frowned and fell silent.

Merritt rescued the moment with real curiosity. "What is this exhibit?"

In his enthusiasm for the subject, Argent neither recognized the awkward silence, nor acknowledged Merritt's assistance. "Bullard's Panorama of New York City." Addressing M directly, Argent added, "I think you will find it both entertaining and instructive. People who have not had the opportunity to visit New York find it engaging, and those who are familiar with the city are taken with its faithful and exact representations, down to the correct number of windows in all the buildings."

M was puzzled by the request, both as some kind of intimate outing and as to the subject matter – she was not drawn to either man in any way (and she was certain the feeling was mutual) and she had no desire whatsoever to see New York, or any city bigger than Louisville. It was an accepted fact that the bigger the city, the greater the crime, filth, despair, and general immorality. Her initial inclination was to reject Argent's offer, but then she considered that accepting it might disarm him – it was obvious the men did not intend to leave her on her own for any but the most personal reasons.

"I have never seen a panorama."

"Then I should be delighted to show you your first. The show starts at half past three, but we should arrive when the doors open – Bullard's is always seated to capacity."

In the lobby of the hotel, M excused herself to speak with the desk clerk. Unlike the clerk in Cincinnati, M had apparently developed something of a cordial relationship with the clerk of the St. Nicholas. He must have remarked on M's pumpkin, because she lifted it up for his appraisal and the man smiled. M wrote something on a piece of paper provided by the clerk (the pen as well), her left hand never leaving the treasured pumpkin. She folded the piece of paper (one-handed) and gave it to the clerk. He nodded and smiled at whatever she said, in addition to her thanks. She lightly tapped the counter three times as if it, too, had pleased her, before heading towards the stairs.

"May I relieve you of your burden?"

M smiled at Merritt, pleased he was pointedly ignoring mentioning the pumpkin. "Am I to be escorted to my very door? I know the way." She was pleased, too, that Argent had remained behind, no doubt to question the clerk as to her request.

"It would simply be my pleasure." Merritt noted M's lack of interest in Argent's absence, but she often feigned indifference to the presence of himself and Argent.

"What did M want with the clerk?"

Argent listened at the door connecting their room with M's before crossing the room and answering in a low voice, "Cosmetics."

"Cosmetics?!"

Argent hissed at Merritt to lower his voice.

Merritt asked in a considerably quieter voice, "What would she want with cosmetics?"

"What does any woman want with cosmetics?"

"M isn't any woman. Are you certain it was cosmetics, that the clerk wasn't misguidedly shielding her privacy?"

"He showed me the list she wrote. Cosmetics."

Merritt was dumbfounded. "I have never seen M wear any cosmetics, or fuss over her appearance in any manner."

Argent had no patience with the subject. "She simply wants to look nice for Easter services. There is no harm in it, or anything unusual, for that matter." Then a bright revelation occurred to him. "Perhaps she does fuss over her appearance, but it is something she forgoes in the spirit of the penitential season of Lent." Argent tried to picture M cosmetically improved, but it escaped him. He shrugged mentally; no amount of facial powder could cover her tanned skin without looking like whitewash.

But Merritt would not let it go. "That pumpkin is involved in this somehow. She was far too pleased with herself, carrying that thing around like a prized puppy."

"I'm sure it pleases her that it stumps you."

Merritt changed the subject. "Did you send a note to Mr. Hughes?"

"Yes, a most emphatic one. He is not to leave M anywhere unless you are with her."

"Me? I had thought you would want to spend the morning squiring her about, in advance of your engagement at the panorama."

"No, I think it had better be you. At some point she will most certainly make a dash for the stables – she was suspiciously silent on Emmett this morning — and I will leave it to you to explain the restrictions that have been placed upon her access to her own horse."

"Because?"

"I think she, in her own way, trusts you in the matter of Emmett."

Merritt laughed. "I think 'resent' more accurately reflects how she feels about me in the matter of Emmett."

"She resents that she trusts you. Please return Miss Warner in time to attend the Panorama at Belvidere Hall."

"How did Miss Warner find Cumberland?"

"A little less attractive in my company, but nevertheless I think she enjoyed her time on the whole. She was particularly taken with the workings of the canal; she stood for quite some time just gazing out over the basins and dam and watching the boats come and go, as she said."

"It's water she'll go to."

"Yes, Mr. Henry did say that. Perhaps, then, if it is the canal that has captured M's attention, it is the canal we should avoid at all costs. I think she prefers older men."

Argent was rooting through the large trunk they had installed in their room, but at Merritt's last non sequitur he straightened up and turned to face Merritt. "I beg pardon?

"M. I think she prefers older men."

"Yes, I heard that, but what made you say it?"

"You know that the canal season is hardly under way and that there have already been some setbacks – minor floods and damages. Yet in this bustling time – and on a Saturday, just hours away from the Sunday closing, when all proper canallers are jostling and scheming to get in the last load and be underway and through as many locks as possible – M managed to find not one but three men – all of them older men – to take the time to explain how the loading docks work, the typical cargo of a canal boat, and how well the mules are taken care of. She seemed particularly concerned for the welfare of the beasts."

Argent ignored M's ranging curiosity and focused instead on the men who satisfied it. "With few exceptions, at her age all men are older men."

"What age do you think that is?"

Argent repeated, "I beg pardon?"

"How old do you think M is? It's a curiosity to me. Sometimes she seems quite oldish, and other times she seems quite immature."

"Most women display such opposing behaviors. My own mother seems quite childish at times, even to me. It is in their nature."

"M's nature isn't natural."

"Neither is this curiosity of yours. A woman's age is of concern to none but her husband." Argent closed, belted, and locked the trunk. "Is all arranged with Mrs. Hughes?"

In making their arrangements for their Saturday night rendezvous, Merritt and Argent had depended on Miss Warner attending some service in the evening, as had been held these last three nights in the Catholic churches in each town where they had stopped for the night. But there were no services this night, possibly because the early morning service had been so very lengthy – the two men had spent a good deal of time waiting outside Sts. Peter and Paul Church, waiting for services this morning to end; Argent had started a third cigarette just before the doors to the church had finally opened, releasing its captive congregation.

"Yes. What time will you be returning? Is it still a four-hour event?"

"It is two hours, and well you know it."

"I should think you know it so well yourself that you have it memorized by now. What is your fascination with this panorama? You are intimately acquainted with New York, without the aid of Mr. Bullard's faithful representation of Broadway."

"I have not seen it for some few years now. I am curious as to any new drop scenes that may have been added."

"And it has nothing to do with a certain young – at the time a very young – lady in the Union Park section?"

Argent picked up his hat from the bed as he headed for the door. "I must be going. It does not do to keep Miss Warner idle and unchaperoned."

M had been careful to keep her interest in the National Road hidden. Mr. Hughes had almost upset the apple cart when, approaching Mechanic Street, he had suddenly blurted out, "Miss Warner, did you not want to see the great Cumberland Road?"

Merritt had been sauntering behind M and Mr. Hughes, surreptitiously smoking a slender cigar, holding it down and behind himself in between pulls. M had heard him toss his smoke to the ground before blowing out his last puff. "But you are on the great Cumberland Road, Baltimore Street being but a segment of it."

"Yes, but Miss Warner had asked about its route out of town." Turning to M, Mr. Hughes had said, "I inquired around the roundhouse, and was told that Mechanic Street leads to the Cumberland Road, on its way out of town."

"Oh?"

M had sensed Merritt's suspicions rise, but she was both proud and ashamed to admit to herself that she had handled the matter deftly. "I wanted to see the Narrows. There is a great deal said about its beauty, in the travel literature."

Merritt's suspicions had melted away and they walked the half mile or so to view the Narrows, and, for M, to judge the character of the bridge she would be crossing alone. M readily acknowledged that the scenery was breath-taking – the Cumberland Road, the B&O, and Will's Creek all shouldering each other as they snaked their way through the floor of the gorge, the lofty slopes to either side rising steeply, in places heavily forested and in others heavy with imposing stone.

Now she was seated next to Argent, before a heavily curtained stage, waiting for the panorama to begin. Argent's desire to arrive early had gained for them seats in the front row, but now they must wait, and while they waited, M considered her escape.

She knew Argent and Merritt had some kind of appointment this evening, the real reason they had suggested lingering in Cumberland; it had nothing at all to do with the great solemnity of Easter and her religious obligations. Still, their need to pause at Cumberland had dovetailed nicely with her plans to leave the private train and return home – they would be occupied with personal pursuits while she wriggled from their constraints and left them far behind and hopefully searching in the wrong direction.

Argent interrupted her thoughts. "I thought you might find this helpful as the panorama progresses," handing her a map, as he sat down. She was not aware that Argent had left his seat.

The map showed what M came to understand was a very small slice of New York City, running along Broadway from The Battery to Union Park. M studied the map, not because she ever intended going to New York, but simply as a device to keep conversation with Argent to a minimum. Occasionally he would lean over, and with his little finger, point out something on the map that he would then proceed to explain to her anything he knew about it, as well as how faithfully it was portrayed in the panorama. Faithful was a word he whispered to her over and over again as the exhibition proceeded.

All light was suddenly banished from the hall – lamps extinguished and curtains at windows drawn – so that for a moment the hall resembled the end of services at church these last few days. Then lights near the stage were raised and a brass band hidden somewhere behind the stage began to play. The heavy stage curtains were pulled back to reveal a large and detailed canvas, at least six feet high and more than three times as wide. The image on the canvas was a bird's eye view of New York City.

M was not certain what to expect from a panorama. The music was certainly unexpected, but she wondered if they were to stare at this large map for the entire presentation. Then a man began to speak from a lectern at one side of the stage, and her heart sank: they were to be treated, he promised them, to *three thousand feet* of canvas, encompassing one hundred and fifty-four separate scenes of vibrant New York life – she was now committed to an interminable presentation, sitting next to a man she could barely tolerate and whom she suspected was an agent of ill will towards her. The narrator began his commentary in earnest, intoning his words like some bored teacher: "We suppose ourselves to be elevated considerably above New York City, looking down upon it." And so began two hours of a narrated travelogue – or excursion, as the narrator repeatedly reminded them – of the southern end of Manhattan Island, only a small part, Argent whispered to M, of New York City.

As the narrator described the different scenes brought before them – either scrolled across the stage by unseen actors and machinery or by separate canvases dropped from above to temporarily replace the scene on stage – Argent would occasionally lean over and whisper some tidbit of information. More often than not, the narrator would almost immediately repeat Argent's tidbit, very nearly word for word. Now and then the narrator would step away from his podium to personally point out on the canvas some detail of particular interest to his commentary. Twice Argent himself pointed out, in abridged motions with his hand and fingers, people personally known to him – a young girl he knew in her later life and a counterfeiter he and Merritt had subsequently captured, though he could not say that he was engaged in counterfeiting at the time the panorama was painted. Argent's obtrusive supplements to the narration finally ceased after several nearby throats were cleared and the narrator himself paused long enough to shoot a warning glance in their direction.

M was appreciative of the skill of the artist and the brilliance of the canvas, and the idea of moving scenes across the stage was very clever, but for the most part she was bored. And she was anxious to return to the hotel; she still had plans to complete for her departure this evening. The only time M truly enjoyed herself was during the scene which depicted the burning of the Crystal Palace. In the middle of the narration describing the loss of the glass and iron building, supposed to be impervious to fire, there ran across the very front of the stage a line of sparks. M applauded the attempt at reality, especially the wafting smoke left behind. Eventually a few others in the audience joined her applause, though not with the same enthusiasm. Argent did not clap, but M assumed that was because he had, so obviously, sat through the performance before. The narrator, however, seemed a little stunned, but perhaps that was because the boy who ran from the stage after lighting the fuse had somehow missed his cue. M thought it was perfectly timed. The narrator never quite recovered during this scene's recitation, limping to the end of it with the sad recounting that one of the precious items lost to the fire was a panorama such as this one — though much longer and of the Rhine — and not one penny of insurance to cover it.

They met Merritt in the St. Nicholas dining hall. Dinner had already been ordered, but not served, as Merritt continuously deferred the meal until such time as M and Argent should return from the panorama. As Merritt did well know, the panorama was two, sometimes two and a half, hours long, but Merritt also knew, all too well, Argent's penchant for remaining behind to speak personally with the lecturer about all the changes in New York these past 20 years that, despite new drop scenes, were not reflected in Bullard's great work of art. Merritt normally did not mind – once, a piece of information Argent learned from Mr. Norton, the lecturer, had helped them in a case that had stymied them for some time in New York – but tonight, they had business to attend to, and they needed M to be safely and securely ensconced in her room for the night. There could be no reason for her to venture out, and so, at least, Merritt would make certain she had her supper.

M had steadfastly refused any drink (and therefore any chloral hydrate) these last two nights, in justifiable honor of these last and holiest days of Holy Week. Therefore, they had engaged Mrs. Hughes to keep a clandestine eye on M from their room – it was a foregone conclusion that M would outright reject any suggestion that Mrs. Hughes stay with M in her own room – until they should return from their errand. For reasons they could not clearly explain even to themselves, Merritt and Argent felt Mrs. Hughes could curtail any plans M may have far better than her husband or any other of the men on the train crew.

Argent finally escorted M to the table Merritt had held for over an hour. Merritt caught the eye of the waiter across the room and waved impatiently to him to begin serving dinner. The look the waiter returned clearly did not appreciate the manner of Merritt's signaling. Merritt was only slightly less impatient when he addressed Argent. "I trust Broadway and lower Manhattan remain essentially unchanged? You will not lose your way the next time we are in town?"

Argent heard the testiness in Merritt's voice and knew it was aimed at himself, though Argent knew the true reason for the delay. Normally Argent would ignore the barb – he certainly would never point an accusing finger at a lady for anything so small as a delayed meal – but he was pleased with himself that he had managed to introduce M to something that had seemed to genuinely interest her. "Miss Warner was quite taken with the panorama. We remained behind some few moments to discuss the mechanisms involved with some of Mr. Norton's associates." M seemed particularly taken with the fire and smoke during the Crystal

Palace scene, but neither Mr. Norton or Argent corrected her that it was some poor and dangerous prank.

Merritt only slightly arched his brows. He knew from personal experience that Argent had indeed detained Mr. Norton – Mr. Norton surely must know Argent by now and no doubt dreaded the after-show discussions Argent pressed upon him – and that 'Mr. Norton's associates' most assuredly meant the menial workers who drove the cranks on the huge drums that advanced the canvas across the stage. Few women would find it respectable to speak to such men. Merritt cocked his head as he considered the situation at the Belvidere – either Argent could not dissuade M from engaging these workers, or Argent willingly let M do so in order to free himself and so satisfy his own desire to reacquaint himself with Mr. Norton. Or perhaps it was a combination of the two.

It was obvious to M that something was transpiring between Merritt and Argent, and that she was being used in some manner that escaped her. She stared straight ahead and waited for the sparring to end. But she felt very nearly as testy as Merritt sounded. Why must every meal with these men be such an ordeal?

For once, Merritt and Argent seemed determined to eat quickly, asking little of M or each other in the way of conversation. Likewise, for once Argent did not press on M a drink to mark the end of another day of travel. As they passed out of the dining room, Argent received yet another of a multitude of notes the men had received these last weeks. M vaguely wondered what could possibly be of such importance that Merritt and Argent were tracked down in nearly every city they visited. Whatever was in the note neither excited nor disappointed Argent.

They arrived at the hotel, and Argent excused himself to send a reply to the note and Merritt and M continued up the stairs. At her door, and though Merritt knew it was pointless to expect a completely honest answer, he nevertheless asked, "Will you be needing an escort this evening?"

"Oh, no. I'm sure Mrs. Hughes and I will be able to entertain ourselves without resorting to the pleasures of Cumberland. We may pray a little."

Merritt very nearly rolled his eyes. So, she had found out about Mrs. Hughes. No matter – now Mrs. Hughes could stay with M in her room. "Splendid. Perhaps you and Mrs. Hughes could pray for a speedy and safe end to our travels."

"I have been praying for that very thing from the very beginning." M winked at Merritt as she closed the door.

~

Merritt was already dressed for their rendezvous – in a suit that had seen better days and had hung on someone else's larger body – when Argent finally returned to their room. If they were to blend in among the saloons, pool halls, brothels, and other places of disrepute, they could not be seen wearing the fine clothes they had been wearing in the company of Miss Warner.

"What was in the note?"

"Our appointed time has been moved up. I sent a note to Mrs. Hughes to come earlier than originally planned."

"But?" Argent had been gone far longer than it would have taken to answer the note delivered to their table and pen a new one to Mrs. Hughes. He must have waited for an answer from Mrs. Hughes.

"But she cannot be here much earlier than we had agreed upon."

"And why is that? She knows – the entire train crew knows – the importance of keeping Miss Warner under surveillance."

"Lower your voice. Do you want her to know we have been monitoring her every move and conversation?"

"I'm fairly certain she already knows that. She at least knows that Mrs. Hughes has been recruited to keep an eye on her. She *winked* at me."

Argent harrumphed. He carefully arranged his vest, coat and trousers on the back of one of the chairs in the room, then he, too, put on the clothes of a man a payday or two away from destitution. Looking at himself in the mirror, Argent groaned. "We will have to slink our way out of the hotel. They will not let us tarry here, looking as we do."

"They will let us tarry here as long as we show our money first. Why can't she come any earlier?" Merritt's tone suggested he knew the answer to the question but needed to be reminded of what he knew.

"She is responsible for feeding her husband and son and every other man on the train. She will be here as soon as she can. She promised me she would even forgo washing the dishes until after we have returned for the night."

Argent dug around in the trunk and offered two hats for Merritt's inspection. Merritt indicated the hat in Argent's left hand. Argent sailed it across the room, then placed the other on his own head. "What do you mean, 'show our money first?' What reason would we have to show our money, especially dressed as we are?"

"For the only reason any man dressed as we are would have to show their money – to refresh the inner man."

Argent considered it for a moment; despite the change in appointment time, they had time to refresh the inner man. "Let us go show our money, then see about this other matter at the Slack Water."

In the hall they passed the porter delivering cosmetics to M's room.

In the lobby, Argent headed into the saloon of the St. Nicholas, where they could both fortify themselves with a smoke and a small drink or two and still keep an eye on Mrs. Hughes' eventual arrival or M's probable departure. Merritt, however, argued for a trip to the Revere House, where they could both fortify themselves with a smoke and a small drink or two and inquire as to any recent messages from their train or telegrams from Washington or New York. They had decided before reaching Cumberland that, in order curb some of Miss Warner's uncanny knowledge of their movements, the Revere House, not the St. Nicholas or wherever they should find themselves staying, should be the point of communication between themselves and Mr. Hughes, as well as the recipient of any telegrams from Grant or Whitley. As Argent, however, had just done so, immediately after dinner, he more than suspected that Merritt's true intention was to visit the bagatelle table in the basement bar of the Revere House. Merritt had never denied his excessive love of the game, but it could not be denied that he excelled at it and, moreover, the game had often served as both a distraction and a lure when, during investigations into counterfeiting and stolen/forged bonds, they installed themselves in the less seedy bars and saloons of middle-class criminals. And Merritt was such a genial bagatelle rival that none resented his skill nor suspected him of being a federal operative. Argent consented to leaving the hotel before the arrival of Mrs. Hughes only after Merritt left strict instructions with the desk clerk to watch for Mrs. Hughes' arrival or Miss Stearns' (M's registered alias) departure, at the event of either of which the clerk was to send a message to the Revere House saloon.

Neither man had subscribed to the temperance crusade, but neither was either man ever accused of over-indulgence. On this night, however, two or three drinks acted on the both of them as would twice that many drinks. They found themselves in the company of three very amiable men, who bought the first two rounds, Argent funding the third, though Argent could not remember if the third round was ever served. Merritt won a few dollars in a bagatelle game from one of the men, while Argent and the other two looked on, offering comments and observations on the game. It was a pleasant diversion with male company, indulging in the small pleasures of men, after spending nearly three long weeks in almost exclusive company of a woman of dubious charms. However, when Argent deemed it was time to leave to keep a previous appointment, the three men protested loudly, so much so that their group drew looks from the other patrons of the bar. It took many professions of thanks and refusals of rounds before Merritt and Argent were able to extricate themselves from the bar and their new friends.

Before heading for the Slack Water, Argent and Merritt somewhat lurched down the street to the St. Nicholas and inquired at the desk as to the arrival of Mrs. Hughes. The night clerk was now on duty. He could say with certainty that a Mrs. Hughes had not stopped by the desk as the note left by the previous clerk had said she would. However, he was not familiar with Miss Stearns and could not say with the same certainty that she had not left the hotel during his shift. This news somewhat sobered the men, as did the unseemly bounding up the stairs to their rooms on the third floor. It was not sufficiently sobering, however, to allow Merritt and Argent to fend off the three men who ambushed them just inside the door to their room.

Cumberland was generally a pleasant town, boasting many big-city amenities, including a police force – recently attired in spanking new blue uniforms with brass buttons embossed with the letter P – that kept crime at a very respectable minimum. However, as in any city that functioned as a transportation hub – and Cumberland served not only the railroad, but the canal as well, and, in a diminishing capacity, the National Road – there was the transitory and sometimes criminal (and even violent) element that came and went with the boats and trains and wagons. And at this time, there was the added influx of defendants and plaintiffs come to town for the sitting of the April session of the Circuit Court, not all of whom were respectable. Usually these people kept to the seedier parts of town. In Cumberland's case, and especially as regards to the canal, this was Shantytown in the southern part of the city, a narrow stretch of second-grade buildings (some of them mere sheds) between the canal and the tracks on the eastern side of the big bend in the Potomac. Merritt and Argent were supposed to be meeting with a fellow agent at a saloon called the Slack Water in Shantytown, chosen for the very reason that very few people cared very little what transpired in that area of town. And if the information they were to receive involved a senator who was rumored to be connected in any way to illegal or questionable activity, that information had to be forwarded in the most anonymous and private manner possible, especially if that rumor proved to be false.

Catering to the needs and wants of the canallers, Shantytown was always a little rowdy, always a little shocking, but never more so than on a Saturday night during one of the canal company's attempts to keep holy the Lord's Day. In its on-again, off-again policy regarding work on the Sabbath, the Chesapeake and Ohio Canal Company directed that no work would be done on the canal between twelve a.m. Saturday and twelve a.m. Sunday. During those hours the locks were shut down, forcing canal boats to tie up for the night. Canallers of every stripe despised the policy. The lock tenders, who should have been glad to indulge in a full night's rest from the duty of locking through boats at all hours of the night during the week, instead found themselves the target of frustrated and angry boatmen, blowing their horns, demanding to be locked through, sometimes damaging the gates, or offering personal harm to the tender himself. Some lock tenders, in defiance of company policy to remove and secure at night the cranks and paddles used to operate the gates of the locks (in order to prevent unauthorized locking through during the proscribed period), left these very devices in places easy to find so that the tenders themselves would not suffer personal injury or insult during those hours of the Sabbath suspension. Owners and crews of canal boats, of course, hated the Sabbath law. In an industry that paid by the load and in which a load usually meant a round trip of 368 miles, every minute tied up was time wasted and money lost. Every canal boat captain therefore tried to make it through to Cumberland (or Washington, at the other end) by midnight Saturday, to be in place at 12:01 Monday morning to begin loading (almost exclusively coal) at Cumberland or unloading at Washington, Georgetown, or Alexandria. Boatmen who laid over in Cumberland naturally sought comfort and entertainment at those establishments especially welcoming to them in Shantytown. And so, Saturday nights were often livelier than any other night of the week.

Robbery, therefore, was the first thing that both Merritt and Argent suspected was happening and remembering the particular geniality of the men they had met in the bar, they also suspected that they had been targeted and 'worked up' for this very act of violence and theft. It separately occurred to Argent, as both he and Merritt were rendered immobile and their guns relieved of them, that their intended meeting in the saloon in Shantytown had somehow been made known and this current situation was somehow related to that meeting. But both theories were exploded when the thug who had Merritt's arms pinned behind his back ordered, "See to Grant's girl." This was no random robbery. It descended into murder when one of the criminals opened the door to M's room and fired twice into the darkness on the other side. Even the extra burst of animation to their muscles that the shock of M's murder occasioned in them was not enough to break them free from their captors. Instead the murderer produced from a coat pocket a bottle and cloth, and Argent caught the sweet smell of chloroform before both he and Merritt were rendered helpless.

It was long hours before they finally reached the Slack Water.

Merritt had the vague feeling of being half-dragged and half-lifted down the stairs of the hotel and down Baltimore Street, and thought he heard the loud and off-key singing of inebriates. Was he one of them? The only distinct memory he had of those hours between M's murder and reaching the Slack Water, was the one serious challenge to his balance, at the corner of Baltimore and Centre, where there was at least a six-inch drop in the sidewalk, merely inconvenient when sober, but which became decidedly more precipitous in his depleted condition. All other memories of those hours were hazy images of bars and saloons with music that was tinny and too loud, and of other men, and even women, who were just as drunk as he was. And they all, himself and Argent included, just kept drinking and smoking. He had no idea how many saloons they had visited, only that as soon as he tried to lay down his head on a table, he was roughly brought to his feet and the whole party stumbled to the door of the next saloon. Finally, someone said they had reached the Slack Water, and they sat at a table in the middle of the room, where someone else started talking, loudly, about counterfeit plates for sale. They were very cheap because they were so very dangerous, and the General Government was so very close to discovering them. Argent said they would not pay one cent for them but would take them, as it was their duty. Argent should not have said that; it was their duty not to tell people their duty; that's why they were the *Secret* Service. Merritt found he didn't care – he was so tired, and feeling sick, and he just wanted to sleep. Even M's murder did not alarm him very much; M, at least, was sleeping. There was a commotion in the saloon – someone new was at the table, talking to the man who had the plates for sale, only he didn't have the plates with him. The man with the plates, but also without the plates, was angry at Argent and shoved the table at him as he left. Then they were on their feet again, because, someone said, they were going to get those plates.

INTER DIEBUS

M had waited in her room for nearly twenty minutes, her ear pressed against the door that led to the hallway, listening for any sign that Merritt or Argent were lingering there, waiting to catch her out of her room. When she cracked open her door, neither man was there, but she had the great good fortune to see one of the hotel porters no doubt on his way to the lobby, having performed some function here on the third floor for one of the other guests. M attracted the man's attention and asked him to wait while she scribbled a note. She asked him to send the note immediately, as the subject of it was of some urgency to the recipient.

Things were falling beautifully into place. The procurement of the pumpkin, especially at this time of year, was great good luck. Her only instructions to the boy had been to find something round, even if it was a rock or lump of wood. She had been ecstatic that the boy had found a gourd, and of such perfect shape and proportions. And now she was able to send a note to Mrs. Hughes, without having to expose herself in the lobby, where Merritt or Argent might see her from the dining room or the saloon, where she was certain they were lurking for just such a purpose. She had heard the men talking in the next room and knew that they had time to 'refresh the inner man,' so they said. She did not know what that meant, but she was fairly certain it involved liquor or women or both. She fancied herself successful at mimicking Argent's handwriting – in truth, his hand had almost no character at all, itself being a perfect mimic of handwriting manuals. She had no doubt that Mrs. Hughes would be deceived. She knew the men had some secret errand to attend to – thus the need for Mrs. Hughes to keep watch over her – and so this was the perfect opportunity to leave the train. She could count on two or even three hours head start before the men returned from both refreshing themselves and the evening errand and discover that neither she nor Mrs. Hughes was at the hotel.

She changed into something more convenient to travel – her trousers and one of the simple but nevertheless handsome shirts Mrs. Müller had made for her, a shirt that was both practical and could also pass for something a woman would wear with a skirt. M was surprised to find that Miss Carrie had packed it – Carrie was openly critical of Mrs. Müller's gifts to M. Upon reflection, M wore over her trousers a simple skirt, and over her shirt one of her old basque-like jackets that M preferred because it was a little too big and afforded her movement. M had left it on the porch upon returning to the house that last night at home, and then had carried it down to the barn and stuffed it, along with her father's gun, into the trunk that was half-packed with apples for Emmett. Her father's gun was still in Cincinnati; she had a court date there; she couldn't think about that.

M then set about packing, then repacking, what little she could take, and what she would most have need of, on her way back home. It had never been her intention to accept any help from Grant's men, but now she was grateful that she had spent relatively little of her own money on any of the expenses of travel. She pulled up her skirt to shove her small stash of money into the pockets of her trousers. It would not be enough for both hotel expenses and a steamer; she would have to sleep on the ground, outside with Emmett. She regretted leaving the bulk of her money in her trunk on the train. There was no time or opportunity to retrieve it.

In the bottom of her grip bag, she laid the laudanum, belladonna pills, and other preparations that helped in the case of some of her worst headaches; she realized she had used quite a lot of it these last two weeks. On top of these she carefully folded and positioned the decent dress that had survived travel so far. Anticipating nights on the ground before she reached Wheeling, and feeling slightly criminal, M took one of the blankets from her hotel bed, carefully rolled it, then stuffed it in her bag. As soon as she had stuffed the blanket in, however, she pulled it out again, not out of guilt, but at a thought of Miss Carrie and her careful packing. M spread the blanket on the bed, pulled her folded dress and cloak from the grip bag and smoothed these out on top of the blanket. Now she carefully re-rolled the blanket, being mindful to keep the clothes at its center as smooth as possible. Miss Carrie could not fault such attention. It still, however, took some amount of cramming to get the stuffed blanket inside the bag.

Once she had finished dressing and packing, M set about turning her pumpkin into a beautiful goodbye surprise for her two escorts. She broke off the stem and set the pumpkin on the table and, using a letter opener, scored the surface, creating a face, and then painted it, using the cosmetics, to more resemble a woman's face. The eyes gave a sense of gratitude and regret, but the mouth she painted was sly and satisfied. M was quite taken with her creation; she giggled out loud. There was nothing that could serve as hair, so M simply turned the pumpkin's face towards the door that her room shared with Merritt's and Argent's room – they would see the ruse the moment they entered the room and lit the lamp. It would have been better if they had been forced to round the bed and then see her trick, but she wouldn't be here, anyway, to reap the pleasure of that extra second or two of their confusion and alarm.

Then M did an extraordinary thing: she unlocked and opened the door between the two rooms. After a second's hesitation, she entered, lit a lamp and examined the room. She did not know what she was looking for, only that she would know it when she saw it. Pockets; she had been thinking of pockets when she had decided to invade the men's room, and now she spied Argent's coat, neatly hanging on the back of a chair. Merritt's clothes lay on the bed, though not so neatly arranged as Argent's. M went through Argent's pockets and found the thing she did not know she was looking for – the manifest for the private train. It was one of at least two manifests that M knew of – Mr. Hughes also had one that she had seen him show to station managers along the way. Even so, the absence of one of the manifests might slow down the train and impede any efforts to follow her, no matter how unlikely. If nothing else, it would annoy Argent.

It had been a bold thing to do, but not as bold as her next act. At the foot of the bed there was a trunk. It was curious to her because the men, like her, had grip bags that were perfectly adequate for a change of clothes and toiletries such as men need – there they were, sitting on the floor near the dresser – and yet the trunk had been delivered to their room in the hotel, not by the hotel's porters, but by Mr. Hughes and his son. It was belted and locked, but M knew where the key was – she had felt it when searching Argent's pockets. When she opened the trunk, her mind stopped; she simply did not know what to think. Two trays occupied the entire top of the trunk, and each tray was full of neatly bundled and separated money, in all denominations and from different banks, but the bulk of the money was in the ubiquitous greenbacks. She did not know what she had stumbled on, but so much money in one place could not speak well of Merritt and Argent. Was Mr. Hughes aware of what he had been pulling behind his engine and now had carried into the hotel?

M removed one of the trays and found a pile of old clothes underneath. M almost yelped, thinking she had come across a dead rat when her hand brushed across one of several false beards and wigs. She quickly replaced the first tray and then removed the second. For the second time since she had opened the trunk, M's mind stopped. There, on top of several wallets and pocketbooks, lay her father's gun, the gun that Merritt and Argent had led her to believe was being held in the sheriff's office in Cincinnati, as some kind of evidence in her upcoming court case. They had as good as lied to her. And the presence of so much money suggested something else to her: they had stolen the gun from her. They were thieves and liars, the very kind of men who would not blink at delivering her to whatever Grant had in mind.

M then thought of her own paltry money in her pockets. She also remembered why she was leaving the company of these men – their intention to keep her locked on the train, watched over by Mr. and Mrs. Hughes, their errand as Grant's men to deliver her to Washington – and now there was the discovery of this deception about her father's gun. She also remembered Argent's own insistence that any expenses incurred were Grant's responsibility, as well as their own honor and pleasure. M pulled two or three bills from the largest stack of money. She did not even note the denomination. She relocked and belted the trunk and dropped the key in Argent's pocket.

The next fifteen or twenty minutes were excruciating, as she waited in her room to receive confirmation that her message had been sent. If it had been intercepted by Merritt or Argent, Mrs. Hughes would knock at her door. Her heart skipped a beat as there was a knock at the door even as she was thinking of it. The porter brought the good news that the message had been sent and received and that the other party sent her understanding of the situation. M thanked the porter, then waited again, listening at the door, before finally venturing out into the hall with her grip bag.

M stepped lightly down the hall, willing the other guests to remain in their rooms. After one flight of steps, M turned to enter the unusual enclosed bridge that connected the St. Nicholas with the Windsor Hotel, across George Street. She would make her exit through the Windsor's back door, then work her way up George Street, recrossing it to reach the large stable in the rear of the St. Nicholas lot, where Emmett was being kept. After that, it was just a matter of making her way to the Cumberland Road. Then she and Emmett could travel as fast as they liked through the night, when few if any would be on the road to judge her style of riding or her manner of dress. She suddenly decided she would continue through the day until noon, find a place to rest until it was night again, and continue on in like fashion until she reached Wheeling where she would buy passage on a steamer down the Ohio to Louisville. She hadn't really needed to steal that blanket after all.

It was while making her way north along George Street that M conceived of the idea to misdirect Merritt and Argent entirely. And she would do it with their money. A train passing on the tracks up ahead suggested the idea to her. She crossed the street near the stables but did not stop until she reached the tracks. She worked her way south along the tracks, following the curve until the tracks led her to the depot. In the shadow of the building, she raised her skirt to extract one of the bills she had taken from the men's trunk. Once her skirt was back in place, and after straightening her jacket, M boldly walked into the depot and bought a ticket for herself and passage for Emmett on the next train west, due to depart a little after midnight. With any luck, the train would be gone before Merritt and Argent looked for her or asked about her at the depot. M was pleased to see a good many people in the depot, even at that hour, and even made pleasant remarks to several of them. She was certain someone would remember her. If only she had thought to bring Emmett — that would have made an even deeper impression in everyone's memories. But all in all, luck had been with her all day.

Her good luck held all the way to the stables, where it finally faltered. Merritt had taken her to the stable to visit Emmett earlier in the day when he had invited himself to join her and Mr. Hughes for a tour of Cumberland. She was aware that the ostler had instructions regarding M's access to Emmett for anything beyond a simple visit. She had forgotten about the ostler; she had not planned for him, or rather, she had not considered it necessary to plan for him – she had thought he would be asleep, available only if the hotel should need him. But lamps were lit in the barn, and as M peered cautiously around the corner of the barn, she could just make out someone relaxing in an old rocker near the entrance. It had been, overall, a warm day – unusually warm for mid-April – and the cool of the evening would be inviting after a long day caring for horses. M knew that Emmett had been stabled in one of the very back stalls – both a testament to his need for solitude and a move to make him as inaccessible to M as possible. For the first time since M set in motion her plan to escape, she panicked. She needed Emmett; she could not leave without him. She was just about to walk in and boldly demand her horse, even if she had to take him at the point of a gun, when she heard two gunshots. Like the porter's knock at the door earlier, this eerie coincidence of thinking of a gun and hearing one at the same instant made her heart skip a beat, then beat all the faster for a moment afterwards.

Though Cumberland in some ways had the look of a western town, gunplay was not an everyday occurrence, as one often thought was the case in towns west of the Mississippi. The sound of shots was novel enough that the ostler stood up, and close enough that he ran towards the hotel at the front of the lot, more than half a block away. M slipped around to the front entrance, saddled Emmett, and pulled him hard to follow her out of the barn. Her grip bag was strapped behind Emmett's saddle and M was ready to begin her long walk to Wheeling. The excitement at the hotel had worked its way to the streets, and M began to hear snippets of information as men exchanged shouts on George Street. She heard the words "murder" and "third floor" and an unexpected terror seized her. She thought of the bundles of money in the men's trunk, more than enough reason to kill. It occurred to her that she was known to have been in their company, and that now she was gone, as was probably the money, the two absences together might seem more than coincidental. She needed to determine just what had happened on the third floor of the St. Nicholas.

She made her way through the dwindling crowd of the lobby to the third floor. After the initial shock of the gunshots, interest seemed to have quickly waned, though she noted the ostler just outside the hotel, talking with a group of men, a bottle surreptitiously passing between them. Perhaps neither Merritt nor Argent had been murdered, nor the money stolen; it was altogether possible that some other guest had been murdered – hotels were often the scene of such crimes, usually involving illicit lovers or questioned honor. Louisville's own hotels had seen such murders. On the third floor, however, M's heart sank – there was a small crowd of people in the area where her room and the men's room were located. As she drew closer, she was surprised to find it was her own room that was the subject of inspection. The manager spotted her and began to demand an explanation, but then immediately declared that damages would be included on the bill, and that she should inform the *gentlemen* of that fact. He had taken a few steps away when he had suddenly turned and thundered at M that she and her escorts were no longer welcome at the hotel; he would not be host to such drunken behavior and whatever else might be happening between these rooms. He had wagged his finger wildly between the doors of their rooms, emphasizing just what he meant by 'between.' M nodded absently as the manager stalked off down the hall. She had been stunned with the accusations of drunken behavior and the suggestion of *liaisons* with Mr. Argent and Mr. Merritt. It was a word she had first come across when reading the newspapers with her father, of scandal in the Bavarian court, involving the Princess Sophia and an artist. It was a word heavy with immorality, and she was mortified to have it applied to her. But something else also stunned her – the manager had called her 'Miss Stearns.' But she could not unravel that now. With the manager gone, the rest of the guests dispersed to their rooms and M was able to enter her room and discover for just what damages Messrs. Merritt and Argent would be paying.

There was indeed a mess in her room and M conceded there was damage that demanded recompense. Her pumpkin head had been exploded and splattered against the headboard and the bed linen. The lamp on the table next to the bed lay in pieces on the floor, the oil staining the carpet. The curtains were torn and shredded in some places by the flying glass of the lamp. But most disturbing of all, there was damage on the wall opposite the door to the men's room – mere feet from her bed – where two bullets had lodged. The door to the men's room was wide open, but the room beyond was dark. M cautiously entered that room, lit the lamp, and saw evidence of a scuffle, but otherwise the room and, more importantly, the trunk were undisturbed. Robbery, then, had not been the motive and the "murder" had been her own. M did not know what to make of it all, only that the need to leave Cumberland and the company of these men was greater than ever. Once again, she left the St. Nicholas via the Windsor.

M ran to the hotel stable. Merritt and Argent were apparently still engaged in their evening errand, but as soon as they heard of the shooting, they would come racing back to the hotel, and if M were not gone, she would never have another opportunity – they would never let her out of their sight, not even with Mrs. Hughes. She needed more time, she needed to make certain the men could not immediately follow her, especially if they did not bite the bait regarding her ticket for the train going west. That ruse would only have worked if their discovery of her absence had been delayed until midnight. That was unlikely now.

Emmett was patiently waiting for her, where she had tied him, pulling tender, spring shoots from the ground. She stood for a moment, pulling at her bottom lip, one hand on the saddle. She could not bring herself to harm the men's horses, and even if she did, they would simply rent other horses. M thought of Mr. Edwards in Louisville. More time could be gained if the men were allowed to advance some distance, then be forced to return for some reason, and then start out anew. M obviously could not refit the horses with loose shoes; it had to be some other deceit. She decided to partially cut through the cinches of their saddles; with any luck, the men would get entirely out of Cumberland before the cinches failed, necessitating a long and time-consuming walk back to any place that could effect such repairs. The trick was not to cut the cinch so much that it would be recognized while the horse was being saddled. Still the cut had to be complete enough so that the cinch broke in a timely fashion. She would have to rely on the urgency of the situation to blind the men to the trickery. She did not have a knife, but she knew that Merritt carried one in a custom sheath on his saddle. She would use it to cut his cinch, and then keep the knife for herself – she may have need of one on the Road. It only then occurred to M the surprising presence of the men's saddles – her note to Mrs. Hughes had directed her to send M's saddle (still in her trunk) to the barn, but apparently Mrs. Hughes had sent the men's saddles as well.

Ill luck initially greeted her again at the entrance to the barn. As she rounded the corner to the front of the barn she heard men talking in hushed and hurried voices. She was not the only one taking advantage of the absence of the ostler – there were horse thieves here. The men were deep in the barn, near where Emmett had been stalled, near where she herself needed to go: Argent's and Merritt's horses had also been stabled in the back with Emmett. She slipped into the first empty stall and pressed herself into the shadow of the corner. From the urgency of their voices, surely they must need to leave soon; then she would slip to the back of the barn, cut the cinches and finally be ready to leave.

Finally, the men began to move towards the front of the barn, urging the horses they were stealing into a faster walk. M could not believe her luck, but also could hardly contain her indignation, as the horses that walked past her stall were Merritt's and Argent's horses, saddled. Their theft certainly cancelled any need to cut the cinches, but it also angered her to see them stolen. Merritt had not only been kind to Emmett but had an obvious tenderness for his own horse – M had seen him several times crooning to his horse and offering him small treats. Merritt's and Argent's loss was her gain, but, still, M regretted that her objectives could not be obtained in some other less permanent manner. If only theft could be semi-permanent. M then decided that it could. She would follow these men only long enough to see in which direction they headed and only close enough until she was able to get an accurate description of their appearance. Once she was home, she would send such information to them, by way of Grant at the White House, and Merritt and Argent could track down their horses on their own. She felt less and less like a criminal herself – even Christian, in light of her good intentions – the more she thought about it.

It was more difficult than M expected. Her good intentions faltered when she realized that the thieves were heading in the opposite direction that she needed to take. She also had to keep a distance far enough from the men that not only could she remain hidden, but Emmett as well. And she had to do it in almost full light. Not all the streets in Cumberland were lit by gas, but even those that weren't – the outlying streets to the east and south that the thieves were taking – were this night illumined by a huge, full moon. M had spent an anxious moment as the thieves collected their own horses on the far side of the barn and then continued down that side to reach George Street on their left. She held her breath as they moved past the back of the barn to gain the street – she had left Emmett on the opposite side of the barn, and a sharp look in his direction would have discovered him. But, again, her luck held.

Like M had done earlier, the thieves followed the tracks of the Baltimore & Ohio, though they crossed the tracks and continued on past the depot, keeping the tracks between themselves and the greater part of Cumberland. Not long after passing the depot, the two mounted men leading the two stolen horses drifted further east from the tracks and struck a wide dirt road. Despite the moon, M was able to keep her distance from the men and keep up with them as well, even though she remained on foot. They had passed the last building of any kind some time ago and M was easily able to keep off the road and in the shadow of woods. But then they were in the area of B&O's rolling mills, newly constructed, and in some places, still being finished, a large complex in a vast cleared area that left little cover for M to employ. A quarter of a mile or so past the rolling mills site, the road began to abruptly rise and once it leveled out again, M found herself almost exposed to discovery. Not far up ahead, the men had stopped near a large clearing that M could see held a racetrack and a few buildings; the area reminded her of the fairgrounds east of Louisville, along the tracks of the LC&L. She darted into the deep shadows of a grove of massive oaks on the opposite side of the road. This would be as far as she would go. It was obvious the thieves were heading south out of town, so there was no reason to follow them any further. However, the cover of the oaks allowed her to get close enough to possibly hear something specific as regarded their plans and possibly even glimpse their faces.

M left Emmett tethered to a large bush, then crept forward, moving from tree to tree, until she was almost opposite the men who had stolen Merritt's and Argent's horses. The thieves were disappointingly silent. This was certainly strange behavior for horse thieves; for all they knew, the alarm had been raised by now and the sheriff and police were tracking them here. M could not say how long they all waited in silence – the two men, still mounted on their horses, still holding the reins to the stolen horses, and M standing in the shadow of a huge oak tree – waiting always made time seem slow. After a time, however long or short that was, a wagon pulled out of one of the buildings on the fairgrounds, pulled up alongside the thieves, and stopped.

M was more confused than ever by the presence of the wagon – horse thieves could hardly expect to escape quickly when slowed down by a wagon. What was its purpose?

The two riders dismounted and finally M heard the men speak.

"Well?"

As he tied Argent's horse to the wagon, one of the men M followed from the hotel stable sounded distinctly disappointed as he answered the wagon driver, "Nothing happened."

The other man, with Merritt's horse, sounded less disappointed, but his words suggested it. "I sent for the others."

That was the end of conversation for a time, as the wagon driver now joined the two thieves in silent waiting, supposedly for "the others." The waiting was apparently expected to be long enough that a leisurely cigarette could be enjoyed. Their smoke drifted lazily over the road towards M. The wagon driver was in the middle of his second cigarette when M heard the sound of several horses approaching. As they crested the hill, M counted three more horsemen, and two of those were leading two more horses. Across these horses were laid two men, tightly hogtied to the saddle. The excessive restraint seemed unnecessary, as the men made no movement of any kind, their bodies given up entirely to the situation.

Joining the group at the wagon, the three new men dismounted and were helped by the men, that M now considered 'her' thieves, in removing the bound men from their saddles and then placing them in the wagon. The wagon driver remained in his seat, finishing his cigarette.

M at first doubted her eyes, but then she realized that, despite the unfamiliar clothes they were wearing, the men who were laid, rather roughly, in the back of the wagon were Merritt and Argent.

"How many saloons did you patronize?" The wagon driver again initiated the conversation, and he put some emphasis on 'patronize' that M did not understand. But the mention of saloons and the condition of Merritt and Argent combined to deliver a judgment to M: Merritt and Argent were drunk, dead drunk. The hotel manager's anger at drunken behavior was justified. She was disgusted with them and sorry she had taken such pains to help them. Her 'thieves,' it now seemed, were merely chums who had taken the liberty of fetching the men's horses for them as they were far too incapacitated to do so themselves; it was an act of misguided kindness, not theft. What was happening here was all somehow part of their secret evening errand, and now here they were out of town and out of sight of disapproving eyes, sleeping it off in the back of a dung wagon.

She should not have been surprised – they were always forcing some drink on her in the evenings. M was so focused on her disgust that she almost missed the next words, but those words slowly prickled her scalp.

Someone answered, "Enough; we ended at the Slack Water."

One of the newcomers – the one without a horse in tow – said in a low voice, "The police never came. There was no news from the hotel."

One of M's thieves, patted Merritt's horse. "They will come, after the canal opens tomorrow night."

M stood, undecided, in the shadows of the massive oak trees, their leaves barely past budding, but their trunks and limbs large enough that she could easily conceal herself behind one and in their shadows cast by the moon. M was not afraid at night among the trees. It was the exposure of the streets, even this desolate road, that gave her anxiety. Most of what she had seen and heard this night spoke of simple debauchery, and it gave understanding to why Argent was so keen to spend a day or more in Cumberland – Cumberland was probably a favorite and familiar haunt to these men. Well, if that was the case, then her plan was made all the easier – she would be far gone by the time Merritt and Argent had slept off this night's liquor.

But these other men had spoken of news from the hotel. There were several hotels in Cumberland; they could have meant any one of them, not necessarily the St. Nicholas. But that there was "no news" nagged at her. Someone had shot at what should have been herself in her hotel bed. Had she been there, it would have been murder; it would have been news. Mere gunshots had sent the ostler from his post, guests from their rooms and beds, and townspeople into the streets. A murder would have run like wildfire through the town. But there had been no murder, so there had been no news, and the police had not been roused.

She chanced one last look towards the wagon and was surprised at what was happening – Merritt and Argent were wrestled free of their coats and vests, and were then being rebound, hand and foot, their gun belts taken and, even more startling, their boots were removed. They were so drunk, they gave no resistance. M now considered that it was possible that Merritt and Argent were at one and the same time guilty of gross overindulgence and also victims of crime. But what was the crime? What would these men want with their boots? It was now obvious that Merritt and Argent were not among friends; friends may be bound on horses for safety's sake, but not bound hand and foot once off the horses. Another thought occurred to M: she had never before seen Merritt or Argent wear gun belts.

M wanted nothing more than to make her way back to Baltimore Street, already familiar to her, then north onto Mechanic to pick up the Cumberland Road. Her suspicions about Grant and Washington pulled her west towards the Ohio and home, but the season of Lent, and this week, Holy Week, in particular, somberly reproached her to help these men, even if she considered them as sometime enemies – no, especially if they were her enemies. The town was just behind her, but even so it would take time to return to the main streets and to find the police and explain the situation. Reflecting on what she would tell the authorities, it sounded ridiculous, even to her own ears: some men were carousing from saloon to saloon, and now they were drunk, and they have taken two of their own out of town in a wagon. Again, just what was the crime?

M returned to Emmett, but before starting out after the wagon, she retrieved her father's gun from the grip bag behind the saddle. With the gun held in her right hand, concealed in the folds of her skirt at her thigh, and the reins in her left hand, M pulled Emmett after her, following the wagon at a very discreet distance. The road was soft from spring rains and Emmett's hoof steps were as muffled as could be hoped, but she would only ride him if the wagon picked up its pace, which was unusually slow – she was easily keeping up just walking. The men certainly did not act as if they were running from anything or were guilty of any crime. Up ahead, the wagon wheels and driver's seat creaked, and the sounds of the other horses easily covered any noise Emmett made.

The unusual warmth of the day had gradually begun to moderate throughout the evening, but now the weather began to swing in the other direction – it seemed to get cooler by the moment, and M suspected rain was on its way. Her shirt and light jacket and the simple skirt she wore over her trousers would not hold back the chill much longer, and she dared not stop to unroll her cloak from her makeshift bedroll in her bag lashed behind the saddle. She did not know this road – the wagon could turn off anywhere and she might miss the turn if she were too far behind.

M could have stayed even farther back, if she had known how few places there were to turn off. She did, in fact, allow herself to fall far behind when the wagon crossed B&O's tracks as they swung east, away from the canal and the Potomac – she wanted to pick her way carefully over the tracks, to be certain Emmett crossed the double tracks safely and without striking any of the rails with his shoes, and she wanted to do it well out of sight of the men with the wagon. She waited long enough for the wagon and its posse to disappear down the road before risking exposure at the wide crossing.

Once across the tracks the road became less maintained, and sometimes she stumbled on a rock jutting above the surface, or a root exposed by soil washed away by past rains. Emmett, however, was sure-footed. They walked for nearly an hour before they came to a covered wooden bridge. M watched the wagon and the mounted men disappear into the tunnel of the bridge and waited long minutes, long enough she hoped that she could cross over the bridge without being heard by the men ahead of her.

M almost did not cross the bridge at all; she feared it led into Virginia. The water the bridge crossed, however, was not the Potomac, but the canal; the other side of the bridge landed her on its towpath. Once across the bridge, however, she panicked at the thought that she had lost the trail; which way did the wagon turn? To the right the towpath led back to Cumberland. Surely that was not their course. She turned left, and very soon found herself the target of some very salty barbs flung through the dark from faceless boat captains in the canal and their mule drivers (some of them very young), objecting to her presence on the towpath, especially since she was traveling in the opposite direction of every single mule team on the path. There was frequent mention of some midnight deadline, and a great hurry to reach Cumberland before the Sabbath suspension of canal operations. M thought that any observation of Sunday should begin with a suspension of all cursing about it. M hurried, pulling Emmett behind her, between teams of mules, slowing down as she passed each one, listening intently for the sounds of the wagon. The crush of mule teams slowly diminished. She stopped after the last team had passed when she heard up ahead the now familiar cursings of some captain whose progress was being impeded by an unwelcome guest on the towpath. The wagon with Merritt and Argent, then, was just up ahead. She would wait and give them time to be out of earshot when her own time came to be berated by the latest canallers.

Since Parkersburg, the moon had seemed to M as if it were growing unnaturally larger and larger, bearing down on her. This night was the full moon, and now it was fully risen and in its full glory. She had never seen the moon so large and bright. She did not like this unfamiliar and aggressive moon that was looming over the towpath. This night she did not want the exposure of the moonlight. Whether she was slipping away on the Cumberland Road or sneaking down the towpath behind this wagon, she preferred a dark night.

Despite the unpleasant obstacles in their path, the men and the wagon had considerably picked up the pace. M would soon have to mount Emmett to keep up. M did not know the hour, but it was not yet midnight – a boat was locking through at the first lock she passed in the towpath, the lock tender and boat captain exchanging relatively mild greetings, only pausing to stare as she hurried by, tugging at Emmett to hurry with her. The stone walls of the lock shimmered in the moonlight, and M thought of the salt works in Athens, so long ago. One of the men called after her, "This isn't a bridle path!"

The towpath now began to descend fairly rapidly. M passed two more locks in quick succession, but there were no boats locking through, or approaching the locks. Just past the third lock, however, there were several boats tied up on the berm side, apparently willing to wait out the Sunday suspension. Lanterns hung on the boats, but they could hardly compete with the white light of the moon. Occasionally M heard coming from the boats the voices of men and women and, once, though the hour was late and surely past bedtime, the piping voice of a child.

It had been some time since M had caught the sound of the wagon – they had either pulled far ahead of her or had finally stopped. The bright moonlight made her cautious and the sudden quiet of the canal made her anxious. She walked slowly in front of Emmett, suddenly realizing anew the strange change in the weather. It was no longer merely cool, but cold. Emmett was glad to slacken his pace; he was tired of this night walk.

M heard the men's voices up ahead, but not their words. She tied Emmett to a sapling several yards off the towpath in the thin woods between it and the Potomac, then moved silently forward until she could better hear what the men were saying. They were spectacularly unmindful of how loud they were, especially given the topic; it froze M's blood.

She distinctly heard the sound of someone drawing on a cigar, then knew it had been tossed away – the sound was incredibly clear under this mysterious moon and the sudden cold. One of them said, "This is just more work. I don't see why we can't just shoot them ourselves. The law doesn't seem to be in any hurry to do it. They don't seem to be overly concerned with murder in Cumberland."

"They're concerned, just maybe not so much when it is a stranger. We need to get the law's attention some other way. He is determined that these men should pay for what they did to him. And what Grant did to him, too."

"Killing them makes them pay, don't it? Who cares if the law does it or we do it?"

"He cares, and he is paying you handsomely to care as well. He wants them ruined on both sides of the grave. We have orders in place for this situation. Nothing gets attention like the disruption of commerce. Then the law will take notice."

"Well, we could have done it at the first lock." The complainer refused to relinquish his claim to whining.

"The first three locks are within spitting distance of each other; we don't want to attract attention to ourselves. We'll let the lock do the work, and it will be discovered in the morning."

"If it's privacy you want, the next lock is seven miles further on." A new voice.

"Maybe so, but this lock is presently unattended."

"Where is the lock tender?" The question had just occurred to someone.

"Cumberland – he hired me to substitute for him. Paid me in advance, too."

"What if a boat comes up, wants through?"

"This lock is closed for the night. Besides no boat can make it through the next lock down and get here in time. They've all tied up for the night. Sunday law."

"Is that on again?" When no one made the obvious answer, the voice asked, "Is it midnight?"

"Close enough."

M crept a little closer, almost to the very edge of the woods that stopped a few yards from a sorry-looking vegetable garden, but it was early in the season yet. M crouched down and watched. A few of the men handed round a bottle, each taking a swig, but none of them was really interested in the drink. They were all standing at the edge of the lock, looking down into it. M could see that the lock was either completely drained or the water was very low, too low for her to see it at all. One man had a hand on his hip, his head bent low, intent on the lock. Finally, he removed his hand and turned toward the wagon. "Let's get started – they're coming around."

M dared raise up a little to look into the back of the wagon. She could not see that Merritt and Argent were rousing; all she could see was the bottoms of their feet. It took three men to handle Merritt and three to handle Argent. Their coats and vests were pulled from the wagon and thrown carelessly on the ground. One man leaned over the side of the wagon near the front and retrieved the boots, and these were just as carelessly dropped on top of the clothes. In contrast to this, the gun belts were carefully wrapped around the holstered guns and laid to the side of the mound of clothing and boots. Merritt and Argent were muscled over the side of the lock and let down as far as possible, then dropped. Bound as they were, they would not be able to break the fall or land with anything like grace or safety. The other men then entered the lock, some of them letting themselves over the side of the lock, as they had done with Merritt and Argent. But the man who had stood with his hand on his hip and one other went down a few inches at a time, apparently on some ladder that M could not see. There was some scuffling and grunting and she thought she heard Merritt attempt to say something, but it came out more like a groan than any articulate word.

A sudden loud grunt was followed by a particularly foul curse amid a few laughs.

"How can there be so much muck in the canal so early in the season?" The voice was unusually loud, amplified by the walls of the lock.

"Stop crying; it will wash off. The question is, how can you be so unsteady after so few drinks. I've had a drink in more than a dozen bars tonight, lugging these two around, and I'm still upright." M was impressed that the man could still speak coherently after more than a dozen drinks.

In his anger and embarrassment, the man who had evidently slipped in the slimy muck at the bottom of the lock attempted to divert the attention from both his clumsiness and his boyish intolerance for liquor, and snapped, "Whatever happened to all the help we were promised from Moundsville?"

"Shut up and mind what you are doing; you almost broke his legs. They are not to be harmed in any way."

Now M was truly confused – why such solicitude for men who are about to be killed? Perhaps she had misheard the earlier talk of murder. More importantly, what was she to do about it? She still had her gun in her hand. She had almost forgotten it over the miles, but now she gripped it harder. There were six of them; she could possibly hit all six of them, but only if they came one at a time out of the lock. She knew this gun, knew its character; every bullet would find its mark.

"Why so much bother to humiliate these two? Looks like they're perfectly able to do it for themselves. Look at them, spread-eagled in the muck and ooze. That girl in town was enough to ruin them and Grant; why all this?" The men were now emerging from the lock, one man's entire backside, as well as his knees and hands, coated in black mud. He must have had occasion to push his hair out of his eyes, because his hair and forehead were also marked by the mud.

The man who had stood with his hand on his hip spoke quietly. "One more word, and you'll be joining them; maybe they won't appear so inept after all." After a pause, he ordered, "Throw the plates in with 'em."

One of the men removed a wrapped package from under the wagon seat, unfolded the wrapping and tossed the plates in the lock; they landed with a thud. It worried M that there were no other noises coming from the lock – except for that one garbled shout, she had not heard Merritt or Argent shout their anger or ask for mercy. M was fairly certain silence would not be her own response, and therefore she assumed the men were incapacitated from too much drink, or – a new thought occurred to her – some other substance.

M was fully crouching again, gripping the gun with both hands. She should start firing now, while she was still hidden, kill them before they killed Merritt and Argent, but she could not see her options beyond her first two or three shots. She was certain she could kill two or three, and it surprised her, in a distant part of her mind, that killing these men did not bother her. While she searched for a strategy beyond after she had exposed herself, she heard the sound of the wagon moving, at the same time that all five horsemen rode past her, on their way back to Cumberland. A minute or two later, the wagon, too, having turned around, passed her. She waited for the creaking of the wagon to die away before she dared stand up. She waited a moment longer before stepping out into the moonlight.

At the lock, M cautiously looked over the edge and saw a curious sight – Merritt and Argent were pinned under an ugly-looking scow of some kind, but it was only half as big as the other boats she had seen tied up along the basin in Cumberland and along the canal itself only an hour ago. It was only half as long as the lock and not so wide as to be snug, like the usual canal boat. She was relieved to see the men not only alive, but alert and actively working to release themselves. It appeared that they were no longer bound, but they were making poor progress, being pinned up to their chests.

Remembering the man who had slipped in the muck, M stepped out of her skirt and laid it across Merritt's saddle. The gun she shoved in the waist of her trousers. She was very likely to get muddy, but at least her skirt could cover her dirty trousers when she was finished in the lock. M saw the grab irons leading down into the lock and let herself over the side and down the rungs.

Merritt and Argent were struggling in vain to free themselves and, as M got closer, she saw that they were struggling to breathe as well; the scow was very nearly sitting with its entire weight on their chests. Only fallen limbs dragged from the woods acting as small make-shift chocks kept the full weight from crushing them.

The scow was in the down side of the lock, about 50 feet away. Still wary of this strangely excited moon, M crept along the western wall of the lock, only stepping out of the thin shadow of the wall when she was directly opposite the men. Even from here, she could smell the liquor and cigar smoke on them. When she crouched next to them and asked, "What is the point of all this?" they both reared up so violently in surprise that they yelped as their chests rubbed against the bottom of the scow with force.

Merritt gasped, "M!" and Argent gasped, "Miss Warner!"

M asked again, "What is the point of all this?"

Merritt regained his composure before Argent. "As the water rises, so will the scow, but not before we're drowned. It's a clean murder, with no witnesses and accomplished long after the murderers have fled the scene."

"Clever plan, but it only works if there is water; the idiots have forgotten to turn on the spigot. I could be a better criminal than these men."

M rose and said needlessly, "Wait here," but Argent's curiosity got the better of him. "How did you come to be here?"

M was already half way to the grab irons in the side of the wall. "I followed the wagon. I'll be back."

Merritt twisted his head and neck to follow M as she left them, and trying to betray as little panic as possible, Merritt called after her, "Where are you going?"

"To find some rope in the tender's house; the horses can pull you out faster than we can dig you out."

M had a foot on the first rung of the grab irons, when a sudden blast of cold wind brought the sound of horses coming down the towpath. She dropped back to the floor of the lock, nearly slipping when she landed, and hurried back down the wall, past the point where Merritt and Argent were trapped under the stern of the boat, crossing at the far water gates to crouch in the shadow of the bow. M prayed that Emmett in the woods did not betray her, then realized a more immediate betrayal lay across Merritt's saddle. It was possible the horses approaching carried friendly, even helpful, riders, but it was midnight and the canal was closed in observance of the Sabbath, and it was more likely that only more trouble was afoot on the towpath.

The wind was coming in ever increasing gusts, blowing clouds across the moon, but the clouds were not so thick or expansive as to completely block its light. M pulled herself closer to the boat and held her breath. She did not dare peek around the bow, but she heard men's voices approaching the lock. They were familiar voices. "Go get the crank."

She heard a boot scuff on the wall of the lock, but the man did not climb down into the lock. She imagined the man standing there, hand on hip, staring down at Merritt and Argent.

M heard several shots in rapid succession, faster than she thought should happen. She heard most of the bullets thud in the muck of the floor, but twice she heard the ping of bullets ricocheting off the limestone walls of the lock. The wind was blowing almost constantly now, and M felt a deep cold envelop her. The shooter had moved away from the edge of the lock, but through the wind she heard him say, "Open it, but only a crack; let them savor their last moments." Then she heard the horses move back up the towpath.

All caution was gone now. She slipped in the muck in her hurry to rejoin Merritt and Argent, terrified that one or both had been shot. She did not see blood on either man, but there was new peril in the water trickling through the partially opened gates. A trickle in a lock, however, could still cover a prone man's head within several minutes.

M tried to clear from the men's shoulders and backs the muck that acted like mortar, but progress was far too slow. Water was spreading over the floor of the lock, seeping into the muck before beginning to gather on top of it. Her hands hurt from scooping the cold mud. She frantically looked around her, even as she continued to scoop muck from under Merritt and Argent. Spying the metal plates thrown in the lock with the men, M hurried over to retrieve one, slipping twice on the way, and going down once, hard. The cold made her clumsy, and now she was almost completely covered in cold mud. The moon was now completely covered, but only somewhat diminished in its brightness; the sky was white with clouds, lit from behind by the moon. In one corner of her mind, the corner where weather was always recorded and analyzed, she thought of snow clouds. It began to drizzle.

M was back with the men, using the plate to scrape great gobs of the muck away from first one and then the other. Abruptly, M worked only around Merritt, furiously excavating under his shoulders and as far down as she could reach on either side. She was making headway, even as the deepening water worked to wash the mud back in place. She began to pray, the Latin tumbling from her mouth so fast that the words jumbled and overrode each other, making the prayers unintelligible.

Merritt rose as high as he could, allowing M to excavate under his shoulders and far down his back; occasionally he laid back to rest his muscles. The water now covered his mouth when he fully laid back. Next to Merritt, Argent was likewise rising up as far as he could to stay above the water, but he, too, occasionally laid back when he could no longer hold the raised position.

Finally, M felt Merritt shift as he raised up; he was freeing himself now by pushing against the side of the scow. M then began to work around and under Argent. Argent had just laid back to rest when a large crack sounded, and water came gushing into the lock. She felt Argent pull up and heard him take a great gasp of air as she herself was knocked over by the force of the water as it broke through the gates, unwilling to enter at such a slow pace. She was on her side and under water. She got to her hands and knees and tried to rise but she could not find purchase on the slippery floor. On her second try, she felt hands grip her under her arms and raise her to a standing position. Merritt pushed her towards the grab irons before he himself slipped and fell under the water. With great difficulty M made her way to the ladder in the wall and pulled herself out of the lock. Her hands and feet were numb, making it difficult to grip the bars with her hands or to keep her feet from slipping off the rungs.

M scrambled over the top of the lock, disoriented as to what to do next. She had not noticed that the drizzle had turned to full rain while she was scraping at the muck in the lock, but now she realized the rain had turned to sleet. She saw Merritt's and Argent's horses standing there, heads hanging in the cold and wet; M's skirt was gone, no doubt blown off the saddle. She didn't bother to look for it. She started up the road to where she had left Emmett, but Emmett had worked loose his reins from the sapling and now came walking calmly towards her on the towpath. M made a weak attempt at a whistle, and enough came out that Emmett began to trot to her. The numbness was spreading to her mind – thinking all need for it had passed, M pulled the gun from her waistband and forced it into her grip bag. It took her three attempts before she was able to pull herself up into the saddle, before heading down the towpath, away from Cumberland. She kicked Emmett into a fast trot, hiding her face from the site of her failure as she passed the lock.

Argent coughed and drew in large hoarse gasps of air long after he and Merritt pulled themselves from the lock. Curiously, Merritt still clutched the plate he had taken from M and that he had used to help clear Argent from under the scow, which now floated quietly in the lock. The earlier violence of the water rushing into the lock was now reduced to the agitation of the sleet diving into the surface.

The men struggled with cold wet hands to wrestle on their boots. It was only slightly less difficult to button their vests and shrug into rain-soaked coats. Their gun belts lay nearby, as if carelessly dropped from their waists before they had, presumably, dived into the lock to recover the plates. Merritt tossed Argent his gun and belt; Argent dropped it twice before taking firm possession of it. Both men fumbled with numb hands to buckle their belts.

It did not take much searching to find Emmett's large hoof prints in the new mud. Merritt and Argent rode as fast as they could in the freezing mud and driving sleet, but it seemed a long time before they first caught sight of M, perhaps a half a mile away, almost black from the mud that covered her. By contrast, Emmett seemed unnaturally white. M had stopped, and in the strange light of this strange April storm, she looked like a dark specter, sitting atop a phantom horse, daring them to approach and challenge her reality. As they drew nearer, M started to dismount, but then slid down Emmett's side to puddle on the ground near his back legs. The specter, having lost the challenge, sank to the ground where mere men walked.

Argent was the first to reach her. She was barely conscious, but Argent could not immediately say why. She was ice-cold to the touch, but even so, it was not so cold, and she had not been cold so long, as to affect her so severely. He laid her back and only after thinking it necessary to do so, opened her jacket and found blood seeping from a bullet wound near her left shoulder. Argent slid his hand along her back to hopefully find the exit wound. M roused slightly and said to no one in particular, "My shirt is wet."

Merritt, ignoring M, asked Argent, "Can you remove it?"

But M would not be ignored. "No, leave it on – I don't have another shirt." Having delivered this directive, M slipped into complete unconsciousness.

Also ignoring M's protests, Argent shook his head, No. Even with the advent of rain and sleet, the sky still was white, and the moon somehow made its presence known. Argent shifted his body to remove his shadow from M. Simultaneously, he pushed on Merritt's chest until Merritt's shadow, too, was removed. Argent cautiously, almost superficially, probed the wound, then sat back. "I can't feel the bullet. It could be anywhere, could have hit her collar bone and taken an eccentric course. Digging around for it here in the dark could just shift it elsewhere, causing even more damage. I need more light than even this moon can give, and I need something more than a pocket knife."

Argent did not like to give voice to the possibility that M would bleed to death before they reached any safe haven, though surely Merritt had considered it as well. Merritt, however, had developed some strange affinity for Miss Warner, though Argent could not call it romantic. Regardless, he would not give Merritt any cause for despair until it was inevitable.

"We can't stay here in the middle of the towpath. As M said, those thugs are idiots; they may have forgotten some other step in their plan and are on their way back to complete the crime or clean up after themselves."

Argent hauled himself up. "Or verify that we did indeed drown. Here, help me lift her up onto Emmett. I'll ride with her. You ride to the next lock and rouse the tender. We all of us need to get out of this storm. Take my horse with you – I have my hands full."

Argent struggled to keep pressure on M's wound and at the same time keep her from slipping out of his embrace while holding the reins and keeping his own hold on the saddle. The sudden cold, along with the drenching in the canal, made his hands clumsy on the reins, yet Emmett seemed to understand his urgency, and they managed a fast walk. Argent dared not ask more of Emmett or M on this miserable night and on this unfamiliar ground that was rapidly turning into a slippery slush. Argent felt the warm ooze of M's blood track down his wrist and arm to his elbow.

He did not know how long they rode or how far they had traveled when he heard horses approaching rapidly from his front. Argent urged Emmett to slow his pace, then carefully transferred the reins to the hand that pinned M in place. It was not until he attempted to remove his gun that Argent realized how numb his hand had become from both the cold and the fixed position in which he had held it since he and M first started down the towpath. He almost dropped the gun, but he had it ready by the time the horse came close enough to be seen through the sleet and, now, the occasional snow.

Merritt pulled up short next to Argent and shouted over the wind; he was also loud in his excitement. "We've stepped into a little luck tonight. There's a bridge across the canal less than half a mile down the path. From there we cross Old Town Road and continue on to a farm about mile and a half beyond the bridge. We can get M help, real help, there."

Merritt turned his horse (pulling Argent's behind), and the group began moving down the towpath, slowly at first. "What about the next lock? Isn't that closer?"

"About the same distance, but the lock tender will not open his door to anyone. I think he has been abused once too often by canal boatmen insisting he operate the lock during the Sunday suspensions. But he told me about the farm — a doctor that once lived there tended to the needs of the canal people when they passed through here."

"Once?"

"Died last year, but his widow – the Widow Lambert – is the town midwife."

"M does not need a midwife."

"The widow also helped her husband in his rounds and services. The lock tender said she was 'very useful' during the war when things heated up around here. Perhaps she has whatever you need to help M."

"Then let us go meet the midwife."

The bridge – one of those compromises the canal accepted when negotiating for land from nearby farmers – was perhaps a little closer than Merritt thought, but the farm was definitely farther than the lock tender stated – by Argent's counting, it was a full two miles from the canal. The farmhouse was, however, dry and warm and commodious, even if the widow was less so. The little group was met a short distance before the farmhouse by a man with a shotgun who demanded to know their business. Once explained (and proven, Argent being required to show the blood still seeping through M's clothes), they were advanced to the door where a woman stood, clearly roused from sleep but given enough time to appear properly dressed (though her hair still hung in disarray behind her back). She was not surprised at Merritt's request for aid, but she was not altogether happy to give it.

M was laid on the bed in a small back room of the house. Unlike the two cots in the back room of M's own house, the bed here was fairly large, leaving room for little else but a night stand and lamp on one side and two tattered chairs opposite the foot of the bed. She was positioned at an odd angle with her head at one corner of the bed and her feet at the opposite corner. She was filthy from the mud of the canal; the sleet had done little to wash it from her. The two men were also dirty, but they had the luxury of relatively clean vests and coats to cover their time in the lock. All three were chilled and numb from an unexpected cold, unexpected even in the chancy weather of mid-April.

The man who had stopped them outside the house now brought in wood and built up a fire in a room which was clearly little used. The widow lit the lamp as soon as she led them into the room, but it was not until the fire took hold that Argent saw just how much blood M had lost.

Even over the black of the muck that caked her clothes, he could see the course of the blood as it had seeped down the front of her shirt and coat. There was blood on her left hand where it had found its way down her sleeve. She was filthy and disheveled, her hair heavy and slick with sleet and mud. She hardly looked human, but, looking at Merritt, Argent realized that he hardly looked much better. Perhaps the widow's chilly reception had more to do with their appearance than with their need for help at such a ghostly hour.

The Widow Lambert peeled away M's coat and the shirt underneath and gingerly probed the wound. Blood was coming at a very slow pace, and even that was discerned only because the widow wiped clean the area around the jagged hole where the bullet had entered, making the blood easier to track. A young woman now came into the room, carrying a leather case. Like the widow, she had the appearance of one who had hastily dressed, obviously woken from the natural hours of sleep. Neither woman showed any excitement, but the younger woman briefly betrayed a disgust at the appearance of the strangers.

The young woman placed the case on the bed next to M, flipped open the lid, and began to pull from it the instruments needed in such a situation. The lock tender may have been mistaken on the distance to the farmhouse, but not on its function – these women had performed services like this before. It occurred to Argent that Mrs. Lambert had a tidy sum of money tied up in these instruments, money that could be had by their sale. Midwifery was one thing but continuing her husband's medical practice could only lead to disaster. Even as Argent was mulling over the presence and value of the surgical instruments, Merritt asked, "Hadn't you better do it?"

Both women looked up at Argent, but it was the widow who spoke. "You have experience in this?"

"Yes." Argent hesitated before adding, "But my hands are numb and filthy besides." The so-called germ theory of disease had appeared in European medical journals for several years now and copied in similar American journals. Earlier, just this year, the theory had found its way into the common newspapers of American cities. The theory seemed to demand attention, though Argent was not convinced that woolen respirators for surgeons, as suggested in these articles, were required to protect patients. And in the heat of battle or its aftermath, it was a selfish luxury to wash oneself between surgeries. Still, it was only courting ruin to perform surgery in such a state as he now found himself. "Are you confident in your own ability?"

The widow returned to laying out her tools as the young woman handed them to her. Without any hesitation, she said, "Yes; the war taught me what my husband would not."

Though M was still insensible, Argent pinned M's legs to the bed, while Merritt did the same with her upper body, practically laying across her torso at an odd angle, pinning her left arm with his right hand. Once again, M roused slightly and tried to struggle against the restraint. More than the pain in her shoulder, the inability to move frightened her and she opened her eyes wide to see a strange woman with a blade poised in her hand. The woman said, "Hold her tight – she will rebel violently at the first cut." M cried out, "Don't," and the woman said sharply, "Turn her face away and hold her." It was then that M heard Merritt; he was above her, calling her name.

"M. Look at me, nothing else."

"Don't."

"It must be done. Look at me, nothing else."

M became frantic. She did not know exactly what was happening – just what was it that must be done? – but she was afraid of her reaction to it. She was afraid she would shame herself by screaming or (worse) cursing. And she was afraid of showing fear to Merritt. A silly thought came to her. "Don't let her cut my shirt. Mrs. Müller gave it to me. It is my birthday gift." The Passion of St. John swirled in her head, like the waters in the lock, and the Roman guards at the foot of the Cross spoke to her. "Don't let them tear it. It is seamless, woven in one piece from top to bottom. Let them cast lots for it." She pushed them from her mind; she should not listen to them; they were Roman guards and crucifiers. Still, she could not remember if there were seams in her shirt. There should be seams – it seems there should be seams.

"Mrs. Müller will make you a new one. Now, M, lay still if you can."

M looked back at the widow and realized it was not only the shirt she intended to cut.

Merritt gently turned her head away from the woman with the blade and slightly shifted himself so that he was in M's sight. "Look at me, M, nothing else."

M instead stared at the arm that pinned her own left arm. She felt Merritt's hand bear down on her right shoulder. Only her head could move – she would have to keep that still on her own. She bit into Merritt's sleeve and prayed for endurance.

M did indeed react violently at the first cut, but the men held her fast, and she mercifully lost consciousness at almost the same instant.

Argent watched the widow at her work and for the most part approved. She was slower than he himself would have been – the war had not taught her speed, though, to be fair, she would never have worked in an army hospital tent, as he had done, where speed was judged on a par with skill, especially when ether and chloroform were not available. She found the bullet with but little exploration and managed to extract it without much digging or further damage. The widow sutured the blood vessels in a manner unfamiliar with Argent (he couldn't say with certainty that it was *wrong*, just not how he would do it). She then rinsed the wound (a step he would not have even considered), and, finally, packed it with lint. Only then did Merritt and Argent relax their awkward holds on M.

Merritt announced that he would see to their horses, now that M no longer had need of his help, but the young woman assured him that Mr. Darnell – the man who had questioned them outside and then had started the fire in M's room – had already taken their horses to the barn and was seeing to their needs for the night. Both Merritt and Argent were at something of a loss as what to do next – Merritt had made himself responsible for Emmett and Argent had considered himself responsible for Miss Warner, and now both men had lost their responsibilities.

After a brief, but failed, struggle with Mrs. Lambert to stay the night with M, the younger woman, now identified as the widow's daughter, led Merritt and Argent to a room they would share. It was a spartan room, like the one where they had taken M, but there was no fireplace. There was one bed in the room, which they would also share. On this bed were laid some clothes, out of date and style but well-kept. Indicating the clothes, the daughter said, "Mother thought you could wear these while your own clothes are washed." Argent began to protest, "We couldn't possibly ask you …" but the daughter blushed slightly before continuing, "There is a cistern out back where you may rinse your clothes of the mud and blood," (particularly indicating Argent's mud-stained vest and shirt where M had leaned back against him on Emmett). "These were my father's clothes.

They may not fit well, but if the day is fair tomorrow, it should not take long for your own clothes to dry."

The daughter left on this optimistic note, but tomorrow was already today, and the storm outside showed no signs of abating. It had now settled into a steady, pounding cold rain. There was little chance of fair weather any time soon.

Merritt and Argent removed their filthy clothes, careful not to let them soil any of the bedding. After searching briefly for a safe place to lay them, they finally opted to simply drop them in a heap in a corner. Merritt's clothes fell with a thud. Argent spun around at the sound.

"What was that?"

Merritt retrieved his coat from the floor and pulled from a pocket the plate he had carried from the lock. Holding it up for Argent to see, Merritt said, "See, the instrument of our salvation. M found it. We both used it to scrape mud from around you in the lock. I had forgotten that I still had it." As Merritt held out the plate he considered it for the first time, and he cocked his head as he recognized it. "This is one of the plates from that counterfeit den we raided last year on Snake Hill. Weren't all the plates sent to New York, with Whitley?"

"Plates and everything else, except the printing press. That was busted up and used for firewood." Argent took the plate from Merritt and examined it himself. "Maybe this is a copy we didn't know about, but there have been no new counterfeits from this plate since the raid. Where did they get it?"

Merritt merely shrugged his shoulders, unable in his fatigue and numbness to care about old plates. He picked a side of the bed, then got under the covers. "You'll get the lamp?"

The widow's husband's shirt fit Merritt well enough, but Argent found the buttons straining to keep a similar shirt closed across his chest. In the end he opted to sleep shirtless (that is, completely naked). Merritt eyed him warily as Argent climbed into bed next to him but said nothing.

Though the lamp had been extinguished and both men were tired from the late hour and still affected by the several (sloppy and incomplete) administrations of chloroform throughout the evening, sleep evaded them both. After some time, Argent spoke, certain that Merritt was still awake. "The President will need to be informed. We were expected tomorrow. Today," he corrected himself.

"No, you were correct the first time. We are expected tomorrow. Today is Easter. We were to have left Cumberland on Monday. M will miss Easter Sunday Mass."

"I'll return to Cumberland and send a wire."

"I'd like to go back to the lock and look around."

"As would I, but Miss Warner is our first concern, though I would hate to see that trail go cold. How did she come to be there?"

"Apparently, she followed us, and it was lucky for us that she did. But an equally important question is, who were those men, and, why did they attack us?"

"It was not for robbery." Argent felt Merritt's head turn toward him on his pillow, and though he could not see Merritt, Argent knew the question on his face. "As for myself, nothing was taken – not my money, not my notebook, not my pocket gun, nothing. You should check your pockets in the morning."

Merritt agreed, then after a moment, added, "I didn't check my pockets. My gun was fired, though. Emptied."

"I didn't think to check mine."

"I did – yours was emptied as well."

"One of our own bullets struck M?"

"Likely."

Argent blew out a breath; he thought of the shape of the bullet the widow had pulled from M – flattened and misshapen. It had either bounced off a bone or, more likely, ricocheted off one of the walls of the lock. M's wound had looked particularly ugly; the bullet, then, was already misshapen when it entered her body. It had never been the intention of the shooter to hit them as they lay there pinned under the scow, just to empty their guns, as any lawman would do in pursuit of criminals. "They didn't know she was there. What was the reason?"

Merritt had only just come around as he and Argent were being muscled into the lock, but he remembered some of their captors' conversation just prior to that – 'spread-eagled' and 'inept' stood out in his mind. "To ruin our reputation, to humiliate us; it has something to do with that."

Both men chased possibilities in their heads for a few moments. Finally, Argent repeated, "I will return to Cumberland tomorrow." Then he turned on his side, away from Merritt.

"No, not yet; let us wait to see how M does, then we will report to him." Merritt, too, turned on his side, both men staring into the darkness of opposite sides of the room.

17 — *Easter Sunday*

It was late in the morning on Easter Sunday when Argent and Merritt left their room. Their clothes were ill-fitting, but they were dry and clean, unlike their persons, which still carried the filth of the lock. Someone, however, had left a water-filled ewer and basin just outside their door, and so they retreated to their room to clean the last of the dirt from their faces, hands, and other parts. Looking to their pillows, Argent saw a great deal of last night's dirt deposited there. He turned them over to reveal the clean side. There was no since antagonizing the two Lambert women at the moment; they would find the deception after the men had left. Their bags and the great trunk were still at the St. Nicholas, and so they were without razor or comb. They made the best of their hair using their fingers, but there was nothing to be done about their incoming beards, but to keep them clean.

They did not immediately go to see M – the widow had said she would call for them if M was *in extremis*, and in this instance, no news was good news. Instead, they went in search of the cistern to rinse out their bloody, muddy clothes. It was still raining, but not so hard that they could not make a dash from the small patch of roof that overhung the back door to the cistern, to fill a couple of buckets with clean water. They took turns doing this, rinsing and rubbing their clothes until the water was dirty, then refilling their buckets with clean water. It was impossible to get out all the stains they had set overnight, something Argent's mother would not have permitted, and he wondered that Mrs. Lambert would allow such a thing in her own home and her guests. He reminded himself that they were not, strictly speaking, guests and that he himself had intimated last night to Miss Lambert that they did not expect to be treated as such; still, it rankled him somewhat. He decided to take the high road.

"We must have presented quite the desperate characters last night. I wonder that the widow consented to help us."

"She consented to help us before she saw you bathed in M's blood. I was merely muddy at the time I made my application." Merritt looked over at him as Argent wrung out the water from his shirt. Argent's borrowed pants, like his borrowed shirt, were too tight, and the legs were too short.

Argent caught Merritt smiling at him. "Fair weather or not, if these clothes aren't dry in two hours, I am wearing them wet."

"Perhaps we could borrow some room and be allowed to build up a fire. That should move things along."

Merritt left Argent to struggle with the considerable blood on his clothes and presented himself at M's door. Miss Lambert, not the widow, answered his soft knock. "How does she?"

Opening the door wide, Miss Lambert silently admitted Merritt into the room. "Well enough. We would like to change the sheets, but mother is tired. We will change them tonight or tomorrow."

"If Argent were here, we could do it now, and save your mother the trouble."

Miss Lambert blushed at the thought of men handling a woman's dirty sheets; perhaps she should not have mentioned the sheets at all. "No, there is no need. It is too early to disturb her; I'm sure mother will want to make sure of the sutures before we move her."

The two women had made considerable improvements in M's appearance. They had managed to remove M's filthy clothes and bathe her as best they could. There was still a considerable amount of dried mud in her hair, but her face and neck were clean, as was the injured shoulder that was bared for easy inspection. M's own shirt had been replaced, but only over the uninjured arm and shoulder. It was a man's shirt – another of Dr. Lambert's lingering wardrobe – but it seemed to adequately fit the purpose of safeguarding M's modesty. He could see the empty sleeve, behind M's left shoulder, hanging over the bedside. It was apparently buttoned up to just over her breasts, but the widow had covered this area with a large cloth, so that truly only the bandaged wound was seen. Mrs. Lambert had also placed M's left arm in a sling, and this also helped to keep M's chest properly covered.

Merritt indicated a bandage on M's forearm, showing from under the sling. "Was there a second wound?"

"Yes, there was large sliver of rock lodged in her arm, but Mother removed it and stitched the gash; it is not as serious as the other wound." Apparently having exhausted all she had to report of the woman lying in bed, Miss Lambert turned to the matter of Argent and Merritt themselves. "After mother has rested and relieves me here, I will be able to feed you. Until then, I left some cornpone and ham on the kitchen table. And, of course, you know where the cistern is, for something to drink."

Merritt glanced at the window and realized it looked out over the yard where he and Argent had been running to and from the cistern. Miss Lambert must have stood there and watched them. Merritt thought of fetching yet more water from the cistern and having only that to wash down his breakfast. He had had enough water to drink last night in the lock and thought ruefully of the coffee he always carried in his saddle bag, which along with everything else they had brought on this trip, remained in their hotel room at the St. Nicholas.

As if she had read his mind, Miss Lambert added, "Darnell has gone into town for some coffee."

Merritt looked sharply at Miss Lambert. "To Cumberland?" Though he and Argent intended to return there themselves, they had intended to do so at night, hopefully reach their rooms quietly and assume new identities before digging into the events of last night. It would not do for Darnell to reveal, no matter how innocently, that the Widow Lambert had under her roof an injured woman and two men who had come to them in the middle of the night, covered in the muck of the canal.

"Cumberland? That is much too far away. No, he has gone to Old Town, but with this rain, he must be a while in returning."

Merritt nodded both his relief and his gratitude. Looking one final time at M, he noticed how pale she was, but at least she was warm and dry. Remembering Argent scrubbing and rubbing his clothes, Merritt asked if there was someplace that would not inconvenience the household where he and his friend could dry their clothes. Despite last night's discomfort at the thought of washing these men's clothes and unlike her modesty where M's sheets were concerned, Miss Lambert did not hesitate to offer the fire and the chairs in the kitchen for the men's use. She also did not hesitate to inform him that they would need to build up the fire in the kitchen, since she and her mother had been busy through the night and Darnell had gone to Old Town. For Coffee.

~

"How did you find Miss Warner?"

Merritt gave Miss Lambert's answer: "Well enough."

Merritt had found Argent in the kitchen, already making himself useful, building up the fire. The seams of his pants were challenged to the utmost as he bent to his task, but at Merritt's rather casual reply to a question of some seriousness, Argent straightened, and the seams sighed their relief. Argent's look conveyed both disappointment and a request for elucidation.

"She is very pale, having lost blood from two wounds." As Argent's brows rose, Merritt explained, "She was also hit in the forearm – a splinter of rock – but the Widow Lambert informed her daughter that it was of relatively light consequence."

"I should look in on Miss Warner and decide that for myself."

Now Merritt's brows rose, but Argent did not respond to the reproach there. "I will start the coffee and set about hanging our clothes on these chairs around the fire. Do we know when we can expect the good widow to make an appearance this morning?"

"She has only recently gone to get some rest, but Miss Lambert holds out hope that her mother will return to M in time for a proper breakfast to be set out. In the meantime, we have been given permission to dry our clothes in here, but I am afraid coffee will have to wait until Darnell returns with it from Old Town."

"Old Town? Are we that far from Cumberland?"

"Yes and no. Miss Lambert indicated that Old Town was much the closer town for such errands, yet it was still some five or more miles away."

"And was Darnell cautioned against mentioning our presence here?"

"Doubtful. I did not ask Miss Lambert; I did not want to inflame any more wariness on the part of the Lambert women. But I doubt it would have occurred to either of them, or Darnell either, that the situation demanded secrecy."

Argent thought for a moment. "I cannot accurately recall: did these men return to Cumberland last night?"

"The wind and the empty lock played havoc with sound, but I am almost certain that I heard the horses return up the towpath, to Cumberland. If they turned toward Patterson's Creek, as we did, they were well ahead of us." Then Merritt added what Argent feared, "They may be at Old Town, but we have no way of knowing."

"Perhaps Darnell could be gently persuaded to reveal all that he hears or sees in Old Town."

"Perhaps, but I don't know when he left, and, as Miss Lambert acknowledged, this rain will slow him. We will have to wait patiently for our coffee and any information."

They had slept off most of the effects of last night's chloroform dosing, and the cold morning rain had dissipated the rest. Now they found themselves famished and they made short order of the small portions of cornpone and ham, and did not mind (not as much as Merritt thought) washing it down with water.

True to his word, Argent did not wait until his clothes were completely dry before divesting himself of Dr. Lambert's binding hand-me-downs. In such heretofore unappreciated comfort, Argent helped Merritt perform the chores necessary to any home in the country. It was determined that Darnell must have left very early indeed, as none of the horses – either theirs or the sorry Lambert nag – had been fed nor the barn cleaned. Unlike the multi-stalled, commodious barn of the Warner farmstead, the Lambert barn was one open space where their one horse roamed at will. One corner of the barn was covered with a scattering of straw, but the family milch cow had claimed this spot. A henhouse of sorts had been built into one side of the barn. Merritt found the feed bag and dropped some corn on the floor a few feet away from the hens, but they refused to take the bait. Getting the eggs while the hens still sat on them proved awkward and, in one case, painful for Merritt, but in the end, he gathered enough eggs for a late breakfast.

The barn itself had seen better days. Argent knew, without ever having met the man, that Mr. Warner would never have allowed his barn to fall into disrepair. The Lambert barn was also much smaller than the Warner barn and seemed to be the only such structure near the house. In fact, the barn and the house formed two very close sides of a square, the other sides being a fenced pasture and a fenced kitchen garden. Only the pasture and garden provided a solid angle in the square – there was an opening between the barn and the house, and the other end of the house and the kitchen garden were separated by the dirt drive that turned off the long road from the canal. While Merritt cradled the eggs to the house,

Argent went in search of the woodshed, which was inconveniently located behind the barn. Here, too, Argent found dilapidation setting in. Mrs. Lambert and her daughter could hardly be blamed, but their man Darnell could certainly be held responsible for the deteriorating condition of the buildings. Argent grabbed an armful of wood before he followed Merritt back into the house.

It was well past noon before Miss Lambert was able to put anything on the table, but the food was surprisingly of good quality and varied, especially given the earliness of the season and the limited resources the widow had to grow any kind of surplus of any crop, to either sell or put up for the winter. The vegetable garden, in fact, had not even been tilled or in any way prepared for the new growing season. Argent realized, even as Merritt said, "We need to pay Mrs. Lambert for her services," that the widow and her daughter lived mostly off what people could pay her for her midwifery and other services. Her patients from the canal could provide her with produce and other amenities not easily found nearby, but easily transported from the Chesapeake area on the boats. Darnell, then, must take as his pay the lion's share of any cash the widow accumulated.

"Yes, I will see to it." Once again, Argent wondered that they had not been robbed at the lock. His own pocket-book was still wet but drying on the bed in the room he shared with Merritt. The money, too, was damp with M's blood, but that could not be helped. "Perhaps you had better see to it; my bills might cause some discomfort."

Merritt nodded. "In the meantime – if it stops raining – perhaps we could start on the repair of the fencing around the pasture." A stack of lumber near the barn and the condition of portions of the fence indicated an intention of repairs.

Now Argent nodded. "What are we to do with ourselves in the meantime?"

They spent the balance of the afternoon carrying wood from the woodshed behind the barn to the small stoop with the overhang at the back door. Argent took two large armfuls of wood to M's room, using some of it to refresh the fire there. He also took the opportunity to see for himself if M was doing well enough. Merritt was right – she was pale from loss of blood, but it did not give her that ethereal look that women longed for and that usually came at great cost of health for those who pursued it. Instead M looked merely sickly, and in the mingled firelight and rain-clouded daylight her skin took on a truly ashen color that somehow also looked greenish. She did not look well at all, but she was alive, though her pulse was weak, and, despite the fire, her skin was cold. The widow reappeared as Argent felt M's pulse, and though she said nothing, Argent felt Mrs. Lambert did not approve of his presence. He left soon afterwards, and he and Merritt were both told at supper that Mrs. Lambert would again stay with M through the night and would alert the men with news of any change in her condition. Miss Lambert delivered this directive with the command of one who had dealt with the friends and relations of her mother's patients many times before. She left the kitchen immediately afterwards, adding on her way out that there would be coffee in the morning – Darnell had returned from Old Town.

18 — Easter Monday

It was as Miss Lambert was pouring coffee at breakfast the next morning that Merritt found an unexpected lump rise to his throat.

"Was your mother up, again, all night, last night?"

"No, she left your friend a few hours ago." She added quickly, quietly, "I am sorry for your loss."

Argent and Merritt looked at each other, and Argent saw Merritt's face pale slightly. He felt his own skin drain of warmth. So, she had not done well enough.

"May we see her?"

Merritt's request was possibly forward, as Mrs. Lambert likely had not had time to prepare the body for burial or for paying one's respects. She was likely worn out with caring for M until the very end. But why had she not called them, as promised? Argent began to feel a sense of propriety misplaced where M's care had been concerned.

"No, mother said to let her alone – all that can be done has been done." Again, the daughter adopted an attitude of command when speaking of her mother and her mother's business. It was, however, a misplaced command – the request was not to see the mother, except perhaps later to ask the usual questions, to satisfy the usual curiosity, that surrounded the dead. Miss Lambert nonetheless perhaps regretted adopting such a tone at such a time. "You must have been very close. Were you related?"

This time it was Argent who spoke. "No, we had only just met, but we had become somewhat attached."

Miss Lambert looked out the small window in the kitchen and watched the rain turn an already muddy yard to a pond. "It must have been horrible – to watch and to be unable to help." The daughter turned from the window. "She feels it very deeply."

Despite just now thinking the widow had somehow overstepped her boundaries, Argent nevertheless came to her defense. "Tell your mother she must not blame herself." Then, despite a growing fear that he had left

M's fate to a mere midwife, he added, as a comfort to the daughter, "No doctor could have done better, or more." In the back of his mind, however, Argent wondered that M's death could have been horrible – she more than likely simply slipped into death from shock and loss of blood.

Argent was lost in his thoughts. Merritt, too, had retreated from the conversation. It was some moments then before Argent realized that the widow's daughter had not moved from the table, that she still held the coffee pot, one hand on the handle, the other supporting the bottom with a towel to protect her from the heat. He looked up to find her staring at him.

"My mother doesn't swim."

Now Argent found himself staring at the daughter. It was Merritt, however, who addressed the strange comment.

"She doesn't swim?"

Something in his voice conveyed to the young woman disbelief, as if it were incomprehensible that anyone should not swim. "She can't swim. She could not have helped your friend – the man who drowned – even if she had been there." As the two men continued to stare at her, she offered, "That's why you were all so wet and muddy – you were trying to save Mr. Argent from drowning. The girl in there spoke in her delirium last night. She feels it very deeply that she was not able to save him."

Merritt asked, again with that same slow tone of disbelief, "She spoke in her delirium."

"Yes, but do not be alarmed. She is sleeping now, truly sleeping. That is why mother thought it safe to leave her bedside and catch some sleep for herself. Mother wanted you to know that the girl —"

"Miss Warner."

"— that Miss Warner is settled, and that we should let her sleep, without disturbing her, for as long as possible. We will change her dressing when she wakes, but for now, everything has been done that needs to be done." After a slight hesitation, she asked, "Was Miss Warner particularly attached to Mr. Argent? Mother is worried a deep loss will affect Miss Warner's recovery."

Argent opened his mouth to speak, but found he was at a loss as to how to begin. Merritt, however, recovered first. For two nights and one day, they had stayed at the widow's house, but they had rarely spoken to her, getting reports of M's progress from the daughter, and spending yesterday bringing in wood and fresh water and seeing to the other business of the property while the owner tended to M, but they had never properly introduced themselves. "We have been grossly remiss in our manners; we have taken your hospitality without giving our names. I am Mr. Merritt, and the gentleman sitting across from me is Mr. Argent, and, as you can see, he is not drowned, but is very much alive. Miss Warner was delirious indeed to think Mr. Argent dead, or that she had anything to do with it."

The daughter visibly brightened, and exclaimed, "I am so glad to hear that Mr. Argent lives. Miss Warner's talk of black water rising and shots in the night and murder was very alarming. Mother will be so glad to know, too. She was worried that she had invited murderers into the house, but now I can tell her it was all delirium, no truth to it at all."

"Pardon me, but if your mother thought we were murderers, why would she allow you to be alone with us?" Argent's opinion of the widow was plummeting.

"Well . . . murderers or not, mother thought your concern for Miss Warner was genuine and that if you offered harm, Miss Warner would be our surety – mother would stop caring for Miss Warner; but that doesn't matter now."

Merritt and Argent spent the morning repeating the chores of yesterday. Despite Darnell's return, they did not see him at any time; he was apparently happy to have Merritt and Argent do his chores for him. The only proof that he had returned was the presence of a second, less sorry-looking, horse in the Lambert barn. It had hardly been brushed of the mud from yesterday's ride. Whatever Mrs. Lambert was paying the man, it was too much. Both Merritt and Argent were back in their own clothes, though the work of the farm and the mud stirred up by the rain did much to render those clothes filthy again by lunch. The widow was awake by then, and had looked in on M, who woke briefly as her dressing was changed, then slid back into sleep. Both Mrs. Lambert and her daughter joined Merritt and Argent for lunch.

After the meal, Mrs. Lambert dismissed her daughter – Ellen by name – and then she began: "My daughter tells me that you are the Mr. Argent of Miss Warner's concern."

"Yes, and though deeply appreciated, her concerns were unfounded; I did not drown."

"Yet you were in water – all three of you – and judging from the mud you bore on your clothes that night, it was the black water of her delirium.

And the bullet in her shoulder speaks the truth of shots fired in the night. Miss Warner's immediate needs two nights ago were such that I did not have time to ask for particulars. I did not even think to ask your names or inquire into your business in this area. Miss Warner's delirium has provided some information that has been verified. The question now remains is this: Was there murder?"

It was an incredibly blunt question to ask, and by a lone woman in the presence of two men she still considered possible murderers. But then the elusive Darnell stepped into the room, cradling a shotgun in his arms.

Merritt and Argent had become, through the nature of their work, accomplished liars. Merritt, especially, showed a talent for lying that had just enough truth to it to make his lies believable – at least in the short run. "There was no murder, and no intent to murder Miss Warner. We are escorting Miss Warner to meet with a family friend. We stopped in Cumberland to spend the night, and we all three found ourselves in the wrong place at the wrong time. The Saturday night revelry spilled from the saloons into the streets and Miss Warner was the unfortunate victim of a stray bullet."

The widow was familiar with the Saturday night revelries of Cumberland, especially of Shantytown, and Miss Warner could well have been such a victim. "It is all these Irish and their love for hard drink. And since the canal board has stopped work on the canal on the Sabbath, there is no reason for the men to remain sober on a Saturday night." Before either man could agree or disagree to the scope of her comment, the widow asked, "And the state of your clothes?"

"Miss Warner's horse bolted, and when she could no longer control him, she was thrown into a rather odious pond. We naturally shared in the mud when we helped her out of the pond."

"And her clothes?" The widow was not one to judge the clothes of other women, but Miss Warner was not wearing women's clothing.

"That is one of the matters on which this family friend intended to speak with Miss Warner. Her father – the last of her family – died several months ago, and Miss Warner now lives alone. Peculiarities that were kept to a minimum under her father's influence have now become pronounced, such as her penchant for trousers, especially when riding." Merritt added, with just the right touch of weary indignation, "And her very dangerous penchant for wandering at night. She had slipped from the hotel unawares and was taking her horse out into the countryside when drunken – pardon me – when revelers very inconsiderately were shooting their guns on the same country road. We had discovered her gone and were following the direction given us by the stable hand at the hotel."

"We did not witness the actual event, but when we eventually found Miss Warner, she was lucid enough to relate the incident to us."

The widow studied the two men before her. They seemed sincere in their concern for Miss Warner, and their story answered all her questions. She looked up at Darnell, who slightly nodded. A different question occurred to her. "Why does she wander at night?"

"She is insomniac. From what we have been told by close family friends, it has been a life-long affliction. At home, on her farm, wandering at night is no problem – she knows her land, and there is none but herself to know that she is not abed or is dressed as she is. She is finding it difficult to adjust to the expectations of the world outside her farm."

"And we are finding it difficult to keep Miss Warner under our protection. Perhaps it would be wise to keep certain articles of clothing out of her reach, especially her shoes."

This last appeal from Merritt did more than any statements before to convince the widow of the truthfulness of the situation. She came to a decision. "She may, of course, stay here until she is well enough to travel. If her condition worsens, however, it would be better if she were under a doctor's care in town. I can recommend you to the doctor in Old Town. I have only the most rudimentary medicines here. And as for yourselves, you are not only welcome to stay as well, but I think perhaps you ought to stay. She needs to know that you are here, especially you, Mr. Argent, and I need to know that if she wanders from her bed, you will be here to retrieve her."

"We are very grateful for the arrangements. One of us will need to return to Cumberland to collect our things and to send word to Miss Warner's friend of her delay, and while there, we can pick up anything you may need for Miss Warner's care and for yourself as well. But in the meantime, we insist that you allow us to pay for our keep with any additional chores or help you may need." Argent also looked up at Darnell. "We have been doing only the most necessary chores, but if there is anything else that needs attention, please tell us."

The widow excused herself to attend to M, and Darnell left, presumably to resume only the most necessary chores, leaving Merritt and Argent alone to sip the last of the morning's coffee.

"Since it was you who offered to perform any chores beyond the most necessary, it will be I who will go into town and leave you to fulfill your offer here on the farm."

"I will count whatever payment the widow asks to be cheap compared to the services she is performing for Miss Warner. I spoke the truth when I said that I had grown attached to her; I was surprised at the sorrow I felt when I thought her dead."

"No more surprised, I'm sure, than when you heard of the sorrow M felt when she thought you dead."

The rain that had settled in the area since the earliest hours of Sunday morning continued. There was really little Merritt and Argent could do, despite Argent's offer of labor; still, they managed to stock more wood for the two fires that were kept going in the Lambert house – the kitchen fire and the one in M's room. April had turned decidedly chilly, and Argent wondered how these women endured the harsh winter temperatures with only those two fires to warm them. And where did Darnell keep warm?

The widow found them on the back stoop as they were scraping their boots of the worst of the mud. They were wet and dirty, but they were making the effort to make themselves presentable. The suspicion of murder still hung over them, and perhaps other crimes as well (as Merritt suggested, two men in the company of a young woman did not present well), and, as every jury knew, murderers and other criminals could often be spotted by the way they dressed and by their manners. It was their very appearance that Mrs. Lambert wished to improve, but she was finding the two men somewhat slow in the matter.

"Miss Warner is sleeping and is doing well – what little fever she has had seems to have left her. Still it would be wise if someone should sit with her while I attend to matters of the house that have been kept waiting." She pointedly mentioned the washing, but the two men merely nodded, presumably their thanks as it certainly wasn't their understanding. Tired with two long nights tending to Miss Warner and exasperated with the presence of two men and all their mud in her house, Mrs. Lambert blurted out, "I cannot abide filth in my house, or in my guests. I know my husband's clothes are ill-suited to you, but you can wear them for the day, while I see to your own clothes."

Merritt and Argent began the usual protests – Argent was the more emphatic of the two – but the widow cut them short, reminding them of their need to return to Cumberland. They would be unpresentable as they are, and therefore subject to suspicions of all kinds. Women, like juries, knew that appearances were everything. As she retreated into the shadows of the house, Argent heard her mutter, "Those clothes should have been allowed to soak all night. Now they will be all the more work to clean."

Once again wearing Dr. Lambert's clothes and, Argent fancied, his authority, Merritt and Argent presented themselves at the door to M's room, and were greeted by Mrs. Lambert, who apparently was willing to let matters of the house continue to wait. "If you'll return a little later, I will have Miss Warner ready for you."

Argent was becoming a little irritated with the widow's dominion over M's care. "How do you mean, ready?"

"I mean that the sheets need to be changed and I am waiting for my daughter to come and help me."

The widow started to close the door, but Merritt placed his hand on it, high above Mrs. Lambert's head. "Many hands make light the work. Let us help."

Mrs. Lambert hesitated – Miss Warner's modesty could be at risk – but then agreed that an extra or two pairs of hands would make things easier on Miss Warner, and the thing could be done discreetly. While she waited for her daughter, Mrs. Lambert neatly pulled the top sheet from under the cover, then tucked in and around M the clean blanket that covered her. The better coverlet that usually laid on the bed had been removed before Miss Warner had been placed on the bed, but the sheets underneath were the same as two nights ago, and they were stained with mud and blood and sweat; the worst of Miss Warner's other bodily functions had been captured on a separate towel placed under her and then removed as necessary. M, however, was for the most part lying on the cleanest part of the bed – the widow and her daughter had repositioned M so that she was more in the position of a composed sleeper and not in that of an inebriate passed out at an awkward angle. Though M's hair still showed her time in the canal, the pillow (or at least the pillow covering) underneath had been changed so that her head rested on clean cloth.

When the daughter at last appeared, they began the delicate task of changing the bed sheets while Miss Warner yet was in them. Mrs. Lambert and her daughter rolled the soiled sheets across the bed until they reach M, tucked tightly into the blanket. A new sheet was advanced to the same point. At a signal from Mrs. Lambert, Merritt and Argent then carefully lifted M – mindful to keep the blanket tucked in around her – while the sheet underneath her was pulled clear and the clean sheet spread in its place. Remarkably, M slept through the whole procedure, though in truth it took only minutes to accomplish.

Argent took the opportunity to examine M's shoulder. He could detect no whiff of infection, but it was still early yet to confidently rule that out. The sutures were holding and there seemed to be relatively little inflammation around the wound. Still, Argent had seen during the widow's surgery where the bullet had tracked, and it had scraped dangerously close to the axillary artery. It clearly had not hit the artery, or he would be examining a corpse at the moment. There was a chance, however, that artery had been bruised by the bullet in its trajectory, and any damaged tissue that might be functioning as the artery wall could at any time slough off, producing an aneurism. Regardless of insult to the artery, Miss Warner would need to be kept still, which would probably prove more difficult than the surgery itself.

Straightening up, Argent found himself under examination by the widow. It was more than mere examination, it was a look of challenge.

"Do you find everything in order?"

"Yes; it was delicate work around the artery, but well done."

The widow did not seem to accept the compliment as it was given. "You have your certificate?"

Argent almost stiffened at this particular challenge. "No, my studies were interrupted by the war. But it was a great and terrible school for surgery."

Mrs. Lambert was not impressed by Mr. Argent's military service, especially as a make-shift surgeon. Her husband had been a true doctor, not a mere butcher, a mere expediency in the slaughters of the late war. Who was Mr. Argent to evaluate her work? She not only delivered the area's babies – and not all of them easy births – she had, and still did, patch up knife wounds and gunshot wounds, gashes to heads and limbs, occasioned on the boats of the canal (and sometimes in Shantytown), men and boys kicked by mules; she also tended to the usual complaints of colds, piles, and other maladies. Judging from his clothes, Mr. Argent had more failure than success to his name, and if he were a physician sufficient to judge her work, he would be better dressed and accepting real cash payment for his services, and not, as she did, coal skimmed from the holds of the boats or hams probably stolen from a neighbor's farm or the useless amenities dragged up the canal from the Sodom and Gomorrah of Washington and Georgetown. The thought of Sodom and Gomorrah left a sickening suspicion behind: perhaps this young woman was not on her way to better family relations or friends but was the plaything of these men. She was dressed little better than they were, and in fact her dress probably allowed them to slip her past most guardians of society – they could register her to stay with them in their rented rooms as a third, younger man; she herself had not known of Miss Warner's gender until she had peeled back the shirt to inspect the injury and had seen the swelling of her breast. She would send Darnell to Cumberland to inquire into the matter, and if this young woman was the victim of their carnal lusts, she would contact the sheriff in Old Town for advice.

Merritt saw the widow's face change from cold observation to challenge to some unknown hard suspicion, and he was certain Argent had registered it as well. There was some battle brewing between Argent and Mrs. Lambert, and Merritt suspected the battleground was M. Before the opponents could truly engage, however, Mrs. Lambert left the field, taking her daughter with her. Though Argent continued to scowl for some minutes after her departure, he unknowingly echoed the widow's own sentiments when Merritt asked how Argent truly felt about M's condition: "She does well enough."

Argent then set about chronicling M's recovery, continuing habits learned, and obeying directives given, during the war when he worked in the field hospitals of the Union Army. From his ill-fitting pants waist, he pulled the familiar notebook that he carried with him everywhere. Randomly choosing an empty page in the middle of the book, Argent began scribbling furiously with his pencil, recording all that had happened to M from the moment (making a credible stab at the time) of M's injury in the lock. Merritt knew better than to attempt to talk with Argent when he was seized with the need to write reports; he stood at the window and looked out over the yard enclosed by the house, the barn, the pasture and the kitchen garden. The rain had stopped for the moment, but the clouds were still pouting, ready to release more rain.

"Merritt, come here. I want you to learn this."

Argent could be overbearing when he was intent on a goal, but he usually had good reason, and so Merritt took no offense. Argent showed Merritt how to take M's pulse, measure her breathing, accurately assess the appearance and feel of her skin, properly observe any movements, etc. Argent had taught these things to Merritt before when his services were needed in the field, and Merritt for the most part remembered them, but he did not resent Argent re-teaching him. Argent demanded accurate information when he was responsible for anyone's care, and Merritt understood. Every hour, both Merritt and Argent – whichever of them was with M at the time – were to make these assessments and record them in Argent's notebook.

Once Merritt had proven himself proficient, he had expected Argent to leave, to perhaps rest a little before returning to watch over M for the night; he had no doubt of Argent's intentions as to M's care – he would not be locked out tonight or any night hereafter. But Argent remained in the room with M and Merritt. The two men took turns standing at the window, watching the rain slowly subside, or sitting in one of the two chairs near the foot of the bed. They spoke little, except to discuss the trip to Cumberland.

"I will make a list of what I want from the chemist's. I hope one of them stocks hydrate of chloral."

Merritt looked at M, sleeping apparently soundly and deeply. "Do you think she needs it?"

"Even more so, now that she is injured. She may be sleeping now, but she cannot be allowed to wander at will, when sleep evades her as the shock wears off. There may be damage beneath the sutures of which we are unaware, damage that will need time to heal. Hiding her shoes may not be enough to keep her still and quiet."

The widow's daughter came and went, softly knocking before entering, then quietly going about her chores, and leaving just as quietly. It was something of a surprise, therefore, when Merritt heard her speak. He turned from the window to see Miss Lambert offering to Argent a slip of paper. Argent was staring at her, uncomprehending. Merritt himself could not recall what Miss Lambert had said, only that her voice had broken the silence.

Finally, Argent roused from his private thoughts, apparently repeating Miss Lambert's question. "Is she dull?"

"Is she slow, or deranged, or confused, in some part? Is that why she wears men's clothing?" When Argent continued to stare, uncomprehending, she urged the slip of paper on him. "I found this in her pocket."

Merritt looked from the widow's daughter to the chest at the foot of the bed where he saw M's clothes, clean and mended and neatly folded. Then he looked again at the paper Miss Lambert still held extended to an unresponsive Argent. It was the list of 'suggestions' for surviving social encounters that he had first seen on the LC&L two weeks ago.

Argent stared at the scrap of paper, more than ever a source of indignation for him, that it should lead anyone to think of M as mentally deficient. He wanted to snatch it from the daughter's hand and burn it, but before he could act in such a rude manner, Merritt stepped from the window and gently took it from her hand, saying nothing, but fixing her with that chameleon stare which seemed to inspire an unspoken response somehow tailored exactly to each one subjected to it. Miss Lambert did not return the rest of the day. Argent himself left soon after, returning just after dark to relieve Merritt.

There was a brief struggle for dominion when Mrs. Lambert also appeared, intending to spend the night with M. Argent stood, as did Merritt, when the widow entered the room. Merritt was astonished, however, when Argent regained his seat without waiting for any acknowledgement from the widow. She, in turn, remained standing by M's bed, without actually tending to M in any way. Merritt looked from one to the other, decided he was out of his depth, bid them each good night and left, happy to be sleeping alone this night.

19 — *Easter Tuesday*

Merritt had half expected to find Argent and Mrs. Lambert in the morning as he left them the night before – staring at each other, Argent sitting and Mrs. Lambert standing, with M sleeping blissfully between them. He found Mrs. Lambert, however, in the kitchen, preparing breakfast. She nodded her greetings to him and nodded as well at the coffee sitting atop the old pot-belly stove. He fixed a cup for both himself and Argent, then headed to M's room.

Argent reported that M spent a quiet night, but Argent looked as if he had spent every moment of it awake, and indeed, it would have been difficult for someone of his height to find a comfortable spot to stretch out in such a small room; even stretching his legs while he sat in one of the chairs would have found him at an awkward angle. As if determined to make her presence known in M's room, the widow entered – without knocking – announced that breakfast was on the table. She and her daughter would change Miss Warner's dressing and tidy her up while Mr. Argent and Mr. Merritt ate – if they could tear themselves away from Miss Warner. Argent sighed heavily and heaved himself out of the chair, took a mug of coffee from Merritt, and led him from the room.

As soon as they sat down at the table, Argent slid a carefully folded paper across to Merritt. It was the manifest for their train, the official B&O document that validated their right to be on the tracks. "Mrs. Lambert gave it to me early this morning. Very early. Her daughter found it in one of M's pockets. Apparently, she meant to give it to us yesterday along with that other document."

Argent said 'that other document' with barely concealed contempt. Merritt chose to ignore it and to address this new document. "Do you think she stole this from Mr. Hughes?"

Argent shrugged. He did not like to think she stole it from Mr. Hughes — they had an almost father-daughter relationship, and Argent did not like to think daughters could be so wicked. "Perhaps he was showing it to her, he was called away, and she kept it, meaning to return it."

"Perhaps; I don't think she would willingly risk his affections." Merritt returned the manifest to Argent, who placed it in the notebook, marking where his notes regarding M's recovery began.

Argent had little else to say at breakfast, instead busying himself with studying his own notes taken during the night. Merritt knew better than to ask if the widow had helped during the night. They ate quickly, and after their meal, Argent handed the notebook to Merritt, repeated his instructions of yesterday, then retired to their room to rest in a bed for a few hours. Merritt poured another cup of coffee before taking up position in M's room.

It was late in the morning when M first woke long enough to speak with Merritt. He was standing at the window, looking at nothing in particular in the yard, except maybe the patter of the light rain on the puddles large and small that had developed from the almost non-stop rain of the past two days. He stood there, hands clasped lightly behind his back, thinking of M straining in the lock, of how she had come out of nowhere to save them, of how much they owe her. He thought back to his conversation with Argent three nights ago. They had wondered then how she had come to be at the lock at that time of night, and they had accepted the unsatisfactory answer that she had followed them. But that only begged more questions: Why had she followed them? How had she known they would need help? And the question Merritt was wild to ask – Why, frankly, wasn't she dead?

Other questions crowded his mind. Why would the attackers, after having murdered M – as they thought they had – remain in town? Though he had been drugged, Merritt hazily remembered being dragged from saloon to saloon, long after they heard the shots that should have killed M. Not only were these men unconcerned with leaving town, they were brazenly exposing themselves in very public venues. It then occurred to Merritt that perhaps the men being exposed – paraded, more precisely – were Merritt and Argent themselves. But for what purpose? Why the long delay before finally leaving a town that would surely see these men hang for murder?

But there had been no murder – M had evaded, somehow, the scheme. She had not been murdered because she was not in her room, as they had thought, as they had all thought. How had she deceived the assassins? How had she known the need to deceive these men? Then it came to Merritt that M was as ignorant at the time of the plot as the men were ignorant of her absence. Her deception was not for the murderers, but for Merritt and Argent; that she had also deceived the assassins was a happy coincidence. Merritt smiled at the thought of M planning her escape. Then his smile faded as he realized the reason for her possession of the manifest – it was to frustrate their own ability to follow her in the train, once she had effected her escape. Was Mr. Hughes yet unaware that M had stolen the manifest from him?

Merritt's indignation, however, wilted in the face of M's actions, in spite of her plan to return home, a desire that he knew, for her, overshadowed almost every other concern. Yet she must have abandoned that plan to follow them to the canal. She had followed them in silence and with stealth. She must have known there was danger, and yet she had come, and she had come alone. Why had she not alerted the sheriff? The thought of the sheriff returned Merritt to the thought of the murder. If there had been a murder, the sheriff would have been alerted immediately – the shots had been in the hotel, other patrons would have reported to the manager, the manager would have investigated, if only to make sure his investment was undamaged, and, upon discovery of the murder, of the body of a woman with two bullets, the sheriff would have been sent for.

Merritt was almost there; he could feel the pieces falling into place. It all had to do with the comment about humiliating Grant, about ruining Merritt and Argent's reputations. He almost had the answer, but something else had been tugging at his attention. Merritt had been almost wholly given over to the puzzle of the canal, but he had also been aware throughout the morning of M's movements in her sleep, and the occasional change in breathing whenever her movements caused the pain in her shoulder to sharpen. After the first few incidents of this nature, he gave them little notice, readjusting his hearing for anything of a more intense noise or motion. He occasionally glanced at her and regularly, according to Argent's schedule, checked her for signs of a rising fever or change in her pulse. Gradually, however, a growing realization of a sound remarkable more for its persistence than for its volume or intensity made him turn from the window.

M had changed position yet again – she truly was a restless sleeper, even when constrained as she was by the sling holding her arm in position. Her head was turned away from him, but even so, Merritt thought he caught a flutter of eyelash. He called tentatively. Again, there was the flex of her eyelash and also the tell-tale sign of her clenched jaw; occasionally, M would swallow.

Merritt moved away from the window and stood looking down on M; from this angle, he could see that her breathing had quickened and deepened. He was fairly certain that she was awake and had heard him. He rounded the bed to stand on the other side. She was awake, grinding her teeth and breathing hard. Merritt offered again, "M? Mary?" She was awake but would not look at him. As he stood there puzzling at her, a tear slid from her eye to drop on the pillow below. The pillow, he noticed, had accumulated a fair number of tears already. How long had she lain there, awake and silently crying?

Though the room and its furnishings were modest, they were not mean or small – the bed was large enough for two, and M had been positioned to lay close to the side next to the window, where the widow could make better use of natural light and the lone lamp on the stand there, where M's shoulder was in easy reach for attention. Merritt gingerly lowered himself to sit on the bed, careful not to jostle M. Taking her right hand, he asked, "Are you in pain?" It was, on the surface, a silly question; of course she was in pain. Merritt himself had experienced such wounds in the war – bullet wounds, knife wounds, bone-deep bruises. What was really meant when anyone asked such questions of the injured was, 'Is the pain less bearable than, say, three hours ago?' M managed a small movement of her head – No.

"M, why are you crying? What do you need?"

Again, there was the slight shake of her head, but she was clearly in pain. Her clenched jaw alone said as much, and the presence of tears only underscored the intensity. "I'll bring Mrs. Lambert."

Before Merritt could rise from the bed, M blurted out in a thick voice, "I'm so sorry," and she sobbed. The tears came more freely now, and she took in great gasps of air between sobs. She refused to open her eyes, refused to look at Merritt. When Merritt attempted to lift her chin and then bent low to her face, she took her right hand from his to hide her eyes.

"M, there's no reason to be sorry if you are in pain; there is no more understandable reason for pain than a bullet wound. Let me call Mrs. Lambert to see to you."

This time, M shook her head savagely. "Mr. Argent! I'm sorry for Mr. Argent! I left him in the water!" She was taking heaving breaths to try to steady herself. "I was afraid, and I left him."

"M, you didn't leave him – I pushed you out. Then I pulled Argent from the water. But I couldn't have done it if you hadn't freed me first. Mary, he isn't dead, he is here in this house."

M's sobs became even more intense; either she did not believe him, or she did not hear him. She continued between sobs, "The water is rising, and he is pinned under water, and my arm hurts so much; I can't help him."

"Those are just bad dreams, nightmares of fever. He is here."

But M had moved on, or rather, she had moved back, back to a comment she had heard. After that first night of complete insensibility in the widow's house, M had become occasionally, distantly aware of movements in the room, of people speaking. There were women here, but she also heard Merritt. The room was filled with water, black water, in which M occasionally bobbed to the surface and heard snatches of conversations. Then she would sink under the water again. At first, she had struggled against the sinking – her skirts were weighing her down and she was unable to swim properly – but then she had learned to succumb to it, searching with her toes for the bottom, and when she found it, she used her feet to launch herself upward again, to break the surface of the water. On one such trip to the air, she had heard Merritt say, "If Argent were here . . ." and then she had sunk again.

She was bobbing again, but quicker now. The water had receded and was shallower. She did not have to sink so deeply before pushing off the bottom. But the more frequently she broke through the surface, the greater her confusion. She heard herself talking and Merritt talking, but she didn't understand what he was saying. He was incoherent because he was grieving his partner, because she had let Mr. Argent die.

Merritt was frustrated. M was inconsolable; she didn't seem to hear anything he said but seemed instead to be talking to herself. "I had to decide who to help first, I just had to pick one, it didn't mean anything, I don't like him less. I had to decide, and my arm hurt." Then, in a strange outgrowth of her misery, she wailed to the room at large, "Who will be his partner now?"

All Merritt's attempts to convince M of the truth met with obstinate guilt and grief. Finally, she cried herself to sleep.

Mid-afternoon, Argent cautiously entered the room to find Merritt dozing in one of the two chairs across from the foot of the bed; his feet were crudely resting on the corner of M's bed. M herself was asleep as well, unaware of Merritt's lack of manners and decorum. Normally, Argent would have reminded Merritt of his manners in the presence of a lady, as well as in the home in which they found themselves guests, by promptly kicking his feet to the ground. However, this was more likely to wake M and aggravate her shoulder than to teach Merritt a lesson he should have learned long ago. Instead, Argent softly cleared his throat.

Merritt opened one eye to acknowledge Argent's presence, before commenting, "You're up early; I did not think to see you until dinnertime."

"It is dinnertime – Mrs. Lambert will be in shortly with M's meal. I wish I had your capacity for daytime napping, but I find it difficult to sleep during the day. How has M spent the morning?"

Argent had pointedly moved to force Merritt to lift his feet, and now stood at the right side of the bed, regarding M. The shirt and the sling (and the large overlaying cloth) was serviceable both to M's wound and her modesty, but in her agitation, M had wrecked this system of safeguards to her modesty that the widow had arranged. Argent straightened the cloth to its original position.

"Peacefully sleeping, on either side of a wrenching episode of guilt and grief over your untimely death. She carries a curious obligation for our welfare in general, and a tender concern in particular for my prospects for a future partner, given your untimely death."

Argent turned to observe Merritt, who was now sitting properly, with his feet on the ground, observing Argent in turn. "You, of course, disabused her of her delirium?"

"I tried, but you know how these tender-hearted women are, once they have succumbed to the tyranny of tears. She was inconsolable, unable to hear me over the sound of her own sobs. I don't know what grieved her more – your death or the burden your death would create for me."

Argent snorted. "She is not so much tender-hearted as she is prescient – she foresaw the cold, hard probability of your solitary service in the future. There aren't many operatives in the force who could be induced to be your partner."

Merritt smiled broadly. "I know; we have M to thank for saving us from that ugly scenario. But first we have to convince her that she did indeed save us, the both of us."

Argent put a finger to his lips, just as Mrs. Lambert entered with M's dinner on a tray. Dinner was probably too grandiose a term for the bowl of simple beef broth that would serve as M's meal. Even that small meal would have to wait a few moments, however. The widow set the tray down on the cedar chest at the foot of the bed, then proceeded to change M's dressing.

Mrs. Lambert loosened the sling at the right of M's neck, pulling the cloth gently away from her shoulder. She worked slowly and carefully, as much to keep M's modesty intact as in deference to the tenderness of her wound. Even so, the sling slipped dangerously low, revealing a great deal of M's left breast, surprisingly white and smooth beneath the angry red of her wound and the darker, tanned skin of her neck and sternum. Merritt's position gave him the most privileged view of M's exposure, but Argent was relieved to see that he had his head down, contemplating the hands folded across his abdomen. Argent wavered between decorously looking away, as a gentleman should, and observing the widow's work, as his medical training demanded. Even doctors, however, had to be very careful to maintain the proper decorum with female patients.

The widow sniffed softly at M's shoulder, then placed a fresh dressing, and finished by retying the sling and rearranging the covers. Straightening up, she found Argent watching intently. She answered his look, "I see no indication of infection, but it is still early yet." She looked down once more at M, then announced, "Sleep is good, but she needs to wake now, she needs to begin eating and drinking to keep up her strength. Has she woken any this morning?"

At last Merritt looked up. "She was awake for some time, but all of it was spent in weeping for the good Mr. Argent here." To forestall any comments from Argent or questions from the widow, he added quickly, "She was awake, but not fully aware – I could not convince her of Mr. Argent's continued good health."

Mrs. Lambert regarded Merritt for a moment, not entirely approving of the light-hearted tone lurking beneath his words. "Then perhaps it is Mr. Argent who should wake her now."

Argent sat where Merritt had sat earlier. Like Merritt, Argent also took her right hand. He called her name softly.

Perhaps the widow was still fatigued from her time watching over M, for a great deal of exasperation leached into her voice. "She just slept through a dressing change, so you'll have to speak louder than that."

Argent winced at the rebuke, but before he could try again, Merritt spoke from above him. "Miss Warner, Mr. Argent is here to see you." Argent twisted around to find that Merritt had left his chair and was now standing behind him.

M's face was still turned toward the wall, and from her pillow she mumbled, "Tired."

Mrs. Lambert intruded loudly, "You need to wake up now, and eat."

M mumbled again, but now her brow furrowed, as she too disapproved of the widow's strident commands. "Not hungry." But M was not hearing the widow. In that strange land between sleeping and waking, M heard her sister calling for her to come down to breakfast. Gretta was insistent, even though M knew her mother probably sent Gretta up to their room with only the barest demand that M appear at table. It was an old fight – M's declaration that she would rather sleep a little longer than eat breakfast and her mother's (ever weakening) determination to maintain some control of the meals. M never challenged her mother like this when her father was home, but he was gone now, on one of his trips; why was Gretta making trouble over such a silly thing?

"Hunger has nothing to do with it," the widow argued. "You need to eat, and you need to wake up to do it." Mrs. Lambert gathered the dirty dressing and Merritt's coffee mug, and at the door, she addressed Argent: "My daughter will be here soon to help her with her meal; see that Miss Warner is awake and ready."

Argent did not approve of the widow's method, but it was effective – M was making the effort to wake. When she finally roused enough to open her eyes, she did not immediately look up. At first Argent thought she was merely staring, still not quite awake, simply looking in the direction the position of her head indicated. But then she pulled her hand from his, and he realized that it was his own hand that had captured her attention.

"Miss Warner? Could you try and take some food now?"

Still she did not answer or lift her gaze from his hand. She returned her hand to his, but not to grasp it. Instead she lifted Argent's hand and turned it over, then laid it back on the bed. Only then did she look up and acknowledge Argent's presence. At first, M paled and took in a sharp breath. Then she stared at Argent, but not in the way that he had come to expect from her; she did not hold his eyes in her gaze, but instead took in his presence in darting glances to every part of his body, always returning briefly to search his face.

After a moment of this, M closed her eyes and breathed out, "Mr. Argent, it's you; I had thought I lost you. It has been a great weight on my soul."

"I would never burden you so, Miss Warner."

M opened her eyes, but quickly lowered them once again to his hand on the bed. "Please forgive me," she whispered. "It was never my intention to leave either of you behind. When the water came, my mind was scattered, and my courage foundered." She raised her eyes once again, and Argent could see the great effort her next words cost her. "I didn't know what to do. I had to make a choice. I only thought that Mr. Merritt would be able to help me free you. I don't know what happened. I never meant to abandon you. I had to make a choice."

"I know, sweetheart. It is the same decision I would have made."

Behind Argent, Merritt frowned. Argent had the occasional habit of calling young women 'sweetheart,' especially young women in distress. Though some few women from "good" families resented the familiarity, most women did not mind, and Merritt had to admit that Argent usually knew the right tone to strike to soothe the female element. But M was not like most of the young women he and Argent knew; she would resent the implied familiarity whether she was poor or wealthy, but Merritt also suspected M would find in the word an implied helplessness or dependency, the two states of being M most abhorred for herself. Merritt was surprised, however, when M made no objection to the word, nor took any notice of it at all. The pain in her shoulder must have been great indeed.

The relief at Argent's survival and the ever-present aggravation she harbored towards Merritt served only to distract and agitate Miss Warner, and so both men were dismissed from the room. Argent's intention to return for the night was swiftly countered by the widow with the observation that Merritt and Argent would need their sleep for the trip into Cumberland tomorrow. And so, with one comment from their hostess, it was decided that both men would return to Cumberland and that they would be doing so in the morning.

Argent was angrily shrugging himself into his own shirt, grudgingly admitting to himself that the widow had been right about the amount of dirt and stains remaining in their clothes after their first own, clumsy attempts at washing them.

"It was supposed to have been a simple fetch and deliver operation – a day or two in getting to the Warner farm, then two, maybe three days, to reach Washington. With sleeper cars, we could have been there in two, the whole matter finished in a week. Now we have to report our own kidnappings, the loss, and then the discharge, of our own weapons by unknown assailants with the murkiest of intentions, and to cap it all off, the very woman we were sent to escort and protect on her way to see the President has instead protected us, and because she has done so she lies seriously wounded in the home of a woman who has all the charm and bedside manner of a drill-sergeant."

Merritt sat on the bed in his own re-laundered shirt enjoying Argent's tirade. Argent had underscored his rant by buttoning his shirt in a manner that somehow conveyed anger, as if each button were an affront to him. Merritt suspected much of Argent's anger sprang from his disapproval of the widow's nearly complete disregard for Argent's expertise in the matter of M's wound. That first night, Mrs. Lambert had been entirely willing to defer to Argent, but she had realized that Argent was not in fact an actual, full-fledged doctor, and she had been steadily growing deaf to Argent's suggestions and questions. A well-placed comment about mere field surgeons had certainly not endeared her to Argent, nor had her obvious distaste for 'conventional medical practices.'

"I can only imagine how our reputations will suffer in the department once word of this gets out."

"Well, it was one of the murky intentions our kidnappers desired, to humiliate us – that much I heard. At least, in that, they can count themselves successful."

Argent's head jerked up from attacking his last button. He let the hem of his shirt fall while he fixed Merritt with an angry stare. "At least?!"

"Think of it from their point of view: it is the only thing that has gone right for them. They failed completely in both their attempted murder of M and our own attempted assassinations. We are in the happy position of being able to reclaim our reputation, being alive and having something of a future within to do so. But I would be very much in error if I didn't think that our would-be assassins aren't at this very moment wondering if their own futures are in doubt. Whoever sent them, must by now be aware of their failures, and anyone so low as to send assassins after two amiable and fair-minded men of the law such as ourselves, and to countenance the murder of a completely innocent woman, would not meet such failure with equanimity."

Argent harrumphed. "Sometimes you make my head ache, though the thought of those scoundrels receiving their just deserts, even from an even bigger scoundrel, dulls the ache somewhat. Regardless of what is happening on the foul side of the law to lessen our pain, what must be happening in the great seat of federal law can only do further damage."

This time it was Merritt who fixed Argent with an angry stare. "What can be happening in Washington to further damage us?"

"My dear Merritt, cannot you not imagine the turmoil Grant has stirred up when he realized – as he surely must have by now – that Miss Warner has gone missing, along with the two men assigned to her safety, two men who came highly recommended by Secretary Boutwell. By now Grant has surely sent out other detectives to locate her, and Boutwell must be stewing at the poor show of two men he recommended." Secretary Boutwell had himself received Merritt's and Argent's recommendation from Chief Whitley, who by now was most certainly regretting it. Argent did not know how it was they had escaped Whitley's house-cleaning when he had taken the reins of the division last year, but he did not see how they could avoid having their letters of appointment revoked now.

The image of the turmoil Argent presented prompted Merritt to return to his earlier musings about M's intended murder. "There should have been turmoil; they were counting on it."

Argent had rounded the bed and stretched out on his side of it, his hands behind his head. He turned to Merritt. "Beg pardon?"

Merritt was still sitting on the edge of the bed, still staring at the spot where Argent had stood angrily dressing for bed. Their shirts would be hopelessly wrinkled in the morning, but there would be no awkward nakedness this night. Now he turned to reply. "What murderer have you ever known to shoot at his victim in such a public place as a hotel and then remain in town, practically asking to be arrested, if not lynched?"

Argent's look of curiosity became one of real interest.

"We were dragged from saloon to brothel to gambling house with the greatest leisure that night, giving plenty of would-be witnesses a chance to see us at our most loutish. They were waiting for the turmoil that M's murder would stir up. But it never came, because she was not murdered. No one sent for the sheriff. There was no lynch mob. They were waiting to turn us over to the law to answer for M's murder. And having frequented such places, no one would have any trouble believing us capable of murdering the woman traveling with us."

Argent was indignant. "It would be their word against ours."

Merritt nodded, but then added, "And their guns against ours."

Now Argent sat up. "They used our guns in their attempt to murder M?"

"How else could they be assured of our conviction? Why else would they remain in town, parading us about as they did? The three men who ambushed us in our room were surely seen at the hotel and seen with us. We heard guns fired, but we never saw it. *I* never saw it." Merritt looked up at Argent to see him shake his head 'no' as well. "Our guns were emptied, but I am certain not all of the bullets were spent at the canal. I am equally certain that if we were arrested, a quick inspection at any time would have shown our guns to be missing one bullet each, while their own guns, most likely recently and thoroughly cleaned, would be shown to be unfired, and, had there been an actual murder, two bullets found in the victim would match our guns." Merritt continued to nod, though he had returned to facing away from Argent. "If we should have somehow escaped hanging, we would be spending the rest of our lives at hard labor in Sing Sing. Our reputations would be utterly and permanently in ruins."

"And the President would have to explain why he had summoned Miss Warner from Kentucky, why federal projects such as the train were being used on his personal errands, and why the two men he had picked to escort her instead murdered her. His reputation would suffer almost as much. He is already fending off attacks on his integrity."

That was true all over the nation, but especially so in the South, and Kentucky seemed eager to lead the way. In the few days they had spent at the Warner farmhouse, Merritt and Argent had been shocked at the vitriolic voice of the Louisville press as regarded the President. Each day, Caleb had ridden to Jeffersontown to collect the newspapers for several farmers near M, who paid him some small recompense for the trouble. Reconstruction was roundly denounced as unduly harsh on the rebel states: Reconstruction governments were destructive, financially ruinous, and upheld at bayonet-point. It was also suggested that Reconstruction was merely a ploy to distract the nation from tariff and other financial questions. Moreover, the Louisville press whipped up fury and fear that Kentucky itself was targeted for Reconstruction, even though she had remained loyal to the Union. All things Grant were decried and ridiculed. It was also presented as Grant's personal joy to torment Georgia, and that Grant's nomination of Bradley to the Supreme Court was given as *quid pro quo* for his unfettered use of the Long Branch property. Those were only the most pointed judgments pronounced against Grant. Every other scandal in the general government was somehow connected with Grant's ineptitude, his avarice, his love of presidential trappings, or his blind loyalty to the hated Republican party. Even his grammar was viciously vilified. And there was no mercy for Grant's father (the querulous postmaster in Covington), who had the treasonous audacity to stump for the hated Cincinnati Southern railroad that hoped to cut out Louisville's railroad concerns by cutting through Kentucky, well east of Louisville, to Chattanooga. Grant appointees also came in for attacks: Commissioner Delano was politely invited to blow his brains out, as an act of patriotism.

Now Merritt laid back, his hands behind his head. "Who could we have so thoroughly offended to have inspired such hatred and vengeance?"

"You were rather rough with that fellow in Parkersburg."

"Hardly rougher than he was with me." Merritt had sported a spectacular black eye for more than two weeks. "That was years ago."

"It was last year."

"Really? It has been a long year. The point is, it must have been someone we have recently offended – this kind of anger doesn't wait to be relieved. I have never known counterfeiters to be so violent." The Parkersburg counterfeiter and his tigress wife had been unusually defiant and desperate when faced with arrest – the liberal use of clubs had been necessary to bring the man to bay, and it had been necessary to bring true physical force to bear on his wife.

"Nor I, but the world is changing fast, and so are the criminals." Argent laid back and closed his eyes. "Whoever it was has failed, and now we are forewarned. We go cautiously for the moment, and when we have safely conducted Miss Warner to the White House, we will have more time and resources with which to solve this puzzle. Something of this nature could hardly be contained; other counterfeiters will have heard of it, and we will pump our usual fonts of information."

20 — *Easter Wednesday*

By morning, the weather had improved, though it was still damp and somewhat on the chilly side, with only the briefest of showers occasionally dripping on the men, the last of the great Easter storm being wrung from the sky. Over Saturday night and into Sunday morning, they had traveled on the towpath of the C&O Canal, first as prisoners and then as escapees, but the towpath had been deserted at that time and, after midnight, no one had accosted them. This morning, however, they returned to the towpath on the slim hope of finding some clue as to the deeds of Saturday night, especially at the lock where they were to have been drowned, their bodies to have been found at 12:01 Monday morning, when presumably the lock tender would be called upon to return to his duties.

Argent could not remember if they had passed another lock after finding M slumped on the ground next to Emmett; it had taken all his strength and concentration to keep both himself and M in the saddle, while keeping pressure on her wound, and also keeping alert to the return of their assailants. But Merritt was certain of himself, certain that there had been no intervening lock between that of their near death and the road that led to the widow's house, and he kicked up a fast walk to hurry them to that lock.

They were not welcome on the towpath, crowded as it was with business backed up from the Easter storm and the Sunday suspension, and it was, after all, not a bridle path. But at the first lock on their way back to Cumberland – Lock 72, as they learned – the lock tender was affable, even as he worked to keep the boats moving in and out of his lock. He was even cheerful, having had the luxury of a short vacation in Cumberland with his family while his lock was tended by a substitute. He had returned Sunday evening, long before the lifting of the Sabbath suspension and, although the substitute had already left, there appeared to be no harm to the lock or the lockhouse. There was the odd presence of a work scow, somehow brought up from Old Town where such equipment was kept, quietly floating in the lock and, odder still, the discovery of a woman's skirt caught in the low branches of a tree. As to the identity of the substitute, the lock tender could not say – it had been an unsolicited transaction and he had not actually met the substitute, but had been contacted by mail, with a letter attesting to the honesty and capabilities of the substitute, signed by no other than Senator Spates himself. Of course he had kept the letter – the lock tender had become suddenly testy at the question – but couldn't the gentlemen see he was busy and didn't have time to go rummaging through papers to find a letter, only to have it taken, it just now occurred to him, by one of those autograph collectors? Merritt and Argent left without a chance to authenticate the signature of Senator Spates or otherwise search the letter for other clues. As they were invited to leave the lock, they were also invited to leave the towpath – it was not a bridal path. It was an invitation that was extended to them several times throughout the morning, sometimes rudely and shockingly so.

In between teams of mules and shouts of insults, Merritt and Argent discounted Spates in any connection to the attempts on their lives or M's. The man may be an embezzler and (only slightly) possibly a counterfeiter, but he was no murderer. The letter was certainly a fraud. The thought of Spates and counterfeiting brought to mind their intended meeting with one of Nettleship's boys; they would have to report that failure as well. Their failure to meet with this man would surely have already triggered some investigation. Perhaps they could find this man and see if he observed anything useful on the night they were supposed to have met with him. Perhaps there would be help already at hand in Cumberland.

Originally, they had thought to travel at night, in order to slip into Cumberland (and hopefully their hotel room) unnoticed, but both the widow and the weather had conspired against them to force a day march. As it was, they were hardly noticeable as Merritt and Argent. They were not only wearing the clothes they had chosen to blend in with the patrons of the Shantytown saloons, but those clothes were now hopelessly stained with the muck of the canal, M's blood, and their own sweat, despite Mrs. Lambert's best efforts. Four and more days without their razors had left them with beards that went a long way to conceal their faces; Argent's beard, in particular, had come in with a vengeance, all his careful grooming of the last few weeks gone for naught. And with slouch hats pulled low over their eyes, there was really little left to reveal their true identities.

In short, they did not look like men who could afford or belonged at a respectable hotel such as the St. Nicholas.

It had been slow going on the towpath, dodging mule teams and ducking the long ropes they pulled. The path itself had slowed them, being sloppy and in places dangerous, from the recent rains. They arrived in Cumberland somewhat later than they had hoped, finding the business of the town fully engaged after the mid-day dinner hour had long since passed.

Merritt still had the key to their room – though their clothes were somewhat shabby, the pockets had been reinforced for the heavy burdens (such as small guns) that they sometimes carried. The seamstress in New Jersey they had engaged for the work had stared at Merritt, much in the same way Merritt himself stared at other people. It was obvious that she wondered at the need for reinforced pockets when the clothes themselves simply needed replacing, but after a moment scrutinizing Merritt, she consented. The key was therefore safe and secure, despite the rough handling of their assailants. The room they had rented, however, was less secure. Workers were putting the final touches on repairs to the damage from bullets and fights, in both their room and M's room, plainly visible through the open connecting door. Even the carpet was being replaced, though Argent doubted the need. Their trunk and other belongings had been removed.

They were directed to the office of Samuel Luman, Esq., on the first floor, for information as to the location of their possessions. It took some amount of patient explaining before the hotel proprietor revealed that their belongings, as well as those of Miss Warner, were no longer in his possession. They were relinquished to the custody of a Mr. Hughes, after that gentleman had paid in full the cost of damages to the rooms. Or, rather, he had caused to be paid such costs, the money being wired to the account of the hotel at the bank down the street. The trunks and bags and the loose clothing left behind had been delivered, at Mr. Hughes' direction, to the B&O depot, next to the Revere House.

Their belongings, however, were no longer at the depot. Their train, too, was no longer in Cumberland. As the station master explained to them, Mr. Hughes had been called to the depot offices to answer a charge of passing a counterfeit bill.

"Mr. Hughes was accused of uttering a counterfeit?" Merritt was almost beside himself with disbelief.

"No, Mr. Hughes was called to the office because one of his passengers on that train of his bought passage on one of the B&O trains with a counterfeit bill." It was clear that the Baltimore & Ohio company employés, despite President Garrett's permission, were still in a snit about the presence of the private train on their tracks, and the transgressions of one of the members of that little train would stain the reputations of all connected with that little train. And unless there was some mistake, the only passenger on that train, beside themselves, was Miss Warner.

Though Argent knew the answer, he asked, "Who, then, bought the ticket?"

The station master looked long at Argent. He was under no obligation to answer these questions, and certainly not to 'gentlemen' dressed such as they. And there was an arrogance about them that rankled the station master, a demand for answers, that in any men dressed more reputably would have been received as confidence or even authority. Nevertheless, if it would remove these men from his office more quickly, he would satisfy their curiosity. What, after all, did it matter? The money was made good by Mr. Hughes and the problem was now his to pursue.

"A young lady." It occurred to the station master that accounts given by witnesses described the young lady as dressed only somewhat better than the men before him; she was possibly connected with them in some manner. "She purchased a ticket for herself and passage for her horse."

"She had her horse with her?" Merritt's disbelief was still there, but it had moderated somewhat; apparently, Mr. Hughes passing a counterfeit was far less likely than the young lady bringing her horse to the station to buy tickets.

The station master blinked before answering Merritt. "Not that anyone reported or noticed."

"Oh, they would have noticed." Merritt smiled broadly at the man, a private joke the man did not understand but in which he had been invited to share. "Where was she bound?" If possible, Merritt's smiled deepened, the private joke having one last laugh in store.

"West, to Parkersburg."

Merritt pivoted on the ball of one foot to include Argent in both his smile and the joke. Argent did not find the situation in the least funny and he glared at Merritt. Without changing his expression or turning to address the station master, Argent asked as much out of habit as out of pique, "Which counterfeit was used?"

"The twenty on the Tradesmen's National Bank of New York. It was a good one, too; we almost didn't catch it."

That particular counterfeit had proven very popular so far this year, but how did Miss Warner come into possession of one? Argent would pass on this information to Whitley, but it was likely an anomaly – Cumberland was not generally a hotbed of counterfeit activity, and Miss Warner could very well have picked it up in Louisville. "Well, as soon as we retrieve our trunks and bags we shall make recompense to the B&O for the fraud."

The station master now assumed a smug expression; he had heard such professions of honesty before, promises to return and pay that rarely happened. The station master saw no need to reveal that Mr. Hughes had already made recompense. "That would be difficult – your trunks and bags are no longer in Cumberland and neither is Mr. Hughes and his train. It was determined that the young lady was connected in some way with a disturbance at the St. Nicholas a few nights since, and when neither she nor the two gentlemen who were her escorts could be found, it was suggested to Mr. Hughes that he take his train to some vacant siding outside of town, preferably outside of Allegany county altogether."

They walked in silence to the telegraph office down the street. Neither man wanted to admit how much he had counted on the presence of the train upon their return to Cumberland. Neither man wanted to admit, either, a certain amount of bitterness at Mr. Hughes' seeming celerity in submitting to a suggestion to leave town; they had, after all, only been missing for a few days, and they had seen him fight with yard masters before for the honor of his train. Honesty did demand of them, however, to acknowledge that Mr. Hughes was under certain obligations to, and at the mercy of, a rather hierarchical authority in these train yards, a hierarchy to which, as a wildcat engineer, he did not belong.

Argent waited outside the office of the Pacific & Atlantic Telegraph Company while Merritt sent information (coded) to both President Grant in Washington and Chief Whitley in New York. It had been decided – without even discussing it – that using B&O's telegraph wires would be suspect to delays (even petty, intentional ones) or even espionage. How else did anyone know about their stop-over in Cumberland or Miss Warner or any connection with Grant? Except for their initial consultation with Grant himself and the lone letter explaining the help waiting for them in Parkersburg, all other communication had been by telegraph, and almost exclusively through the B&O lines. Telegraph companies were serious about the security of their clients' messages – their business would suffer irrevocable loss of confidence otherwise – but Argent was not certain such a high priority was placed on the private messages sent over a railroad's wires. Operatives in the Secret Service soon learned who in telegraph offices throughout the nation could be trusted for both speed and accuracy and discretion, and George Deetz in B&O's Cumberland office was one of those operator-managers respected and trusted since the days of the war. He had helped devise the ciphers that kept military information safe as it traversed the wires of the B&O, and he had been instrumental in keeping those wires up and operating between Cumberland and Martinsburg during the strife. If there was a breach in security in the B&O wires, it was not because of Deetz and it was doubtful it was at Cumberland. Still, more caution than less was needed here, and so they found themselves at the P&A, using a private code they hoped the President would know to seek out Whitley for understanding.

Merritt joined Argent on the sidewalk. "The messages will be sent as soon as possible."

"The operator is aware these messages claim priority? Government business directed to the President and Chief Whitley?"

Merritt sighed and very nearly rolled his eyes. "Yes, they are aware, and I did my best to underscore the priority. They say the wires are crowded." The operator had looked at Merritt and taken in both his dress and the seemingly incoherent message scribbled on the form, to be sent to the President of the United States, as well as an equally incoherent message for Chief Whitley of the Secret Service in New York City. Merritt knew the operator saw him as just one more over-excited citizen sending 'important' telegrams to the President, full of crucial advice for the leader of these United States in these rocky Reconstruction times.

"Perhaps I should have a say with them."

Merritt lightly grabbed Argent by the arm, forestalling Argent's storming of the telegraph office. "They hardly took me seriously, given my manner of dress. You would cause positive alarm. We need to stay low to the ground while we are here, if we are to effectively – and safely – conduct our investigations."

Argent was reluctant to let any disrespect from the operator go unchallenged. "There has been a decided change in attitude among these operators since that strike earlier this year."

Merritt was not about to let Argent's frustration turn into a long-winded diatribe about duty and the common good, not on an empty stomach at any rate. "I'm hungry; let's find something to eat and a place to bed down for the night, then we'll return here to learn the status of our messages."

The thought of accommodations for the night, and possibly tomorrow night as well, brought the men up short against their financial situation. They had boarded their horses at a livery stable on George Street as soon as they had reached town, and that had already taken a small bite out of their resources, as had (and will) telegraph expenses. There would also be – and maybe most importantly – expenses for medicines for M. They could not afford the comforts of the better hotels, and given their appearance, despite the considerable efforts of the Widow Lambert, no respectable landlady or landlord would accept them as boarders. That left them with the less savory and limited accommodations of boarding houses near Shantytown.

They supped at one of the saloons on Mechanic Street, then returned to the telegraph office. Their messages had been sent, but no reply was waiting for them; it would likely take some time for the President to track down someone to help him with the cipher. They were fortunate to find a decent boarding house, also on Mechanic, being referred there by the proprietor of the saloon where they had their dinner. As suspected, upon applying at the door, the matron of the house had initially denied their patronage, but upon giving the saloon-keeper's reference, they had been grudgingly admitted. They had been shown to a very small room in the back of the house, evidently a hastily and poorly constructed addition to the house. They would again be sharing a bed. As unaccommodating as their room was, it did afford them a great deal of privacy and a separate entrance to the house. Late in the evening, after Merritt and Argent had gone to bed, someone tried to enter their room from the outside door, turning and re-turning the knob with vigor and pulling hard at the door, swearing under his breath at his lack of success. Both men pulled their guns – reloaded before leaving the widow's house – from their respective coats, hanging from the bed knobs at the head of the bed. They had not worn their gun belts to Cumberland, but they carried more bullets in other pockets. Though both men rose silently from the bed, it was Merritt who approached the door and loudly warned the intruder away, promising a deadly defense if the intruder did not comply.

It was apparent, only moments later, that the room they occupied belonged to the saloon keeper, who in turn belonged to the landlady. It was the son who had tried to access his room, a lean-to added on to the house in order to free his boyhood room for boarders. He had almost as little success at the front door as he had at the side door, but apparently had succeeded in waking his mother to let him in. She could be heard berating her son in loud, angry whispers in the hallway outside their door that if he wanted a place to sleep, he shouldn't have sent two desperate-looking men to her home. She couldn't rest for fear that they would kill them all in their sleep. Her son could just sleep here at the foot of their door. If they stumbled over him on their way to nefarious acts, he would at least have done them all some small service.

21 — *Easter Thursday*

There were no windows in their little make-shift room, and being on the western side of the house, morning did not come early to Merritt and Argent. Only Argent's acknowledged experience with elderly ladies and last night's absence of foul play persuaded their landlady to allow them a late (though decidedly cold and diminished) breakfast at her table. They had washed up as best they could at the small tin pitcher and basin in their room, without benefit of a mirror. Even so, they had managed to remove most of yesterday's mud spatter from their time on the towpath, from both their persons and their clothes (beating their coats and pants with their hands), and with their hair roughly tamed by finger-combing, they appeared far less alarming in the morning light.

They planned their day as they walked Mechanic Street, but once they turned up Baltimore, they adopted silence, not even exchanging parting words as Argent continued up Baltimore while Merritt stepped up into the offices of the Pacific & Atlantic.

It had been decided that Argent should interview the ostler at the St. Nicholas stables. Merritt had dealt with the man in making arrangements for Emmett as well as their own horses, and therefore was known to him. However, Argent had never visited the stables and so could approach the ostler with complete anonymity. It was the mid-hour of the morning, and all the early chores being done, the ostler was sitting just outside the barn door, his chair tipped back to lean against the wall, enjoying the continuously improving April weather. The man did not stand at Argent's approach or answer Argent's hail, but he did let his chair drop to sit squarely on the ground.

The man scrutinized Argent, taking in his dress and semi-kempt appearance. Argent, for his part, adopted the air of a man assessing a possible investment, craning his neck to inspect the interior of the barn and the overall environs. "What are your arrangements for horses that board here?" Argent, indeed, sounded like a discerning man, particular about the care of his horse, a horse that at the moment did not exist, as far as the ostler could tell.

When the ostler continued to stare at him, Argent informed him, "My horse is currently at the stables down the street, but I am not altogether happy with his care. I find the feed inferior and the stalls unnecessarily dirty. The flies are legion."

Now the ostler showed interest beyond his bored suspicions. "You get what you pay for. I am not the cheapest stable in town, but no place takes better care of the horses." Returning to his critical scrutiny of Argent and doubting both that the man owned a horse or could afford to stable one, the ostler flatly demanded a week's payment in advance; any overpayment would be returned to the owner at the time the horse was reclaimed. "I have been stung by the perfidy of better dressed men, and I will no longer allow my generous nature to be fodder for crows."

Argent drew himself up and allowed his natural pride in his reputation as an honest man to swell. "The perfidy of others, no matter how well-dressed, cannot be attached to me. What days are these when a working man, doing a noble day's work, can be so jilted by his patrons that his natural affinity for his fellow man is stripped from him?"

This was high talk from a man dressed as Argent was. But he spoke a truth that softened the ostler's jaded spirits. It was true, he performed a noble service for a noble beast, but he was rarely given credit for it. He once again inspected the man standing before him. His clothes perhaps bespoke hard times more than neglect, and he did appear clean in his person. The ostler relented. "I have been jilted of late, and it has made me guarded."

"Perfectly understandable. I have money to pay in advance." Argent pulled from his coat his pocket book, and from this he partially pulled one ten-dollar bill, chastely peaking above the seamed leather, not committing to one expense or another. After exposing his tender tender, Argent gently pushed it back into its cloistered pouch and replaced the pocket book next to his breast. "But this perfidy you speak of worries me. A man who would cheat his horse's keeper may not be above cheating another man of his horse altogether. And I am rather attached to my horse."

"Not only men, but women, too."

"I beg your pardon?"

"Last Saturday, there was a disturbance at the hotel."

"This hotel?" Argent hooked his thumb over his shoulder, indicating the St. Nicholas. Then to emphasize his disbelief, he turned to fully face the grand edifice behind him. He turned back to the ostler with wonder on his face.

"Yes, sir. Even the best hotels are not safe from the riff-raff that ride the rails and go from town to town, living free and easy on other men's hard work."

"What happened?" Argent's interest was not hard to feign — he was truly curious to know how the events of last Saturday night were seen by those not involved.

"Well, sir, it seems there was some lovers' quarrel. Some fallen girl had been ruined by two professional gamblers; some say she was abducted from her home for their own sinful pleasures. Now beyond this, the story departs, depending on who does the telling. Some say that two or three of her brothers caught up to these outrageous men and after a fight in their hotel room, dragged them out of Cumberland, where they dealt with them as any family men would do for the honor of their sister."

Argent had paled at the story being circulated about them and Miss Warner. Where had such salacious details come from? Argent realized his mouth had dropped slightly open; he made the effort to close it, then cleared his throat. "And what do others say?"

"The two or three men who tracked these gamblers to the hotel were not brothers, but this poor girl's first ruiners, come to reclaim their baggage, so to speak. But it ends the same. The two gamblers are dragged from their room and out of town and dealt with, as criminals deal with, one to the other."

"And the young woman?"

"She was either hauled back home with her brothers, to face family love and punishment, or she was reunited with her first despoilers. Either way, she is ruined for marriage and decent society."

Argent stood for a full moment, struck dumb with the accounts swirling around themselves and M.

The ostler took Argent's silence as a true Christian's shock at the wickedness of the world. Enjoying his role as sensationalist, he added, "And the worst of it is, President Grant is somehow involved."

"President Grant!?"

"Yes. These two gamblers, you see, were on their way to call on the President. That much is clear, though no one could speculate as to the purpose."

Argent pulled a hand down his face. It was bad enough that their own reputations had been besmirched and that Miss Warner had been dragged into the muck, but President Grant absolutely could not be associated with such stories, no matter how fabricated. With great effort, Argent pulled his mind back to the point. "How did such an unfortunate unraveling of life at the hotel come to bear down on you?"

"These two gamblers – dressed well, you see, and able to pay, so I thought – boarded their horses with me. Very particular in their instructions, written out on heavy stationery. The girl wasn't to come near the horses, especially the great draft horse, as if any woman could handle such brute size and power. I realized after all was said and done that they were keeping her from escaping their foul designs."

"Yes?" Argent was finding it hard to keep leading the man back to the point. He was anxious to find Merritt and relay the unsavory stories constructed around their abduction from the St. Nicholas last Saturday. The mention of the President was proof that there was some break in the security of their communications.

The ostler repeated, "These two gamblers boarded their horses with me." He said it slowly, perhaps a little annoyed at Argent's impatience. "But they did not pay me."

Argent regretted that his agitation had seeped through his voice. He immediately changed his tone to one of slowly dawning shock. He spoke almost as slowly as the ostler had done. "They refused to pay?"

The ostler regarded Argent with a squint. "No; they didn't have the chance to refuse, did they? Being dragged out of town to their just deserts. No, they did not pay in advance, and so I was not paid. That is why I now require an early deposit on my labors."

"But, if these men were dealt with accordingly, either by the lady's brothers or her paramours, you still had the horses to sell, did you not? As well as the saddles?" Finally, they were coming to it.

"But there's the rub, as they say: I don't have the horses to sell, or the saddles. They were stolen that night, right from under me. I still don't know how the thing was done."

Now Argent squinted at the ostler, not believing such a thing could be done. Emmett could be heard walking from quite a distance – he, at least, was not spirited away, not while anyone was in hearing distance of his massive hooves. As he came to the realization that the ostler was lying about his part in the 'theft' of the horses, Argent's eyebrows slowly shifted until his left brow began in a little curve to the far left then rose up to swoop magnificently over the eye before diving to a point just above his nose; the right brow furrowed over its eye, the thick black hairs of the brow crushed together in the upheaval of doubt, disapproval and growing anger in Argent's mind. It was the look that often broke the resolve of counterfeiters, forgers, smugglers, and others of their ilk when pressed about their crimes. It was now the look that bore down on the ostler, and in that moment Argent seemed taller and heavier even than he really was, and any consideration of Argent as a lesser man than the ostler completely vanished.

The ostler found himself confessing to Argent that he had left the barn – only for a few minutes – to satisfy his own curiosity about the disturbance at the hotel. He admitted, also, to having shared a nip or two with a few men who found themselves outside the hotel, seeking to satisfy the same curiosity. There had been something of a carnival atmosphere in the street in front of the hotel, spilling around the corner onto George Street. Shots had been fired, Argent was to understand, an occurrence that was relatively rare in Cumberland. When all the commotion had died down – perhaps the ostler had stayed in the street longer than a few minutes – he had returned to the barn. In a last fit of truth-telling, the ostler ended by saying that he had not realized the horses were missing until the next morning, when he woke, feeling somewhat crapulous.

"I see." Argent did not, in fact, see everything, but some things were becoming clearer. The struggle in the hotel room served a second purpose other than M's attempted murder and his own and Merritt's abduction. Whether intentionally or not, the now famous disturbance at the hotel also served to distract the ostler while a second group of criminals stole their horses. M must have been in the barn at roughly the same time, 'stealing' her horse for the escape that the particular and written instructions had indeed been given to the ostler in order to foil. She in all likelihood had seen their horses stolen. Is this when she decided to follow the criminals? Or was she simply following the horses?

Argent realized the ostler was still staring up at him. Clearing his throat once again, he announced, "I am sorry. I'm afraid I cannot commit my horse to the questionable care of this establishment." With that, he stalked off in the direction of George Street.

Merritt was waiting for him at the corner of George and Baltimore. He knew instantly that Argent had news, and Argent likewise could see that Merritt's time at the telegraph office had been productive, but in an unsettling way. Merritt suggested they have lunch at the basement bar in the Revere House, and Argent merely blinked in assent. Otherwise they walked in silence, as they had earlier in the day.

They ordered sparingly, but Argent ate the lion's share while Merritt played a lackluster game of bagatelle. If Merritt had hoped to learn anything about their time in the same bar last Saturday night, he was disappointed. The flair for play and conversation that had always assured Merritt partners at the table and observers at the bar was absent today. And, at this hour of the day, the bar was lightly populated; there would have been few takers even if Merritt had been at his dazzling best. Argent thought perhaps Merritt should sit and share in the meal, but Merritt was ready to leave and merely grabbed a piece of meat from the plate, which he shoved in his mouth on the way out.

Argent led Merritt back down Baltimore Street, leaving him on the sidewalk to contemplate his poor performance at bagatelle, while Argent stepped into L. Fevre and Son, chemists and druggists. Here, he largely ignored the list the widow gave him and instead had prepared for M medicines he considered best for her. His order included a good supply of chloral hydrate. He intended to keep M in bed while her wound healed, and in her car, once they reached the train, for the duration of the trip. If he had to dose her horse with the chloral, he would do that as well.

Once again walking down Baltimore, Merritt casually remarked, "I have news."

Argent looked pointedly at the several newspapers under Merritt's arm. "Yes, I see." Merritt apparently had visited one or several newsstands while waiting for Argent. "We need to make inquiries in Shantytown. But first I would like to drop by our room and pack up these medicines." After a few more steps, he added, "We can talk in private there."

They made a great show of entering the boarding house by the front door, talking loudly of nothing in particular, except the desire and intention to read the day's papers. Merritt stopped in the kitchen to ask the landlady if it would be possible to have a cup of coffee or two in their room. Having survived the night with Merritt and Argent under her roof, the landlady was more inclined to accommodate the gentlemen, especially given Merritt's twinkling blue eyes and winning smile. Perhaps there was no harm in them after all.

Argent removed all his purchases from the package, tore a handkerchief into strips, then carefully wrapped each medicine in one of the strips of cloth before distributing them among the pockets of his vest and coat, while Merritt divided the newspapers between them. By the time the landlady brought them their coffee – a full pot with a small plate of cookies Argent suspected came from the confectionery they had passed on Mechanic – the newspapers were spread over the bed and on the floor. After the landlady left the room, with the hope that the gentlemen enjoy their *leisure time* as well as the coffee, Merritt listened a moment at the door. "She really is a sweet lady. Do we know her name?"

Argent shrugged with his eyes. Pouring himself a cup of coffee, he asked, "What news do you have? I have found nothing from these papers." The newspapers Merritt had gathered were old editions from Easter Sunday and the next two days. There had been no mention of any peculiar doings in Shantytown or at the lock. Even the "disturbance at the St. Nicholas Hotel" received only scant coverage; the greater part of the papers was given over to descriptions of the Easter services in the town.

Merritt took Argent's cup of coffee before Argent had a chance to take the first sip, and before taking his own first sip, informed Argent, "Nettleship never requested a meeting with us, never sent any of his men to relay to us any correspondence, reports, or investigations."

"Someone wanted us at the Slack Water on Saturday night."

"Yes, and we would have been there, willingly and on time. Why the need to kill M?"

"Something changed, some new factor was thrown into the equation, some new element that changed the balance."

"But not the outcome: we would still have been disgraced, whether M was involved or not." A revelation occurred to Merritt. "M herself is the new factor, the new element."

Merritt's revelation ended there, but Argent picked up the thread. "We would have been disgraced whether Miss Warner was involved or not, and so, indirectly, would the President and the Service. But add Miss Warner's death to the mix and the President becomes personally and directly involved and disgraced, as does the Service, being used as an escort, as a special favor to the President, a President whose administration is somewhat tarnished by scandal." After a brief pause wherein this new realization matured, Argent added, "M's murder would have been a far blacker eye for both the President and the Service than a mere bungling of a baseless investigation into long-retired counterfeit plates."

Argent poured another cup of coffee and blew on it. He stood a long moment, holding the cup to his mouth, but not drinking, searching his memory of last Saturday night. "So, it was a work up job, just not how I thought." A somber realization came to him. "Then, no one has missed us until now, no inquiries have been made, nothing is in motion."

"Until now, no."

Argent looked up. "You have news of help coming?"

"I wouldn't call it help, and they are not coming to Cumberland." Merritt took a deep breath before delivering what appeared to be painful news. "Marshals are being sent to the train."

The subject of the United States Marshals was a touchy one for Merritt. He chafed under their greater exercise of authority, especially where the power of arrest was concerned. It seemed absurd to Merritt (and to more than a few other operatives of the division) that the Secret Service – charged with protecting the nation's money supply, and with thwarting smuggling, illicit distilling, land fraud, tax fraud, and other criminal activities that threatened the nation's economy, and now, added to these infractions against the Federal Laws, were investigations into the Ku Klux Klan – did not have powers of arrest when directly confronting these matters. It was the operatives who did the investigating, who spent long hours watching suspects, keeping notes for later trials, doing all the work that led up to the actual arrests. But it was the marshals, with court ordered warrants, who would swoop in to claim the arrests. Merritt hated the system – "Begging to do our jobs," as he put it.

The marshals, of course, were happy with the system – they were paid, individually, a fee for each warrant served and arrest made, and they weren't about to share that with the upstart Secret Service. Moreover, marshals could make even more money if the criminals they were sent to arrest could outbid the court, so to speak, and buy their freedom. Losing such a lucrative system, being paid at one end by the courts or at the other end by criminals, was not in the marshals' best interest. The marshals were, therefore, not only happy to make arrests for the Service, they were absolutely adamant that only they should do so.

That system, however, was avoided whenever possible, which was often. The frustration of applying for a warrant for arrest, waiting for the court to order it, and then waiting further for the marshal to execute it, was largely a thing of the past. To avoid the frustration and the wait (and admittedly the professional humiliation), operatives now made liberal use of the citizen's arrest. Since no citizen needed a warrant when, in the witnessing of a crime, to make an arrest, Secret Service operatives simply waited (and often enticed) the intended arrestee into committing the crime, while a second agent – who happened to be nearby to witness the crime – stepped in to make the citizen's arrest. It had been satisfying for a while – to evade the marshals in this way – but it had only served to make it that much harder to have warrants served when the citizen's arrest could not be used. Merritt's creativity in employing the citizen's arrest had made him a particular object of the marshals' contempt since the ruse had gone into effect.

Operatives also cultivated working relationships with the local police, which offered the option of having the police present at the raid or place of crime, allowing the arrest to be executed by the police without warrants (or marshals). The marshals, for their part, resented these professional subterfuges: their incomes relied heavily on the fees collected for executing warrants and arrests. Every arrest made by Secret Service operatives was money out of their pockets.

The broader conclusion was that arrests were being made in as efficient a manner as possible, and usually without the smug and avaricious involvement of the marshals. Even so, Merritt maintained a petulant attitude about the marshals, who, outside the activities of the Service, performed admirable and necessary tasks for the general government.

Argent cleared his throat, and adopted a gentle, comforting tone to his voice. "There can be no harm in having a little help. As we have seen here in Cumberland, an extra gun or two would have made all the difference at the St. Nicholas." Unwilling to coddle Merritt any further, Argent cleared his throat again, and addressed what Merritt's news meant, beyond the obvious point of help, however unwanted or resented. "If marshals are being sent to the train, then that means they must know where the train is."

Without abandoning his sulk or acknowledging Argent's attempt to soften the blow of the marshals' 'interference,' Merritt pulled from a coat pocket several slips of paper and held them out to Argent.

Taking them, Argent read each one in quick succession, before reading them aloud, then deciphered: "The train is at Patterson Depot. The train has been moved to Green Spring. The train will be at Little Cacapon, until further notice." Argent dropped the telegrams on the bed. "At this rate, we'll have to take passage on one of B&O's fine trains to catch our own train at Martinsburg."

Merritt brightened at the thought. "Perhaps we should. It's a far shorter ride for M to Green Spring than to Little Cacapon. And once we're on one of B&O's fine trains, there is no reason to leave it. It is only eight hours' ride to Washington; we would be there long before midnight. It would be a silly waste of time to switch trains."

Argent was not about to indulge Merritt in his fantasy. "And what of our horses? What of Emmett? Having seen Emmett's elegant accommodations on our own train, Miss Warner is hardly likely to allow him to travel in any other manner, nor be parted from him while he is transported on some later train in a cattle car. And don't forget – our funds are low, and our trunks and saddle bags, wherein we keep our monies, are on the train, *the* train. As it is, we can hardly afford train fare for ourselves, much less for Emmett, nor the payment in advance for stabling our horses here until we can return to claim them."

"In advance? Since when is the horse itself not surety for the return of the owner and payment therefrom?"

"Since our own horses and Miss Warner's left the care of the St. Nicholas stables without making good the bill. It seems the ostler was somewhat put out about the whole affair and it has soured him on future clients."

Merritt's disappointment at the news of the marshals completely disappeared. "What did you learn of M?"

"Of facts, very little. Of rumors, a great deal, all of it very disturbing. It would appear, from the ostler's statements, that M took advantage of the disturbance at the hotel to liberate Emmett and herself from our care."

"Then M was already at the stable when the disturbance occurred."

"Very likely. The ostler admitted to being absent from the barn, being drawn to Baltimore Street by the disturbance, and remaining there to join the 'carnival-like' crowds and share a drink or two with fellow revelers."

"Let no man's death go uncelebrated."

"Oh, but we weren't presumed dead yet. Rumor did have it, however, that we – thought to be hardened gamblers and despoilers of young women – were on our way to certain and ignominious death at the hands of either Miss Warner's brothers, come to avenge her dishonor, or her keepers, come to reclaim their chattel."

It wasn't often that Merritt was without some remark. It took him a moment before he said, "M can never know of these rumors, and these rumors can never be attached to her name." Last Friday, Argent had registered himself as Joseph Hunt, Merritt as Dennis Matthews, and M as Miss Stearns. Merritt never asked Argent where he got the names he used as aliases, only what name he himself should answer to. They had never bothered to tell M of her alias – Argent was convinced that, with close supervision, Miss Warner would never have reason to have to answer to her alias. Argent also admitted to a dark suspicion that once Miss Warner had accepted one alias, she would not be shy about using a second alias at some other time to thwart their efforts and duties to escort and chaperone her.

"Agreed. We must somehow plant the seed of some less objectionable rumor before we leave."

"Is there some objection to the truth? That two men were merely escorting the young lady to relatives or friends when they all three became victims of ruffians?"

"Too much of the truth is already exposed. It is somehow known that we were traveling to see the President. The President's honor is now involved. He must be completely expunged from the story. I admit that I was so shocked at the outrageous nature of the rumor that I did not think to stop it there and then, to supplant that rumor with one less indecent and at least as believable."

"At least as believable?"

"Think on it, Merritt. What circumstances, other than immoral and disgraceful ones, could account for gunshots in our rooms and the sudden disappearance of all three of us, plus our horses? What innocent story could possibly account for those facts, without exposing both M and the President? No, the truth will not do here."

"Well, we will have to think of something, but I know of no better place to plant our rumor than with the landlady of a boarding house, who also has a son who works in a saloon. From these two sources alone, a vast number of people will hear our rumor. We have until tomorrow to come up with one. For now, it is time to revisit Shantytown."

They locked the bedroom door to the hallway, then slipped out the outer door of their room. They spent the rest of the afternoon and early evening making the rounds of the Shantytown saloons, where they learned very little beyond what they already suspected – that they had been put on display in these saloons so that every barkeeper in the area remembered the two men who could not hold their liquor, but whose friends paid with large bills and never stayed for the change. No one could remember with any certainty the appearance of these friends, but every barkeeper remembered – and remembered with good humor – the two men who were obviously in their cups and then some: in every saloon and gambling den the two men had ordered a brandy smash. It had been uproariously funny, and even after the large party had left, the rest of the night someone would shout out "A brandy smash here, please!" and the saloon would find itself in stitches again. Merritt found some small consolation in the revelation – drawn out from the fourth saloon they visited, but with evident reluctance from the barkeeper, who thought such information ruined the humor of the situation – that Merritt and Argent did not, in fact, directly order such a fancy drink in such rough-and-tumble places, but that the drinks had been ordered for them. The barkeeper assured them, however, that the order came from the two inebriates – one of their friends bent low to the men (their heads already hanging low with drink) and after whispered consultation, relayed the order to the bar.

It was at the Slack Water, however, where the most interesting information was learned. As usual, there was the silly order of a brandy smash for two men in a party of five or six and there was the same payment in a large bill for a relatively small order. But this time, the group of five or six did not simply leave without waiting for their change. An unknown man, but obviously another of the group, had rushed in, making a great noise and hullabaloo looking for his friends, found them at their table and with wild gesticulations and loud but indecipherable whispers imparted some news of great import. This occasioned great excitement at the table, the men rising as one, except the two inebriates who had ordered the brandy smash – they had been hauled to their feet and exhorted to look lively; there was money to be made. As the others in the group lurched out the door, the last one pulled payment from the wallet at his belt and told Maggie that he couldn't wait for her to change the bill – he and his friends were fast on the heels of a counterfeiter with important plates that they intended to capture. He had winked at Maggie knowingly as he pushed the twenty-dollar note into her bosom – far down into her bosom.

"Was it on the Tradesmen's National Bank of New York?"

"The plates?"

"No! The twenty!" Argent was near the end of his patience with Shantytown in general and the bartenders in particular. However, at the nod from the barkeeper, Argent made the effort to keep his agitation out of his voice as he pressed further. "Do you still have it?"

The barkeeper bent low under the bar and produced a cash box that he opened with a little key fished from a pocket in his dirty apron. There was a great deal of poking around in the cash box before the twenty-dollar bill was produced, though Merritt was certain it was the only such denomination in the box. The bill was laid on the counter but fixed firmly under the thumbs of the barkeeper. Merritt and Argent examined the bill in turn and both determined it was one of the counterfeit twenties that had been circulating since last November. The barkeeper indignantly pulled the twenty from their scrutiny once informed of its spurious nature. Though he denied that such was the case – and how would these gentlemen know, anyway? – it was certain that he would pass the bad bill onto the next person he could, and the bill would blow its way through Cumberland and probably down the canal or over the rails until someone would finally be caught with it and only then would it (maybe) be taken out of circulation. It was a very good counterfeit, well calculated to deceive, as all the counterfeit detectors and newspapers were fond of saying.

The barkeeper lost his affability once his prized bill had been denounced. To be fair, the saloon was beginning to fill up and he didn't have time to talk to men who had ordered one beer between them. When Argent asked to speak with the woman who had been paid with the twenty, the barkeeper baldly told him that Maggie was working upstairs tonight, and most likely wouldn't be available until morning. He was welcome to put his name on the dance card, so to speak, but both Argent and Merritt declined.

"We were supposedly chasing plates that when found with our bodies on Monday morning would prove to be of no value whatsoever, having been taken out of circulation almost nine months ago." Merritt's amusement at M's trickery at the B&O office had steadily given way to his warming anger at the assault on his reputation, on every facet of his reputation – as a mostly sober man, as a deliberative and thinking man, as an operative of the Secret Service, as an honest man. They had walked in silence until they were well out of Shantytown – word of two men going from bar to bar asking the same questions had surely circulated by now, and they wanted to make certain they were not followed and that their subsequent conversations were private.

Argent suddenly pulled Merritt into a narrow alley between two buildings just south of Baltimore Street. "Let me see that plate again." The light had mostly faded from the sky, and the alley made things all the darker. Merritt held a match as Argent studied the plate. Long after the match fizzled out Argent stared at the plate, lost in thought. Finally, he said, "This plate, and the others thrown into the lock, may not be as valueless as we thought." He continued in thought another moment, then asked, "Do you remember what distinguished the counterfeit from the genuine?"

Merritt thought back on the hot day last July when he, Argent, and several other Secret Service operatives raided a counterfeiting den on the second floor of the county road house, near Hudson City. They had approached the road house at night, a strange journey across the marshlands of New Jersey, the abrupt, dark prominence of Snake Hill silhouetted against a slightly less black night sky. The plates and the amount of counterfeit paraphernalia captured that night had surprised everyone, but outstanding from them all had been the 60-pound tobacco revenue stamp. It was very nearly a perfect replica of the genuine. Only later, after intense scrutiny, laying the counterfeit next to the genuine, and using powerful glasses, could the differences be discerned. A circular from Whitley had given the particulars, and from this Merritt remembered, "The 'i' joins the 'n' in the word 'Continental' so that it looks like an 'm'; the hatched cross lines on the bale in the genuine are only single lines in the counterfeit; over the mane of the horse, there are four dots in the counterfeit, but straight lines in the genuine." Merritt seemed like he had more to say about the counterfeit, but then confessed, "I can't remember the rest."

"It's enough. This isn't the same plate." Argent held out the plate for Merritt's inspection as, this time, Argent held a match.

The counterfeit plate they had captured at Snake Hill had been a very good, a dangerously good, effort, but this plate appeared to be extraordinarily well done. It, too, would take a great deal of critical examination before any flaws could be detected. The discovery of the Snake Hill and, subsequently, Staten Island plates had forced the treasury to begin the process of creating new revenue stamps of all kinds, the 60-pound tobacco stamp and the one-cent proprietary stamps being prominent among them. There had been a shocking amount of the one-cent stamps; even Whitley had been stunned to find that there could be so much profit in counterfeiting a stamp of so little value. Henning & Bonhack, the match concern in New Jersey, had made liberal use of these counterfeit one-cent stamps; both Messrs. Henning and Bonhack were currently being held on a hefty bond for this revenue fraud. The Internal Revenue Bureau had moved quickly to smother any further counterfeiting of all revenue stamps, arguably the single greatest source of income for the nation. New and multiple colors as well as different vignettes were being added into the designs of the new stamps.

This plate, however, would still be usable until the new plates were ready and the new stamps printed and sold. The government sold these 60-pound (class 32-cent) stamps to tobacco manufacturers for $19.20; counterfeit stamps were only $3, a huge savings to tobacco manufacturers, suppliers, and proprietors, a savings that was certain to create a large and willing market for the counterfeits. Why would any counterfeiter pass up an opportunity, no matter how short-lived, to sell their product? Especially such a product as this plate could produce, and especially given that such a plate represented a great deal of investment. The principals of the counterfeiting rings rarely disposed of their plates, keeping them for possible future use (future adjustments) and keeping them sometimes simply because they owned them, despite their possible use as evidence against them. No counterfeiter merely tossed their plates away.

"The new stamps are already being designed and contracts have been awarded to the printers and engravers. But even at best estimates, they won't be ready for sale until July. There is still plenty of time to make use of this plate." Argent released the plate into Merritt's keeping.

"Someone must hate us very much, if they are willing to throw such valuable sources of fraud away." Merritt sounded slightly proud to have generated such hatred; it was almost patriotic to be hated by such criminals. Merritt secured the plate in one of the reinforced pockets in the lining of his jacket, then led Argent out of the alley.

It was late into the night before Merritt and Argent made it to bed. They had reached the boarding house after the dinner hour, by way of their private door. At first the landlady was adamant that she could do nothing about their supper – hadn't she knocked and knocked at their door to remind them of the hour? – but little by little, she relented, bringing out, first, coffee and a few more cookies, then some cold meat, then reheating side dishes one at a time, as Merritt or Argent praised the dish before them. By the time her son came home from his job at the saloon, Merritt and Argent had eaten a full meal, though piecemeal. The son was grateful that the food was already out and the stove warm enough to fix himself a decent meal as well. Rather than leave the table as the son sat to his own meal, Merritt and Argent accepted the landlady's invitation to stay and repeat what they had heard about the disturbance at the St. Nicholas last Saturday night. Without waiting for either Merritt or Argent (known as Messrs. Lambert and Darnell) to tell their tale, the landlady launched into the particulars. It seems that Miss Stearns was not a fallen woman at all, but the niece of the engineer of that strange little train that came through here last week. When the son protested that the young woman had been intimately connected with the two men, Merritt assured him that he had it on good authority that the young woman's only connection with the two men was their connecting rooms at the hotel, which, Argent was quick – a little too quick – to inform was a mere coincidence. Any inquiry at the hotel will satisfy one's curiosity that such accommodations were not requested. And, furthermore, Argent could assure them, the door between the two rooms was locked at all times, the key in the lady's possession. Such assurances seemed questionable coming from someone newly arrived in the city and not connected with the event.

"With the event, no, but I am related to the young lady, and I do assure you her innocence and morality is without question or stain." This was more than Merritt and Argent had agreed upon for their story, and Merritt looked askance at Argent.

"But why was the woman at the hotel with the men, at all?"

The landlady looked expectantly at the two men. Her conversation with them had not covered that point, and she waited to see how they would answer her son's question.

Merritt resumed the original line of their counter-rumor. "Miss Stearns and her aunt, the engineer's wife, simply wished a night or two off the train and were to take a room together at the St. Nicholas. Miss Stearns went ahead with the two gentlemen, where she would wait for her aunt to join her later. Miss Stearns was in fact not in her room when the disturbance occurred but was at devotions with her aunt. When they returned and saw the commotion and learned that there had been gunfire in the vicinity of their room, they immediately returned to the train. Miss Stearns was so distressed that she refused to leave the train again." This was more wishful hoping than any statement based in past experience.

"But who were the two men?" The landlady had seen a lapse in information and had pounced on it.

Merritt said with an absolutely straight face, "As to that, I cannot say."

"But they were on the same train as your cousin."

"His cousin." Merritt nodded to Argent, both for the landlady's benefit and also indicating that Argent, as cousin, should reply to the objection.

Argent started, as from a deep introspection. "I only know that they were men of means, means enough to charter a private engine and private cars. As to the rumor that these men were on their way to request an audience with the President, I cannot say where the basis for such a rumor lay. My aunt never told me any such thing."

"Why were your aunt and cousin on the train?" At first accepting of everything Merritt and Argent had told her, the landlady was now showing a bothersome need for detail.

"My aunt often travels with her husband; they are an inseparable pair. And it was suggested that Miss Stearns accompany her aunt and uncle on the trip in order to visit with relatives, somewhere in Virginia, I believe."

"Don't you know?"

"Ma'am?"

"Don't you know where your relatives live?"

"Oh, not our shared relatives, but her relatives, on her father's side."

"Well, that's understandable. I can hardly keep up with my own relatives, much less my departed husband's."

There was another half hour or so of pleasant talk – of the new rolling mill the railroad company was building and her son's hope of obtaining a job there, of the recent fires in the city and the arsons who escaped the jail, of the odd weather of the past several days, and, of course, wasn't it exciting to have Mr. Spates back in town.

When Merritt and Argent finally stood to excuse themselves, the landlady made one last foray into the story of Miss Stearns. "Isn't it odd?"

Both Merritt and Argent were bleary-eyed and foggy-brained. "Mm?"

"Isn't it odd that your aunt and uncle and cousin were just here a few days ago, and now here you are."

Argent recovered first. "Well, I knew my uncle's train was headed for Cumberland, and I had hoped to reach here in time to catch a ride with them to Baltimore and spend some time with them along the way. But as it was, Mr. Darnell and I ran into some difficulty on the way here and we missed the train."

"Oh, dear. Difficulty?"

"Yes." Argent stumbled a moment, then inspiration righted him. "We were waylaid on our way out of Wheeling and treated rather roughly." To underscore the difficulty, Argent took in with his glance Merritt's clothes and his own.

"How awful! I imagine those brigands came out of Moundsville. There's a penitentiary there, you know, and there was a riot there, just this week. Very hard men there."

"Yes ma'am.

22 — *Easter Friday*

The men again rose later than intended, and the landlady, one last time, afforded them a late meal. Merritt retrieved their horses while Argent stopped by the telegraph office where he sent a telegram to Whitley, regarding the new counterfeit plate in their possession and the others, temporarily safe in the bottom of the lock, and received a telegram from Grant, amending his telegrams of yesterday to include stern admonitions that Miss Warner not be moved until absolutely well enough to do so. Also, there had been some delay in finding marshals free of their other duties to accommodate the President in his request to help Merritt and Argent.

Argent met Merritt on the street, leading both horses. Argent took the reins to his own horse. "We have one stop to make, and then we can be on our way."

"Two stops."

"Has something changed?"

"Not at all; I only wish to express my gratitude to the Lambert ladies, to pick up a little something as a thank-you."

"We have little enough money left as it is. We have a long ride ahead of us once Miss Warner is able to travel, and some of that money needs to be spent on at least one canteen. Miss Warner, especially, cannot be asked to go any length of time without water. We cannot be spending it on gewgaws and fripperies and frumperies. It is time to leave." Once Argent had made up his mind to move on to the next subject, job, or town, he could become cranky and impatient.

Merritt ignored Argent's clock thumping. "I have my bagatelle money. I want to get something for the ladies, and maybe something for M as well, in addition to a canteen."

"Those few dollars you won last Saturday have already been spent."

"I won more than a few dollars." Merritt handed his reins to Argent as he stepped up into a store advertising everything from fancy and staple dry goods to gents' furnishings to ladies' furs and hosiery, &c.

As it was, they needed to make only the one stop. Merritt emerged some long moments later and held up in one hand two canteens, and in the other a rather gaudy reticule, sparkling in the late morning sun.

"Is that for M?"

"No. Of course not. This is for Miss Lambert. And these," pulling from the reticule a pair of white gloves, "are for Mrs. Lambert."

"Nothing for Miss Warner?"

Merritt's face fell slightly. "No; she is devilish hard to shop for. But it occurred to me that the excitement of receiving a gift such as these" – Merritt held both the bag and the gloves up higher – "might prove too much for her in her reduced condition."

"Adeptly reasoned. Might I suggest that to keep excitement of another kind from Miss Warner that you make your gifts to the Lambert ladies privately and far from M's room." An only child, Argent had nevertheless grown up in a household of women — mother, aunt, and female cousins — and nothing had caused more excitement than if one received a gift and another did not.

Having no saddlebag in which to carry his treasures, Merritt returned the gloves to the bag and hung the bag from the horn of his saddle, where it bounced and glittered as they turned down Mechanic on their way to Old Town Road. Merritt smiled and tipped his hat to everyone who passed, unaware of the odd looks and second looks that were given to the reticule adorning his saddle. Argent, however, was supremely aware of it, and was glad when the road became less crowded as they moved farther away from Cumberland.

The sunshine and pleasant temperatures and his recent triumphs at the notions store had buoyed Merritt's spirits, but after a mile or so he returned to the subject of the marshals.

"Perhaps we could stop by Patterson Creek – send a telegram – and suggest to the President that there is no hurry to send any marshals."

Argent was a little put out by Merritt's pettiness in this matter and was still smarting a little that Merritt had withheld money that could have gone towards a proper bath and a trim of hair and beard.

"It's no use crying over spilt milk or spent bullets. At any number of points along this trip, a little luck could have avoided all of this; luck just was not with us this time."

Merritt sulked at this new thread of thought. Luck had certainly not been with them; he could not recall such a string of bad luck, coincidences, mis-timings, and multiple collisions between man, nature, and technology. He was quite willing to believe the marshals had conspired to create it all. His peevishness suddenly matured into a serious musing on their mishaps. It was, of course, ludicrous to suspect the marshals – he did not doubt they would love to humiliate and undermine the Service, but he seriously doubted even they could wield such power to maneuver events in this way. Who did then? And who would have the motivation to do so?

"Does it not strike you, though, that things seem to have been moving us in a decided direction and with a dogged determination?"

Merritt had not spoken for so long that Argent had thought the matter closed. "Merritt, this personal grievance you have with an entire group of men, most of whom you have never even met, smacks of a kind of paranoia."

"I am not speaking of the marshals, but of some unknown force of will. This trip has been remarkable not only for the number of delays but for the variety of them as well."

"Not only is it a pointless exercise, but a frustrating one as well, to catalogue and bemoan and sigh with 'What ifs' the ill-luck and missteps of one's journeys." Merritt remained silent staring straight ahead. Argent sighed. "But I shall consent to indulge you until we reach the widow's. And no further."

Merritt considerably brightened. "Thank you, Argent. It will help to pass the time."

"Perhaps M could school you in some of her father's exercises to help you pass the time."

Merritt smiled. "I am certain of it. But for now, let us catalogue the ill-luck and missteps of our journey; we can bemoan and sigh later. Our first delay came in Cincinnati."

"Yes, that regrettable, but hardly scripted, incident at Spring Grove."

"No, no, no, Argent. You are getting ahead of yourself. Our first delay was that torrential week-long rain storm that very nearly swamped all of

Cincinnati. Now," and Merritt held up his hand to forestall Argent's argument even as he said, "Oh, come now!"

"Now," Merritt repeated, "we have to decide if it was orchestrated or a natural act." Merritt waited for Argent to decide, then agreed with his unspoken answer. "I think we can both agree that all that rain and the consequences of it were of natural origin."

Merritt again waited for Argent, but Argent's participation in this began and ended with his permission to pursue this exercise.

"Next there was the matter of Miss Warner herself." Merritt rushed to include Miss Warner in the column of delays of natural origin. "Miss Warner, of course, had her own reasons for delaying, and also, I think we can both agree, brings to bear on her cause a dogged determination."

Argent was equally dogged in his determination to remain silent.

"After Miss Warner's substantial resistance was overcome, we were met with an hour's wait on the L&N from Nashville."

"Trains are late all the time. Although aggravating, there is nothing nefarious in it."

"Are you certain? Do we know why the train was late? It certainly served to delay us."

Argent offered nothing further on the delay in Louisville.

"Shall we put a pin in here, then? Next, we have our tarrying in Covington, a direct result of the L&N delay in Louisville. But once we reached Cincinnati, I think the delays take on a more coordinated character."

Merritt heard Argent shift in his saddle, but Argent remained silent. Privately, Argent thought Merritt had missed the matter of Miss Warner's horse nearly being sent to Paris – if Merritt was going to pursue this exercise, he should commit to it fully and completely. In his own independent exercise, Argent put a pin in Paris.

"We arrived in Cincinnati to find ourselves summoned to a court case we thought would not be heard for at least two weeks."

Argent could not help himself. "That was no delay but a quickening of an event."

Merritt did his best not to smile at Argent's inability to refrain from engaging in a puzzle. "At first glance, yes, but it did serve to delay us in Cincinnati for several days. And now we come to that regrettable incident at Spring Grove."

"Regrettable, but hardly scripted."

"I am not so certain."

"How could such a thing be directed? It was an unpredictable reaction in a random crowd to an unusual visitor on an unplanned visit."

"I submit that the reaction was entirely predictable, as well as the crowd, especially when the element of an unusual visitor is introduced."

"Explain yourself."

"The crowd may have been random in its makeup, but Spring Grove by its nature attracts crowds, and given its spiritual character and its place in Cincinnati's pride, the reaction of any crowd there, when confronted with a presumed insult to the grounds, would be predictable."

"But Miss Warner herself is unpredictable. She did not know herself, until that morning, that she would be visiting Spring Grove."

"But once she did know, it became known to several people."

Argent conceded the point by naming a few of them. "At least two hotel clerks and the ticket agent at Pike's Opera House."

"Pike's Opera House?"

"There are only two places to purchase tickets – Pike's Opera House or the first toll-gate on the road. Since her route did not take her past the first toll-gate, she had to have gone first to Pike's Opera House." Argent felt smug in his knowledge until his smugness was replaced with one of astonishment and disappointment. "Merritt, have you yourself never been to Spring Grove?"

Merritt sheepishly admitted that time had never permitted.

Argent stared at him, then appeared to have something to say, then stared some more. Finally, he said, "I see I shall have to take you there myself the next time we are in Cincinnati."

"I think M would be a better companion, but I should like to tag along with the both of you. But back to M. Others were aware of her intentions, and at least one of them had reason to spoil her visit there."

"Agreed, but how could he have orchestrated such vengeance in such short time. He did not strike me as overly ambitious or remarkably intelligent."

"That was M's estimation of him as well. No, I do not think it was the clerk who orchestrated M's infamy at Spring Grove, but what if someone else was able to do so for him, someone who might pay for any information regarding Miss Warner's movements during the times we were busy in court? What if this someone knew that our initial undertaking in coming to Cincinnati was to escort Miss Warner to Washington?"

"I thought we were going to forego the 'what ifs' for the time being. You are straying from facts."

"Not at all. Someone did know of our charge from the President to escort Miss Warner. U. S. Attorney Bateman somehow knew of Miss Warner's summons to Washington to see the President. How did he know? In all the confusion and hurrying at the time, we never thought to ask him. Moreover, his telegram to President Grant could easily have been made known to anyone with enough money to bribe a telegrapher, or who has a telegrapher in his shadowy employ. Don't forget – quite a few telegrams were reportedly sent to us at Louisville and Covington, telegrams we never received."

"This is all very circumstantial. Each new brick in your theory is circumstantially weightier than the last, and so necessarily predicated on a weak foundation. Your theory will fall in on itself."

"Perhaps, but if it falls in on itself, what is the loss, except a blow to my pride? And even if my theory can be taken as true, what can we do except know that the orchestration exists? Until we know the conductor, we have no options to act."

Argent pulled in a deep breath, then slowly let it out. "Then let us have the rest of your bricks and see what it is you have built."

Curiously, Merritt did not appear relieved or grateful to have Argent's blessing to continue. If what he was building stood against Argent's arguments or the evidence of events, then it was likely to be a structure that would not collapse in on itself, but one intentionally designed to do them some harm. The nature of the harm and the reason behind it were as unknown as the conductor.

"And let us not forget the mysterious absence of Mr. Hamper on the day of the Spring Grove incident."

"I admit it was mysterious, but hardly a delay."

"Unless his absence allowed Miss Warner to embroil herself at Spring Grove, and thus creating the delay of her arrest and court appearances. We have never been disappointed in Mr. Hamper before."

Argent paused to absorb this, then offered, "A pin for Mr. Hamper, then?"

"Please. So. Someone is watching our movements, and in order to delay us, he is also watching M's movements. If telegrams reportedly sent to us were intercepted in Louisville, then this plan or design was being put into operation even then. When we arrived in Cincinnati, it was known that our plans were merely to take the M&C as soon as possible, to our ultimate destination in Washington."

"Which with the best of luck would take a mere two days."

"That is too early or too quick, for whatever reason. We must be delayed in Cincinnati. So, first there is the early trial, but that is still not enough time for some unknown purpose. Miss Warner makes her intentions known to visit Spring Grove and this nefarious designer, who is able to manipulate the telegraph office, can surely manipulate circumstances at Spring Grove so that M is exposed in her unusual attire in front of a crowd . . ."

". . . whose reaction is predictable. And the law takes over from there, so that M is mired in Cincinnati's labyrinthine court system, and we are delayed yet again. That takes care of Cincinnati. What is next?"

"The bridge at Chillicothe was burned."

"Too early — it was repaired by the time we went through."

"The wreck near Chillicothe."

"Wrong direction — we were not delayed."

"Could have been a miscalculation in timing – the train was early coming in to Chillicothe, and by mere minutes." Argent's face remained doubtful, so Merritt moved ahead. "There was the freight train off the tracks near Athens. We were delayed a good while."

Argent hesitated before speaking. "It was just after Athens when our compartment was visited by the man looking for the water closet."

"Yes." At first Merritt seemed to have nothing further to say about the man, but then he added, "A coincidence we must keep in mind. Another pin."

"Athens was the site of another coincidence that bears pinning. There were the two emergencies that did not actually exist – the fire that preceded the jail break and the vague emergency at the train that called our porter away and allowed the intrusion into our apartment."

They rode in silence for some time. "Mr. Hughes was adamant he had thoroughly checked the train, yet the axle rod was cracked." Argent had been musing about the event at Tray Run, but did not realize he had spoken. As if considering what he himself had just said, Argent paused before continuing. "At the time, I had uncharitably assumed negligence on his part or the part of one of the crew."

"And now?"

"And now, having observed Mr. Hughes for some days and under some trying circumstances, I no longer assume that." Not only had Mr. Hughes proven himself dedicated to his duty and his engine, he was also curiously dedicated to Miss Warner's safety and comfort. Had he been negligent before, he would not be so as long as Miss Warner was a guest on his train. "There were also the curious comments made by both engineers during the incident at Tray Run."

"How curious?"

"At the time, I did not consider them at all, but both men specifically remarked that the axle had snapped in two, in the very middle. Later, however, as we waited for help, I returned to the comments. Mr. Hughes hoped he had not given me cause for anxiety – axles, unfortunately, break all the time – but he was simply surprised at the position of the brake. As Mr. Hughes will tell you, in great detail, the rod is thinnest at the center, and therefore, one would expect breaks to occur there all the more frequently. However, the opposite is true. It is not impossible for an axle to break in the middle, just very unusual for it to happen in that location."

"Perhaps the axle had been tampered with. Did he retain the two pieces?"

"No, someone in the repair crew tossed them into the Cheat River." Mr. Hughes had looked at Argent with mild amazement at the question – why would a broken axle be retained? It was, after all, made from scrap metal, and it was likely the core of it was corrupt. "Mr. Hughes, however, coupled his curious observation of the axle with an equally curious observation that luck had nevertheless been with us."

"Luck?"

"Had we been going at a faster speed the train would very likely have jumped the track."

"Thank goodness M was not aware of that."

"Oh, I'm quite sure she was very aware of that, as she was very aware of our position, perched precariously atop Tray Run Viaduct." Argent recalled M sitting in the middle of the floor of her car, looking up at him.

Suddenly Argent exclaimed, "Emmett!" and Merritt echoed him in return.

They had ascribed the vexing problem of Emmett's transfer to a freight train as one of the vagaries of riding the rails. But now it took its place as one more brick in Merritt's theory. The wait for Emmett to rejoin them had kept them in Parkersburg an entire day. And now Argent returned to his first pin, the pin in Paris.

"Before the problem with Emmett on the M&C, there was the near problem with Emmett on the Kentucky Central. Had Emmett been sent to Paris, it would have cost us a day in waiting for his return. This mysterious wealthy man in Louisville who promised M princely care for Emmett – did you see his horse or see the man himself in Covington?"

"Neither. But I cannot say that there wasn't a horse or that the man did not travel to Covington; he may have remained in Louisville and sent the horse forward." The thought of Emmett had brought to Merritt's mind another incident, though it did nothing to delay them. "There was a man at Fort Boreman."

When Merritt seemed stopped in his thoughts, Argent urged, "Yes?"

"M had wanted to watch the ferries cross the river, as we waited for you and Emmett to rejoin us. A man, one of several people enjoying the return of spring weather on the hill, had overheard her." Merritt had been studying some spot on his horse's mane as he remembered the morning at Fort Boreman, but now he turned to Argent. "He knew that M had only recently arrived in Parkersburg."

"Parkersburg is a small city – he may have simply been familiar with all its inhabitants and would recognize her as a stranger."

"No, he mentioned that he had arrived several days before us. How could he be certain that M was not herself a citizen of Parkersburg?" After he had intruded upon their conversation, the man had drifted away, and Merritt had not seen him again. Merritt rubbed his chin; he was beginning to find it difficult to differentiate between an innocent exchange and an intentional interruption.

A thought darker than delays crept into Argent's mind. "If Emmett was indeed another intentional delay, it is possible this force of will of yours knew more than the mere facts of Emmett's presence. Any other owner of livestock . . ."

"Emmett is more than livestock – he is her pet and sometime companion. And he is the pet and companion given her by her father."

"Exactly, and someone knows this. Any other owner of such livestock would have simply sighed at the inconvenience and continued on, expecting their livestock would eventually catch up with them."

"But not M."

"No, not M. Someone knew she would not budge until she was reunited with him. Someone knows her or knows about her, enough to use her to delay us."

"More likely, someone has come to know her or about her, since she has come to know us."

"I think we need not add any more bricks to your edifice — it has assumed form enough to know its function. We were to be delayed until such time that we could be publicly disgraced, having murdered a young woman, and conveniently hanged for it by incensed citizens."

"That could have happened in Cincinnati. Why wait until Cumberland?"

"The police are well-established and well-distributed in Cincinnati; a lynch mob over one more murder there is unlikely to form and hold under such a force. Cincinnati is also the seat of the District Court and a good many learned and practiced lawyers. We could well be exonerated. This force needed a smaller town, one with a weaker hand on the tiller of the law, and far away from all the learned and practiced lawyers in Baltimore, who hone their practice in the highest federal courts."

"There are other smaller towns with much the same characteristics. Chillicothe, for example."

Both men mused on Chillicothe's failures as a venue for free and unfettered murder. It was Merritt who spotted the flaws there. "Chillicothe doesn't have a Shantytown or Walnut Bottom in which men with a criminal bent could hide, either before or after the deed. Such men could be brought in to Cumberland by this force of will, at any time, and await our arrival."

"Brought in from somewhere like Moundsville, perhaps."

"There were no escapes." Merritt patted the day's newspapers – read at breakfast – in his saddlebag. "And our abductors were disappointed at their absence. But it does fit – they were waiting for escapees from Moundsville. That means the prison conspiracy was known and perhaps orchestrated from the outside. A date was set, for some unknown reason, and we had to be detained until that date, until escapees could make their way to Cumberland." Merritt sucked in his breath. "It is a great deal of work to disgrace and kill such humble servants as ourselves."

"You mean federal underlings."

Merritt smiled for the first time since their deliberations began. "I stand corrected."

Argent's comment had a tinge of bitterness to it, but it served to prompt him into higher understanding. "We may be federal underlings, but the President most certainly is not. He is the highest federal employé and it may be that he is as much a target as we ourselves, maybe even more so, and that we are being used to reach him as much as M is being used to reach us. A target like the President would make such machinations necessary and ultimately justifiable."

"They were aware of M's relationship with the President. 'Grant's girl.'" Merritt said the last with heat and indignation – despite his own loyalty to Grant and the government, Merritt felt some loyalty to M as well, and knew she would detest being referred to in such a way. In a more normal tone he said, "We still don't know the architect."

"No, but we know his goal, and as you said, now that he has failed in that goal at the lock, he will be frustrated and angry and will try again. As soon as Miss Warner is able to travel, we take her with all speed to Washington, no matter what delays are put in our path. We take another train, if necessary, or the canal, or ask a ride with some farmer. She will not be used in this way. And we say nothing to M."

"That goes without saying."

Though the route home via the Old Town road was shorter than the winding towpath, their late start at Cumberland kept them from reaching the widow Lambert's house until the evening. They turned their horses out on this fine spring evening before washing up at the pump. Merritt was anxious to present his gifts to the ladies of the house.

Their return to the house was greeted with lukewarm enthusiasm until Merritt produced his gifts, which elicited great delight in Miss Lambert and reserved gratitude in Mrs. Lambert. It did produce in both women a greater willingness to put food on the table long after the women themselves had eaten. Argent wisely waited until after they had eaten to give to the widow the medicines he had bought in Cumberland, medicines starkly lacking in those Mrs. Lambert had requested for Miss Warner. Mrs. Lambert received them with barely contained irritation, which burst its thin boundaries when she espied the chloral hydrate.

"What is this?"

"Hydrate of chloral, a new compound highly recommended among doctors for keeping a patient calm and rested and for promoting sleep. Miss Warner has a history of poor sleep." Without waiting for the widow's reactions or objections, Argent said with an authority Merritt rarely heard when Argent addressed ladies, "See to it that she gets it tonight."

23 — *Easter Saturday*

There was a stony silence that met Merritt and Argent as they emerged from their room the next morning, neither Mrs. Lambert nor her daughter being found in the house. Merritt briefly considered that it must be Sunday, as the silence reminded him of M's farm three weeks ago, the silence of Sunday services observed in town, in this case, the tiny village of Spring Gap. Argent corrected him, assuring him it was most definitely Saturday. Merritt was certain, however, that Sunday or no, the effect would have been the same – Argent's short-tempered handling of Mrs. Lambert the night before could only have left her stung and seething, and a stony silence would have been their just reward. Merritt had reproached Argent last night, but Argent had countered – admittedly, not without justification – with the absolute need to keep Miss Warner from wandering (escaping), especially now that it was very nearly established that she had become the target of some bitter retribution against Merritt, Argent, and possibly, the President. Merritt had to agree, but he thought that perhaps there could have been a softer way to ensure the widow complied with his wishes.

"With kid gloves, perhaps?"

"It couldn't have hurt."

Argent's only regret about last night had been his forgetfulness, in his pique, to ask after Miss Warner. Miss Lambert had knocked on their door some time after Argent had stormed out of the kitchen, trailing Merritt, to thank them for the beautiful handbag. Argent had asked then if Miss Warner could receive him, that he might satisfy himself as to her health, but Miss Lambert had assured him that Miss Warner was doing well, and that she was at that moment asleep. Argent longed to ask if Miss Warner had been given the chloral, but his pride stayed his tongue.

Miss Warner had been asleep at the moment when Argent asserted his authority in Mrs. Lambert's kitchen, but she was soon woken, out of something like spite, to be dosed with the chloral. But it wasn't only the chloral at work producing such a dreamless and yet somehow restless sleep. Late Wednesday afternoon M had asked for her grip bag. Miss Lambert had cheerfully informed her that it had been under the bed all this time, Mr. Darnell having brought it in that first night. Miss Lambert offered to retrieve anything from the bag for her, but Miss Warner assured her that she merely wanted to know its whereabouts. Soon after Miss Lambert left, M had pulled herself out of bed and retrieved the bag. A great relief came over her when she confirmed that her father's gun was still there. The men, then, had not searched her bag, had not relieved her of the gun, had not discovered the stolen hotel blanket nor the remainder of the money she had taken from their great bank of bills. They were not aware, then, of her intention to leave. She shoved the gun among the rolls of the blanket and dress, well out of sight and secure against shifting when the bag was being handled.

In the very bottom of the grip, carefully wrapped in one sock and stored in the other, M found what she immediately wanted, the laudanum. Her shoulder wound ached, but it was her headache that cried out for the drug. The total relief from her headache and the pain in her shoulder was so complete that M slept through dinner and into the early hours of the morning on Thursday. She had taken another, though smaller dose, Friday after dinner, and so Mrs. Lambert had some trouble waking M to take the dose of chloral as Argent prescribed. M was awake but struggling to focus when Merritt knocked softly at her door, asking admittance. M did not answer, hoping Merritt (and she supposed Argent, as well) would respect the boundary of the door and leave her in peace.

Merritt and Argent found her sitting up in bed, but her eyes were closed, her right hand loosely holding an empty cup. Her recovery had progressed enough that her left arm had been admitted to the sleeve of Dr. Lambert's shirt; the shirt may even have been a different one than she had contorted about her on Wednesday morning when they left. Some attention had been given to her hair; at the very least, it had been brushed clean of the caked mud and muck from the canal. She had evidently been reading – several newspapers were neatly stacked on the bed to her right. Merritt cleared his throat, and M sighed inwardly before opening her eyes.

"Oh, Mr. Merritt, you're back. I hope you concluded your business satisfactorily?"

Merritt stood near the door, watching her with that mild amusement that so irritated her. Argent moved into the room and seated himself in one of two chairs near the foot of the bed. He crossed his legs; for some reason this signaled to M that this morning's visit had some import other than to announce themselves returned and possibly to ask after her health. Merritt then took the chair to Argent's right, nearest the door.

Argent began. "Miss Warner. How do you do this morning?"

"Fine, thank you for asking."

"And last night? Did you sleep well?"

"Perhaps too well." Her sight was still bleary, and she felt another headache slowly sprouting from a knot at the base of her skull.

Argent smiled, then recrossed his legs. "Good."

M waited for Argent to introduce the other subject that was hanging in the air between them. Argent and Merritt also waited, their eyes never wavering from M's face. This was a technique both men had found successful in eliciting confessions or information from suspected counterfeiters or other criminals; Argent was especially effective at the expectant gaze. In this case, however, they found themselves outmatched in the waiting game – M was profoundly more experienced, and naturally adept, at sustaining and enduring an awkward moment. And in this case, also, M's bleary sight was an asset – she could not precisely see the men's faces and so was less affected by their stares.

Merritt began. "In the course of our work, we are required to file reports with our superiors."

"I am very sorry to hear it. It must be dreary to constantly rehash the day's happenings and frame them in an official language. It reduces the day to mere sequences."

Merritt gave a dry laugh. "Yes, well, the point is, we don't have all the information we need to complete our report regarding the events at the lock on Saturday night."

"Or the hotel. For instance," Argent shifted in his chair, "we are at a loss as to how you escaped certain death at the hotel."

"Yes, you see, one of the rogues who assaulted us entered your room. We heard two shots, and he seemed quite sure of himself that he had killed you – or some thing in your bed – and, yet, here you are." Merritt was almost smirking at her. "It is almost as if you weren't even in your room at the time."

"Perhaps those criminals were merely bad shots – they very nearly botched your own assassinations. Clearly they were not a higher class of criminal." Something was tickling at the back of her mind, but Merritt's smirk was distracting her.

"There is nothing high class about a man who would shoot a woman asleep and defenseless in her bed."

Whatever had been lurking just outside her memory had retreated even further at Argent's unexpectedly heated reply. M did not like the tone in Argent's voice. "Bed is one of the most defenseless places on earth."

Merritt heard M raise her guard. Though Argent's indignation at M's attempt at levity on such a heavy subject was justified, it had clearly made her defensive, and Merritt had learned in their few weeks together that one of M's greatest defenses was absolute and iron-clad silence. Merritt attempted to bring the conversation back to the point. "So, it follows that you were not in your room or in your bed."

M remained defiant. "I don't like to be defenseless."

"Clearly. Please don't misunderstand – we're," Merritt placed his hand over his heart in the manner that M found overly dramatic, "very happy that you survived the attempt on your life, but – again – we have these reports to file, and our superiors insist on accuracy and detail." Then Merritt allowed his eyes to widen as he feigned an epiphany. "M, were you running away?" Despite his disapproval of Argent's heavy-handedness with M, he failed to realize his own effect on M as a smirk again settled on his face.

So, they were aware of her intention to leave. "No, I was returning to home, not running away from home."

"Running away doesn't always mean running away from home. Take this case in particular." M particularly disliked this imperious attitude that seemed to be ever present in Mr. Argent.

"It always means that. Everything you are or have comes from home or starts at home. Whenever one runs away, it is always away from something at home or from home. I was returning to home, and I take exception to Mr. Merritt's insulting suggestion. I am no coward; I don't run away."

Merritt seemed genuinely chastised, as all amusement left his face. Whatever could be said of M, she certainly was no coward. "Withdrawn, with apologies. But, for our reports, at what point were you in your return home, when the incident under discussion happened?"

M scrutinized Merritt to determine the sincerity of his apology. Apparently satisfied with what she saw, M decided she could reveal a little something of Saturday night. "I was in the barn with Emmett." What had been tickling at the back of her mind abruptly came to the front: the discovery of vast amounts of money in the men's trunk, of her father's gun in their possession, and the memory of the lie they had let her believe about the gun, of the hotel manager's charges of drunken behavior and improper relations, of an alias obviously given to M in the hotel registry, of the restrictions they had placed on access to her own horse, of restrictions placed upon her. Other than the gun and the money, she had not thought of these things since she left the hotel for the last time. The few kindnesses shown to her by these men had led her to following their horses and then to following the men themselves. In the excitement of their imminent death at the canal lock, everything had flown from her mind. And now it all came racing back and prickled her scalp like the return of feeling in a leg or arm fallen asleep and then revived. Half-formed suspicions about these men began to take on new shape. She had to be careful what she told them and subtle in eliciting from them information that might prove useful.

Argent saw her complexion pale suddenly and at the same moment that she seemed to forget that she was talking. He had taken her word that she was fine but had done nothing to confirm it for himself. He moved to take her pulse, but M waved him off. He stood by the bed a moment looking down at her. Now her complexion was flush, but she returned his gaze with a clear and unwavering eye. Behind him, Merritt cleared his throat and shifted in his chair; Merritt wanted Argent to break off his tardy examination of M's health.

"Are you unwell? You seemed to pale just now."

"If I paled it was at the memory of a request made of me and that I neglected. The hotel manager asked me to relay to you the urgency of payment for our time at the St. Nicholas. I assured him you would see to it. You will see to it?"

"It has already been seen to. Set your mind at ease." Argent reseated himself.

Merritt nodded his thanks to Argent, then prompted M, "You were saying."

"I was in the barn with Emmett when there were shots fired. The ostler ran towards the hotel and I followed a few minutes later when he did not return." M stopped here, having answered, she felt, the original query into her whereabouts at the time of the incident at the hotel.

Merritt looked to Argent, but he was stonily staring out the window. Merritt resumed the questioning. "What did you find at the hotel?"

"Your room had been disordered, but mine showed considerable more damage."

"How so?"

If Mr. Merritt wanted details, she would give them to him, and make him see how ineffective he was as an escort for her. "The curtains were torn and in places shredded by flying glass; the lamp had been shattered. Oil from the lamp was staining the carpet. Bullets had damaged the wall next to the bed."

The recitation of damage seemed to have come to an early end. Merritt prompted her once again. "Nothing more?"

M paused, considering Merritt. "My pumpkin was monstrously abused."

At this, Argent choked as he took in a breath of air. He managed to croak out, "Your pumpkin?"

Merritt leaned forward. He knew that pumpkin had some part to play in all this.

"Yes, my pumpkin. And yours, too. I had carved and painted a most becoming visage for you, a face I hoped would convey my regret, for your sakes, that you would be continuing on to Washington on your own. I had thought it would soften our parting when you found it the next day. But the face was completely destroyed and now you will never see it." M seemed to lapse into speculative sorrow.

"Perhaps you can recreate it for us at some later date."

"No. No, it was an original piece and is committed to God's memory now. I had hoped you would find it in the morning light and that it would convey a sense of gratitude for your help so far."

"You are grateful, then?"

M didn't like Merritt's attitude about her pumpkin. She felt he was smirking again, though he kept it from his face. "No. I was just being polite. But it was a happy carving because I was happy to be returning home."

Finally, Argent took the conversation in hand. "How did you come to find us?"

"Oh. When I saw my room and the disorder in your room, it occurred to me that you just might not be a couple of carousing drunkards spending the taxpayers' money on debauchery."

"You thought that?" Now Argent was diverting from their purpose; he was genuinely concerned that she should think well of him. Merritt gave him a sidelong glance.

"I was told that, by the hotel manager." She did not tell them of the other things the hotel manager said to her. "I was also witness, however, to similar behavior or, rather, results of similar behavior when you were brought, unable to ride your horses, to the wagon." M's eyes dared the men to contradict her memory of that night.

"You are mistaken, Miss Warner." Argent was determined to defend his honor – he was not one to drink excessively at any given time, and certainly not when he was on duty, of any kind. But at M's challenging look, he added, "Through no fault of your own. We were rendered insensible first through the use of chloroform, and then through the introduction of some unknown stimulants."

Merritt stared at the floor at his feet. Though the events of that night were mostly hazy, Merritt remembered drinking and often, so that some of the stimulants they imbibed that night were not unknown.

M privately did not relent in her opinion of Merritt and Argent as sometime inebriates. If chloroform was used, other facts remained the same: these two men closed every evening with a drink, inviting, almost insisting, M to do the same; they had made arrangements to keep M under surveillance so that they could keep some nighttime meeting; their abductors had reported – almost reveled in – visiting more than a few saloons, with Merritt and Argent; and she had smelled the liquor on them – they must have spilled quite a bit on themselves, must have had so much to drink they could not handle the glass.

"M, why were you at the wagon with these men, and why did you follow it, and us, to the lock?"

It had been an impulse of guilt and gratitude, inspired by the religious fervor of Holy Week. Some of her suspicions and reservations sloughed away as she thought back on Saturday night. She opened her mouth to speak then shut it again as she considered how to begin. She did not know why, but she could not look at the men as she admitted her gratitude to them; she absently realigned the edges of the papers next to her.

"You have shown a great deal of consideration in the matter of Emmett, a great deal of consideration for my feelings in the matter." M paused again, her old resentment at being restricted in her access to Emmett at the hotel stable rising before her. However, that had not crossed her mind on Saturday night when she had decided to follow the men's horses, and so it should not be part of her story now. "I was in the barn when the men came to steal your horses. You have been solicitous of Emmett's accommodations," – M looked up briefly at Merritt only – "and so I thought you might have more than practical feelings for your own horses. It would be a great loss to me, if Emmett were stolen. My first intention was to follow your horses to watch the general direction in which they were taken, and then I would send word to you of this. Then I considered that more information would be needed, and so I followed hoping to overhear something or catch a glimpse of the men's faces to give you a better grasp of where your horses might be."

"That was an incredibly dangerous and, might I add, foolish, undertaking."

Merritt took in a deep breath at Argent's disapproval. It was just the sort of comment that would seal M's lips. M, however, seemed to take no notice of Argent's tone or the insult. She seemed, in fact, eager to change Argent's mind.

"There was no danger; I stayed well back of the men, and they were making so much noise of their own, I doubt they would have heard us if we were right behind them." M had stumbled slightly at the word 'and' — she had almost said, 'and I had my gun.' She had almost revealed her own criminal act of going through their trunk and stealing both the manifest and the money.

Both Argent and Merritt marked M's transition to some other thought in mid-sentence. Merritt resumed his questions before Argent could aggravate M by commenting on the transition. "You initially intended only to gather information for us, before taking the train home. But where you found us is ten miles from Cumberland. Why would you follow us so far? Why did you not alert the police in Cumberland for help?"

M's heart gave a little leap of joy — the men had taken the bait about her purchase of tickets at the B&O depot. She may be able to salvage her plans, after all. She would dismiss the men, then return to Cumberland and resume her plans to take the Cumberland road to Wheeling. Let them ride up and down the B&O looking for her, if they liked. But for now, she would answer their questions; hopefully, being able to complete these reports would make the men more amenable to returning to their other duties, before more reports about their time with her would be required. A small shadow of suspicion about these reports raced across her mind to settle in the knot in the back of her neck – what were they reporting about her, and to whom? Grant, certainly, but who else was included in these superiors to whom they were reporting?

"What should I say to the police? That two drunken men are being taken out of town in a wagon? What would be the alarm in that? I suspect that drunken men are carted off by the wagonload in most cities."

There was no disputing that, though Argent objected to being included in that unsavory group of men.

"As you say, it happens. What made you continue to follow us if you thought we were merely drunk?" Merritt was determined to know the rest of the story.

"They spoke of events at the hotel. They were disappointed that the police did not come. And they took your boots."

"They took our boots?" It wasn't often that Merritt showed genuine surprise, but Argent heard it now.

"It was a curious thing to do, and I was curious as to why."

"You followed a gang of men down a road at night to an unknown destination to know why someone took our boots?"

Unlike Merritt's question, Argent's was not one of surprise, but of anger, and M resented it. She was not about to tell them that she followed them out of some kind of gratitude or Christian obligation. Those were the justifications of last week, when the fervor of Holy Week excited her. The ancient homily she had heard that day had been reverberating in her mind – *Something strange is happening* . . . – and she had somehow equated that with the strange happenings on the road and towpath that night. It sounded silly, and slightly blasphemous, when she thought on it now; it could only sound worse if said out loud. She resented that Argent made her doubt her actions, doubt herself. Regardless of how they viewed it, she had done the right thing. She had kept them from being murdered, and now she was finished with them. "You need not write that in your reports, if it causes you shame."

Argent had obviously angered M, but Merritt hoped to bring her back to the matter at hand and back to a less defensive posture. "Was your curiosity satisfied?"

M blinked slowly, once, twice, before bringing her gaze to settle on Merritt. "I saw nothing more, as I was following at a discreet and safe distance. I believe you were sufficiently recovered to hear all that I did, at the lock."

That was it, then; Argent's outburst had so offended M that she returned to her habitual reserve. It seemed, moreover, that all their hard work of the last few weeks to gain her trust had suddenly evaporated; they were meeting, once again, the Miss Warner they had first met on the porch on the first day of April.

If Merritt was disappointed and angry with Argent before, it was doubled at Argent's next words.

"For the remainder of the trip, I must insist you stop all such wandering. Surely, you will be able to control yourself for the space of a day."

Merritt held his breath. It was uncharacteristic of Argent to coat his words with sarcasm, and absolutely unheard of for him to do so when speaking with women. Merritt knew Argent was weary with the constant realigning of his duty with M's peculiarities, but now was not the time to change tactics. Couldn't Argent see the shift in her attitude, a return to her original attitude towards them?

"The space of a day?" M's resentment at Argent's attempt to shame her into obedience took the form of a challenge.

"Eight or nine hours, to be more precise; the time it will take us to reach Washington."

Merritt rushed in to forestall the inevitable response to such a statement. "When, of course, you are able to travel."

"When I am able to travel, it won't be to Washington."

Merritt sighed. This conversation should not have taken place until M was indeed ready to travel. Why had Argent jumped ahead to a conversation certain to bring out the worst in M?

"Miss Warner, this childish defiance —"

At last the widow Lambert made her appearance, without the courtesy of knocking. She took one look at the patient in her bed, whose face was an alarming mixture of pallor and blush, with glassy eyes. M had indeed become flushed at Argent's accurate though stinging assessment. With more diplomacy than Merritt thought the woman could muster in Argent's presence, Mrs. Lambert said, "I think Miss Warner has had more than enough excitement for the time being."

Both Merritt and Argent nodded their assent, though not their satisfaction, rose, and left the room. Mrs. Lambert closed the door firmly behind them.

In the barnyard, Argent pumped water to rinse his face. It, too, was an alarming shade of red. After a moment, a cooler and calmer Argent expressed regret at losing his temper, especially with a convalescent, but then he exploded anew with frustration. "Miss Warner is exasperating and stubborn, and there is no reasoning with her."

"We were warned of her volatile nature."

"It is not only her nature that is changeable. Have you remarked how her" – Argent's hand circled the air looking for his next words – "level of understanding of matters seems to wax and wane? In some matters, she seems absolutely erudite, and in others she seems ridiculously naïve. It is as if she was sometimes a child and sometimes a wizened old woman. Do we even truly know her age?" Argent's earlier admonition that a woman's age was between her and her husband apparently did not apply to himself.

"It is certain she doesn't. If she is as young as she acts at times, she ought to know to obey her elders. If she is as old as she seems at times, she ought to know better how to behave. Her behavior has been erratic, but I ascribed it to her grave losses, homesickness, and a regrettable unacquaintance with life outside the farm. Regardless, she must have reached her majority, else she could not be managing her farm and herself on her own."

"Miss Carrie made mention of an institution. Do you think her instability is of a permanent nature, and she needs to be under strict supervision?"

Merritt scratched his head. "I don't know what to think of her. She'll save your life at the risk of her own but won't accord you the natural respect due to a gentleman or officer of the law or expected from someone of such a strict and reasonably accomplished upbringing. She avoids common conversation with people, but willingly engages in verbal sparring, at the slightest provocation. She can hardly live on her own, but steadfastly rejects company or help."

Argent was glad to finally give voice to his observations, to add to Merritt's litany of M's faults. "She can't fix her hair, but she can saddle a horse, shoot a gun, work a plow, and follow an engineer's drawings. She's obviously intelligent, yet she doesn't seem to have the simplest understanding of social propriety. She can seemingly induce herself into a trance with great ease, but she can't seem to focus on anything in front of her."

"She can't be left alone." Merritt took his turn at the pump. "It looks as if we'll be returning to Kentucky."

"At which point, we'll be returning to civilian life. Any hopes of joining Colonel Ackerman's group will die the minute we head back west. We can expect only disapprobation from Grant and —"

"— and a dogged reputation for being herded and broken by either a young woman or an old girl."

24 — *First Sunday of Easter*

The house was silent again the next morning, but appropriately so, it being Sunday. The Lambert ladies were gone to attend services in Spring Gap, Mr. Darnell taking them in the small wagon that sat behind the barn. A note was left on the table explaining this, with the promise of a proper breakfast upon their return. A pot of cold coffee was left on a cold stove, but Merritt soon had both warming. Argent steeled himself for the task of assessing Miss Warner's health; it could go very badly if she was awake.

M, thankfully, was still asleep when Argent examined her shoulder and arm. There was some inflammation in the shoulder, but nothing to overly concern him. The other wound was trifling in comparison and showed perfect intention of healing. Argent was also pleased with the effects of the chloral (the widow had evidently followed his orders in administering it) – M did not rouse at all during Argent's inspection.

Merritt and Argent drained the pot of coffee while they commiserated on the problem of Miss Warner. The marshals were on their way, if not already installed on the train at Little Cacapon bridge. They had to somehow convince her to at least accompany them to the train. Once there, it would be impossible for her to merely dismiss both themselves and the marshals. Merritt was loath to rely on the marshals to accomplish their task, but when it came to choosing either his pride or Miss Warner's safety, Merritt did not hesitate. Merritt also did not hesitate to upbraid Argent for his lapse in control during yesterday's interview with M. Argent was very contrite and promised to better monitor himself in future.

After taking care of the morning chores in the barn – Merritt took especial care of Emmett, in the time it took Argent to attend to both his and Merritt's horses – the men headed in to begin the delicate task of steering Miss Warner to the idea of meeting the train at Little Cacapon.

They found M not only awake, but sitting up, and, moreover, sitting in one of the chairs across from the windows, at the foot of the bed. She was wearing her own clothes, both her pants and shirt having been cleaned and mended by Miss Lambert. Her arm was still in a sling, but also fully in the sleeve of her shirt. Completely dressing, and on her own, must have cost some amount of pain and patience, but she seemed more at ease.

She laid aside the newspaper she had been reading and greeted them pleasantly enough, but Merritt and Argent already had enough experience of her to detect a ready heat bubbling just below the surface. Yesterday's unpleasantness still reverberated through her.

Argent sat in the chair to M's right while Merritt sat on the cedar chest at the foot of the bed. After an awkward moment of silence, Argent expressed pleasure at seeing M feeling so well as to leave bed.

Merritt was watching M again, as he had so long ago in her front room. Uncontrollably and illogically, she began to feel the need to check her left shoulder for a sagging dress. She fussed at the sling on her shoulder. M made a genuine attempt at pleasant conversation. "It seems very pleasant out today." M nodded towards the only window in the room.

Argent looked over to the window; how had she managed to open it? Merritt, however, ignored the offer to inspect the weather; his gaze on her remained constant. Argent rose to close the window. "It is pleasant out, but this may prove too drafty for you."

"Please leave it open – I enjoy the fresh air." There was a hint of irritation in her voice.

Argent returned to his seat. He repeated, "It is pleasant out."

"I need to find my shoes. I would like to go out and enjoy the weather; sunshine always raises my spirits, and I have been too long indoors."

"I've never known a lack of shoes to be an impediment to you."

Argent immediately forestalled any further encouragement, no matter how cynical, of walking outside. "I don't think trying her health out of doors is the appropriate course at this time."

"She has no intention of trying the outdoors. She enjoys trying our patience."

This was not how Argent thought they would be approaching Miss Warner. They were to be coaxing her into compliance, not stoking her ire.

"Apparently I don't have to try very hard. I hope asking when you intend to leave won't tax your patience too much."

Argent attempted to cool the sudden heat in the room. "We'll be staying a little longer. We promised Mrs. Lambert to help Mr. Darnell with some of the more burdensome chores in exchange for her hospitality."

"Fortunately, you have this very pleasant day in which to accomplish your chores. Perhaps we'll see each other in the course of our separate outdoor activities." As long as Miss Warner's shoes remained in the barn, where Merritt had taken them before leaving for Cumberland, all her talk of outdoor excursions remained just talk. They could afford to indulge her in this desire as long as it could not be fulfilled.

As agreed, Merritt returned to the thorny discussion of yesterday; today, he would be the target for all her anger and bile. "We would be happy to conduct a search of the house for your shoes, but after we have settled the business between us. We were interrupted yesterday by Mrs. Lambert." Merritt paused a moment, allowing M to recall that moment when Argent had called her childish and defiant; though it had been poorly timed and recklessly worded, it had been true, and Merritt wanted M to reflect on them. M, however, showed no reaction at all. "We still hope to see you safely to Washington, but if you are inflexibly opposed to this, we intend to see you safely back home. But either way, we need to regain the train, waiting for us at a siding not far from here. And either way, I hope we can part amicably."

M had been watching Merritt intently, looking for any signs of duplicity, and finding none, she turned to study Argent. He was beginning to accept this gaze, not as a sign of rudeness, but as a sign of an intense desire to understand the person under her gaze. She abruptly broke her gaze from Argent, and returning to Merritt, she said simply, "Agreed." Like Argent, she had realized that the tone of yesterday's conversation did not serve her interests; she would be agreeable until it no longer suited her purposes.

Merritt clapped his hands lightly. "Now, would you like to step outside? I'm sure your shoes can be found."

After the shoes were retrieved and after a prolonged, one-handed struggle to secure her shoes to her feet, the men escorted M outside into the barnyard. She absolutely refused to take the arm of either man, and walked, fairly steadily, under her own power. Emmett was enjoying his leisure time in the field across from the house. Merritt whistled, and both his horse and Emmett raised their heads. Merritt called for Emmett, but at first the horse ignored him, feigning not to have heard his name. He remained standing, staring past the barn while he lazily chewed the fresh greens of the field. Merritt called again, and this time, after a shorter interval of rude disregard, Emmett walked to the fence. M was a little jealous at Merritt's ease with Emmett — that Emmett had come at all made her resent Merritt's care of her horse.

She forgave Emmett's betrayal, tenderly stroking his great nose and head, speaking quietly to him, words that neither Argent nor Merritt could make out. Emmett was not, generally speaking, an emotional horse, and when he had had enough of M's attentions, he trotted back to his original position, and resumed the contemplation of his surroundings. M leaned a long time on the fence rail, watching Emmett, then turned her head on the rail, full to the sun, and closed her eyes.

The sun was warm on her cheek and she felt herself quiet and peaceful, even in the presence of Merritt and Argent. She was aware that they had moved away; she could hear boards of lumber being dropped one upon the other as the men moved them from some place in the yard to stack them against the barn. It was a pleasant noise, a familiar noise, and in her dozing, she was back on her farm, and her father and Mr. Henry were stacking wood against the barn there. They would be replacing the roof of the barn soon. The disgruntled voice of the widow broke the spell. M rolled her eyes beneath her lids, then opened them to see Merritt and Argent, suspended in their work with the lumber, watch the widow stride across the barnyard.

"What do you think you're about, walking around with your shoulder barely healed, the stitches still in?"

M raised her head from the railing and blinked at Mrs. Lambert once, twice, three times. Past Mrs. Lambert, M could see Merritt and Argent walking towards her. They arrived just in time to hear M transfer the widow's anger to the men.

"I tried to tell them we should consult with you first, but you know how men are – they always know what's best, even when there's an acknowledged authority right in front of them. My brothers were all like that. But, please don't be angry with them. I did express a wish for fresh air, and I feel much stronger for it."

Mrs. Lambert did indeed transfer her anger to the men, Argent in particular, turning to glare at him, but she did not address either Argent or Merritt. She said to the barnyard in general, "Dinner will be ready soon." Then she turned back to M and grudgingly admitted that M did seem better. "I've certainly never heard you say more than two words at a time."

"I know I've been very fortunate in your care, and it is to your credit that I'm able to stand here in the sunshine so soon. It would be the very epitome of my convalescence if I could take my dinner outside."

Merritt very nearly rolled his eyes at such an ingratiating manner, especially, for some reason, from M.

"You do seem better and there is finally some color in your cheek. I'll have my daughter bring your dinner out here to you. The gentlemen can join you." Argent sighed; the widow was still in a snit over the chloral, though clearly M was sleeping better and, as the widow had observed, there was some color in M's cheeks.

"Yes, ma'am; that would be delightful." Merritt smiled and bowed as Mrs. Lambert swept past them.

Merritt waited until Mrs. Lambert was in the house before he slowly turned to face M, who was leaning smugly against the railing and sporting a wickedly triumphant smile.

Argent watched both Merritt and M as they observed each other, a little jealous at some unspoken understanding. Merritt finally smiled and extended his arm to M. Her jubilant smirk broadened and transformed into a genuine smile at the gesture, not of social convention, but of acknowledgment of a well-scored point. M took Merritt's arm, and as they passed Argent, she winked at him.

Merritt steered M towards a small trestle table under the soft, early-season shade of a tree near the house, but M had spotted a crude swing hanging from another tree nearby, and this is where she seated herself. Merritt and Argent then resumed their work transferring the lumber from a jumbled heap near the kitchen garden to a neat stack near the barn. M wondered at the intended use for the lumber, though, in truth, everything was in need of repair. M also wondered that Mr. Darnell would allow Merritt and Argent to do all his work for him. He had seemed more considerate than that; he had brought her newspapers from Old Town.

It was not long before Miss Lambert called the men to dinner. It was surprisingly large and varied meal, but, Merritt had to remind himself, it was Sunday and Sunday meals were always the capstone to the week. Miss Lambert made several trips, some of them obvious attempts to pay special attention to Merritt. They had seen little of her mother since the unfortunate clash of wills Friday evening, but Miss Lambert had seemed to be always nearby, available and willing to see to their every need. She had been particularly flattered by the reticule, mentioning it often. Argent had warned Merritt that Miss Lambert had possibly misinterpreted the meaning of the gift; gaudy and refractive gifts seemed to indicate to the ladies an unspoken contract. In truth, Merritt had simply sought to soften his earlier rudeness to Miss Lambert when he had taken the slip of paper from her, without a word.

It was obvious after several trips between the house and the table that Miss Lambert had no more food to bring out, nor utensils, nor pitchers of milk or water, but still she hovered near the table. Finally, Argent asked Miss Lambert to join them, and she happily sat next to Merritt. She had conveniently slipped an extra plate under Mr. Merritt's and this she now retrieved for her own use.

M sat on the bench directly in front of the tree, and occasionally she leaned back against its trunk. Argent took note. Occasionally, he stole a glance at her as Merritt and Miss Lambert chatted. She seemed suddenly tired, though she still had color – perhaps too much color; but she was making an effort to eat.

Every now and again Argent added to the small talk, but his attention was largely on Miss Warner, whose usual silence had taken on a worrying aspect – she was staring dully and though she held her fork in her hand she had stopped eating.

Miss Lambert addressed M twice before M roused. "I beg pardon?"

"I said, I'm so glad you are doing better. Mr. Merritt tells me you are on your way to Washington City. That must be so exciting. What will you do there?"

Miss Lambert was, for some reason, speaking slowly and a little loudly. M wondered if she was a little slow. She certainly giggled incessantly at Merritt, an undoubtable sign of low intelligence. M hated to admit it to herself, but she was very tired, and she did not care to make the effort at pleasant banter.

"Initially, the purpose of the trip was to see the President, but my plans have changed."

"The President! How wonderful for you! But could you be sure of an audience? He's awfully busy, running the country."

M was already tired of this ninny but recognized her debt to Mrs. Lambert and her daughter. She made a valiant effort to remain civil and patient.

"Yes, an audience was assured; I was traveling there at his insistence. I'm sure he wanted to discuss matters of great importance with me." This last bit of sarcasm, M could not help, but it was not directed at the daughter.

"I'm sure he did, and I'm sure you'll make it to Washington eventually. Isn't that right, Mr. Merritt?" She was simpering at him, which M found tiresome. Everything was becoming tiresome.

M answered for Mr. Merritt. "Not likely. Traveling doesn't agree with me."

"Well, that's the beauty of pretending, isn't it? You just go on to the next dream."

"Pretend?" M looked curiously at Merritt and Argent and noticed that both men were looking at their plates. She was missing something here, but she was just too tired to ferret it out. This girl was pitiably unsophisticated.

"Oh, there's nothing at all wrong with it. I wish I had your imagination." At this last, Miss Lambert reached across the table as if to comfortingly pat M's right hand, but being unable to reach it, she patted the table in front of M instead. Miss Lambert then turned to beam at Merritt, who continued to stare at his plate. "You can imagine yourself wearing just the best dresses and jewels, and never spend a penny. And you'll never have to worry about the dangers of traveling, either, like those desperate men who escaped from Moundsville just the other day."

At this, Merritt and Argent both looked up. Moundsville was being mentioned quite a bit of late.

"No one escaped from Moundsville." M had read the newspaper from town about the uprising at Moundsville Penitentiary and the plot to escape *en masse* of nearly fifty convicts. But an inmate informed on them and the plot was foiled. There was only one injury, one of the conspiring convicts was shot and seriously injured by someone in a town mob gathered at the prison. The two guards who were overpowered and stripped of their uniforms, of course, suffered injured pride. But the story running wild over the AP wires was the only thing that escaped from Moundsville.

Apparently, Miss Lambert had not read the recent newspaper; where had she gotten her information in the first place?

"Oh, but someone did!"

"Not according to the paper from town." M did not like having her facts disputed.

Miss Lambert sucked in her breath, and after what appeared to be a moment of panic, said, "You must be right. But even so, you are very lucky to have these two gentlemen to protect you from other dangers of travel, whether you are going to Washington or just the next town over, or whether you have lovely jewels or a pair of worn out shoes."

M was completely at a loss and could only stare at the girl across the table. Apparently, Miss Lambert's performance for Mr. Merritt was concluded; she withdrew her hand, and asked Merritt if she could get him anything else. She sighed and said before leaving, "I'm afraid I live in the humdrum world of chores and plain dresses. You're such a lucky girl."

M leaned back against the tree, and closing her eyes, said, "She's fortunate she's pretty – marriage will save her from starving, unless she can pretend up some other means of living."

It was a mean, spiteful thing to say, especially about a young woman who had opened her home to all three of them and who had helped M in her incapacity. For once, Argent was willing to ignore M's bad manners. He was more interested in the newspapers M had been reading. The newspapers they had seen lying on M's bed had aroused no curiosity in either man until this moment, when M had recent information regarding the prison break at Moundsville.

"Miss Warner, how did you come by the newspapers in your room?"

M opened her eyes and turned her head to consider Argent. Then, as if answering some other question, she said, "Oh, because of what those men said at the canal." She closed her eyes again and dismissed the subject. "No one came from Moundsville because no one escaped."

Argent looked expectantly at Merritt to try his luck. "Yes, but, M, where did you get the newspapers? How did you get newspapers so soon after such a recent event?" News, and newspapers, traveled freely up and down the canal and along the tracks, but the Lambert house was set well back from either, and could not expect to see fresh newspapers on anything like a regular basis.

This time M did not bother to open her eyes. "Mr. Darnell brought them back from Old Town yesterday." M crinkled her brow in disbelief at her own words. "No, three days ago. He knew I was bored lying in bed all day. He said he would bring more today."

Darnell had gone to Old Town early last Sunday, an innocent trip in search of coffee for unexpected guests. But more deliberate reflection would question the need to go so early when it was likely no stores were open until after the conclusion of Sunday services, if at all on a Sunday, especially in such a small town where Sundays were sacrosanct. Trips for supplies were the tasks of weekdays, when stores were sure to be open and business was expected to be conducted. Moreover, having just gone to Old Town for supplies on Sunday, why would he need to return again so soon as Thursday? And where was Darnell now? He had taken the Lamberts to town for church, but he had not been seen since their return.

Argent signaled to Merritt an end to further questioning Miss Warner. They quietly left the table to resume their work in the yard. They did not speak of Darnell, though they kept an eye out for him. Argent, in addition, kept on eye on Miss Warner. After such a propitious beginning to her recovery, she seemed to be faltering. He should not have allowed her to leave her bed, no matter how adamant she was nor how large a leverage it was in exacting a promise from her.

Miss Lambert had left some time ago, taking her own plate in with her, but she had not returned to gather the other plates and dishes. It was her mother who performed this chore, and it seemed to Argent that she was not particularly quiet about it, especially given that M was dozing against the tree, at the table. Finally, M stirred, and the widow complained loudly that M had not made a better effort to eat, that she had wasted good food. Both Argent and Merritt stopped in mid-stoop as they were raising a board. Argent was furious that Mrs. Lambert should visit on M the spleen she felt for himself. Argent laid down his end of the board and walked over to the table. He meant to shield M from the widow's bad temper. Merritt followed, determined to shield the widow from Argent.

What both men heard surprised them.

"You did not eat your meat on Friday and precious little yesterday and again today you have eaten none. It is meat that gives you strength. And now you are out here doing greater mischief to your injury. You can blame none but yourself if your recovery is slow. I, for one, would have your recovery speedily done."

M looked truly contrite and chastened and a little confused. "I am very sorry. I mean no insult to your cooking or your efforts. I had thought my appetite returned yesterday, but today it has left me again. But on Fridays, I must refrain from meat. I should have told you."

The widow was in the motion of lifting a dish from the table, but at M's confession, she stopped. After a long pause, she asked, "You are Romish, then?"

"Romish? Not at all; I am Kentuckian."

M's attempt to deflect the coming prejudice fell flat. The widow rephrased her question. "You're a papist, then?"

M's gaze was unfocused as she looked across the table to the field beyond. She blinked – once, twice, three times – then turned to look up at Mrs. Lambert and corrected her. "Catholic."

The two women regarded each other, unflinchingly, for a long moment, then the widow retreated into her house.

M announced to no one in particular, "I will sleep with Emmett tonight."

Merritt sat across from her. "I am sorry."

M sat very still, staring at the field where Emmett grazed, unbothered by M's religious affiliations. M was aware, of course, of the murderous anti-Catholic rioting in Louisville more than a dozen years ago, but she had been very young and had no personal memory of it. But, occasionally, echoes of the Know Nothing Party were heard; recently, there had been rumblings in Cincinnati between Catholics and Protestants there regarding which Bible, if any, should be used in public schools. Protestants were suspicious of the separate Catholic schools, incubators, they were certain, of popish propaganda, and Catholics who did not send their children to these incubators resented that their children were subjected to the heretical King James Bible. M did not know if it had all been resolved – reading about it to her father had upset him in those last weeks and months, and she had not bothered to pick up the thread after he died. She was aware of the extreme prejudice and even hatred many in the country bore towards her faith, but she had little personal experience of it. As if she had said all this out loud, she continued, almost as a confession, "I stay within Catholic circles, my acquaintances are Catholic, I patronize Catholic merchants – mostly because they are parish members and I know them. I never thought to ask you if traveling with me, with a Catholic, would cause problems or if it was personally objectionable to you. And for that I am sorry, and also for not considering your own religious needs, if you would like to stop on a Sunday to visit your own churches. I meant no disrespect; it was only ignorance born of habit. I am rarely with anyone who isn't Catholic."

Now Argent sat at the table, but this time to her right. "M, we served with many Catholics in the war, and they were some of the bravest soldiers, on either side. Most of them were as pious as you could wish, praying daily and often. And the priests who came to the battlefields knelt down by Catholic and Protestant alike as they lay dying or said a prayer over them after death had claimed them. The only one guilty of ignorance are those who hate without knowing or understanding. But I will not see you sleep in a filthy barn because of some woman's bile."

"It is best not to stir things up any further. I have slept with Emmett before."

"We will come to some arrangement with Mrs. Lambert. As soon as you are able to travel, we will politely and quietly take our leave."

M brought her gaze to focus on Merritt. "Does Washington feel the same way? Did my father work among such suspicion and hatred and fear?"

Merritt managed to say convincingly "Washington is much less concerned with religion. Mr. Warner did not labor under any such bigotry."

M continued to search Merritt's face, then apparently accepted what he said. "He worked hard for this country. He was absent from home often in its service. I would hate to know that he could be so ill-used that this nation would take his energy and intelligence by day and repay him with hatred for his faith by night."

Argent took M's right hand as much to comfort her as to feel her pulse. "I can only tell you, Miss Warner, that not everyone feels as the widow does, and that Merritt and I don't feel that way. Your faith never gave us a moment's pause, and I hope you never feel unsure of our help in seeing you to services on Sundays or any other days of religious importance to you."

M did not answer but returned to gazing at Emmett in the field.

"Miss Warner?"

M pulled her gaze back to Merritt and retrieved her hand from Argent. "I am sure of you. I don't want to keep you from your promises to Mrs. Lambert."

Argent stood. "Let me take you in to rest."

M shook her head. "No, I am truly enjoying being outside. I'll go in later, if she'll let me, when the day is done. I'll decide tomorrow what I'm going to do." There was no rancor in her voice, only fatigue and finality.

Merritt and Argent finished transferring the lumber to the barn, then fixed some broken fencing and cleared brush around the kitchen garden. The sun sank behind the woods beyond the farm's few fields, tingeing the sky behind the widow's house with soft purple and pink and bright orange. Merritt and Argent cleaned up at the pump, rinsing and wringing out their shirts. They had thought it safe to do so, they had thought M returned to sleep, but as they approached the table, they saw that she was awake and waiting for them. There was the real possibility that she had seen them stripped to the waist, but she said nothing about it.

Someone had removed the remaining dishes from the table, though neither man had seen it happen. The air had grown cool, but M insisted she was not cold, nor was she tired or hungry. In the fading light, Argent could not tell if she spoke the truth.

Merritt sat at the table and kept M company while Argent went inside to bargain with Mrs. Lambert as to M's immediate future on the farm. It was inconceivable that the woman would deny a sick person succor simply based on a religious difference, but despite Merritt's and Argent's words of comfort, both men knew of brutal instances where religion decided between basic respect and indifferent neglect and intentional harm, between who died and who lived.

M was curiously quiet. She answered Merritt when he spoke to her, but her voice was softer than usual and there was a quality to it that Merritt could not quite pin down. She was calm, resigned, wistful.

Argent returned in a happy mood. He assured M that everything was fine; Mrs. Lambert had softened since her earlier reflexive comments and had agreed to allow them to stay as long as they needed. Argent studiously avoided Merritt's questioning glances. The two men helped M to her room and even arranged the pillows so that she might sit up a little in bed. She thanked them, and when they promised to be back with supper, so that they could take their meal together, she earnestly begged them to eat without her – being back in bed made her suddenly feel sleepy, and she did not want them to wait on her to eat. Again, Merritt noticed a calm resignation tinged with sadness. Argent promised to look in on her later. M merely nodded in response.

In their bedroom, Argent told Merritt that the widow was intractable – M had to leave the next morning; she would have not have papists under her roof. She had done all she could for them and now they must go. Despite her sudden dislike for M, Mrs. Lambert was curiously concerned about M's wound. She urged, repeatedly, that they should return to Cumberland where a proper doctor could oversee her continued convalescence. That they must go was settled; where they should go seemed to cause her great apprehension, but Argent could not elicit anything else from her.

Miss Lambert knocked to let them know a small supper was on the table for them. She hoped that there would be nothing else they needed as she and her mother were retiring for the evening. It was a vastly different Miss Lambert who spoke to them at their door than who had joined them at the trestle table just hours ago. Argent's only request was that Miss Lambert make certain that Miss Warner receive her medication for the night.

Argent looked in on M one last time before he himself retired for the evening. She had fallen asleep as they had left her, except that she had managed to kick off her shoes. Argent covered her with the blankets that Merritt had turned down when they had brought her to the room. Before he turned down the lamp, Argent shut the window against the night air, then shut the door as he left the room.

25

Merritt and Argent were up before first light, saddling the horses and making last minute preparations. Mrs. Lambert was absent again, but Miss Lambert made herself completely available to the men and Miss Warner. She had breakfast ready and on the table when the men came in from the barn and field, with plenty of strong, hot coffee. While they ate, she changed the dressing on M's shoulder, helped her dress for the day, fixing her hair in a simple braid, and finally, rearranging the sling on her shoulder. M's jacket, brushed as clean as possible of the muck from the canal and still sporting blood stains, lay on the edge of the bed. Roomy enough on any other day, it had nevertheless proven too closely-fitted to pull over M's sore arm.

Everything had been conducted in almost complete silence. Merritt and Argent said very little, even to each other, but even those few words were spoken in low tones, in deference to some crouching presence that was sensitive to noise. The usually spritely and talkative Miss Lambert remained largely mute, speaking only to say that she would attend to Miss Warner, before leaving the men to their breakfast. And there had been no word at all – of or from – Darnell.

Argent, therefore, felt as if he had broken some code or indulged in some irreverence when he spoke aloud in Miss Warner's room. "Miss Warner, are you ready? We are leaving early today."

Upon knocking and then entering her room, Argent had found her fully dressed, but barely awake. She was sitting on the side of the bed nearest the door. She had not acknowledged Argent's knock nor his entrance, but at his voice, she looked up dully at him. "Mr. Merritt has hidden my shoes again."

Argent looked down at her feet and saw that she indeed was without shoes. "I see them." Last night, he had left them near the bed but now they were under one of the chairs; Mrs. Lambert must have looked in on M during the night and moved them. Argent retrieved the shoes and, kneeling on one knee, began to work the shoes onto her feet. M roused enough to protest such help; she even tried to push him away, but she was too weak to budge him in the least. Argent said nothing but finished as quickly as he could. As he made the last fastening, Argent spied M's grip bag under the bed, and pulled it out, bringing it up with him as he rose. After her first protest, M had become quiet again, but at the sight of her grip bag, she became agitated until Argent set it on the bed next to her.

Miss Lambert returned to the room, with a cup that she then handed to M. Spying the bag on the bed, Miss Lambert opened it and wrestled with it to make room for the useless jacket. M had not moved since she had been handed the cup and now Miss Lambert knelt in front of her and urged her to drink its contents. The first sip did not agree with M, but Miss Lambert pushed the cup against M's lips and persuaded her to drink it all. "It will help you endure the ride to the train."

Argent carried M's bag with one hand and with the other he guided her out of the house and into the yard where their horses were waiting for them. It was still dark, but Miss Lambert followed them a few minutes later, carrying a lantern and a package. Merritt had managed to set up a series of steps and had tied Emmett to the fence railing next to them. Of the few things discussed this morning was the determination that Argent should ride with M on Emmett, large enough and powerful enough to carry the both of them the entire distance to the train.

Argent handed M's bag to Merritt to secure behind Emmett's saddle. He mounted first, then waited as Merritt helped M up the steps. While Merritt steadied M on her right, Argent helped guide her left leg over the saddle horn. Argent did not approve of women riding astride, but this would cause M far less pain than if she were to ride side-saddle in front of him. It would also be far easier on him, as he tried to manage Emmett and keep M from falling off. Miss Lambert's draught had turned M's initial dullness into grogginess, a worrisome state on a horse.

Argent shifted a little in the saddle, feeling for the best position, then gently pushed M forward, allowing himself as much room as possible on such a crowded saddle.

"This is not my saddle." M's speech was slurred, but she was confident in her statement.

"No, I prefer my own."

"But this is Emmett. My saddle should be on Emmett."

Argent gave her the simplest excuse that would cause the least objections from her. "My horse has thrown a shoe. I thought we could ride together."

It seemed perfectly reasonable to M, and she gave her assent by a mere, "Oh."

Miss Lambert had remained nearby, holding the lantern high all the while. Now, with Argent and M settled on Emmett and while Merritt mounted his own horse, she moved closer to speak with Argent. She stood looking up at him for a moment before abruptly mounting the steps. As she leaned in to lay a package in M's lap, she whispered to Argent, "Please take Miss Warner and yourselves to Cumberland. Mother says it means Miss Warner's life." Then she pressed into his hand what appeared to be a sachet, tied with a delicate ribbon. At Argent's questioning look, Miss Lambert explained, "The chloral; you left it on the nightstand."

Argent could hardly remonstrate with the daughter for the actions of the mother, but he thought bitterly that if Mrs. Lambert was truly concerned for M's welfare, she would not have forced such an ill-timed removal; it was obvious now that after a promising beginning to M's recovery, she was suffering some reversal. M should be in bed, but if she was forced to ride, it would have to be to the closer source of help – it was some fifteen miles to Cumberland but, by their best estimates, Little Cacapon bridge was less than ten. M would have to endure today in the saddle, then they would see her comfortable on the train. Most importantly, she would be on her way to Washington where Grant could procure for her the best medical help.

Argent merely nodded, pocketed the chloral, and then handed the package to Merritt to his left. As they turned out of the yard to the dirt drive between the house and the kitchen garden, Argent glanced back and saw the widow standing in the doorway, watching.

The sky was fully light by the time they reached Spring Gap, though the sun had yet to make its appearance above the trees. They were through Spring Gap before they realized they had entered it, and now began the long ride to Old Town. They, of necessity, set a slow pace, aware that every step of Emmett's would jar M's wound and that a faster pace would only increase her misery. A long ride was thus made longer; it was a full five hours before they reached Old Town.

Not all of that time, however, was spent in the saddle. M had made a valiant effort to sit up straight in front of Argent, but Miss Lambert's draught was pulling her forward to slump. As soon as they left the Lambert yard, Argent had offered to M, "Lean back, if you like," but M had resisted the offer. Just before they turned onto Old Town road, at the end of the long lane that led from the widow's home, M finally succumbed to the draught and she slowly sank against Argent's chest, and, just as slowly, her head drooped forward. Argent had then slipped his left arm around her waist, just under the sling, to keep her in position, and with this hand he pulled the flap of his coat around her right shoulder and arm to provide some warmth against the chilly morning air. M slept soundly for much of the time, occasionally rousing enough to ask a question, but often falling back into a doze before hearing or registering the answer; she sometimes asked the same question in between stretches of sleep. They had traveled roughly halfway to Old Town when M sat up suddenly, almost butting Argent's chin with the back of her head. She began furiously patting Argent's right hand on the reins, and commanded, almost in a panic, "Let me down! Let me down!"

M barely waited for Emmett to stop before she flung her right leg over Emmett's head, wiggled out from Argent's grip around her waist, and slid from the horse. She nearly collapsed as she reached the ground, but she immediately righted herself and ran to the woods on the side of the road. Argent dismounted and, throwing the reins to Merritt, followed her. He found her, crouching next to a young tree, her right arm encircling it for balance, as her stomach revolted in one dry heave after another. Argent could do nothing but stand helplessly nearby, praying that the spell would pass quickly. After several minutes, the body-wracking spasms slowed and finally ceased altogether. M leaned her head against the tree, still hugging it one-armed, exhausted from the exertion.

Argent returned to the road, where Merritt silently handed him one of the two canteens they purchased in Cumberland and filled at the widow's pump. M dropped into a sitting position, though she still clung to the tree for support and as a head rest. She was still breathing heavily when Argent returned. He pulled from one of his many coat pockets a handkerchief, folded though not as clean as when he had first placed a small stack in the pocket many days ago. He poured a little of the precious water onto the handkerchief, thoroughly wetting it, then handed it, dripping and still folded, to M. She had to release her hold on the sapling to accept it, but she was grateful to be able to wipe her face and mouth. Turning it over to the cleaner side, she held the wet cloth to her forehead. When her breathing calmed, Argent handed her the canteen. At first, M drank tentatively, uncertain if her stomach would tolerate even water, but then her thirst took over and she drank lustily.

"Slowly, M." But she was already resting the canteen on her knee, the mere act of drinking having tired her.

Behind him, Argent heard Merritt bring the horses just inside the woods, securing them against wandering. In a moment, Merritt was standing just behind him. "There is a comfortable log just a few yards away."

M handed the canteen to Argent and began to haul herself up, using the sapling for support. Argent, in turn, handed the canteen to Merritt, then helped M to her feet, supporting her as Merritt led them to his comfortable log. It was indeed an agreeable place to sit, the log having fallen and settled next to a rather large rock, creating a backrest for the weary.

M sat on the log, leaning against the rock, occasionally wiping her face, folding the cloth over and over to find a cool spot. Argent noticed her hands shook as she did so.

Argent sat on the log next to her, but Merritt remained standing, dividing his attention between M and the horses. They remained this way for some minutes until M broke the silence.

"Where are we going?"

Merritt glanced at Argent; he had heard M ask this question more than once already. Merritt decided it was his turn to answer. He crouched in front of M, so that she would not have to look up. "We're going to meet the train, at a siding not far from here."

"How far have we come?"

Merritt again looked to Argent. They were about halfway to Old Town which was itself about halfway to Little Cacapon; they were making miserable time. Merritt did not like lying to M, but he did not want to burden her either. He opted for a half-truth. "Not quite halfway."

M closed her eyes in disappointment and dread of more nauseating time in the saddle. She resumed folding and refolding the handkerchief, though she no longer wiped her face.

Argent suspected the reason for M's reaction. "We can rest here as long as you like, but when you are ready to continue, I have more of the medicine. It seemed to help you sleep through the worst of the ride."

M carefully shook her head. "I think it was the drink that made me sick. I may not make it off Emmett fast enough the next time."

Argent gravely considered this possibility, especially since he will be sharing with Emmett the danger of M's sudden sickness. "Well, we'll return to that later." Argent took the handkerchief from M then held out his hand to Merritt for the canteen. He first handed the canteen to M, allowing her to take a few sips. Retrieving the canteen, he rinsed the handkerchief clean.

As he was returning the cloth to M, she asked, "Did Mrs. Lambert have a change of heart?"

Argent was caught off his guard and covered his momentary surprise by carefully corking the canteen. "Not at all. Merritt and I knew how much you wanted to be on your way. The time seemed right to catch our train, so to speak."

"You must put more effort into your lies, Mr. Argent, if you wish to deceive."

Argent made an unnecessary show of sitting up straighter; though he had indeed lied to Miss Warner, he did not like for her to think him a liar. Most women would know to accept the fiction as a kindness and let it pass, but Miss Warner was blunt in her comments, one of her many social shortcomings.

"Oh, you're not hearing him at his best." Merritt was smiling broadly, as much at M's brazen critique of Argent's aptitude for falsehoods as at Argent's indignation. "In Cincinnati, he convinced a lonely widow that he loved her and courted her hand in marriage."

Argent's indignation quickly transformed to one of warning anger. "That was in the line of duty, and well you know it."

"Oh, yes, the Widow Rogers. I have heard this story before." M did not sound interested in hearing it again.

"Not all of it, not the better portion, by far."

Merritt's obvious anticipation of the story distracted M from her fatigue and the ache in her shoulder. "Oh?"

Rather than let Merritt embellish the tale, as he had so often done in the retelling of it among their colleagues, Argent stepped in to take control of the narrative. He turned full to M to explain. "The Widow Rogers, if you will remember, ran a successful and injurious counterfeiting ring in Cincinnati, and it fell to my lot – it was my duty, my unpleasant duty – to gain her confidence in any way possible in order to infiltrate the ring."

Argent was certain that such toying with a woman's affections – even though the woman was a criminal – would cause Miss Warner discomfort, as well as inspire a natural affinity with the abused woman. However, after a moment's search of his face, Miss Warner burst out laughing, a most unseemly reaction. Argent was grateful they were in the seclusion of a woods on the side of a lightly traveled road. His indignation deepened and did not subside even as Miss Warner's laughter diminished to a silent shaking of her body.

Merritt was grinning at him foolishly, which provoked Argent into an outburst of his own. "The woman practically threw herself at me. At one point, I thought she was going to disrobe right there in her front parlor." Argent stabbed the air in front of him, as if the parlor were there to confirm his fears.

At this, M held her stomach and laughed silently until tears came into her eyes, both from the story itself and from the pain the act of such intense laughing caused in both her shoulder and her raw stomach.

Now Merritt took over the story. "We had settled ahead of time on an alarm to signal for help – a bobwhite call that Argent is particularly good at. He must have whistled bobwhite a dozen times and as loud as he could. We all thought he was at gun point, but when we burst into the widow's parlor, it was just him and the widow and her bustle full of counterfeit notes. Argent was practically cowering by the door."

"I was not cowering. I was maintaining a respectful distance." Argent's petulance was something M had not heard before and it redoubled her glee.

It was evidently a well-worn tale, for Argent wore the look of a man weary and used to the laughter. M shook even harder with laughter, and finally gasped out, "Please, stop."

Argent finally joined Merritt in grinning, enjoying M's good humor despite the ride, the wound, and the vomiting.

When she finally regained her breath, M patted Argent's knee, consolingly. "You should be proud of your work. Besides, I suspect the job fell to you because your charms are utterly inescapable."

Given her general and stated disregard for himself and Merritt, this was an obvious bit of social fiction on M's part. Argent, however, accepted it and beamed at M, and gloated a little at Merritt.

"It is a shame you couldn't be more successful with this late widow."

Argent's disapproval of Mrs. Lambert bubbled to the surface. "I don't think I could muster the stomach it would take to even falsely court that woman."

M's good humor extended even to the Widow Lambert. "Oh, don't be too hard on her. All her bile is wasted on me. She should have waited for a better Catholic to despise."

"A better Catholic?" Merritt's smile had faded somewhat, but now it was mixed with a challenging confusion.

"Almost any Catholic is better than I."

"How so?" Argent, too, seemed to challenge M's assessment of herself.

M regretted making the observation and the comparison, and sought to change the subject. "Oh, just accept my word on the matter. I hope this unscheduled stop has given the horses a chance to rest and eat a little. Should we be on our way?"

Merritt rose from his crouch and looked toward the horses. They were enjoying the tender green shoots, but they should be allowed to drink at the next creek or water source. "Do you feel ready to ride again?"

"Yes, I think I can manage Emmett now."

"That is not what I asked. You may ride either with me or with Mr. Argent."

M sighed, though she was inwardly grateful that Merritt had denied her the option of riding alone. The thought of riding at all exhausted and nauseated her. "Unless he needs a rest from the extra burden, I shall stay with Mr. Argent. He has gotten me this far, and Emmett seems accustomed to him."

Merritt brought Emmett to the log, and Argent steadied M as she stood on the log, the better to reach the stirrup and haul herself up. Even so, it took both men to help M settle in the saddle. M started to kick her foot free of the stirrup to allow Argent to mount, but he laid a hand on her foot. As he shortened M's stirrup, he said, "I think I would like to walk for a bit. Emmett could use a rest from double riders and I could use a stretch of my legs." Argent nodded to Merritt on the other side of the horse and M felt him shorten the other stirrup and place her foot in it. "You will let us know when you can no longer sit the saddle." It was more of a command than a request.

The story of Argent and the Widow Rogers had lifted M's spirits and she had truly thought she could finish the trip without too much help from either man. But now her general discomfort was not dulled by Miss Lambert's draught, and despite her best efforts, small groans or gasps sometimes escaped her. Argent walked beside Emmett, always close enough to grab the reins or Miss Warner if the need should arise. Merritt rode a little farther ahead, trailing Argent's horse after him. After only an hour, however, Argent called to Merritt that it was time to halt for their meal. Merritt raised his hand in acknowledgement and kicked his horse into a slightly faster pace, to scout up ahead for a likely place to stop.

It was more than half an hour before Argent and M caught up with Merritt at the intersection with some private farm road. There was a creek that ran nearby, easily accessible for the horses, but just as important, there was a stone ledge over a shallow, (currently) dry tributary to the creek where M could sit comfortably in the shade.

M was stiff and pale when the men helped her off Emmett. She did not answer Merritt when he asked how she did, but he took no offense. While Argent did his best to make M comfortable, Merritt took the horses down to the stream for a long drink. The day had warmed considerably, and in the sun, it was hot, but in this deep shade, M shivered a little. Argent laid his coat over her shoulders, but she did not acknowledge it or thank him. She seemed uninterested in what he was doing, allowing him to move her and adjust her into a comfortable position. M merely obeyed Argent when she heard, "Lean back, if you like." Her eyes were closed but she was not sleeping. Her mouth was drawn tight, and Argent knew she was gritting her teeth.

Merritt returned from settling the horses along the bank of the creek. He removed his coat as well and, doubling it twice, placed it behind M's head. He then took from M the handkerchief that she had been clutching since their last stop. He rinsed it clean in the cold waters of the creek, then returned it to her hand. M never opened her eyes, never acknowledged Merritt's kindness nor thanked him for it.

Merritt and Argent spoke quietly of nothing in particular – of the pleasant spot for their lunch, of the (exaggerated) progress made so far in their trip to the train, of anticipating Mrs. Hughes' cooking. The package that Miss Lambert had given Argent, and that Merritt had cradled in his lap for the entire ride, was found to include several smaller packages of food rolled in rude napkins, all of them wrapped together in a small cloth, which Merritt now spread on the stone ledge as a kind of table cloth. One by one the smaller packages were unrolled, and the different foods revealed and spread on the cloth. There was bread and cold meats, dried fruits packed in a tin cup, boiled eggs, and a huge slab of loaf cake. Argent stepped down to the horses and relieved them of the canteens. He dumped the warm, hours-old water, replacing it with the clear, cold water of the creek. He handed a canteen to Merritt and kept one for himself, to share with M.

Argent pulled from his coat yet another handkerchief and, using it as a kind of plate, placed food on it for M and laid it at her side. At both his and Merritt's urging, M managed to eat most of it, but she drank far more than she ate. She seemed always to be thirsty of late.

They stayed at the creek for some time, enjoying the lull of the moving water, the cool shade, and their simple meal. M said nothing, but she was aware of the men talking and of their movements as one or the other left the stone ledge to attend to the horses or refill the canteens. Eventually, M dozed, an uneaten piece of loaf cake in her hand.

Argent roused M and convinced her to try the medicine again. It was his opinion that she would be able to tolerate it better, now that she had something on her stomach. M mechanically took the proffered tin cup of water mixed with medicine and drank it down without any further prompting from Argent.

Merritt brought Emmett to the stone ledge and handed the reins to Argent, quietly asking if he needed a rest from double riding. Argent merely shook his head. By now they had all become familiar with the process of seating M on Emmett, and it went quicker and more easily this third time. Argent mounted first and from the height of the stone ledge M was almost able to simply step over onto Emmett. Merritt led them back onto the road, then remounted himself, again taking the lead.

Once again, M tried to sit straight in the saddle, but she lost the struggle much sooner, slumping against Argent within minutes of regaining the road. She was fully asleep soon after that, her left ear resting against Argent's chest. By the time they descended the road into Old Town, Argent's right arm and hand were aching from the unchanging position of holding the reins, but he feared that switching to his left hand would cause M pain. He kept his left arm around her waist to steady her in her sleep.

It was hot, and any time their path led them into the sun, Argent felt himself sweat. Merritt had reclaimed his coat, but Argent's still hung on M's shoulders. She must be close to broiling from the sun, the coat, and her contact with Argent, but she slept on. Argent's own shirt was wet with sweat beneath his vest, where M leaned against him. He cautiously felt M's forehead. She was hot, but whether from the day's heat or fever, he could not tell. Merritt had turned in his saddle – as he had done periodically the entire ride – and caught Argent's movement. He looked the question at Argent, but Argent answered with both a shake of his head and a small shrug of his shoulders – he couldn't tell.

They left Old Town road just as it was going through the town, turning their horses south towards the C&O Canal and the Potomac. They crossed the canal at one of the three locks at Old Town, though neither man could say which one. A boat was locking through, giving the captain and the lock tender a few idle minutes to stare at the short parade of horses making use of the lock's bridge — one rider with a horse in tow and the other sharing a saddle with what appeared to be a drunken confederate, though, to be fair, one arm was in a sling and perhaps this was why the man could not ride his own horse.

At the bank of the Potomac, both Merritt and Argent paused. This was the easiest – the only – place to ford the river within miles, but still it would take a great deal of caution. Argent tightened his grip around M's waist, then nodded to Merritt. He waited until Merritt had crossed, making note of exactly each step of Merritt's horse, then he followed, carefully retracing Merritt's crossing. Both he and M were wet by the time they reached West Virginia on the other side, but still M did not wake.

Perhaps a quarter of a mile away they struck the tracks of the Baltimore & Ohio Railroad at Green Spring. While Merritt stepped into the station to inquire into any telegrams that might be waiting for them – especially as regarded the latest position of the train – Argent waited patiently outside, enduring the stares of people wondering at the coatless man propping up a dissipated youth in front of him. Merritt returned with a shake of his head, and they moved out of the little town, following the tracks for roughly two miles where they came up against the South Branch of the Potomac. Crossing here, without benefit of ford or ferry, would have been their greatest challenge even if Miss Warner had not been injured. The flow here was not particularly rapid nor the water particularly deep, but it was dangerous nonetheless.

"How shall we proceed?" Merritt had been waiting for Argent and M to reach him. He had gone ahead and searched along the bank for a likely place to cross and settled on a spot where two small spits of land intervened between the banks. Less than two hundred feet downstream was the B&O's bridge. "We could try the bridge. Only four hundred feet to cross and a line of sight down either side of half a mile or more. It could be done."

Argent gazed at the bridge. He should not even consider it. "No, if something goes wrong up there, it is certain death. We'll take our chances with the river."

"You should wake her now, so that she may prepare herself. It will take me a while to cross and return; that will give her enough time to be fully awake and aware."

Argent had so much trouble rousing M, he thought he might have to resort to slapping her, but at length she woke and was able to understand Argent.

"Miss Warner, we need to cross the river."

"We have already crossed the river. We are still wet."

"We have forded the North Branch, but now we must swim the South Branch. Once across we are only an hour or two from the train. Do you understand?"

"Yes." M sat up straight and looked out across the river. It was nothing like the Ohio at Louisville, her standard for rivers. She was not alarmed at the prospect, but she was concerned for Emmett. "Get down. I won't ask Emmett to carry both of us across."

"Nor would I."

Once on the ground, Argent began to unbutton his vest while Merritt did the same. Argent tossed his vest to Merritt who added it to his own vest and coat and rolled them all tightly together, with the package sent by Miss Lambert snug in the middle. With his and Argent's neckties he tied the bundle in two places, then handed it to Argent, who secured it to the back of Emmett's saddle. Socks and boots were secured on top of the saddles.

Merritt slid down the steep bank with his horse and waded with him into the river. Both man and horse swam to the first spit of land, where Merritt emerged from the water just long enough to indicate to Argent that the first section of the river was safe, then he returned to the water to swim beside his horse to the next tiny island. This little piece of land was larger than the first and would take several long strides to cross, but neither Merritt nor his horse felt the need to stop here, and soon they were on the other side of the river, walking up a much more gently sloping bank.

Merritt took the saddle off his horse and then tied the horse to a bush before he returned to the river to swim back to Argent and M. He took a minute to catch his breath before coming to stand next to Emmett, releasing Argent and his own horse to cross the river. Neither one bothered to stop at either island. Once across, Argent likewise removed the saddle from his horse and tied it nearby Merritt's horse. Then Argent, too, recrossed the river.

Within a few minutes of rejoining M and Merritt, Argent was ready to cross the river one last time. Before they began, however, M insisted that she carry her bag herself. She did not want to risk its contents getting wet. No argument would move her in this – she was adamant that she could both maintain her hold on the reins with her left hand and hold her bag out of the water with the other. It was only when she offered her bag to the men's clothes as well that they relented, but with the admonition that the first thing she should abandon, should there be trouble, would be the bag. "It is not a very big river," was her parting salvo to their arguments.

Argent made one last arrangement. He removed his coat from M's shoulders, then held it for her to wear. M gingerly removed her left arm from her sling, then allowed Argent to help her into his coat, even to buttoning it in the front. It was not a coat that he was proud of or even needed, but it had served to keep M warm, and they still had several miles to go. She might have need of it, and there was no sense letting it slip off her shoulders and into the river.

Merritt coaxed Emmett down the steep bank as slowly as possibly while Argent remained on the other side, his arm out to grab M if she should become unbalanced. At the water's edge, Merritt asked, "Ready, M?" and without waiting for an answer, pulled Emmett out into the river. Merritt and Argent flanked Emmett, one on either side, ready to help M out of the saddle if she proved too much for her horse, but Emmett was supremely indifferent to the change in circumstances and easily carried M, saddle, bag, and all, to the other side.

M had not spoken to Emmett at all as they crossed the river, but once on the far bank, she was effusive in her praises, and while Merritt unsaddled him, she retrieved the bundle from her bag. Peeling away the outer layers of the men's clothing, she found the slab of loaf cake, which she then offered to Emmett, neglecting to offer any to the other two horses. Too late she realized the partiality of the act and walked off to gather bunches of the tenderest greens to offer Merritt's and Argent's horses in recompense.

The men rested until their clothes were mostly dry and ate from the leftovers of their lunch. The excitement of crossing the river had energized M, and she spent the time, while the men and the horses rested, performing odd jobs that, of themselves, were not strenuous, but which were all the harder being done one-handed; she would not have the men know, but the simple effort to hold Emmett's reins while crossing the river had reawakened the soreness in her shoulder and arm, and she avoided using that arm at all. She spread the men's coats and vests over small shrubs both to air out and to keep them off the damp, almost muddy, ground. She spent a good deal of time exploring the area for treats for the horses. In between these errands, she retrieved from the men's second picnic the emptied napkins, shook them free of crumbs, then carefully folded them and stuffed them in her bag. She did not want them to take it upon themselves to make use of her bag – she could not risk them discovering her father's gun that was in her bag and no longer in their secretive trunk.

At last Merritt and Argent returned socks and boots to their feet and re-saddled the horses, and M's bag was once again secured behind Emmett's saddle. Argent urged M to take a third dose of the medicine, but she absolutely refused. She did, however, agree to return to the use of her sling. M then argued that she was able to ride the last hour or two on her own, but this was an argument she would not win, so once again she shared a saddle with Argent.

All through the day, they had heard the sounds of trains coming and going on the double tracks far below the road, but now they rode within spitting distance of the great beasts, their passages raising a breeze – sometimes from the front and sometimes from the back. M could feel their trundling through Emmett's great body, and it worked to lull her into sleep again. Despite the settled heat of the day, M had never offered to return Argent's coat to him, and the warmth of it also helped to subdue her efforts to remain awake.

The horses behaved admirably, given their proximity to such loud and large distractions, but occasionally it was thought best to pause while an unusually fast or long train passed. Though their path was cleared for them by the needs of the tracks, Merritt still rode ahead of Argent and M, scouting for any difficulties in the way. The trickiest problem was the crossing of the several creeks and rivulets that intervened between the South Branch and the Little Cacapon. In each case, they had been obliged to leave the level land near the tracks and pick their way carefully over the streams. Once, Argent had waited some minutes before Merritt was able to report that he had found a safe crossing. Then, once he had seen Argent and M across the creek, Merritt pulled out ahead again.

Whenever he returned to warn Argent of anything on the ground that might cause Emmett to stumble or shy or in any way disturb M, or to advise him of the need to cross a creek, Merritt spoke in a low voice and always informed Argent of M's status. For more than two hours since leaving the South Branch, he had always reported, "Still sleeping." When Merritt returned a final time to announce one last creek ahead, and that the siding was just beyond it, he saw that, while her position had not changed – her head against Argent's chest and facing the river – M's eyes were now open but staring. If M saw Merritt approach, she gave no notice.

"We're very close, perhaps half an hour." Then in an even lower voice, Merritt added, "She's awake."

Argent spoke softly. "Miss Warner, how do you?"

M replied equally softly, but without moving at all to address him directly; she continued staring into the woods that lined the Potomac. "Well, I thank you." Her voice sounded wooden, hardly the sound of someone doing well.

Argent pulled Emmett to a stop. Merritt walked his horse around to look at M. "Do you need to stop?"

M focused her gaze on Merritt. "No, if we are very close, there's no sense in stopping now." Though she had shifted her gaze, M had not raised her head from Argent's chest to address Merritt.

Merritt nodded, then handed her his canteen, which she gratefully accepted, but she took only a small sip. It was obvious that M was near the end of her reserves – that burst of activity at the river bank was telling on her. Merritt then offered the canteen to Argent, who accepted it with some difficulty – he was stiff and his movements awkward from the day's ride spent in one unwavering position, his right hand on the reins, his left around M's waist. Somehow, even though she could not see his movements, M could feel Argent's discomfort.

"I can take the reins for this last bit." Her voice sounded disembodied, a projection from some distant object.

Argent assured her he, too, could continue as they were, but M removed his left arm from her waist and put the reins in his left hand, and when he was finished with the canteen, she placed his right arm around her waist. Argent accepted the change of position gratefully, but offered, "Let me know if this hurts your shoulder." In reply, M merely patted the back of Argent's right hand with her own right hand, then left it there, both their arms laying against her waist.

They crossed the last creek and entered the last soft curve of the tracks, just before the bridge over the Little Cacapon and the siding where the train was waiting for them. The sun was almost directly behind them and low to the ground, and it created a glare on the tracks that momentarily stunned Argent's sight, and for a wild second, he feared the train was not there, that it had been moved yet again. He did not think M could endure any more. But his vision cleared and there sat the train. He did not expect the relief he felt at the sight of their little train. M must have sensed it, for she at last pulled herself up from Argent's chest. That, too, was a relief for Argent.

Just as they reached the siding, Mr. Hughes jumped down from the engine and came running towards them. The train, which was sitting far back on the tracks, was facing towards them, towards Cumberland. Though there had been no news for them at Green Spring, the engineer informed them that he had the latest instructions from Washington: they were to take off immediately — whether the marshals were here or not.

This gratified Merritt immensely. "Then let us take off."

"Before they can possibly arrive."

Argent's wry addendum to Merritt's enthusiastic suggestion was not lost on the engineer, and he hastened to give the reason. "It seems there have been inquiries in Old Town about two men, and an injured third, who were taken in by a widow lady in the area. The marshals have been dispatched to look into the matter and to ferret out how such information came to be bandied about town."

Merritt shifted in his saddle. "There was only one person who knew we were staying with Mrs. Lambert."

"It seems Darnell has been busy gossiping during his several trips to Old Town."

"There's something else, Mr. Argent. There were other inquiries, in Cumberland, about drownings of two men in the canal. Parts of the canal near the ten-mile lock were dredged, but nothing came of it. The descriptions of these men were very like yourselves. I don't mind admitting, Mrs. Hughes and I were worried for you. And Miss Warner, of course."

All during his delivery of the news, Mr. Hughes had stolen glances at M. She, in turn, focused her sight on him, but Mr. Hughes wasn't certain if she was hearing anything. He gave M one last look, then announced that he would alert Mrs. Hughes to their return and the need for her help. Merritt and Argent heard him shouting to his fireman to stoke the engine, well before he actually reached the train. As they drew nearer, they noted a small flurry of activity: Mr. Hughes knocking on the side of one car – apparently the car wherein was his wife, for she came out immediately afterwards – the brakeman appearing on the top of the first car, the great engine quickening to life, the puffs of steam from her bonnet growing larger and larger as she gained the strength needed to force her great wheels into motion.

Merritt dismounted as soon as Mr. Hughes returned to his train, and now walked the two horses, this time behind Argent and M, who remained seated atop Emmett. Merritt stopped at the stock car, but Argent urged Emmett on to the end of the train. Behind him, he heard Merritt pull out the ramp for the horses. Mrs. Hughes hurried ahead of them, and was ready to help M out of the saddle onto the steps of the platform attached to the back of the caboose. M immediately sank to the top step, holding onto one of the balusters and resting her head against it. Mrs. Hughes sat next to her and, after a moment, carefully unbuttoned the old coat M wore to reveal her left arm in a sling.

Argent handed Emmett's reins to Merritt as soon as Merritt reached the caboose but spoke to Mrs. Hughes. "Miss Warner will need help with a fresh dressing."

Before Merritt started off with Emmett to the stock car, M commanded, "Give him an apple; he deserves that much."

"I'll give him two apples, since he did double duty today."

Argent snorted. "You're as bad as she is about spoiling that horse." Argent realized too late that he had spoken aloud, but M surprised him with her mild reaction to his criticism of her horse and her handling of him.

"Don't be jealous, Mr. Argent." She stood and called out as Merritt retreated with Emmett, "Bring back two apples for Mr. Argent. He has done double duty as well." Merritt raised his hand in acknowledgement, though he never turned around or stopped walking.

Argent held out his hand to help M down the step, but she ignored the gesture. Mrs. Hughes took up position on M's left, while Argent walked to her right. They passed the caboose and the two older, shorter crew cars. Argent naturally paused at the fourth car, Miss Warner's car, but Mrs. Hughes continued on with M, who apparently was paying little attention to where she was going. Argent cleared his throat. "Mrs. Hughes?"

The engineer's wife turned at her name. M had stopped with Mrs. Hughes but remained facing forward. Mrs. Hughes said nothing but waited for Argent to speak further.

"This is Miss Warner's car." Now M turned around, finally aware, like Argent, that she had passed her own car.

Mrs. Hughes stared at Argent, then seemed to come to herself. "Oh, no, sir. Begging your pardon, I completely forgot that you are not aware of the new arrangements. That is now your car, and Mr. Merritt's, of course. Miss Warner's is now the car next to the stock car."

Argent hesitated a moment, considering the two cars. Though they were generally alike in structure and of the same size, the 'gentlemen's car' did not have a clerestory, whereas Miss Warner's car did. This, therefore was definitely Miss Warner's car and the car to which Mrs. Hughes was leading them was his and Merritt's car. If there had been a change in arrangements, it was not a mere switching of the two cars. He beckoned Mrs. Hughes to proceed, then followed.

At what was now Miss Warner's car, Mrs. Hughes removed Argent's coat and handed it to him. "Miss Warner's trunk is here. I'll find something suitable for her to wear." And with that, Argent was dismissed.

It was sometime later before Merritt joined Argent in what was now their car. "Mr. Hughes awaits our signal. Is all ready?" At Argent's nod, Merritt stepped out onto their platform and waved their readiness to Mr. Hughes, leaning out of the cab of his engine, awaiting this very signal. Within seconds they felt the abrupt jerk forward as their car was pulled in its turn. Upon re-entering the car, Merritt continued, "We will need to return to Cumberland, of course, to make our turn, but Mr. Hughes informs me that – barring unforeseen traffic or other problems – we will still be able to make Grandiflora well before midnight. We will stay the night there and be in Washington tomorrow."

Argent gave the smallest nod. He and Merritt had ridden the Cincinnati-to-Washington rails often and were fairly intimate with all the towns and water and coal stops along the way. It only now occurred to him how few places there were to turn around. He could not think of any such place between Martinsburg and Cumberland; both were equipped with roundhouses and repair shops as well as room and rails for changing directions. It seemed ridiculous that there should be no Y or other accommodating system for turning these great engines around. How many times in these last few days had Mr. Hughes been obliged to run all the way between Martinsburg and Cumberland to make the turn as he was ordered from one siding to the next, with the sidings occurring on opposite sides of the tracks, leaving the train facing in opposite directions?

What had taken all day on horseback at a snail's pace was accomplished, and more, by the train in little more than an hour. At Cumberland, there was the slightest delay, as they waited a chance and a place to make their turn. In that space of time, Argent hurried down to M's car to give Mrs. Hughes the chloral crystals. Mrs. Hughes answered his knock but did not invite him in.

"Please see to it that Miss Warner is given a mixture of these crystals in some drink at bedtime. It will help her to sleep through the night." Argent untied the ribbon on the little bag, which was simply a square of cloth, its corners brought together. As the corners fell away in his hand, he found not only the vial of chloral, but also a small folded piece of paper. Pocketing the paper, he handed the vial, cloth, and ribbon to Mrs. Hughes, indicating the amount of crystals to be dissolved in M's nighttime draught. Then he hurried back to his car, reaching the platform just as the train began its maneuvers.

"How is M?"

"I did not see her, nor had time to inquire. Mrs. Hughes has assumed watchdog privileges over her."

Merritt smiled; one more older woman was thwarting Argent's natural authority over M. "What do you think of our new lodgings?" Merritt was sitting across from Argent, his arms flung wide over the back of his couch.

Argent looked up from emptying the pockets of his coat, annoyed. "Were you aware of the change in accommodations?"

"Mr. Hughes told me, while I was brushing Emmett. Apparently, M's – shall we say, discomfort – at the furnishings of her car were not lost on Mr. Hughes. Upon advising Mrs. Hughes of his suspicions, that good woman's initial injured feelings gave way to a burst of charitable activity in which much of what was once in this car alone was disbursed between our car, Miss Warner's, and the car that the Hughes make as their home on the rails."

Argent looked around, truly noticing the car for the first time. There were far less dressings on the windows, tables, couches and other surfaces than he remembered when M occupied the car. "I hope she kept some comforts for Miss Warner."

"Oh, you needn't worry. We won't be sharing a bed this night – the large bed that once graced the bedroom in this car is now ensconced in our old car, and, likewise, our simple but separate cots await us behind the fireplace. What do you have there?"

As Merritt spoke, Argent had pulled from his pants pocket the folded piece of paper that had been included with the chloral. He unfolded the paper and held up for Merritt's inspection a medallion of St. Jude. Merritt reached across, took the medallion, and turned it over in his palm while Argent read from the paper, "My mother found this pinned to the inside of Miss Warner's shirt while we were cleaning and mending her clothes. Please return it to Miss Warner with our wishes for a speedy recovery."

Argent retrieved the medallion and studied it in his turn. "Something is not right about this."

"You are an expert in Catholic medallions?"

"Something is not right about this gesture on the part of the Lambert ladies, about the tenor of the note. They are at complete odds with the widow's blunt disapproval of M's religion." Argent considered the medallion and the note one last time, then shoved both back into his pocket. Standing, he announced that he would wash up and change into some clean clothes, his own clothes, for the first time in more than a week. "Our trunks are with us?"

Merritt merely indicated with a jerk of his head that the trunks were in the other room. When Argent reappeared later, a cleaner and happier (and shaven) man, Merritt decided he, too, could stand a cleaning and a change of clothes. When he returned, it was to find Argent stretched out on his couch, deeply asleep. The day's ride had been a strain on Argent, though Merritt knew he would never admit it, even to himself.

Merritt considered Argent for a moment before returning briefly to the bedroom. He re-emerged holding rolled maps retrieved from their work trunk. He lit a lamp near the little table in the corner next to the fireplace, keeping the wick low, in deference to Argent. He spread one of the maps on the table and began a careful retracing of their trip. The chain of events that led them to this point were certainly connected in some manner other than random sequence, and the men who had launched the most recent events in Cumberland were still out there, and still a potential threat to everyone on this train. Merritt intended to be ready for them, but first he had to understand all that had gone before.

Merritt woke with a start, his head jerking violently as his chin slipped from his hand. At first, he was confused, having fallen asleep as he studied the maps; the canal, not the train, was on his mind. But now he found himself on a train. Slowly, he was able to focus his mind and he realized that the train had stopped. Merritt turned to find that Argent had also woken at the sudden stopping of the train, and was sitting up, with a wild confusion on his face. Merritt suspected his own face looked much the same. Argent's eyes searched the car, finally finding Merritt in the corner at the table. In that instant, Merritt remembered what it was that had woken him – he had heard gunshots. Apparently, these same gunshots had woken Argent, and with one look between them, both men rose, intending to make investigation into the source of the noise.

Though he was further away, Merritt reached the door first. Just as he reached for the handle, he was knocked backwards as the door was violently flung open from the outside. His head bled alarmingly from the gash where it had met the door, but he was on his feet immediately. His efforts were wasted, however – several men burst through the door, and quickly overtook Merritt and Argent. Their hands were tied behind their backs and they were then shoved roughly to sit on the couch that faced the old cylinder desk. The intruders wore no masks, nor attempted to hide their identities in any way. They spoke freely, and both Merritt and Argent recognized the voices of some of these men as belonging to those at the canal.

Two of the three men they had met at the bagatelle table in the basement of the Revere House were dispatched to search the room behind the fireplace. They could be heard ransacking the room. One of them now returned and reported that there was no one in the next room, and in an aggravated, disappointed tone, added, "They live like monks – there's nothing of value in there."

The other man now appeared and corrected his friend. "There's a trunk in there, belted and locked. Couldn't find the key." Though his friend was disappointed in the spoils of the bedroom, this man carried Merritt's best coat and a well-worked pair of boots.

"We'll get to that later."

"I thought these were wealthy men, rich enough to own a train or charter one. I thought there would be booty. There was nothing at the farm and there is nothing here either."

"We'll get to that later." A dangerous warning had crept into the man's voice.

Argent gave a dry laugh. "You were lied to, my friend. We are not wealthy men, and this is not our train." Argent's truth was repaid with a blow to the face.

The leader – not the same man as at the canal – began barking orders before any other awkward truths could be revealed. Three men were singled out. "Make sure of the other cars. Go through everything. Secure the horses. Kill everyone but the engineer and the brakeman." As the three men turned to leave, the leader added, "Make sure the woman is dead this time – bring me her body."

"I tell you she was dead. She was in her bed; I saw her look at me. She is not an attractive woman; it was not a face I could forget – ghoulish-looking." M's erstwhile murderer resented the implied failure.

For a brief moment, everyone in the car paused to stare at the man who could not hit his target mere feet away. He had become the butt of their jokes these last few days, but now they were tired of his protestations, of the obvious lie of two bullets to the head. The leader was tired of him, too. "Go with them and see how it's done." As the last of them filed out of the car, the leader had a change of heart. "Wait. Don't kill her yet, but chain her up if you have to; we don't want her wandering away this time, not just yet."

Merritt and Argent struggled to rise, to mount some kind of defense, but they were held fast to the couch by the men pinning them from behind. In the midst of their struggles, they heard shots from further up the train, then silence. They had been hopelessly, unforgivably unprepared, and now the train was at the mercy of these mysterious brigands. First Argent, then Merritt, realized the futility of struggling, and they slowly left it off.

The leader leaned against the wall next to the cylinder desk and pulled back the curtain at the window. He stood this way for some minutes, then with a gesture of his chin indicated two of the remaining men. "Go see what is taking so long."

A flicker of hope, or at least of the satisfaction of seeing an enemy's plans falter, flared in Merritt's mind. "It's never a good sign when things go off schedule." Argent noticed Merritt's slurred speech. It may have been the product of concussion, but he shared Merritt's sentiment.

The two men chosen to look into the matter hesitated. The leader countered Merritt's insinuation. "Perhaps they have had better luck with loot." He rephrased his order. "See what they have found."

When the men left, a little more eagerly at the thought of wealthy, train-owning men's treasure, the leader turned to Merritt and smiled. If Merritt had hoped to goad the man, he had misfired.

"The whole point is to go off schedule. When this train doesn't reach Martinsburg, when you fail to report in to Washington, a second wave of marshals will be dispatched to find out just why you are delayed yet again on this simple escort trip. What they will find are your decaying bodies, the sad victims of mistaken identity, a disappointed robbery turned to murder. But no one will mourn you – what will they think of you when that crazy, tall, tomboy pet of Grant's is discovered, murdered like you, but with all the markings of repeated outrage upon her person. Prison has kept me from life's simple pleasures for some time now, and I am in sore need of the pleasure a woman can provide, even if she is dressed like a man. It just takes a little longer to get to the prize. And the boys, well, the boys are always spoiling for it. They'll be glad of the old woman until I have finished with Grant's girl."

At this Argent stood so suddenly and violently that he broke free of the hands on his shoulders. Using the seat of the couch facing him, he propelled himself over its back, intending to take down the man at the window by the sheer size and force of his body. He had no real chance to succeed. The leader neatly sidestepped Argent's charge, and as he did so, he pushed Argent, slamming him hard into the desk. Argent fell to the floor, unmoving.

Merritt also stood, momentarily throwing off his captor's hold on him, but he was struck from behind, and Merritt also sank to the floor. But as darkness overtook him, he heard a gun speak twice. His last thought was, I wonder which of us was shot first.

Merritt was having a hard time swimming to the surface of the canal. He did not remember the canal being so deep, nor water being so *thick*. He hoped Argent had made it to the surface, and he was certain he had gotten M out in plenty of time, if she had left when he told her. But he heard Argent calling M's name urgently. Something was wrong. Had she fallen back into the lock? Argent again called her name; this time, he was practically shouting. Something was wrong with Argent. As Merritt slowly broke the surface of the water, he found he was not in the canal, but in the "parlor" car, M's car, sitting on the couch with its back to the cylinder desk. As his eyes focused, he could see M seated at the table in the corner, her head laying in the crook of her good arm, a gun laying limp in her hand. Again he heard Argent shout, "Mary!"

That was what was wrong with Argent — he never called her Mary; he rarely referred to her as anything but Miss Warner.

Merritt was stupid with concussion and could not quite understand the situation. He turned to Argent sitting next to him on the couch and asked, almost disinterestedly, "What's wrong?"

Argent turned to him with obvious relief and concern at the same time. "Are you all right? How's your head?"

Merritt had to think back, hard, and remembered the raid on the train, and, like a train picking up speed, memory flooded in on him – Argent falling senseless, the blow to his own head, two shots.

"I heard two shots. I thought we were dead."

"You heard more than I did, then," Gingerly, he nodded towards M at the table, unmoving.

Merritt's eyes widened, and whispered, "Is she —?"

"No, I can see her breathing, but I can't rouse her."

It wasn't until then, when he moved to simply get up and go to M – why hadn't Argent thought to do so? – that Merritt realized he was still bound, as was Argent. Only now their feet were bound as well. But Argent had been on the floor by the desk, and Merritt had fallen – he was fairly certain – on the other couch. How did they come to be seated together on this couch?

Merritt called to M, and Argent joined him.

"Argent, hold off a minute." Then Merritt said to M, not shouting, but loudly, "M, Emmett needs you. He won't come to me." He waited a second or two, and repeated, "Emmett needs you," several times.

At last, M responded to Emmett's needs, and slowly raised her head. She blinked three times, then said, "Merritt, your head is rattled. Emmett is on the train. He's fine, I made sure of him before we left."

Merritt realized, then, another thing: the train was moving and at a fast pace, though it was night and the engineer had often voiced his opposition to traveling at night through these mountains and valleys, in the presence of other, faster express trains and other, much heavier freight trains.

"Miss Warner, you're bleeding." She was, in fact, not bleeding, but Argent saw fresh blood on the sleeve of her shirt, her right sleeve.

Merritt saw it now, too, and asked, "Are you hurt?" Then remembering the threat of violations, he asked in a lower and tentative voice, "Did they *hurt* you?"

Argent looked at Merritt; he too remembered the threat and the black rage that had overtaken him.

M looked down as if seeing the blood for the first time, then remembering the injury, said, "It isn't bleeding anymore. A bullet broke the skin is all. And," indicating Merritt, "you're not bleeding anymore either." Mrs. Hughes had shown her how to hold a compress to the head and eventually Merritt had stopped bleeding; there had been so much blood. She looked at Merritt with concern. "I hope your head does not grieve you overmuch."

Merritt was only just now beginning to feel the slow rising of a headache, promising to grieve him very much indeed.

"Miss Warner, untie me and I'll look to Mr. Merritt and to you, and see what's happening with the train."

Merritt stepped in with a question. "How did we come to be here, together, on this couch? The last I saw, Argent was on the floor by the desk."

M, though fully awake, seemed to be struggling with a headache of her own. She spoke quietly, with strain, and often rubbed her temple. "Oh, he was, and you were lying in a very awkward position on this couch. But I had the last robber right you and place you both on that couch." It seemed to occur to her as an afterthought to explain further. "And tie your feet."

"The last robber? And tie our feet?"

"You had him put us here?"

Argent and Merritt had been speaking over each other, but they both finished at the same time and with the same question. "Why?!"

"To make you listen, to open negotiations. I want to re-negotiate the" – M closed her eyes, weary, searching for the right word – "boundaries of this trip."

"I'd be happy to discuss boundaries, but first untie us."

Argent seemed to miss entirely M's reason for having them bound. Merritt, however, responded as if these were normal circumstances under which negotiations would be conducted. "What boundaries do you wish to discuss?"

Argent looked at Merritt, stunned, that he would be so complaisant in this situation. Clearly, he was suffering diminished mental capacity. Merritt ignored Argent's stare.

"I know that you have been dosing me with your vile concoctions at every opportunity."

Argent became angry, with both M and Merritt. "Now is not the time to play this game. Untie us and let us assess the situation and make our deliberations."

M answered with anger of her own. "This is no game; you very nearly got me killed, having Mrs. Hughes put so much tonic in my drink. If it weren't for this headache, I may very well have been asleep and unable to defend myself, and coincidentally, help defend you. And you assume a great deal in claiming any deliberations exclusively for yourselves."

"The course of deliberations is not only —"

Merritt cut in before Argent could put dynamite to the discussion with his certain arguments as to whose claim to deliberations were more valid. "We, both Mr. Argent and I, put those drops in your drink to help you sleep. There was no devious intent. M, you're bleeding again. Untie us and let us help you."

"The only help you consider is for yourselves." M spoke with a child's anger and hurt, something they had not heard in her voice before. "I know you put those drops in my drink, so I would sleep, and you wouldn't have to bother with me." Suddenly, she was close to sobbing. Words now came pouring out, curdled with emotions, more words than she had ever spoken together at once. "I have tried to do everything right – I have said the right things, asked the right questions, avoided bad topics." Her voice rose in her own defense. "I followed the list." She swallowed at the memory of the humiliation of these men reading her list, of knowing her need for such a list. "But it still wasn't good enough. I see the looks people give me. I see the looks you give each other. No matter what I do, it isn't good enough. You intended to keep me locked in that car, in that box, only to let me out to eat and occasionally see Emmett. I know that's why we left Mrs. Lambert's – to bring me back here and lock me away again. Miss Carrie said, *Go to Washington, get out of this house, meet new people, end your loneliness, these men will be your friends.* But I have never been so lonely as I have been on this trip. It is less lonely in that big house back home with all the empty rooms and the stripped beds and the dust of disuse. I know I've lost my temper and I know I've made mistakes and I know I've made you work hard, but you've made mistakes, too, but no one locks you up at night or tells you when you can visit your horse or anyone else on the train, or whether you can have a drink or not." M's misery made her defiant. "I *will* go to Washington, I *will* see Mr. Grant. But I won't get there if I'm dead, so the rest of this trip will be on my terms and I will see to my own safety. If there is a key to the car I now occupy, I will have it. I come and go as I please when the train is at rest. You don't presume" – this was said with particular heat – "to tell me when or how much I should drink or eat or sleep. You no longer slip tonics of any kind into my food or drinks. In fact, I think it is better that we no longer eat together. When we stop at towns, we go our separate ways; I will ask Mr. Hughes the time of departure and I will be back in time. And if you can't treat me as anything more than an assignment, we finish this ill-begotten trip in silence."

Merritt and Argent sat, stunned at the grievances laid before them, but, worse, at the obvious pain M had held at bay for three weeks.

Merritt spoke, but quietly. "How would you like to be treated?"

"As if I were your brother."

"Why not as if you were our sister?"

"I have been a sister, and I find it wanting. And you don't know how to treat a sister. A brother isn't so irritatingly polite. A brother wouldn't leave his sister alone for hours in a locked car. A brother would say, it's a fine morning, let's go hunt. A brother would say, you're getting fat – you eat too much pie. A brother would play cards with me in the evenings. My brothers would do those things. I miss those brothers. Miss Lambert was right – I do pretend, but not about traveling or jewels. I pretend in order to keep my sanity, and when we started out from Louisville, I thought that – for a few days – I could pretend to have new brothers. All I have left is remember and pretend, and I thought it would be enough to get me through this trip, but it isn't. You have to pretend, too. So, we either pretend together, or endure our separate realities."

There was another long silence, and again it was Merritt who broke it. "M, I sincerely apologize for us both. We never meant to ignore you. We thought you valued your solitude; we didn't want to intrude. And as for the sleeping drops, it was not to keep from being bothered by you, it was to help you sleep through your injury and headaches. And we would never, never have done anything we thought would put you in danger. And not just because it is our duty or an assignment." Merritt gambled that the sleeping drops M referred to did not include those given before the events at the lock.

M ignored the apology but softened her tone. "One final item: these men that keep dogging you – whatever grievance they hold against you, you need to settle things one way or another. I can't spend all my time rescuing you; it's exhausting."

M pushed herself up wearily from the table. "I can't believe I left my dogs for this." She picked up the gun and moved towards the bedroom door, obviously having forgotten this was no longer her car.

"Miss Warner?" Thinking perhaps a brother would not address his sister so formally, Argent started again. "Mary? Will you untie us?"

M stopped and raised her hand to her head, the gun still in her grip. "I am sorry. I forgot you were still bound."

She laid the gun on the table, then knelt before the men, untying the ropes around their feet. It took more time than it should have, but her hands were clumsy. Argent only now noticed that her left arm was no longer in a sling. She rocked back on her heels and closed her eyes for a moment then got slowly to her feet.

Addressing Argent, she commanded, "Stand up and turn around."

Argent obediently stood but when he turned to present his tied hands to M, he gasped. Merritt looked up at Argent, and first turned to his left and then to his right, when he, too, betrayed surprise. In the corner of the car, near the door, sat a man, spread-eagled and eyes wide-open, a bullet in the center of his forehead. Merritt turned again to face M.

M knew what had made them draw in their breaths, but she did not look up from attacking the knots at Argent's wrists. Merritt and Argent exchanged glances, then realized they were guilty as M had charged, for doing so.

Once Argent was finally free, he sat M on the opposite couch, then freed Merritt's hands. Merritt stepped out onto the platform, hoping to make sense of where they were on the tracks. But he returned saying, "We just have to trust that Mr. Hughes knows what he is doing."

Argent was almost as concerned for Merritt as he was for M. His speech was still slurred, and he teetered when he walked. Merritt sat heavily across from M and closed his eyes. "I wonder that no one at Little Cacapon depot heard the gunplay and came to our assistance."

"We were not near Little Cacapon depot. Mr. Hughes was instructed to proceed past the bridge to the siding near Rockwell Run, the 140th mile siding."

Merritt opened his eyes, though he did not raise his head. "How do you know this?"

"Mr. Hughes told me . . . when he helped me kill that last man there." M indicated the dead man in the corner. "He received word in

Cumberland of our new destination. We were waylaid when we stopped for the night at the siding."

"Where are headed now?"

"Sir John's Run. Mr. Hughes hopes to wait there until the marshals come."

Merritt closed his eyes again. "They are to meet us there?"

"When Mr. Hughes telegraphs for them. He doesn't know where they are at the moment."

Merritt groaned; the presence of the marshals could only make his head ache more.

Argent could tend to Merritt later, but for now he sat next to M. "With your permission." At M's nod, Argent carefully, respectfully, pulled back M's shirt to reveal her shoulder. The wound that had done so well last week was now angry-looking and inflamed, and hot to the touch. He left M for a moment, disappearing into the room behind the fireplace. The room had been thoroughly upturned, but he was able to find a clean washcloth and douse it in the pitcher of water, surprisingly still standing in its basin on the washstand. Returning to M, he placed the cloth on her shoulder, which made M gasp.

Argent held the cold cloth to M's shoulder for a moment, then turned it over and replaced it, the cooler side against her skin. M did not react this time.

"I am sorry, truly sorry, that we – that I – have been the source of so much pain and loneliness. It was never our intention."

M had been studying her feet all during Argent's examination and while he held the cloth to her shoulder. She should hold it there herself, but she was suddenly exhausted and did not think she could raise her arm to do it. "I laid the full blame on shoulders that were only partially at fault. I suspect Grant was less than forthcoming about your task."

"Yes, he was."

Argent said this in such a forceful manner that M regretted some of her earlier words. Perhaps Merritt and Argent had been tricked into accepting this duty. "If you had known all the particulars, would you have asked to be excused?"

"Yes, but only because I would have thought myself inadequate for your needs." M appreciated his honesty, but it stung nonetheless, that

Argent saw her as someone who needed extraordinary attention or care. "I am grateful, though, that he did not give me the option to refuse."

"Is it acceptable to lie to be polite?"

Argent considered M. She had called him out on a polite lie earlier today. She was blunt, but it was not rudeness that prompted her comments. She seemed genuinely lost in simple conversations.

"I was not lying."

M studied his face to appraise his sincerity. From somewhere deep in her memory came the appropriate response. "That is very kind of you."

Argent left briefly again and returned with a second damp cloth, replacing the one at M's shoulder. He left it there, and with the first cloth he cleaned and examined the wound on M's right arm. He was relieved to find that it was indeed a superficial wound; the bleeding had all but stopped. As he tied the cloth around her arm, he returned to the subject of Grant. "I know that what is between you and President Grant is private." Argent paused, uncertain of the propriety of his next words. "Is there anything I can do to help?"

M had closed her eyes against the pounding in her head, and Argent thought that perhaps she had dozed off, but now she opened her eyes to study him once again, this time for a very long moment. Argent was about to apologize for intruding when M finally answered him.

"My father and the General were colleagues and more than colleagues. Dad admired the General greatly, and I think the General returned the esteem. When I knew Dad was in his last illness, I sent the General a telegram. I said, *Come visit him; it would mean so much to him to see you again.* When Dad was *in extremis*, I sent word to the General." Her voice began to betray the deep and bitter anger and betrayal she felt. "I said, *Come say goodbye to your friend.* When he died, I said, *Come help me bury my father.* But he never came, he never answered. I stood by the grave while Dad's box was lowered into the ground. I stood there alone. Grant should have been there. He should have acknowledged Dad's passing." M swallowed hard several times before she continued, but her voice was no longer shaking. "Grant is my godfather, a promise he made to my father. He owed it to me, but more importantly, he owed it to my father. He should have been there. I can never forgive him for the slight to my father. I can never forgive him for his neglect of duty. Once the war was won, he didn't need Dad anymore, he didn't care about us anymore."

Argent could not imagine why the President would not have answered M's telegrams, but he knew this president in particular could not possibly attend all the personal events to which he was invited. Argent knew Grant was beseeched daily by soldiers who had served under him, by wives asking for help collecting pensions due them in the name of the loyalty and duty given by their deceased husbands, by favor-seekers with only the slightest acquaintance with him. Argent said as gently as he could, "The President is a busy man —"

M was swift and savage in her denunciation. "He is busy, but not as a President. He is a busy show-dog, taking his laps around the country, lapping up ribbons and prizes and sycophantic honors, posing and prancing for whatever crowd gathers around him. On the day my father died, he was busy on a pleasure trip, on an *excursion*, in a private car provided him by the Erie Railroad. Of course he was too busy to attend a dying friend – a funereal trip to a farm in Kentucky could not possibly contend with a pleasure ride through a pro-Grant state in a gilded kennel."

Argent should have been shocked at M's diatribe; he should have rebuked her for such a vicious assault on the man who held the office of President of the United States, the office to which he owed complete fealty, no matter who occupied it. But he knew that M's bitterness had been given too long to fester, with no other target for her bile than Grant, and with no one to counsel her in taming her anger. But he also knew that if Mr. Warner was indeed a close friend and associate of the President's, as close as M believed, then Grant should have acknowledged his passing in some way, should have sent condolences and comfort to Mr. Warner's last surviving child. M had been left isolated in her grief, and it had proven to be the perfect condition in which to cultivate her utter and complete rejection of Grant, a loathing that she had apparently not yet plumbed.

"You are right. He should have acknowledged your father's passing; he should have been there."

M's anger turned to surprise. She had not expected agreement from one of Grant's own men.

Argent took her left arm and examined the other wound from the canal. "I don't know why he wasn't there, but it wasn't because he doesn't care. He desperately wants to reconcile with you. He gave us two commands: don't take no for an answer and spare no expense – make her comfortable and happy. I am afraid we have failed to make you happy."

A little of M's old spark flared briefly. "Most people fail at that. I am hard to please."

She was pale and in obvious pain, but Argent suspected it was more than her shoulder and the two other trifling wounds. "At least let me make you comfortable. I have promised not to dose you without your knowledge, but I can see that you suffer. It was a long day in the saddle and a longer night fending off thieves. I have some morphine in my trunk —"

M waved him off decisively. "Dad told me never to use it. He said it ruined soldiers who took it."

"It is true, many soldiers became addicted to it, but they were often given it unsupervised and, unfortunately, simply to help keep entire hospital wards calm and quiet while doctors were busy with other soldiers. That won't happen with you. I won't let it happen. Just a little, to take the edge off, to help you sleep. And Merritt and I will keep watch the rest of the night."

Her head was pounding, and she did not know when the train would stop, when she would be able to return to her car and retrieve the laudanum from her bag. She relented, with the caveat, "Only a very little."

"I'll be just a moment." Argent left a third time for the bedroom, where he retrieved from his personal trunk the box wherein he kept a few basic instruments and medicines, to give what help he could to his colleagues in the field, until more authoritative help could be obtained. From this box he took a syringe and needle and a vial of morphine, that most sovereign of all remedies. He screwed the needle onto the syringe, and then drew the precious liquid into the barrel.

M's eyes were closed when Argent returned, but she opened them when she felt him sit next to her. "Where is the morphine?"

"Here." Argent held up the syringe and noted M's reaction. He mistook her simple fear of the needle for a renewed concern of addiction. "I promise to keep you from the dangers of this drug."

Without any further explanation other than "Don't move," Argent straightened her right arm and held it tight, but then he lowered the syringe as the train jerked suddenly. The train jerked several times more as it slowed in sudden increments before finally coming to a halt with one last, relatively soft jerk. Argent held M's arm until he was sure that the train had indeed stopped, then finally injected the morphine. M quickly became groggy, but Argent was able to help her to her car before she completely succumbed to the drug.

26

The little train arrived at Sir John's Run depot in the wee hours of the morning. Exhausted as they were, Merritt, Argent, Mr. Hughes and his son, the fireman, stood sentry against a second attack that never came. The brakeman – their only brakeman – had been killed in the attack. Mr. Hughes had, therefore, been obliged to employ a medley of maneuvers to make the stop at Sir John's Run, including engaging an experimental variation on Creamer's emergency brakes. The Baltimore & Ohio Company would be pleased to know that these brakes worked admirably. Mr. Hughes had immediately sent telegrams to Washington and Baltimore, advising the separate presidents of circumstances in their separate realms. President Grant sent a personal reply, though not until after breakfast; President Garret sent an immediate reply, though it is unlikely he was actually awakened to respond personally at such an hour. Both responses, however, acknowledged that the entire scheme and schedule were in tatters and that the attack against the train was an alarming development. Separately, both presidents advised that the little train should remain at Sir John's Run – thankfully not yet experiencing the rush of the summer season at nearby Berkeley Springs – until further notice.

During their time guarding the train in the pre-dawn dark, Merritt and Argent had been able to piece together a complete account of the raid on the train. That this raid was an extension of events in and near Cumberland was indisputable to Merritt and Argent, though Mr. Hughes seemed to think that events of last night were of some random nature. The brakeman, stationed on the caboose as usual, had been the first (and only of the crew) to die. Argent had suggested that the attack, then, had come from behind, though what the significance of the orientation of an attack on a siding was unclear. Mr. Hughes had added, however, that the engine was taken over at the same time as the caboose, so that the attack had been spread over the cars of the train. There were, then, more members of the gang than Merritt and Argent saw in their car, though the leader was clearly there.

Mr. Hughes himself could tell them little of what happened after he and his son had been rendered harmless by the attackers. Mrs. Hughes, however, had told him quite the tale, as she tended to her wounded son and helped stoke the engine as they sped to the safety of Sir John's Run. It was the two women who had saved the day (or night, the engineer was pleased to offer this small crumb of humor). As the train came to a stop, Mrs. Hughes had looked out the window of her car and had narrowly missed being seen by several men on horseback, just beyond the tracks. She had immediately made sure the two guns and one shotgun in the car were loaded, then tucked the two handguns into the waistband of her skirt. She heard men walk along both sides of the car, then someone from the engine yell, "All clear!" and she watched as the men on horseback left their horses and headed for the gentlemen's car. She had then quietly let herself out of the car and headed for Miss Warner's car. After that initial walk along both sides of the train, the attackers stayed on the side of the train farthest from the main tracks.

"She heard some of what transpired in your car, as she crept along the side, but it was Miss Warner she was worried for, you see." Mr. Hughes seemed to find it necessary to explain his wife's actions.

"Of course. Miss Warner was the most vulnerable on the train."

"But that's just the thing, Mr. Argent. She wasn't the most vulnerable. My wife told me she found Miss Warner outside her car with a gun of her own, loaded and ready."

"Where did she get a gun?" Merritt's curiosity had a tinge of humor to it.

"My wife gave it to her, before we left Little Cacapon bridge. Miss Warner said that events of the last week or so had impressed upon her the need for protection. I hope Mrs. Hughes did no wrong?"

"We can hardly argue the outcome, though perhaps we should be advised of any future arming of Miss Warner."

Mr. Hughes nodded to Merritt, both his relief and his acknowledgement. "Well, sirs, my wife said that while she was willing to do whatever was necessary to rid the train of these ruffians, she really had no idea what to do. But Miss Warner seemed quite certain what to do, and she gave my wife instructions just as if they were both in the army. Mrs.

Hughes was quite struck by how natural command seemed to come to Miss Warner, and that she herself so readily submitted to it. She said Miss Warner seemed somewhat removed from the situation, like she was herself receiving commands from someone else. But that's just how my wife talks, sometimes."

Mr. Hughes paused here a moment, as he considered the way his wife talked sometimes or perhaps it was the person of Miss Warner he considered, but if Merritt hadn't prompted him, the pause would have lasted a great deal longer. Brought back to the conversation, Mr. Hughes continued. "Miss Warner decided they needed more guns —" Argent nearly choked "— given the number of desperadoes attacking the train. So, they slipped back past your car, if you'll credit it, and gathered what guns they could find in the crew car — the boys like to hunt a little when the opportunity provides."

"Naturally." Mr. Hughes waited, as if needing an invitation or some indication to continue, which Merritt provided. "They gathered more guns."

"Yes, sir. Miss Warner said the ruffians would be looking for her, and that she and my wife would have to act quickly, before it was known she was not in her car."

"She said that – they would be looking for her?"

"Yes, sir, but she didn't tell my wife why." Mr. Hughes paused to consider Argent. "Were they looking for her? Do you know why?"

Argent contemplated how much to tell Mr. Hughes, then decided this was an excellent opportunity to underscore the need to keep Miss Warner under watch. "Miss Warner may have become a target as a result of her association with us. She should never be allowed to leave the confines of the train alone, and without notifying either me or Mr. Merritt."

Mr. Hughes nodded his understanding, then at a motion from Argent, continued. "They left a gun under your car and Miss Warner's car, then Miss Warner left my wife with a gun on the track side of the stock car. My wife did not like to get under the car, like Miss Warner told her to do, but she crouched low." Mr. Hughes did a fair imitation of his wife crouching by the side of the stock car.

Argent was losing his patience with Mr. Hughes' long-winded account of the ladies' exploits. "I am certain she acted admirably under the circumstances. But how did they come to secure the train?"

"I'm getting to that, sir. Miss Warner left a second gun under the stock car, but as she started forward for the engine, my wife said they heard men coming from your car, looking for Miss Warner." Mr. Hughes stopped, then lowered his voice. "I don't like to repeat what those two ladies heard about themselves. I can hardly blame Miss Warner for what she did next."

"We are aware of what these men intended for Miss Warner. And your wife. I assure you, if we had been able, they would never have left our car."

"I'm sure of it, Mr. Merritt, and I appreciate your sensibilities including my wife." Mr. Hughes paused in a kind of salute to Merritt's sensibilities, but then a kind of wonder came over his face. "Do you know what my wife told me next? Miss Warner said, 'I will be damned' – begging your pardons, sirs – 'if I will be murdered a second time in as many weeks.' What do you suppose she meant by that? Then she said, 'It is time these men learn they aim at a Kentuckian at their own peril.' Then my wife said Miss Warner strode down the car, bold as you please, stepped up on the coupling, and fired three times. When Miss Warner returned, she told my wife to hand her the gun under the stock car, that her plans had changed."

The engineer looked at Merritt and Argent in turn and in a voice of fearful admiration said, "Miss Warner has such a tender understanding of trains and mechanics. It is difficult to balance that with someone who can be so cold and ruthless with a gun."

Despite the gravity of the subject, Merritt was somewhat amused at Mr. Hughes' confused admiration for Miss Warner. "I suspect it was her tender regard for the train that drove her to defend it with such ruthlessness."

Mr. Hughes brightened considerably, relieved to be able to salvage his esteem for Miss Warner. "I'm sure you're right, sir. She is very fond of this train."

"And yet she is constantly trying to escape it." Argent muttered this under his breath, but more audibly he prompted, "What happened after that?"

"Here is where I can tell you of my own part in the fight. As I told you, my son and I were overcome by these desperadoes, unable to come to your defense or that of Miss Warner's. But when Miss Warner fired her gun, why naturally our captors stuck their heads out of the cab to see what was the hullabaloo. That's when my son and I kicked them from behind and out they tumbled, right under the guns of my wife and Miss Warner.

While my wife untied my hands, one of the men on the ground made a move – I didn't see it, but Miss Warner did – and she cocked the gun and said – you won't believe it, sirs – she said, 'There are three corpses three cars down. Those men had intent to disrespect me. Do you intend to disrespect me?' It made my blood run cold to hear her, but that man never moved a muscle after that. While Miss Warner and my wife held guns on them, my son and I tied them up as neat as you please, and gagged them, too, and took their guns. Miss Warner said she had a headache and that their mere breathing was bringing it on to pound, so she and I left the engine and started towards your car. We heard more men coming down the other side of the train, so I moved down towards the end of the car, but before I got there, I heard two shots. When I crossed the coupling and looked around the corner, I saw two men on the ground. Miss Warner came running towards me and asked for one of the guns I had taken off my captors. She said she had only one bullet left. She must have hit those men from forty feet or more, and in the dark; the moon was not risen at the time, as it is now. She has dead aim, I do assure you."

Mr. Hughes stopped again, no doubt lost in a struggle between admiration of such skill and fear of such skill in a woman. Finally, Argent prompted, yet again, "And what happened in our car?"

The engineer opened his mouth to speak, thought better of it, then reversed yet again that decision. Rubbing his chin, he said sheepishly, "Now I hope you gentlemen don't keep me in low regard for what happened next, but Miss Warner was like a force of nature last night. There was no denying her."

The engineer had stopped again, rubbing his chin and regarding the ground at Argent's feet. This time, Merritt prompted Mr. Hughes. "I assure you, we understand the pressure Miss Warner can bring to bear and the localized storms she can produce."

"Well, sir, she told me to take the far door, and she would enter through the headend door, and that way we would have the varmints covered at both ends, the better to rescue you. Now, I'm no military man, but I expressed concerns about each of us being in the other's line of fire, if you follow my meaning. But Miss Warner said that she had no intention of firing any more guns tonight, that her anger had passed on, so that I needn't fear from her. I argued, 'What if I were to hit you?' She's a curious woman, Mr. Merritt; she said, 'I have shot, and I suppose killed five men tonight, shot them before they even raised a hand against me. If you should by chance hit and kill me in that car, it will be but just punishment for such heedless anger and wanton killing, though I don't know how else I could have kept my own life. I only ask that you take me home for burial with the rest of my family.' I can't credit such thinking in the middle of an action and from someone so young. She is surely not yet twenty-five?"

Argent was staring at Mr. Hughes, and Merritt thought he saw something like fear in Argent's face.

"I think she indulges in such thinking often."

"Yes, sir." Mr. Hughes answered as if Argent's statement required affirmation. "We entered as planned. I burst through the door," – the engineer was animated here, swinging his arms forward violently, to underscore the ferocity of his entrance – "but they never fired a shot at me. But when Miss Warner entered from the other door, one of them shot straight at her, and she would be dead, if she hadn't entered crouching. She shot that fellow right between the eyes. The other fellow shot at almost the same time, but he had seen that she was low, and nicked her in the arm. I put my gun to his head and he dropped his own gun. The third man offered no resistance whatsoever."

A final time, Mr. Hughes paused, then confessed, "I wanted to tie them both up right there and then, but Miss Warner flat out told me 'not yet.' That's when she told the two of them to set you up right on the couches. Make them comfortable, she said, but then she told them to bind your feet. I can tell you, they didn't know what to think about that, but they did it – we each had a gun on them, you see. Then we had the one bind the other, and then I bound the last one while Miss Warner covered me. I made sure they were both good and tight, then we marched them right off to the caboose, where they are yet. I am very ready for the marshals to come take these men off my hands and off my train."

Mr. Hughes finished his story by relating to Merritt and Argent that he had brought his wife down to the parlor car – "that's Miss Warner's name for the car, sirs" – to see to Merritt's head, which was still bleeding. When Mrs. Hughes had seen the men trussed up as prisoners, she asked Miss Warner the reason. Miss Warner had replied, "For their safety."

Mrs. Hughes had heard a different purpose in Miss Warner's tone that her husband had not and had merely nodded before seeing to the two gentlemen. She had shown Miss Warner how to care for Merritt's head and what to watch for in both men when they regained consciousness.

When husband and wife left Miss Warner with Merritt and Argent in the parlor car, Mr. Hughes had asked his wife what Miss Warner had meant about safety. She had told him – either in complete ignorance or complete understanding of her husband's reaction – that keeping the gentlemen bound would protect them from further injury, from rolling around, whenever the train should lurch.

"Lurch, she said! This train never lurches, not under my control! Every engine must fight against train resistance when starting, and I hope people will find my operation at starting smoother than most." Mr. Hughes was highly indignant at his wife's rather left-handed reproach.

Merritt and Argent assured the engineer that this was the case. They had ridden under many engineers and they had found no fault with him, in the ordinary operation of this train. Mr. Hughes had been gratified to hear such confirmation, but the retelling of his wife's betrayal had soured Mr. Hughes on further communication. He abruptly announced that it was time (without consulting his watch) to move the train to make room for the 6:13 fast train and strode off to his engine. Argent consulted his own watch, and sighed — it was only 5:45, but they boarded their car anyway, and waited for the inevitable, and completely understandable, lurching as the train pulled off the depot siding and onto the main tracks.

Mr. Hughes had been obliged to move his train several more times that day, first moving forward onto the main tracks to wait for a scheduled train to unload its passengers or mail, or take on new passengers, then backing up his train, returning to the depot siding, while the scheduled train did the same onto the main tracks, before continuing on its way. In this see-saw manner, the little train was able to maintain its position, and yet allow the regularly scheduled business of the Baltimore & Ohio to flow along the tracks.

The marshals did not come until shortly after noon, but Merritt and Argent were relieved soon after the first morning train, allowing them to get some much-needed sleep. The carriage company that serviced the trains at Sir John's Run, transporting passengers and their baggage from the depot to Berkeley Springs, two and a half miles away, had learned of the little train's difficulties and had then offered several of its employés to stand guard while the crew and passengers recovered.

So it was that, despite the desperate events of the night before and despite being wary of a repeat of such events, Merritt and Argent could be found resting in their shirt-sleeves in the early hours of the afternoon, having woken only an hour or so earlier. They had been roused by the marshals, had given their reports, and then had shown the marshals the prisoners, bound and locked in the caboose, sharing the space with their dead brethren. The brakeman's body was preserved separately in the crew car, but it also was given to the marshals to make arrangements for its return to his family. In turn, the marshals – or, rather, deputy marshals – gave their report – or, rather, information that had been given them to relay to Merritt and Argent. After waiting at several destinations and tired of being shunted from one siding to the next, the first marshals sent out to find the gentlemen and Miss Warner had gone to the widow's farm, hoping to move things along. It was apparent that these first marshals – and the two deputies standing before Merritt and Argent – considered the task at hand not so much a matter of escorting of a young woman to the White House but one of rescuing her from the inept efforts to do so by the Secret Service. Merritt and Argent had been grateful to see the backs of these deputies as they rode off to Hancock to procure jail cells for the prisoners and pine boxes for the dead. Before they departed, however, Merritt advised them that there were at least five more dead somewhere up the line, near the 140th mile siding near Rockwell Run, that would also need their attention. Oh, and also the horses that brought these men to the train.

Merritt was satisfied that the marshals would be occupied for the rest of the day. In the meantime, he and Argent had the news of the deputy marshals to consider. In addition to the thinly veiled insult to Merritt and Argent in particular and to the Service in general, the deputies had reported that the first marshals had found Mrs. Lambert's farm in ashes and both women dead among them. Darnell was conspicuously absent from that report. The marshals who had discovered the tragedy had gone to Cumberland to report the deaths to the sheriff there and to make their investigations into the fire and any connections it may have had to Merritt, Argent, and Miss Warner, as the widow's recent guests. When Mr. Hughes sent his early morning telegram to Washington, it was received after the first marshals' telegram reporting the farm, where Merritt, Argent, and Miss Warner were staying, completely destroyed by fire. The first telegram lay undelivered to the President, being considered too distressing to disturb his sleep; if Miss Warner was dead, she would still be dead in the morning when the President woke. Mr. Hughes, in his understandable agitation and not knowing of the earlier telegram intimating Miss Warner's death, had not specified that all three – Merritt, Argent, and Miss Warner – were alive and with him on the train; he had only relayed that the train had been attacked and was awaiting further orders from both President Grant and President Garrett. Mr. Hughes' telegram, therefore, had lain with the earlier telegram as just more bad news that could wait until after President Grant's breakfast. The delay in informing the President had resulted in a delay in dispatching more marshals which had, in turn, delayed their arrival and assuming charge of the situation. Uninformed and unaware of the size of the situation, too few deputies had been dispatched, and now those marshals were off soliciting more help and spreading out to contain the situation, which covered ten or more miles of track and almost as many men (dead and alive) and their horses.

But the news of Miss and Mrs. Lambert's deaths was disturbing on several levels. Of course, they regretted the deaths of two women who had helped them. They had done so much for them, but especially for Miss Warner, tending to her wound and her most intimate needs, washing and mending her clothes, clothes that those two ladies were certain to find objectionable for one of their own sex.

Argent bolted upright in his seat. "I said – did I not? – that something was not right about that. And now I know what it is."

Merritt had been mildly surprised by Argent's sudden movement, and it somewhat slowed his understanding of Argent's statements. But now he thought back on yesterday when Argent had first said something was not right. "You mean about the St. Jude medallion. What is it that you now know?"

Argent fished the medallion from his pants pocket and again offered it for Merritt's review. Merritt, however, was currently nursing a dull, but persistent, headache, and he lay on one of the sofas, his arm flung over his eyes, seeing nothing.

"This medallion was found whenever Miss Lambert or her mother washed and mended Miss Warner's clothes."

"They were washed and mended by Monday afternoon. I saw M's folded clothes on the chest at the foot of the bed. Miss Lambert must have found the medallion at the same time that she found that abominable list." Merritt spoke disinterestedly, merely relaying facts that did not at all intrigue him.

Argent waited. After a moment, Merritt turned his head towards Argent on the opposite sofa, wondering what had stopped the conversation. Argent raised his eyebrows in expectation that Merritt would make the connection. Eventually, finally, Merritt did make the connection and sat up, though not nearly as quickly as Argent had.

"Mrs. Lambert knew by Monday, within two days of our arrival at her house, or suspected by that time, that M was Catholic. So, then, why did she wait until two days ago to mention it and make it a reason to expel M and us?"

"I think the better question would be, what happened in Spring Gap to prompt Mrs. Lambert to use Miss Warner's religion as an excuse to expel M and us?"

Merritt considered the question. "She was genuinely concerned for M's welfare, yet she was insistent that we leave, knowing that M should not travel."

"The widow was insistent, if you'll recall, that we return to Cumberland." Argent leaned forward. "Miss Lambert whispered to me as we left yesterday morning, 'Please take Miss Warner and yourselves to Cumberland. Mother says it means Miss Warner's life.' At the time I was merely annoyed at the whole situation, at the pointless necessity of making Miss Warner travel. But now I wonder, how did the widow know we were *not* going to Cumberland?"

"I think another question would be, where would she think we were going, if not to Cumberland?"

Argent stared out the window behind Merritt. Then closing his eyes, he remembered. "The train. She knew we were going to meet the train. Miss Lambert said, 'It will help you endure the ride to the train.' I was barely listening at the time, but I hear it now."

"The only people who knew we were to meet the train were the person who sent the telegram, the marshals we were to meet, Mr. Hughes, and the telegraph operator who took the message."

"And Darnell. It had to have been Darnell. He took the ladies to Spring Gap for Sunday services, Mrs. Lambert returned – her will turned against Miss Warner – and Miss Lambert returned knowing our destination. And now the widow and her daughter are dead, because they could not steer us towards Cumberland, as they were threatened to do by someone in Spring Gap."

Now Merritt leaned forward and took from Argent the St. Jude medallion, turning it over and over, considering it. "What if . . ." Merritt stopped and closed his eyes, suddenly dizzy. He sat back and began again. "What if the widow was not threatened to steer us to Cumberland, but threatened not to steer us anywhere at all? Consider that the widow was to keep us at the farm, that we and M were to be at the farm to perish in the flames, that she expelled us in order to save us, and that she hoped going to Cumberland would be safer than going to the train."

Argent nodded, slowly. "If the widow and her daughter knew about the train, then whoever threatened her in Spring Gap knew about the train, and she knew we'd be riding into a trap." It made sense of Mrs. Lambert's sudden turn against Miss Warner. Rather than turning Miss Warner out, endangering her health, the widow had sent Miss Warner away from certain death. Argent had badly misjudged the woman. Then he closed his eyes again. Miss Lambert had included the St. Jude medallion and the note in the package with the chloral, separate from Miss Warner's clothes; she had wanted Argent to know, in her own way, that she harbored no ill will towards Miss Warner.

"There's no need to tell M of this."

"No, no need. But we keep a tighter watch on her for the few hours we have left of this trip."

"The sooner she is off this train and in the White House with the President, the better."

It was with a great deal of effort, therefore, that Merritt and Argent controlled their anger when they learned of Miss Warner's recent excursion into the woods behind the depot at Sir John's Run. One of the young boys from Berkeley Springs who loitered most days around the depot after school had been employed by the station master to deliver a telegram to the gentlemen's car. Merritt tipped the boy, then, adding another small coin, asked the lad to inquire of Mrs. Hughes if Miss Warner was able to receive them.

"I'll ask her myself, sir, if you like. I'm just on my way to join her and my friends. She has taken her great horse out to exercise him and let him graze."

After a moment's stifled rage, Argent managed to sputter, "She is riding her horse?!"

"Oh, no, sir; only walking him. She said she is not able to ride him yet. Her arm is hurt, you see. Is it true her great horse can jump the Potomac here?"

Argent pulled a hand down his face. Merritt intervened before Argent could unload his spleen on the boy, who promised to be a well-source of information. "Miss Warner is with your friends, you say?"

"And Mike, the fireman from your train." The boy gave a sly smile. "We think he's sweet on her."

"Please inform Miss Warner to join us here, in our car, at her earliest convenience. And tell Mike to return Miss Warner's great horse to the stock car. We may be asked to leave at a moment's notice."

"Oh, no, sir. The train will not leave until tomorrow morning. The marshals have said the train is not to be trusted to leave without them, and they are busy cleaning up the mess of last night. Was it a great battle?"

"Very great." Merritt shoved the boy out onto the platform and closed the door after him.

Argent muttered, "The only thing great about that horse is its appetite."

By the time M made her appearance at the door of the parlor car, both Argent and Merritt had cooled their anger and were able to receive her with something like their usual equanimity. In view of her recent exertions on their behalf, and the trust she had shown in them in unburdening herself about her feud with Grant (which Merritt confessed he had overheard), and in view of the contents of the telegram, they had agreed to ignore M's lack of judgment where her horse was concerned and where her own safety was concerned.

Argent was relieved to see Miss Warner was dressed appropriately, though he had not seen her wear any but the simplest dresses. As with the shirts she wore, her dress had an open collar that belied the modesty Argent knew Miss Warner guarded. He and Merritt rushed to reclaim their forgotten coats, but M forestalled them. "Oh, please don't do that on my account. I promise you, the sight of you in mere shirt sleeves neither excites nor offends me. I mean only to stay a moment, to answer your summons and, if you will permit, to unburden myself."

Both men hesitated, with arms half-way into their coats, then by wordless agreement, both men discarded them. Argent gestured that M take a seat, but neither man joined her, on either couch. Despite her protestations for the men's comfort, M seemed herself ill at ease. It wasn't her dress – despite her general complaints about them, she seemed as completely at home in a dress as in trousers. She was still without her sling, of which both men disapproved, but she had fairly successfully covered the wound in her shoulder by means of a scarf, tucked into and peeking out (rather artfully, Argent thought) the entire perimeter of her collar and neckline.

M had come prepared to ask forgiveness for her outburst last night, but the sight of the belted and locked trunk, serving as a table between the two sofas unnerved her. It wasn't there last night. Is this why she had been summoned to this car? Had Merritt and Argent discovered her crime, that she had reclaimed her gun and stolen both the manifest and money? A worse thought occurred to M: now that they knew she was aware of their obvious criminal activity, what were their plans for her?

Merritt saw M pale as she took her seat, and some of the anger he had vowed to set aside returned. "You should not have been out, romping with that great horse of yours, your arm out of its sling. You are not yet fully restored."

M found relief in Merritt's anger; perhaps their concern, their unwarranted concern, for her was all that was at the heart of this interview. In her relief, she did not argue Merritt's point, but neither did she agree with him or acknowledge his concern.

In an unusual turn, it was Argent who intervened before Merritt's disapproval spoiled their visit with Miss Warner. "You said you wished to unburden yourself."

M shifted on the couch, folding and refolding her hands. She did not like having to divide her attention between Merritt at the desk in front of her and Argent before the mantle to her left. "I wish to make my apologies for last night, for my intemperate words and for, in a fit of pique, having you doubly bound by those scoundrels. I would have done it myself, but I could not trust the strength of my hands." At this, Merritt's anger floundered, and he smiled as M's apology took on a unique flavor. "I hope you will accept them, and in your charity assign to last night's behavior the impetus of fatigue, homesickness, a pounding headache, and a little over-indulgence in my emotions."

She had obviously practiced this apology, for she said it rapidly and with the delivery of a child reciting lessons with a wish to dispense the lines quickly ahead of a fading memorization.

Merritt shifted as he stood leaning with one elbow on the cylinder desk. M thought perhaps Merritt was standing out of some social deference to her and that he was uncomfortable. Perhaps he should sit, in deference to his head. M could empathize with an aching head. "Do you do better today?"

"Yes, very well, but your apology gives me some discomfort. There was nothing you said last night that requires an apology."

M looked from Merritt to Argent. Argent, then, had told Merritt of their conversation regarding Grant, while Merritt had seemingly slept.

"Mr. Merritt heard everything. And he is correct – you need not apologize." Argent cleared his throat and pulled straight his vest. "Now that we are clear of that subject, there is another that we wish to broach."

M took a deep breath and willed herself not to betray, again, her fears about the trunk sitting at her feet.

"It has come to our attention that tomorrow is your birthday."

"Is it?"

"You don't know your own birthday?"

M did not care for Merritt's incredulous smile. Birthdays were once a special occasion in her family, more at her father's insistence than her mother's. But ever since the death of two brothers on the *Sultana* five years ago – had it been that long already? – the deaths, on her birthday, of two brothers who had made it through the war – the day had been not celebrated but mourned. Her father had come home to attend the funerals and burials of his sons, to commission the headstones, and then he had left again. M folded and unfolded her hands as she thought of Ernst and Joseph, always so close, always together; they had enlisted together, had survived the war, and then had died together in a steamboat explosion on the Mississippi. This was a private matter, a family matter. She took a deep breath and concentrated on her present disdain for Merritt.

"Certainly I do. I simply don't know if tomorrow is it; I am not quite certain what today is."

"That is easy enough to remedy – today is April 26."

M was glad to be able to answer Argent and not Merritt. "Then, yes, tomorrow is my birthday. How came you by this information?"

Merritt picked up from the desk a telegram, which he waved at M, but did not show her. "We have received word from President Grant, asking us to fête you in his stead." Left unsaid was the awkward fact that Grant, having waited more than three long weeks for Miss Warner to join him in Washington City, would no longer be there to greet her. He had attended to his duties as President, of course, during that three-week-long wait, attending General Thomas' funeral at Troy and joining General Sherman and others at the reunion of the Army of the Potomac in Philadelphia, both earlier in the month. But now he was taking his family to spend a few days at West Point, to visit his son, a cadet there. Perhaps he had intended to invite M to join him on that visit, but more traveling for her would surely not be recommended. Merritt and Argent, therefore, were to keep her "secure," as it was phrased in the telegram, ostensibly recovering from her injury, until Grant returned from West Point next Monday. Next Monday would be May; they will have been on this particular assignment for more than a month. Whitley could not have been happy about this latest delay, but his silence on the matter spoke volumes of Grant's interference on their behalf.

M grew stiff, glad that her anger at Grant could so completely engulf the thoughts of her family. "You needn't bother. The current affairs between General Grant and myself do not permit me to accept anything from him. I especially reject any well wishes from him on my birthday."

"Then please accept them from us and allow us to mark the day with you."

"Is this an invitation from federal operatives?"

Merritt's smile broadened; he knew the word that was truly on M's lips was 'underlings.' "Not at all. Consider us two brothers celebrating a birthday with a younger brother."

"Why do I have to be the younger brother?"

"Because you are younger. Now," – brooking no more argument on the matter of relative ages – "we thought we would start with breakfast. There are several places in Grandiflora where a solid breakfast can be had."

"Grandiflora?"

"The next town over – after a brief stop in Hancock – only a few miles."

"Why are we stopping at all? I am told Washington is only a few hours away."

Merritt looked to Argent. They had not discussed this question from M. M saw the look but did not know what to make of it.

Argent straightened his vest once more. "Given the current state of affairs between you and President Grant, we thought you would enjoy the day out of Washington rather than in it. We will stop in Hancock only long enough to divest ourselves of the odious fellows who attacked us last night."

M studied each man in turn; the explanation seemed perfectly plausible, especially given her very forward expressions on the subject of Grant. "We breakfast in Grandiflora. Are we to lunch in the next town and enjoy our supper in yet a third?"

Argent merely smiled; it was Merritt who answered. "We thought we could have a pleasant picnic near a sweet little stream not far from town. We could take Emmett – there is plenty of shade and tender grass for his comfort and enjoyment."

"It has been a long time since I have been on a picnic."

"After the picnic, we could sample the admittedly few shopping establishments, where you could pick out a gift." It was obvious Argent thought the offer of a gift would cement M's cooperation.

"Gifts are out of the question; I hardly know you."

"Hardly know us? We have traveled together these many miles." Argent cleared his throat, even as Merritt realized his mistake – reminding M of a long-overdue termination to this trip was not the best way to gain her compliance to yet one more delay. He corrected course. "We are brothers, after all."

"Well, I can hardly contradict my own demands, and my brothers always gave me brilliant gifts, so I suppose it is in the best interest of continued good will that I accept."

Argent slowly let out a breath. It was obvious that Miss Warner was relieved at being so easily outmaneuvered on the matter of gifts. She was greedy for gifts, and, with the death of her father, the prospects of receiving any in the future were surely grim. "Wonderful. We may then end the day with a leisurely supper, and perhaps a hand or two of cards and a goodnight toast to the birthday girl."

"I could not ask for a more attentive birthday, and it seems you have done a great deal of planning and scheduling, but I wonder at the rather large gap of time between breakfast and picnic. Or do you intend to proceed to picnicking immediately after breakfast?"

M spoke lightly, but she couldn't help but feel something was afoot. In the short time that she'd known these men (in the many miles they had traveled together) every time they conducted a conversation in this see-saw manor – first one speaking, then the other, almost as if rehearsed – there was always some unpleasant surprise waiting for her. She was also feeling a little worse for the wear – the dizziness of last night had returned and she had become suddenly tired.

"The time between breakfast and our picnic provides an excellent opportunity to visit a doctor to have your shoulder and other wounds given some attention." Argent spoke out of turn; it should have been Merritt.

"And to have your heads examined. You must be addled indeed if you think I intend to spend any moment of my eighteenth birthday with a doctor, especially a doctor in a backwater coal town —"

Merritt straightened at the desk, his eyes wide. M thought that perhaps she had gone too far in insulting West Virginia doctors in particular, or maybe it was coal town doctors. Instead of the remonstrance she expected and deserved, Merritt repeated, "*Eighteenth* birthday?" Then turning to Argent, he exclaimed, as if Argent had just entered the car, "Giles! She eighteen!"

M did not understand Merritt's astonishment, but she was glad to have him diverted from the subject of doctors. She was not about to let him slip back to it. "Seventeen. I won't be eighteen until tomorrow. If your dates are correct."

Argent sat, slowly and deliberately, on the couch across from M, as if the act of sitting required all of his attention. He was stunned at the revelation. Suddenly, so much of M's behavior was explained: the list of instructions for the simplest social encounters, the petty exchange of insults with the clerk in Cincinnati, the childish anger and hurt of the previous evening, the almost manic concern for her horse, her unusual acquiescence to Mr. Henry and Miss Carrie in her own home, the titanic bursts of rebellion, the Homeric feud with Grant, the constant reversals between her intention to return home and her intention to confront the General. These were all more indicative of a lack of experience and of immaturity than of an indulged personality. She had brought on this trip all the world-weariness of a veteran of loss and grief and responsibility, but also a nearly complete innocence of propriety and an unexercised social discipline. There was nothing in her stature or demeanor that suggested her youth. Even her height had conspired in this counterfeit; she was taller than most women and many men; it suggested a fully matured body, a fully matured mind, a greater age. She moved with confidence and decisiveness, not the with the timid dependence on direction of most girls her age. And she did not have that girlish voice that so often attends women well into their twenties. She was a child, legally an infant, and would remain so – if Kentucky was like most states in this regard – for three years more, or until her marriage, when her status would change to *feme covert*.

Argent searched over the past four weeks for some clue that should have told them, that would have indicated her age. He had been staring at M as the shock of her age washed over him, but now he closed his eyes as he realized that he could have known as early as Cincinnati. When M was first being processed for the workhouse, all pertinent information would have been collected from her, including her age. The sheriff's words came back to him: I am not clear what your relation is to Miss Warner, but at the very least, her father should be advised. The sheriff knew M to be a child, but neither Argent nor Merritt had thought to inspect any records kept about her, because they had simply assumed she had reached her majority. How else could she be living on her own, managing the farm on her own? But that was a question for another day. And now Miss Carrie's words came back to him: She is an angry child, in an ailing woman's body. At the time in her life when most girls were learning their place in society from mothers and aunts and other female relations, M had navigated life alone, her mother worn out with grief and exhausted with M's admitted peculiarities; she had spent her formative years without true guidance. M's rages and rebellions were childish because she was still a child.

And yet, at seventeen she had endured with grace a harrowing time in jail and in the justice system of a strange town, as well as a serious wound that most men outside of war would have no knowledge of; and in following himself and Merritt to the lock, alone, she had shown a courage and coolness he had little seen in men outside of a group. She had easily discarded any deference she might owe to Merritt and Argent based on her age and sex and spoke to them with the casual assumption of expected respect that a much older woman would have developed. She had been running the family farm on her own for the last few years, since the advent of her father's illness. Argent was further astonished at the realization that M would have been but fifteen when her father began to turn the reins over to her. She had nursed her father in his final illness and decline, without benefit of mother or the help of sisters. She had been living alone and on her own since her father's death. In every way she was an adult, except in age.

Whatever her age – or, more than ever, because of her age – Argent was responsible for her well-being. With this new understanding of her vulnerability and his responsibility, Argent returned to the subject of a doctor. "Miss Warner, I saw your shoulder last night. It looked angry and inflamed then, and I am certain it is worse now." Indeed, when she first entered the car, he noted her high color and he noted now that it had not subsided, even though M had been sitting quietly for some time, after having ceased her romping with her great horse, as Merritt had put it.

M marked the change in Argent's demeanor towards her, and the old frustration with arbitrary authority flared up in her. "Not half so angry and inflamed as I am, at having my own birthday used as bait for an unwanted and unnecessary confrontation with a doctor of unknown worth and reputation."

"Why does it have to be a confrontation?"

Argent turned to stare at Merritt. Both he and M were stupefied at the points Merritt chose to magnify. Merritt merely gazed back at them, innocently, obviously expecting an answer. After his initial shock at the disclosure of M's age, he seemed to be entirely indifferent to it.

Argent broke the stalemate first, and to his credit, did not rise to match M's angry tone. "Miss Warner, you were forced to ride all day far too soon after your injury, and then you – very commendably – spent a good deal of the night defending the train and everyone in it against attack. Circumstances have not been such that you are permitted to heal. I can see from here that you are unwell."

M, in fact, did look unwell – her face was flushed long before the current argument began, and purple-red circles were camped beneath her eyes, which were beginning to take on a sunken look. Argent was fairly certain the wound was in the beginning stages of infection, and from sad experience in the war, he knew that could end disastrously. Evidently, Merritt was thinking the same thing, for he threw his weight behind Argent.

"M, we've both seen what infection can do to a body, and that's something we just will not allow to happen, certainly not merely to mollify your fears."

Argent winced – this, surely, was not the best way to convince M to see a doctor.

M rose, though, surprisingly, less angry. "I, too, have seen what infection can do to a body. And I have seen what incompetent medical treatment can do to a body as well. I will make this concession to you." Argent moved to object to any negotiations in the matter, shaking his head, but M spoke over his expected objections; she indeed assumed a right far beyond her age to speak with them this way. "If my shoulder is worse tomorrow than today, I will consult with the doctor in Grandiflora, but I reserve the right, unto myself, to reject in part or in whole any treatment he suggests. That is non-negotiable. I am not so gullible as to think a doctor is all knowing about my or anyone else's body."

"By virtue of his degree, he knows more than the patient about the body."

"Just because a man carries a gun doesn't make him a marksman; just because a man hangs a degree on his wall doesn't make him competent. Now, if you will excuse me, I promised to help Mrs. Hughes with her chores – she is worn out tending to every injured person on this train, yet she is still responsible for feeding the marshals and the prisoners."

"Miss Warner, a moment, please." Argent indicated that she should seat herself again. M hesitated; she did not want to resume this conversation. Argent, sensing her hesitation, assured her, "We are finished speaking of doctors for the moment. Please, sit."

After M reseated herself, it was Merritt who began the next conversation. "Last night, you made a comment that we would like for you to clarify."

M thought back on last night but could not think what comment needed elucidation. "I have already apologized for my comments and behavior."

"Yes, and as we have said, without need. But we were intrigued by the suggestion that these brigands had a grievance against us. What makes you think so?" Though they had discussed the probability, they had no way of proceeding without more information, and M may have overheard something.

M looked at them with mild confusion. Didn't they know? "The brigands themselves said so. They made reference to some grievance – though they did not clarify – a mighty grievance that required your utter destruction. Oh, and Grant's, too. I felt some sympathy with them – I know how Grant can aggrieve someone – though I would never stoop so low as to murder him or his federal underlings to relieve my grievance."

Argent smarted once again at her barb. Despite what he thought was a rapprochement these last few days, apparently Miss Warner still held her disapproval of them just below the surface.

Merritt smiled to hear M restored to her stinging humor. Perhaps she was feeling better already. "When did you hear this?"

"When you were drunkenly incapacitated in the wagon in Cumberland and near the lock; mostly near the lock. One of them wanted to kill you then and there, since the law in Cumberland wasn't interested in murder, especially if it was a stranger. They wanted to ruin you on both sides of the grave, for economic reasons. It makes no sense, though someone was paying them; perhaps that was the economic reason. He wanted to make you and Grant pay for what you did."

"Who wanted to make us pay?"

M was having trouble understanding Merritt today, and it took her a brief moment to consider what he said. "They didn't say a name, only that he gave orders for this situation, the situation when the law didn't care." Then M cocked her head as a new thought occurred to her, as if this new thought had knocked her head to the side. "Did you kill someone? A criminal with an angry brother?" She didn't seem overly alarmed at the thought of traveling with killers. On the contrary, she seemed to look at them with new regard. Killing someone who inspired such loyal vengeance seemed to bolster her regard for them, perhaps even to elevate them to some hierarchy above 'federal underlings.'

Merritt slid a look towards Argent who had visibly stiffened at the inquiry. "I hardly think that is a topic for mixed company."

Now M stiffened. "If you will recall, it was at your own instigation that this conversation began. That the initial topic of brigands naturally enough led to crimes, theirs and others', is hardly my fault." With that, M stood, then left, summarily closing all conversation.

Merritt smiled lazily at Argent, enjoying M's parting shot. But Argent had his own parting shot as he, too, left, to make certain the prisoners remained secure, in the absence of the marshals.

"Merritt, I shall have to put you to bed – your speech does not improve. I find it may be an impediment to appearing with you in public."

They did not see M again until after dark, until after the train had made its brief stop at Hancock, shedding the weight of several prisoners and newly deputized marshals. One of the marshals, however, remained on the train, helping Mike with his duties as fireman, and a new brakeman joined them (assigned to the train, fresh in from Martinsburg), so that stopping for the night at Grandiflora was not nearly so jarring an event as stopping at Sir John's Run and Hancock had been.

Argent found it had not been necessary to put Merritt to bed, as Merritt had done so himself, soon after M and Argent left the car. As the train pulled into Grandiflora, Merritt woke and pronounced himself very hungry. When the train stopped, he and Argent presented themselves at M's door, intending to ask her to dinner with them. But it was Mrs. Hughes who answered their knock. She did not speak but led them to M's bed. The inside of the car had been renovated for its new occupant. No doubt, if he had had time, Mr. Hughes would have erected a wall and fireplace between the back of the car and the front, as was done in Miss Warner's original car. Instead, Mr. Hughes built and hung a large swing where such a wall would have been, and Mrs. Hughes had somehow managed to cobble together some of the heavy cloths from the parlor car to create a curtain that hung behind the swing, acting as a wall, giving Miss Warner some semblance of privacy within her own car. Argent thought of Miss Warner's swing on her front porch in Kentucky; what had prompted Mr. Hughes to build a swing, how had he known? Mrs. Hughes led them past the swing, heavily bolstered with pillows and fabrics that once adorned the parlor car, and into the bedroom behind it.

M was asleep but definitely in fever. Mrs. Hughes gently pulled away the scarf from M's dress to reveal a very angry-looking wound. There was no need to speak, the fever and the inflamed half-formed scar spoke for itself. Leaving Mrs. Hughes to sit with M, Merritt and Argent struck out for Grandiflora, perhaps a mile from the tracks. If a doctor could be found, Argent would gladly abdicate M's care to him. Argent did not think Miss Warner's fever was a harbinger of anything decidedly disastrous – fevers were expected after such an injury, though generally manifested much sooner – but the timing could be advantageous to the situation. It would be expected, even by someone so rebellious as Miss Warner, to spend a day or two recuperating from a fever. It would be a ready-made reason to detain Miss Warner until such time as President Grant was able to receive her. Argent was ashamed that the thought occurred to him.

Grandiflora was a town without an identity or a purpose. Though there was a siding nearby, it was more to service the tracks over the creek that fed into the Potomac than to service the town. There was, in fact, no depot to announce the existence of the town, only a finger signboard with the name "Grandiflora" printed in Gothic script. Hoping to become the next resort town of West Virginia, to compete with Berkeley Springs, Grandiflora had been the dream of a man of accidental wealth. He had laid out its streets, built its one hotel, funded its several quality shops, then had waited – in vain – for the envisioned onslaught of summer visitors. Though the view up the Potomac, of North Mountain and Sideling Hill in the distance, was magnificent, there was little else to commend the area for tourists and their money. There was a spring that watered the town, but there were no mineral springs nearby, no bathhouses in which the weary or the truly sick could immerse themselves. Nor was the elevation of the spot particularly high, certainly not high enough to promise the rarefied and healthy air one thought of when considering resorts. There was no industry here, either – coal had not been found, the clay pits were closer to Martinsburg, and the timber concerns were not interested in the scrub pine and swamp white oaks that proliferated in the area. There was a perfectly good creek nearby, but no mills had been erected because there were few nearby farms in need of having their grain milled. Nonetheless, the town survived from year to year, with a steady infusion of funds from the accidentally wealthy man, who enthroned himself as mayor of the town. Even the late war had left Grandiflora untouched, as the battles raged all around it, in the perpetual tug-of-war over West Virginia and the B&O as it traveled through that newly-birthed state.

Merritt and Argent had tracked an engraver here a few years ago, a man of only middling talent, but he had been recruited to engrave counterfeit plates on the nation's new money supply and, as such, he represented a threat. Merritt and Argent had been surprised to find the town – they had ridden over these rails many times, but they had never noticed the signboard. In this particular instance, their work had brought them to Grandiflora, and it had taken a great deal of arguing with the engineer (while at Hancock) to stop the train on the siding to let them off. The arguing, it turned out, had been completely unnecessary, as the engineer would have made the stop anyway, in response to a lady's scarf hung on a leaning pole about a mile from the siding. It was later explained to them in the town that this was a signal to obliging engineers to stop and pick up the person or persons wishing a ride to Martinsburg or Harper's Ferry and points beyond both. The brakeman would yank the scarf from its pole as the train passed; whoever boarded the train at the siding reclaimed the scarf from the brakeman so that it may be returned to the clerk of the Grandiflora hotel for its next use. Neither Merritt nor Argent could quite work out how tickets were purchased, but the system seemed to work for the good people of Grandiflora, and surely the Baltimore & Ohio would have objected if fares were not paid.

They had caught their man, assiduously working in one of the hotel rooms – he had specifically asked for a room with a southern facing window, for more light for his "artwork." The owner of the hotel (who was also the owner of the town) had briefly been under suspicion of working with the engraver – he had openly supplied the engraver with whatever paper and inks the engraver required (from the book and stationery store, which the hotel owner also owned), and, moreover, had given the engraver his room and board free of charge. Merritt and Argent learned, however, that the hotel owner had provided all these necessaries *gratis* because the engraver had misrepresented himself as an artist who would put the little town on the map, so to speak, with sketches of the hotel and the few other buildings of note, as well as of the surrounding beautiful scenery, something in the vein of Porte Crayon. The town's founder had been so grateful that scandal had been avoided (Merritt and Argent had been able to catch their man discreetly) that he had insisted he repay Merritt and Argent in some way. They, of course, had to decline – they could not accept anything that might whiff of a bribe or personal enrichment – but they had noticed the owner's two daughters, and had made a point of returning to the town a time or two since, to avail themselves of the attractions of the town, as private citizens. That next day, a lad of the town had been sent to hang the scarf on the pole, and Merritt and Argent had stood by the siding in the rain, the engraver in handcuffs between them.

This night, of course, they would not need to convince the engineer to make the stop, nor hope for the coincidence of a scarf on the pole. Mr. Hughes knew of the siding, but not of the town (it was not on the list of sidings, depots, and stations he had been given at Baltimore, several weeks ago), so that the only convincing was that of assuring him of its existence. There were no carriages here, awaiting their pleasure, as there would be at Sir John's Run or Hancock, so Merritt and Argent walked to the town along the little used wagon road.

There was only one main street in the town, and this was oriented roughly east to west. Argent and Merritt entered the town near its center, the wagon road widening out into a sort of welcoming gap between the buildings. They were familiar with Grandiflora and at ease on its few streets, but this night they were sensitive to observation – the report of the deaths of the Lambert women and of inquiries about them in Cumberland made even sweet little Grandiflora suspect. Though it was not very late, it was dark, and most of the town had already retired for the day. Even so, as they walked down the main street, Merritt was aware of being watched.

The hotel was at the far western end of the street, an odd placement for what was arguably the only reason for the town's existence. It was much too big for a town with little to offer. Argent led Merritt down a short side street two or three blocks before the hotel. "I seem to remember a physician's office down here. I think he also serves as the town's undertaker."

"That will not inspire M's confidence."

"Miss Warner's confidence needs to be taken down a peg or two."

Argent found the office, but it was, as expected, closed for the day. The restaurant across the street, however, was not closed and was, at that hour, heavily patronized. Grandiflora boasted perhaps seven hundred inhabitants and an unusual number of restaurants and saloons to serve them. In the restaurant on the corner and obliquely across the street from the doctor's office, it was obvious to more than one of the inhabitants

Merritt's and Argent's object. Merritt's hunger had never left him, and now he led Argent across the street to the restaurant. Merritt noticed a man watching them from the window. "Argent."

"I see him; he has been watching us since we entered town. Not making any effort to hide it either."

Before taking a table, Argent took the opportunity to ask a patron, an older man, as he was passing on his way out, about the physician whose office was just across the street. The man was enthusiastic in his praise of Dr. Culver. The praise included a rather detailed account of the relieving of the man's bladder by the introduction, if you please, of a catheter – a number 7, silver! – right up the shaft of his penis, easy as pie. Merritt visibly paled and even Argent, with his relatively extensive knowledge of the profession, found the story unsettling. But in Grandiflora, everybody's business was known to everybody else, and the man's story provided no more reaction than an appreciative nod or two by those rude enough to be listening to another man's conversation. Argent replied that, happily, that service was not needed; privately, both men prayed that it never would be. To Argent's request as to when the good doctor would return to his offices, the bladder patient replied with all the confidence and information of one who frequently consulted with the doctor.

"Doctor Culver arrives at eight every morning but Saturdays and Sundays – Saturdays he's in at nine, Sundays, not at all. Sometimes he is in his rooms earlier if he has scheduled patients. Do you need to schedule an appointment?"

"Well, that would be ideal, but since his office is closed, I don't see how that is possible."

"Oh, more than possible! There he sits, yonder, at that table." Argent's informant waved to the man at the window table. "Got some patients for you, doc!"

Argent thanked Doctor Culver's satisfied patient and he and Merritt made their way to the table where the doctor sat waiting for them. Removing his hat, Merritt opened the conversation. "We're very sorry to bother you, doctor, especially when you are at table, but we'd like to make an appointment for the morning, first thing, if possible."

"Please, sit. I've been watching you two peering into windows and reading signboards. I was wondering if you would make it down as far as my door." A waiter appeared at the table, asking if the gentlemen joining the doctor would like anything to eat or drink. Merritt ordered whiskey and water with a deferment on the food until their business with the doctor was concluded; Argent declined to order anything. "I'd advise you to skip the drink as well, Mr. ?"

"Please excuse me. It's Merritt, and this is my associate, Mr. Argent. Why should I skip the drink? It seems like a respectable establishment and at least one town doctor isn't afraid to patronize it."

"Oh, it's a fine establishment; I recommend it highly. They serve some of the finest whiskey available, but a man suffering concussion should not drink."

Merritt was dumbfounded, but Argent was excited. "How do you know he has a concussion?"

"The bruise on the side of his temple is as plain as day, even in this low light, and now I see the cut above it, just at the hair line. And he holds his head gingerly, slightly to one side. I suspect there is a second injury to the neck. His walk is occasionally off-balance, and I detect a slurring of his speech. Now, both of these last two symptoms, if you will, are also indicative of drunkenness, but I think I can confidently dismiss that. No, the bruise on the temple was the deciding factor – from a distance, that is. I could be completely mistaken, though – many situations could be the cause for his symptoms, independent of a head trauma."

Argent could hardly contain his excitement. "No, no, you're absolutely correct. He was hit, not once, but twice, in the head, in the same evening." Merritt was beginning to sympathize with M's irritation at having her medical situation discussed without being consulted.

"Was he intentionally hit, or was this the result of drunken falls or other accidents?"

"Come to think on it, the first blow was an accident, though it could conceivably be determined as intentional, but the second blow was definitely delivered with malicious intent."

"And did he lose consciousness?"

The waiter had returned with Merritt's drink, which Merritt gratefully sipped, despite the doctor's admonition.

Argent thought back on the attack on the train, speaking slowly at first, as the memory clarified. "I don't believe he did with the first blow, though he was very groggy. He definitely lost consciousness with the second blow, and for quite some time."

Doctor Culver observed Merritt, disapproving Merritt's drinking, in defiance of his professional advice. Merritt gazed dreamily in return; maybe sometimes it does have to be a confrontation.

"For how long, exactly?"

Merritt finally spoke up, regarding his own concussion. "Mr. Argent cannot answer that, exactly, because he himself was unconscious."

Doctor Culver sat back fully in his chair. "Is that so? And how did Mr. Argent come by this state?"

"Like my own, Mr. Argent's blow to the head was partly that of an accident and partly that of an intentional injury. I would like to take this opportunity to point out, however, that while my associate succumbed to unconsciousness at one blow to the head, it took two to subdue me. Clearly, mine is the harder head and thus the lesser cause for concern and scrutiny."

Doctor Culver observed Merritt. "That remains to be seen. Well, it is a curious situation to have two men concussed, both accidentally and intentionally, in the same evening, but we can sort that out tomorrow at your appointments." He rose and gathered up his hat. "I shall see you at 7:30."

Argent also rose, but Merritt was determined to finish his drink, and remained seated. "No, you misunderstand. The appointment is not for either of us."

"You should reconsider that."

"We have, in our care, a young woman who suffered a bullet wound to the shoulder."

The doctor started at this. "Then why have we wasted time on your concussed heads?"

"Please, doctor, let us explain." Argent motioned for Doctor Culver to regain his seat. "This young woman suffered this injury more than a week ago."

"And did a physician attend her at that time?"

Argent looked briefly at Merritt, then admitted, "No, circumstances at the time did not permit, but the wound was admirably treated, nonetheless."

Merritt knew that admission came at something of a cost to Argent. He raised his glass to both Argent and the late Widow Lambert.

"And you are just now consulting a physician?"

"She appeared to heal at first intention, but these last few days have challenged her recovery to the point that we now fear the wound is infected."

"Where is this young woman now? I must see her immediately."

Despite bristling briefly at Doctor Culver's implication that he had postponed proper treatment for Miss Warner, Argent became once again enthusiastic. "We can show her to you. She is on our private train on the siding just outside of town."

"The siding? Did you walk here?" At Argent's nod, the doctor rose again. "We'll stop by the hotel stable for a carriage to take us to your train."

Merritt and Argent both rose with the doctor; Merritt swayed slightly. Doctor Culver observed this and sniffed. "I told you not to drink that. Well, come along and you can explain to me, on the way, how it is that a young woman receives a bullet to the shoulder while under the care of two gentlemen wealthy enough to own a private train."

During the drive to the train, Argent explained – without revealing the events at the canal – that Miss Warner was a victim of a ricocheted bullet from a nearby shooting, involving Saturday night revelers. He reported in detail the surgery and care of the widow (which impressed the doctor) and gave a brief account of the day's ride in the saddle (which received the doctor's thorough disapprobation), and finally, Argent disclosed the events which saw them both concussed while Miss Warner worked to thwart a train robbery (which left the doctor speechless). Argent also gave a detailed record of the types and amounts of medication given to Miss Warner during the course of her convalescence. Merritt noted that Argent omitted the almost constant use of chloral hydrate since Cincinnati. Merritt, however, said nothing, being aware of his lack of professional knowledge in the matter and also now keenly self-conscious of a slurred speech.

Upon knocking at M's car, Mrs. Hughes met them with a pistol in her hand. Argent introduced the doctor, but even this did not loosen her grip on the weapon. Doctor Culver noted it but said nothing. While the doctor made his examinations, Argent asked the engineer's wife how Miss Warner had passed the last two hours.

"She has hardly moved."

Argent nodded, and Merritt commented, "A sure sign that she is unwell." At this, the doctor turned from M, to fix Merritt with a stare. "She is normally a restless sleeper."

The doctor continued to stare. "She is a confirmed insomniac?"

Merritt was reluctant to so completely condemn M's sleeping habits, and amended his earlier statement with, "Perhaps it is only trains that disrupt the natural order."

Argent cleared his throat behind the doctor and admitted that, by their own observation as well as by statements of those closest to her, Miss Warner was chronically sleep-deprived, and that they had tried chloral hydrate at the suggestion of other physicians, but with mixed results. Though Argent had spoken, the doctor continued to stare at Merritt, then abruptly returned to finish his examination.

After only a few minutes, the doctor rose and instructed the men to bring her to his office at 7:30. He suspected the cause for the fever, and did not think it forebode any dire outcome, but he was concerned, as any doctor would be, of settled insomnia, especially in females. It was well known that persistent insomnia was often the early symptom of insanity. A woman's health, alas, was generally dictated by her womb, and any derangement there more often than not directed a derangement of the mind. He was a sad observer of many such cases; manual correction of the womb was often a woman's only recourse.

Mrs. Hughes, who had lowered her gun and hid it in the folds of her skirt, now brought it back in sight, resting it at her waist. Doctor Culver noted it but said nothing.

Argent escorted Doctor Culver from the car, and as he helped him into the carriage Argent begged a moment for a final word. "I would be remiss if I did not inform you that Miss Warner has an avowed aversion to doctors. She may not be the most cooperative of patients."

"Leave that to me – I know how to handle surly patients, be they male or female. I will send a carriage for you in the morning."

Merritt joined Argent outside as the doctor disappeared in the darkness towards town. Argent remarked, rather cattily, "I noticed you said precious little."

"There was no need – you were amazingly forthcoming with all kinds of information."

Argent turned towards Merritt. "Now Merritt, don't be angry. I thought his diagnosis of you from across the room was the proof we needed of his competence. It was an amazing stroke of good luck running into him."

"More amazing than his diagnosis of me from across the room was his missed diagnosis of you right across the table."

"Come, now; your slurred speech and shambling gait is no reflection on your manhood. Some of us can simply handle our concussions better than others."

27 — *Wednesday, M's Birthday*

M made it through the night without crisis, but she was still feverish in the morning when the men came to collect her. Mrs. Hughes had stayed with her all night, and should have had M ready on time, but Merritt and Argent were made to wait outside the car for nearly fifteen minutes. They reminded Mrs. Hughes several times, as they stood and knocked at the door, that they had an appointment to keep. Each time, Mrs. Hughes answered in an increasingly irritated tone that she was having trouble helping Miss Warner dress. Argent muttered under his breath, "She does know this is a doctor's appointment and not a ball that we go to?"

When Mrs. Hughes finally opened the door, they were astonished at M's appearance. She was, indeed, not dressed for a ball, but neither was she dressed for an appointment in town. Mrs. Hughes had dressed M in a heretofore unseen skirt and one of M's better shirts, though not a shirt one would expect a woman to wear with a skirt. In fact, M was dangerously close to being in a state of incomplete dress, having no basque or any other jacket placed over her shirt. Acknowledging the looks from Merritt and Argent, Mrs. Hughes explained, "It will be so much easier for the doctor and Miss Warner if her shoulder were more easily available. The skirt is mine; Miss Warner brought precious little in the way of clothes"

Upon closer inspection, Merritt could see that the skirt was too wide in the waist for M and far too short in length. Mrs. Hughes had attempted to remedy these problems by pinning the waistband to better fit M and by sitting the waistband as low as possible on M's long torso. M remained uncharacteristically quiet while being reviewed like a cadet. Remembering Doctor Culver's talk last night of deranged wombs and manual corrections, Argent suggested that perhaps Mrs. Hughes should accompany Miss Warner. Mrs. Hughes regretted she could not, as she was needed on the train, "But, you tell that doctor that Miss Warner is not deranged in her mind or anywhere else, and that he should keep his attention and his hands on her shoulder and nothing else."

It was arguably the most Mrs. Hughes had ever said to them, and it was certainly the first she had ever spoken to them in the voice of command. Argent was beginning to think that there was no woman left who respected a doctor's opinion.

Mrs. Hughes had replaced M's sling, so that she was one-handed once again, and with the added weakness of her fever, she needed considerable help gaining a seat in the carriage. Her initial grogginess gave way to the considerable pain aroused by riding over the rough and rutted wagon road. She was fully awake now, but her attention was completely given over to enduring the jostling of the carriage, the growing nausea, and the misery of her rising fever. Her concentration was such that she hardly registered that the carriage had stopped and that she had been helped out of it. Eventually, she was able to focus enough to realize she was being abandoned, judging by the smell, at a doctor's office. She heard the doctor say, "Return in two hours. She will sleep for some time afterwards." From the back room where she found herself laying on a cot of sorts, she called, "Return in five minutes." When no one replied, she added, "I mean what I say: five minutes."

The doctor returned to the room, introduced himself, then promptly rendered her senseless by means of sulphuric ether, introduced on a towel, freshly laundered and folded according to the latest medical specifications, soaked with the anesthetic.

Standing under the doctor's shingle on the walkway outside, Merritt and Argent were experiencing the pangs of parents leaving their child in the care of someone else for the first time. They had both heard M's command to return in five minutes. Argent had turned to console her, but Merritt had held him back, though he, too, felt the pathos behind the plea. As they stepped down into the street, Merritt was hit with inspiration: "Let us go buy her something." This considerably cheered Argent, and they started off to scour the local shops for something truly special for the girl turning eighteen on their watch.

They returned to the doctor's office as told, exactly two hours later. They were, in fact, twenty minutes early, but they hid their anxiety by waiting the twenty minutes in the restaurant across the street where they had met Doctor Culver the night before. Precisely at the two-hour mark, the two men exited the restaurant, leaving behind two coffees, ordered, but untouched.

Merritt and Argent entered the office in somewhat exaggerated good cheer, adopted for M's sake, but the bluster was wasted. Doctor Culver was there, but M was not. The doctor explained that everything had gone well: he had drained the blooming infection, debrided some tissue in the wound, and removed several small slivers of necrosed bone that had failed to work their way through the skin, the source, he suspected of the infection. Otherwise, the wound looked good and he expected a full and satisfactory recovery. As to Miss Warner's whereabouts, he was uncertain. He had left to look in on a patient nearby, certain that Miss Warner would still be under the effects of the ether but had returned to find her gone. Doctor Culver then sent out a few of the older town children to search for Miss Warner, with the promise of a nickel for the one who found her, but none had yet reported back. Rather unnecessarily, he intoned, "She should be resting and not wandering about, creating fresh havoc for her person."

Argent, who had so recently proclaimed the doctor's competence, took issue with the doctor on two points: one, at leaving a patient unattended, no matter at what stage of insensibility, and two, at the choice of ether over chloroform. Merritt and Argent were both witnesses, he informed the doctor, to the common use of chloroform on the battlefield, and Argent wondered that a private practitioner should eschew the example of army surgeons steeped in four years of hard surgical experience. Doctor Culver heatedly replied that battlefield surgeons were often mere butchers, hardly worthy of the title 'doctor,' lopping off digits and limbs with the greatest abandon, and as to their preference of chloroform over ether, there was no preference at all – any doctor worth his salt is aware of the potentially fatal consequences of chloroform and equally aware that ether carries almost no such potential; chloroform on the battlefield was a mere administrative and logistical choice based on convenience, in that chloroform requires less baggage room than ether.

Merritt remained silent during this exchange, but for reasons other than vanity. He thought Argent was overreacting and wondered at the real cause. After all, what did either of them (even Argent) really know of chloroform or ether, other than its use in the war and the sickly-sweet odor it carried? The sweet smell of chloroform was often mingled with the sour and putrid smells that wafted with it from every hospital tent and ward. Merritt felt slightly ill.

Argent stormed out, declaring that Miss Warner was perhaps not entirely wrong in her estimation of doctors. Merritt remained behind to thank the doctor and to pay him for both his services and the regimen of medication he prescribed for M. These included chloral hydrate and laudanum, medications as much for her shoulder wound as for what he called "Miss Warner's hysterical manifestations" – a diagnosis prompted by Mrs. Hughes' comments and supported (through keen extrapolation) by several comments Merritt and Argent made regarding the young lady's unusual circumstances and predilections.

Merritt joined Argent on the sidewalk outside, still fuming. His anger, however, was not all directed at Doctor Culver. "This penchant of Miss Warner's for unauthorized and premature departure is becoming a bad habit, and we must break her of it, or President Grant will find himself spending all his time running after Miss Warner instead of running the country. She has too long assumed an independence far beyond her age and sex and far beyond the confines of her farm." Merritt said nothing, but grabbed Argent's elbow and steered him down the street to begin their search for M. It was a middling sized town, by West Virginia standards, and well laid-out. Merritt tried to smooth Argent's ruffled feathers by expressing the opinion that it shouldn't be too hard to find M.

They found her almost immediately. Argent had caught sight of her, out of the corner of his eye, as they passed a book store – a woman wearing a sling, obviously tall, though she was seated by the window. She was leafing through a book that was of doubtful interest to her. More likely, she was interested in sitting in the chair she had found inexplicably abandoned among the shelves of books. She had dragged it over to the window, and then had picked up books at random to peruse as she rested. The proprietor was on to her ruse – not many women would read a book on geology, moreover one in German, and he was suspicious that any woman dressed as poorly as M could afford a book. When Merritt and Argent entered the shop, the bookseller was insisting that M either buy something or leave.

Argent dismissed the man, promising that he would take care of the situation. Before the bookseller was barely out of hearing, Argent commenced an apparently long-simmering lecture on Miss Warner's irresponsibility which in turn reflected on his own responsibilities, a lecture delivered in the sternest terms and tone possible when addressing a young lady. If Argent was angry with M for leaving without permission, among a multitude of other missteps these last few weeks, it was more than matched by her anger at finding herself alone in a strange establishment, against her very clear intentions, expressed only yesterday, with a fresh pain in her shoulder, and no idea where to find the train. Argent was clearly unprepared for such a vehement counter-offensive, and quickly sought to staunch M's freshet of fury. At the first break in the exchange, Merritt casually remarked that M seemed to be feeling better; in particular, her fever seemed to have fled. Argent paused, realizing the import of what Merritt said, but M merely regarded them both coolly. "As I said it would." And with that thoroughly unsatisfactory end to the argument – for both contenders – M left the bookshop, handing to the proprietor the book she had been paging through – *Mineralogia Polyglotta*, Merritt noticed. She paused at a table long enough to read the title of a treatise on the West Virginia tobacco trade, and as she passed through the door, she threw over her shoulder, "You Virginians are deluding yourselves hoping to compete with Kentucky white burley."

"West Virginians," the bookseller called after her.

Merritt and Argent caught up with her in time to hear her mutter, "Maybe today, but who knows which way you'll lean tomorrow?" In an even lower voice, she added, "Fickle people. How many times have they changed their capital?"

Merritt admonished her, "M, you must stop comparing the whole of the nation to Kentucky; not everyone is lucky enough to be born or live there."

M visibly softened. "It is uncharitable of me, when I have been so lucky in that regard. But how will they know their misfortune if they are not made to see?"

"Perhaps the rest of the nation should be allowed to wallow in its ignorant bliss."

"Nonsense. By that logic, we should leave the ignorant pagan in a graceless state. Still, perhaps I shouldn't broadcast too widely the alluring seeds of Kentucky's merits – the state could be quickly overrun by foreigners far and near. God help us if the Hoosiers migrate south! Do you know, there will soon be a second bridge across the Ohio at Louisville? All this congress between our shores can only come to grief."

Both M's and Argent's anger seemed to have dissipated, but M had no intention of remaining in their company. As far as she was concerned, they had already reneged on her birthday breakfast, disregarded her decisions in the matter of the doctor, had abandoned her – without her consent or knowledge – at some quack's door, then had the audacity to remonstrate with her on leaving under her own power upon waking.

M was walking at what she hoped was fast enough to lose her two escorts, but they took up position, one on either side of her and kept pace with her, quite easily.

Argent offered, "You are feeling better."

"Yes."

"Splendid! Then you'll be able to attend our picnic, as planned."

M stopped so suddenly, the men continued on a step or two beyond her. "I had forgotten about the picnic. I'll go fetch Emmett." She turned her head this way and that, looking around her. "Where is the train?" Spotting the hotel, she turned to retrace her steps, hoping to find the information she sought there; she had no doubt she would get anything but delays and demurs from these men.

Merritt moved to physically intercept her, blocking her way. "I would be glad to bring Emmett, but we're not quite ready yet. Argent and I have yet to procure the food and blankets, dishes, etc. In the meantime, there is a pleasant hotel just down the street – we've had occasion to stay there – with a very commendable larder. Let us secure a room for you, where you may rest, and some food can be sent up to you. You must be hungry – you slept through dinner last night and missed breakfast this morning."

"I have no intention of spending my birthday in a hotel room." M was beginning to feel trapped, and she was not about to admit that she was indeed hungry. Also, although M had woken rather abruptly and completely from her surgery, she was now finding it difficult to focus her thoughts. She was fruitlessly searching for a way to rid herself of Merritt and Argent when the solution presented itself.

From across the street came the shouts of two women. "Shaw! Giles!"

Merritt and Argent turned at their names, and M saw a change in the men's attitude that she had never seen before, nor understood. It was obvious the men and women knew each other, and well enough that the women called the men by their Christian names. Still, M could not name what she observed in the men – was it a kind of appreciation? or was it appraisal? – a word that had simply appeared in M's mind.

The two women were already crossing the street to greet them, as M teased apart the confusion in her mind. Merritt and Argent greeted them warmly, and for the moment seemed to have forgotten M was with them. It would have been the perfect opportunity for M to slip away, but she was fuddled at the moment, and did not recognize her chance.

"We didn't know you were in town! Why didn't you let us know?! Which train brought you here?"

Already, M decided she did not like these women. They were tightly corseted, over-dressed, over-coifed, and – worst of all, if M's first impression held true, and it usually did – they were silly, punctuating every statement with importance and emphasis usually reserved for only the most passionate of subjects. As M considered the women, she felt her dislike of them grow beyond her acknowledged reasons, and her dislike of Merritt and Argent grew along a parallel trajectory in her mind, but she could not see its terminus. She heard Merritt answer the first woman.

"This was an unscheduled stop, or we would certainly have given notice."

M noticed that Argent was unusually quiet, and that Merritt had failed to mention that their unscheduled stop coasted in on a private train. M, finally seeing an opportunity to escape, uncharacteristically entered the conversation. "Are you friends of Mr. Merritt and Mr. Argent? They told me they have had occasion to stay at the hotel here." A strange instinct had come over her, and she noticed with satisfaction – though she did not understand why – Merritt's slight blush and that Argent looked almost alarmed.

The two women seemed to notice M for the first time; they pointedly took in her sling and rather shabby attire. The second woman now spoke. "Shaw, aren't you going to introduce us to your friend?"

"Oh, we are not friends." M's new instinct was forging ahead, clearing a path for her away from these men and these women. "Mr. Merritt is my older brother." Merritt turned slightly, to shield from the women the wicked look of warning he flashed at M. "My name is Em," and M offered her hand, which each woman took, awkwardly, in turn.

"Shaw, you never told me you had a younger sister."

"So much younger as to be hardly related at all, isn't that right, Mr. Merritt?"

The first woman laughed. "Why on earth would you call your brother Mr. Merritt and not Shaw?"

Merritt's look of warning took on a smug aspect, enjoying the fatal error M had made. Argent, however, was looking anxious.

M smiled sweetly at Merritt and was gratified to see Merritt's smugness fade considerably. Despite her recent round with ether and her earlier dullness, she began thinking at least one move ahead of Merritt and Argent. In fact, she felt her mind begin to race with the possibilities the unexpected presence of these two women provided. Something of M's excitement must have shown in her eyes, for Merritt was now looking as anxious as Argent.

"I'm afraid I've mis-stepped. Mr. Merritt is what Wrenny insisted we all call him." Merritt was surprised that M had remembered his name – though offered to her, she had never called him anything but Mr. Merritt. "I barely remember it, of course; he's so much older than I, but I've heard the family stories so often, I just naturally call him that – Mr. Merritt."

Now the second woman laughed. M realized that Merritt's and Argent's discomfort was so complete that they had yet to introduce the two women. "We must hear these family stories. Shaw is usually so taciturn, we rarely get anything of value out of him."

M also laughed, but at Merritt. "I imagine they whipped all manner of silliness out of him at the reform school he attended, especially frivolous conversation." Argent pinched her just above her right elbow. To her left, she felt Merritt settle in for the battle.

"Reform school." The second woman seemed slightly alarmed at M's information.

"It was a private reform school; only the best for our Wrenny. But please don't be alarmed. It wasn't because he was violent – believe me, he can hardly defend himself." Merritt and Argent both smarted at that. M saw the hit go home, and smiled sweetly at Merritt a second time while she also moved out of Argent's pinching reach. "No, he needed discipline of the mind. He was forever pretending that he was a government operative, entrusted with all manner of important state affairs. That's why he insisted we address him formally, as all government men are addressed."

M carefully observed the women's reaction and rejoiced to see them nonplussed. Argent stared straight ahead, but Merritt smiled at M, a smile that accepted her challenge.

M continued. "But they didn't quite break him. He sometimes still likes to indulge in his old fantasies. This trip, for instance. The entire time all I've heard is government this and government that, and rules and regulations. I confess it to be very tiresome." M said this last devoid of the gay little sister tone she had adopted for the women's sake. Argent knew she was loading the final shell in her barrage. "I'm so glad he and Mr. Argent have someone here in town to share their company. I have never been here and would love a chance to wander and enjoy the quality of the town. I am very glad to have met you." As she stepped off the sidewalk, she whispered to the second woman, but loud enough for Merritt and Argent to hear, "Ask Mr. Merritt to show you his private train." M followed this barb with a theatrical wink.

She was half-way across the street – she was so close to slipping loose, at least for the day – when Merritt called after her. "Em, you know the family has entrusted you to me on this trip. You know this is my last chance to prove myself to them, especially to Uncle Sam. Please don't take that from me." The pleading in Merritt's voice sounded almost sincere. It certainly stirred the two women standing with him to clasp their hands to their hearts and bite their lower lips in suppressed emotion.

M slowly pivoted on one foot and considered Merritt long and hard. Standing in the middle of the street, she was narrowly missed by an on-coming carriage, whose driver shouted at her loudly and disdainfully. M never flinched, but Argent turned away to hide his relief. M slowly, almost leisurely, returned to the little group on the sidewalk.

"You know no one blames you – not really – for that unfortunate incident in Cumberland. I'm sure you've learned your lesson about the evils of too much drink. This is an opportunity for both of us to *move on*." M turned a second time to leave, but Merritt cleared his throat to speak again. M performed a creditable about face.

"You know I promised, particularly, our Uncle Grant to keep you safe. It will be difficult enough to face him with your arm in a sling." Turning to the two women, who watched the interplay between M and Merritt with growing interest, Merritt informed them with what M thought was cloying sentimentality, "We've all overindulged her." Merritt turned pointedly to include M at this point. "But she's only a girl, after all." M's eyebrows shot up, and Argent anticipated an escalation that would ensure he and Merritt could never stop in this town again, but Merritt was continuing, recklessly so. "I should have been firm with her, and had I known she had developed such a reckless disregard for her own safety – doubtless, you witnessed it just now, in the street – I would never have allowed her a gun. In short, the worst of circumstances converged, and she visited injury upon herself."

The two women gasped and cried out, "No!" M endured the women's deep concern for her and protestations that she must consider the consequences of her actions, if only in deference to the deep love her brother so obviously carries for her. Argent saw with sickening certainty that M endured this – the shrill alarms and the stroking of her arm that peeked out from her sling – endured this because, as the smile threatening to break at the corners of her eyes and lips indicated, M had already formulated her next salvo, and the wicked stare she was favoring Merritt promised it to be of apocalyptic proportion. But Merritt wasn't finished. He broke in on the women's cacophony of censure and care.

"That's not the worst of it."

"No! It can't be worse!"

"Yes, it can. She refuses to take proper care of herself even in good health, and now I find – and it is somewhat difficult to reveal," Merritt said this with just a touch of derisive, condescending laughter, "my little sister is afraid of doctors."

"Why, that's silly. Of course, certain things need to be endured, but it's all for the best."

Argent thought this was going too far, and apparently so did M. Her complexion, so nearly recovered from the morning's fever, had burst into flame, and she lowered her eyelids, a sign of modesty in most women, but in M it was a warning of danger ahead. Argent thought of a cottonmouth ready to strike.

"No, it's true. It is why we have made this unscheduled stop, to find help for my Em here. We just came from Doctor Culver's, only to find she had run away like a little child." Argent pleadingly tugged at Merritt's coat sleeve. "I don't know how we'll convince her to return for tomorrow's appointment."

M drew a deep breath, the harbinger of a mighty typhoon on the rise, but Argent stepped in to halt this crazy one-upmanship of shame. "Well, that's all in the past now, and there's no need to rehash anything else." Argent looked directly at M, and was able to somehow convey a sense of pleading and warning at the same time. "We will sort through tomorrow's schedule later." Argent paused a moment, to congratulate himself on diffusing this strange standoff between M and Merritt, though M continued to glare at Merritt, as Merritt continued to gaze good-humoredly at M. In that pause, however, the first woman, with the best of intentions, attempted to soothe M.

"You must obey your brother in this. He only wants what is best for you."

M retorted, without breaking her smoldering glare at Merritt, "My brother only wants what is easiest for him. If he could do so without fear of total societal censure and just condemnation, he would have me in a collar on a chain – that is, when he deigns to allow me to take the air during our evening stops. Otherwise, his promise to Uncle Grant apparently means committing me to solitary confinement for hours at a time."

"M, I thought we had decided to —"

Merritt interrupted Argent with that maddening smirk. "Please forgive her. She's normally the sweetest of girls" – said with the greatest exaggeration – "but her recent injury and its ill effects have rendered her somewhat shrewish and unruly."

Argent now stepped in with a voice that could only be described as shouting. "And since it is Em's birthday, we are planning a picnic in her honor, and we were just working out the details when we were so delightfully interrupted."

"A picnic!"

"Your birthday!"

M turned to the women a face so full of loathing that Argent wondered at it. But M was remembering her brothers – her real brothers – who had died this day. There was no reason to hold these women responsible for anything – certainly they could not know the solemnity of the day in M's family – but M held them damnable nonetheless for their frivolity and silliness on this day.

Merritt had regained the conversation. "Only, Argent and I still have the errands to run beforehand, and we were just trying to convince Em to rest in your father's hotel. Could we prevail upon you ladies to keep her company while we attend to the details of the picnic?"

Argent realized then, that all that had gone before might have been forgiven, but not this, not committing M to any length of time with total strangers, especially women of dubious intellectual merit. They were sweet women and well-meaning, but completely and deliriously vacant, and loquacious in their empty thoughts. Argent closely watched M as the sisters – the Floss sisters, that Argent just realized had never been properly introduced to M – pledged their help.

"Oh, it would be our true pleasure. We will see to it that she rests, but Shaw, it's her birthday – could we please buy her something a little more festive to wear?"

Merritt was smiling broadly – the smile that melted Alice Floss's heart – either unaware of the deadly silence M had adopted or thoroughly reveling in M's complete rout at his hands. "I was hoping you'd see to that very thing. She has asked often that I take her shopping, but I'm afraid I'm just a bull in a china shop at the ladies' boutiques. Please pick out something pretty and ladylike for her."

The Floss sisters were ecstatic at the prospect of dress-shopping, and with open credit, no less, as Merritt handed them a promissory note with his signature, allowing them to tap his apparently considerable credit here in town. The two sisters had already moved down the sidewalk, talking excitedly about which shops to visit, and so enthralled with the mission before them, that they failed to notice M had not moved off with them. She had continued to glare at Merritt until the sisters had prattled past her. Only then had she moved toward Merritt and Argent. She did not stop when she reached them but passed them until she came to a crate at the door of the shop behind them. With one foot she neatly overturned the crate, so that it bounced up from the ground, easily caught it with her good hand, then returned to face Merritt. Dropping the crate at his feet, she stepped up on it, so that she was nearly three inches taller than he. Merritt watched it all with open amusement, unwilling to hide it even as he was forced to look up at M.

"I will break your bank." M fairly hissed at Merritt.

Merritt had a reputation of being somewhat reckless himself, but Argent had never seen Merritt so careless in his actions as now, when he casually reached into his coat pocket, retrieved a slender cigar, and lit it, all the while smiling that idiot smile that M so detested.

The Misses Floss, finally realizing they had forgotten M, called to her from the corner, calling her Miss Merritt. M stepped down from the crate and, after a last glare at Merritt, she warned Argent, "I shall attend to you later."

"Me? What did I do?"

"No one likes a *neutral*, Argent."

As M stalked off to begin her birthday purgatory, Argent reflected that M had never before referred to him as merely 'Argent.' In the distance, he heard one of the sisters introduce themselves as Alice and Abigail. They added that it was ungentlemanly of Merritt and Argent not to have properly introduced them, but that they would take them to task at "our picnic."

"It is gratifying to see her feeling so well again."

Argent continued to stare after M, apparently unaware of Merritt's comment. "A Kentuckian is the last person who can comment on the neutrality of others."

Merritt laughed over his cigar. "Nonsense; a Kentuckian comments on others' neutrality from the expertise of personal experience. It would be unwise, though, to make like comments to a Kentuckian."

The picnic was far less tense than Argent had anticipated, though M was unusually quiet, even for her. He occasionally glanced at her to look for any indication of a returning fever, but she seemed only tired, and it was certain that her shoulder was sore. M was very polite to the sisters and even seemed genuinely attentive to their babble. She ate was put on her plate by Abby, but Argent wasn't certain she enjoyed it or could even taste it.

After their meal, M announced that she was going to visit Emmett, who had indeed been invited to the picnic and retrieved from the train. Emmett was quietly enjoying the lush grass that grew by the creek. M was wearing a new dress, one that fit better than any they had seen her wear thus far. It was short on embellishments, but the color – a kind of bluish pink – suited her. The sisters had even managed to fashion for her a more stylish sling than the old white dinner napkin she had been using. It reminded Merritt of the scarf that had been hung on the pole outside of town, a few years past, when he and Argent had need of a train, after the capture of an engraver.

M struggled a little with rising, but Merritt was instantly up to help her to her feet. She accepted his help without comment, then walked, at first unsteadily, to visit with Emmett.

"You were never in a reform school, were you?" Abby asked the question in a tone that acknowledged the answer.

"No. We like to tease each other, and I'm afraid I may have carried things a little too far this morning. I shall make my apologies tonight when I present her with the birthday gift we found today." Merritt pulled from a pocket a beautiful silver chain. The sisters admired it and pronounced it a wonderful gift, and sure to sweeten his apology.

"And did she really inflict that wound on herself? It was frightful to see. She was odd about it, though. She didn't seem to mind the scar so much as she minded being helped into and out of dresses. One wouldn't think she'd be so terribly modest, given how she was dressed this morning, with her collar open and no jacket over her shirt."

Both Merritt and Argent were stretched out on their sides, propped on their elbows, Merritt's head near Alice's lap and Argent's head near Abby's. Merritt twisted his head to regard Alice as he considered her question, but it was Argent who answered. While Merritt''s back was to M, Argent had a perfect view of her. Watching her, he said, "I think in her own mind, the way she dresses is more modest than what is considered proper. She has her own view of the world."

Abby returned to the wound, obviously unperturbed by Argent's continued surveillance of M. "But did she shoot herself?"

Now it was Argent who twisted to look up at the question. "No, of course not. It was just a terrible accident. She was in the wrong place at the wrong time."

Alice lightly tapped Merritt on the head. "It was wicked of you to say such a thing, Shaw. I'm sure I should be odd, too, if I had such a brother."

Merritt looked to Argent, but Argent refused to acknowledge Merritt's obvious invitation to defend M. "You think Em is odd?"

Alice blushed slightly. "I meant nothing by it. She's very sweet, shy even, but she is strangely quiet, and it was almost as if she had no interest in the dresses she bought. Which, by the way, Shaw, she bought quite a few. Don't let me forget to give you the receipts."

Merritt gave a short laugh. "I think she enjoyed at least part of her shopping today." Merritt turned to lay on his back with his head in Alice's lap. Alice idly fingered his hair. Abby's fingers were also busily exploring Argent's hair and the back of his neck and the chest beneath his vest. She leaned forward and met his lips in a familiar kiss. When they parted, Argent looked up to see Abby smiling warmly at him. She was pretty and kind and not so proper or school-girlish as to blush at a picnic kiss. He lay back with his head in her lap, ready to submit to a well-deserved nap. He glanced over to see Merritt with his eyes already closed, one hand flung carelessly over his head, one finger slowly stroking the palm of Alice's free hand, the other resting lightly on his chest. It was a perfect picnic. As a matter of recent habit, Argent searched beyond Merritt to find M. She was standing in the distance, holding Emmett's simple halter, watching her birthday picnic from afar. There was no expression on her face, except maybe acceptance. Slowly she felt Argent's gaze upon her, and she returned it before leading Emmett to the creek.

Argent finally did drift off into sleep, the sweet sleep of a spring nap, but like all such naps, it was too short. Merritt and Argent helped the Floss sisters pack up, then while Merritt re-hitched the rented horse to the rented wagon and tied Emmett to the back, Argent headed for the creek, to tell M it was time to go.

When he first awoke, Argent suffered a flash of panic, realizing that he and Merritt had both left M to her own devices while they slept. She could have easily slipped off to anywhere in anger and defiance, and it would have served them right. Argent had never felt such shame as when he realized that he had usurped M's birthday picnic for the company of a sometime girlfriend, and, worse, that M had realized it, too. Merritt's face on waking had also had that look of momentary panic, but he had immediately spotted M's skirt draped over the side of a huge tree root, overhanging the creek.

Argent slowly rounded the tree to find M asleep in the crook of the root. He hated to wake her – she was in such need of sleep. He left her there, to wake her at the last possible moment. He returned to the wagon to see how far along preparations to leave had progressed. Merritt, upon seeing Argent alone, asked with real concern, "Where is M?" Merritt had imagined a scenario wherein M had somehow exchanged her dress for other clothes, leaving the dress, tantalizingly draped as a deceit, while she escaped. "She slipped off again?"

"No, that is, yes. She has slipped off to sleep. I hate to wake her."

"We'll have to wake her sometime. Soon; we have dinner plans."

From the creek, they heard Alice and Abigail in their high-pitched voices calling to them. "Shaw! Giles! Here she is! She's asleep!"

"Not likely anymore."

Merritt shrugged his shoulders; she would have been woken anyway.

M rode in the back of the wagon with Alice and Abigail, the blankets, and the picnic basket. She wedged herself in the corner directly behind Merritt, who had the reins. She was seated on the floor, using the walls of the wagon to stabilize her body against the jostling of the wagon as they rode over uneven ground not in any way improved as a road. Alice and Abigail faced each other across the bed of the wagon, each seated on a hay bale, chatting amicably. Argent sat next to Merritt, but often turned to enter into conversation with the sisters. Each time, he chanced a look at M, whose earlier resilience had considerably slackened. Her shoulder was obviously paining her, and she was tired. Perhaps surgery, shopping, and picnicking were too much for one day.

Merritt stopped in front of the hotel, and, with Argent, helped the ladies off the wagon. Argent was especially careful helping M down. She thanked him, as she had the three other times that afternoon when he had helped her in and out of the wagon. She thanked him, but said nothing more, nor did she look at him. Merritt took the wagon to the stables in back of the hotel, pulling Emmett along behind, to be stabled in the town for the night.

On the sidewalk in front of the hotel, Argent made his farewells to the Floss sisters, at least for the moment. Happy as ever, and absolutely oblivious to anything else but their own entertainment, Alice and Abby promised to dress quickly and return to the hotel for M's birthday dinner. Argent saw them off, but when he turned to address M he found her gone. He opened the hotel door just in time to see M climb the last step of the stairs and watched as she opened the door to her room, enter, and shut it with a quiet click.

Argent was waiting in the lobby when Merritt returned, intending to discuss plans for the night. But Merritt was in high spirits, anticipating the night's dinner with Alice, planning to walk her home the long way afterwards. Argent could not wedge a word in anywise. Merritt clapped Argent on the shoulder as he passed, bounding up the stairs to clean up before dinner. Argent followed Merritt, though more slowly, hating to broach the subject that would subdue his friend's mood. In their room, Argent suggested that perhaps M was too tired to attend dinner and that it might be a good idea to keep things quiet for her sake. But Merritt would hear nothing of it because, he said, it was certain that M would hear nothing of it. She would resist and rebel at any sign of trying to curb her in any manner or matter, so they might as well not try. If she tires, she could certainly excuse herself, as she has before. They could flip a coin over who would then stay with her, leaving the other to enjoy a deserved night out after three weeks of unrelenting M duty. He promised to abide by the fate of the coin. Argent waved his hand; if it came to that he was happy to release Merritt to his much-anticipated walk with Alice. He was certain Abby would understand.

Soon after, they received word that the Floss sisters had returned and were awaiting their pleasure downstairs. As they descended the stairs, Merritt remarked on how becoming M looked in her new dress. "And did that sling remind you —?"

"It was very like."

In the hotel dining room, the two couples were seated, but they informed the waiter that they awaited a fifth party, so that they would not be ordering just yet. It was pleasant to sit at table with these two young women, companionably chatting with them, remembering past visits. Nonetheless, Argent was determined that M should be the center of the dinner, that he would give her his every attention, even at the risk of offending Abby. He was just about to advise Abby of this very intention, when the waiter returned, unbidden, removing the empty fifth chair from the table. Argent reminded the waiter that a fifth party would be joining them, but the waiter informed him that the young lady in question – the fifth party – sends her regrets but finds that she is unable to attend. "She also sends hopes that you will understand and also sincerely wishes that you enjoy your evening together." The waiter stood, expecting to take their orders, but Merritt asked for one moment more.

There was a long moment's silence at the table; even the usually unintuitive and chatty sisters fell quiet. Merritt and Argent looked down at empty plates, knowing their guilt. Alice spoke first, acknowledging the guilt, though slight compared to that of Merritt and Argent, that she and her sister owned in the matter. "I'm afraid that we've unforgivably intruded on your time with your sister, Shaw."

Abby added, "No doubt she's feeling worn out from everything that has happened today. You should both spend a quiet evening with her."

After the Floss sisters left, Merritt called the waiter over to order three meals, to be delivered to their rooms. In the hallway upstairs, they knocked on M's door, but she did not answer. They called her name, but she did not answer. Merritt looked to Argent, but he was hesitant to force the door. Only when Merritt reminded him that M had a habit of running did Argent consent. Merritt announced that he was coming in, then waited before trying the knob. It turned easily but he could not open the door. Only when Argent added his weight to Merritt's were they able to force the door open a few inches. But M had barricaded the door well, and they could make no more progress, certainly not without creating a stir in the hotel. And unless M was in some dire trouble, they would not risk another rumor like the one circulated in Cumberland.

Argent was nonetheless impressed. "How did she move all that by herself?"

"She draws a lot of strength from her anger. M, let us in; move all this away from the door."

Still, M would not answer. There was no light in the room. Merritt remembered another dark room, in Cincinnati, when M had wanted to be left alone. That time, Merritt had been able to push his way in, by the mere force of his hand. M had learned from that time; there would be no unwanted admittance this night. Argent lowered his head and his voice to suggest gathering help from the staff. Merritt had hardly considered a reply when the door was quietly closed, and they heard the key turn in the lock.

In their room, next door, the staff set up dinner for three then quietly exited, leaving Merritt and Argent to face food they no longer wanted. As a precaution – as a matter of standard procedure on this trip – Merritt sent word to the clerks at the registration desk to alert them immediately if Miss Warner left the hotel. But they later had reason to believe the precaution was unnecessary — more than once during the night, they could hear M stifle a sob.

28

In the morning, Merritt left the room to try M's door once again, gingerly turning the knob, but it was still locked, like it had been the several other times he and Argent had tried the knob during the night. He returned to find Argent fully dressed and resolved to try his luck at M's window. Merritt stepped over to their own window and leaned far out to assess the situation. There was no balcony or other structure, just a ledge that ran the perimeter of the building between floors. It was an unnecessary feature, decorative only, but one deemed a requirement nonetheless for any resort hotel. Merritt pulled his head back in the window and appraised Argent.

"No. I will do it. If you fall and are hurt, you will be at the mercy of Doctor Culver and his ready-to-hand catheters. If I fall, I will have you to nurse me. And M still has need of you."

Argent had stiffened as Merritt had first made his pronouncement, but now he considered the rest of Merritt's comments. To give added support to his decision, Merritt added, "I think she will trust you more than any doctor in a backwater coal town."

"She should not have said that."

They had been whispering, sensitive to M's extraordinary hearing. Argent had barely spoken above the sound of his own breath last night when he had suggested rounding up reinforcements, and yet M had heard him, and had locked the door against them. Now, all speaking ceased as they prepared to breach M's ramparts via the window.

Merritt stepped fully out onto the ledge, facing the wall, then grabbed one of Argent's hands as Argent himself placed one foot on the ledge and used his other hand to grab the side framing of their window, providing a counter-balance for Merritt. As Merritt sidled along the ledge, Argent leaned as far out the window as possible without losing his own footing or his hold on the window frame. Just when Argent thought he could give no more length of his body to him, Merritt whispered, "It is locked." At that moment, Merritt's hand slipped from his and Argent himself almost fell from the window. Righting himself, Argent felt his heart skip a beat as he searched the ground below for Merritt. Then, to his right, Merritt called to him, and Argent saw him leaning out of M's window, with that silly grin on his face. "I'm in."

Merritt turned from the window to more properly assess M's room. She had only been at the window long enough to unlock and open the window and grab Merritt's vest as he temporarily lost his balance. As soon as his position seemed stable, she had left him, and now he saw her seated, cross-legged, on the bed, which she had pushed against the wall, creating a kind of couch with the wall as the back. She was still wearing the lavender dress from yesterday's picnic, having obviously slept in it. Merritt noted the sling missing from her arm, carelessly tossed on the floor. He realized that M had steadied him with only her right hand – she was incredibly strong, for a woman; her left arm she still favored. Against the door, M had pushed the dresser, the washstand, and two chairs. Laying across the two chairs were a dozen or more dresses of all colors and cuts – Grandiflora was fashionable, even if a year or two behind the fashions of bigger cities. Merritt, a serious student of ladies' fashions, suspected Grandiflora's boutiques of selling ladies' ready-made clothing that was more than likely the used and discarded dresses of wealthy women loath to wear the same dress two years in a row.

M was placidly observing Merritt; there was no evidence of last night's misery or justified anger.

"Are those the dresses I bought for you?"

M did not answer but continued to observe Merritt as he sifted through the dresses. A knock at the door interrupted Merritt's appraisal of his purchases. He gathered them all together, then tossed them on the end of the bed. M remained as she was – sitting cross-legged at the head of the bed, imperial, like some eastern princess – neither acknowledging the knock nor forbidding Merritt to answer it. It was all beneath her – Merritt, the dresses, the interloper at her door.

"Just a minute." Merritt reached across M's barricade to unlock the door, then shoved the furniture away from the door just enough to admit Argent. As Argent squeezed through the opening, he took in the state of the room – the furniture in disarray, the discarded sling, the disorganized pile of dresses on the bed. He brought his visual sweep of the room to settle on M, sitting erect and silent on the bed, wearing the same dress as yesterday, now hopelessly wrinkled. She was gazing at Argent, her face completely unreadable. It was her eyes, however, that arrested Argent's attention – he had never before seen them so green and clear. At this moment, despite her disheveled appearance, no one could believe her to be only eighteen – she was ageless and eternal in her regal wrath. Argent was certain she could remain this way indefinitely, but he was uncertain how to begin to apologize.

As if waiting for it, the very instant Argent spoke his first syllable, M said, "Allow me to apologize," then she stopped.

Again, as if waiting for it, the very instant that Merritt attempted his first syllable, M said, "I was in error. You do know how a brother treats a sister. You know, however, exactly how an arrogant, selfish, domineering, manipulative brute of a brother would treat a sister. I commend you on your quick study of the subject."

Argent thought, *She is magnificent in that wrinkled dress, sitting like a swami.*

To her left, Merritt tentatively started a word, then waited to see if M was going to pounce again on his sentence. M blinked slowly at him, a priestess giving permission for the unwashed to address her in her holy sanctuary.

"M, we are very, very, *very* sorry for the disappointing birthday we gave you yesterday."

Argent winced inwardly. Even at his most sincere, Merritt sometimes gave the impression of suppressed amusement. M would surely notice.

M continued to regard Merritt as if he were some servant delivering a message, but, having done so, lacked the proper training to leave.

Standing amid the chaos of M's barricade, Argent also apologized. He was desperate for the penance that would appease this goddess risen from the cyclone of M's anger and bitterness. "I can't possibly express the shame and regret I feel. Merritt should never have baited you like that or forced you into the unwanted company of the Floss sisters." Merritt's eyes widened at this self-serving partitioning of blame, but he had the good sense to remain quiet. "And we should never have invited the sisters to a picnic we had promised to you. Please. You must let us make it up to you."

M remained silent and still a moment longer, then asked, "Are you opening negotiations?"

Merritt sighed and, grabbing the chair at the secretary, swung it around in front of him, to sit, straddled, with his arms resting on the chair's back. Argent let out a breath he did not know he had been holding, and answered (a little too quickly, Merritt thought), "Yes."

Again, she held her position and her gaze for a moment longer. "Preliminary business: I want it now and forever held to be true that I am *not* afraid of doctors." Merritt hung his head in mock regret, hiding his smile; he looked up from under guilty brows. "I do, however, view them with great prejudice and hold them to higher standards than they apparently hold themselves, especially in regard to pharmacopeia, in which field they seem to adopt a prescribe-and-pray approach to illness." Merritt's smile faded as he remembered the package of medications purchased for M's prescribed use. Although M began this preamble in a slightly defensive and petulant tone, it was obvious her regards to this aspect of the medical profession was serious and deeply held. M thought of her father, enduring a constantly changing regimen of medicines, none of which helped, and most of which made him ill and weak.

Merritt answered as if seconding a motion at a board of directors. "So held."

Argent merely nodded, though he was watching M intently.

M drew breath to continue. "I do, however, admit to being terrified of these railroad bridges we cross, and seem to be crossing with ever increasing regularity." With this very human confession, the goddess-priestess disappeared and there was only M, leaning forward to smooth the expanse of her dress in her lap, suddenly uncertain of her position and power. Still considering her dress, and with a final smoothing, she returned to the negotiations. "I propose . . . in lieu of compensatory birthday events . . . that I be allowed . . . to occupy the parlor car during the normal operation of the train." Having started out slowly and hesitatingly, like a train laboring uphill, she finished this last thought rapidly and all in one breath – the train triumphant, whooshing downhill.

Neither man answered immediately, both incredibly relieved and shocked at such a small request to cover such a large debt or sin. M took the pause as a measure of their unwillingness to accede. She pre-empted what she was sure would be a negative response, listing the caveats that she hoped would make the proposition more appealing. "You'll find me to be an easy roommate: I have plenty of books to draw my attention; I promise not to initiate conversations; nor to enter any between you unless expressly invited to do so; I will not explore the contents of the parlor car, its cabinets, storage boxes, the locked trunk, and, of course, your sleeping quarters are off limits. I need only a chair and a quiet corner."

M paused, still looking at her lap, crossing and uncrossing the fingers of her clasped hands. Merritt and Argent remained silent, stunned that M would think it necessary to impose such terms on herself. M, afraid to look up, added quietly, "I need the comfort of distraction, even if it is only to share a space with someone." With that final admission, she dropped her hands to lay quiet in the lavender field of her dress, and finally looked up, between hunched shoulders, at Argent. She didn't risk looking at Merritt – she couldn't bear to see the derision and triumph sure to be camped on his face.

More than ever, Argent was ashamed at how grossly they had misjudged M – Miss Warner – in almost every aspect: that her need for privacy and quiet nullified her need for human contact; that her peculiarities in dress and habit and thought precluded any natural and usual feminine predilections; that a demanding and assertive approach to her own circumstances prohibited a generous and forgiving approach to that of others; that a fearless, even risky, character would not allow for fears of any kind; that frank, direct, even bald comments cancelled out the possibility of shyness. They had even misjudged her age, and so had underestimated the range of experience and maturity of emotion that she had brought on this trip. Merritt must have felt much the same way – he remained with his head down, his hands hanging limp off the back of his chair.

For once, Argent did not attempt to treat M as he would any other woman, of any age. He instinctively knew that further apologies or reference to bridge fears would only agitate her more, that M was a creature of direct and unpretentious manners, thought, and feelings. He answered for both himself and Merritt. "The parlor car is at your complete and unregulated disposal."

For the first time in days, M smiled with genuine happiness and relief. She chanced a side-long look at Merritt, and found him also smiling, as genuinely as was possible for him.

"I think I'm entitled to see my purchases properly displayed."

M made a strange sound, that neither man had ever heard her make. "Ach!" M made a face of distaste, perfectly matching the distasteful sound. "So much work, first thing in the morning, and after hard negotiations."

"Well, then. How about breakfast first, then we can have a look at the dresses."

Breakfast was brought up to the room, which Merritt and Argent had restored to its former placid arrangement, except for the bed, which M insisted remain lodged up against the wall, where she invited them to join her to take their meal. Merritt and Argent at first protested the propriety of such a seating arrangement, especially if they were expected to sit cross-legged as M was. They only agreed after M wickedly referred to the arrangement as a sort of picnic indoors. To make room on the bed, the dresses were returned to lay, lifeless, across the backs of the chairs.

As they sat together, companionably eating from plates alternately held in hand or balanced precariously on crooked knees, Merritt regarded the dresses spitefully purchased with his credit. Pointing with his fork at the far chair, he asked, "What merit did you see in that dress?" A remarkably gaudy dress, dripping with lace of all kinds from a livid red coarse material, lay atop one pile.

M swallowed before answering. "None at all. That was the first dress I bought. I thought it was particularly hideous, as I was in a particularly hideous mood. I planned to wear it if you and I should ever be out together, and I would tell everyone we met that you had picked it out. I thought it would bother you more than me, but seeing it now, divorced from a vengeful mood, I see it would be impossible to wear for any reason."

"Did you buy any dress that could stand the light of day, divorced from a vengeful mood?" Argent was thinking back on Miss Carrie's suggestion that M avail herself of Mrs. Grant's help in procuring proper dresses for her time in Washington.

"Yes." M waved a piece of bacon in the general direction of the dresses. "After the first few dresses, I lost heart in the strategy. No one raises the ire as quickly as Mr. Merritt, nor as quickly depletes one's natural resources. There are a few dresses buried beneath that mountain of piece goods that are serviceable."

Merritt, skipping over the comments regarding himself, asked, "Only serviceable?"

"It's all I need."

"Nonsense. You'll have need of something more than serviceable while in Washington. But perhaps the shops of Grandiflora are not the source for more appropriate attire."

The silence that met this remark reminded Argent that the impending trip to Washington was still a sore subject for M.

A knock at the door salvaged the awkward silence. One of the kitchen girls had come to collect the dishes, but upon entering and seeing the two men and young woman, seated so ridiculously and possibly inappropriately, quite pushed dishes from her mind. As she stood there stammering her apologies, Merritt was struck with an idea. Without warning, he bounced up, nearly causing Argent to upset his plate. He took the young girl by the wrist, while still holding his plate in his left hand, high and out of reach for some reason.

"Would you do us the greatest kindness?"

The girl tried to pull away from Merritt, stammering that she had to get back to the kitchen, but Merritt promised payment for her services, at which the girl paled alarmingly.

"For heaven's sake, Merritt, you've frightened the girl out of her wits." Turning to address the girl directly, Argent sought to calm her. "I have no idea what he has in mind, but I assure you it does not involve a surrendering of your honor or morals." Returning to Merritt, and more for his own peace of mind than the girl's, Argent asked, "Does it?"

Merritt was almost embarrassed at the implication. "Oh, I see the confusion. No, not at all. Our . . . my sister there has injured her shoulder" – M obligingly turned down her collar as proof; the girl gasped at the jagged scar. Argent gave M a disapproving look, but Merritt was delighted – "and cannot properly display the dresses she purchased yesterday. May I impose upon you to try them for us?"

After much cajoling, and a trip on Merritt's part to the hotel manager, the girl consented, at first timidly, but then grew to enjoy the experience of trying on so many new dresses in so short a time. Another servant passing in the hall was also employed, and the two young women took turns helping each other in and out of dresses in Merritt's and Argent's room next door.

There was a noticeable lag time between showings, and M remarked on the need for a second pair of hands just to get dressed in the morning.

"There must be some other way of fastening than all these buttons and eye-and-hook affairs."

Merritt suggested a second pair of hands could always be found in a husband.

"Fat little you know of husbands – they are rarely home." M spoke almost reflexively; she had been staring at the dresses, contemplating the phalanx of fastenings involved.

"I guess that's true as far as you know. I understand your father travelled often."

"As do you – the value of your own hands in marriage are very much in question."

Argent was not certain this conversation was headed in a proper direction. He stole a glance at M but saw nothing there to suggest any unseemly meaning to her words. Argent noticed that Merritt was also considering M and had also concluded she was completely innocent of any double meaning.

Realizing both men were considering her, M sought to turn the scrutiny on them. "Of course, the Misses Floss present a brilliant solution to such a situation."

Argent did not at all like where this was headed. "Oh?" He sounded a little faint, even to his own ears.

"When the four of you are wed, and you and Merritt are off redeeming the nation of its baser proclivities, the sisters will be able to button each other's dresses in the mornings and unbutton them in the evenings."

Merritt leaned back and crossed his arms in disapproval, but Argent objected, "I think perhaps you misunderstand the nature of our relationship." Apparently, despite M's parlor car proposal *in lieu* of compensatory birthday events, she intended very much to exact payment in other forms for yesterday's unfortunate *faux pas*.

M ignored this as Lizzie (the kitchen girl) entered the room modeling one of the dresses. Lizzie was nowhere nearly as tall as M or as broad in the shoulders, but the dress fit her decently, which led Merritt to ask, "M, did you even try on these dresses?"

"Hardly any. After the first two my shoulder was aching, and I sat while Miss Alice and Miss Abby tried on dresses for me, but the shop owners assured me all these dresses could be tailored to fit my 'singular proportions.' This dress for instance was picked out by Miss Alice especially because she thought you would favor it, Mr. Merritt. It happened to be in her size."

Merritt leaned his head back against the wall and caught Argent's eye. It was becoming clear just how trying a time to which Merritt had condemned M. Sore and angry, she had had to contend with two silly sisters whose attentions to M were becoming suspect, as well as what had to be cutting comments on M's height and frame.

They sat through all the dresses, out of which there really were only two or three that all agreed suited M, both in color and cut. When the two hotel girls brought all the dresses back to M's room, M leaned in close to Merritt and whispered, "Can we give them each one of their choosing? I think it would make them so happy." Merritt regarded her with something like confusion but nodded his assent. M smiled broadly, patting his arm, then wriggled off the bed with as much decorum as a dress allows, and approached the two girls.

There was a shared squeal of delight from the pile of dresses, and M turned to smile at Merritt, shrugged her shoulders and mouthed 'Thank you.'

By the time they had eaten breakfast and viewed all the dresses, the morning was mostly spent, and Merritt and Argent told M they needed to return to the train. The bed was returned to its original position, and the men returned to their own room next door to gather their few things. Lizzie made one last call at M's room to give her the receipts for the returned dresses. She offered to help M change from her wrinkled dress into one of the new ones, but M told her they all needed the hems let out — the dress she was wearing had been altered in a hurry yesterday. Lizzie held up her hand, signaling M to wait, left briefly, then returned with a sharp knife. Lizzie brought the mint green dress to the bed, then began to let out its hem. M thanked her but protested there was not enough time; the gentlemen were surely waiting on her now. Lizzie assured her there was time, as one of the gentlemen had gone to the telegraph office and would surely be gone for some minutes yet. Lizzie measured the hem of the lavender dress M had on, and very quickly basted a new hem on the mint green dress. She helped M change dresses, then promised to send the other dresses to the train. Lizzie opened the door to Merritt and Argent on her way out.

"I see you couldn't wait to put on a new dress."

M snorted at Merritt's intended insult. "Apparently the wrinkles excited much comment between Lizzie and Martha. It's a shame – I favored the lavender dress more."

"As did I." This earned Argent a smirk from Merritt and something like embarrassment from M; but Argent was still remembering M, regal and unreadable in her lavender dress.

M handed Merritt the receipts for the returned dresses and thanked him for the opportunity to earn the ones she kept.

"Earn them? M, they were gifts."

"They can hardly be considered gifts when I had to shop for them, listen to endless commentary on the merits of this collar vs. that collar; the current thinking on bustles, the absolutely mortifying discussion on undergarments, and of course enduring the ordeal of twisting in and out of dresses almost uniformly too small for me. The next time you want to improve my wardrobe, I'll give you my measurements and you go and pick out and buy a dress."

"Well, then, you haven't been given a birthday gift at all." Argent produced a small velvet pouch from his coat pocket that he handed to M.

Like a greedy child, M wrenched open the bag, which she promptly dropped as she pulled a beautiful silver chain from its mouth. She was clearly taken with it, watching it writhe and sparkle in the sun from the window, but after a few moments of guilty pleasure, she retrieved the pouch from the floor and returned the silver serpent to its lair. She handed it back to Argent, saying, "It's too much."

Argent objected, "Not at all."

Merritt, however, wasn't interested in another of M's protracted and convoluted arguments. Grabbing the pouch from Argent, he said, "We don't have time for this," took the chain from the pouch and commanded M, "Don't move." He clasped the chain around her neck, put on his hat and announced, "We have a train to catch."

Watching Merritt leave the room, she looked at Argent while fingering her new silver necklace and said, "That is how a brother gives a sister a gift," and she followed Merritt from the room, leaving a very confused Argent to follow in his own time. As he approached the desk in the lobby, he heard a woman request that the scarf be put out for her tomorrow. After she left the hotel, the clerk announced, to no one in particular, "Mrs. Preston is going to Martinsburg."

Merritt had not been quite truthful when he stormed about catching a train. He waited outside the hotel for M and Argent, and together they walked toward the tracks north of town. M was exceptionally proud of her new chain, fingering it often, but slowly she came to realize that Merritt and Argent were anxious about something. The cause became clear when they turned down one of the streets and halted in front of Dr. Culver's office.

"Is one of you feeling poorly?" M was seething, knowing full well why they were there. She was particularly angry that Merritt and Argent had led her here after she thought there had been some rapprochement. She began to see the chain as a kind of bribe or pretty distraction.

"M, you know that isn't the case. This is a simple stop to make sure everything is progressing as it should. It won't take five minutes." M seemed to remember something about five minutes yesterday, but she was more distracted that Argent had referred to her as M.

"Come, I'll hold your hand the whole time."

"You will hold my hand under threat of losing it. Give me your watch."

Merritt handed over his watch out of equal parts amusement and unthinking obeisance to M's command.

M took it, made sure it was working, then snapped it closed, instructing, "Stay here." She strode to the door, tripping only slightly on the uneven hem. As she shut the door behind her, Merritt and Argent heard her say, "You have five minutes."

She was out in three minutes, and Merritt couldn't resist asking, "Now, was that so bad?" Over M's head Argent shot Merritt a look that asked, *Why are you baiting her?* Merritt returned the look with the smile that so infuriated M.

M, striding to escape Merritt's teasing, tripped again, this time with enough loss of balance that Argent leapt forward to grab her arm to keep her from falling. M let out a sharp cry of pain, that surprised her as much as it alarmed Merritt and Argent. Argent realized too late that he had pulled M up by her left arm. Merritt was on her right to take her weight, as Argent released her on the left.

M was more embarrassed than hurt – though the initial pain was sharp and intense, it had quickly returned to its habitual deep ache – but the men insisted on making a fuss. It took several minutes and more than a few threatening looks from M before Merritt and Argent began to relent, but it was the advent of M's cursing – "It is this damned hem on this damned dress!" – that finally released M from their ministrations. It was this condemnation of the mint green dress that impressed upon Merritt and Argent, more than anything that she had said or done, the utter frustration M felt at the constant concessions she had had to adopt so far on this trip, but especially since her injury, an injury suffered in their defense. Her dependence on anyone for the simplest tasks was a sore trial for her. M may have been stoic in the face of her pain, but she was monstrous at the feet of her dependence.

As promised, M rode the rest of the day in the company of Merritt and Argent in the parlor car, but M was brooding over her outburst, and Merritt and Argent were a little intimidated by it, having rarely seen such raw reaction in a woman. The bridges which precipitated M's admittance to the parlor car were crossed largely unnoticed.

Despite Merritt's bluster about hurrying to their train, it did not leave the siding until late in the afternoon, waiting on the return of the marshal, who had sneaked off to town to enjoy himself, and waiting, too, for the arrival of M's new dresses. M was definitely looking and feeling better, but fatigue still dogged her, and she must have dozed off, for she found herself looking up into Argent's face.

"Miss Warner." From his tone, Argent was evidently repeating himself. "We've stopped for the night; we're going into town for dinner."

M stared at him, uncomprehending for a moment, but then allowed herself to be helped up from the couch where she was sure she had started out sitting, but apparently had toppled over to lay stretched in sleep.

Merritt held out Argent's hat for him, while doffing his own. "We'll wait outside for you to get ready. Take your time." Merritt held the door open for Mrs. Hughes to enter carrying M's lavender dress, free of wrinkles, then the door closed quietly behind Merritt and Argent as they left the car.

They had stopped in Harper's Ferry for the night, having made some twenty-five miles since leaving Grandiflora. Washington was only sixty miles away, as the crow flies, but the B&O did not fly as the crow, and Baltimore (or nearly Baltimore), eighty miles away, would be their last stop before Washington, forty additional miles, via the Washington Branch. For this night, their train settled on the tracks near the old armory. Some of these tracks were recent additions, as the B&O slowly encroached on the government lands that once housed the old musket factory.

They shared a simple dinner at the best inn the town had to offer. Merritt and Argent talked of the weather (of course), the distance traveled versus the distance yet to cross, the marvels of trains, the new lines being developed out of Washington (including the highly anticipated Metropolitan Branch, which would save some 40 miles and two hours over the current route), and of course the absolute adequacy of their dinner. M contributed little to the conversation; she was brooding over a conversation, half-heard, between Argent and the tardy marshal, a conversation that involved keeping M secure until such time as the President could manage her. It had stirred in her half-buried fears and threats of asylums, of being managed. The suspicions about the true meaning of this trip surged up in her, and she began to see and hear – in every gesture and word – the threat of the asylum, of being caged, far from home. She had been correct from the beginning; why had she allowed these men to trick and herd her? The headache that had begun yesterday morning, as she was dragged from dress shop to boutique by the Floss sisters, also began to surge in great waves. She wanted to return to the train; she wanted the peace of the laudanum.

Even as she suspected Merritt and Argent of complicity in Grant's plans, she acknowledged that a new reserve towards her had developed in them. In the back of her mind, M played over and over again her shocking outburst on the street, and running constantly, like a subterranean molten river, were her words 'damned hem, damned dress' over and over again, until it simply became 'damned, damned.' The old familiar desire to erase the memory of all her missteps washed over her – not only her own memory, but those of anyone who had ever known her, had ever heard her, seen her, or been told of her. Only when she was dead could she be free of the shame of her memories and the humiliation of occupying anyone else's memories. And she could only rest in death and eternity when anyone with memory of her was also dead. And the longer she lived, the more time there was for more inappropriate words, inappropriate behavior, outbursts of anger, cringing apologies, and for more people to be witness to them. Sometimes, she didn't think she could endure it. Her self-imposed exile on her farm was meant to avoid further stains on her memory, and the events of this trip bore out the necessity and the sagacity of that exile.

She realized Merritt had spoken and expected an answer. "I beg pardon?"

"I said, shall we go? We thought we could take a short stroll down Shenandoah street . . . if you like."

Was Merritt intimidated by her? Had she so shocked Merritt and Argent with her anger and curses that they approached her with caution on the simplest subjects? M only wanted to retreat to her car, even willing to brave the bridges alone and in silence, if she could just put distance between herself and these witnesses to her shame.

M decided this was but just punishment. She properly accepted the invitation to walk, even enduring Merritt's helping her from her chair, the over-solicitation for her shoulder, and silently accepted Argent's draping his coat around her shoulders against the cool night air. She would take her medicine and take it with grace.

Upon their return to the train for the night, Argent escorted her to her door and helped her up the stairs. Merritt left them momentarily but returned with a small glass in his hand. Mrs. Hughes greeted them at the door, ready to help M out of her dress. Merritt extended the glass to her, which she slowly reached for, looking a question at him. "Dr. Culver wants you to take this every evening, to help you sleep."

"And M," Argent added, "You'll let us know if your shoulder requires attention?"

They were so cautious around her now. She would, indeed, have to take her medicine. She decided, though, that this would be the last night she would allow herself to be dosed. What did it matter what they thought of her, how she was reflected in their eyes, if they would be parting soon, never to meet again? She would stand firm after tonight, no matter how shrewish she appeared to them.

She meekly took the glass and drank its contents, then handing it back to Merritt, thanked them both for a pleasant evening, then retreated behind her door. Mrs. Hughes helped M undress and then made M lie down before she left. As soon as Mrs. Hughes left, however, M rose, found the bottle of laudanum in the bottom of her grip bag, and took a dose. Sometime during the night, Mrs. Hughes returned to find M still awake.

"I don't know what that Dr. Culver prescribed for you, but it isn't working. This seemed to help a few nights ago." Mrs. Hughes urged M to take a dose of the medicine Mr. Argent had given for M on the night of the attack on the train. M was united with Mrs. Hughes in her distrust of Dr. Culver; she began to think that Mrs. Hughes was the only one she could truly trust.

M's headache begged for another dose of laudanum, and after swallowing it, M waited for both the laudanum and the second sleeping draught to take possession of her. Instead, she spent a miserably fitful night, full of night demons and flashes of very real visions of Merritt and Argent angry with her and leaving her chained underground, never to see sunlight. Sometimes she was able to master her screams and other times she found her terror silenced by an involuntary paralysis of her vocal chords – no matter how hard or loudly she tried to call for help, little more than a croak escaped. She finally dropped off to sleep not long before Mrs. Hughes entered the car, first thing in the morning.

"I'm afraid we did little better entertaining M tonight than we did yesterday."

Argent nodded. "I confess I could not keep my mind from those poor souls in Richmond."

Even though it was not immediately on the line of the tracks, Grandiflora was nevertheless able to obtain the most recent news, and Argent and Merritt had seen the morning papers filled with particulars of the tragedy – at least fifty dead and dozens more were injured in Richmond, when the balcony in the courtroom of the Capitol building collapsed; a courtroom packed beyond capacity to hear Chief Justice Chase give his decision in the mayoralty case, whether Mayor George Chahoon, appointed by the military governor, would remain mayor or be replaced by the popularly elected Henry Ellyson. As the crowd waited for all the judges to arrive, timbers supporting the balcony had suddenly and simply snapped, the sound of it said to be that of the report of a gun, and within seconds, the floor had given way and the crowd had dropped twenty-five feet to the chambers below; and then the ceiling had followed. M, who had proven to be a voracious reader of newspapers during this trip, had not seen the papers, and the men had decided that, in her delicate health, she should not share in the national shock.

"M seemed to feel it all the same. She was very quiet, even for her."

"She is tired – has been tired for many days – and we pushed her too far yesterday. She will sleep tonight."

29

Mrs. Hughes reported the next morning, as she delivered breakfast to the gentlemen, that Miss Warner did not respond well to Dr. Culver's prescription. She did not report that she supplemented said prescription with more of Argent's concoction – Mr. Argent, after all, was well aware of what he had given to Mrs. Hughes and the instructions he had provided; what need had she to report it? Mrs. Hughes had found Miss Warner wide awake a little after midnight but had found her asleep some five hours later when Mrs. Hughes stopped by Miss Warner's car before setting out to do the morning's shopping for breakfast. Miss Warner was still asleep when last Mrs. Hughes looked in on her two or three hours ago.

Over Mrs. Hughes' ample breakfast and strong black coffee, Merritt and Argent began the delicate task of planning the delay of Miss Warner's descent upon Washington. Argent had already spoken to Mr. Hughes about the possibility of remaining in Harper's Ferry for one or two days, and Mr. Hughes had promised to ask the station master here for the favor of a siding for such a length of time. Argent thought they could take M on a tour of Harper's Ferry, including John Brown's fort, as well as a walk up to Maryland Heights, for a picnic, perhaps.

If they could not keep M here for more than the day, there would still be Baltimore, with all its attractions, to occupy her until Grant returned from West Point and was able to properly welcome her to the White House.

"What would you show her in Baltimore?"

Argent felt that Merritt was challenging him in some way. "Why, the usual places and sites that excite newcomers to the city. A tour of the monuments, perhaps – the Washington monument and the statue of Taney; the Cathedral, certainly; Druid Hill Park, the lake and spring there; the old Post Office building; the *Sun* iron building. Oh, the new gateway at Patterson Park."

Merritt's smile seemed indulgent to Argent, and slightly derisive.

"Well, what would you show her?"

"The docks and piers, the great B&O enterprise at Locust Point – the grain elevators, etc.; Greenmount Cemetery; the Mount Clare shops – although, Mr. Hughes may want to show her that."

"You would show her the very means by which she could yet effect her escape? The ships and trains?"

"Calm yourself, Argent. She would never take the ships – they go to Europe or South America; she would never leave her beloved farm behind. As for trains, should she attempt to leave by that means, there are depots all along the way where she may be apprehended, and telegraphs strung all along the rails where news of her escape may be sent well ahead of her."

Argent resented Merritt's suggestion of excitement on Argent's part. Nevertheless, he pointed an admonishing finger at Merritt. "'It's water she'll go to.' Remember Mr. Henry's words. Keep her away from the docks and piers."

Merritt continued to smile, but he did nod his assent. "But we go ahead of ourselves. We do not know if we will need to tarry long in Baltimore."

The last of the morning passenger trains pulled out of Harper's Ferry. There had been several freight trains and one passenger train during the night, and then had begun the morning traffic – four passenger trains, beginning at 6:30. All the trains were attended with the usual screeching of wheels slowing and stopping, bells clanging and whistles blowing, as well as the low grunting of the engines as they began anew their labors after stopping briefly in Harper's Ferry. No train passed by at speed – no train could, either after or before crossing that contorted bridge arrangement spanning the Potomac, with its wicked curves – but still, the trundling of the cars on the tracks managed to transfer to the siding to somewhat shake the cars of the little train. Argent wondered how Miss Warner had managed to sleep at all during the night. He had certainly struggled to remain asleep. Perhaps they should leave Harper's Ferry sooner rather than later, for everyone's sake.

Mr. Hughes made his appearance just as they were finishing the last of their morning coffee. Merritt and Argent were in good humor, having the luxury to finish their morning coffee at some leisure, since Miss Warner would in all likelihood sleep late this day. Mr. Hughes declined the offer of a cup, being in something of a hurry. Mr. Wood, the station master, had relayed to Mr. Hughes the B&O's instructions to remove his little train to the freight siding at nearby Sandy Hook, with the added suggestion that such accommodations could only be had for one night. Harper's Ferry had always been a small town – and now greatly reduced since the late unpleasantness between the states – but even so, it was a busy railroad station. There were more than a dozen passenger trains throughout the day (servicing patrons of both the B&O along the Potomac, and the Winchester & Potomac along the Shenandoah) and there were freight trains as well. In short, the little train simply could not take up any sort of permanent residence on the sidings in or near town. It was rather forcefully suggested that Mr. Hughes take his train directly to Baltimore, where facilities there were far more expansive and able to accommodate a protracted presence.

"Is it still your intention to remain in Harper's Ferry?"

Merritt shrugged the question to Argent. "Yes. If they have given us one night, let us take it."

Mr. Hughes lingered just inside the doorway, turning his hat over in his hand. "Should we not continue on to Washington? Miss Warner expresses an eagerness to be finished with traveling."

Merritt looked to Argent, not to answer the question, but to gauge his reaction. This was fairly presumptuous, coming from Mr. Hughes.

Argent stared blankly at Mr. Hughes for a brief moment, then started, "Miss Warner . . .," but then he stopped. A second start found him replying to Mr. Hughes from a different direction. "We have been directed to delay Miss Warner's arrival in Washington. The situation has changed; preparations are being re-made for her there. The White House will not be ready to receive her until Tuesday."

Mr. Hughes felt properly chastised, though for what, even he was not certain. He replied, "Yes, sir," as he bowed himself out the door.

A few minutes later, the engine roared to life and Merritt and Argent felt the train slowly make its way across the bridge over the Potomac. Within a very short time the train stopped on a siding at Sandy Hook, barely a mile from Harper's Ferry. Merritt announced he would walk the settlement and see about grazing the horses for the day; M would surely want to give Emmett some time off the train. As he picked up his hat to leave, Merritt commented on Mr. Hughes. "He means no offense, you know. He is attached to M in a fatherly way. He only wants to see her happy, in any way that he can give it to her."

Argent reflected on Merritt's words a moment or two after Merritt left, then decided he should have a further word with Mr. Hughes. He was surprised to find Merritt not only still at the train but discoursing with the engineer. Argent felt a resentment rise in him, if Merritt had taken it upon himself to make some kind of amends or excuses on Argent's behalf. As he neared, however, Argent realized the conversation was not about Argent but about Miss Warner and her apparent absence from the train.

"No, sir! I would never allow Miss Warner to go about on her own!" Taking in Argent as he approached, Mr. Hughes added, "Did you know, sirs, she is not but eighteen years? I would no more allow her to walk the town alone than I would allow my own daughter, if I had one. She is with Mrs. Hughes, taking in the shops, I believe."

Merritt turned to Argent, not particularly alarmed at Miss Warner's unauthorized removal from the train. "You return to Harper's Ferry and find Miss Warner. I'll join you as soon as I see to the horses."

"If I may, sirs? I would be happy to see to the horses, but I was wondering if I may borrow one of them, to visit a fellow engineer here, up on Maryland Heights." Before either Merritt or Argent could respond, Mr. Hughes continued, "If we are to stay the night, or at least the day, that is. The train will not be unattended – my son knows well enough how to operate a train, if the yard master here should need it moved; he is training to become an engineer himself – soon he hopes. And there is the marshal and the brakeman to help see that the train is unmolested."

"Take my horse; he is sturdy enough for these elevations." Argent realized that Mr. Hughes and his wife had also been inconvenienced by the setbacks and delays of this trip, and neither had complained nor asked for any favors. Why shouldn't Mr. Hughes be afforded the chance to visit with a colleague? "We will return to the train, with Miss Warner and Mrs. Hughes, before nightfall. We leave as early as permissible in the morning."

Merritt and Argent left a grateful Mr. Hughes to find pasturage for the horses and struck out down the county road that led back to Harper's Ferry. It was a pleasant walk, though the morning was cloudy. The road, the tracks and the C&O canal all shared a narrow ledge at the base of the mountain. Boats in the canal were already backing up before the next lock, waiting their turn to lock through. They heard the usual banter among the canal captains and the lock keeper and saw more than a few children tethered to the canal boats on which they lived with their parents, the tethers preventing that most lamentable and preventable of childhood deaths – drowning. They started their walk as a long freight train, of six engines, was passing Sandy Hook, and they reached the bridge just as the last of that train snaked across it. The road they walked extended past the bridge, to the north, along an abrupt rise in the mountain, but at the bridge, Merritt and Argent crossed the canal, with the tracks, onto the bridge that both trains, wagons, and pedestrians shared in crossing the Potomac. Looking up the road to the north, Argent saw a tall white stone building, just across from the next lock on the canal. It looked like it was built out of the mountain itself, it was so close to the cliff that towered behind it.

They found M and Mrs. Hughes on Shenandoah Street, where most of the town's shops could be found. M was definitely not happy to see them. She was still without her sling and it was evident she had slept little last night. Mrs. Hughes greeted them cordially enough, though there was a reserve in her as well.

"Mr. Hughes has moved the train then?"

Mrs. Hughes must have known that was so, but Argent knew how to handle older women – it was best to ignore them except when complimenting their cooking or clothes or when they were in need of consoling. "We have promised him to see that you and Miss Warner are safe and enjoying yourselves, and to have you back at the train before dark. We have an early departure in the morning."

"And has Mr. Hughes gone to visit Mr. Smith?"

"He has gone to visit a colleague, though he didn't give a name."

M had said nothing yet, not even to bid Merritt and Argent good morning, but at this, she turned to Mrs. Hughes and, with something like excitement, asked, "Christian Smith? The engineer?"

"Oh, yes! I met him this morning while doing my shopping for breakfast. He was in town, selling his butter to the groceries here. I bought from him directly, enough to last us for several days." This last was said in a cryptic tone that neither Argent nor Merritt understood, but apparently made some sense to M.

Merritt ignored the subject of butter. "Who is Christian Smith?"

M barely glanced at Merritt before replying. "He was the engineer to first enter Harper's Ferry when the tracks were first laid here. He has a farm somewhere nearby."

"Up on Maryland Heights, dear." Turning to Merritt, Mrs. Hughes explained, "Mr. Smith and I exchanged pleasantries and he told me that he wasn't always a farmer but had been an early engineer for the Baltimore & Ohio. 'Oh,' I said to him, 'My husband, Mr. Hughes, is an engineer, though not for the B&O. We have special permission to use their tracks, for a private train, not just a private car.' 'How curious,' says he, 'Mr. Hughes must visit me at my farm across the river, up on Maryland Heights.' So I told Mr. Hughes, 'You must go visit Mr. Smith; he insists on it.' But, of course, he could only go with your blessing. And I suppose you have given it."

"Yes, ma'am, and Mr. Argent has given him his horse as well. I hope he enjoys his visit." Merritt was hoping the mention of horses would spark M into joining the conversation more fully, but she ignored his bait. It was somewhat troubling that M did not inquire after Emmett.

Both M and Mrs. Hughes were holding packages, the spoils of their day so far in Harper's Ferry, though M's was much the smaller. Argent offered to relieve the ladies of their burdens, but only Mrs. Hughes accepted the offer; M did not even acknowledge it. Argent took the package from Mrs. Hughes then promptly handed it to Merritt.

"Where do you ladies go now?" Argent knew better than to ask permission to accompany them, as Miss Warner would most assuredly decline. His question, as asked, left no room for misinterpretation: he and Merritt would be going wherever the ladies were going.

"We thought to visit St. Peter's, up the steps there. Then, of course, we must see Jefferson's Rock. Miss Warner would like to visit the cemetery – it looks to have a splendid view of the town and the mountains round about."

For the first time, M seemed uncomfortable with Mrs. Hughes' comments; M clearly wished to keep her intentions and wishes private.

"Perhaps we could have a little something sent up the hill a little later and enjoy a picnic, while we enjoy the view."

Merritt thought, perhaps, mention of picnics was not the best topic so soon after M's birthday. M clearly thought the same, ignoring the suggestion and looking down towards the Shenandoah River. Mrs. Hughes, however, despite her earlier reserve, thought it a wonderful idea. If she had known a picnic was to happen, she would have gladly made a little something to bring along, but now she supposed they would just have to do with whatever could be had from the groceries and perhaps the confectionary here in town.

Argent excused himself to make the arrangements for the picnic, promising to rejoin them before they left St. Peter's. Merritt returned Mrs. Hughes' package to Argent – he was sure Argent could find some place safe to store it until they were all ready to leave town.

St. Peter's Church was literally built on a rock, as St. Peter himself was the rock upon which Christ built His church. The stone foundation jutted out from the mountainside, three of its walls built sheer to its very edge. It faced east, the three arched windows waiting to receive a morning sun that, as far as M could tell, likely didn't crest Maryland Heights until well after sunrise. M did not know how anything grew on this mountainside – there could not be much soil on top of all this rock, not enough for decent roots. Yet there were some trees growing in the area, clinging to the hillside.

Merritt was waiting outside the church when he heard Argent huff his way up the stone steps that led, steeply, from High Street below. He offered Argent a draw from his cigar, which he gratefully accepted. His breathing restored, Argent asked, "The ladies are inside?"

"Yes, they have gone to light a candle for a successful conclusion to our trip, whenever that may be."

"They said that?"

"Mrs. Hughes did. I think they are aware of our need to delay entry into Washington."

"But Miss Warner did not speak."

"No. But, if she is aware of these new delays, it could very well account for her silence, which is as stony as this hill."

Argent sat down on one of the four stone steps that led into the church. "How did they find out?"

"M has incredible hearing. Or maybe Mr. Hughes told Mrs. Hughes, who, quite naturally, told M."

"I had intended to tell Mr. Hughes to keep that particular news to himself, but we left immediately after our initial talk. I did not think he had time to tell anybody anything."

Merritt shrugged, but Argent did not see it. They remained this way for some time – Merritt standing, smoking, and Argent seated on the stone step, both men lost in thought amid the spectacular views afforded them. Argent suddenly stood as Mrs. Hughes and M opened the church door. Mrs. Hughes was talking with great enthusiasm with someone just inside the door, but Argent could not see who until the man stepped out of the church altogether. He was a priest, a clean-shaven, good-looking man, about his own age, though if he were being truthful, the priest was closer to Merritt's age than his own.

"Mr. Merritt, Mr. Argent, this is Father Kain." Mrs. Hughes was fairly gushing with the simple act of introductions. Merritt and Argent both shook hands with Father Kain, though neither said much beyond the normal comments made during an introduction. Father Kain bade M and Mrs. Hughes good-bye and hoped the gentlemen would excuse him, as he had a great many things to do to get ready for the weekend rounds of the parishes under his ministry. M alone said nothing during the introductions.

Without further addressing Merritt or Argent, Mrs. Hughes took M's right arm in hers and together they started off for Jefferson's Rock, above and behind the church. All the way up to their destination, Merritt and Argent could hear Mrs. Hughes talking excitedly about their visit to St. Peter's and, of course, their great good luck in running into Father Kain there. Argent was amazed at Mrs. Hughes' sudden loquacity and animation, and even more so as they were climbing a steep and winding path – the woman rarely stopped to draw breath. Occasionally, M answered whenever Mrs. Hughes directly addressed her, but her voice was low and her answers short, so that neither Merritt nor Argent could catch what she said.

At Jefferson's Rock (a misnomer, since there was more than one rock involved in the formation), it took both Merritt and Argent to help Mrs. Hughes up onto the base rock upon which sat, at an angle and supported by red columns, a flat slab, yearning towards the south. M did not wait for help from either man but managed to climb onto the rock herself. Neither woman, however, ventured to climb any further. M stood as near the edge as she dared, her right arm hooked around one of the columns, and looked out over the Shenandoah River, to Loudoun Heights, and upriver to the great curve that took the stream out of sight. Down below, hundreds of feet, was Shenandoah Street and the Winchester & Potomac Railroad. There were buildings – dwellings and shops – on the far side of the railroad, in danger of being crushed, should any of the boulders that clung to the hillside be dislodged and go rolling down to the river. Close to the river's bank was Virginius Island, a place of mysterious flooded tunnels whose waters moved the turbines that provided power to the industries located on the island. It was a sublime view, and M could have stood there, she thought, forever, watching the river and the turn of seasons, waiting for the great rocks beneath her to finally succumb to gravity and tumble into the water.

Behind her, Mrs. Hughes voiced her decision to picnic here, but another group of people was climbing the stone steps for their turn at the view, and the spell was broken. M turned and scrambled down the great rock, even as Merritt and Argent warned her to wait for them to help her. At the stone steps there was a general discussion about where to have their picnic, but when asked, M merely replied that she had no preference in the matter. What she really wanted was to escape these men and even Mrs. Hughes, who would not stop going on about Father Kain, the picnic, and dinner tonight. M did not sleep well last night, and her fatigue was fueling a headache that was nearly constant now. She wanted to go somewhere private, dark, and cool, take some of the laudanum she had purchased this morning, along with some other medicines Mrs. Hughes had suggested. She still carried the bag with her purchases and realized that she was clutching it in a death grip. Her hand was cramping.

There was not much level land in the immediate vicinity, but there was a cemetery nearby that could perhaps provide a flatter and less stony venue for their picnic, and hadn't Miss Warner wanted to see the cemetery? Merritt's suggestion of the cemetery was voted down by Argent (as inappropriate, and he privately thought Miss Warner should stay away from cemeteries) and by Mrs. Hughes (as uncomfortable – the allure of Jefferson's Rock had been its ready ledges for seating; Mrs. Hughes was not looking forward to lowering herself to the ground and then struggling to rise, no matter how helpful the gentlemen would be). They settled, instead, on the bombed ruins of a church not far from St. Peter's, though neither Argent nor Merritt could say which church or denomination it was. As they were descending the path that led back towards town, they met the boy sent from the grocer's, with their picnic. Argent and Merritt divided between themselves what the boy had carried alone; Merritt tipped him handsomely in tribute to this accomplishment.

Inside the broken and empty walls of the church, Mrs. Hughes directed where and how to set up the picnic, selecting a spot that had several random building stones nearby. With a little grunting and determination, Merritt and Argent moved and stacked enough of these stones so as to create both seating and a makeshift table of sorts, though it was very low and uneven, basically a collection of stones of different heights, upon which Mrs. Hughes placed the different dishes. M sat on her stone stool and waited for some improvement in her headache. As the men had pushed and shoved and levered stones into place, Mrs. Hughes had rummaged through M's package and pulled out the particular drug that she had suggested at the apothecary's as wonderful for headaches. M had taken it mechanically, washing it down with a hasty sip from the wine bottle.

It was not the grand picnic that had been set out for her birthday – there were no china plates and crystal glasses borrowed from the hotel (as a personal favor to Merritt and Argent), as there had been at Grandiflora – but it was pleasant enough, and there was some camaraderie in sharing a bottle of wine by simply passing it around. M's headache did ease some, though she attributed it more to the wine than to Mrs. Hughes' particular drug; M found that the more she drank, the better she felt.

M's attention drifted in and out of the conversation. She heard Mrs. Hughes explain that Miss Warner was nursing a headache, and not to make too much of her silence. There was talk of the near-complete destruction of this church while St. Peter's, not a stone's throw away, had been spared during all the fighting in and around Harper's Ferry during the war. "St. Peter's salvation," Mrs. Hughes had said. M knew that somewhere in that comment was a smug satisfaction that it had been a Protestant church that fallen into rubble. Argent added that John Brown's Fort – the old engine house of the armory – had also escaped destruction. After their meal, they could walk down to have a look at the building. M absently nodded her assent.

As the wine lifted her spirits and deadened her headache, she began to relax her attitude towards Merritt and Argent. Upon waking, she had gone to look in on Emmett. Mike, the fireman, was there grooming Emmett. He had acted sheepish when she had found him there, but she was grateful for his help; though she was righthanded and it was her left shoulder that was wounded, sometimes even doing tasks with her right hand and arm aggravated the pain. Mike had shown her what he thought was a concern in one of Emmett's hooves; she had suggested Emmett could be seen by whichever farrier was going to see to Mr. Argent's horse. Mike's confusion at her suggestion soon became her own when Mike informed her that there was nothing wrong with Mr. Argent's horse – no, the horse had not thrown a shoe or had any other problem that Mike knew of. Mike had then shown her each of the horse's hooves, and they were all securely shod. That had turned her anger at yet more delays into a fresh resentment at being lied to – at the necessity of being lied to – a return to her old suspicions of motives for the trip, a rekindling of old fears of what was waiting for her in Washington. And then had come the news that Argent's horse was able enough to scale Maryland heights with Mr. Hughes. Her dull headache had become a fierce pounding, a triphammer dropping on her skull over and over again.

Merritt and Argent were watching her now – they were always watching her – and it raised her hackles anew. But she could not let that show, she could not bare her teeth — she was more than an animal, she could think beyond the immediate attack. She must lull them into thinking her complaisant. Let them think that, but she would not go to Washington. She would not be diverted this time. They had not discovered her ruse in Cumberland. She would try again, buy a false train ticket at the office here in Harper's Ferry, but this time she would take the canal – there were offices somewhere across the Potomac; she could buy passage there on a packet boat, back to Cumberland – and while Merritt and Argent were scouring the trains, she would be making her way back by water, and then onto the Cumberland Road to Wheeling. Maybe a packet would be too exposed; maybe she should hire out Emmett to one of these other boats that hauled coal and God knew what else – these canal boat captains would be glad to have a strong horse like Emmett pull their boat, and she would be glad to walk beside Emmett on the towpath, the towpath that had few bridges and none of them very high. And Emmett's absence from the train would make the men divide their time between the trains and county roads, thinking she might be riding Emmett home.

M realized they were all waiting for her to answer. She made the effort to will the anger to drain from her eyes. "I would be interested to see John Brown's Fort."

There was an awkward moment's pause and M saw concern — or was it justification — in Merritt's face, and anger in Argent's.

Mrs. Hughes put a hand on M's knees. "We are speaking of dinner. I told the gentlemen that we have been asked to dinner by Father Kain, that it is a great honor and that we cannot decline. The gentlemen are – kindly enough – concerned about our return to the train."

Dinner; M had forgotten about dinner. "There is no need for concern." M was almost curt. "I would welcome the walk back to the train after dinner, and we have Mrs. Hughes' gun for protection."

At Argent's alarmed look, Mrs. Hughes smiled and patted her handbag. "After that unpleasant business on the train the other night, I have decided I should not be surprised again. I intend to carry a gun with me at all times."

Merritt, too, was disconcerted at this news, but also a little confused that it was Mrs. Hughes and not M who carried the gun. Then Merritt suspiciously eyed M's bag. Just what was she carrying in it, that she would not let it out of her hand? "Ladies, there is no need for that. Mr. Argent and I will simply have our dinner at the Potomac House and await your pleasure at the church. We will walk you back to the train."

Merritt was rarely this forceful, and to contest the matter further would only have aroused their – his and Argent's – anger. With the end of that discussion came the end of the picnic, and they descended to High Street, where Mrs. Hughes announced that if they were to leave early in the morning and she was to be out somewhat late tonight, she had better purchase a few items that would make tomorrow's breakfast easier and quicker to make. Merritt offered to escort her and to make sure her purchases were sent to the train, and Argent and M continued on to John Brown's Fort.

Argent spoke of John Browns' raid as they walked, and M listened with only half her attention, but when they turned the corner onto Potomac Street M was sobered by the sight. When she left the train last night and this morning, the town was still shrouded in shadow and her mind was shrouded in dark thoughts, undercut by the pounding in her head. This morning, she had noticed little of the town until she had found herself in the apothecary's shop on Shenandoah Street. The difference between Shenandoah and Potomac streets was notable. The shops and dwellings on the former had been repaired – a few were even newly built – but

Potomac Street and the federal lands below it was in ruins, still, these five years after the war. Little had been done to even clear away the rubble of destroyed buildings. The federal armory buildings had new roofs and were rudely patched, but even these did little to dispel the overall sense of desolation. Opposite the tracks along the federal canal, north of the engine house, could be seen the foundations of the musket factory. What must have once been an attractive stone and iron fence now straggled, gap-toothed, around the perimeter, most of the iron pickets missing, and even some of the stone posts were blasted or missing. A great chimney rose out of the flat and barren ground.

A train whistled, announcing itself as it slowly made its way across the Potomac. As she followed its progress onto the West Virginia shore, M was surprised to see how elevated the tracks were, sitting on a long stretch of trestles, themselves resting on two stone walls on the very edge of the river. She could not remember how she and Mrs. Hughes had descended to the street.

Argent was still talking about the war, about all the different battles and skirmishes here, about the different generals and majors and captains, on both sides, who had fought here, won, and then lost here. It was too much to remember. It all came down to whoever could command the heights – across the Potomac in Maryland, across the Shenandoah in West Virginia, and behind the town itself. M looked back up to Bolivar Heights, past the houses and buildings, stacked one upon the other up the hillside, past St. Peter's. From this view the mountain looked shaggy, growing a stubble of new trees to replace those cut down during the war for use by the troops or merely to clear away possible hiding places for the enemy. M turned in a full circle and took in all the mountains surrounding Harper's Ferry – they all looked the same – ashamed and shorn.

Argent had truly warmed to the subject, and hardly noticed M's half attention. He was pointing out – with wide sweeps of his arm – the positions of batteries on Maryland Heights, when M suddenly asked, "Where is Sandy Hook? Where is the train?"

Argent stopped in mid-sentenced, his arm still outstretched, pointing to the treacherous cliffs of Maryland Heights, which goats, not guns, now commanded. Slowly he let his arm drop; perhaps Miss Warner was not as interested in the war as he thought. "It is across the bridge, in Maryland, about a mile east of here." Argent followed M's line of sight and realized she was contemplating the bridge. Perhaps she was concerned about the walk across the bridge; she had been nearly incapacitated with private and silent fear as they had crossed the bridge into Cincinnati, but that was a much higher and longer bridge. She had admitted, just yesterday, her fear of bridges. How to reassure her without igniting her monstrous pride was a problem.

"What is there, what is at Sandy Hook?"

Argent blinked. He had been prepared to comfort her fears about the bridge, but that, apparently, was not what was on her mind. M had a manner of asking questions that sounded more like a demand than an inquiry; when she wanted information, it was rarely an idle curiosity. "It is a very small settlement, mostly a place for warehousing freight from both the railroad and the canal. The rail yard there is small, but there was more room for us there than here. You see the limited facilities here."

M nodded as she looked out over the river. It wasn't the bridge that interested her, but the canal on the other side. The bridge, of course, would have to be crossed, but she could walk fast and focus on the opposite side; she could endure it for a few moments.

A loud whistle brought both M's and Argent's attention to the area that used to be the launch for the old ferry that Mr. Harper and his heirs used to operate. Merritt was there, holding open the door of a shabby carriage. Mrs. Hughes had decided that she could not possibly dine with Father Kain dressed as she was and so it was also decided to hire a carriage to return to the train. This same carriage was contracted to carry them back to Harper's Ferry in time for dinner at the rectory. Despite crossing the bridge, M found the motion of the carriage and the sound of the horses comforting and was surprised to find that she had almost drifted off to sleep in the short ride to Sandy Hook. Mrs. Hughes, Merritt, and Argent all suggested she rest before dinner, which irritated her, even though that was what she intended to do. But sleep nor rest came, only a resurgence of her headache. She allowed herself a dose of laudanum, and when that did not work, she took another dose of Mrs. Hughes prescribed drug. When Mrs. Hughes called on her later to help her dress, M was more fatigued than ever, and her headache was only slightly better.

Dinner was not the trial M feared it would be. Father Kain had invited several ladies and gentlemen to dine with him, so that M was easily able to limit her conversation without appearing rude. Merritt and Argent had ridden back to Harper's Ferry with the women, had their supper at the Potomac House, and were waiting for them on the stone steps when M and Mrs. Hughes left St. Peter's. There was another short ride back to Sandy Hook where Argent again presented M with the vile medicine prescribed by Dr. Culver. M declined; she needed her head clear, and these concoctions that Argent was forever giving her only clouded her thinking. She was so tired, and she needed to make her move soon. She could not remember how long they intended to stay here, at Sandy Hook. There was some mention about it, but she could not remember what was said.

Argent was still standing there with the glass in his hand, and now Merritt was standing behind him, on the steps of her platform. When had Merritt joined them? Argent insisted that M take her medicine, and at that M's latent anger, suppressed all day, immediately blossomed, and she fairly shouted at him, "It is doing me more harm than good. I don't want it."

Argent took on an authoritarian posture. "Miss Warner, the doctor has prescribed this for you, and you must follow his dictates; you cannot merely say no."

M shot back, "I am not obligated to follow his dictates. He was consulted, I tried his regimen, and now I reject it. Saying no is always an option, even to authorities."

Surprisingly, it was Merritt's anger that now exploded. "Take it and swallow it, and I will hear no more of these arguments. If you knew what was best, you would be the doctor."

Ever since learning of her true age, Merritt and Argent had begun to treat her like a child. Had she known their original assessment of her age, she would never have revealed the truth. They were beginning to treat her like a child and, worse, an invalid. After leveling at Merritt a glare heavy with loathing, M took the dose proffered by Argent and swallowed it in one gulp, then promptly entered her car, slamming the door.

When they descended from the platform, Argent and Merritt realized their argument with M had been loud enough to pull Mr. and Mrs. Hughes from the car near the caboose and Mike from the tender at the other end; both the marshal and the new brakeman had poked their heads out from the stock car where they were playing cards on the hay bales. Argent waved away the concern at the headend of the train, while Merritt did the same to Mr. and Mrs. Hughes.

In their car, Argent expressed concern that the gains M had earned through Dr. Culver's surgery were quickly evaporating, as she appeared more and more fatigued, and her anger more and more easily triggered and creeping ever nearer to the surface. He disclosed that he had increased the last two doses in the hopes M would receive more benefit from the prescription. Tomorrow they would be in Baltimore and he would consult the doctors there. In the meantime, they would have to keep a tight watch on Miss Warner.

In her car, M relived in her mind yet another of her outbursts. She clasped her hands between her knees, beseeching God or anyone else who might be listening to forgive her her faults, to release her from them. Why could she not be like other women, like other people, knowing what to say and how to act. M looked up at the arched roof of her car; there was no clerestory there, no windows, no way for her prayers to escape her car and make their way to anyone who might care. For the first time she thought of her car as a tunnel or a tomb. This train was burrowing through the mountains; the train itself was a tunnel, a moving tunnel, that would lead her to her tomb. She wanted out and a breath-robbing panic overtook her. She opened her door only to find the marshal stationed outside. He turned around and smiled at her, but it was a knowing grin, a sly grin. She closed her door again.

She walked up and down the length of her car, going from the back of her bedroom at the headend of the car to the door at the other end. She packed and repacked her bag, preparing for a trip she did not know how to begin. More than once, she pulled her father's gun from the bottom of the bag and stared blankly at it. She needed to leave but she did not know how it could be accomplished. For the first time, she considered that she might have to leave Emmett behind. The very idea wrenched a sob from her, and soon after the marshal knocked on her door and asked if she was well. She sent him away, then called him back. Could he find some ice? Her head needed ice.

A little later, there was another knock at the door, but this time it was Mrs. Hughes. The marshal had obviously roused her after he had somehow found ice, no doubt begged from one of the warehouses nearby. Mrs.

Hughes said nothing but pulled M into the car with her. She made M sit down, then handed her the ice wrapped in an old towel. Mrs. Hughes then mixed one of her headache powders into a cup of water and silently handed it to M. Once M had taken the elixir, Mrs. Hughes made her lie down, placed the iced towel on her forehead, turned down the lamps, then silently left the car. After a moment, M got up only long enough to lock her door. She wanted no more guests tonight.

M finally drifted off and fell into nightmare. She dreamed of total and complete loss of freedom, of being locked in a room and forcibly dosed day and night. The memory of Argent injecting her with morphine became a nightmare of unknown drugs introduced in the same manner. In her dreams, she had a terror of such needles and procedures. She gasped and panted in her sleep as she was torn from her farm, never to see Jack and Morty or Emmett again. She watched in horror as Captain James criss-crossed the farm with tracks going nowhere. She saw the family cemetery, neglected and disrespected. But worst of all, she dreamed of riding in a sideless railroad car, with nothing to hang on to as the car, under its own motion, climbed and climbed and climbed a bridge whose incline was so steep that she could not see any tracks beyond the end of the car, making it appear as if the car could at any moment simply ride off the tracks. M felt herself slide to the back of the car, helpless against the gravity, and felt herself try to scream for help, but all she heard was a scraping sound in her throat.

Finally, the car did fall with a sickening lurch to land in the yard of a hospital in Washington, the name above the door a familiar one – the Insane Asylum of which she heard mentioned late at night as her parents spoke quietly downstairs. Then she did scream, or rather, shout for help, for she knew with ice-cold certainty that Merritt and Argent were escorting her to Washington, not to see Grant, but to commit her to this hospital. All their kindnesses, all their attentions and gifts and friendly teasing were a viciously clever cover for the darkest of deeds.

Argent, asleep in his bed, heard Miss Warner shouting, begging for mercy, pleading over and over again, "No, please don't, please don't." Throwing on some pants and an unbuttoned shirt, Argent, and Merritt just behind him, ran to M's car. She was still crying out in anguish for help. Argent tried the door, but it was locked. He banged on the door, calling to her. Almost immediately the gargled screaming stopped. Argent continued banging, insisting that the door be opened. After a long moment, a haggard M, wearing only the slip that women wore under their dresses, answered his knock. Terror was still in her eyes, though receding quickly and being replaced by an openly wary regard of Argent. Her gaze shifted beyond him to take in Merritt. Her wariness deepened and hardened and even took on a hint of hatred. Her pupils were completely dilated, so that her eyes appeared black and wild; she seemed a different person altogether. Below the platform, other members of the train were gathering. The brakeman, Mike, and the marshal were to have split the night standing guard at Miss Warner's car, but the brakeman had fallen asleep, had even slept through the worst of M's screams.

"Miss Warner, what has happened? Are you all right?"

M's eyes were constantly shifting between Merritt and Argent. "Yes, I am all right. I'm sorry I disturbed you. It won't happen again."

"Our concern is not about being disturbed —"

"It won't happen again." M shut the door, bolting it from inside, another modification, courtesy of Mr. Hughes. Mrs. Hughes asked to enter, but the door was tightly shut to everyone.

Argent dispersed the little train community, and Merritt had a stern word with the three men tasked with keeping Miss Warner safe and secure, then followed Argent back to their car.

In the parlor car, the lamps remained lit until a very late (or very early) hour. The exchange with M had left both men very concerned, but neither Merritt nor Argent gave voice to the nearly hysterical suspicion they saw on M's face. They argued about a course of action – clearly, something needed to be done. Whatever peculiarities M exhibited on her farm in Kentucky were clearly compounded by the stresses of this trip, not the least of which was a bullet taken in their defense.

"She was never this bad until she started taking Dr. Culver's prescriptions." Argent was pacing but stopped long enough to run both hands through his hair, clutching at the ends.

"You don't know that. We only saw her for a short time on her farm; we can't know what is normal for her based on such short acquaintance. And Henry did allude to her 'states.'"

"If this were normal for her, do you think Miss Carrie and Mr. Henry would have sent her with two strange men without acquainting them of the problem, and, moreover, without instructing them in the management of the problem? And more to the point, none of this is normal, for anyone. Her sleep problems, her peculiarities of character, her isolation, and her grief have all been allowed to fester and poison every facet of her life. She is invalided by it; she is a cripple without a crutch."

Merritt winced at Argent's description of M as a cripple. There was no doubt that M moved haltingly in society, but he did not like to think of her in that term. "We're almost there. We keep a closer watch on her – either keep her distracted here in the parlor car or we insist Mrs. Hughes stay with her. When we reach the White House, we'll advise the President of the situation, of our experiences with M, and know that he'll get her the help she needs."

Argent sat heavily. "I feel more responsible for her than merely dropping her off at the White House steps."

Merritt replied with some heat, "That is not what I said. I feel responsible for her, too. She saved us both – twice – and I have no doubt that much of this recent trouble stems from her injuries. Traveling does not agree with her – she spends half her time in white-knuckled, clench-jawed terror of train wrecks, bridges, and now brigands nipping at our heels. She should never have been asked to make this trip. President Grant should have gone to her." Merritt stopped suddenly, a little alarmed at his presumption to criticize the President. Argent was a little alarmed as well; he had never heard Merritt make any such comment about Grant or any of his other commanders. After a moment, Merritt continued in a cooler voice. "We lack the knowledge to help her. We can only get her to the people who can. But I will tell you this: I will be advising Whitley that I will require some personal time – I mean to accompany M to every doctor appointment and hold her hand, if she will allow it, until I see her back to her natural balance, or at least back on her farm, where she belongs."

"I fully intend the same. In the meantime," Argent drew a breath before admitting, "I find myself in agreement with M – the current regimen of medications is doing her no good. The morphine only seemed to give her any respite. On Tuesday, I will report that I have done so at my own discretion; you need not involve yourself."

"Agreed. No more of these reckless, new drugs, but I will stand with you for any condemnation for this course of action."

30

M finally dozed off just before daybreak, exhausted in mind, spirit, and body. She was surprised and a little leery, upon waking, to find that the train had not begun the day's transit. She peeked out her door to see the same vista as the night before – she had not slept through a day's travel.

At her feet she found an envelope addressed to her. In the enclosed note, Merritt and Argent explained that they have delayed the train, giving her the chance to complete some much-needed sleep. When she was ready to depart, she need only come to the parlor car, where they have kept breakfast for her. In a post script, Argent had added that they did not intend to visit the events of last night, but that they hoped she would be open to suggestions for the rest of the trip.

M studied the note, and, in her exhaustion and fear, saw betrayal and entrapment; 'suggestions' to her was code for incarceration and more of Dr. Culver's poisons, possibly even a prolonged state of senselessness, via Dr. Culver's ether kerchief, which he has doubtless provided to Merritt and Argent – she would wake already committed, beyond the reach of the few friends she had not completely alienated. No one would know where she was, no one would come to her defense. She would spend her days in tears and screaming, and at the mercy of an indifferent staff. The threat of asylum had loomed over her for almost as long as she could remember, and she had read every article she could about these institutions. There was no such thing as a comfortable, happy jail. For the condemned, there was only one way out of a jail or an institution. M made her decision.

M dropped the note. In the bedroom, she again pulled her father's gun from her grip bag and made certain it was loaded. She saw the dress she wore yesterday draped across the stuffed armchair near the bed. It was one of the dresses Merritt had purchased for her; she felt disgust at the sight of it. In her trunk, she found the dress Mrs. Müller had made for her, the dress she was wearing when she was attacked in Spring Grove; it held a warrior's charm for her. Once dressed, she found the old dinner napkin that had been her first sling and returned it to that use. With the sling in place, M placed in it the loaded gun, facing towards her elbow and securely wedged between her forearm and stomach. She arranged the cloth of the sling, so that the gun was fully hidden. Finally, she scribbled a hasty note, and left it on the swing where Mrs. Hughes would find it.

At the parlor car door, M was admitted to solicitous remarks about the reappearance of her sling. *They are only pretending to care.* Merritt and Argent herded her to sit on the couch with its back to the cylinder desk. *They do not want me to easily reach the door.* She assured them it was a very temporary setback, having wrenched her arm attempting to dress too quickly this morning. Merritt attempted a little humor, reminding M of her comments regarding a second pair of hands. *He is insincere; he is mocking me.*

"I think we can squeeze in ahead of the next train. I'll let the engineer know we're ready."

As Merritt left the car, M thought, *Of course, the engineer must be complicit, and his wife. He has gone to finish preparations.*

Argent was watching her, smiling, but she could see he was anxious to be going. *He is almost finished with his task, a task that has taken far too long. They will deliver me, then go back to their lives.* M made a true effort to match his smile; she mustn't let on that she knows, not yet.

Argent stirred from his observation of her, suddenly remembering, "We have set aside some breakfast for you. Mrs. Hughes made it especially for you – she knows your fondness for bacon and pancakes, and Merritt went into town this morning to get the first milk off the wagons. He even found some ice, though it is mostly melted now, but there is enough left to cool your milk . . . how you like it."

Mrs. Hughes knows my fondness — it was significant — she knows my fondness. The import of the words was colossal, though M could not understand why. The train in her brain kept circling, chugging out the words *It is significant, it is significant.*

Argent fussed about, setting out a plate of food, covered to keep it warm, and the utensils wrapped in a napkin. M watched from the couch and only realized she was frowning when Argent turned to beckon her and asked, "M, do you feel unwell?" She must mask her face and her movements; the timing must be exact.

"No; I was only thinking that Mrs. Hughes should not have gone through any extra effort on my account, for, truly, I am not hungry."

Argent's face fell, and M thought she saw a flicker of – what? Anger? Frustration? Argent recovered quickly, however, and came to sit next to her. The barrel was pointed at his vital midsection. He turned toward her and with a very good imitation of concern asked, "Answer honestly: does your shoulder give you pain? There is still the morphine left, and it would take only a very little. It might even help you relax – I know how you hate the bridges."

"I answer you honestly – my shoulder does not give me pain, not in the sling, only if I move my arm too suddenly or too expansively. The sling reminds me of those limits today."

Argent smiled warmly, and M's heart sank a little. How could perfidy be so pleasant? But then she remembered the story of how Argent fooled the Widow Rogers into believing him in love with her. He has been fooling M all along. She hears him say in her mind: *'It was my duty — my unpleasant duty — to gain her confidence in any way possible.'* Other lies came to her: Argent had lied about his horse throwing a shoe; Merritt had easily lied to the Floss sisters about his supposed relationship with M (though she herself had birthed that particular lie, Merritt easily adopted it and presented it to women he apparently held some affection for); they had lied to her about Emmett nearly the entire time they rode on the M&C; they lied to her about her father's gun. She suspected them of other lies, but ones she could not prove – all the mysterious errands to the telegraph office or the desk clerks in the different hotels, sending messages and receiving messages, one of them always gone somewhere, doing secretive things. And there was the great trunk that they kept with them always, under lock and key and strap, the trunk with the bundles of money and false beards and wigs. She did not really know who these men were. Argent was a liar, a good liar – they both were – and she had been silly enough to believe them. They were actors, they were acting, they were lying. Their friendship and concern for her were only lies employed in the cause of their mission, to complete their roles in the production.

"I am very glad to hear it, and glad to see you adopt such a sensible strategy. But you must be hungry; it is after noon. Merritt and I have been remarking on how well your appetite has rebounded. We're a little proud of ourselves – we've been especially attentive to what foods you favor and have been asking Mrs. Hughes to fix them for you."

M's eyes widened and she involuntarily gasped. She understood now – they had been encouraging her to eat, even past her hunger, by providing food sure to entice her. They had been poisoning her, to subdue her for an easy delivery to Grant and his plans for her commitment. They have been preparing her from the very beginning, even in her own home, maybe even with the help of Carrie, so ready to be rid of M. And their insistence, every night, of a drink to mark the end of the day – what was in the drinks? From the first such drink in Cincinnati, she had been almost constantly ill, beset by headaches and unusual fatigue.

Argent was alarmed at her reaction. "Miss Warner, what is it? Are you unwell?"

She almost tipped her hand but after only a little stammering, she managed to mumble at being humbled to have people so attentive to her quirks.

Argent outwardly accepted this, though he was clearly not convinced of her lie. He was still looking at her with worry. "You're pale, and I can see you are shaking." He reached across to take M's right hand to find her pulse. He very nearly brushed the gun hidden in her sling, and the near discovery sent her heart racing. Argent, alarmed at her rapid pulse, stood, declaring they will not leave until she is feeling better. He moved to leave to countermand Merritt's earlier message to the engineer, but M grasped at his hand as he turned from her.

"Please. Please. It is nothing. I hate all this fuss. I hate the bridges. I hate the delays. I only want to get started. Please, let it all be over soon." M released Argent's hand. "Give me your watch."

Argent looked at her dubiously but handed her his watch. Her hand was shaking, but she managed to open the watch. Concentrating on the second hand, she soon closed her eyes to concentrate on the tick-tick-tick. Argent noticed that her hand stopped shaking and her breathing visibly evened. Merritt entered the car, but M was so intent on the sound of the watch that she did not register his entrance. Once again, Merritt and Argent exchanged glances, though this time M did not see.

After a moment or two, M opened her eyes, saying lightly, "See, it was nothing." The familiar lurch of the train straining against its inertia made M relax; it would not be long now.

Taking a seat across from her, Merritt asked, "What was nothing?"

"A silly womanish response to the kind efforts of everyone on this train."

"Not every womanish response is silly. You're sure it is nothing else."

"Quite sure." Merritt sitting across from her with his amateurish philosophical observations and Argent standing above her peddling false concerns whetted her anger, putting steel in her resolve. The first shock at understanding the vehicle by which they have been controlling her had been intense, but she had recovered and needed only to remain firm for a little while longer.

Argent told Merritt, "I have been trying to tempt M with some of Mrs. Hughes' breakfast, but it won't be long before we'll be forced to move on to the excellent lunch she has packed for us. I always say, *No great enterprise ever began on an empty stomach.*"

"Yes, you always say that, ever since we first met." M was eying him with new suspicion; how could she have missed this ploy? He'd been plying her with food and drink from the very first. How long had they been poisoning her?

"Perhaps if you sat at the table, the aroma of the food will awaken your appetite."

She was going to have no say in the matter. Merritt was lifting her by her right elbow, while Argent hovered near her left. She would have to allow herself to be corralled at the table, or they would discover the gun prematurely. She sat before the plate but could not bring herself to eat any. Merritt and Argent sat at table with her, drinking coffee, but eating nothing themselves.

The train was gaining momentum, and let out a long blow of its whistle, joyful in its own power. M thought of Argent's offer of morphine. She thought of her mother, thought of the whispers about her death and the large doses of morphine said to have been left by the doctor to alleviate the pain of the sick of the household, rumors that said the children had died so suddenly, there had been little chance to use the morphine, and yet it was all gone. When the doctor had returned to check on his patients, all the morphine was gone, and all the patients, too. M wondered how much morphine was needed to induce death, but Argent had offered just enough to let her relax; would it be wrong to accept it? She was beginning to doubt her courage; but her decision was pure, so the courage or fear that she brought to bear on it must be pure, too. Her mind could not be clouded any more.

M had been staring for some minutes at Argent's watch on the table where she had laid it. When she at last blinked, Argent remarked, "You've been thinking quite a lot lately. What were you thinking just now?"

"I was remembering."

"What?"

M turned to Merritt. "My mother. And others. What do you think about? Do you think about what you will do once we reach Washington?" This was skating too close to the edge, but M needed to screw up her courage. She needed to hear them talk of their lives beyond the train, of how they will forget her and forget their part in her fate. She wanted her resolve to flare in the face of their indifference for her.

"As a matter of fact, Argent and I were talking just yesterday about spending some free time just roaming Washington City and the areas around it. We were hoping we could show you some of it."

"Do you know Uniontown? My father spoke of the area sometimes."

"Oh, yes; it is one of the areas we had wanted to take you. You will like it – lots of shade trees, still very rural. There is a wonderful vista of Washington City from the tower of a nearby institution. You will like it."

An Institution. The Institution her parents had talked of. They wanted to take her there. Argent had told Mr. Hughes preparations were being made for her, but they were not ready for her yet. What preparations? Ready for what?

M did not know how much longer she could continue in this mockery of companionship. She looked down at her cold breakfast, remembering breakfasts at home at the big table, the chaos of dinners, the inevitable crime of etiquette she would commit and the hot tears that would follow sharp words from her mother, and laughter from her brothers and even, after they were older, her younger sisters. Her memories did not bring her feelings of loss, but feelings of eternal humiliation and shame and unworthiness. She can never outgrow or outlive odd little Lally, and now she must add to those memories, new ones of odd Miss Warner and her life at St. Elizabeth's Hospital, the institution for the deranged. She was overcome by her thoughts, and without realizing it, let out a despairing sob and dropped her head into her hand.

Merritt and Argent both were alarmed at this unprovoked display. Argent left the table and crossed the room to one of the cabinets by the door. Merritt also left the table and moved to the cylinder desk across the room. The train blasted out the signal that indicated they were approaching a tunnel. Though the day was overcast, no one had thought to light a lamp, and as the train entered the tunnel, darkness entered the car. M stood, disoriented. The sound of the wheels as they clicked over the rails reverberated off the walls of the tunnel. The sound became a pounding in M's head, a great triphammer falling from greater and greater heights. She felt the gun hidden in her sling. The wheels beat out a tempo that formed words in M's head: triphammer and trigger, triphammer and trigger, triphammer and trigger.

One of the men lit a lamp, just as the train was leaving the tunnel. The day outside was growing darker; they would be riding into rain soon. Argent looked up from the lamp as he blew out the match and noticed M had stood.

"It was only a tunnel, Miss Warner. I promise to let you know when we reach a bridge." Argent returned to his rummaging in the cabinet by the door.

Merritt turned towards M as Argent spoke, but he, too, returned immediately to his task at the desk.

M moved to stand before the mantle. It was time. Despite what Argent said – he was a liar – M knew, without seeing it, that they were about to cross a bridge, the bridge of her nightmare, the prescient nightmare that she understood in a flash that Randy has sent to her. He had not visited her in her dreams for years now, and she thought he had abandoned her in disappointment, but he was always the most forgiving, and he sent the vision to her to give her courage, to prepare her. It will happen on the bridge, between courage and fear. How could anyone call it cowardice while she straddled a bridge on the mighty B&O? She would stop the nightmare at the point of her own choosing. She would do this on her own two feet, and not cowering in a corner in the presence of cold, poisoned food. She would not be dragged to terrifying heights to plummet to hell. She would not suffer the final humiliation.

The car darkened again as the train entered a second tunnel. Merritt was bending over the desk, scribbling a note in the low light of a single lit lamp. "We'll stop at the first opportunity, and I'll . . ." Merritt suddenly straightened at the desk and turned towards Argent, instinctively knowing the silence was wrong. He had been hearing Argent rummaging in the cabinet – he knew Argent kept smelling salts in there, somewhere – but all sound from Argent's corner had suddenly ceased. Argent was standing with the smelling salts limp in his hand, staring ahead, and deathly pale. Merritt turned yet again and saw M standing in front of the mantle, her sling on the floor nearby, a gun in her right hand.

"M, what are you doing?"

She placed the gun to her right temple, halting Merritt's initial move toward her. She said, simply and without emotion, "Maybe in fifty years, I will finish dying," and pulled the trigger.

By the time Argent regained his feet, the train had stopped moving, a dead thing surrounded by dead rock. Merritt was already moving toward the mantel. M was lying face down on the floor, a pool of blood spreading from under her head, joined by a second stream of blood running across her forehead to drop to the floor. The gun was still in her hand, still pointing to her head.

Argent carefully removed the gun from her hand and found no pulse in her wrist. Incredulously, though, he detected shallow breathing. Merritt had likewise found no pulse at her neck and had let his fingers slide away from the disappointment there. Argent gingerly explored the source of the blood at her exposed temple. When Merritt pulled the emergency break, M's hand had jerked up as she fired, and the bullet merely seamed her scalp. It was ugly and would leave a scar, but it was not deadly.

Merritt looked to Argent, desperate to see hope and action there, but Argent, too, seemed lifeless. Throughout their service together – in the war and since – Merritt and the other men of their particular circles had tacitly acknowledged Argent as the medical authority in the absence of professionals. Argent had been expected to follow his father and two uncles in the medical arts – he had the aptitude, the intelligence, and even the interest at the time. But Argent's was a restless mind and body; he was soon enamored of the expanding west, the rapid explosion of technology of all kinds, and the freedom they afforded. The war found him first, indeed assisting doctors at the edge of battle, but, though he was not a squeamish man, he found it frustrating to work in the almost hopeless aftermath of battle. Argent's father had died during the war, and with him had died Argent's desire to become a doctor, or perhaps his father's death had freed him from the preordained destiny. Certainly his two uncles continued to press him to return to his studies, but Argent, now his own man, resisted. Now, Argent felt Merritt's eyes on him, expecting him to help somehow, relying on him to do the doctoring.

Argent met Merritt during the war. Merritt had brought in a man, carried on his shoulders, unconscious, and with a leg wound, a tight tourniquet applied against further bleeding. He had brought the man straight to Argent – thinking him to be a doctor – dropped the man unceremoniously, and instructed, "Bring him around." Argent was standing among many injured, doing little more than presiding over the deaths of those deemed too injured to survive. Those most likely to survive were already in the surgeon's tents, their moans and the occasional scream suggesting that surviving was of questionable desire.

Argent had quickly assessed the man – injured, certainly, but in this war of outrageous abuse on the human body, this man had less claim on Argent's time than these other poor dying souls. "Take him to the next group over." Then Argent had turned away from Merritt, disgusted with everything.

Argent was then surprised to feel his shoulder gripped as he was roughly spun around. The young man who had dropped the injured soldier to the ground was staring angrily at Argent. The young man, Argent noticed, was himself injured, blood slowly dropping from a slice in his arm. He was hot, dirty, and his eyes were completely bloodshot. Tickling at the back of his mind, Argent wondered at a soldier with a knife wound in the middle of a battle where guns were the universal weapon. Even bayonet wounds were rare, despite some commanders' almost romantic loyalty to the virtue of the bayonet, and their unfounded propensity to order the bayonet charge. Some units had even blatantly disregarded the order to fix bayonets.

"I said, bring him to his senses."

Argent was a little alarmed at the vehemence of the young man. "Look, son, your friend doesn't belong here. Look around you – there is no hope here." With a nod toward the tents and the moaning, Argent directed the young man, "Take him over there where proper doctors can help him."

"He isn't my friend, and I don't give a damn if he dies. In fact, I'm the one that shot him, but in my anger for this slice he gave me, I shot him in a vital spot. I brought him here because I need privacy with him, and these fellows here will tell no tales. After I've interrogated him, you can cut the tourniquet loose and let him bleed, for all I care. But right now, I need you to bring this man to consciousness."

"Interrogate him?"

"He's a spy, a double-agent, and he has valuable information that my commander desperately needs. I've been tracking him for days, and he tried to lose himself in the turmoil of the battle."

When Argent still hesitated, Merritt ascribed it to medical ethics, but Argent seriously doubted the sanity of the wild-looking young man before him. Merritt suddenly appeared weary. "If you want to stop this" – waving his hand at the field of dead and dying – "if you want a chance to stem the magnitude of this, if you want to stand in the middle of a smaller harvest of bodies, you will help me get out of this man what I need."

Something shifted in Argent, and he pulled out of a pocket of his apron smelling salts, and, motioning Merritt to take up his burden and follow, led him to a break in the line of bodies – the boundary between those still dying and laid side by side, and those already dead and stacked like cordwood. Merritt dropped the man again, but this time Argent saw it was not out of anger, but because his injured arm precluded any gentler movement.

Argent revived the man, then moved away at a motion from Merritt. He heard Merritt's voice low and even – a softer interrogation than his previous anger indicated he was capable of conducting. After several moments, Merritt rose, tucking a folded paper in his breast pocket. Looking down, Argent saw that the man had died, considerately saving Argent from the awkward decision to prolong the life of a spy sure to be hanged upon the instant he could stand.

The young man mumbled his thanks and turned to move off. Argent called after him and insisted on tending the arm. The cut was moderately deep and had obviously bled a goodly deal. Calling to an orderly to cover his duty, Argent took the young man to his own tent, cleaned the wound, and stitched it together, admiring the young man's ability to keep his own arm still. Many men could stifle a scream, a moan, a gasp, but few could control the urge to flinch and draw back. He gave the young man his cot, and, promising to bring him some food and water as soon as he could, left to return to his duties. When he returned with a plate of food and a tin of coffee, however, the young man was gone, and in his place was a note: If you want to help stop the bleeding, let me know. At the bottom was the name of his regiment.

Three months later, Argent had buried his father, and upon his return from furlough, Argent decided to 'stop the bleeding' and to find the young man with his regiment.

They had been working together ever since. Argent had unexpectedly proven adroit at espionage, going to the very heart of the Confederacy, to Richmond, and in three short months providing the Union with invaluable information on Confederate defenses along the Rappahannock and other nearby waterways, including detailed sketches and maps. He had quickly become something of an expert in torpedoes. Argent had grown his hair long and then had paraded himself behind enemy lines as Dr. Largo, alternately of New York City and Wilmington, North Carolina. The want and suffering he saw throughout the South doubled his determination to help stop the bleeding for the poor rebels of the Confederacy as well as the true-blue Union soldiers. He had finally been caught and arrested as a spy just as he was crossing the Rappahannock one last time. Merritt, addressing himself as Conrad Sterling, had been Argent's contact, receiving the intelligence gathered and relaying it directly to the War Department. Even when Argent was held in Richmond's Castle Thunder, facing the all too real possibility of hanging, Merritt was close-by, planning and waiting for the opportunity to free the man he had talked into a life of spying.

The desperation Merritt felt at that crisis, among so many crises in the war years, flooded in on him. He was desperate again now, but unlike that time in Richmond, there was nothing Merritt could do; it was out of his hands. He looked to Argent to solve this crisis, but Argent seemed stunned, unthinking, useless.

Argent's mind was blank, or rather it was arrested – he could not move beyond the image of M on the floor. Over and over his mind said, *The bullet missed; she should not be without a pulse.* Sudden death like this occurred in infants and older adults, not a young woman. There was nothing to be done for her – no bullet to extract, no tourniquet to be applied, no wound to stitch, no fever to abate. She had no pulse, but she was breathing, barely.

Finally, Argent stirred and motioned to Merritt to help him turn M onto her back. There had been no reason to do so – it was no precursor to action – but Argent had needed to do something. Merritt thought Argent had decided on a course of action, but realized Argent had no plan at all, had no hope.

A wound on her left temple was the primary source of the pool of blood on the floor, but blood was no longer escaping from this wound, where she'd hit her head on the great trunk that sat between the sofas.

M's breathing had rapidly deteriorated; she was taking short, shallow gasps, very few to the minute. Occasionally, her chest would heave as her body gasped for a large gulp of air. Soon it would cease altogether. Because she had no pulse.

Merritt sat back on his heels, his face unreadable. He reached forward to pull a strand of hair off her face, but otherwise remained silent and staring. Argent looked up, helpless, at the younger man. Merritt always had an alternative, never gave in to failure, always stood by with an amused private smile, never empty of encouragement. But now Merritt was resigned. There was no point to this death. On the battlefield, they had witnessed many friends and comrades die, but there was always a target to move on to, a reason behind the deaths and the fight. Here was M, dying, for God knew what reason. Why had she done it?

Merritt reached out a final time to feel the artery at M's neck. There was no change, he had not been mistaken. Argent's mind simply stopped; he was numb with shock and guilt and a kind of grief that had never accompanied the dying before. As he listened to M's body struggle to breathe, the pointless thought occurred to him, *If she were drowned, I'd know what to do; she wouldn't be struggling so hard to breathe.* He remembered M's own very real sorrow at what she thought was a failure at the canal, when she thought she had left Argent to drown, pinned under a work scow. She had not failed him, though; he was failing her.

Argent bowed his head in defeat, but his mind kept thinking about drowning victims, and he automatically reviewed all the tracts and treatises he had read with mild interest in the days of his presumed medical career. There were several variations of the re-animation process, but all agreed on the artificial introduction of breath via the mouth – midwives had long claimed success at reviving newborns in this manner.

Argent made a fanciful connection between M and newborns. A strange thought, a silly play on words, had lodged in his mind: M was not a newborn, but she was an infant, a legal infant. It was some odd connection that Merritt would make, but Argent could not remove it from his mind. In desperation more than any deference to any clinical trial, Argent leaned over M's face and blew hard into her mouth. Merritt was a little alarmed at his friend's action, but he, also in desperation, hoped it portended something productive. Merritt saw Argent's eyes begin to oscillate at a frenzied rate. He worried about having to tend to Argent as a victim of some kind of fit.

Argent remembered that the Danish prescribed a combination of chest massage and artificial ventilation. Argent had abandoned a medical career, but he remained interested in the subject, reading any articles about new procedures or theories being advanced in the medical community. Galvanic batteries could be used in some cases to re-animate the heart in patients whose hearts had stopped during surgery. But there were no galvanic batteries at hand. Her heart had stopped, and because her heart had stopped, she was drowning, struggling to breathe. How to shock a heart without a battery? Would any kind of shock do? Concussions were shocks to the brain; he needed to concuss M's heart.

Merritt's fears for Argent seemed to be validated as he watched his friend lean over M once again and then strike M, hard, on the chest. Merritt was stunned, as if Argent had struck him, as well as M. Still kneeling over M, Argent began to bear down on M's chest with great force, over and over again. Argent's face was hard, almost angry. Merritt grabbed at an arm and tried to pull Argent from M's body. But Argent was the larger man, and Merritt had never really appreciated his raw strength until that moment when he could not budge Argent from this frenzy.

Merritt tried to reach his friend another way: "Argent, leave her alone; she's gone."

Argent was pushing harder and harder, and faster and faster, sweating with the exertion. He had no idea of the pace he had adopted; it merely matched the frenzy of his desperation. Had he remembered his readings, he would have been shocked at how far he had diverged from the recommended pace of compressions – that of normal respiration.

"Argent, stop! Get off her!"

Merritt grabbed again at his arm, and this time managed to pull his arm mere inches across M's chest. Argent stopped only for a fraction of a second, long enough to look up at Merritt with murderous warning in his face, then returned to his compressions.

Merritt said softly, "Giles, you can't help her."

"She's drowning." Argent spoke equally softly, though as if to himself.

Merritt now truly feared his friend was suffering from some mad grief. "No, Giles; she was sick, and she tried to kill herself. She fell; she didn't drown."

From his labors, Argent told Merritt in a voice that conveyed more emotional than clinical conviction, "The symptoms are the same. Breathe for her." When Merritt didn't respond, Argent shouted at him, "Put your mouth on hers and breathe in, and keep doing it until I tell you otherwise." All the literature said efforts had to be maintained for at least forty minutes. It occurred to Argent, in some distant part of his mind, that he had given his watch to M, and she would have been happy to keep the time for him.

This was a rarely seen Argent – angry, authoritative, menacing – and Merritt did what he was told, if only to mollify this strange version of Argent until this fit had passed.

After a few minutes, Merritt was gasping for breath of his own. Argent was also breathing heavily and sweating. He instructed Merritt, "Check for a pulse."

Miraculously, Merritt found one at her neck, and looked up with excitement. "There's a pulse."

"Yes."

Merritt resumed breathing for M, but he was becoming light-headed. Argent was terrified of leaving his position artificially pumping M's heart, but it would do her no good if Merritt passed out. In one of his more courageous acts, he switched places with Merritt. Even while he breathed into M, he kept watch on Merritt's work, ready to correct him; but Merritt had been watching Argent and he matched Argent in intensity and pace.

It seemed like they worked together this way for hours, but Mr. Hughes, who had run down the side of the tunnel to find out just what was going on, and who had walked into the parlor car to find the two men committing he-didn't-know-what acts upon Miss Warner's person, swore to them it was no more than twenty to thirty minutes from the time the brakes had been engaged.

Finally, M coughed and drew a long scraping breath of her own into her lungs, and began to breathe again on her own, her heart also keeping its own pace.

Mr. Hughes asked from the galley way door, "What has happened?"

Merritt looked up, red in the face and sweating, to acknowledge the engineer's presence. Rising unsteadily, he said, "Get this thing going now and don't spare the steam. Lay on the whistle and bell for any train that slows us down. No more stops."

"We'll have to stop at least once for fuel and water. I'll have our train given priority." After a moment he added, "Will she make it?"

From the floor, Argent answered, "She'll make it," as if he were commanding M to obey.

At Frederick Junction – Merritt still called the station Monocacy, which Argent attributed to a natural stubbornness – they took on more coal and water. Mr. Hughes immediately went to the office there and took the extraordinary measure of telling the dispatcher to clear the tracks for his little train. When the dispatcher began to assert his indisputable authority in these matters, Mr. Hughes had cut him off. If the dispatcher wished to waste precious time telegraphing to Mr. Garrett, that was all well and good, but Mr. Hughes intended to push his engine to its fullest and woe to any train that got in his way. Mr. Hughes was out of the office before the dispatcher could form a reply. Just as Mr. Hughes was ready to pull out of the station, a messenger ran up and begged his patience while a pilot engine was readied to lead his little train. Everything from Frederick Junction to Baltimore had been side-tracked, the way was cleared, and the pilot engine was being dispatched to make certain all trains had received the instructions.

They covered the fifty and more miles to Baltimore in very respectable time, even given the steady rain that had settled over the entire area and the slick tracks it produced. Mr. Hughes kept up his speed – urging the pilot engine to accelerate by following it a little too closely – only truly slowing down when they reached Baltimore. Mr. Hughes followed the pilot engine to the Mount Clare station, where it was forcefully suggested to relinquish control of the train to one of the yard's engineers. But before the little train was parked in one of the most inaccessible areas of the yard – there would be no more of this foolish commandeering of the tracks by wildcat trains – an ambulance was sent for, and M was carefully lifted into the conveyance.

Merritt and Argent were maddeningly proprietary and exacting in their instructions to the orderlies. Upon entering the car, the two orderlies found a young woman supine on the floor, the entire perimeter of her body lined with rolled sheets and blankets, acting as bolsters of some kind. The walls and tables and other surfaces had been stripped bare of anything that might fall or roll or break. Had the two men looked in the bedroom behind the fireplace, they would have seen a room in complete disarray. The beds had been stripped of all bedding, even the mattresses. Everything loose in the front room had been thrown carelessly in the bedroom, and then locked against escape and threat to the woman insensate on the floor. Why had they not simply moved the woman to one of the couches? But these were apparently wealthy people, and the wealthy often did not act with any kind of natural sense; it had been bred out of them.

Argent insisted on the transfer of M's head himself, cradling her head and neck in the most immobile fashion possible. Once M was secured to the stretcher to Merritt's and Argent's satisfaction, M was transferred to the waiting ambulance. The two men who arrived with the ambulance took it all in stride – they had loaded enough sick and dead to know their job – but they were somewhat annoyed when Argent clambered into the back of the wagon, apparently presuming he had a right to accompany the young woman to the hospital. But Argent did presume that right and a great deal of authority as well. Argent sat near M's head and directed one of the orderlies to join him in the back. Argent would personally keep M's head absolutely still during the ride, while the orderly would keep the stretcher as immobile as possible. Merritt joined the other orderly in the front. From the back, Argent gave the order to *festina lente.*

The closest hospital to the Mount Clare station was the University Hospital, staffed by the Sisters of Charity, at the corner of Lombard and Greene streets. There was no trouble at all keeping to the *lente* part of Argent's command – the streets were clogged with Saturday afternoon traffic, despite the rain, and the ambulance crawled the few blocks to the hospital. All the while, Argent kept M's head absolutely immobile. The orderly who sat in the back with Argent and the young woman was irritated with Argent's over-attention to her. She was unconscious, it was true, and with an obvious head wound, but there was no need for all this excessive attention. There had been a lot of blood on the sheets and pillows around her head, but head wounds always bled a great deal; it could be alarming, but the blood was the least of the problems.

At the hospital, Merritt and Argent gave a detailed account of M's injuries, as well as they knew them. Between them, they had pieced together flashes of images from the moment M put the gun to her head to the moment she lay senseless on the floor. The sudden brake on the forward motion of the train had not only mercifully changed the trajectory of the bullet, but unfortunately had thrown M backwards against the mantel where it was assumed she had hit the back of her head, and as she fell from this event, she had hit her left temple on the corner of the large locked trunk between the couches. They described the moments immediately after the injury, the presence of jagged breaths but no apparent pulse, then the event of death.

At this point, the doctor stopped them, and amended, "You mean the approach of death."

"No, sir, she was dead, without pulse or breath."

The doctor regarded the two men, and concluded they were serious in this narrative, but he knew better than to contradict men in the throes of grief as they were, especially men apparently sleep-deprived and, judging from their wild looks, capable of great damage. He bade them go on.

Argent took over the narrative. "I reanimated the heart through vigorous massage" – Merritt lowered his eyes at this massive understatement of Argent's pounding compressions – "and while I continued to apply a pumping motion to the chest, I directed Mr. Merritt to provide breath for Miss Warner."

"Provide breath for Miss Warner? How do you mean?"

"Midwives have long sworn to the usefulness of breathing into the mouths of infants to start normal respiration." Argent sounded defensive. Upon reflection, he realized that he had far diverged from standard procedures.

"You did not pump her arms between compressions?"

"No, it escaped my memory." It did not escape Argent's memory; he had simply discarded the necessity of it. If the result of pumping the arms was to introduce breath, then that goal had been provided by Merritt. Argent could not say that he had made the decision based on that reasoning at the time; he had simply acted – Merritt would breathe for M and Argent would pump her heart.

The doctor regarded the men. It was the steady pumping of the arms that was thought to excite respiration. The arms pulled first above the head, then pushed back down, expanded the ribcage allowing for air; on the downward pump, the arms were to be crossed over the stomach of the patient, where pressure was to be applied; the process was to be repeated for at least forty minutes. This man standing before the doctor was that most dangerous of bystanders – one who knew enough to be dangerous. His partial understanding and execution of the process could have cost the young woman her life. "And how came you to this course of action?"

"I recalled several treatises on drowning, which instructed both chest compressions and ventilation intervention. I applied the same procedure as I remembered it to Miss Warner."

"Miss Warner was not drowning."

"No, but death looks remarkably the same whether from drowning or sudden cessation of the heart." Realizing how petulant and fantastical that sounded, Argent added, "She was dead – it could do no harm to try."

"No, and it seems no harm has been done. And you have done well to keep her head immobile. Even so, these are serious injuries, and I can hold out no great hope for a successful issue."

Merritt and Argent then endured an agonizing wait before they were allowed to visit M at her bedside. The marshal on their train had been detailed at the Mount Clare station to advise the President of the situation, of this latest situation. A simple telegram from the President of the United States had reached the hospital and insured M would not only receive the best care, but also that she would be afforded a private room, where she now lay on a simple, almost cot-like bed. Merritt and Argent felt like they were attending a visitation – M lay utterly still on the bed in the middle of a quiet and unpopulated room. Except upon close examination, it appeared as if M was not breathing. Her breaths though regular and even did not appear to be deep.

Merritt and Argent felt like intruders now, her care someone else's responsibility. Merritt sat for a while and held M's hand. Argent remained standing, hat in hand, willing her eyes to open. After having waited so long to see her, they left after less than half an hour. They met with the doctor again, briefly, before they left the hospital.

M had reasonably good vital signs, was young, apparently strong, and had no other detectable physical or medical problems. These were all in her favor. However, the doctor warned Merritt and Argent, that individuals who visit violence upon themselves with the intent to commit suicide often will themselves to die in spite of proper care and the best of care.

"And should she survive this attempt, provisions will need to be made for her constant care and vigilance against her desire for self-destruction." The doctor suggested the mental hospital near the Anacostia neighborhood in Washington City. He understood there was some connection with the president; perhaps this would be a favorable arrangement for them both.

There had been no glossing over the history of these injuries, not to a doctor, not as they had done with her shoulder wound with the Floss sisters. The doctor was correct to warn them of the part M's will could play in her recovery, and of the prospect of lifelong care.

The two men walked in silence for some time, taking no notice of the rain. Merritt, normally the taciturn one, found Argent's silence challenging and worrisome. He led Argent into a saloon, and they were well into their third drink when Argent finally spoke.

"She knew that place."

"What place?"

"The insane asylum in Washington that the doctor recommended. She specifically asked if we knew that neighborhood; and I told her it was where we wanted to take her, that she would like it."

"Yes?"

Argent stared hard at him. "Merritt, you are one of the best detectives the department has, but, by God, sometimes you are thick. She thought we were bringing her to Washington to place her in that hospital. It was the last thing we talked about before . . ."

"Why would she think that? How many times did she herself talk about meeting with Grant, having words with him?"

"Yes, but how many times did she mention Grant at all since Grandiflora? Ever since I doubled her dose of chloral hydrate, she became erratic. I think she was suspicious that we meant her harm. She was suspicious that we weren't taking her to see Grant at all, but this was all some ruse to put her away. It's the thing she fears the most – the one thing – 'the hotbox waiting for her, and the people who want to put her there'. In Athens, we two walked towards the new asylum being built there, but as soon as she learned its purpose, she abruptly turned around. And today, when she asked about Anacostia, I mentioned the institution there, and she paled. She must have heard of it some time ago – she referred to the area as Uniontown." Argent paused before continuing in a lower voice. "You noticed the look on her face last night?"

Merritt ignored the question; he did not like to remember the look M had turned on him. "If she survives, though, more than likely she will end up there or somewhere similar, at least for a while."

"That can't happen. We can't let it happen. It would destroy her, or she would destroy herself in an attempt to escape."

"Argent, I feel deeply responsible for what happened, and I'll testify to high heaven that her attempted suicide came after taking chloral hydrate, that we forced upon her in increasing doses, but we aren't blood relatives; only they have say in her future."

"The president is her godfather." Argent said it quietly, conspiratorially.

"The president is her godfather," Merritt agreed with vigor. And for the first time in two days, Merritt and Argent smiled. Though he was not a blood relative, it would be a bold hospital superintendent that did not afford considerable weight to the wishes of the President of the United States and a wildly popular war hero. Argent intended to petition him to exercise that weight, and to offer his and Merritt's help in any way in M's care.

EPILOGUE — Several days in May

Updates were sent daily to the White House, which were usually answered with a simple, *Thank you; maintain your posts*, probably sent by some unknown secretary to Grant. Their own telegraphs had been appended with *Relay to President Grant*, but Merritt and Argent could not be certain this was done. Maintaining their posts was what they fully intended to do, but it was not something that Whitley cared for. Two of his agents – two out of an already small force expected to cover all of the United States and its territories – had been out of the field for more than a month, and he chafed at the current reason: sitting at the bedside of an insensate girl may have been noble, but it was hardly productive. Only the fact that the President wished it kept Whitley from issuing an outright order to return to work. He needed the President's support against a growing murmur of discontent aimed at the Service, but he also needed his men to produce the results that would help to alleviate that discontent.

At the hospital, the fantastic and highly-doubted tale of Miss Warner's resuscitation was attracting visits not only from the hospital staff, but from doctors in private practice and from other hospitals in the city and neighboring areas. A few even came from hospitals and practices in Washington. No one doubted that she was alive and obviously had suffered grave injuries, but few medical men believed she had truly been dead, and for so long. After all, the word of these men who purportedly resuscitated her was suspect on professional grounds – they simply were not doctors. And if the engineer could be believed, the chest compressions applied by the two gentlemen were unforgivably rapid. Established and recommended practice demanded chest compressions equal to that of normal respiration. If the girl had indeed died, it was at the hands of these two boobies, smashing away at her chest like madmen. Any resuscitation happened in spite of their actions.

Merritt let loose a torrent of cursing and threats both believable and remarkable (revealing a soaring creativity Argent did not know he possessed) when it was discovered that the bulk of the medical men parading in and out of M's room were mere gawkers, attendees at a medical sideshow, each with their own explanation that unmasked the true nature of the specimen in bed before them. Argent enjoyed Merritt's fireworks – when properly motivated, Merritt was an artist in volubility. Merritt's theatrics may have been entertaining, but it was Argent's quiet suggestion, that such invasion of Miss Warner's privacy would surely not sit well with the President, that truly sent these 'observational' doctors packing. The doctors grumbled that it had all been mere allusions to resuscitation. There would be no papers written about M or presentations given to medical societies. The whole affair was the mere deluded memories of two laymen, understandably confused in the heightened emotions of the moment. It was folly to have ever taken their reports under serious consideration. To the certified and practicing doctor, laymen were only slightly less reliable than research 'scientists.' One doctor even recalled a similar claim for another Kentuckian earlier in this very year – carried in papers as far away as New York – of the German wife-killer, hanged for his crime, pronounced dead by the gaol surgeon, and then supposedly reanimated (by the galvanic process). The hubris of these Kentuckians extended even to claims of conquering death.

As if waiting for the medical men to leave, M slowly recovered her senses. Argent was grateful for the absence of those senses during some of the more intimate procedures deemed necessary for her recovery. He knew she would never consent to the enemata by which nutrition and some medications were introduced into her body (and also, of course, to cleanse the bowels), her bladder relieved by a catheter, and the cold and clinical examination of her body would have mortified her, especially those earlier examinations conducted as a kind of afternoon lecture series for fellow doctors interested in M's case. It had been this callous disregard for her modesty that had triggered Merritt's harrowing of Baltimore's University Hospital. Surprisingly, the good sisters afterward became very attentive to Merritt.

The hospital staff, at first moved by the concern Merritt and Argent obviously carried for Miss Warner, began to dread their frequent and long visits. Argent, especially, questioned every procedure and every drop of medication extended to Miss Warner. He expected the staff to accept unquestioningly his right and duty to scour M's charts and other records kept regarding her. Argent often invoked the presidential interest in this patient to underscore the necessity of staff obedience in these matters. As M gradually emerged from her coma, Argent began to keep an even more diligent presence and vigilance over her care. When he overheard the suggestion of chloral hydrate after M had spent a restless night, he absolutely forbid its administration in any form. When the doctor, summoned by a frightened nurse, challenged Argent's authority, either legal or medical, in this instance, Argent boldly and (Merritt knew) fraudulently asserted his authority was sanctioned by the President himself. When the doctor seemed still unconvinced, Argent thundered, "Need I bother the President of these United States, the Commander in Chief, our duly elected leader, the Hero of Appomattox, to procure yet another directive in the cause of this young woman?" Normally the doctor would not respond to such bullying, but Congress was reorganizing the Marine Hospital Service and the Secretary of the Treasury, who now held the purse-strings for that Service, would soon be naming a new supervising surgeon, and it did not hurt to have the patronage of the President of the United States when such a position was being filled. M's doctor relented but noted his objections in his private entries in hospital records.

The next day, however, either because M's case had failed to maintain the level of *cause célèbre* that the hospital had hoped for, or because the incessant presence of Merritt and Argent began to wear on the doctors, M was transferred to Providence Hospital in Washington. Merritt and Argent were told Miss Warner's condition had stabilized to the point of safe transportation and it was their wish to have the patient near the President, under whose authority, apparently, Miss Warner's care fell.

The private train was called into service again to transport M in her own car, with Mrs. Hughes and Argent in attendance, to the hospital in Washington. The doctors had wired ahead informing Providence of the coming patient and her condition, and also warned them of the approaching irritation that attended the patient at all times.

As the train made its tortuous way to Washington, Merritt sat alone in the parlor car and reflected on Argent. Twice Argent had seemed to swell physically, both times in frantic defense of a helpless M. First when Merritt himself had tried to interfere with Argent's chest compressions and Argent had turned that primitive raw challenge on him (Merritt would never forget that face), and the second time when M was threatened with a second round of choral hydrate, the mischievous drug which they both believed had been a factor in her extreme behaviors. But when Argent sat next to M, as she lay quiet and subdued in her hospital bed, he had seemed to shrink.

The first signs that M was truly emerging from the dark of her mind occurred on her first evening at Providence Hospital, and these were her reactions to physical stimuli. As Argent predicted, even mostly unconscious, M objected to enemas and catheters and medical probing. She was sensitive to cold hands on her body but seemed not to react at all to the presence of Merritt's or Argent's hand in hers. She began to grab at her sheets and push them off. Argent cowed a poor young sister who attempted to thwart M in this by tucking the sheets so tightly that M was essentially bound.

When movement was detected beneath M's eyelids, the doctors and nurses began to speak to M, but she did not respond. It was then that Merritt and Argent began to present some value to the hospital staff. They encouraged the men to take turns sitting with M and talking constantly, even if it was only reading from the newspaper. Merritt and Argent were grateful for the meaningful work, and the staff was grateful to have the gentlemen's attention turned from staff duties and fully focused on Miss Warner.

The sisters caring for M noticed that Miss Warner seemed more relaxed when the gentlemen were with her, reading to her, and this was reported to Sister Beatrice, the superior who directed the nursing staff. Sister Beatrice, in turn, reported this to the White House, which by now promptly relayed all such notes directly to the President, who had returned from West Point late on Monday. The President then promptly requested of Chief Whitley the favor of Merritt's and Argent's continued presence at the hospital. Chief Whitley replied that it was his pleasure to extend to the President any help the Service could offer. Merritt and Argent, unaware of these communications, wondered when Whitley would be recalling them to their primary duties, but neither man was willing to go so far as to volunteer to return.

It was apparent that M was trying to open her eyes but was just beyond success. After two days and nights of fruitless talking, cajoling, reading, and praying, Merritt and Argent were, if possible, even more frustrated.

They were maddeningly close to communication with M. In some ways, it had been less agonizing when she was completely insensate.

Late on the third night in Washington, Merritt and Argent sat together on overlapping shifts, on opposite sides of M's bed. There seemed to be nothing left to say about M or to do for her. They were now old veterans of M's injuries and her hospital room and the regimen of her care – they knew when she was bathed, when her linens were changed, when the doctors made their rounds, when her medications were dispensed and in what form. Thus, they spoke like old campaigners, often repeating the same worn comments and memories, and even understanding with a look between them that one such comment or memory need not even be spoken. Nonetheless, Merritt repeated a favorite observation.

"It is hard to believe we were once on a farm in Kentucky, and that we promised to bring her safely home in two weeks, in time for Easter."

Argent nodded absently. Merritt continued. "You were worried about a boring, tedious trip with an old woman who would insist on afternoon teas and frequent stops. She was nothing we expected."

"No," Argent agreed absently.

Merritt recognized this mood in Argent and knew better than to hope for real conversation. He stood to take his leave, then remembered the note in his pocket. "A letter came today from Mr. Henry and Miss Carrie. I'm not sure what more we can tell them. They have asked leave to care for M, should she recover her senses." Out of the blue, Merritt said, "I have been trying all afternoon to remember M's middle name. One of the sisters asked if she had one. I think they're ready to transfer her to a private home, someone President Grant knows here."

Argent looked up at the word 'transfer,' then slowly lowered his gaze. Transfer meant the doctors had exhausted all options; transfer meant no hope. Listlessly, he answered Merritt, "We were never told her middle name; some awful family secret, I suppose."

Merritt heard caustic resentment and bitterness in Argent's voice, but at least he was talking. Merritt countered, "No, no, her middle name was spoken. We just couldn't hear it because M shouted over Carrie every time it came up."

Argent mused over the comment; he regretted they had never asked about it. "What could be so awful about a name that M couldn't bear it to be spoken? . . . Lally. But that wasn't her middle name. That's what the family called her: Lally."

On the bed, M stirred, and Merritt and Argent held their breath.

"Lally." Argent said her name again, but this time without the bitterness and regret.

M tried to part her lips, but they were dry and sealed closed. Merritt dipped a clean cloth in the ewer next to her bed and lightly ran it over her lips. She bit the cloth and sucked the water from it. Merritt looked up at Argent, like a child delighted with a Christmas toy. Argent felt himself suspended.

Argent took a shaky breath and asked, "Lally, are you thirsty?"

From a far distance, 'yes' traveled down a dark tunnel, bouncing between the walls like a bubble, finally to pop into a hoarse whisper at her lips: "Yes."

Merritt dipped the cloth over and over again to let M suck from it the cool water. In his joy and eagerness, Merritt dripped water on her chin, from where it traveled down her jaw and under her ear to wet the pillow. M raised her hand and moved it toward her mouth but missed the cloth. She just missed touching her chin, then let her hand drop, exhausted by the effort.

Argent scolded Merritt. "You are dripping water everywhere. She does not like it."

Merritt was abashed, and tenderly and thoroughly wiped away his carelessness. M took a few more sips from the cloth, but then turned away when she was finished.

Argent picked up her right hand from where it had dropped and laid it back by her side. He called to her twice more, but she was asleep – merely asleep, Argent was convinced of it – drinking having worn her out. Merritt had intended to return to the hotel room he and Argent shared, but he was far too excited to leave. Twice more during the night, M had roused and responded to Merritt and Argent's questions – no, she was not cold; yes, she was tired.

When the sisters came to give Miss Warner her morning bath and change her sheets, they found the two men, coatless and disheveled and sprawled in awkward angles asleep in the chairs. While the sisters tended M, Merritt and Argent reported the night's events to the doctor doing rounds that morning. He was very nearly as excited as they were but cautioned them over too much enthusiasm.

The sisters emerged from M's room and reported that M had briefly opened her eyes – with great effort, it appeared. Merritt and Argent nearly fought the doctor for first admittance to the room. M was freshly washed, and her hair brushed back off her neck and face – Argent had seen her pull her hair away from her neck constantly as she lay in the back room of Widow Lambert's house, and he had made sure every nurse knew to arrange it so for her.

Argent, by unspoken consent, called to M: "Lally, are you awake?"

"Li'l," she mumbled – there was not enough room in the bubble or the tunnel for so expansive a response as "Yes, a little."

The doctor blundered in. "Miss Warner, I am Dr. Grayson. I'd like for you to answer a few questions for me."

Dr. Grayson was one of the staff doctors assigned to M's care by Dr. Toner, the chief house physician. He was a young man, clearly only recently certified, assigned to those cases where he could do the least harm until maturity and gradually-offered experience prepared him for more difficult cases. He spoke to M gently and he meant no harm, but it was a poor beginning with this particular patient.

In her most forceful bubble yet, M answered with a clear "NO." The tunnel almost collapsed under the force which her answer had been propelled forward. M breathed hard with the effort.

Merritt immediately hooked the doctor by the arm and firmly propelled him, backwards, out of the room. In the privacy of the corridor, he instructed the doctor that, at least for now, while M was still so fragile in her understanding, he was not to reveal that she was in a hospital or attended by doctors and nurses, and, upon further thought, all due respect for her modesty must now be strictly imposed – everyone was to assume she was conscious and aware of her body. The doctor was at first indignant but relented under the firm grip and icy stare of Merritt's insistence. Baltimore had warned the Washington staff of just such interference as this, but until now the two gentlemen had been subdued and bothersome only in their constant presence. Argent, suspecting the conversation underway in the corridor, reinforced the strictures by casually mentioning, upon the doctor's re-entry, the patient's relationship as goddaughter to the President. This piece of information was new to the doctor, and its import showed properly in his face. Everyone on the staff knew that Miss Warner was in some way connected to the President, but none knew exactly how. Instinctively, Argent had withheld this small, but powerful bit of information from the very beginning, and now knew the time was ripe for revelation.

M's interview progressed more easily. She was, with great effort, able to give both her first and last name, and after that, she was asked only questions that required a simple yes or no:

Could she open her eyes? Yes (but she declined to do so – Merritt smiled; even nearly incapacitated, M was rebellious.)

Could she feel this? Yes (each toe was explored, as were her ankles, calves and knees. In keeping with Merritt's very recent admonitions, it was taken as given that she could also feel her thighs, and other parts best left covered.)

Could she squeeze his hand? Yes (again, M elected not to follow an affirmative with a demonstration). Merritt, in a great show of exasperation for the uninitiated, said, "Lally, please squeeze the hand," which she did, but with little strength

Did her shoulder hurt? No.

Did her neck hurt? Lil.

Did her head hurt? Lot.

Was she hungry? Tired.

The doctor tried another tack. "Would you eat something, if someone helped you?"

"Tired."

The interview was at an end. As the three men moved towards the door, Merritt turned and asked, "What, Lally?"

Back at the bed, M opened her lips several times, stoking the tunnel for heavy traffic. "'met. . . Jack . . . Mor'y."

Merritt sat by the bed and took M's left hand. "They are well and cared for. Emmet gets two apples every day; he'll get three today. Jack and Morty are fine, too. They want you to wake up and come down to the barn."

Argent was sure he saw a slight smile. "'morrow," M answered, then surprised everyone with a clear giggle and, almost as clear, "Silly boys."

M's progress over the next few days was erratic and unpredictable. The only measurably consistent progress was in her steady increase in time spent awake. She opened her eyes for longer and longer stretches of time, though whether she always perceived or understood what she was seeing or hearing was questionable. Merritt and Argent continued their vigil at the foot of her bed, one or both of them always present for whenever she should wake, whenever she should speak.

Though sometimes it seemed that M was following the conversation in the room, she rarely spoke, even if directly addressed. Gradually, however, she began to answer the doctors' litany of questions fairly regularly, and with bored accuracy. Spontaneous discourse, however, remained elusive, though occasionally M produced unprovoked, singular comments. Late one night, as moonlight spilled through the window, she said, "*Supra lunam sunt aeterna omnia.*" It was Argent's turn to stay the night with her, and for a moment as she spoke he thought he saw a wistful wonderment in her stare, but then it was gone. Another time, she raised her head and said, angrily and with an odd authority, "Creek," then laid her head back on her pillow and closed her eyes. These rare occasions of speech were maddening to Merritt and Argent, who had thought M's first rousing indicated a complete and permanent return to awareness (though Argent certainly knew better). Even so, M's cryptic announcements gave them something to discuss and analyze during long stretches when she was uncommunicative.

Mary, however, enjoyed the drowsy state where every object had a white haze and every sound mimicked that distant quality of noise under water. She did not recognize the place where her sleepy mind had taken her, but it did not alarm her. Even at those times when the place and the people in it threatened to be real, she felt herself safe behind a kind of transparent membrane that nothing could penetrate. And always there was the lulling quality of sound under water. She often felt as if she were lying in the creek below her home, where the water was shallow enough to do so, her hair carried back and waving in the flow of the stream. There was enough water to cover her ears and up to her chin. Sometimes, in her dreamworld, the water would surge slightly, and she felt herself slightly buoyed up. It was during these surges that she heard clearly the sounds and conversations of her dream and that she saw with clarity the room beyond the creek. Once when her dream was particularly insistent upon her attention, she raised her head out of the creek and told her dream, "You are not allowed in the creek." Then she laid her head back down, her ears below the water.

Usually she could command this dream she was in, but sometimes she found segments of the dream repeating over and over again, and she could not regain the murmur of the water until she had forcefully entered the dream to move the scenery forward. One or another of the hazy people in her dreamland was always demanding the most inane information from her, and she could not enjoy the soft flow of the water or the susurration just below the surface until she had satisfied these demands.

There was night and day in the dream world, where men and women floated in and out, leaving behind their garbled sounds, but Mary did not bother to measure their passings. She was not even certain if the cycle of day and night followed the natural order. Sometimes it seemed like day succeeded day and other times night succeeded night; but in the creek it was always bright day, the water was always warm and gently rocking, but never wet. Although she noted these facts, she did not wonder at them, until a searing flash of lightning made her bolt from the creek, and the accompanying blast of thunder shattered the membrane through which she watched and heard the strange world of her dreams. When she looked out over the creek from her new place on the bank, she saw the sun glinting on the water, but heard nothing – no birds or insects or wind rifling through the leaves. On the ground she saw a strange pattern of shade made by the leaves, as if the leaves had all taken on a half-moon shape, all of equal size. The pattern on the ground puzzled her, until she gazed upward to gauge the leaves, but the leaves were unchanged. It was the sun, however, that was casting these strange shapes on the ground – a sun partially eclipsed by the moon. Then she blinked at the eclipse and it was gone, and so was the creek and the soft hum of its movement.

Preceding this event, Mary had experienced a few occasions of a kind of shifting of her awareness, the feeling of slabs of bedrock of varying sizes slipping back into place after a monumental upheaval. The occurrence of the thunder and lightning marked the greatest such shift. The magnitude of this event was such that Mary experienced it as a great and disorienting wrenching apart of several great slabs of bedrock, into which an even greater piece forced its way upward. She woke deep in the night to find herself in a strange bed in the room of her dreams. She was sweating and breathing hard but shivering with the sudden change and loss. Someone called her name, a foreign sound after months and maybe years listening to the murmur of the creek. She did not want to acknowledge her name, to acknowledge anything about this place, but after a moment a man's face came into sight. He asked anxiously, "Are you unwell? Are you in pain?" Then the man added, as if she was a child, "It is only a storm; it will pass."

She stared wildly at him, then against all hope that he could help, she said, "I want to go back." Though she longed to recover the peace and comfort of the creek, she could never find her way back among the boulders and the cracked and scored granite floor that once was the creek.

The next day, there was an almost miraculous change in M. Her speech returned to that which Merritt and Argent remembered, in pronunciation, vocabulary and application of grammar; she no longer spoke in the short simple sentences that had marked her communication since she first roused from her coma. She spoke, however, with her eyes closed; speech exhausted her. Merritt and Argent were exhausting themselves, staying day and night with M, loath to miss even the smallest milestone in her recovery. The doctors finally felt it time to politely request that the two men abandon their night shifts. The patient seemed out of danger of death, and the men were only exhausting themselves (and the night staff); surely they could do Miss Warner more good by getting their own proper rest. Remembering a like suggestion from the widow, Merritt and Argent acquiesced.

Responses from the White House to their daily bulletins now included clear notes of relief: *Thank God; our prayers are answered; keep her spirits up.*

This last request was sure to prove difficult to achieve. As M came to understand where she was, she equally understood where she was not. It could no longer be hidden that she was in a hospital, and therefore not home, where the creek awaited her. She began to ask questions, the answers to which were sure to upset her: *Why am I here? How long have I been here? How did I get here? When can I leave?*

At first it was easy to distract her or satisfy her with evasive or partially true answers, but she eventually realized that she was being patronized. She became angry and defiant and withdrawn. She would end the day exhausted and defeated. She waited in the dead of night for the sisters to finish their rounds, when she could quietly, quietly weep.

Very gradually, Mary had been allowed to sit up in bed, and this was another source of frustration for her. She was not used to looking up to any but the tallest people, and now she found herself constantly on the lower end of visual contact. It underscored her grating helplessness and she was determined to at least meet the people coming and going from her room on as equal a visual footing as possible. The timetable set by the doctors for this accomplishment was much too slow for Mary's liking, and one morning she took it upon herself to haul herself into a complete sitting position.

She was shocked at how weak she was, and how dizzy just sitting up had made her. Her spinning head brought on nausea that narrowly avoided the need to vomit. She was panting and pale and shaking and sweating with the effort. However, eventually her head slowed down considerably, taking with it the nausea, and she stopped shaking. But she could not shake the fatigue from the mere effort, and so dozed a little.

When she next opened her eyes, it was to see the same two men who had been coming for as long as she could remember being here. She did not think they were doctors, yet they seemed to be able to direct the doctors. She once overheard the taller, broader man scold a doctor outside her doorway for frightening Mary – which he had – with talk of transfers to private care.

Provisions, he had informed the doctor, were in place for her care when she was ready to leave this hospital. She was not sure that the provisions mentioned by this man would be any less frightening, but she did not want to alienate such an obviously powerful ally, a possible means of leaving this place.

The two men sat, as they always did, on either side of her bed, just near her feet. She never thought about her feet, or moving them, until the men brought attention to her feet by sitting there. They had been kind and solicitous, but she wasn't sure of their purpose. Why were they always there? And always, always talking – to each other, to the sisters, to the doctors, and to her.

Every day, a doctor came in and asked her name, her age, where she lived, the names of all her siblings, her parents' names. (The first time she had listed their names, at that time long ago when it was such effort to talk, the doctor had asked, "And where are they now?" Mary had said, "Gone." No doctor had ever asked that question again.) At each repetition, whatever doctor had conducted the interview, always turned to these two men to confirm her answers. Mary suddenly realized this bothered her. Why should her answers about herself ever need to be confirmed in the first place and by two complete strangers in the second place?

This day was one of those days in Mary's recovery on which she felt a sudden wrenching back into place of some part of her mind or memory. As the doctor turned to confirm her age with the two men, the one with the light eyes had the audacity to correct her answer, and Mary realized that she had been hearing him do so for days.

Her dander was up. From the full regal height of her pillows, Mary forcefully challenged both the doctor and these men. "I beg your pardon. Why do you consult with these strange men on matters that are particular to me? And, for heaven's sake, why don't you write down my answers, so you don't feel the need to consult with strangers and I won't have to re-tell you day after day after weary day?"

These were the most words she had strung together since she first began her verbal responses a week ago. All three men stared at her with varying degrees of surprise.

The doctor was quick to answer. "I know it seems pointless, but with injuries such as yours – to the head – it is important to keep track of your mental progress or decline. Comparing answers from day to day indicates consistency or inconsistency of memory and knowledge. I ask these gentlemen to confirm your answers as a sort of check against both your memory and our records. I assure you it is standard practice." After the slightest pause, he continued, "I take it you do not know these gentlemen?"

Mary suddenly felt a trap closing. What was the answer they wanted? How would it affect her at this place, how long she had to stay, the manner of her stay? Suddenly, she was frantic to get out, to leave and go home.

Something of her panic must have shown on her face, for the taller, broader man with the dark eyes spoke softly to her. "There is no penalty or repercussion, no matter what your answer. Do you know me?"

"No."

Gesturing to the other man with him, he asked, "Do you know this man?"

"No."

The dark-eyed man smiled, saying, "I know this has been difficult for you."

"Was I correct? Should I know you?"

But it was the other man who answered. "We only just met, before your accident; it is reasonable you would not remember."

The taller man stood. "We don't want to tax your reserves any more. We have taken the liberty to see how you do while our business has kept us here. We wish your continued rapid recovery."

Argent gathered up Merritt and they left the room. In the corridor, Merritt began to protest this strategy, but Argent took his friend by the elbow and led him further from M's door – he had become aware of how clearly conversations in the hall could be heard in M's room.

"We have been recalled to our duties. The Clarke case comes to trial."

Merritt rolled his eyes; it was hard to take the Clarke case seriously. "Again? It will just be postponed again."

"And if it is, it won't be because the government can't produce these two witnesses. We have enough time to pack our belongings and catch the next train to New York."

Merritt was clearly not pleased at being called away from M just as she was truly becoming communicative, merely to sit in Judge Benedict's court, as they had several times before this, to hear of yet another delay in the process. Colonel Clarke had been arrested amid an overwhelming cache of evidence of counterfeited revenue stamps, and the means to produce them. They had him dead to rights, yet somehow the prosecution had been unable to slip the noose over his head. The defense had proven very adept at weaving and dodging to keep the colonel's head free of the noose. This had been going on for months, since Clarke was first arrested early last November. Merritt had lost count of just how many times they had been pulled from one assignment or another to offer testimony, only to return to the field for a week or two before being summoned again. Merritt could only surmise that Colonel Clarke's position in New York society was proving to be of great benefit to him.

Argent saw the frustrated disappointment on Merritt's face. Two months ago, Merritt and Argent would have been eager to move on to the next assignment – even to return once again to Judge Benedict's court – but that was when they had thought escorting a Mrs. Warner to Washington was going to tax their patience. But Mrs. Warner had turned out to be Miss Warner, and she had surprised them both, and in a strange twist, it had been she who had protected them. Now they were loath to leave her, and they knew that Grant had been advocating their presence here with Miss Warner. Even President Grant, however, could not forestall the inevitable forever; there was work to be done, and precious few men in the still fledgling Service to do it in the great expanse of the nation.

Argent continued, "This seems tailor-made to cover our exit and absence. Why leave her with a sense of confusion regarding us? She may yet remember us, and we'll have occasion to find out when we return in a few weeks. She is where she needs to be for the moment, and close enough for the President to easily send for her when he receives word of her ability to travel."

"She is on the verge of remembering everything. What if removing ourselves now from her attention forever buries her memory of us? That cannot be acceptable to you."

Argent observed Merritt harshly. "What is acceptable to me is not for you to suppose. Nearly two weeks of constant vigil has yielded no memory of us. Two or three weeks of absence can do no worse, and it may be that our sudden reappearance will create a bridge between her most recent memory of us and her lost memory of us."

"M fears bridges."

"I'm beginning to fear them, too."

www.ingramcontent.com/pod-product-compliance
Lightning Source LLC
Chambersburg PA
CBHW021928110726
47901CB00003B/749

* 9 7 8 0 9 6 0 0 6 4 9 0 8 *